W9-ABU-334

THE LADY OF THE SORROWS

THE BITTERBYNDE · BOOK II

The Bitterbynde Trilogy:

Book 1: *The Ill-Made Mute*

Book 2: *The Lady of Sorrows*

Book 3: *The Battle of Evernight*

THE LADY OF THE SORROWS

THE BITTERBYNDE · BOOK II

CECILIA DART-THORNTON

WARNER BOOKS

An AOL Time Warner Company

WARNER BOOKS EDITION

Copyright © 2002 by Cecilia Dart-Thornton
All rights reserved. No part of this book may be reproduced in any form or by any electronic or mechanical means, including information storage and retrieval systems, without permission in writing from the publisher, except by a reviewer who may quote brief passages in a review.

Cover design by Jon Valk
Cover illustration by Daniel Craig

Aspect® name and logo are registered trademarks of Warner Books, Inc.

Warner Books, Inc.
1271 Avenue of the Americas
New York, NY 10020

Visit our Web site at www.twbookmark.com

An AOL Time Warner Company

Printed in the United States of America

Originally published in hardcover by Warner Books

First Paperback Printing: April 2003

10 9 8 7 6 5 4 3 2 1

For my friend and muse, Tanith Lee

CONTENTS

Synopsis

This is the second book in THE BITTERBYNDE trilogy.

Book 1, *The Ill-Made Mute,* told of a mute, scarred, amnesiac who led a life of drudgery in Isse Tower, a House of the Stormriders. Stormriders, otherwise known as Relayers, were messengers of high status. They "rode sky" on winged steeds called eotaurs, and their many towers were strewn across the empire of Erith, in the world called Aia.

Sildron, the most valuable of metals in this empire, had the property of repelling the ground, thus providing any object with lift. This material was used to make the shoes of the Skyhorses and in the building of Windships to sail the skies. Only andalum, another metal, could nullify the effect of sildron.

Erith was randomly visited by a strange phenomenon known as the shang, or the unstorm: a shadowy, charged wind that brought a dim ringing of bells and a sudden springing of tiny points of colored light. When this anomaly swept over the land, humans had to cover their heads with their taltries—hoods lined with a mesh of a third metal, talium. Talium prevented human passions from spilling out through the skull. At times of the unstorm, this was important, because the shang had the ability to catch and replay human dramas. Its presence engendered tableaux, which were ghostly impressions of past moments' intense passions, played over repeatedly until, over centuries, they faded.

The world outside the Tower was populated not only by mortals but also by immortal creatures called eldritch wights—incarnations wielding the power of gramarye. Some were seelie, benevolent toward mankind, while others were unseelie and dangerous,

The drudge escaped from Isse Tower and set out to seek a name, a past, and a cure for the facial deformities. Befriended by an Ertish adventurer named Sianadh, who named her Imrhien, she learned that her yellow hair indicated she came of the blood of the Talith people, a once-great race that had dwindled to the brink of extinction. Together, the pair sought and found a treasure trove in a cave under a remote place called Waterstair. Taking some of the money and valuables with them, they journeyed to the city of Gilvaris Tarv. There they were sheltered by Sianadh's sister, the carlin Ethlinn, who had three children: Diarmid, Liam, and Muirne. A city wizard, Korguth, tried unsuccessfully to heal Imrhien's deformities. To Sianadh's rage, the wizard's incompetent meddling left her worse off than before. Later, in the marketplace, Imrhien bought freedom for a seelie waterhorse. Her golden hair was accidentally revealed for an instant, attracting a disturbing glance from a suspicious-looking onlooker.

After Sianadh departed from the city, bent on retrieving more riches from Waterstair, Imrhien and Muirne were taken prisoner by a band of villains led by a man named Scalzo. Upon their rescue they learned of the deaths of Liam and Sianadh. Scalzo and his henchmen were to blame.

Imrhien promised Ethlinn she would reveal the location of Waterstair's treasure only to the King-Emperor. With this intention, she joined Muirne and Diarmid and traveled to distant Caermelor, the Royal City. Along their way through a wilderness of peril and beauty, Imrhien and Diarmid accidentally became separated from their fellow travelers, including Muirne. Fortunately they met Thorn, a handsome ranger of the Dainnan knighthood whose courage and skill were matchless, and Imrhien fell victim to love.

After many adventures, followed by a sojourn in Rosedale with Silken Janet and her father, these three wanderers rediscovered Muirne, safe and well. Muirne departed with her brother Diarmid to join the King-Emperor's armed forces. Recruits were in demand, because rebel barbarians and unseelie wights were mustering in the northern land of Namarre, and it seemed war was brewing in Erith.

Imrhien's goal was to visit the one-eyed carlin, Maeve, seeking a cure, before continuing on to Caermelor. At her final parting from Thorn she was distraught. To her amazement, he kissed her at the last moment.

At last, in the village of White Down Rory, Imrhien's facial disfigurements were healed. With the cure, she regained the power of speech.

Two of her goals had been achieved. She now had a name and a face, but still, no memory of her past.

END OF BOOK ONE

THE LADY OF THE SORROWS

THE BITTERBYNDE · BOOK II

The Known Countries of Erith

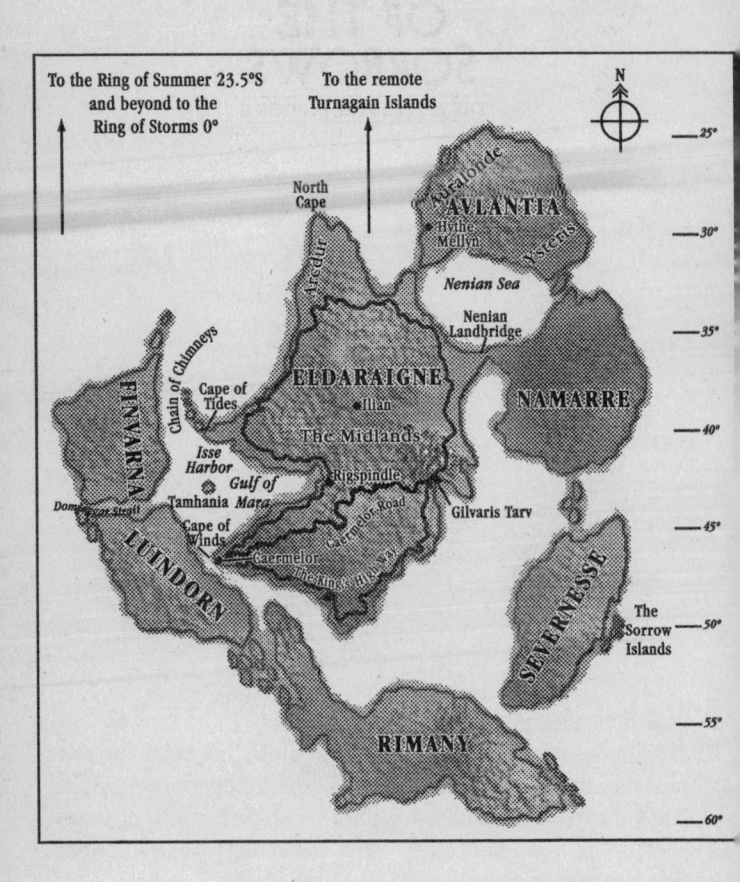

To the Ring of Summer 23.5°S
and beyond to the
Ring of Storms 0°

To the remote
Turnagain Islands

N

— 25°

Abralonde

North
Cape

AVLANTIA

Hythe
Mellyn

Ysserris

— 30°

Aredur

Nenian Sea

Chain of Chimneys

Nenian
Landbridge

— 35°

Cape of
Tides

ELDARAIGNE

NAMARRE

— 40°

Illan

FENVARNA

The Midlands

Isse
Harbor

Gulf of
Tamhania Mara

Rigspindle

Damorcas Strait

Caermelor Road

Gilvaris Tarv

— 45°

LUINDORN

Cape of
Winds

Caermelor

SEVERNESSE

The
Sorrow
Islands

— 50°

The King's Highway

— 55°

RIMANY

— 60°

1
WHITE DOWN RORY
Mask and Mirror

Cold day, misty gray, when cloud enshrouds the hill.
Black trees, icy freeze, deep water, dark and still,
Cold sun. Ancient One of middle Wintertide,
Old wight, erudite, season personified.
Sunset silhouette; antlers branching wide—
Shy deer eschew fear while walking at her side.
Windblown, blue-faced crone, the wild ones never flee.
Strange eyes, eldritch, wise—the Coillach Gairm is she.

SONG OF THE WINTER HAG

It was Nethilmis, the Cloudmonth.

Shang storms came and went close on each other's heels, and then the wild winds of Winter began to close in. They buffeted the landscape with fitful gusts, rattling drearily among boughs almost bare, snatching the last leaves and hunting them with whimsical savagery.

The girl who sheltered with the carlin at White Down Rory felt reborn. All seemed so new and so strange now, she had to keep reminding herself over and over that the miraculous healing of her face and voice had indeed happened; to keep staring into the looking-glass, touching those pristine features whose skin was still tender, and saying over and over, until her throat rasped:

"Speech is mine. Speech is mine."

But she would discover her hands moving, as she spoke.

Surrounding the unfamiliar face, the hair fell thick and heavy, the color of gold. Lamplight struck red highlights in the silken tresses. As to whether all this was beauty or not, she was unsure; it was all too much to take in at once. For certain, she was no longer ugly—and that, it seemed for the moment, was all that mattered. Yet there was no rejoicing, for she lived in fear, every minute, that it would all be taken away, or that it was some illusion of Maeve's looking-glass—but the same image repeated itself in placid water and polished bronze, and it was possible, if not to accept the new visage, at least to think of it as a presentable mask that covered the old, ugly one—her true countenance.

"I kenned you were mute as soon as you fell through my door," said the carlin, Maeve One-Eye. "Don't underestimate me, colleen. Your hands were struggling to shape some signs—without effect. And it was obvious what you were after, so I lost no time—no point in dilly-dallying when there's a job to be done. But 'tis curious that the spell on your voice was lifted off with the sloughed tissue of your face. If I am not mistaken you were made voiceless by something eldritch, while the paradox poisoning is from a *lorraly* plant. Very odd. I must look into it. Meanwhile, do not let sunlight strike your face for a few days. That new tissue will have to harden up a bit first, 'tis still soft and easily damaged.

"Tom Coppins looks after me, don't you, Tom?"

The quick, cinnamon-haired boy, who was often in and out of the cottage, nodded.

"And he will look after you as well, my colleen. Now, start using your voice bit by bit, not too much, and when 'tis strong you can tell me everything: past, present, and future. No, the glass is not eldritch. Come away from it—there is too much sunlight bleeding in through the windowpanes. And there's shang on the way—the Coillach knows what *that* would do to your skin!"

Not a day, not an hour, not a moment passed without thoughts of Thorn. Passion tormented the transformee. She whispered his name over and over at night as sleep crept upon her, hoping to dream of him, but hoping in vain. It seemed to her that he was fused with her blood, within her very marrow. Ever and anon her thought was distracted by images of his countenance, and conjecture as to his where-abouts and well-being. Longing gnawed relentlessly, like a rat within, but as time passed and she became accustomed to the pain, its acuteness subsided to a constant dull an-guish.

Late in the evening of the third day, the howling airs of Nethilmis stilled. Maeve dozed in her rocking-chair by the fire with a large plated lizard sleeping on her lap. Imrhien was gazing at her own reflection by candlelight, twin flames flickering in her eyes. Tom Coppins was curled up in a small heap on his mattress in a corner. All was still, when came a sound of rushing wind and a whirring of great wings overhead, and a sad, lonely call.

Quickly, Maeve roused and looked up. She muttered something.

Not long afterward, a soft sound could be heard outside the cottage, like a rustling of plumage. Maeve lifted the lizard down to the hearthrug and went to open the door. A girl slipped in silently and remained in the shadows with the carlin. Her face was pale, her gown and the long fall of hair were jet black. She wore a cloak of inky feathers, white-scalloped down the front. A long red jewel shone, bright as fresh blood, on her brow. Maeve spoke with her, in low tones that could not be overheard, then began to busy herself with preparations, laying out bandages and pots on the table.

The carlin's activities were hidden in the gloom beyond the firelight, but a sudden, whistling, inhuman cry of pain escaped the newcomer, waking Tom Coppins. Maeve had set straight a broken limb and was now binding it with splints. When all was finished, the swanmaiden lay quivering in the farthest corner from the fire, hidden beneath the folds of her feather-cloak.

"Pallets everywhere," muttered Maeve, leaving the dirty pots on the table. "I shall have to take a bigger cottage next year."

"You heal creatures of eldritch, madam?" Imrhien's voice was still soft, like the hissing of the wind through heather.

"Hush. Do not speak thus, when such a one is nigh. I heal who I can where and when I am able. It is a duty of my calling—but by no means the beginning and end of it." Maeve fingered the brooch at her shoulder; silver, wrought in the shape of an antlered stag. "Carlins are not merely physicians to humankind. The Coillach Gairm is the protectress of all wild things, in particular the wild deer. We who receive our knowledge from her, share her intention. Our principal purpose is the welfare of wild creatures. To protect and heal them is our mandate—care of humans is a secondary issue. Go to bed."

"I have another affliction. You are powerful—mayhap you can help me. Beyond a year or two ago, I have no memory of my past."

"Yes, yes, I suspected as much. Do you think I haven't been scratching my head about that? But it's a doom laid on you by something far stronger than I, and beyond my power to mend. For the Coillach's sake, come away from the mirror and go to bed. You're wearing out my glass. Don't go near her, that feathered one—she is afraid of most people, as they all are, with good reason."

The saurian jumped back onto the carlin's lap. She scratched its upstanding dorsal plates as it circled a couple of times before settling.

"I would have liked something less armored and more furry," she murmured, looking down at it, "but bird-things would not come near, if I had a cat. Besides, Fig gave me no choice. He chose *me*."

It was difficult to sit still inside the house of the carlin, within walls, and to know that Thorn walked in Caermelor, in the Court of the King-Emperor. Now the renewed damsel was impatient to be off to the gates of the Royal City. At the least, she might join the ranks of Thorn's admirers, bringing a little self-respect with her. She might exist near him, simultaneously discharging the mission she had taken upon herself at Gilvaris Tarv: to reveal to the King-Emperor the existence of the great treasure and—it was to be hoped—to set into motion a chain of events that would lead to the downfall of those who had slain Sianadh, Liam, and the other brave men of their expedition.

Maeve, however, was not to be swayed.

"You shall not leave here until the healing is complete. Think you that I want to see good work ruined? Settle down—you're like a young horse champing at the bit. Even Fig's getting ruffled." The lizard, dozing fatly by the fire, adeptly hid its agitation. In the shadows the swanmaiden stirred and sighed.

Three days stretched to five, then six. The weather raged again, battering at the walls of the cottage.

At nights a nimble bruney would pop out from somewhere when it thought the entire household asleep, and do all the housework in the two-roomed cot with amazing speed, quietness, and efficiency. Under Maeve's instructions the girl feigned sleep if she happened to waken and spy it. Its clothes were tattered and its little boots worn and scuffed. When it had finished, it drank the milk set out for it, ate the bit of oatcake, and disappeared again, leaving everything in a state of supernatural perfection.

Tom Coppins, the quiet lad with great dark eyes, was both messenger and student to the carlin, performing errands that took him from the house, aiding her in preparing concoctions or helping her treat the ailments and vexations of the folk who beat a path to her door: everything from gangrene and whooping cough to butterchurns in which the butter wouldn't "come," or a dry cow, or warts. Someone asked for a love potion and went away empty-handed but with a stinging earful of sharp advice. From time to time Maeve would go outside to where her staff was planted in the ground and come back carrying leaves or fruit plucked from it—potent cures. Or she would tramp out into the woods and not return for hours.

More and more, the carlin allowed Imrhien to wield her voice; it was exhilarating to converse freely; such a joy, as if the bird of speech had been liberated from an iron cage. Little by little she told her story, omitting—from a sense of privacy if not shame for having been so readily smitten— her passion for Thorn.

When the tale had been recounted, the old woman sat back in her chair, rocking and knitting. ("I like to be busy with my hands," she had said. "And it sets folk at ease to see an old woman harmlessly knitting. Mind you, *my* needles are anything but harmless!")

"An interesting tale, even if you have left out part of it," Maeve commented. Her patient felt herself blush. Maeve's perceptiveness was disconcerting. "So now you still have three wishes, eh? Isn't that right? That's how it usually goes—yan, tan, tethera. No, there is no need to reply. You wish for a history, a family, and something more—I see it in your eyes. Mark you—remember the old saw, *Be careful what you wish for, lest—*"

"Lest what?"

"Lest it comes true."

The carlin completed a row of knitting and swapped the needles from hand to hand.

"Now listen," she continued. "I do not know who you are or how to get your memories back, but I do ken that this house, since five days ago, is being watched."

"Watched? What can you mean?"

"I mean, spied upon by spies who do not know they have been spied. And since they began their enterprise not long after you arrived, I deduce that it is you they are after. Nobody gets past my door without my allowing it—the world knows that. Therefore, these observers must be waiting for you to come out. What think you of that, eh? Are they friends of yours, wanting to protect you, or are they enemies?"

It was like a sudden dousing in icy water. All that had happened to Imrhien since her arrival at the carlin's house had driven out thoughts of pursuers. Now the recent past caught up with a jarring swiftness. These spies might be henchmen of the wizard, the slandered charlatan Korguth the Jackal—but more likely they were Scalzo's men who had somehow tracked her down. She had been traced right to the carlin's door! If they had come this far, across Eldaraigne in search of her, or if they had sent word of her approach by Relayer to accomplices in Caermelor or even at the Crown and Lyon Inn, then it was obvious they were determined to catch her before she went to the King-Emperor explaining her detailed knowledge of Waterstair's location. Danger threatened. Desperate men might resort to desperate methods to prevent her from reaching the Royal City.

The carlin's eye was fixed intently upon her guest.

"How do you estimate these watchers? Take care with

your reply. A false decision might bring disaster. What comes next depends on what you say now. Your tongue is new to you. Use it wisely."

"I think they are evil men," the girl replied slowly. "Men who wish me ill; brigands led by one called Scalzo, from Gilvaris Tarv, who slew my friends. They will try to stop me from reaching the Court."

"That may be the case. I am not in a position to judge. If 'tis true, then it is perilous for you to depart from here un-protected. With this in mind I have already asked my patient Whithiue to lend you her feather-cloak so that you might fly out in the guise of a swan and send the cloak back later. She would not hear of it of course but it was worth a try—she and her clan owe me many favors. Yet I have an-other plan. If those who watch are your enemies, then they will know you chiefly by your hair and by your name. My advice is this—when you set out for the Royal City, go not as Imrhien Goldenhair. Go as another."

The needles clattered. A ball of yarn unrolled. The lizard watched it with the look of a beast born to hunt but re-strained by overpowering ennui.

"Change my name?"

"Well, 'tis not your name, is it? 'Tis only a kenning given you. One kenning is as good as another. I'll think of something suitable to replace it, given time. But you *cannot* go to Court with that *hair* and not be noticed. By the Coil-lach, colleen, know you how rarely the Talith are seen? Only one of that kindred resides at Court—Maiwenna, a cousin of the long-defunct Royal Family of Avlantia. In all the lands, there are so few human beings of your coloring that they are always remarked upon. Feohrkind nobles can rinse their tresses in the concoctions of carlins and wizards and dye-mixers as often as they like, but they can never copy Talith gold. Their bleached heads are like clumps of dead grass. No, if you want to mingle unmarked, you must change the color of your hair as well as your kenning. And for good measure, go as a recently bereaved widow and keep that face covered."

"You know best," said Imrhien slowly in her whispering tones, "for I know nothing of the ways of the King-Emperor's Court. But who would recognize the face I wear now?"

"Folk from your past, haply."

"Then that would be wonderful! I should meet my own folk, discover all!"

"Not necessarily. Who left you to die in the rain in a patch of *Hedera paradoxis*? Not folk who were looking after your interests. Safer to remain unknown, at least until you have delivered your messages to the King-Emperor. And if you cannot tell His Majesty himself, why then you would be equally well-off to confide in Tamlain Conmor, the Dainnan Chieftain, or True Thomas Learmont, the Royal Bard. They are his most trusted advisers, and worthy of that trust, more so than any other men of Erith.

"If you manage to leave my cottage unmarked and reach the Court, you will likely be richly rewarded, you understand. Gold coins can buy security, or at least a measure of it. When all is done and your work discharged, then you shall have leisure to decide whether to doff the widow's veil and show yourself, and risk all that goes with being Imrhien of the Golden Hair."

"There is good sense in what you say," the girl admitted to the carlin.

"Of course there is. And if you had your wits about you, you'd have thought of it yourself, but I expect you've lost them in that glass. By the way, are you aware that you speak with a foreign accent?"

"Do I? I suppose it is Talith."

"No. It is like no dialect I have ever heard."

"Am I of the Faêran? It is said that they lived forever . . ."

The carlin cackled, true to type. "No, you certainly are not one of the Gentry. Not that I have ever set eyes on any of them, but there is naught of the power of gramarye in you. If there were, you would know it. You are as mortal as any bird or beast or *lorraly* folk. None of the Fair Folk would get themselves into such scrapes as you manage. And yet, your manner of speech is not of any of the kingdoms of Erith. Your accent's unfamiliar."

"The Ringstorm that encircles the world's rim—does anything lie beyond it?"

"Let me tell you a little of the world. Some say that it is not a half-sphere but an entire orb with the Ringstorm around its waist dividing Erith from the northern half. That is why the world has two names; 'Erith' for the Known Lands, and 'Aia' for the three realms in one, which comprise the Known Lands, the unknown regions on the other side of the Ringstorm, and the Fair Realm. Of those three realms only Erith is open to us. Many folk have forgotten the Fair Realm. Some say it never existed at all. People believe what they can see. Furthermore, it is commonly held that nothing lies beyond the Ringstorm, that it marks the margins of the world, and if we were to pass further than that brink, we would fall into an abyss."

"Mayhap there is some path through the Ringstorm."

"Mayhap. Many have tried to find one. The shang winds and the world's storms are too much for any sea-craft. The Ringstorm's borders are decorated with broken Seaships."

"Mayhap there is a way through to Erith from the other side, from a land on the other side where they speak differently . . ."

"Too many 'mayhaps.' Let us to the business in hand."

"Yes! Madam Maeve, I am concerned for your safety. Should I depart hence under an assumed persona, the watchers will believe Imrhien Gold-Hair bides yet here, and they may keep watching for a time until they tire of it and assail your house."

"A good point." Maeve thoughtfully tapped her ear with a knitting needle. "Ah, but if they *think* they see Imrhien Goldenhair leaving and they follow her, then find out it was a ruse and rush back here and see no sign of her, they will think she escaped during their absence. In sooth, she will have. An excellent plan—nay, ask no questions, it will all be clear to you soon. Meanwhile, I had better rouse Tom— he has errands to run for me in Caermelor. We shall need money to carry out this scheme. How much have you?"

"Madam, please accept my apologies. Your words remind me that I owe you payment for your healing of me, and my board and lodging. What is your fee?"

"My fee," said the carlin, shooting a piercing glance from her bright eye, "is whatever those who receive my services are prepared to give."

"What you have given me is valuable beyond measure— worth more than all the treasure in the world."

"Have I given it, or was it already yours by right? Do not be thankful until you have lived with your changed appearance for a moon-cycle or two. See how you like it then. "

"I cannot be otherwise than happy!"

"Ha! The measure of happiness is merely the difference between expectations and outcomes. It is not concerned with what one possesses—it is concerned with how content one is with what one possesses."

Imrhien had taken out her leather pouch. The pearls she had left in Silken Janet's linen-chest, the ruby she had given to Diarmid and Muirne, but there remained two more jewels and the few gold coins she had saved when she ran from the caravan. In glittering array she spread the stones and metal before the carlin.

"This is all I have. Please, take it."

Maeve One-Eye threw her head back and laughed.

"My dear," she said, "you will never survive out in the wide wicked world if you do this sort of thing. Have you not heard of bargaining? Such an innocent. And how would you fare with no money to spend on your way to the City? This I shall take." She leaned forward and picked up the sapphire. "The mud from Mount Baelfire is costly to obtain. And blue is one of the colors of my fellowship, the Winter shade of high glaciers and cold water under the sky. Leave the emerald out of your purse—it is of greater worth and will fetch a high price. It is necessary to sell it to pay for the purchases Tom shall make in Caermelor on your behalf. But put away the sovereigns and doubloons and the bit of silver. You may need them someday. And be more careful to whom you display your wealth—fortunately, I can be trusted, but not all folk are as honest as Maeve One-Eye!"

Her thicket of albino hair bristled untidily, like a rook's nest in a frost—her guest suspected that it was in fact inhabited by some pet animal—and she leaned back in her chair, chuckling. The needles resumed their *click-clack*.

"True to Talith type, you possess the darker eyebrows and eyelashes—those I will not need to alter. What color of hair want you? Black? Brown?"

"Red."

"A canny choice. Nobody would ever believe that any clear-headed person would *choose* the Ertish shade, thus they will think that you soothly *are* of Finvarnan blood. I take it you will not mind being despised as a barbarian in Court circles?"

"I have had my fill of contempt! I have been despised enough for twenty lifetimes. Not red, then. What is the fashion for hair at Court?"

"Black, or straw yellow—save for the salt-haired Icemen that dwell among them; their locks do not take kindly to dyes, nor do they wish to alter them, being a proud race."

"It seems I must choose black. But I will not stay long at Court—only long enough to deliver my news, and then I will be away."

And long enough to find someone.

"Be not so certain. You may not obtain an audience with the King-Emperor straightaway. He is busy, especially at this time of strange unrest in the north. As an unknown, you will be seen as inconsequential enough to be kept waiting— if necessary, for weeks, despite the fact that I am going to transform you into a lady of means for the mission. If you successfully reach Caermelor and then obtain permission to pass within the palace gates, you may have to wait for a long time. And if you are eventually granted an audience, the next step must be verification of your news. They may ask you to lead them to this treasure."

The carlin paused in her handiwork, holding it high for a better view. "Cast off, one plain, one purl," she muttered obliquely. With a thoughtful air, she lowered the needlework to her lap. "So. A name you will need." She hummed a little tune. "I've got it! 'Rohain.' A tad Severnessish-sounding, but it suits you. And you must say that you come from some remote and little-known place, so that there is small chance of meeting any person who hails from there and might betray you. The Sorrow Islands off Severnesse are such a place—melancholy, avoided whenever possible. Tarrenys is an old family name from those parts. Yes— that's it. Ha! *Rohain Tarrenys* you shall be—say farewell to Imrhien Goldenhair, Lady Rohain of the Sorrows."

"Am I to be a lady? I know nothing of the ways of gentlefolk. I shall be discovered."

"Methinks you underestimate your own shrewdness. Hearken. Should a peasant wife arrive at the palace with a story of discovering great wealth, that woman risks her life. There are those at Court who are not as scrupulous as the Dukes of Ercildoune and Roxburgh; those who would wish to take the credit to themselves for such a discovery, and to silence the real messenger. It is possible a commonwife would not be given the opportunity to speak with the Dukes before she was bundled off with a few pennies, maybe to be followed, waylaid, and murdered. Howbeit, a *gentlewoman* must be treated with greater scrupulosity."

"Who, at Court, could be so perfidious?"

"It will become clear to you," said Maeve briskly. She changed the subject. "Have you a potent tilhal for protection along the way?"

"I have a self-bored stone, given me by Ethlinn."

"A worthy talisman," said the carlin, examining the stone with a lopsided squint. "You might well have need of it. Many malign things wander abroad these days. Doubtless you have heard—it is said that one of the brigand chieftains of Namarre has grown strong enough to muster wicked wights in his support. There is no denying that some kind of summons, inaudible to mortal ears, is issuing from that northern region. Unseelie wights are moving across the lands, responding to the Call. With an army of lawless barbarians, aided by unseelie hordes, a wizard powerful enough to summon wights would be an opponent to be reckoned with. They say such a force might stand a goodly chance of overthrowing the Empire and seizing power in Erith. If that should come to pass, all the lands would be plunged into chaos. It would mean the end of the long years of peace we have known."

A chill tremor tore through the listener.

"These are uneasy times," continued the carlin, with a shake of her head. "Even creatures who have not revealed themselves for many lifetimes of men have lately reemerged. It is not long since I heard a rumor that Yallery Brown has been seen again."

She returned the stone to its owner.

"What is that?" asked the girl, tucking the tilhal beneath her garments.

"Yallery Brown? One of the wickedest wights that ever was or is—so wicked that it is dangerous even to befriend him. Have you not heard the old tale of cursed Harry Millbeck, the brother of the great-grandfather of the mayor of Rigspindle?"

"I have heard many tales, but not that. Pray tell it!"

"He was a farm laborer, was Harry," said Maeve. "On a Summer's evening long ago, he was walking home from work across fields and meadows all scattered with dandelions and daisies when he heard an anguished wailing like the cry of a forsaken child. He cast about for the source and at last discovered that it issued from underneath a large, flat stone, half-submerged under turf and matted weeds. This rock had a name in the district. For as long as anyone could remember, it had been called the Strangers' Stone, and folk used to avoid it.

"A terrible fear came over Harry. The wails, however, had dwindled to a pitiful whimpering and being a kind-hearted man he could not steel himself to walk on without rendering aid to what might have been a child in distress. With great trouble, he managed to raise up the Strangers' Stone, and there beneath it was a small creature, no bigger than a young child. Yet it was no child—rather it looked to be something old, far older than was natural, for it was all wizened, and its hair and beard were so long that it was all enmeshed in its own locks. Dandelion yellow were the hair and whiskers, and soft as thistle-floss. The face, puckered as lava, was umber-brown, and from the midst of the creases a pair of clever eyes stared out like two black raisins. After its initial amazement at its release, this creature seemed greatly delighted.

" 'Harry, ye're a good lad,' it chirped.

"*It knows my name! For certain this thing is a bogle,*

Harry thought to himself, and he touched his cap civilly, struggling to hide his terror.

" 'Nay,' said the little thing instantly, 'I'm no bogle, but ye'd best not ask me what I be. Anyway, ye've done me a better service than ye know, and I be well-disposed towards ye.'

"Harry shuddered, and his knees knocked when he found the eldritch thing could read his unspoken thoughts, but he mustered his courage.

" 'And I now will give you a gift,' said the creature. 'What would you like: a strong and bonny wife or a crock full of gold coins?'

" 'I have little interest in either, your honor,' said Harry as politely as he could. 'But my back and shoulders are always aching. My labor on the farm is too heavy for me, and I'd thank you for help with it.'

" 'Now hearken you, never thank me,' said the little fellow with an ugly sneer. 'I'll do the work for you and welcome, but if you give me a word of thanks, you'll never get a hand's turn more from me. If you want me, just call *"Yallery Brown, from out of the mools come to help me,"* and I'll be there.' And with that it picked the stalk of a dandelion puff, blew the fluffy seeds into Harry's eyes, and disappeared.

"In the morning Harry could no longer believe what he had seen and suspected he'd been dreaming. He walked to the farm as usual, but when he arrived, he found that his work had already been completed, and he had no need to lift so much as a finger. The same happened day after day; no matter how many tasks were set for Harry, Yallery Brown finished them in the blink of an eye.

"At first the lad augured his life would be as leisurely as a nobleman's, but after a time he saw that matters might not go so well for him, for although his tasks were done, all the other men's tasks were being undone and destroyed. After a while, some of his fellow laborers happened to spy Yallery Brown darting about the place at night and they accused Harry of summoning the wight. They made his life miserable with their blaming and their complaints to the master.

" 'I'll put this to rights,' said Harry to himself. 'I'll do the work myself and not be indebted to Yallery Brown.'

"But no matter how early he came to work, his tasks were always accomplished before he got there. Furthermore, no tool or implement would remain in his hand; the spade slipped from his grasp, the plough careered out of his reach, and the hoe eluded him. The other men would find Harry trying to do their work for them, but no matter how hard he tried he could not do it, for it would go awry, and they accused him of botching it deliberately.

"Finally, the men indicted him so often that the master dismissed him, and Harry plodded away in a high rage, fuming about how Yallery Brown had treated him. Word went around the district that Harry Millbeck was a troublemaker, and no farmer would hire him. Without a means of earning a living, Harry was in sore straits.

" 'I'll get rid of this wicked wight,' he growled to himself, 'else I shall become a beggar on the streets.' So he went out into the fields and meadows and he called out, 'Yallery Brown, from out of the mools, come to me!'

"The words were scarcely out of his mouth when something pinched his leg from behind, and there stood the little thing with its tormentil-yellow hair, its pleated brown face and its cunning raisin eyes. Pointing a finger at it, Harry cried, 'It's an ill turn you've done to me and no benefit. I'll thank you to go away and allow me to work for myself!'

"At these words, Yallery Brown shrilled with laughter and piped up: 'Ye've thanked me, ye mortal fool! Ye've thanked me and I warned you not!'

"Angrily, Harry burst out, 'I'll have no more to do with

ye! Fine sort of help ye give. I'll have no more of it from this day on!'

"'And ye'll get none,' said Yallery Brown, 'but if I can't help, I'll hinder.' It flung itself into a whirling, reeling dance around Harry, singing:

Work as thou wilt, thou'lt never do well.
Work as thou mayst, thou'lt never gain grist;
For harm and mischance and Yallery Brown
Thou'st let out thyself from under the stone.

"As it sang, it pirouetted. Its buttercup tresses and beard spun out all around until it resembled the spherical head of a giant dandelion that has gone to seed. This thistledown orb blew away, disappearing into the air, and Harry never again set eyes on Yallery Brown.

"But he was aware of the wight's malevolent presence for the rest of his life; he sensed it opposing him in everything to which he turned his hand. Forever after that, naught went aright for poor Harry Millbeck. No matter how hard he worked he couldn't profit by it, and ill-fortune was on whatever he touched. Until the day of his death Yallery Brown never stopped troubling him, and in his skull the wight's song went ceaselessly round and round, '. . . for harm and mischance and Yallery Brown thou'st let out thyself from under the stone . . .' "

"That's a terrible injustice!" cried the listening girl.

"Aye," said Maeve, "That's the way of unseelie wights and that one is among the wickedest."

The carlin gave detailed instructions to Tom Coppins, who went off to Caermelor on a pony and returned three days later laden with parcels.

"What took you so long?" Maeve said impatiently.

"I was bargaining."

"Hmph. I hope you got the better of those rapscallion merchants. How much got you for the emerald?"

"Twelve guineas, eight shillings, and eightpence."

"And what purchased you with that?"

"Shoes, raiment, and trinkets such as you asked, and a hired carriage to be waiting at the appointed place at the appointed time."

"Good. Keep half a crown and give the rest to my lady, Rohain of the Sorrows."

Tom Coppins was accustomed to unquestioningly accepting curious events. That a yellow-haired monster should have entered the cottage and been transformed was no more strange than many things he had seen while in the service of Maeve. He loved the old carlin with unswerving loyalty—whatever she needed, he would fetch; whatever she asked, he would do, and without question. He was an astute lad and warmhearted. In the time he had been in Maeve's service, he had seen beyond the aspect of a simple old woman, the aspect the world saw. He had been witness to the carlin's true dignity and power made manifest.

That night, Tom washed Imrhien-Rohain's hair with an iron-willow mordant. He rubbed in a thick mud of pounded and soaked iris-roots, then rinsed the hair again with the mordant, as Janet had done to Diarmid's locks in the valley of roses. The black-haired girl shook out her sable tresses in front of the fire.

The swanmaiden's eyes gleamed from the shadows. Maeve brought food for the wight-in-woman-form, speaking to her in a low, foreign voice.

The next morning, at *uhta,* the eldritch maiden departed. Before she left, Imrhien-Rohain saw her standing framed in the doorway, her fair face and slender arms gleaming white against the nightshade of her cloak and hair. The lovely wight offered a single black feather to Maeve. Then she slipped behind the doorpost and vanished. A moment later, with a rush and a whirr, dark wings lifted over the house-roof. There came a plaintive, mournful cry that was answered from far off.

Maeve stood on the doorstep, her face raised to the sky.

"She rejoins her flock at a remote mountain lake," she said at last. "She could not bear to be enclosed any longer within walls. The limb is not yet properly healed but it might be she will return for my ministrations, now and then, until it is whole. They always know where to find me, in my wanderings. And soon I must wander again—I have stayed here long enough and Imbroltide draws nigh."

Consideringly she looked at the long black feather, before swathing it in a swatch of linen.

"Now it is but sixteen days until the turn of the year, the most significant time of all—Littlesun Day. There is much to be done."

She set a fiery eye on her other visitor. "Take this swan's plume with you. The swans of eldritch sometimes give a feather in token of payment. When the feather's holder is in need, the swan is bound to help, but once only. Her calling-name, potent only for the duration of the bitterbynde, is *Whithiue*. This is a gift of high value."

A bitterbynde. Imrhien-Rohain recalled hearing that term when she dwelled in the House of the Stormriders. The betrothal of a daughter of that House, Persefonae, had been pledged on the day she was born. A vow, or geas, laid upon a subject willing or not; a decree that imposed bitter sanctions upon its breaking, and demanded stringent, almost impossible conditions for its removal—that was a bitterbynde. In the swan-girl's case, she was bitterbound to come to the aid of whomsoever grasped the feather and summoned her.

"Now," said Maeve earnestly, folding the linen package

firmly into the hand of Imrhien-Rohain, "it is your turn to go forth."

So it was that on the fifteenth of Nethilmis, before the early gathering of morning, a cloaked and taltried figure, mounted sidesaddle, rode swiftly from Maeve's door. White stars arrayed a fretwork of black boughs, and the green star of the south was a shining leaf among them. Thin chains of mist fettered the trees. Every leaf and twig seemed carved from stone. The rider, awkward and uncertain, continually glanced from right to left. The long skirts kept tangling with the stirrups, but, as if in haste, the rider urged the pony on. Not far from the house of the carlin, dark figures sprang from among the trees as the steed cantered past. The rider cast a glance backward, then, with surprising alacrity, threw one leg over the pony's back and, giving a shrill cry, surged forward. As the pony's hooves clattered away, other figures ran from the trees bringing up horses with muffled hooves. Soon they were galloping in vigorous pursuit.

The pony, although swifter than an ordinary mount of its kind, could not outmatch the long strides of the horses. Yet for a time it seemed the pursuers did not want to catch up, but merely to follow from a distance and mark their quarry, as though biding their time. Suddenly they rounded a bend and were forced to rein in their horses so sharply the steeds reared on their hind legs and screamed their indignation. Right in their path, the pony had halted. It wheeled, then, and faced them. The rider flung back the hood, revealing the face of a dark-eyed lad. His hand dipped beneath his cloak and he flung out a powder that exploded in the faces of the pursuers with a dazzling flash, followed by billowing smoke. When they finally fought free of the thick fog, he was gone.

Back, then, they rode like a storm. When they returned

to the house of the carlin, the windows and doors stood open, sightless. No smoke wisped from the chimney. The place was empty and all trails were cold.

A quarter-moon danced overhead. The Greayte Southern Star hung like an emerald set in onyx, and falling stars peppered the night sky.

Imrhien Rohain ran along a narrow woodland path leading northwest, clutching her purse of coins to prevent them from clashing together. She had the advantage of a secret start, and carried a potent tilhal of Maeve's as protection against things of the night that dwelt around White Down Rory. A Stray Sod had been let fall behind her at the beginning of the path to mislead any mortal who stepped thereon, and a sudden, temporary thicket of brambles camouflaged the path's entrance. Despite these precautions, terror spurred her pulse as she fled through the black trees. The glimmering footpath seemed enchanted—no root reached across to trip her up, no wight crossed it or started up alongside. Without pause, she hastened on, casting many a backward glance, as if the mysterious riders who had watched the house might spring out of the darkness. At last, lacking breath, she slowed to a swift walk.

The money from the emerald had been well-spent. Rohain of the Sorrows, an elegant lady, would become a widow as soon as she unfolded the silk mask across her face to hide her grief, in the fashion of bereaved women. By her ornaments and garments, she would appear a noble widow of considerable means. The silk domino, blue as night, was worked with scarlet. Jet beads sparkled in her long dark hair. Matching needlework, dark red and azure on midnight blue, drenched the full bell-sleeves of her gown, slashed to show contrasting lining, and dripped down the voluminous skirts from below whose picoted hems several petticoats peeped demurely. Her waist was cinched by a crimson leather girdle, housed within silver filigree. A long, fitted fur-lined traveling cloak, frogged down the front, covered the yards of fancy fabric. A fur-lined velvet taltry topped the outfit.

She went forward. Hours passed. A soft noise like the wind in an Autumn wood came rustling. She thought it strange, for there was no wind, and all around, stark boughs plowed black furrows into the fitful moonlight, unmoving. A tall, pale figure glided past; some wight in almost mortal form. It groaned and soon passed out of sight. The susurration of falling leaves went on and on. Suddenly the moon shone out radiantly and the sounds changed to faint murmurs of laughter and ridicule that continued for a while, then faded.

Down among the tree roots, tiny lights were moving. The path climbed a final slope and came out on the Caermelor Road as the sky began to pale. Farther down the Road, to the left, squatted a white milestone. It was there that the coach waited, its coach-lamps glowing like two amber flowers. The horses' breath steamed, a silver mist combed to shreds by the sharp and bitter cold.

The coachman had received an enticing down payment on the understanding that his services were to be performed with confidentiality—*not* that the noble lady passenger had held a clandestine tryst in the woods with a bucolic lover, *of course*. Simply, she desired privacy and no questions. Given his utmost discretion, the pecuniary reward at the end of the journey would exceed even the down payment.

He saw a slender, cloaked figure materialize out of the darkness, silent as a moth.

Bowing, he murmured, "Your ladyship." Her name was unknown to him.

She nodded. He could not see her face behind the decorative blind. Handing her into the carriage, the coachman stepped up into his box-seat and shook the reins. His bellowed "Giddap!" harshly interrupted the night.

With a sudden thrust forward, the equipage bowled rapidly along the Road to Caermelor.

Light wooden caskets were waiting in the coach. With a sense of excitement, the passenger opened them. One was filled with sweetmeats and refreshments for the journey, one contained a most risible headdress, another an absurd pair of shoes, and a fourth accommodated an ermine muff and a pair of gloves. With difficulty inside the cramped and jolting compartment, the "widow" added these items to her person.

The wide headdress was fashioned from a thick roll of stiffened fabric trimmed with sweeping carmine plumes, beaded, latticed with silver. It possessed a crown rising to a point draped with yards of azure gauze. Altogether, the dainty, fragile shoes, the voluminous sleeves, the stiff, embroidery-crusted fabric of the gowns, the heavy girdle that made it difficult to bend forward, and the wide headdress that made it impossible to approach any wall seemed most onerous and impractical, not only for travel but for everyday living. These garments and accoutrements would impede the simplest of tasks. Could it be that such strange raiment was truly the fashion at Court? Had her benefactress and the lad been mistaken, out of touch? Quickly she dismissed the thought. Nothing escaped the carlin's notice—the costume would be correct.

Her heel kicked against a heavy object sitting on the floor—a foot-warmer. Tom Coppins had thought of everything. Housed in its elaborately carved wooden case, the brass container with its pierced lid gave off a welcome warmth from the glowing charcoal in its belly. The passenger propped her feet thereon and sat back against the padded leather upholstery.

Yet the new Rohain could not enjoy the comforts of this unaccustomed mode of travel. She fervently hoped that all she had heard about the Court had been exaggerated—the tales of the refined manners, the complicated rules of etiquette, the forms of speech. Between the fear that the carriage would be overtaken by her enemies, the dread of what was to come, and constant battles with the unwieldy headdress that threatened to slide off, she made the journey in great discomfort and alarm.

Throughout the Winter's day, the carriage rolled on.

Days were short. At its zenith, the sun had risen only marginally above the horizon, where it glowered from behind a dreary blanket of cloud.

Emerging from the woods, the Road ran through farming lands patched with fields, hedge-bordered. Here and there, a house topped with smoking chimneys nestled among its outbuildings. After passing through a couple of outlying villages, the Road began to climb toward the city walls.

The buildings of Caermelor clustered on the slopes of a wall-encircled hill that rose four hundred feet out of the sea at the end of its own peninsula. To the south, the sea had taken a deep bite out of the land to form a wide and pleasant bay fringed with white sands. The far side of this bay was cradled in the arm of a mountainous ridge reaching out into the ocean to form a second, more rugged peninsula, its steep sides clothed in forest.

Eastward, an expansive, flat-bottomed valley opened out. Through the middle of it ran the river that drained the encircling hills, flowing until it reached the sea to the north of the city-hill. There, salt tide danced to and fro with fresh current. In the estuary, waters ran deep enough for the draft of the great-keeled Seaships. Wharves, piers, docks, and jetties jutted from the northern flank of the city-hill, stalking into the water on thick, encrusted legs.

Atop the highest point, the palace overlooked all—the vast sweep of ocean to the west, the curve of the bay with its long lines of lace-edged waves, the blue-folded shoulders of the ridge dropping sharply to the water; north, the ocean stretching to distant mountains; northeast, the river-port teeming with business, forested with tall masts. Eastward, the city spread out over the plain, dwindling to scattered farms and the backdrop of Doundelding's hills on the horizon.

But blind ocean was not all that could be seen to the west, for a tall island rose up, perhaps a quarter of a mile offshore, directly opposite the city-hill. At low tide, the waters drained from a causeway that connected it to the mainland. At all other times it was completely cut off by water. Here stood the Old Castle, much like a crag itself, jagged, gray, and gaunt. Of yore it had been the fortress to which citizens had retreated in times of war. Now it stood, stern sentinel, silent guardian, facing the palace on the hill.

Late in the afternoon the coach halted at last before the city gates. There was a knock on the front wall of the compartment. Imrhien-Rohain slid back the little window that opened onto the coachman's box. His eyes appeared, goggling like a fish's.

"Where to now, m'lady?"

"To the palace." Her new voice had crisped to a clear, ringing tone.

"Very well, m'lady."

She slid the window shut, like a guillotine chopping off the outside world.

Guards lounging under the portals had a word with her coachman. Through the windows they eyed the passenger with curiosity as the vehicle went by. Imrhien-Rohain drew the curtains against their intrusion. Beyond, voices rose and fell, wheels rattled, seagulls mewed. Children yelled. In booming tones a town crier shouted, "Hear ye! Hear ye!"

She had come at last to Caermelor.

2
CAERMELOR, PART I
Vogue and Vanity

Euphonic fountains splash, by arbor walls
where climbing roses, red and yellow, cling.
Proud peacocks strut on sweeping, verdant lawns
and nightingales in gilded cages sing.
Glass carriages with plumed and matching teams
roll on amidst this royal plenitude,
By ornamental lakes where sleek swans glide,
reflecting on their mirrored pulchritude.

The silk and satin ladies with their fans
incline upon the marble balustrade.
The night will see them dance like butterflies,
when they attend the Royal Masquerade.
Fair jewels gleam on ev'ry courtly peer:
bright rubies, sapphires, diamonds, and pearls.
The costliest of velvets, plumes, and furs
adorn dukes, viscounts, marquesses, and earls.

Prosperity and luxury abound;
sweet music plays as nobles feast and sport.

The rarest beauty and the greatest wealth
are found within the Empire's Royal Court
FASHIONABLE SONG AT THE COURT OF CAERMELOR

Caermelor Palace had been originally constructed as a castle stronghold and still retained its fortified outer structure. Machicolated watchtowers, siege engine towers, stair turrets, a mill tower, round mural towers, square mural towers, and numerous other outjuttings thickened the twelve-foot-deep walls at varying intervals.

The road into the parklike palace grounds crossed the moat by means of a drawbridge. Beyond the drawbridge bulked the garrisoned gatehouse and the barbican. The main outer gate was constructed of solid oak, studded with iron. It could be barred, if necessary, by an iron portcullis that remained raised in times of peace and was lowered only for the purpose of oiling the chains and maintaining the winches.

When this outer gate was shut, persons on foot might enter by a smaller postern set into it, whereupon they would find themselves in a long chamber set within thick walls, with a gate at either end—the gatehouse, a solid edifice specifically dedicated to the purpose of providing a space between the inner and outer portals. Peepholes in the walls allowed guards in side passages to inspect purportedly innocent visitors. Those approved visitors might pass through a second gate. It opened onto the outer bailey, which in recent years had been filled with walled gardens and leafy courtyards. A third gate led to the inner bailey with its stables, barracks, parade grounds, kennels, pigeon-lofts, coach-mews, and falconry-mews. It was bordered by the King's Tower winged with fluttering standards, the arsenal tower, the Great Hall with its pentise, two tall Mooring Masts, the solar, and the keep. The windows of the internal buildings had been enlarged from cross-slitted arrow-loops and narrow arches to gracious fenestrations of latticed glass, and greater opulence reigned within them than in former days. The transformation from fortress castle to residential palace had also involved the creation of ornamental gardens around the keep.

Somewhere within the vitals of that keep, Tamlain Conmor, the Most Noble the Duke of Roxburgh, Marquess of Carterhaugh, Earl of Miles Cross, Baron Oakington-Hawbridge, and Lord High Field-Marshal of the Dainnan—to name only his principal titles—strode into the richly furnished suite he always occupied when at Court, calling for his junior valet and his squire.

"Ho, John! Where is my lady wife?"

"The Duchess Alys-Jannetta is at her bower with her ladies, Your Grace," piped the valet.

"So. Have you laid out some clean clouts for the evening?"

"The scarlet hose or the puce, Your Grace?"

"I care not, just as long as they are serviceable enough that they don't split along the crotch seam and let my backside hang out. Wilfred, is Conquest well-polished?"

"Conquest is oiled and polished, sir," replied that young man.

"Give him here." The Dainnan Chieftain stroked the broadsword lovingly; held it up to the light.

"Good." He handed the weapon back to his squire. "See that the new scabbard is maintained as bravely. Who's that at my door? Enter."

A footman opened the sitting-room door. A messenger ran in, went down on one knee before the warrior and bowed, offering a silver salver on which a leaf of parchment flapped. Roxburgh read the note, scratching his bluff chin.

"Very well." He sighed. "Conduct this lady to the Cham-

ber of Ancient Armor. She may await me there. My wife is
at her bower, you say?" Crumpling the parchment into a
ball, he threw it at John, who ducked too late. The messenger bobbed his head in answer and ran out.

As the sun dipped, the clouds in the west parted, allowing a gleam of bronze to lance the lofty windows of the
Chamber of Ancient Armor. The room overlooked a walled
courtyard of fountains and statues. Across the tapestries on
its walls, scenes from history and legend spread themselves, all with a bellicose theme. Here, two cavalry
brigades charged at one another, pennants streaming, helmet plumes, manes, and tails flying, to clash in a tangled
mass of armored brawn and rearing, screaming war-horses.
There, Dainnan archers in disciplined rows fired a deadly
rain of darts, the back line standing with legs astride, braced
to shoot, while the front, having spent its arrows, reloaded.
On another wall, Warships locked each other in combat
among a ferment of storm clouds above a city. Farther on,
the infantry of the Royal Legion raged about a trampled
field. Their enemies lay thick on the ground and the colors
of Eldaraigne fluttered high above.

Afternoon light spilled like brandy across an acorn-
patterned carpet at the daintily shod feet of the visitor who
sat waiting in a chair heaped with brocade cushions. A page
boy in the livery of Roxburgh, gold and gray, stood stiffly
at her shoulder.

Filigree brass lamps hung on chains from the ceiling and
jutted in curled brackets from the walls. A servant scurried
about, kindling them to amber glows. Disappointed, the last
of the sunrays withdrew. As they did so, a white-wigged
footman entered, wearing black pumps and an iron-gray
tail-coat with gold trimmings. He bowed.

"Your Ladyship, His Grace will see you now."

He held the door open. The dark-haired, masked widow

passed through and was guided deferentially to a larger chamber: the Duke of Roxburgh's audience-room. In a loud voice the footman announced, "Lady Rohain Tarrenys of the Sorrow Islands."

The visitor was ushered in.

A hearthful of flames flung warmth into this room, cheerily bouncing their glow off polished walnut furniture and silver-gilt. A pair of cast bronze andirons with eagle motifs supported a burning giant of the forest. They matched the decorated fender, the pokers, the tongs. Crossed swords, broad-bladed hunting knives with deer's-foot handles, and other trophies of arms enlivened the walls alongside a mounted boar's head with formidable tusks and the masks of other game.

The fire's light was supplemented by three hanging lusters and, atop a table, a bronze urisk holding a massive bouquet of bell-flowers whose cupped petals were candle-sockets. Two more goat-legged wights in marble supported the mantelpiece, which in turn bore a set of equestrian statuettes in malachite and agate. On a bearskin rug before the hearth lay a pair of lean hounds.

Conmor, Duke of Roxburgh, stood by the window. He was still in the field-dress he had worn that day: loose-sleeved shirt, leather doublet slit to the hips, belted loosely at the waist, embossed baldric slung across the shoulder, suede leggings, and knee-boots. Firelight burnished his shoulder-length, unbound locks to dark mahogany.

At her first sight of the Dainnan Commander, a muffled gasp escaped from beneath the visitor's veil.

Thorn!

But no. Of course not—it was just that she had not been expecting to see a tall figure wearing the subdued Dainnan uniform here in the palace suites, where braided liveries stalked alongside jeweled splendors. This man with brown hair tumbling to his shoulders was not Thorn, although he came close to him in height, and if she had not first seen Thorn, she would have thought the Commander exceedingly comely. He was older, thicker in girth, more solidly built, his arms scarred, his thighs knotted with sinew. At the temples his hair was threaded with silver. Proud of demeanor he was, and stern of brow, but dashing in the extreme.

The warrior leader's hazel eyes, which had widened slightly at the sight of the visitor, now narrowed. Somewhere in remote regions of the palace, something loose banged peevishly in the rising wind.

"Go and see to that shutter, will you, lad?"

The momentary distraction allowed Rohain-Imrhien to recover her poise. She curtsied and awaited tacit permission to speak.

"Rohain of the Sorrows," repeated Roxburgh, "pray be seated and remove your widow's veil. Here in the palace we are joyed to look upon the countenance of those with whom we hold converse."

His guest inclined her head.

"As Your Grace's servants have many times assured me, sir. But I am uncomfortable without it. I have made a vow—"

"I insist," he broke in; a man used to having his demands met and impatient with those who would not cooperate. There seemed to be no choice.

She unhooked the mask and drew it aside.

Her eyes never left his face. She read all that passed across it—the look of surprise, the turning away, then the avoidance of her eyes. What could it mean? This was the first test in the outside world of this new face she wore. Was it then so strange?

"Wear the veil if you must," the Dainnan Commander said briskly, throwing his shoulders back as though regaining control of himself after a lapse. "Wilfred, have refreshments brought for Her Ladyship and myself."

Murmuring compliance, Wilfred withdrew.

"For you must be weary, m'lady," continued Roxburgh, "after your journey. The message I received from the Doorkeeper indicated that you have traveled to Caermelor on an errand of importance, with news that you will entrust only to the King-Emperor."

Rohain-Imrhien fastened the mask back in place.

"That is so, Your Grace."

She perched on the edge of a velvet-covered chair. Roxburgh remained standing, occasionally striding up and down in front of the hearth.

"Have you any idea," he said, "how many folk come knocking upon the King-Emperor's doors with the same message as you? Petitioners, beggars, would-be courtiers, social climbers—most of them do not get as far as an audience with me. You have been fortunate, so far, due to your apparent station. I have many calls upon my time. His Imperial Majesty the King-Emperor will not hold audience with you. It is a busy time for all—meaning no discourtesy, my lady, but His Majesty has no spare time these days. Our sovereign's waking hours are devoted to the urgent business at hand. As one of His Majesty's ministers I am empowered to speak for him and take messages on his behalf. Now, what are your tidings of import?"

A page in gray-and-gold livery came in bearing a laden tray. He set it down on a table with legs carved like sword irises and inlaid with mother-of-pearl, then bowed to his lord and to the lady.

"Thank you—"

Her host glanced at Rohain sharply. Obviously she had made a mistake by thanking the lad. It appeared that those born to be served by others did not consider it necessary to show gratitude to the servants here in the palace. She must avoid such errors. To survive here among the denizens of the Royal Court, one must do what all newcomers must do in a strange country—copy the behavior of the inhabitants. If she observed them closely, if she followed their customs and manners, then she might pass undiscovered.

"My tidings are for the ears of the King-Emperor," she repeated. The Dainnan Chieftain frowned. He seated himself opposite her, leaning back in the chair.

"Well, my lady of the Sorrows, it seems we can discover no common ground. Pray, partake of wine and cakes before you depart. I am sorry there can be no commerce between us."

Ethlinn and Maeve had said that Roxburgh could be trusted, but it would be better to see the King-Emperor himself. She must try for it.

"I *must* speak with the King-Emperor."

"And I have told you that it is impossible."

He handed her a goblet, silver-gilt, enameled in mulberry.

"To your health."

"And to Your Grace's."

She raised the vessel, lifted the veil, and drank. The liquor was the essence of peaches, on fire.

"'Tis a pity to travel so far only to leave with your mission unrequited," remarked the Duke conversationally, lifting one mightily thewed shank akimbo and resting a boot on his knee.

"Yes, a pity."

"How do they speak of us, in the far Isles of Sorrows?"

"Highly, sir. But no words I have heard spoken do justice to the wonder and wealth of the Royal City. The name of Conmor, Duke of Roxburgh, is also famous in far-flung places, of course."

"And no doubt many a story is attached to it."

"All are gestes of valor."

"And honor?"

"Most assuredly!"

"If Conmor of Roxburgh is spoken of, perhaps you are aware that he has little time for secret messages, being more concerned with the safety of the Empire. It is no secret that war is gathering on the borders. Our spies reported large movements of armed barbarians in northern Namarre last month near the Nenian Landbridge. Yesterday the Royal Legions began deploying five hundred troops to the north as part of the King-Emperor's moves to guard against possible military action by Namarre. I am needed there. I sally forth on the morrow."

"I know nothing of such matters, sir, but perhaps a show of strength may be all that is required to make these rebels think again."

"Precisely. Otherwise, they shall know the fury of the King-Emperor's Legions."

"It is said that they are allied with immortals—unseelie wights of eldritch who are moving northward in answer to some kind of Call; formidable foes."

"In sooth, but so-called immortals only live forever unless they choose to die or are slain."

"I have heard that if they are wounded so sorely that their bodies become incapable of sustaining existence, they are able to transmute and thus live on in another shape?"

"Some possess that power, yea, but they must take a weaker form, threatless."

Conversation petered out.

The Dainnan Commander quaffed the remaining contents of his goblet. Rohain-Imrhien sipped her own, replaced it on the inlaid table, and stood up. Roxburgh also rose to his feet.

"You are leaving so soon?"

"I will not squander more of your time, sir—Your Grace

is a busy man, I know. Thank you for sparing me a moment."

"But your tidings . . ."

"Will Your Grace take me to the King-Emperor?"

"Before you stands his sworn representative. Is that not enough?"

"No, sir."

She curtsied. Beyond the palace walls, out in the gulf of night, the wind raged, hammering at the windows.

"Good speed," said Roxburgh, smiling slightly.

Rohain-Imrhien guessed he would not truly let her leave without divining her purpose.

She paused by the door, where two footmen of matching height stood poised to escort her. Then she turned and looked over her shoulder. The war-leader stood with his feet apart, arms folded. He nodded curtly. She walked back into the chamber.

Her bluff had not worked.

His had.

"I will tell you, sir," she said, since there was no option.

The wind sucked along corridors. It sang weird harmonies, flinging doors open and shut with sudden violence and setting every hound in the Royal Kennels to howling.

A sleepy young footman went around the Duke of Roxburgh's audience-chamber, lowering the gleaming lamps on their chains and trimming the wicks, lighting a score of candles slender and white like young damsels, now yellow-haired. In the tall hearth, the flames had simmered down to a wary glow, enlivened now and then by a sudden gust down the chimney. The hounds by the fire twitched, dreaming perhaps of past hunts.

Rohain fell silent, her story told. Long before this night, before she had become Rohain, she had held an inner debate on what she would say, should she ever reach Court.

To reveal the existence and whereabouts of the hidden treasure was her purpose, and to uncover the corrupt Scalzo and his adherents so as to be avenged. But to disclose her own identity—insofar as she knew it—was not her intention. In truth, she was nothing but a homeless waif who had forgotten a past that possibly was best left forgotten. She was a foundling, an ex–floor-scrubber, a serf, a stowaway, a misfit, and an outcast. Now a chance to begin afresh had fallen like a ripe plum into her lap. The lowly part of her life could be swept away and hidden. With a new face and a new name, she who had first been nameless and then been Imrhien might indeed become Rohain of high degree.

To begin living a lie did not sit comfortably with her, but so many reasons made it the choicest path. A noblewoman could wield so much more influence than a servant. That power might be used to help her friends. With influence, she had also some chance of finding Thorn again, of at least seeing him, from a distance, one more time. Thirdly, having once tasted dignity and luxury, it would be hard to relinquish them.

And so she had told her story to Roxburgh not as it was, but as she wished it to be heard. He had listened closely throughout, and when she had finished had asked several pertinent questions. He was no fool; she guessed that he perceived some flaws in the web she had woven, but, perhaps out of tact, he chose to overlook them.

The story went that she had left the Sorrow Islands and begun a journey across Eldaraigne in a small, private Windship. A storm had wrecked the craft over the Lofty Mountains. She and a crew member had been the only survivors of the disaster. Wandering destitute and in danger through the wight-ridden forests, they had come accidentally upon a treasure hoard of unsurpassed magnificence, at a place they named Waterstair.

"A treasure hoard? You say that it contains much sildron?"

"Vast quantities, sir."

"Did you bring any with you?"

This might be a trick question.

"Knowing that all newly discovered sildron is the property of the King-Emperor, I did not take any from this trove—nor did my companion. But those who discover such wealth are entitled to a share of it in reward, or so I am told. We took jewels and coin, to help us, should we find our way out of the wilderness and regain the lands of men, for we were destitute, as I have recounted."

"May I see these valuables?"

"All is spent." She added hastily, "We took so very little—we could not carry much."

"Spent? Where?"

"In Gilvaris Tarv, when we reached it. Of course, my first thought was to send a message by Stormriders to the King-Emperor, to inform him of this find. However, I held back at the last moment. I was reluctant to let such precious knowledge pass out of my hands—not that I do not trust our most worthy Stormriders, but accidents may happen. I decided, then, to journey to Caermelor, in person, with the news. As I was preparing for the journey, disaster struck. My unwonted spending, and that of the aeronaut who had helped me survive in the forests, had not gone unnoticed. He was abducted, with a number of his friends, by a gang of perfidious knaves. They forced him to lead them to the trove, and there he was betrayed, slaughtered before the very doors of the vault. One of his companions escaped to tell the tale, but later perished. I barely escaped with my own life. Through adventure and misadventure I made my way across Eldaraigne until I came here, to Court. Even as we speak, those black-hearted murderers, Scalzo's men, may be raiding the King-Emperor's treasure at Waterstair—

not for the first time—while the bones of brave fellows lie rotting in the grass."

"The name of this aeronaut?"

"Oh—the Bear, he was called," she stammered, fearing she might somehow betray Sianadh by revealing his true name.

"The Bear, indeed?"

"Yes."

"And the haunts of these brigands?"

"Gilvaris Tarv, near the river. On the east side. I know no more."

The Dainnan Chieftain called for more wine. He leaned forward, resting his elbows on his knees.

"But if all is as you say, my lady, then this is a very serious matter. We are talking of treason."

She made no reply.

"Treason, perpetrated by those who have concealed and appropriated the property of the Crown. The punishment for that is severe."

"As I imagined."

"You will understand, my lady, that you must remain, as it were, under royal protection until your story can be verified. This is for your own safety as well as for reasons of security."

"Of course."

This had been half-expected. Besides, where else would she go? It had been in her mind to ask her coachman—by now no doubt comfortably ensconced in some downstairs pantry with a tankard in his hand, waiting for her—to take her to the nearest reputable inn for the night. Beyond that, she had formed no plan.

"You must bide here, at the palace, until transportation to the Lofties can be arranged. Since you know the way, you must lead us there. Your reward shall be substantial— more than a few jewels and coins easily spent."

Untruthfully, she said, "Sir, knowing that I serve my sovereign is reward enough. Nevertheless I accept your offer with gratitude. I hope for every success in tracking down the treasoners."

He laughed humorlessly. "So, 'tis retribution you are after!"

Truthfully, she said, "Yes, but that was not my primary goal. I came here to fulfill a promise to a friend, and that I have done."

He shrugged. "I will have that wag Wilfred call your servants to bring your accoutrements. Your horses and carriage shall be accommodated in my own stables, your coachman in the grooms' and equerries' quarters behind the Royal Coach-Mews, and your maidservant in a chamber off the suite to be prepared for you."

"I have no handmaiden. The coachman and equipage are hired."

"What? No maid?"

The Dainnan scowled. He left his seat and again paced restlessly before the fireplace.

"My lady Rohain, you are a most singular noblewoman. You come here, unannounced; nobody has ever heard of you. You come masked and maidless, bearing a most extraordinary tale. You speak with disarming plainness, unlike a courtier or any member of the peerage. Are you in fact a spy?" On the last word, he spun on his heel and glared at her accusingly.

Outraged, Rohain jumped up. Her overblown skirts knocked the table. A goblet fell to the carpet, scattering its contents like spilled blood. Angry words sprang to her lips in the heat of the moment.

"Now you accuse *me* of treason! Indeed, sir, it seems you have been in the King-Emperor's service for too long—you have become suspicious of all strangers who set foot in the palace. I have come here in good faith, to carry out my duty, only to be called an infiltrator. My mask disturbs you? Well then!" She tore off the domino and threw it on the fire. Was it a sigh of the wind she heard, or the sudden intake of her host's breath? The hounds lifted their heads, snarling.

"If I speak too plainly for your Court manners," she cried, "teach me otherwise! And as for your treasure, I will prove that it exists. What more would you have me do?"

Her knees trembled. Abruptly, she sat down. The blood drained from her face. How had she possessed the temerity to dare such an outburst? What would happen now—would she be hanged for insolence? She fixed her eyes on the fire. The fragile mask had already been consumed. She was exposed, vulnerable.

Out across the city, a bell tolled. Unquiet fingers of air slid under the door and plucked at the curtains.

"Your pardon, lady," said Roxburgh at length. "I stand chastised." He bowed. His visage softened. "Pray do not think me unkind. It is my way, to test others at first meeting. Surely I have this night learned not to taunt the ladies of the Sorrows, should I ever meet another! Prithee, rest by the fire awhile." He paused for another moment, as though savoring some anomaly or bizarreness, then summoned his pages. "Lads! See to Her Ladyship's belongings and pay off the driver. Have lodgings made ready. Find a lady's maid."

Two or three young boys hastened to do his bidding.

This Dainnan lord speaks forthrightly to say the least, thought Rohain-Imrhien. *He is a man to place faith in.*

"You are His Majesty's guest now," Roxburgh informed her.

And prisoner? What if my ruse were to be discovered?

"Gramercie. I am weary."

"Wilfred—play."

The multiskilled squire took up a lyre, checked the tuning, and began expertly to coax a melody from the strings.

The wine, the warmth, and the music were sweet. Rohain may have dozed; it seemed no time had passed before a knock was heard at the door. There entered a damsel of her own age, perhaps seventeen or eighteen years, her hair corn yellow, half-encased in a crespine of gold wire. She curtsied, peeping at Rohain out of the corners of her eyes, blinking.

"Mistress Viviana Wellesley of Wytham at your service, Your Grace."

"You are to be servant to the Lady Rohain Tarrenys," said Roxburgh.

"Even so, Your Grace."

"Lady Rohain," he said, "I beg you to dine in the Royal Dining Hall tonight."

"Sir, I am honored."

Roxburgh again addressed the lady's maid. "Miss, is the suite of chambers ready?"

"Yes, Your Grace."

"Then pray conduct Her Ladyship to them with due consideration!"

Accompanied by a footman four paces behind to the right and the new personal maid four paces behind to the left, Rohain-Imrhien was verbally guided through a gridwork of resplendent corridors to her lodgings. The footman waited outside the door, holding it open for them to enter. She caught him staring at her and he blushed to the roots of his powdered wig.

A small, neat woman awaited them in the rooms, a bunch of jangling keys attached to her belt. She curtsied. Her mouth hung open, until she snapped it shut like a frog catching flies. After an awkward pause, Rohain concluded that servants were not permitted to speak first.

"Speak," she offered, lamely.

The Chatelaine of the King's Household introduced herself and indicated an anteroom where a bath awaited. Rohain dismissed her without thanks. The little woman bustled out with a rattle and a clash of stock, ward, and barrel. The footman closed the door and the sound of his steps echoed away.

Sixty candles lit the scene, rising from their brackets like tall yellow flag-lilies. Rohain stood staring. The opulence of the palace suite forced Isse Tower's decor into insignificance. These rooms burgeoned with decor in shades of emerald and gold, from the patterned carpet like a soft expanse of lawn studded with buttercups, to the gilded walls covered with plaster frescoes and the velvet hangings in apple green and lemon, their lush tassels dangling in bunches like ripening fruits. The bed's four posts were carved in the likeness of flowering wattle-trees whose boughs soared to a canopy of green brocade fringed with round gold beads above a matching coverlet and cushions. The windows were draped, swagged, and pelmetted in green and gold; daffodil tiles framed a niche wherein a fire blazed bravely, gleaming on a burnished grate and fire-irons. Rohain's fur-lined cloak, which had been urbanely subtracted by a butler as soon as its wearer had entered the palace, had been placed on a gilt chair next to her few pathetic belongings—the boxes from the carriage and, absurdly, the foot-warmer.

A soft clearing of the throat from the new personal maid drew Rohain's attention.

"Ah—what was your name again?"

"Viviana, m'lady. Vivianessa, in sooth, but I am called Viviana."

"Well, Viviana, would you—ah—put away my traveling cloak?"

This was all that came to mind, on the spur of the moment. What in Aia was she to do with this girl? Were the Court ladies expected to be incapable of dressing and undressing themselves? What a nuisance, to have someone constantly bothering and fussing around!

The young servant folded the cloak carefully into a camphorwood chest carved with woodland scenes. Rohain went into the small room indicated by the Chatelaine. Therein stood a copper tub on lion's feet, lined with white cambric that draped over the sides like falls of snow. The tub was filled with steaming water tinct with sweet oils and strewn with unseasonable primrose petals like flakes of the sun.

A marble washstand held a matching toiletry set. There was a pair of highly decorated enameled porcelain globes on high foot-rims, pierced all over to allow moisture to drain and evaporate. One contained scented soaps, the other a sponge. These were accompanied by somewhat superfluous porcelain soap stands, soap dishes and soap trays, ewers, jars, pots, candle-branches, and a vase overflowing with hothouse-forced snowdrop blossoms. Incongruously, a shoehorn lay on the floor. Made of pewter, it was mounted in ivory with carved and inlaid handles in the shape of herons.

The lady's maid spoke. "Wishest donna mine that sas pettibob shouldst lollo betrial?"

"I beg your pardon?"

The girl repeated her strange sentence, twisting a fold of her skirt in her fingers, gazing hopefully at her new mistress.

"I don't know what you are talking about. Please speak the common tongue."

The girl's face fell. "Forgive me, m'lady. Methought Your Ladyship might like to practice slingua for this night. I asked only whether Your Ladyship would like me to test the bathwater."

"Slingua?"

"Yes, m'lady—courtingle, some name it, or courtspeak.

Lower ranks call it jingle-jangle. Does Your Ladyship not have it?"

"No, I do not have such palaver."

It had sounded like childish babble, yet the girl seemed to hold great store by it. Could that curious string of quasi-words be part of the social fabric of Court?

"I will bathe now."

By this phrase, Rohain had meant to indicate that this Viviana should leave her alone. Instead, the girl stepped forward.

"Let me unfasten Your Ladyship's girdle—"

"No! I can do it myself. Leave me!"

With a look of despair, the lady's maid rushed from the room. Rohain's conscience was stricken. The girl had only been trying to do her duty as she saw it—but how annoying and confusing it all was! Rohain almost wished herself back in the woods with Sianadh and the wights. Existence had seemed simpler then: It was life or death—none of these perplexing customs and slangish vernacular.

A sound of stifled sobs emanated from the outer room.

What a featherbrain of a girl! Fancy having nothing better to cry about than a sharp word from her mistress! To one who had faced the Direath and the Beithir, it all seemed so superficial.

Rohain removed her girdle of leather and filigree, and struggled with the gown's difficult fastenings. Presently she peered around the door.

"Viviana, will you help me unlace?"

The lady's maid came willingly, red-eyed. Together they battled the endless buttons, the petticoats, the pinching, mincing little shoes.

Timidly: "Does my lady wish that I should soap her back!"

"No. I bathe alone." *Providence forbid, that the girl should see the whiplash-scars.*

Nervously: "Then shall I lay out Her Ladyship's raiment for the evening?"

"I have no other clothes—only what you see."

The girl's face crumpled as though she were about to cry again.

Rohain gathered her wits and said quickly, "Naturally, I shall require a more extensive wardrobe. You must soon expedite some purchases on my behalf." *It is fortunate that so much money remains to me from the sale of the emerald.*

The servant picked up her skirts and effected a dismal bob of acknowledgment.

Beyond the walls, the wind wailed.

Bathed and dressed, Rohain sat before a many-mirrored dressing-table in which she could scarcely recognize herself, while Viviana brushed out her coal-black locks. The courtier was subdued, doleful. Recalling only too well her own servitude, Rohain's heart went out to her. Anthills could appear to be mountains if one were an ant oneself, condemned to live among them daily. Softly, she said, "I come from a faraway place where Court customs and ways are not known. This seems to trouble you. Why so?"

"Indeed, my lady!" Viviana blurted out. "It troubles me, more than all the wights in Aia, because it will trouble you, my mistress!"

"Why should my tribulations be yours?"

"As your servant, your standing reflects on me. I shall suffer for it."

"You speak with honesty, if not tact. How shall my plain manners trouble me?"

Viviana spoke earnestly. "My lady, there is a way of going on that is not commissioned by those holding office, yet it has grown up in our midst. Here at Court, there is a self-styled elite Set or Circle. The Royal Family and the dukes and duchesses are not part of this courtiers' game, but many nobles below the degree of duke are counted Within the Set or Out of it, with the exception of the very old and the very young. If one is regarded as being Within the Set, one must fight to retain one's hold, for if one is Cut, which means cast Out, there is little chance of regaining one's place."

"Is it so terrible, to be Out of this Set?"

"Indeed, I would say that life is scarcely worth living! Until she witnesses with her own eyes, my lady will not know of what I speak. But by then it may be too late. If my lady is not included in the Set, she will want to leave Court and then I shall be sent back to be maidservant to the unmitigable Dowager Marchioness of Netherby-on-the-Fens! I'd as lief die, in honesty. 'Tis unspeakable, the manner in which the Marchioness treats us. She is continually finding fault and slapping us with her broad and pitiless hand."

Rohain assimilated this information, staring unseeing into the mirror.

"Tell me more."

"My lady, as the daughter of an earl, you shall be seated amidst the cream of the Set at table tonight—the very paragons of Court etiquette."

"What makes you think I am the daughter of an earl?"

"Oh, simply that your finger displays no wedding band, ma'am—despite that I caught a rumor you were a widow— and to be called by the title of 'Lady,' you must be the daughter of at least an earl, a marquess, or a duke. Yet since the name Tarrenys is not familiar at Court, methought it must be an earl, begging your pardon, Your Ladyship."

This was encouraging. Viviana possessed a certain acuity of mind, then, despite her frail emotional state. It seemed that during her stay at Court, no matter how brief, Rohain would need an ally. She studied the lady's maid in the mirror, seeing a rounded, dimpled face, a turned-up nose, a spot of color on each cheek, hazel eyes with brown lashes that did not match the bleached hair. A pretty lass, Viviana was clad in a houppelande of sky-blue velvet, with a girdle of stiffened wigan. In addition to the girdle, her waist was encircled by one of the popular accoutrements known as a chatelaine, from which depended fine chains attached to a vast assortment of compact and useful articles such as scissors, needle-cases, and buttonhooks.

"And I reckoned that my lady came from a faraway place," the girl chattered on, wielding the hairbrush, "because of the way m'lady thanked the Duke for his dinner invitation."

Rohain swiveled in alarm.

"Said I something incorrect?"

"Yea, verily, m'lady. A dinner invitation from a duke is a command. One must reply, 'I thank Your Grace for the kind invitation and have the honor to obey Your Grace's command.' I don't know what he thought, forsooth, but likely the lack of form did not irk him, for those of the Royal Attriod are above such matters."

"But you say that I will be scorned and reviled by others if I am ignorant of these complicated forms of etiquette?"

"In no small measure, m'lady! The cream of the Set can hang, draw, and quarter the ignorant, in a manner of speaking. Those they have scathed never prosper in Society. But 'tis not merely the forms of address and the slingua—'tis the table manners and all. Entire libraries could be devoted to them. Coming from a high-born family, Your Ladyship will have all the table manners, I'll warrant."

"Not necessarily."

Unbidden, images formed in Rohain's mind; the table at Ethlinn's house—everyone seated around, plucking food from a communal dish with their hands and wiping their greasy fingers on the tablecloth; Sianadh clutching a joint of meat in his fist and tearing at it with his teeth; thick bread trenchers used as plates, to soak up the gravies and juices and to be eaten last.

Rohain chewed her lip. To be catapulted from shame to glory and back to shame would be more than she could bear. And what if Thorn should attend this dinner, to witness her humiliation?

"Do the Dainnan attend the Royal Dining Hall?"

"Sometimes m'lady, when they do not dine in their own hall."

"Are you acquainted with any of the Dainnan?"

"Not I, m'lady."

"Viviana, why do the noble courtiers insist upon this? These dialects, these intricate manners you hint at—why are they necessary?"

"Marry, I vouch it is to show how clever they are, how much they deserve their station because they are privy to secrets of which the commoners know naught. Yet again, those of the highest degree do not concern themselves with slingua and such codes—they do not have to prove themselves worthy."

"Viviana, you are wise. I believe I have misjudged you. Teach me, that I may not be made an outcast this night."

"My lady, there is no time!" From somewhere down the labyrinths of corridors, a hum mounted to a reverberating crescendo—the sounding of a gong. "It is the dinner gong! In a few moments, a footman shall come to escort Your Ladyship to dinner. And then we are both ruined!"

"Calm yourself. Listen, you must help me. When I go to the table, stay beside me at all times. I will do as others do. Prompt me if I err."

"But my lady's hair is not yet coiffed appropriately!"

"Shall I wear the headdress to conceal it?"

"No, no—that design is not suitable for evening wear."

"Then attend to my hair."

"It will take long—"

"Nonsense! Do the best you can. We have moments, do we not?"

"Verily, m'lady."

Determinedly, Viviana swapped the hairbrush for a polished jarrahwood styling brush inlaid with colored enamels, its porcelain handle knopped with crystals. She twisted the heavy tresses, looping some of them high on her mistress's head. Securing them with one hand, she fumbled at the legion of assorted knickknack boxes, bottles, and jars set out on the dressing-table, fashioned from silver, ivory, wood, and porcelain. Rohain lifted a few lids, unscrewed several caps, to reveal pink and white powders, black paste, pastilles, gloves, buttons, buttonhooks, ribbons, decorative combs of bone, horn, or brass inlaid with tortoiseshell, silver pique barrettes, enameled butterfly clasps, scented essences, aromatic substances.

"What seek you?" Rohain winced in pain as Viviana in her haste tweaked a strand of hair.

"I seek pins for the coiffure."

A carved ivory box fell open, spewing jeweled pins. Viviana snatched them up and began thrusting them ruthlessly into Rohain's cloud of curls.

"Ouch!"

"Forgive me . . ."

"What is the purpose of these paints?"

"They are for the beautification of the face. Kohl for the eyes, creams and colored powders for the skin; rouge made from safflowers . . ."

Suddenly panicking, Rohain clapped her hands to her cheeks. In the looking-glass, her new visage had seemed unobjectionable to her, but how could she be certain that this was not merely wishful thinking? Her heart began hammering.

"Should I be using them?"

"Many courtiers do, but you need not, m'lady."

"Why not, if 'tis what others do? My face—is it acceptable? Tell me truly!"

"My lady already has the look that others wish to achieve—she needs no paint."

"What do you mean?"

Viviana halted her furious burst of hairdressing activity and planted her hands on her hips.

"Does my lady jest?"

"No. I do not jest. I wish you to tell me if my features are acceptable. Tell me now, and if they are not, I will not venture into that Hall this night, command or no command." Butterflies roiled in Rohain's stomach.

A loud rapping at the door startled them both. A voice called out imperatively.

"Yes, m'lady, yes they are!" Viviana squeaked hastily. "Quickly—to be late for dinner is an unpardonable lapse. M'lady would be Out before the first forkful."

"Then let us go."

The decoratively painted plaster walls of the great Royal Dining Hall, here and there covered with tapestries, soared to elaborately carved cornices and a domed, frescoed ceiling. Six fireplaces, three on either side, threw out enough warmth to fill its vaulted immensity. In a high gallery a trumpeter stood like a stalagmite dripped from the plaster ceiling plaques and chandeliers. He was one of the Royal Waits, wearing scarlet livery and the ceremonial chain of silver roses and pomegranates.

Along the walls, edifices of polished wooden shelves lit by mirror-backed girandoles displayed ornamental silverware, tempting platters heaped with fruits and cakes, covered cheese dishes disguised as little milk churns or cottages, silver chafing dishes with ivory handles, and glowing braziers of pierced brass ready to warm food. Liveried butlers and under-butlers stood at attention beside every board. Broad trestles ran down the length of the Hall, draped with pure white damask cloths, lozenge-patterned. The High Table, set up at right angles to this, stood upon a dais at one end. Its snowy wastes were bare of tableware, save for a quartet of surtouts, the seasons personified; grand sculptures in silver-gilt. Spring, her hair garlanded with blossom, caught butterflies. Summer, laurel-wreathed, held out her dainty hand for a perching lark. Autumn, twined with grapevines, dreamed by a corn-sheaf, and Winter, crowned with holly, danced. Candlelight glittered softly from their frozen glory.

The long tables, loaded with dinner service, made the High seem by comparison austere. Myriad white beeswax candles in branched candelabra reflected in fanciful epergnes of crystal or silvered basketwork, golden salvers lifted on pedestals and filled with sweetmeats or condiments, sets of silver spice-casters elaborately gadrooned, their fretted lids decorated with intricately pierced patterns, crystal cruets of herbal vinegars and oils, porcelain mustard pots with a blue underglaze motif of starfish, oval dish-supports with heating-lamps underneath, mirrored plateaux and low clusters of realistic flowers and leaves made from silk.

Quiet music wafted from an overhead gallery where a trio of minstrels fifed and strummed, ignored by the dour-faced Wait. A stream of noble courtiers flooded through the doors at the lower end of the Hall. At first glance they seemed not to be human, so fantastic was their raiment.

Not one of these ladies seemed to be clad in fewer than three garments at once: a shorter surcoat, a longer half-sleeved kirtle worn beneath, and a full-length tight-sleeved undershift, the three contrasting hems and pairs of sleeves all tailored to be cleverly revealed. Their outer sleeves either fitted at the shoulder and hung in loose folds to be gathered into a tight band at the wrist, or they were tight, with a roll or gathered puff at the shoulder, or bell-shaped, sometimes turned back to the elbow, showing the fur lining, sometimes gathered into a bunch at the shoulder and left to fall in deep folds under the arm. So ridiculously long and full were many of the sleeves that the lower sections had been tied in great knots to prevent them dragging along the floor. Rich embroideries covered every yard of fabric. From the ladies' girdles and chatelaines, harnessed with silver and gilt, hung keys and purses and little knives in pretty sheaths to match the armbands, brooches, and jeweled pins of these human peacocks.

Their headdresses were exaggerated affairs: horned, steepled, gabled, flowerpot, or resembling wide, fretted boxes. Taltries being unnecessary within dominite walls, the lords burdened their heads instead with large beaver hats or generously draped millineries of velvet and cloth, or cockscombs of stiffened, scalloped fabrics. Liripipes of impractical length twined around their owners' heads and shoulders like strangler vines. There were hats with tippets dangling and flapping about, hats with coronets, hats with bulbous crowns, hats with long and voluptuous plumes and painted hoods. Dagged, jagged gorgets fell in a profusion of ornamented folds over the shoulders of the lords. Wide and embroidered tippets trailed to the ground.

With painted faces floating above brilliant damasks, velvets, figured satins, samite, keyrse, tisshew, cloth-of-gold, shot silks, saffian, cambric, gauze, partridge, and baudekyn, this magnificent crowd milled around the trestles and chairs of carven oak. They stood by their accustomed places with their squires and pages and other personal attendants keeping guard at their backs. Some courtiers carried their pet cats on their arms: highly bred miniature lynxes, caracals, and ocelots, trained to sit demurely at plateside and daintily share the feast.

"An it please my lady, wait behind the doors until the assembly be seated," the escorting footman had said. "The Steward of the Royal Dining Hall will proclaim my lady's name as she enters, in order that she may become known to all."

A trumpet sounded.

"Bide," whispered Viviana, attending close at Rohain's elbow. She added unreassuringly, "Ah, would that there had been time to enamel m'lady's fingernails—they look so *overgoren* bare."

Between fanfares, the voice of a steward or herald announced the arrival of various aristocrats of the upper echelons who took particular precedence. When these were seated, the rest took their places with a scraping of chairs and a murmur of conversation.

"Lady Rohain Tarrenys of the Sorrow Isles!"

Rohain entered the Dining Hall.

Like a lens concentrating light beams, the appearance of a newcomer drew immediate and intense attention. Aware of the covert glances, the open stares and whispers, Rohain felt the blood rush to her face. The Hall seemed overheated and stifling.

"This way, m'lady." An obsequious under-steward indicated an empty place and helped the new arrival arrange herself and her wayward petticoats into it. Rohain courageously lifted her eyes and nodded politely to those seated in her vicinity. Not one of them met her gaze for more than an instant, although she knew they scrutinized her intensely when she looked away. Her eyes scanned the faces of the rest of the company. Thorn was not among them. The under-steward introduced her to the young men seated on her left and right but she scarcely heard, so awed was she by the dazzling landscapes of the tables.

Another trumpet blast seemed to be a signal. At its sound, ewerers approached the tables bearing fish-shaped aquamaniles with spouted mouths, and proceeded to pour perfumed water over the diners' hands. The water fell into small porcelain bowls with perforated lids, and was thus hidden from view, being now polluted. Serviettes for drying were proffered, then whisked away along with bowls and ewers. Following the handwashing, a formidable procession of servants carried in massive covered platters that were set down in the few available spaces.

The High Table, with its canopy over the tall chair in the center, was so far removed that it would have been difficult to make out the faces of any seated there. However, it remained empty of diners and food. The small silver tools chained to Viviana's chatelaine jingled softly as she leaned to her mistress's ear.

"They will now begin the Credence and the Assaying. Your Ladyship need only wait."

"Why is the High Table empty?" murmured Rohain.

"The Royal Family and the Attriod, and others of the highest degree, frequently dine privately, in the Royal Dining Chamber or one of the parlors. The Lord Chamberlain, the Master of the Horse, and the Lord Steward have joined them this night; also the King-Emperor's Private Secretary, the Crown Equerry, and the Keeper of the Privy Purse. Many lords who were staying at Court have returned to their own estates, what with the threat from the north and all."

When the courtier referred to the northern menace, her tone became grim. Her flow of information abruptly ceased. Rohain sensed the undercurrent of apprehension behind the words, and her queasiness doubled. Namarre—that strange, wild land seemed so far away, and yet its very name loured like an airborne pestilence over the Royal City.

"And the Dainnan?" Rohain's gaze roved among the knights in white satin tabards seated along trestles at the far side of the Hall.

"Their tables are poorly attended. Only one *thriesniun* dines with us this night."

One of the courtiers seated nearby shot Viviana a censorious glance. She drew back and stood respectfully to attention as before.

At the top end of the long tables were arranged the earls and countesses, the viscounts and viscountesses, and one marquess. There, among side tables, moved the Tasters, who were commissioned with the job of dying if the food should be poisoned. They swallowed morsels with grace, deliberation, and an air of the utmost insouciance. Assayers touched the food with serpents' tongues, crystals, agates, serpentine, and jewels from toads' heads, all of which would change color or bleed should poison be present.

"With all these boats at table, one imagines that the Cook has arranged something diverting in the way of marine vittles for the second course," drawled the drooping-eyed courtier seated to the left of Rohain. Detached sleeves were tied at his shoulders with the laces they called "points." Beneath them, the sleeve of his doublet was slit up to the shoulder to reveal a third set of sleeves, those of his silken shirt.

Noting the nautical salt cellars, the sailing-ship serviettes, and the scallop-ended cutlery, Rohain forced a smile. "One would imagine so."

"Does my lady intend to stay long with us at Court?" casually enquired the long-jawed fellow to the right. He wore a short gown with bagpipe sleeves and a harness with bells attached, slung across his shoulder.

"I am uncertain, at this time . . ."

Butlers serenely poured wine: rose, white, and gold. Crystal goblets enhanced the brightness and color of the liquids. The rituals of Credence and Assaying seemed to be taking a long time. Making small talk was like mincing on a tightrope. Rohain felt that at any instant she might speak a false word and plunge into an abyss of condemnation. Catching her eye, Viviana nodded encouragingly.

"Ah, the 1081 vintage Eridorre," said Droop-Eyes, admiring the wine. "A good year. And at last, the Tasters cease. One might expire of thirst."

Yet another brazen fanfare clove the air.

The elderly marquess at the head of the table levered himself to his feet with difficulty, being stout and dreadfully gouty. Three long thin cords hung ornamentally from the yoke of his gown. Weighted with beads, they became entangled at the back, causing his page utmost concern. Heedlessly, the plum-cheeked aristocrat raised his goblet.

"Let the cups be charged for the Royal Toast!" he bellowed. The courtiers rose and looked around, holding high their goblets and drinking horns.

"To the health of the King-Emperor—may His Majesty live forever!"

With one voice, the company loudly echoed the marquess's sentiment. Crystal rang against crystal. At a nudge from Viviana, Rohain noted that all the other ladies were holding their goblets by the stems rather than by the bowls. Quickly she changed her grip, but not before someone snickered daintily. All then lifted their drinking vessels, tasted, looked around once more, and sat down.

"Let Dinner be served!" boomed the Master of the Dining Hall. "The Soup! Green turtle, lobster bisque, and cream of watercress!"

The elderly marquess at the head of the tables leaned back slightly. His squire draped a large and luxurious napkin over his left shoulder, it being a breach of etiquette to demolish the starched linen ships. At this signal, the other bodyservants followed suit. Silver domes were whipped off tureens of steaming liquids. The first course commenced.

"Much good do it you," the courtiers wished each other as they fell to, imbibing without a single slurp, with the exception of those at the head of the table where rank obviated the need for manners. By scrupulously imitating the other diners, Rohain won through the soup course. When the soup bowls had been removed, the top layer of the sanap was taken away, revealing a clean, unspotted layer beneath.

The seafood course was duly announced and launched with applause. It comprised a magnificent sturgeon that was carried around to be viewed before serving, to the accompaniment of a flute and violins played by musicians dressed as chefs. Two kitchen-hands wearing knives carried the horizontal nine-foot ladder upon which the whole baked sturgeon was laid out on leaves and flowers; beside them walked four footmen bearing flaming torches. The procession was led by the Head Porter, marching with ax in hand. After being paraded once around the table, the dish was borne out of the Hall for carving. During the entremet, the diners were entertained by acrobats and a couple of overdressed mortal dwarves riding wolfhounds.

At the actual serving of the marine fare, the diners picked up their silver fish forks in their right hands. With the edge of the implement, they cut off a small piece, then impaled it with the tines, raised the morsel to their mouths, and delicately closed their lips around it. The fork was put down while each piece was chewed, and taken up again to prepare the next bite.

Rohain had been accustomed to eating only with hands and knife. She had glimpsed forks once, in the Dining Hall of the Tower—more common had been the sight of the larger versions used to pitch hay up to stacks. Now she picked up the fork and held it as others did, with her index finger pointing toward the root of the tines. So intent was she on managing this with grace that she did not notice, until alerted by tittering, and an agonized whisper from Viana, that all others held their forks with the curved tines pointing downward. The newcomer had been in fact partly spearing and partly scooping, using the fork like a spoon. It would seem wantonly perverse to deny the fork its useful ladle-like qualities, yet that was exactly what was expected. Hastening to turn it over, she dropped the offending instrument. It clattered boorishly against her plate. Another gaffe. She found it impossible to eat flesh anyway, and only picked at the garnishes.

Across the table from Rohain and a little to the right sat a strikingly handsome lady, surrounded by many admirers. The ornate roll on her head, eighteen inches high and a yard in circumference, was bent around into a heart shape, the front worn low on the forehead, the sides raised to reveal gold-fretted nets covering her ears. Her fur-edged, cutaway surcoat revealed a contrasting, skintight kirtle. Huge quantities of fur had been lavished in the wide cuffs of sleeves that reached to the floor. Having ignored the newcomer up to the middle of the seafood course, she now tossed a flashing smile in her direction, saying,

"Dear Heart, how well you look, considering the travails of your long journey. Don't you think she looks well, Lady Calprisia? Isn't she just the prettiest thing? Lord Percival Richmond thinks so, don't you, Percival, you've scarcely taken your eyes from her all evening! Don't be alarmed, Dear Heart, Percival shall not bite, at least I don't think he shall!" She followed this with a chiming laugh. Others joined in.

"That is Lady Dianella," whispered Viviana. "Beware."

"Speak up now—don't be shy," continued the Lady Dianella. "How do you like our maritime theme for this evening?" The lady's smile was as brilliant as the jewels flashing at her throat, waist, and fingers.

"I—ah, it is wonderful," offered Rohain weakly, bedazzled.

The laugh carilloned.

"Wonderful, is it? Wonderful, she says, did you hear it? Marry, but she *does* have a word to say for herself after all. Such charming wit—can you believe it, Lord Jasper? I suppose you know far more about Seaships than we poor land-lovers, you coming from the Sorrow Isles. I am given to understand that those unfortunate lands are so named due to the number of shipwrecks which have occurred on their rocky shores, am I not correct? Is it true that the ship-wrecked mariners are welcomed into the arms of the ladies of the Sorrows?"

As if this beauty had said something infinitely scintillat-ing, her section of the table burst into loud guffaws, the an-tithesis of the restraint practiced in the Tower. Tear-eyed with mirth, Dianella added, "Do you like sailing, Lady Ro-hain?" which provoked a further outburst of merriment.

Rohain burned. "I know nothing of sailing," she said.

"La! Of course not, Dear Heart, your time would be de-voted to much feater accomplishments, naturally! Do you sing?"

"No."

"Perhaps the Lady Rohain plays a musical instrument," put in a lady with fake seashells and ropes of pearls bedi-zening her horned headdress, her hair having been drawn through the hollow horns and falling in waves from the ex-treme ends.

"No, I do not play."

"Do you then dance? One would suppose that you dance blissingly! We should like to see it," said the one referred to as Calprisia, taking her cue. Her dainty face was framed by a steeple headdress delicately painted with black lacework, from which trailed a starry veil.

"I am sorry to disappoint you—"

"Oh come! Do not be so modest! Hide not your talents—we only wish to encourage, in good sooth," said False Scallops.

"I can only applaud the talents of others."

"La! What must they do with their spare time in the Isles!" Dianella exclaimed. "One can scarcely begin to imagine!"

"And do they all wear their hair like yours?" asked Calprisia. " 'Tis a most intriguing style, so simple yet so . . . ah—"

"Simple!" said Dianella innocently, and to the amusement of her friends.

Rohain sensed credibility slipping like sand from her grasp. How should she respond—should she meet affront with austere civility? Exhibit disdain or try to match them at their game?

"Of course you likely find us complete scoundrels, here at Court," added Dianella. "No doubt you think us utter reprobates! What brings a polished lady like Rohain Tarrenys to our midst?"

"My business is with the Duke of Roxburgh."

That set her tormentress back, but the respite was only temporary.

Turning to the lord beside her, Dianella said, "Athal selevader chooseth sarva taraiz blurose."

"Fie! Aura donna believeth sa mid-uncouthants es," he replied, laughing.

"You must know I do not understand your slingua," said Rohain, flustered. "Why then do you speak it in front of me?"

She knew at once that she had erred again. Dianella's smile dropped from her face like a mask. She arched her eyebrows in a look of exaggerated surprise.

"Marry, because we are not *speaking* to you, that is why! La! Is the lady endeavoring to eavesdrop on our conversations? How churlish! Selevader taketh baelificence, Lord Percival."

"Dianella, really . . ." The droop-eyed lord protested halfheartedly.

"Pash com grape-melt es—sildrillion et gloriana. May aftermath sault-thou, et storfen-thou!" responded the other tartly. The rest went off into hoots of laughter. Lord Percival sulked throughout the remainder of the meal. Rohain sat drowning in misery.

"The Roast Beef!" roared the Master of the Dining Hall. The third course arrived. The Carver, a comely man with his knives in hand, walked into the Hall followed by the Taster, the Assayers, the Cup-Bearer, the Head Butler, and the Head Panter, all flanked by torchbearers. For the diversion of the company, he carved the meat in front of them, performing with the dexterity and flair of a juggler. He divided the beast into sections and speared entire joints on the carving fork, before lifting them into the air and shaving pieces off with a keen knife. Thin slices of meat fell to the trenchers in organized patterns, slightly overlapping. Swiftly, he used the knifepoint to place final touches to the arrangement. Salt was sprinkled over the dish before it was presented to the potential consumers. The courtiers served themselves from chased oval chafing dishes of vegetables, side dishes, and patés up and down the tables, and boats of thick sauces and gravies. Some allowed themselves a sprinkle from the personal nutmeg graters they carried at their belts: small silver boxes with a steel rasping-surface and a hinged lid at the top and bottom.

Through the croon and purr of shallow conversation pricked by the tinkle of crystal and artificial laughter, a far-off, eldritch howling sent sudden shivers through the assembly. Then a deeper note rumbled, so deep that it was felt, not heard. The bass vibration rumbled up through their feet and set the wine to rippling in the goblets. The small table-dogs about the floor began to yap. The pet cats bristled. As exclamations of astonishment flew like angry

wasps around the tables, the tall windows snapped alight
with a white blaze. Cries of alarm pierced the air, followed
by laughter.

"'Tis only the beginnings of a natural storm," the
courtiers reassured one another. "I heard the cry of the
Howlaa."

But what a storm.

It was as though some great pent-up anger had been un-
leashed, which threatened to pound the city to rubble and
shake the palace to its very roots. The wind sang in a multitude of voices, like the keening of women lamenting lost
lovers and the deep groaning of old men in pain, like the
yowling of wolves baying at the moon and shrill pipes
whistling in the chimneys, or the boom of some monstrous
creature of the deep oceans. The banners and standards atop
the palace had to be hastily lowered, for fear that they
would be ripped to tatters. Slates tumbled from the roofs,
smashing in the courtyards below. The trees in the gardens
bent low, moaning. Their boughs whipped and cracked.
Sudden whirls of leaves gusted by.

In the Royal Dining Hall, servants covered the light-
stabbed windowpanes with heavy draperies, but no fabric
seemed thick enough to banish those incandescent flashes.
Bolts came hurtling out of the sky, one after another. The
trio of musicians increased its volume, trying to be heard
over the rain, the wind, and the thunder.

A fire-eater and a stilt-walker endeavored to attract attention. A juggler performed amazing feats with plates and
balls and sticks and flaming brands to while away the next
entremet. He was largely ignored, except when he dropped
something on his foot and hopped about clutching it,
squawking. The Court thought it the best part of the act and
applauded.

The fourth course, a pair of swans, was brought into the
Hall on a silver dish by two comely young serving-girls in

plumed costumes. The birds had been flayed carefully so as to leave their feathered skins intact, then stuffed and roasted before their feathers were sewn back on, their heads replaced complete with jeweled collars, and their feet gilded.

Visualizing the swan-girl at the cottage of Maeve One-Eye, Rohain recoiled in horror, then tried to disguise her reaction, dabbing at her mouth with a tiny kerchief presented by her lady's maid. *But wights cannot be slain,* she recalled with a rush of relief.

The counterfeit swanmaidens presented their dish to the elderly marquess and it was then expertly divided up into modest morsels by the Carver.

During the dispatching of the swans, Dianella and her friends conversed with each other almost exclusively in slingua. Their eyes frequently flicked over the stranger among them. Sometimes they giggled behind their hands. Rohain toyed with her food, pretending to eat, sick to her stomach. She could think of nothing to say and only wished to leave the Hall and retire to the solitude of her suite.

Out beyond the dominite walls, thunder rolled its iron ball along the metal tunnel of the sky. Wind laid both hands on the palace roof and tried to wrench it off.

In readiness for dessert, the last layer of the sanap was removed to reveal the chaste tablecloth. Now the ladies of the heart of the Set, bored with each other, flung an occasional retort at the shrinking violet in the midst of their convivial bouquet—sweet words, sharp-edged and biting, liqueur laced with poison, swords beneath silk. Airily, they tossed her dignity from one barb to another, until it hung in shreds.

Lucent jellies, glossy syrups, smooth creams and blancmanges, cinnamon curds, glazed pastries, and fruit tartlets followed the last entremet. Rohain pictured the oleaginous scenes necessarily taking place in the sinks of the palace sculleries.

"When are we permitted to depart?" she murmured to her handmaiden. She felt nauseous, but not due to fancy's images.

"Not until my lord the Marquess of Early has left the table."

"I hope he lives up to his name."

"Won't you tell us what you are whispering about with your maid?" entreated False Scallops, the Lady Elmuretta.

"Yea, prithee, tell us!" chorused others, eagerly, eyes shining as they scented a further delicious opportunity to savor somebody's discomfiture and win one another's approval.

"Naught of importance."

"Oh, how provoking!" they cried, in tones of astonishment.

"Fie!" Elmaretta wagged a gilt-nailed, admonitory finger. "You must out with it. No whispering at table!"

"And besides, Dear Heart, everything you say is of importance to your friends!" added Dianella sweetly.

"Well," said Rohain boldly, "I was merely telling Viviana what the fox said to the ravening hounds."

"Oh? And what was that, pray?"

" 'When you have devoured me, let the weakest among you look over his shoulder.' "

The ladies exchanged glances.

"Is that intended for a joke?" queried Calprisia. "Marry, 'tis not very amusing."

"No, it is not amusing," her friends agreed. "What a very odd thing to say!"

"Are you sure you've not partaken of too much wine, Dear Heart?" said Dianella. "Or maybe not enough! Look, she's scarcely touched a drop. Butler! Fill up my lady Rohain!"

Several people laughed bawdily.

Rohain held her temper in check. To lose it would be the

final humiliation. Having scored, Dianella appeared to lose interest and turned away.

After distending his bloated belly a little farther by way of the inclusion of frumenty, the gouty old Marquess of Early was helped to his feet and made his exit with ceremony. Dinner, mercifully, was over.

Outside, the storm raged on.

The wattle-gold rooms were a haven.

"The lords had not such viperish tongues as the ladies," muttered Rohain wearily. "Not one of them said a word to degrade me."

"The lords have their own reasons for courtesy, my lady."

Rohain climbed the steps of the bed and sank into the feather-stuffed mattress.

In a small voice, Viviana said, "Your Ladyship ate very little. To be of modest appetite is considered chic."

"You are kind," returned Rohain, "and supported me as best you could against overwhelming odds. But I know how it is. I have failed. I shall never be included now. I am Out before ever I set foot Within."

It seemed a terrible disgrace, as though the world's weight had been set on her shoulders.

Having helped her mistress to bed, Viviana went to dine on the leavings, with the other maids of the lower ranks.

A pair of inhuman eyes, red coals piercing the gloom of a drain.

A stench of rotting matter and feces, stifling. A skittering and a chittering and a squeaking in the shadows, which were alive, running, slithering clumps and humps, black shapes climbing over one another and surging forward in a terrible, living tide. They were everywhere, in increasing numbers—under the bed, in the folds of the curtains and the canopy, falling with soft, heavy plops from the damask pelmet and the frilled valance like malignant raindrops, jammed, wriggling in corners, swarming up the elegant brass legs of the firescreen, smothering the matching firedogs, crawling up the gold-inlaid piers of the lacquered table, upsetting the bowl of oranges upheld on its silver pedestal by four winged babies.

They were rats, and they squeaked.

Their stealthy, filthy claws scratched and scratched. As they drew near, she saw that they wore the spiteful faces of courtiers. Soon they would come running, in long black streams, up the steps of the bed and across the embroidered eiderdown, along her arms to her face. Then they would cover her with their warm, stinking bodies and begin, with those needle fangs, to gouge, to gnaw, burrowing through the newly emptied eye sockets into the brain, until her flesh was devoured and blood gouted all over the silken pillows and ran down to pool on the meadowy carpets and all that remained was a sightless, staring skull.

Screaming, Rohain woke up.

Pale, pearly light suffused the windows. The pillars of the wattle-tree bed grew protectively all around. Her eyes roved the chamber. The fruits in the dish were not oranges but pears, onyx pomegranates, pastel-dyed marzipan plums, enameled porcelain apples, amethyst grapes.

Of rodents, there was no sign. Her hand brushed her forehead. Her breath came and went in shallow gasps, her skin felt damp with perspiration.

Viviana ran in, full of concern.

"My lady, what is it?"

"'Tis naught. Only a dream."

The windows rattled. Viviana went to them and pulled back the lace curtains. Bright sunlight streamed in. The storm had cleared.

Outside on a green hill near the garden wall, albino pea-cocks swaggered, unaware of their status in the eyes of the Royal Carver. Nannies monitored overdressed children freed from the Palace Nursery, frolicking with their wooden hobby-horses, their whipping-tops, their pet dwarf-horses the size of small dogs. Citizens of Caermelor peered in through the bars of the iron fence, past the shoulders of the Royal Guards, hoping to catch a glimpse of royalty. The se-questered children stared back, equally fascinated. A diminutive son of an earl drove past the window in a child-sized carriage drawn by sheep. Savagely he wielded the whip.

"What do you fear?" Rohain asked suddenly.

"I do not understand my lady's meaning," the court ser-vant parried uncertainly.

"I have a fear of rats," explained Rohain. "A fear most intense and unreasonable. After all, they are only small an-imals, relatively harmless, easily slain by foxes and lynxes. Why I should hate them so is beyond guessing."

"My cousin Rupert is in dread of the sound of tearing cloth," said Viviana.

"How strange!"

"Methinks it is not strange, m'lady. When he was but an infant, Rupert had a crooked hip. They used to bind it tightly so that it would grow straight. The binding was most painful for him—he used to wail when they did it. They would rip long pieces of linen to use as bandages, and this was the signal for his terror. So his fright remained, despite that he has now grown to manhood. My mother used to say everyone harbors at least one unreasonable dread, for it is human to do so. Mine is fear of spiders."

"Spiders? But they are lovely creatures, so clever, so delicate . . ."

Viviana shuddered. "Even to speak of them, ma'am, sets me atremble."

"Why must we have these fears?"

"I know not, m'lady, but it is said they begin early in childhood."

"Then," whispered Rohain to herself, "my childhood was troubled by rats."

Viviana glanced again toward the window. "Was that not the most fearful storm last night, my lady?" she asked, "It has weakened now, but the wind's still with us, although it is past noon."

"Past noon? I have slumbered too long. I would have been better off without those last moments."

"It is well that Your Ladyship woke now," Viviana said, with the air of one who has hitherto suppressed exciting news for the purpose of surprising her listener. "The Duke of Roxburgh's footman came here earlier, with a message, but I would not waken you. The Duke has already boarded a Windship bound for the north, but he left a message bidding my lady be ready to depart from Caermelor at sunset."

"So they are casting me out already?"

"Nay—my lady is to be taken aboard a Dainnan patrol ship, a swift craft of the air, for a voyage to the Lofty Mountains under the protection of Thomas Rhymer, Duke of Ercildoune. I have been instructed to attend Your Ladyship on this voyage." Her voice rose with exhilaration. "My lady, I have never traveled on a Windship before. This is the blissiest thing that's ever happened to me!"

"I am glad of it."

"Your Ladyship, I am utterly delirious to be accompanying you from this palace. I will be well away from the clutches of the Dowager Marchioness, at least for a time." The servant-courtier bobbed a small but exuberant curtsy.

"For longer than that, perhaps," smiled Rohain. "I will not give you up easily! Let us prepare."

"My lady, you shall require several changes of attire, as befits your rank," Viviana informed her. "I have taken the

liberty of notifying the Court tailors, who even as we speak
are altering several ready-made garments in accordance
with my estimation of m'lady's measurements. It will be
necessary, nonetheless, for you to summon them to a
fitting-session at the earliest opportunity."

"Well done, Mistress Wellesley!" said Rohain in admiration. "Have they told you the price?"

"Of course, m'lady! And 'twas not over-high, either. I
haggled somewhat," she added modestly.

"I shall straightway give you the money to pay these tailors."

Despite the frenzy of preparations that day, vision of the
rats did not crumble away for hours. Rohain knew it had not
been a dream, but a snippet of memory.

The Dainnan frigate clove the air at speed, with a following wind strong from the west, at around twenty knots.
Her timbers creaked. The decks rose and fell, lifted by rising currents on the windward slopes of the foothills and
tossed by turbulent downcurrents on the lee slopes. The
sweet fragrance of wet leaves rose from below, and the
twitterings of a multitude of roosting birds. Behind the vessel, across the sea, penduline clouds blackened the long, in-
fernal forge-fires of the guttering Winter sun. The sails'
shell-scoops glowed fuchsia for an evanescent moment before graying to somberness, scoured out by the raw and
grudging westerly. Soon the stars would appear.

Clutching the lee rails in one hand and her taltry-strings
in the other, Rohain of the Sorrows stood on the open deck.
She was looking back through the lower rigging at the
dwindling lights of Caermelor on the hill: the buttressed dominite palaces, dark and massive on the heights, their
crenellated shapes squatting among their battlement-
crowned turrets and spangled with many eyes; the fragile,
latticed columns of Mooring Masts like a forest of webby

trees; the spires; the sudden skyscraping upthrust of Caermelor Tower, the fortress of the First House of the Stormriders.

In the darkening courtyards and gardens of Caermelor, fountains would be tinkling unheard. Indoors, out of the cold, lords and ladies would be drinking mulled wine by their fires, serenaded by bards with harps and lutes. The watcher's heart ached with an abstruse longing—but not for *them*.

The ship having just entered an airflow of a greater velocity, the wind—traveling faster than the ship it drove—swept the dark tresses from Rohain's face. Long strands fluttered out on the airstream. Aloft in the rigging where shadowy sky-blue canvas cracked taut, Dainnan aeronauts called out to one another. The sails were constantly being trimmed. The men working them from the decks were standing in a snakepit of hemp and manila. The aeronaut on watch at the bows stood by the bell ready to sound warning of any ships sighted to port or starboard, ahead, above, or below. Crewmen coiled rope on the decks, checked gear and rigging for chafing, and often, in the course of their duties, strode past the two passengers at the taffrail, the only women aboard. Others of the Brotherhood voyaged aboard the Windship; a *thriesniun,* a detachment of seven-and-twenty Dainnan under their freely elected leader, Captain Heath. Thorn was not among them, and Rohain feared to inquire after him lest she besmirch his name by association, or appear to be brazen. And what would she do, should she be brought into his presence? Confess her passion? He had protected her and Diarmid on their journey across Eldaraigne, as was his duty. As a Dainnan he must safeguard the lives of citizens. The journey was over, the task done. The entwined cords of their lives had split and unraveled. But each time a tall olive-green–clad warrior strode by, her heart lurched like a ship windhooked. From sheer habit, the

Lady of the Sorrows pulled her sumptuous taltry closer around her face.

The ship heeled. Viviana staggered at her mistress's elbow. She looked pale.

"Come into the chartroom, m'lady. If the air or the ground should become bumpier, there is a goodly chance of being tossed overboard."

The courtier sidled like a crab across the deck, fell against a wall, and tiptoed back with involuntarily quick, light steps. Rohain watched in surprise. Personally, she found it little effort to compensate for the ship's movement.

The chartroom was lit by oil-lamps on hooks, sunflowers of light that swayed in a rhythmic dance with the shadows. Thomas Learmont, called the Rhymer, the Most Noble Duke of Ercildoune, Marquess of Ceolnnachta, Earl of Huntley Bank, Baron Achduart, and Royal Bard of Erith (to name only his principal titles) scratched his red goatee. He was poring over a map, alongside Aelfred, the ship's navigator. Lamplight glanced off the Bard's shoulder-length silken hanks of hair, turning them wine red against the robin's-egg blue velvet of his raiment. Around his neck coiled a torque of gold with sapphire eyes: the bardic snake-sigil.

At their first meeting, Rohain had almost mistaken him for Sianadh, not having expected to see red hair at Court, after all she had heard of the place. This man with the neatly trimmed *pique-devant* beard and dapper mustaches was not Sianadh, although he matched her lost friend in height and girth. The features of his freckled face were strong and pronounced, the eyes deepset and hooded beneath bushy eyebrows. Winged keys were stitched in gold all over his costume. A demi-cloak swung from his left shoulder, fastened by a zither-shaped brooch. True Thomas, as he was commonly called, had not questioned Rohain concerning the story she had told to Roxburgh. He was no fool, either; shrewdness dwelt behind those twinkling eyes. But for whatever reason, he took her at her word, for now.

The Bard's pale eyes now turned toward the visitor. He bowed and kissed the back of her hand.

"My lady."

She curtsied. "Your Grace."

"Thirty-four hours should see us at the Lofties, given that this fair westerly keeps up. We sail by night and day." He turned to his apprentice, a downy-chinned youth in the Bard's blue-and-gold livery. "Toby, is the rosewood lute re-strung?"

"Yes, Your Grace," said Toby, handing it over.

The Royal Bard appreciatively stroked the shiny rosewood and plucked a few strings, which gave out soft, bell-like notes.

"Good." He handed the instrument back to the apprentice. "See that it is kept tuned. As I do not have to remind you, new strings stretch, particularly in the changeable airs at these altitudes. Gerald, bring supper and wine. Roll up your maps, Master Aelfred—the lady and I shall dine here anon, with the captains. But first we shall stroll together on deck, if that is to m'lady's liking."

"My servant tells me I am likely to be tipped over-board."

"There is little chance of that for the duration of the next watch, m'lady," said Aelfred with a bow. "The ship will be passing over smooth and level territory. Turbulence is improbable."

"Then I accept Your Grace's kind invitation," said Rohain, exulting yet again in her newfound powers of speech.

Quarreling over the best perches, the birds settling in the treetops beneath the hull made noise enough for a dawn chorus. The celestial dome arching high overhead glowed softly with that luminous, aching blueness that is seen only at twilight, and then rarely. The rigging stood out in ruled black lines against it. The moon, just over the half, floated, bloated like a drowned fish.

"What a strange time of night—or day," mused Rohain politely as they stepped along the gently canting deck. "Is it day or night, I wonder? The moon and the sun are in the sky both at once. Birds carol as though they greet the morning. It is a *between* time—neither one nor the other; a border-hour."

Her companion offered her his arm and she reached past the wide perimeter of her petticoats to rest her hand lightly on his lace-cuffed wrist. The Duke of Ercildoune, Royal Bard and Rhymer to the King-Emperor, was a man of courtesy and learning. She had warmed to him at their first meeting.

"Speaking of borders," said the Bard, "puts me in mind of a very old tale. May I tell it to you? There are few pleasures greater, it seems to me, than indulging in storytelling on such an evening, at such an altitude."

"I would be honored, sir, to be told any tale by the Bard of the King-Emperor."

He inclined his head in a gesture of dignity and courtesy.

"There was once a fellow," he began, "named Carthy McKeightley—a braggart who took to boasting that he could best any wight in a contest of wit. These brash words eventually came to the ears of Huon himself . . ."

Panic seized Rohain. She struggled to conceal it.

"And," Ercildoune continued, gazing out over the starboard side without noting her distress, "being of a sporting nature, the Antlered One challenged McKeightley to play at cards with him, a challenge which McKeightley, to uphold his words, must accept. To make it interesting, the life of the loser would be at stake.

" 'Be certain!' said Huon the Hunter, lowering his great antlers threateningly. 'If I outwit you, your life shall be forfeit, whether you be within your house of rowan and iron or without it. If you run I shall come after you with my hounds, the Coonanuin, and I swear that I shall take you.'

"To this, McKeightley blithely agreed."

The storyteller paused. Having recovered her composure, Rohain smiled and nodded.

"Wily as McKeightley was," said Ercildoune, "Huon was craftier. The game lasted for three days and three nights and at the end of it the unseelie wight was the winner.

" 'Now I shall devour you,' he said.

"But McKeightley jumped up and fled to his house, locking the rowan-wood doors and windows with iron bolts. It was no ordinary house, built as it was of stone, with walls four feet thick. Every kind of charm was built into it.

"The Antlered One came to the door like a dark thundercloud, with eyes of lightning, and said, 'McKeightley, your iron bars will not stay me. You have pledged me your life, both outside your house and within it. I will devour you.'

"With that, he struck a mighty blow on the door. Every hinge and lock in the place shivered to pieces and the door burst apart. But when the mighty Huon strode in, McKeightley was nowhere to be seen.

" 'You cannot hide,' laughed the unseelie lord. 'My servants will sniff you out.'

" 'Oh, I am not hiding,' said a voice from somewhere near the chimney. 'After such a long game I am hungry. I am merely sitting down to dinner.'

" 'Not before I eat,' said the Antlered One.

" 'I fear I cannot invite you to join me,' said the voice. 'There is not enough room for a big fellow like you here in the walls where I now dwell, *neither within my house nor without it.*'

"Huon gave a howl of rage and disappeared with a thunderclap!"

"But how clever!" said Rohain with a smile. "Did McKeightley spend the rest of his days living in his walls?"

"No, for he had in fact outwitted the Antlered One and so had won the contest. He had a sort of immunity from the creature from then on, and his boastfulness became legendary. He infuriated a good many more folk of many kinds, but surprisingly, lived to a ripe old age; overripe, really, almost rotten.

"The wrath of Huon was, however, formidable, and upon other mortals he wrought vengeance for this trick. I always air this geste when Roxburgh wishes to dispute my tenet that the brain is mightier than the thew. Do you not agree the tale indicates, my lady, that wit wins where muscle fails?"

"Why yes. The walls—how astute!"

"Yea, verily," said the Bard, nodding his head. "Walls and borders and marches are strange situations—neither of one place nor the other."

Rohain looked up at the sky, now colorless. To the west, cumulus clouds converged, boiling in some disturbance of the upper atmosphere. She half-expected to see dark shapes sweep across them, howling for blood.

"Pray, tell me of the Unseelie Attriod," she said in a low voice. "Where I come from, they will not even speak of it, believing that the mere mention brings ill fortune."

"They may be right," replied Thomas of Ercildoune, "under some circumstances; for things of eldritch mislike being spoken of and have ways of listening in. But I'll vouch we are safe enough here, mark you! In times past the Unseelie Attriod was the anathema of the Royal Attriod, of which I am currently a member, as you must be aware. An Attriod, of course, consists of seven members, one of whom leads and two of whom are the leader's second-in-command."

He slid a jeweled dagger from a sheath at his belt and

with the point scratched a pattern on the upright panels of the poop deck.

"This is how an Attriod is shaped. If the leader is placed at the top and the others in a triangle, with four along the base, a very strong structure will be created—a self-supporting, self-contained framework with the leader at the pinnacle, at the fulcrum, from which he can use afar. It may be seen as an arrowhead, if you like. Each member must contribute particular talents to the whole, such that when locked into position, the structure lacks nothing. As Roxburgh and I now stand at the left and right shoulders of the King-Emperor, so, in macabre travesty, Huon the Hunter and the Each Uisge, the most malign of all waterhorses, once long ago flanked their leader."

"Who were the others?"

"They were four terrible princes of unseelie: Gull, the Spriggan Chieftain; the Cearb who is called the Killing One—a monster who can shake the ground to its roots; Cuachag of the fuathan; and the Athach, the dark and monstrous shape-shifter. That is—or rather, *was* the Unseelie Attriod, whom some called the Nightmare Princes."

"What of their leader?"

"The Waelghast was struck down. They are leaderless now, and scattered. Many centuries ago, the Waelghast made an enemy of the High King of the Faêran, but eventually it was a mortal who struck the deciding blow, putting an end to the power of that Lord of Unseelie."

For a few moments a thoughtful silence hung between them.

"Yet these Hunters are not the only scourges of the skies, sir," said Rohain at last. "Mortal men can be as deadly. Do pirates frequent these regions?"

"None have been seen. If we encounter them 'twill be they who have the worst of it, for this frigate is heavily armed and those who sail in her are not unskilled in war-riorship."

"There is a place . . ." Rohain hesitated.

"Aye?" prompted the Bard.

"There is a place in the mountains, a deep and narrow cleft. The sun rises over a peak shaped like three standing men. To the west stands a pile of great, flat stones atop a crag. As the sun's light hits the topmost stone, it turns around three times. Pirate ships shelter in that place."

Ercildoune revealed no reaction to this astonishing news, not by the merest facial twitch.

"A ravine, you say, between the Old Men of Torr and one of those un*lorraly* formations in stone they call a cheesewring," he replied, "of which there are said to be several in the Lofties. This knowledge may prove to be of great use. How you came by it is your own affair, my dear. Be assured, it will be acted upon. But let us speak no more of wickedness. Let us to the cabin—the night grows cold."

Just before they bent their heads to pass though the low door, Rohain saw the Bard glance over his shoulder, to the northern horizon. It was a gesture that was becoming familiar to her since her arrival at Court. The awareness of strange and hostile forces gathering in Namarre was never far away. It was always felt, even if not voiced.

Besides Captain Heath of the *thriesniun,* another Dainnan captain sailed aboard the frigate *Peregrine.* He was the ship's captain, a skyfarer with the Dainnan kenning of "Tide." These two took supper with Ercildoune and their lady guide, dining in the Ertish manner, with total disregard for forks.

Conversation in the captain's mess was dominated by the kindly Bard, who was never at a loss for words. As she grew to know him better, Rohain noted some indefinable similarity between him and the Duke of Roxburgh.

"How describe they us, in the Sorrow Isles?" he asked her.

"With words of praise, sir. The name of Thomas, Duke of Ercildoune, is well-known and highly regarded."

"And no doubt many an anecdote is told thereof."

"All are tales of chivalry."

"And musicianship?"

"Most assuredly!"

"Since Thomas of Ercildoune is spoken of, perhaps you are aware of the geas he carries with him," subjoined Sir Heath.

"Is it true, then?" asked Rohain, recalling one of Brinkworth's histories concerning the Royal Bard. "I feared that to ask about it would appear discourteous."

"Yes, 'tis true," answered the Bard. "I never utter a lie. This virtuous practice, if virtuous it can be called, is a bitterbynde I have sworn to, and shall never break."

"Such a quality," said Rohain, "must be as a two-edged sword, for while His Grace's word is trusted by all, he likely finds himself in an unenviable position when obliged to comment upon the charms of a noblewoman whose aspect has not been graced by nature."

The Dainnan captains grinned.

How glibly the words came to Rohain's lips! By rights, she thought, her tongue ought to have rusted from disuse. Wordsmithing came very easily, considering that she had been for so long mute. With the birth of a new persona, she could become whomsoever she pleased. But what manner of woman was she, this Rohain of the Sorrows? Given the power of speech, she had already used it to lie and flatter, to vent anger. Could this be the character that memory had suppressed?

"Zounds, you are sympathetic!" The Bard smiled broadly at his demure guest. "Indeed, when it comes to flattery, I am not in the contest. As for hawking my own wares, exaggerated boasting is impossible—only in song and poesy have I license to give rein to fancy. Over the years, I have learned to avoid awkward dilemmas. Never was I a liar or a braggart, but I have come to be of the opinion, since I was gifted with this bitterbynde, that a little white lying, like a little white wine, can be good for one's constitution. Unfortunately, I am incapable of it." He reached for the rosewood lute, and as an afterthought added, "Of course, there is a curb on truth as there is on every facility of man. That is, one can only speak the truth *as one believes it oneself.* If you were to tell me a lie and I were to believe it, I should repeat it to another as a veracity." He plucked a string of the instrument. "I am for some song—what say you? I have one that I think shall please you."

"I should like to hear it!" exclaimed Rohain.

Experimentally, the Bard strummed a few chords, then began to sing:

One holds to one's ritual customs, one's intricate, adamant code;
One's strictly correct with one's manners, in line with the mode.
Real ladies are frugal when dining; to bulge at the waist would be vile!
Their forms must be slender as willows—of course, it's the style.

One's speech is quite blissingly novel—'tis far from colloquial brogue!
And common folk don't understand it; they're not in the vogue.
One's raiment's expensively lavish and drives ev'ry suitor quite mad.
One's tailors are paid to keep up with each glorious fad.

One's hairstyles defy all description; each strand is coiffed
    right to the end.
One needs to put up with the anguish to be in the trend.
We carefully choose whom to cherish with fine and
    fastidious passion;
'Tis seemly for one to be seen with the doyens of fashion!

Between each verse he led a facetious chorus of *fal-lal-
lals* in which, after the first time around, everyone joined,
masters and servants alike. The song concluded amid general merriment.

Later, talk among the Dainnan captains turned to weight-
ier matters, such as the strength and numbers of the rebels
in the unquiet north. Rohain could only listen in growing
consternation, untutored as she was in the ways of warfare.

"And how do their tactics serve the barbarians of Namarre?" asked Sir Heath.

Ercildoune replied, "Reports say they are but loosely organized under their several chieftains. They shun pitched
battles. Instead they use their speed and horsemanship to
ride swiftly from location to location, assailing isolated de-
tachments, intercepting convoys and plaguing columns on
the march. Until they feel confident of winning, they try to
avoid full-blown conflict."

"I have heard additionally," said Sir Tide, "that their
light horsemen also use the classic tactics of feigned flight,
luring our troops into ambushes or doubling back at a pre-
arranged position and charging the pursuers."

The Bard nodded and went on to describe other maneu-
vers performed by the rebels in their constant harassment of
northern Eldaraigne by land and sea. Of the unseelie wights
being drawn to Namarre by a Summons undetectable to
mortalkind, little was discussed. By this omission, Rohain
guessed the true depth of the men's unease. The ways of eldritch wights were alien, often incomprehensible. Who

could guess what horrors might come of such an unprecedented mustering?

Thus in conversation the evening passed, until it was time for the passengers to retire to their cabins.

The role of bard was one of the most important and highly regarded functions in society. Historian, record-keeper, songmaker, entertainer: a bard was an exalted figure and a good bard a treasured auxiliary to any person of high birth. "Second only to jesters in consequence," Thomas of Ercildoune himself had drily proclaimed.

He being probably the most learned man in the five kingdoms, later in the voyage Rohain tapped him for information about the Talith: how many were known to dwell in Erith, where they were located, whether any Talith maidens had been reported lost or taken by wights during the past year or so. He gave her many details about the yellow-haired people, yet although he spoke at length, nothing he revealed gave any clue as to her origins.

But he was merry company, and the Dainnan captains, if sterner and more watchful, were also quick to smile and exchange banter. In song, story, and discussion of the foibles and quirks of courtiers, the voyage passed swiftly.

An unstorm came casting its crepuscular veil and lighting the dusky forests with jewels of multihued fires. By night, the *Peregrine* wandered through a cloudscape of long white ridges and blue-gray valleys, smooth snowfields like bleached velvet, frosted mountains, blue abysses and hoary cliffs occupied only by silent towers of ivory and flocks of teased-wool sheep. The rising sun crayoned bright gold edges on them all.

Before dawn on the eighteenth of Nethilmis, the Windship reached the snow-tipped Lofties and was onhebbed to a lower, more perilous altitude so that Rohain could view the dark landscape. The sky, pure violet in the zenith, shaded to pale gray in the south. Northeastward, the low red rim of the sun burned, rayless. The snowy peaks glistened brilliantly in appliqué against the dull sky.

When at last they drifted over the shadowy pine forest wherein she and Sianadh had been lured by the malignant waterhorse, Rohain was able to get her bearings. Rugged Bellsteeple reared its glistening head in the north. Below it, the line of the distant escarpment was dimly visible across the terrain. Westward, wild, wide *cuinocco* grasslands stretched as far as the eye could see. There was the gleaming slash of the river-gorge, gouged by the Cuinocco Road on its route to the Rysingspill in the south.

On board the Windship, all attention was directed toward Rohain.

"This is the waterway we called 'Cuinocco's Way,' which springs from Bellsteeple. Where the land begins to rise"—she stretched out an arm and pointed—"that is the Waterstair."

Now the vessel flew up the river, directly above it, the hull's sildron repelling the shallow riverbed but unable to affect the water. In such narrow confines, Captain Tide ordered all sail to be furled. The *Peregrine* ran only on her quiet, well-oiled sildron engines. Progress was slow but inexorable. Below, jacarandas reached crooked fingers skyward, their cyanic glory now vanished. The firmament unrolled overhead like a sheet of beaten pewter.

Every memory of Sianadh threatened to overwhelm Rohain. She saw the river redgum trees lining the western shores where the walls of the gorge subsided; at this season the river, deprived of its lifeblood by ice's iron grip in the higher altitudes, ran at a low mark. Farther along, the treebridge still lay across the channel. There she and Sianadh had fled to safety and she had brought him water in a boot. Her mood grew melancholy.

In silence and despondence the refugee from Isse Tower came, for the second time, to Waterstair.

"Before daylight grows," said Sir Tide, "we shall onheb down to fifty feet and bring her in behind the trees. If any keep watch on this Waterstair, this ship shall not be seen by them."

The wind dropped. Light as ash keys, the winged, wind-dispersed fruits of ash trees, the *Peregrine* settled down amid tall firs. The port and starboard anchors were tossed out noiselessly in the brittle air. Landing-pods were rolled down on ropes and Sir Heath led his *thriesniun* forth. Like shadows they melted into the greenwood.

The sun stepped a little higher, but no rays bristled forth to pierce the greenery of a thousand shades in the cold, leafy galleries where the *Peregrine* bobbed, camouflaged by her mottled hull.

A Dainnan knight materialized silently below, the sage green of his raiment scarcely visible against the vegetation. Climbing a rope ladder as easily as another man might run up a stair, he came before the Bard, and addressing him by his honorary Dainnan kenning, delivered a message.

"My Lord Ash, the place is found. Prisoners have been taken. Lookouts have been posted through the forest. The way is clear."

Now the other passengers descended and made their way alongside the river.

The water's loquacious tongues muttered softly. Bushes and grasses beside Cuinocco's Way lay trampled and crushed. Vines lay shriveled at the cliff's foot. Rohain searched there for any signs of Sianadh—a fragment of clothing, perhaps; a belt buckle or an earring. She found nothing. Scavengers would have dragged away any carcass left aboveground to rot. His bones would lie scattered somewhere. She had heard it said that hair was an enduring thing, that in graves opened centuries after their occupation and sealing, even the bones had crumbled to dust but the hair yet remained undecayed. Would ruby filaments hang upon twigs here and there, blowing in the wind, all that remained—besides memories—of a true and steadfast friend?

She learned from Captain Heath all that had taken place on the ground while she and the Bard had been waiting in the Windship. Perhaps a dozen of Scalzo's men had been left to guard the doors of Waterstair. Their lookouts had not perceived the approach of the Dainnan, who moved as quietly as wild creatures. Some of the eastside men had been stationed around the skirts of the rocky pool into which the cascade poured—Sianadh's "porridge pot." There they had lolled unwarily. The Dainnan warriors had crept up unnoticed under the cover of the waterfall's noise and taken them without trouble.

However, beneath the water curtain it was a different story. Several of the guards had managed to seal themselves inside the cavern, having slipped through the doors when the surprise attack was launched. They had pulled the doors shut behind them.

The massive, decorative portals would not budge. The Dainnan, having discovered the stone game pieces atop the cliff, had as yet embarked upon no course of action. Twelve of their knights stood ringed around the wet stone platform in the cavern facing those impossibly tall doors, which glimmered green-gold under the gaze of the carved eagle. The ever-descending torrent at their backs cast its illusions on the eyes of those who watched them. As they stood braced, the knights seemed to be moving upward.

An indication of his calm faith in Dainnan prowess was given by Captain Heath, who allowed the lady passenger to accompany the Bard beneath the falls. Now Thomas of Er-cildoune stood before the doors of Waterstair. His eyes, squinting with intense concentration from beneath his embroidered taltry, moved across the motifs of twining leaves to the runes. Abruptly, the solemnity of his mien was broken by a flashing smile. He nodded at Sir Heath, who signaled his men. The Bard's chest expanded. He shouted out a single word, which rose above the cataract's thunder. Smoothly, as they had been designed to do, the doors swung open.

Instantly the Dainnan were inside. The tussle was brief; Scalzo's mercenaries had no chance of matching the King's warriors. The Dainnan took the armed guards without drawing their own weapons, in a spontaneous display of speed, strength, and force. In a short time, all were disarmed and restrained.

The treasure at last lay revealed.

So mighty was the mass of the hoard that although it had been despoiled, it seemed to Rohain there was no change in its magnitude. There lay the jeweled caskets, the candelabra, the weapons and armor, the cups and chalices, the gold plate, the coffers and chests overflowing with coins, the spidersilk garments. Over everything burned the cold, crystal flame of the swan-ship. Certainly no change had been wrought in the beauty and wholesomeness of any of the artifacts. So much beauty—and so much blood had been spilled for it.

Laying eyes on the preternatural ship, Captain Tide said, "Now I have seen the fairest ship in Aia." He wandered long on her decks and vowed that one day he would take her into the sky.

"All this is of Faêran make," said Ercildoune in amazement. "I trow it's lain here for many lives of kings—since the Fair Ones went under the hills. The door runes have kept their secret for a long time."

"How did you open the doors?" asked Heath.

"The password was plain to discover, for those who have studied the Faêran tongue, as I have. Written on these walls is a riddle. Loosely translated, it reads:

*In my silent raiment I tread the ground, but if my dwelling
is disturbed,
At whiles I rise up over the houses of heroes; my
trappings lift me high,
And then far and wide on the strength of the skies my
ornaments carry me over kingdoms,
Resounding loudly and singing melodiously, bright song.
Wayfaring spirit, when I am not resting on water or
ground.*

"The answer? A swan—*eunalainn,* as the Faêran would
say. That word is the key."

Now that her work had been completed by guiding the
King-Emperor's men to the hidden cache, Rohain was able
to withdraw to the sidelines. In the bitter chill of the morning, the captured eastsiders were brought in chains to the
hold of the Windship. Sir Heath and his Dainnan took over
with energetic efficiency, thoroughly exploring Waterstair's
cavities and cliffs, leaving nothing undisturbed, loading objects onto the Windship under the direction of the Bard,
with the use of sildron hoisters and floating transport plat-
forms.

"Behold," Ercildoune pointed out to Rohain, "no war-
harness exists here. All these most wondrous armors are intended for ceremonial purposes only. The Faêran had no
need of bodily protection in battle. They loved it for decoration but their fighting skills precluded the need for body-
shields. Also, while the Faêran could be diminished, they
could never be destroyed."

Among the booty was a set of thronelike chairs, each
adorned with carvings of flowers: marigolds of topaz and
crocodilite, roses of pink quartz, hyacinths of lapis lazuli,
their leaves cut from chrysoprase, olivine, jade. With a

spasm of pain, Rohain watched the poppy and lily chairs being loaded aboard. Visions from memory sprang to mind.

Settling himself back in the poppy throne, Sianadh took up a brimming cup, sampled it with a satisfied air, and watched the girl over the rim of it. She repeated every sign, almost to perfection.

"Ye left the fat out of the pig part."

Having corrected this he went to check on the helm of fruit juice, which, optimistically, he was trying to coax to ferment into something stronger. The girl idly flipped gold coins in the sunlight; they winked light and dark as they spun.

"This brow ought never to be plowed with sorrow," quoted Ercildoune as he drew Rohain aside, leaving Viviana alone to admire each new piece being hoisted on deck. They stood beneath the lichened arches of a melancholy willow that wept green tears at the water's edge,

"I grieve for departed friends," said Rohain, to explain her frown.

"Who does not? Yet such grief is merely selfishness. Hearken, Lady of the Sorrows, and be no longer of them. What we have uncovered here is as you promised, and more. This is a wealth of vast import. It might have been whittled away at the edges, pilfered by petty thieves over time, but you have rescued the greater part of it for its rightful owner. You have done the King-Emperor a great service and therefore you shall be appropriately rewarded. An it please the King-Emperor, you shall receive honors. I myself shall nominate you for a peerage in your own right. Lands and more shall be bestowed upon you, I'll warrant."

"I have only done my duty."

"Do not underestimate your deed. By nightfall, this lusty little bird of a frigate shall be loaded to her ailerons and ready to lumber through the sky like an overfed duck. Then we shall to Caermelor go in haste, leaving a goodly company of Dainnan behind to protect the King's interests. We shall arrive in triumph and in good time to make ready for the New Year's celebrations! Now, if that does not make your smile blossom, then you are not the sweet-tempered wench I took you for!"

His jollity being infectious, she smiled.

"Ha!" The Bard laughed, flinging his cap in the air. "All is well! I feel a song coming on!"

3
CAERMELOR, PART II
Story and Sentence

As warmer seasons wear away and nights begin to lengthen,
The power of the eldritch ones shall waken, wax, and strengthen.
Blithe heat and honest, artless light from all the lands shall wane,
Shadows shall veil what once was clear. Unpleasant things shall
  reign,
And mortal folk should all beware, who brave the longest night,
Of wickedness and trickedness—of fell, unseelie wight.

FOLK-CHANT

The Dainnan patrol frigate returned to Caermelor with its
cargo on the evening of the twenty-first of Nethilmis,
having waited twenty-four hours in the mountains for a favorable wind and then been blown off course by its fickle-
ness.

News from the north greeted them at the Royal City.
Roxburgh had returned already. Tension at the Namarran
border had recently eased somewhat. It seemed that for the

time being, at least, activity in Namarre had ground to a standstill. Insurrectionary lightning-raids had ceased and no spies had been seen for some time. An impasse had been reached, a breathing space in which the seditionists halted their mustering and proceeded to work only on fortifying their groundworks. As for the Imperial Legions, with most of the heavy equipment already in place, troops were kept busy performing military exercises.

This mortal state of affairs, however, did not apply to unseelie entities, which continued to be drawn, by degrees, into the north. What mortal or entity possessed the power to summon them could only be guessed, but it boded ill for the peace and stability of the Empire. A mood of suppressed fear insinuated itself throughout Caermelor, but the citizens endeavored to go about their daily lives as usual.

New Year's Eve drew nigh. This being the Midwinter festival, Imbrol, and the most important annual feast-time in Erith, the populace spared no effort to realize every traditional custom for the decoration of their surroundings and the entertainment, gratification, and nourishment of themselves. Here was a good reason to set aside their apprehension for a time and immerse themselves in jollity. All over Erith, in hovels and bothies, in cottages and crofts, in marketplaces, smithies, and workshops, in barracks, taverns, malt-houses, and inns, in manor houses, stately homes, and Towers, in halls and keeps, castles and palaces, they set holly garlands on rooftrees, ivy festoons around inglenooks, sprays of mistletoe above the doors and strobiled wreaths of pine and fir and spruce on every available projection. They chopped dried fruits, mixed them with suet, honey, and flour, wrapped this stodge in calico and boiled it for hours, then hung the lumpy puddings like traitors' heads, high in their butteries and spences. These and numerous other things the folk of Erith did in preparation for the Winter Solstice and the birth of the New Year, 1091.

This was the season when young lasses, whose hearts were stirred by something beyond the walls of the mortal world, dwelled upon the frightening and attractive possibility of going out into the wilderness during the long, enigmatic nights of Dorchamis in case the Coillach Gairm, the blue crone as ancient as Winter, as terrible and as miraculous, should choose to come silently, unannounced, and offer to them a coveted staff of power in exchange for whatever mortal asset she might wish to take for herself.

But that way was not for Lady Rohain of the Sorrows. She had no desire to wield eldritch powers through the Wand and would rather retain any human powers of which she found herself in possession. Having lived without several, she now valued them all too highly to risk forfeiture. That was for others to choose. Those who would be carlins generally carried that ambition from childhood.

Although Rohain knew where her future did not lie, she was uncertain as to where it did. In the city, festive splendor was the order of the day. Amidst the bustle and business of the preliminaries to Imbrol, Rohain learned that Ercildoune's nomination for her recognition by a peerage had indeed been sanctioned by the King-Emperor. Creation of a new peerage was a long-drawn and tedious affair; first the Letters Patent must be prepared, after which the new title would be posted and proclaimed. The appointment would be complete when she received the accolade personally from His Majesty. The scribes of the Lord High Chancellor were also arranging the handing over of titles to a modest but choice Crown Estate in Arcune, with a return of two hundred and seventy guineas per year, which was to be bestowed at her investiture. Meanwhile she, as treasure-revealer, had already been gifted with eighty golden guineas (most of which lay locked in the Royal Treasury for safekeeping, but some of which already weighed down the purses of city tradesfolk), and a casket of personal jewelry from Waterstair: rings, bracelets, fillets, torques, gorgets, pins, girdles, the value of which could only be guessed. The amnesiac lackey from the House of the Stormriders had become wealthy beyond all expectation, exalted beyond all hope.

The days leading up to Imbrol took on an insubstantial quality. It was all too much to absorb at once. Later, Rohain could not have explained what her feelings were at that time. She was conscious of performing all actions automatically, of being swept along by a tide of events she herself had set in motion, with visits to the tailor's, the milliner's, the shoemaker's, with Viviana fussing and exclaiming, dramatizing and exaggerating everything in her joy at knowing that at last she was free of the threat of being relegated to the service of the dreaded Dowager Marchioness of Netherby-on-the-Fens, and as if paying for this sense of relief by means of exerting her imagination, sculpting her mistress's hair into ever more fantastic designs and decorating it in ever more novel ways. She was well-intentioned and good-natured, this lady's maid; a lass who had lived a sheltered life, whose most feared hardship was a scolding, whose thoughts skimmed like swallows over the shallows, yet every so often dived deep and shrewdly, whose hands and chattering tongue were always fretting to be busy.

Testing the new powers springing from wealth and recognition, as a youth suddenly waking to manhood would experimentally flex expanded sinews, the prospective Baroness Rohain Tarrenys inquired discreetly after her friends. Messengers were dispatched, returning with the news that both Muirne and Diarmid had been accepted for military service and were training at Isenhammer. Farther afield, of the itinerant Maeve One-Eye there was no sign, which was not surprising, given the current season: Winter was the tenancy of the Coillach Gairm. Inquiries at Gilvaris

Tarv resulted in a message via Stormriders that the carlin Ethlinn Kavanagh-Bruadair also had ventured abroad in response to the subliminal call of the Winter Hag, or possibly only from habit. Her whereabouts were unknown. Roisin Tuillimh still dwelt at Tarv, hale and hearty. To Roisin, Muirne, and Diarmid, Rohain anonymously sent gifts. She wished to share her good fortune without revealing a past identity that, certainly at Court, would transform her into the subject of scandal and possibly revulsion.

Of Thorn, she dared not inquire, even discreetly, for she guessed that the Dainnan knights had ways of knowing what was whispered about any of their number. She existed in a paradoxical state between fear of meeting him again and hope of it. While her face had been masked by ugliness and there had been no question of her feelings being reciprocated, to adore him in secret had been the only possibility. She had been able to say to herself, "He cannot look upon me with favor; I am not worthy, but if I could be otherwise, he might look again." Now that a fairer face was revealed, she was vulnerable. If he should look upon her and dismiss her, it would be a rejection of the best she could be, rather than the worst, and thus the ultimate rebuff.

There was no doubt that Thorn had been kind to her, but kindness was of his nature. Besides, that benevolence had also been extended to Diarmid. Of the meaning of the parting kiss, she could not be certain. Had he bestowed it out of pity or—against logic—out of liking? On impulse, but with enough forethought to do it where no other eyes could bear witness? If the latter, then he would have regretted it afterward, in which case he would not wish to be reminded of his folly by a stranger who had infiltrated Court by means of deception. No: Her past association with the dark-haired Dainnan warrior was like a jewel of the most rare and precious kind, but so fragile that should the rigorous light of day fall upon it, it might crack asunder, crumble away. It must be locked away in the darkness of her mind's vault, to be cherished and kept entire, even though its loveliness could never in actuality be enjoyed again.

Without meeting him, the potential existed for happiness. There could be no risk. Yet she looked for his presence everywhere, as a lost wanderer would scan for any sign of water in a desert wasteland. The first glimpse of long black hair flowing over broad shoulders never failed to make her heart turn over. All sweetness, all joy, all light existed by his side, wherever he might be, and to be without his voice, the sight of him, the proximity of him, was to secretly live in wretchedness.

Sad longing dwelt on an inner level. Only a heart of stone could remain cold amid the festive revelry that day by day ascended toward its height. What was more, Rohain found herself surrounded by convivial company. Chief among these were Viviana, the irrepressible Thomas of Ercildoune, the Duchess Alys-Jannetta, Roxburgh's wife, with whom she had formed a friendship, and, in a surprising turn of events—or perhaps not so surprising—her erstwhile foe Dianella and that lady's faddish coterie. Now that she was to become a peer in her own right, was feted for her role in adding to the Royal Treasuries, and moreover appeared to be glaringly in favor with the King-Emperor and the greatest aristocrats at Court, Rohain had been accepted Into the Set.

Whether due to this fact or some other, a goodly number of dashing sons of peers both In and Out of the Set seemed to find her companionship to their taste. They were constantly begging her to wear their favors upon her sleeve when they fought their rivals with rapiers, at dawn, in secluded places. Like fighting cocks they tiresomely challenged each other to illicit duels over trivial hurts to their pride—contests that seldom eventuated. Some excuse was usually discovered at the eleventh hour, some pretext that

allowed both parties to retire with dignity and intact flesh.
Rohain scarcely had more than a moment to spare for each
of these heroes. Invitations from Dianella, Calprisia, Elmaretta, Percival, Jasper, and the rest of the trend-setting
circle continually bombarded her. Would she come gathering ivy and spruce in the King's Greenwood? It would be
such an amusing jaunt, with just enough danger to spice it,
although only seelie wights were said to dwell there and the
excursion would be guarded by outriders and carriage dogs
accompanying the barouches! Would she come glissanding
there, or hunting? Did she like to ride to the hounds? Would
she come and view the new dress Dianella's tailor was
sewing for her to wear on New Year's Eve? Would she
come fishing upon the sea, or ice-skating on the frozen
mountain lake where they were going in the Windship of
the Lord High Wizard Sargoth? And so on.

Not to appear unsociable, Rohain accepted their entreaties for her company, and they drew her into their so-
phisticated, butterfly crowd with joyousness, teaching her a
smattering of slingua so that she could become truly as
they. Their activities, in fact, turned out to be novel and diverting; their chatter boring. Rohain was glad enough of Ercildoune's frequent presence as an excuse to desert them.

Taking advantage of a break in the inclement weather,
she strolled with him in the Winter Garden, their attendants
keeping a discreet distance among the trees. Caermelor
Palace boasted a garden for every season of the year, each
walled off from the others so that its individual theme could
be enjoyed.

"You shall, of course, remain at Court until well after
Imbrol," said the Bard. "Much time may elapse until your
new title, Baroness of Arcune, is invested. Nothing can be
done to advance the proclamation of your title and the securing of your estate until after the festive season."

"I understood, sir, that one is normally presented to the

King-Emperor *before* residing at his Court. I have not yet been granted the honor of an audience with His Majesty."

"You speak knowledgeably, my dear, but these are troubled times. With the situation as it is in the north, with all this to-ing and fro-ing, councils and moots and so forth, normal procedures fall by the wayside. The King-Emperor is busy now as Imbrol approaches, and who knows but that at any time there may be a sudden escalation of belligerence in Namarre, leading to further need of his attention at the borders. Howbeit, it is not necessary for these military matters to hinder the bestowal of honors upon you. The title can be officially recognized merely by issue of Letters Patent granting full privileges of the honor and the posting and proclamation. Still, in good sooth, 'twould be a pity not to receive the peerage from the hands of our Sovereign himself, with all due pomp."

There were no fountains in the Winter Garden. The walks were lined instead with marble pedestals whose bases, dados, and entablements were richly carved. Atop these pedestals, great bowls of stone cupped living fires whose flames leaped like the petals of giant stained-glass magnolias.

Evergreens spread resinous boughs or stood virgate, as if upholding the sky, or else modestly wept. Barberry and cotoneaster hedges popped with ripe scarlet spheres. Here, too, grew laurels with dark purple fruit, and firethorns with their startling orange.

"I suppose I shall remain," said Rohain after some thought. Like a shimmerfly cloyed with honey, she felt herself to be trapped by a kind of inertia, mired in the sweetness of the luxurious Court environment. Indecision played a major part in her proposal to linger.

"Marry," said the Bard poetically and somewhat whimsically, "had you other plans? To return to the Sorrow Isles and tell your people of your fortune?"

"No."

"I confess, I am glad of that," he said suddenly. "A con-firmed bachelor have I always been, and vowed to remain, for I love the fair sex too much to restrict myself to the company of only one of their number. Despite this I find myself half inclined to pay you court."

His companion turned to him in astonishment.

"Look not askance, my lady! Am I not but one more in a long line of suitors?"

"Indeed, no!" she said emphatically.

"Then, what say you? Or is your heart already given, as I suspect?"

"Well, since you ask it—yes, my heart is already given."

"Alas."

His chest heaved with a gentle sigh. Subdued, they walked a little farther along the lakeside path where sharp-eyed robins bounced like plump berries, past a stone gazebo whose pillars repeated their symmetries and patterns in the water. Rohain could scarcely believe what she had heard—that she should have received homage from one of the high-est in the land.

"Then," said the Bard, "I will not speak of courting again. However, if you should chance to receive your heart again, will you think of me?"

"Most certainly, sir."

"And meanwhile, shall we remain friends?"

"Indeed! And sir, you honor me too much. I am not wor-thy."

"Alas," sighed the Bard once more, "I was ever a slave to a fair face."

Rohain stopped in her tracks, confused.

"A fair face?" she repeated.

"As fair as any I have seen," he said. "And when ani-mated, so that hectic roses bloom in the cheeks and a sparkle sets fire to the eyes, why, 'tis above all others most comely. 'Pon my troth, you are exquisite in every measure!" He laughed. "Like all women, my lady of the Sorrows loves praise, and it comes sweeter from True Thomas, verily, for 'tis not flattery but truth."

The girl leaned out over the still surface of the lake. Like quicksilver, it gleamed.

"Mind!" he warned. "Do not fall! 'Tis not the season for swimming!"

She did not hear him. Her taltry-enclosed face looked up at her from the water, framed by branches of evergreens, backed by the metallic sky.

"I cannot see it myself," she said with a frown.

"What? Brazen modesty?"

She straightened and turned to him.

"Nay!" he said, and it was his turn to be surprised as he read the honesty in her expression. "Not false humility. You see no special virtue in your own features. Odd! But charming. Let me assure you, my dear, that you are alone in your opinion. Ah, Rohain, I understated just now, thinking that you would know I jested, but I am too accustomed to the complex cerebrations of courtiers. Let me now do you justice—hearken—for yours is a beauty more radiant than a flame, more perfect than a snowflake, more enchanting than music, more astonishing than truth, and more poignant than the parting of lovers who know not whether they will ever meet again."

"You mock me, sir!"

Soberly he shook his head. "Not at all. When I look at you, my eyes are filled with a beauty to ache for, to make tyrants and slaves of men, a beauty to beware of. Be aware of it; others are."

"Gramercie," she stammered, nonplussed.

It was a revelation.

* * *

Once, between engagements, Rohain borrowed Ercil-doune's coach-and-four. His coachman drove her to Isen-hammer. From high on the hill overlooking the town, the drill, parades, and training exercises of the recruits for the Royal Legion Reserves were clearly visible below. Having descended, she moved among the young cavalrymen, foot soldiers, and archers, escorted by her lady's maid and two footmen.

The feeling of tension among the recruits was almost palpable. It was like the pulled-back string of a bow, on the point of letting the arrow fly. They executed their drill with extreme dedication and concentration. Sometimes, involuntarily, their eyes slid toward a certain horizon, their heads turning, in the gesture Rohain knew so well. The north: What dire events were brewing there, so far away?

Diarmid and Muirne, in cadet uniform of the Legion, appeared hale and content. They did not know her, nor did she wish that they should. She had no desire to receive thanks for the costly gifts she had sent them, nor did she want to behold the aloofness or perhaps distrust that would appear in their eyes should she reveal her identity.

It was not that she shunned her friends, but that she did not see how she might fit in with their chosen life-paths. It was her intention to ask them to share her new estate when the procedures were finalized. For now, she wanted to ensure that they dwelled in comfort, lacking nothing. She returned to Caermelor without having spoken to them.

Imbrol drew nigh. Meanwhile, Viviana Wellesley seemed to be enjoying her latest role.

"It is quite a feather in m'lady's cap, to have been invited to meet the Lady Maiwenna," she raved enthusiastically. "She does not mingle with many people at Court, for her manner is quite reserved. When I saw the two of you together, I thought you looked almost like sisters in some respect."

Rohain's spirits had been lifted by eager suspense when Ercildoune introduced her to the Talith gentlewoman who was said to be the last of the Royal Family of Avlantia. Yet her hopes were shattered. No recognition had registered in the green eyes of that golden damsel.

Her own hair was showing the slightest trace of a golden glimmer against the scalp, but this had not yet become apparent to anyone but herself. The elaborate, close-fitting headdresses fashionable at Court concealed her hairline. Her maidservant, busy chattering and clattering about with jeweled combs during the tedious coiffing sessions, had remained oblivious of the color contrast. By the way she habitually held her hand-work at arm's length, squinting, Rohain suspected her of long-sightedness or poor vision.

"Howbeit, no one can compare with my lady, of course," Viviana prattled on. "Upon my word, if I may take the liberty of saying so, my lady's face and figure are the envy of the Court. Such elegant limbs—no wider than my wrist, I'd swear—and a waist the size of my neck!"

Rohain ignored these compliments. Her new servant chattered more than necessary, yet she continued to prove herself a cornucopia of information about Court matters.

"When I told Dianella she would look well in green," said Rohain, "why did she exclaim, 'Odd's fish, how revolutionary!'?"

"My lady, the green is not to be worn. Not as a main color, anyway—only in bits for decoration, and then not the proper leaf green."

"Why not? Is it forbidden?"

Viviana was taken aback. "Wear they green in the Sorrow Isles then, m'lady?"

"No, no, but tell me."

"It is not forbidden, exactly, but it is not done to wear the green."

"The Dainnan wear it—a kind of green, at least."

"Begging your pardon, m'lady, it is not exactly green that Roxburgh's knights wear, but the color *dusken*. 'Tis as if a dyer mixed together brown paint, a little grayish, with mayhap a pinch of saffron—"

"And a good helping of grass green,"

"—and perhaps a hint of green. *Dusken* is not truly leaf green or grass green, m'lady, 'tis in the shades of dusty bracken-fern."

"I see. What of green furnishings?"

"They are allowable."

"And what of emeralds?"

"Green jewels ought to be worn with discretion. Royal purple is forbidden, of course," added the lady's maid warily, anxious not to offend her mistress by implying she was ignorant of such matters.

"Of course," replied her mistress. "But royal purple is reserved for royalty. Why should green be held in reserve?"

"Oh well, it was the color most favored by Themselves, and old customs die hard, m'lady. It was unlucky for mortals to wear it. Green was only for the Faêran."

The subject of the Faêran interested Rohain. For further information she went to Alys-Jannetta of Roxburgh, the wife of the Dainnan Chieftain. The Duchess, a level-headed gentlewoman of assertive spirit, liked to ride and hunt and shoot with a bow. On her chief estate she had a rose garden that she often tended with her own hands, not being afraid to dirty them. Rohain found her bold bluntness refreshing.

"I will give you one view," said the Duchess, "and others will give you another. For my part, I hold no good opinion of Themselves—as a race, that is—and I think it well that the Fair Realm was sundered from us so long ago. The old tales tell all. It was one law for mortals and another for the Faêran. A haughty folk they were, proud and arrogant, who thought nothing of stealing mortals who took their fancy. But if you would hear tales, why, there is only one man who knows them all and tells them so well, and that is our Royal Bard, Thomas. Come, we shall attend him."

It was Ercildoune who opened up the subject of the Faêran for Rohain as never before; he who possessed an inexhaustible supply of stories concerning them, he who awakened her interest in their lore and history and taught her of their beautiful, dangerous, vanished world: the lost kingdom, the Fair and Perilous Realm of the Faêran.

The Bard's palace suite was decorated to a musical theme. Across the tapestries on the walls of the Tambour Room, scenes from history and legend spread themselves. Here, seven maidens harped beneath flowering horse-chestnuts. There, a youth played a gittern to charm an evil lord into sleep, that the musician might recover his stolen wife. On another wall, a virgin beneath a green oak tree sang a unicorn to her side. Farther along, a row of trumpeters sounded a fanfare of triumph to a flower-strewn parade.

The room was crowded with crested arks and dark cabinets thickly carved with leaves, rosettes, and lions. A clear, red fire burned in the grate, beneath a chimney piece whose side panels were a carved marble relief depicting the beautiful water wights, the Asrai, lyres held in their slender fingers. Inscrutable footmen in the pale-blue-and-gold livery of Ercildoune stood to attention at the doors.

The Duke of Ercildoune welcomed his guests and settled them near the hearth. His apprentice Toby strummed softly. A small lynx purred on a ragged appliqué cushion that it had previously shredded with its claws. Five tiny moths flitted along the ornately carved friezes and architrave moldings, then fluttered down to the thickets of candles to dance with death. Viviana arranged her mistress's skirts. The Duchess of Roxburgh toyed with a tasseled fan, occasionally glancing at the velvet-draped windows that looked out over the Winter Garden, across the city to the ocean. A chill mist was rising from the river. The first star of evening had already punctured a sky both clear and dark. In the still and crystalline air, frost threatened.

To the Bard, Rohain said, "Your Grace, in these days I have passed at Court I have heard somewhat of the Fair Realm, and it has whetted my appetite, for I have little knowledge of the place or its denizens. Will you tell me more?"

Ercildoune's demeanor altered subtly at her words. From being the jovial host, he seemed to metamorphose, to become a stranger, remote, staring now into the fire.

"The stars," he said suddenly. His visage sharpened to a wistful look.

Rohain waited.

After a pause, he continued: "The stars. So beautiful, so mysterious, so alluring are they—so unreachable, pure, strange, and glorious that they could only be of Faêrie. Go into the wilderness on a clear night and look up. Look long. Then you will have seen something of Faêrie." His voice roughened to an uncharacteristic huskiness. "Or behold, at dusk in Springtime, drifts of white pear blossom glimmering palely through the gloom, for the turn of the seasons is evanescent as the beauty of the Fair Realm, which slipped through mortal fingers like handfuls of seed-pearls. The power of the Fair Realm cannot be comprehended."

He gazed into the fire's red world. Eventually he added, "The Realm is a place with no frontiers."

"You speak with longing and love, Your Grace," said Rohain wonderingly.

"Anyone would long and love, who had heard even a tenth of what I have heard."

"Yet is it a place? Did it exist?"

"Fie! Never say that it did not—I will not brook it!"

"Forgive me! I did not seek to denigrate that which stirs your passion."

"Nay," the Bard replied hastily, "you must forgive *me,* Rohain—I spoke too harshly just now."

"Well then," she answered lightly, bantering in the manner she had learned at Court, "if I am to forgive you, you must give me a tale about the Faêran, so that I can come to know them better."

"Gladly, for this is a subject dear to my heart."

He drew his chair closer to the hearth.

"The Faêran," he began, pronouncing the word as if he spoke some ancient, arcane spell, "had many names: the Gentry, the Strangers, the Secret Ones, the Lords of Gramarye, and other kennings. Their Realm had many names also. Some called it the Land of the Long Leaves. Before that, it was called Tirnan Alainn.

"Most of the Fair Folk were well-disposed towards mortals, but there were those who harbored ill-feeling, for, dare I say, the deeds of mortals are not always courteous. Of all the faults of Men condemned by the Faêran, they despised spying and stealing most of all.

"Long ago, before the ways between the Fair Realm and Aia were closed forever, there were places in Erith which the Faêran favored above others. Willowvale, in northern Eldaraigne, was one of these. At night, the Faêran would ride out through a right-of-way that used to lie under the green hill called the Culver, and go down to Willowvale. There they would bathe in the river and sing in harmony with the water as it flowed over its rocky bed, glinting beneath the moon's glow.

"One blossom-scented twilight in Spring, a little girl who was gathering primroses by the waterside heard the sound of laughter and music coming from the Culver, so she walked up the hill to investigate. The right-of-way lay open and she dared to peep inside. There she saw a sight to gladden her spirits: the Faêran folk, in their beauty and their gorgeous raiment. Some were banqueting, others were whirling about in graceful, lithesome dances. The child hastened home to inform her father, but the good farmer could not share her delight, because he knew that the Faêran would come for her. They guarded their privacy jealously. Any mortal who spied on them would either be sorely punished or else taken away to dwell forever with them, and he did not doubt that they would choose to take a little girl so fair and mild.

"Because he cherished his daughter and could not bear to upset her, the farmer did not tell her what would happen to her for spying on the Faêran. He went straight to a carlin who knew something of the laws of the Gentry.

"'They will come for your daughter at midnight tonight,' she told him, 'yet they will be powerless to take her if utter silence is maintained throughout your farmstead. When they come, you must ensure that there is no noise, apart from any made by the Faêran themselves. Even the faintest sigh, the softest tap of a fingernail, will shatter the charm.'

"Away to his house went the farmer. That night, he waited until his daughter had fallen asleep in her bed. Then he herded all the geese and hens into their coops, removed the bells from the necks of the milch-cows before shutting them into the byres, and locked the horses into the stables. He gave the dogs such a large dinner of bones and scraps that they lay down to sleep at once, their stomachs distended. He tied down anything that could sway and squeak in the slightest breeze. Then he came indoors, and laid the rocking-chair on its side, that it would not rock, and doused the hearth-fire so that there should be no spitting or snapping of sparks, and he sat down in the dark, cold, silent cottage to await the Faêran.

"At midnight they came.

"The latch on the garden gate went *click* and the hinges creaked as it swung open, then the farmer heard the clopping crunch of horses' hooves coming up the path. When they discovered the place so soundless and frozen, the riders hesitated. The farmer sat motionless and held his breath, lest they should hear even the slight whisper of the exhalation. The silence deepened, the minutes lengthened. The blood pounding at his temples sounded to him as loud as a blacksmith's hammer. Then there came the clatter of hooves turning around—the Faêran were leaving. He let go of his breath with no noise at all, but alas, he had overlooked one thing. At the sound of the Faêran horses beneath the window, the little spaniel that slept at the foot of his daughter's bed jumped up and barked. The charm was shattered. Instantly the farmer hastened up the stairs, his heart bolting, only to discover his worst fears realized. The bed was empty. His daughter was gone.

"Devastated by his bereavement, he resolved to try everything in his power to regain her. So wild was he with this anguish that straightaway, without waiting for the dawn, without eating or drinking, he went again to consult the carlin.

" 'Even in this extremity I can give you advice,' said she. 'Nonetheless, the challenge will be fraught with difficulty. You must take a sprig of rowan for protection and go to the Culver every night and lie down on top of it. Should they Themselves come to inquire your purpose, you must ask them to give back your daughter, but I warn you, what they may ask in return may not be easily guessed.'

"The farmer did as she had advised and on the third night the Faêran appeared before him and asked him why he should be so bold as to lie down on top of the Culver.

" 'I am come to ask for my daughter, who you took from me,' he said.

" 'Well then, you shall have her back,' they said, 'if, before Whiteflower's Day you bring to us three gifts—a cherry without a stone, a living bird that has no bone, and, from the oldest creature on your farm, a part of its body given without the shedding of any blood. If you come back with those three things, we will give you your daughter.'

"Hope sprang afresh in the farmer's heart as he departed. But then he asked himself, 'How can there be a cherry without a stone, save that I should cut the stone out of it? But I am certain that is not what they mean. As for the bird, I could kill a hen and take its bones out, but how shall I find a living bird with no bone? And what of the last part of the riddle—could it mean milk from my old cow, Buttercup? Yet milk is not really part of an animal's body. What if I cut off the tips of her horns? But wait—is not Dobbin the carthorse older than Buttercup?' He tormented himself looking for the answers but could find none, and the carlin could not help him further. Unable to rest, he took to roaming through the countryside, asking himself those questions over and over, and querying whomsoever he met, but with no success at all, and Whiteflower's Day was coming closer."

The Bard leaned to caress the soft fur of the lynx. Taking advantage of the interlude, the Duchess of Roxburgh said, "Whenever I hear this tale I wonder at the thickheadedness of that farmer. How could anyone not guess the answers to such simple riddles?"

The Bard smiled, saying, "Not all folk are as clever as Alys of Roxburgh."

"Hmph!" she returned, feigning a slap at him with her folded fan. "Go on with the tale!"

"Barely three weeks remained before Whiteflower's Day," resumed Ercildoune, "when, as he trudged along the road, the farmer met a beggar.

"'Prithee, sir,' said the ragged fellow, 'can you spare a crust? I am famished!'

"'A crust and more,' said the farmer feelingly. Opening

his leather wallet, he generously handed out bread, cheese, and apples. 'I know what suffering is,' he said sadly, 'and I would alleviate the distress of others if I am able.'

"'You have succored me,' said the beggar as he took the food, 'and in turn I will give you aid. The answer to your first question is: A cherry when it is a blossom, clasps no stone.'

"In amazement the farmer stared at the beggar, but the old fellow just walked away, smiling. Although he seemed to walk slowly he was along up the road in a trice and quickly disappeared around the corner. The farmer ran to catch up with him but when he rounded the bend all that he saw was the long, empty road stretching away to the distance, and no traveler upon it.

"Marveling, the farmer walked on. He was passing a spinney of chestnuts when he saw a thrush trying to escape from a kestrel, which stooped to kill it. Momentarily setting aside his woes, he seized a pebble from the roadside and hurled it at the hunting hawk. The kestrel fled, but the thrush returned. It fluttered down to perch on the bough of a thorn bush, regarding its rescuer with a bright and knowing eye.

"Seeing such a look, the farmer was hardly surprised when the bird opened its beak and spoke to him in melodious tones.

"'You acted in kindness. Now I will reward you with the answer to your second question. If a broody hen sits on an egg for fifteen days, that egg will hold a chicken without a bone yet formed in its body.' The man gaped at the little brown bird, but it trilled three musical notes and flew away.

"The farmer was vastly encouraged. 'Two answers!' he said triumphantly to himself, 'Two answers have I!' Then he thought, 'But what good are they if I cannot find the answer to the last question?' And he almost despaired.

"As he tramped on his way, frowning and cogitating

about the third riddle, there came to his ears a pathetic wailing. In the hedges bordering the road, a rabbit was trapped in a wire snare. Its crying moved the man to pity. Crouching beside the creature, he gently set it free, expecting it to run away forthwith.

"Like the thrush, it focused its gaze upon him. This time, he was not astonished, yet a sense of wonder welled in him.

" 'Sir,' piped the rabbit, 'you have done me a favor, therefore here is the final answer you require. If you cut off a lock of hair, it will come away from the body without shedding one drop of blood. As for the oldest creature on your farm, why the looking-glass will answer that.'

"When the farmer blinked the rabbit was gone, but he threw his cap into the air and ran jubilantly home. Hurrying to the chicken coop, he placed an egg under a broody hen. When fifteen days were past he took the shears and chopped off a lock of his own hair. Then he went out into the orchard and gathered a great bough of pink-and-white cherry blossoms. Throwing his cap in the air, he whooped for joy.

"He could hardly wait for night to fall. At sunset, he stuck a sprig of rowan in his cap and went down Willowvale and up to the top of the Culver. There he sat down and bided his time, and the stars came out over his head, and the night was warm and still, and yet he kept vigil. After a time he heard music and laughter, which seemed to be coming from beneath the hill, and soon the Faêran came. They were annoyed to see him there, but they could not touch him because of the sprig of rowan, and they could not abduct him because he had failed to transgress their code. When he showed them the blossom, the egg, and the lock of hair, they had to give him back his daughter. At first she gazed at her father in bewilderment, as one who has woken from a dream, but then she gave a cry of happiness and threw her arms around him. They returned home together, and never again did she try to spy on the Faêran."

With a discordant twang, a string broke on Toby's lyre. At the sound, the listeners started.

"The Faêran had their own laws," continued Ercildoune after a sidelong glance at his apprentice, "as this tale shows. And when those laws were broken, they meted out their own forms of punishment. Yet they were not unmerciful. First, they gave the farmer opportunity to reclaim his kin. Secondly, they tested him to see if he was worthy of reward. Because he showed kindness, they themselves gave him the answers to the riddles. Kindness in mortals was a virtue which they esteemed highly."

"Also great courage," Alys contributed.

"Aye, and neatness and cleanliness, and true love, and the keeping of promises," added the Bard.

With a practiced air, Toby removed the broken string from his lyre and unrolled a new one.

"I have learned," said Rohain, "that they delighted also in feasting, dancing, and riddles—a merry race, it seems they were, but also dangerous."

Ercildoune, leaning on his elbow, called for a page.

"Bring piment!" he said. "Does m'lady like piment?" he added, turning to Rohain.

"I know not what it is."

"A brew of red wine, honey, and spices."

"I am certain it would please me."

The Bard snapped his fingers and the lad hurried away. Toby plucked a rising scale of liquid notes to tune the string as he tightened it.

"Did they live under the hills?" pursued Rohain. "Was their Realm underground, in caves?"

Ercildoune laughed. "Not underground, not under water, not under or over anything. Faêrie lay elsewhere. It was Away. The traverses that linked Aia and the Fair Realm—

some called it the Perilous Realm—used to lie in such places as eldritch wights now see fit to haunt. There was an access under the Culver, as under certain other hills. These green mounds were known by many names, such as *raths, knowes, brughs, lisses,* and *sitheans* or *shians,* but passage existed also under lakes, in coppices, in wells, in high places and low. So you understand, Rohain, the little girl gathering primroses did not look into an underground cavern—she looked through a traverse into the Realm itself."

"Well," said Rohain, "abduction seems severe retribution for an unwary glance."

"It seems so to us," agreed Ercildoune. "Howbeit, bearing in mind that the Fair Realm could be a place of delight, the Faêran may have seen it merely as a way of preventing the child from telling others all that she had seen, and thus preempting an influx of human gawkers. Generally, they considered mortal spying to be an outrageous crime and they were swift to avenge, as I shall relate. But first allow me to provide you with a further example of traverses and mortal transgression."

A hallmarked lore-master, ever enthused by his trade, the Bard launched into another story.

"There was once a Faêran right-of-way at Lake Coumluch in the mountains of Finvarna. Coumluch is a solitary lake with a mist of white vapors ever on it and lofty cliffs rising all around. For most of the year the lake waters were unbroken by any reef, rock, or isle, but every Whiteflower's Day there would be an island in the lake's center, and at the same time a Door would appear in the face of the cliffs. The Door stood open, and if anyone should dare to enter they would follow a winding stair descending to a long, level passageway. This traverse beneath the lake was a right-of-way into the Fair Realm. At the top of a second stairway, a Door led out onto the island. Fair and stately was this domain, with its long, verdant lawns, its great drifts of per-

fumed flowers like clouds of colored silks and confetti, its
arbors dappled with freckles of golden light and lacy shade.
The Faêran made their bedazzled guests welcome, bedeck-
ing them with garlands of flowers. They plied them with
dainty viands and refreshing drafts, which were not of the
Fair Realm but had been brought—stolen, perhaps—from
Erith; for the Fair Folk did not wish to capture their guests,
only to entertain them, before letting them go. Neither
would they allow the Longing for Faêrie to come over
them. Eldritch wights struck up tunes on their fiddles—
Faêran musicians rarely played for the amusement of mortals—and the guests were invited to join the dancing. In
mirth and revelry the day fled by, and as evening drew in
the mortals must take their leave.

"The Faêran imposed only one condition on their visitors: that none should take anything from the island. Not so
much as a blade of grass or a pebble must be removed. The
gifts of flowers must all be put aside before the guests went
down the stairs to the passage beneath the lake.

"For centuries, this condition was met. Eventually, however, one man's curiosity overcame him. Just to see what
would happen, he plucked a rosebud from his garland before he put it aside, and slipped the bud into the pocket of
his coat.

"Down the stone stairs beneath the lake he went with the
rest of the departing crowd. Halfway along the passage he
felt in his pocket, but the rosebud was no longer there. At
this, terrible fear gripped him, for he guessed that the
Faêran had ways of knowing about transgressions like his.
He hastened to the Door in the cliff face, and passed
through it, and all the jovial crowd with him. As the last
guest passed out of the right-of-way, a voice cried, 'Woe to
ye, that ye should repay our hospitality with theft.' Then the
Door slammed shut and, as usual, not a crack remained to
show where it had been.

"But from that day forth, the island never reappeared on Whiteflower's Day, nor was there ever again any sign of the Door in the cliff face. The Faêran of the Isle never forgave mortals for that theft. They withdrew their annual invitation and closed that Gateway forever. One of the traverses to the Fair Realm was closed, never to be reopened, but it was only the first. Later, at the time of the Closing, all the rights-of-way were barred forever."

"Why?" asked Rohain.

"Mortals have done worse than steal flowers from the Fair Realm. Some of the Faêran were greatly angered by the deeds of our kind. They wished to have no more commerce with us."

"And you say that these traverses were barred forever? Can they not be reopened?"

"No."

"Perhaps it is for the best," suggested Rohain. Alys nodded.

"Never say so!" cried the Bard, now heated. "Aia has lost its link with a world of wonder such as mortals can only dream of. The Fair Realm was and remains a perilous land, aye, and in it were snares for the unwatchful and prison towers for the foolhardy, but it was far-reaching and unfathomed and lofty and filled with many things: all kinds of birds and beasts, shoreless oceans and stars beyond measure, beauty that is spellbinding and dangerous, gramarye both rich and strange, joyousness and sorrow as piercing as any Dainnan blade. In that Realm a man may have considered himself lucky to have roamed."

A lonely thread of music arose from outside in the night. Somewhere, someone was playing a reed flute. The thin piping in the key of E-flat minor jarred with Toby's recommenced strumming in some major key. Eventually the swooping notes and trills trailed off into silence.

The Bard said loudly, "Where's that piment?"

Two pages came hurrying in, one with a tray of goblets, the other with a steaming jug and a towel. The fragrant brew was poured. They drank a toast to the King-Emperor, then Ercildoune commenced his next tale.

"If you wish to understand more about the Faêran," he said, "you must hear the tale of Eilian."

Rohain inclined her head.

"Back in those olden times, an old couple came to Caermelor from the village of White Down Rory, to get a maidservant at the Winter Hiring Fair. They saw a comely lass with yellow hair standing a little apart from all the others and they spoke to her."

"A Talith maiden?" murmured Rohain.

"Aye, a Talith maiden, brought low by circumstance. She told them her name was Eilian, and she hired herself to them and came to their dwelling. In the villages thereabouts it was customary for the womenfolk to while away the long winter nights by spinning after supper. The new maidservant used to take herself out to the meadow to spin by moonlight, and some passersby said they saw the Faêran gathering around her, singing and dancing. Springtime came. As the days grew longer and the hedgerows budded and the cuckoo came back to the greenwood, Eilian ran away with the Faêran and was not seen again. To this day, the meadow where she was last seen is known as Eilian's Meadow, although folk have long forgotten the reason why.

"The old woman who had been Eilian's mistress was a midwife, and her reputation was such that she was in great demand all over the countryside, but she did not get any wealthier because those she tended were as poor as herself. About a year after Eilian's flight, on a cold, misty night with a drizzle of rain and a full moon, someone knocked at the old couple's door. The old woman opened it, to see a tall gentleman, wrapped in a cloak, holding by the bridle a gray horse.

" 'I am come to fetch you to my wife,' said he.

"Suspicious of the gentleman's exceptionally comely countenance and not altogether pleased by his haughty tone, the midwife was about to refuse, but a strange compulsion came over her. Despite herself, she gathered her gear and, getting up behind the stranger on his horse, rode with him until they came to Roscourt Moor. If you have ever been to Roscourt Moor you will have seen the rath they call Bryn Ithibion, the great green hill rising in the center of the moor. Bryn Ithibion resembles a ruined fort or stronghold, crowned with standing stones, with a large rocky cairn on the north slope. When the midwife and the stranger reached it, they dismounted and he led her through the side of the rath into a large cave. Behind a screen of donkey's skins at the farther end, on a rude bed of rushes and withered bracken, lay the wife. A smoky wood fire smoldered in a small brazier, hardly taking the dismal chill off the place.

"When the old woman had helped the wife to give birth, she sat on a rough wooden stool by the fire to dress the baby. The wife asked her to stay in the cave a fortnight, to which she agreed; her old heart pitied the wife, you see, for the birthgiving had grievously worn and pained her, and her surroundings were shoddy. Every day the tall stranger, the husband, brought them food and other requirements, and every day the child and the mother grew more healthy and robust.

"One day, the husband came to the old woman with a curiously carved little box of green-hued ointment, telling her to put some on the baby's eyelids but forbidding her to touch her own eyes with it. She did as he bade, but after she had put the box away, the old woman's left eye began to itch and she rubbed it with the same finger she had used on the baby's eyes.

"Instantly she saw a wonderful sight. The cave had disappeared, and in its place was a marvelous paneled chamber, decorated in green and gold, fit for royalty. Instead of being seated on a wooden stool before a guttering fire in a brazier, she found herself in a high-backed, carved chair near an open hearth, from which a glorious warmth was blazing. Deep-piled rugs covered the polished floor, gorgeous tapestries adorned every wall, and a gold framed mirror spanned the mantelpiece. Stifling her gasps of amazement, she crept across to where the lady lay asleep, no longer upon rushes, but on a featherbed endowed with sheets of ivory silk, the most luxurious pillows, and the richest of embroidered counterpanes. None other than the lovely yellow-haired Eilian lay sleeping there! The baby too who had before seemed a very ordinary little chap, was the comeliest child the midwife had ever nursed.

"Even more extraordinary was the fact that the old woman could only see all these marvels with her left eye. When she closed that eye and looked with her right, she saw everything as it had first appeared: the rough stone walls, the humble couch of rushes, the crude, unplaned furniture, and the floor of beaten dirt.

"Prudently, she did not mention her acquired faculty of vision, but while she dwelled in the cave she kept her left eye open during her waking hours, although it was sometimes confusing, and she must repeatedly wink with the right—and in this fashion she came to acquire much information about the Faêran.

"At last it was time for the midwife to go home. The tall stranger took her on horseback to her door, and once there he pushed into her hands a purse bulging with coins. Before she could thank him he was up on his horse and galloping away. Hurrying indoors she poured the money out on the kitchen table. A hill of gold gleamed before her eyes, and in great excitement she counted it. Soon she realized she had enough gold to keep herself and her husband in ease for the rest of their lives.

"What with her wealth and her power of seeing through Faêran glamour, the old woman considered herself fortunate indeed. Wise enough to know that having the Sight and the gold would put her neighbors in awe of her and cultivate jealousy amongst them, she said nothing about it to anyone. Besides, it was well-known that the Faêran would be vexed if any kindness of theirs was revealed to all and sundry. She even concealed her faculty and her fortune from her husband, in case he should inadvertently betray the secrets.

"Sometimes in Spring she would see the Faêran lords and ladies in the orchards, walking among the apple-blossom, or in Summer dancing within grassy rings under the night sky, and once she beheld a procession of lords and ladies on a Rade."

"A Rade?" interjected Rohain.

"That is the term for a cavalcade of the Faêran, on their way to some entertainment, or else taking horse merely for the pleasure of the jaunt. The old woman would see them riding through the fields at dusk, with a gleam of light dancing over them more beautiful than sidereal radiance. Their long hair seemed threaded with the glint of stars and their steeds were the finest ever seen, with long sweeping tails and manes hung about with bells that the wind played on. A high hedge of hawthorn would have kept them from going through the cornfield, but they leaped over it like birds and galloped into a green hill beyond. In the morning she would go to look at the treaded corn, but never a hoof-mark was imprinted, nor a blade broken.

"One day she happened to go earlier than usual to market, and as she went about her business amongst the booths and stalls she rounded a corner and came face-to-face with the tall stranger who had knocked at her door on that misty evening. Trying to cover her surprise, she put on a bold front and said, 'Good morrow, sir. How fare Eilian and the bonny young boy?'

"The stranger politely replied, with favorable tidings of his wife and child. Then he asked conversationally, 'But with which eye do you see me?'

" 'With this one,' said the old woman, pointing to the left.

"At that he laughed. Producing a bulrush, he put out her eye and was gone at once. She never saw any of the Faêran again."

"Fie!" exclaimed Rohain, sitting bolt upright. "Another severe and brutal punishment for a small fault. After all, the woman meant no harm—she merely rubbed her own eye, and that without forethought or malice! Why should she be blinded so painfully?"

"Terrible was the revenge of the Faêran angered," said Ercildoune, taking a draft from his goblet.

"The tale only serves to illustrate my point," said the Duchess of Roxburgh.

Ercildoune laughed. "Alys views the Faêran race as through a black crystal," he said. "To each his own thought. Mine is the opposite view."

"Ercildoune would discover benevolence in the Each Uisge himself," rejoined the Duchess drily.

"The girl Eilian must have thought well of the Faêran," said Rohain.

"That is likely," replied the Duchess. "In the end, though, she was exiled from the Fair Realm for some minor transgression, and pined away to a miserable end."

"A harsh fate," said Rohain presently.

"But you must not judge without knowing all," said the Bard. "That pining was not put on Eilian by the husband or, indeed, by any of the Faêran—it was the inevitable effect of the Fair Realm on all mortals who entered it. No mortal could dwell for more than a short period within the Fair Realm and return to Aia without languishing thereafter, yearning ceaselessly to return, being filled with unutterable longing. The longer the stay, the fiercer the craving. This affliction was called the Langothe. Wilfred, bring more piment. Another story will illustrate."

The lynx on the cushion stood up, yawned, disemboweled its bed, and settled again. Its master began another tale.

"Perdret Olvath was a very pretty girl who lived in Luindorn. Being from a poor family, she made her living in service. It is said that she was a girl who liked to indulge in flights of fancy, or romance, as some would call it. Conscious of her own comeliness, she was also rather vain. Pretty women have a right to vanity, in this gentleman's humble opinion, but others would not agree. Perdret would take great care to dress herself as well as possible, in colorful, flattering clothes; she twined wildflowers in her hair and attracted the attention of all the young men, to the envy of the other lasses. She was also highly susceptible to flattery, and, being unsophisticated and without education, was unable to conceal this fact. If anyone praised her looks, her eyes would light up with pleasure.

"Perdret having been without a situation for some time, her mother was anxious to see her employed. No positions were available in the local area, so she told her daughter that she must look further afield. The girl did not want to leave her village, but there was no choice. She packed her few meager possessions and set off.

"She walked a long way, and everything seemed to be going well until she came to the crossroads on the downs, when she discovered that she knew not which road to take. She looked first one way and then another, until she felt mightily bewildered; should she choose some path at random or return home or stay where she was? Unable to decide, she sat down on a granite boulder and began in dreaming idleness to break off the fronds of ferns which grew in profusion all around. She had not sat long on this stone when, hearing a voice near her, she turned around and saw a handsome young man wearing a green silken coat covered with ornaments of gold.

" 'Good morrow, young maiden,' said he. 'And what are you doing here?'

" 'I am looking for work,' said she.

" 'And what kind of work seek you, my pretty damsel?' said he with a charming smile.

" 'Any kind of work,' said she, quite dazzled. 'I can turn my hand to many things.'

" 'Do you think you could look after a widower with one little boy?' asked the young man.

" 'I dote on children,' said Perdret, 'and I am used to taking care of them.'

" 'I will hire you,' he said, 'for a year and a day. But first, Perdret Olvath'—Perdret gaped in wonderment when she discovered the stranger knew her name, but he laughed. 'Oh, I see, you thought I didn't know you, but do you think a young widower could pass through your village and not notice such a pretty lass? Besides,' he said, 'I watched you one day combing your hair and gazing at your reflection in one of my ponds. You stole some of my perfumed violets to put in your lovely hair.'

"Seduced by his winning ways, the girl was more than half inclined to accept his offer, but her mother had trained her to be careful. 'Where do you live?' she asked.

" 'Not far from here,' said the young stranger. 'Will you accept the place and come with me?'

" 'First, I would ask about wages.'

"He told her that she could ask her own wages, whereupon visions of wealth and luxury rose before Perdret's eyes.

" 'But only if you come with me at once, without returning home,' he added. 'I will send word to your mother.'

" 'But my clothes . . .' said Perdret.

" 'The clothes you have are all that will be necessary, and I'll put you in much finer raiment soon.'

" 'Well then,' Perdret said, 'we are agreed!'

" 'Not yet,' said the stranger. 'I have a way of my own, and you must swear my oath.'

"A look of alarm spread across Perdret's face.

" 'You need not be afraid,' said the stranger very kindly. 'I only ask that you kiss that fern-leaf which you have in your hand and say, "For a year and a day I promise to stay." '

" 'Is that all?' said Perdret, and she did so.

"Without another word he turned and began to walk along the road leading eastward. Perdret followed him, but she thought it strange that her new master went in silence all the way. They walked on for a long time until Perdret grew weary and her feet began to ache. It seemed that she had been walking forever, and not a word spoken. The poor girl felt so exhausted and so dispirited that at last she began to cry. At the sound of her sobs, her new master turned around.

" 'Are you tired, Perdret? Sit down,' he said. Taking her by the hand, he led her to a mossy bank. Overwhelmed by this display of kindness, she burst out weeping. He allowed her to cry for a few minutes before he said, 'Now I shall dry your eyes.'

"Taking a sprig of leaves from the bank, he passed it swiftly across one of her eyes, then the other. Instantly her tears and all weariness vanished. Perdret realized she was walking again, but could not remember having left the bank.

"Now, the way began to slope downwards. Green banks rose up on either side and the road passed swiftly underground. The girl was not a little apprehensive, but she had struck a bargain and was more frightened of going back than forward. After a time, her new master halted.

" 'We are almost there, Perdret,' he said. 'But I see a tear glittering on your eyelid. No mortal tears can enter here.'

"As before, he brushed her eyes with the leaves. They stepped forward and the tunnel opened out.

"Before them spread a country such as Perdret had never before seen. Flowers of every hue covered the hills and valleys; the region appeared like a rich tapestry sewn with gems which glittered in a light as clear as that of the Summer sun, yet as mellow as moonlight. Rivers flowed, more lucid than any water she had ever seen on the granite hills. Waterfalls bounded down the hillsides, fountains danced in rainbows of brilliant droplets. Tall trees in belts and thickets bore both fruit and blossom at once. Ladies and gentlemen dressed in green and gold walked or sported, or reposed on banks of flowers, singing songs or telling stories. Indeed, it was a world more beautiful and exciting than words could describe.

"Perdret's master took her to a stately mansion in which all the furniture was of pearl or ivory, inlaid with gold and silver and studded with emeralds. After passing through many rooms they came to one which was hung all over with snow-white lace, as fine as the finest cobweb, most beautifully worked with flowers. In the middle of this room stood a little cot made out of some beautiful seashell, which reflected so many colors that Perdret could scarcely bear to look at it. Sleeping in the cot was the sweetest little boy she had ever seen.

" 'This is your charge,' said the father. 'You have nothing to do but wash him when he wakes, dress him and take him to walk in the garden, then put him to bed when he is tired. I am a lord in this land and I have my own reasons for wishing my boy to know something of human nature.'

"Perdret began her duties and did them well and diligently. She loved the little boy and he appeared to love her, and the time passed away with astonishing swiftness. Strangely, she never thought of her mother—she never thought of her home at all. Dwelling in luxury and happiness, she never reckoned the passing of time.

"But the period for which she had bound herself finally ended, and one day she woke up in her own bed in her mother's cottage. Everything seemed unfamiliar to her and she appeared unusually abstracted or foreign to all who saw her. She could evince no interest in meat or drink. At night, instead of sleeping, she would go out under the stars and gaze up at them. Sometimes she would wander all night, barefoot, only to be found exhausted on her bed in the morning, unable to rise. She grew pale and thin and was hardly ever seen to smile. Numerous wise persons were called in to try to cure Perdret's ailment, and to all she told the same tale, about the Faêran lord, and the beautiful country and the baby. She being known for her fanciful turn of mind, some people said the girl was 'gone clean daft,' but at last an old carlin came to the cottage where Perdret lay on her bed.

" 'Now crook your arm, Perdret,' said the carlin.

"Perdret sat up and bent her arm, resting her hand on her hip.

" 'Now say, "I hope my arm may never come uncrooked if I have told ye a word of a lie." '

" 'I hope my arm may never come uncrooked if I have told ye a word of a lie,' repeated Perdret.

" 'Uncrook your arm,' said the carlin.

"Perdret stretched out her arm.

" 'It is the truth the girl is telling,' said the carlin. 'She has been carried away by the Faêran to their country.'

" 'Will my daughter ever come right in her mind?' asked the mother.

" 'I can do nothing,' said the old woman, shaking her head. 'Perhaps she will, in time.' "

The Bard having finished his soliloquy, the Duchess added, "Anyway, it is told that Perdret did not get on very well in the world. She married, and never wanted for anything, but she was always discontented and unhappy, and she died young."

"Verily," said the Bard, "some said she always pined after the Faêran widower. Others said she pined after the Fair Realm itself. No matter the reason, it was the Langothe that plagued her."

"And was that the same Faêran lord who had been husband to Eilian?" Rohain inquired.

"I think not. The first tale happened subsequent to the second. I have told them out of order. Over the course of time, more than one fair mortal maiden has been taken away to the Realm."

"Did the Faêran steal mortal men as well as maids and wives?" asked Rohain.

"Most certainly," came the Duchess's quick reply.

"Well," declared Rohain, "it seems to me that the Strangers were a dangerous race, selfish and arrogant, cruel in many ways, excessively wanton and proud in their immortality."

"Yet theirs was a conditional immortality," observed the Bard sharply.

"What do you mean?"

"Age and disease could not slay them, but they could be defeated by violence."

"Even then," amended the Duchess, "they could only be diminished, not destroyed."

"Yet what mortal violence could defeat the gramarye wielded by the Lords of the Fair Realm?" argued Rohain. After a silence, she added, "Is it possible that any folk of their blood remained in Erith—perhaps children of mixed races, both Faêran and mortal, like the child of Eilian?"

"Historically," said the Bard, "very few Half-Faêran have been born—perhaps a score, that is all. None have walked our world since the Ways were closed. They chose to stay on the other side."

"What of their progeny? The children of the Half-Faêran?"

"There is no such issue. The Half-Faêran were all barren."

"Is it possible that one of the Faêran could be stolen by a mortal?" Rohain asked.

"Indeed!" responded the Duchess. "There were ways, if one knew how. Many a mortal man has been drawn into desperate love after setting eyes on a Faêran damsel. To see the Faêran was to be attracted to them. In truth, some Faêran damsels who desired mortals—I will not say 'loved,' for I believe they were all incapable of love as we know it—allowed themselves to be caught as brides." She paused, then added, "And it was possible for Faêran brides to be taken by men."

"But surely, never against their will!" exclaimed Rohain.

"Only once," said Thomas, "has an abduction like that occurred, and only because, as in the tale of the swan-maiden, foolish chattering wights gave away the secret of how to do it. They revealed the rules to a man of our race who, smitten with the sickness of love, was able to capture a Faêran bride." A troubled shadow fleeted in the depths of his eyes. "That particular tale is another example of our race stealing from the Faêran—perhaps the most significant example of all. The theft of a Faêran bride by a lowly mortal greatly roused the ire of some of the Fair Realm's greatest lords. Thereafter, one Faêran prince in particular began to take pleasure in the company of unseelie wights whose delight was to plague and torment mortals."

"But how could a mortal man steal a Faêran damsel?" wondered Rohain.

"They could not be stolen in the same way as wightish brides," explained Thomas, "as, for example, power is gained over merrows by taking their combs, over swan-maidens by stealing their feather-cloaks, over silkies by purloining their skins. But there were certain words and deeds which could force the Faêran to remain in our world, at least for a time."

"But not for long," interjected the Duchess, nodding sagely. "And after she left him, he pined away to, if you'll excuse the cliché, an early grave. As ever, all love between immortals and mortals was doomed. In the end, all unions between Faêran and humankind ended in tragedy."

Groups of peasants stamping in the cold went about Caermelor singing traditional songs on street corners and before the doors of townsfolk, to be rewarded with coins or wrapped cakes and common flagons of mulled ale. Carts rumbled along the streets bearing great logs cut from the forest to supply the Imbroltide fires. Marketplace trade rose to fever pitch. Lanterns burned all night in workshops as tradesmen hurried to meet deadlines on orders for the no-bility, the exchange of gifts being one of the most eagerly looked-for customs of Imbrol.

Colored lamps had been strung along the streets, vying with glowing garnets of charcoal in the braziers of the hot-chestnut vendors. Under the Greayte Southern Star, Caer-melor bustled late into the freezing nights and scarcely slept, despite rowdy winds that knocked the lamps about and blew out the charcoal fires, despite the lightning that danced like green skeletons all across the western skies.

This was angry weather, uncharacteristic of Imbrol. Some people were blaming it on the gathering of unseelie swarms in Namarre. "'Tis *their* doing,' they muttered darkly. "'Tis but a premonition of the first assault. Wicked wights allied with barbarians! How are such enemies ever to be defeated?" Beneath the outward merriment, horror flowed through the thoroughfares of the city.

New Year's Eve.

When the bells tolled the last stroke of midnight, Misrule would reign until dawn on Littlesun Day. The tradition of Misrule entailed the annual turning of the tables that saw lord trade places with footman and lady step into the shoes of chambermaid, so that, for a few hours, the world would be topsy-turvy and Foolery would be the order of the night until cock-crow.

But hours before all that, there was the Feast.

Grander and far more expansive than the Royal Dining Hall, the Royal Banqueting Hall boasted eight fireplaces, in each of which burned a massive tree trunk, the traditional Imbrol Log. Coincidentally, eight Waits stood vigil in their splendor to fanfare the courses. The High Table on its dais was so far removed from the opposite end of the Hall that those who graced it could scarcely be expected to discern the countenances of those seated at the lower trestles, or even the central ones—a state of affairs that, despite the blaze of countless girandoles, lusters, and candelabra, was exacerbated by the soft haze of steam and incense filling the air. Below the high dais lay a second platform, innocent of furniture. Here, some of the entremets would be played out between courses.

All plate was of gold or the harder, more brilliant silvergilt. White light dazzled over its myriad surfaces. Not a gleam of silver, copper, brass, or bronze winked forth. For ornament, there were golden surtouts in the shape of fruiting and blossoming trees. Cakes had been fashioned and frosted to resemble white castles, cities of dough and Sugar, glittering coaches-and-six, peacocks in full display, sprays of lily of the valley, bouquets of roses, the traditional spinning wheels of Imbrol, snowy ducks and geese. The sideboards struggled to support pyramids of ripe and luscious fruits from the Royal Conservatory, forced to grow out of season, all surrounded by garlands of evergreens and berries. For the occasion, the salt cellars took the shape of ceremonial snow-sleighs, hung about with tiny gold bells and emblazoned with the King-Emperor's insignia. The linen serviettes were folded in enchanting forms of snowflakes. Superfluous napkin rings, garlands of holly and other winter leaves individually crafted in gold, lay empty next to every place setting.

More accustomed now to the dangers of mistaking blade, prong, and scoop, Rohain silently reviewed the different uses for each piece included in her place setting: the oyster fork nestling in the soup spoon; the marrow scoop; the pairs of knives and forks each dedicated to the fish, the meat, and the poultry; the dessert spoon and fork; the fruit knife; the tiny bonbon tongs. Beyond the boundaries of her place lay the cutlery to be shared: the suckett forks, condiment spoons, Sugar shells, mote spoons, pickle forks, butter picks, nut picks, cheese scoops, horseradish spoons, and various others, not to be confused with the soup ladles, fish slicers, jelly servers, snuff spoons, and wick scissors to be wielded by the servants.

Most of the courtiers were already drunk when they entered the Royal Banqueting Hall—Rohain among them. They had been junketing all day, insisting that she match them deed for deed, and, loathe to relinquish her new status, she had acceded. Unaccustomed to imbibing liquor, she had succumbed to it more swiftly than they. The Hall swam before her eyes.

Everyone was standing beside their chairs. The High Table filled last of all—the lords of the Royal Attriod and the chief advisers of the King-Emperor's Household entered with their wives, preceding by several minutes the young Prince Edward. When the King-Emperor appeared, an awed hush settled on the assembly, yet in good form, none regarded their sovereign directly. His Majesty took his seat in the tall chair overshadowed by its richly decorated canopy, after which everyone else followed suit.

Now Rohain noted that one of the long tables was occupied entirely by Dainnan warriors in dress uniform: thigh-length doublets overlaid by tabards emblazoned with the Royal Heraldry. She strained to view them. Some were positioned with their backs to her. Of those she could descry, none were Thorn, but her gaze fastened on that table and it was difficult to look away.

Pages and ewerers came to pour scented water for the handwashing. Rohain looked up. The face of the boy holding the ewer for her seemed familiar.

"You!" blurted Rohain suddenly, and not particularly distinctly.

"I beg your pardon, m'lady?"

"You! Where have I seen you before?"

"I am sure I do not know," stammered the lad, embarrassed.

"I have seen you. Oh yes, I know now—"

She checked herself. Realization had dawned. This was the cabin boy from the merchant ship *City of Gilvaris Tarv.* He would not recognize her. Joy welled in her heart—he, then, had been saved. What of his shipmates?

"You were once in the employ of a merchant line, the Cresny-Beaulais, were you not?"

"Aye, m'lady, but—"

"Your ship was scuttled by pirates. What happened to the crew?"

Nonplussed, the boy stammered, "Some were slain, m'lady. Others escaped. The captain, he was ransomed. Others were sold as slaves, methinks."

His eyes showed his obvious desperation to ask how she knew so much about him, but he was too well-drilled to question a high-born lady.

"And you escaped?"

"Aye, m'lady."

Rohain peeled a ruby-encrusted bracelet from her wrist. It matched her outfit—tonight she was clad all in crimson and gold, with a hint of jade. Viviana had braided silk rosebuds into her crimped locks. A vermilion plume within the circlet of a band of cornelians nodded over them. Tiny red roses had been appliquéd in lace all over the watered silk of her houppelande. Her bodice was scalloped, edged with appliquéd rose leaves, her waist was clasped by a scarlet-purple girdle harnessed with gold beads and lattice. The sleeves fell in lacy folds to the floor.

"Take this," she said, proffering the bracelet. "It pleases me to give it you. Sell it, if you wish. If ever you need help, ask for me. If ever you require a position, ask at the Estate of Arth— Argh— that is, Arcune. I am to be Baroness of it, y'know." Unaccountably, her tongue seemed to have thickened. It appeared to be reluctant to shape words.

"By the Powers, my lady! I thank you."

"'Tis nought. You deserve it."

A lad as acute as the erstwhile cabin boy might have been expected to complete his task in haste, in case his benefactress should sober and reverse her benevolence. Instead he performed the rest of his duties slowly and wonderingly, then bowed and withdrew.

Servitors ported trays laden with hunches of fluffy white bread up and down the tables, beginning at the top. Each diner was served, with a flourish and a pair of tongs, accompanied by a loud declaration of his title and honor, whereupon he stood up and afterward sat down again. Simultaneously, the Credence and the Assaying took place.

Wines were dispensed by footman-bees, filling with nectar the goblet-flowers. Snow floated in the wine jugs.

"'Tis going to be ever such a capital occasion tonight!" cried a lady in a turquoise surcoat of figured satin and a lavender kirtle with an upstanding collar of stiffened wigan. "I adore play-acting at Misrule, don't you? I intend to be an ever so slovenly scullery maid, and make my footman a prince!"

"Don't take it too far, my dear," rejoined another in an embroidered gable headdress and an apricot-colored gown of shot silk. "One never knows what a prince may ask of a scullery maid!"

"Faugh! Jenkin would never overstep the mark with me!"

"Unless you beg him," Dianella said sweetly. Her friends shrieked, to High Collar's thinly disguised discomfiture. Dianella turned to Rohain. "Zounds, Dear Heart, quot wroughtst-thou un sa manfant pove? Mi sugen esprait quill overgrand pash-thou es." *What have you done to that poor lad? I should say he is mightily in love with you.*

"Ta ferle-fil?" *That page boy?* replied Rohain offhandedly. "Quot sugen cheyen-mi al ins?" *What should I care for him?*

She had learned to answer Dianella's audacity with stoicism.

That comely doyenne of innuendo, her beautiful head encased in a pointed turban topped with clusters of golden baubles, turned to those seated near her and began to converse in rapid slingua. Shadowy tresses fell loose across her smooth white shoulders to the damask bodice, the heavy diamond necklace.

The Waits trumpeted fiercely. Far across the room, at the High Table, someone rose up from behind the table-decorations to propose the Toast. Rohain could make out a tall, distinguished figure across the tables. When he spoke,

his reverberant voice revealed him to be Thomas of Ercildoune. The Royal Toast and the Loving Cup were attended
to in due order, after which Rohain seemed to see many
more accoutrements upon the table in front of her than had
been there previously. She knew she had taken too much to
drink, but to refuse the traditional pre-dinner drafts would
have been uncouth. This insobriety hampered her efforts to
discover Thorn among the Dainnan and her ability to converse in a sprightly manner.

With utmost pageantry, the Soup was revealed and consumed. There followed the first entremet of this Imbrol
Feast—a score of dancers in sildron harness, costumed as
the cicada-like species of creatures called the Five-Eyed.
They had encased their faces in masks with convexities of
glass for the large eyes and a triad of jewels for the small.
Helmets clasped their heads, bronze cuirasses covered their
chests and backs. Wings of gauze and silk like rippled
glass, spangled with sequins, expanded from their shoulders in sapphire blue, gold, and emerald green. At their hips
they wore factitious tymbals, and their heels were spurred.

To the rattle of nakers and other percussive paraphernal-
lia, these exotics performed a gliss-dance of prodigious
gymnastic skill, floating above the heads of the diners,
grasping each other by the arms to change direction or
pulling on streamers and crosiers; spinning and gliding,
pushing off the walls, somersaulting, flying. At the conclusion the diners applauded enthusiastically and the next
course was served: golden carp suspended in colored
gelatins and whole baked dolphins on beds of oysters, complete with pearls. The butlers built pyramids of balancing
goblets and poured wine into the topmost ones. The torrent
splashed lavishly down from layer to layer in a spectacular
cascade of pale gold.

A display of swordsmanship next entertained the Court.
A hefty purse having been promised to the winner, the com-

batants treated it as no light matter. Three dueling pairs, all accomplished professionals, fought with foils, sabers, and épées. In a fine exhibition, they footed it up and down the lower dais in front of the High Table. Through the milky airs, beyond the candle-flames that shifted and jumped, beyond the gleams that glanced off dinnerware and played ocular tricks, Rohain dimly descried figures leaning on their elbows, watching. At the far-off tables that stood nearest the High Table, the only identifiable faces belonged to the comely Lady Rosamonde, eldest daughter of the Duke of Roxburgh, the balding Dowager Marchioness of Netherby-on-the-Fens in her incongruous and outrageously expensive wig of real Talith hair, and the young Talith noblewoman Maiwenna, her good looks framed by naturally acquired gold.

Nearer at hand, a group from Rimany, born of the Ice-Race called the Arysk, sat like a row of lilies or plumy white birds, wearing the feathers of albino peacocks and ibis. Ivory of skin were they, their locks of pure white silk framing grave faces and eyes of palest blue. Like the trows, they favored silver for adornment, and as for apparel, they chose only white silk and gauze and cloth-of-silver, ice blue or sea gray. Sudden blood-red, like a stab wound, was the only bright hue of their decoration, deepest carmine velvet edged with sable. They kept to themselves—Rohain had been introduced to only one of their number, the Lady Solveig of Ixtacutl. The candlelight had described in her eyes ice-pinnacles tinged by a flame of sunset.

Blood having been shed, the swordfighting event closed in time for the ensuing dish, which appeared to consist of a bloated ox. In roasted state, surrounded by glazed worts, parsley, nasturtiums, and sausages, the beast was wheeled in on a golden cart drawn by skittish reindeer, to be presented at the High Table. As the cart halted before the dais,

Roxburgh stood up. His voice roared out across the Hall. A horrified silence fell abruptly over the assembly.

"What's this? An ox for dinner at Imbrol? And look at it! Is this fit to be presented to His Majesty? Has it not even been gutted and stuffed? Are we to chew entrails? Bring the Master Cook. We'll see him hanged for this incompetence!"

The Royal Cook was dragged sniveling and groveling from the kitchens. On his knees before the High Table he begged for mercy, rolling his eyes hideously.

"Your Majesty! Your Highness, Your Graces, have pity! I did my best, but there was no time—"

"Silence!" roared Roxburgh. "I'll see *you* gutted instead!"

"But sir," said the Cook, "I'd rather show you the beast's innards than mine."

With that he drew a long knife from his side in with one easy movement slashed open the ox's stomach. A cheer went up from the diners as an entire roasted cow rolled out. A slash along the cow's abdomen revealed a baked doe. Inside the venison was a nicely cooked sheep, stuffed with a pig, crammed with a turkey that contained a pigeon packed with forcemeat. By now the audience was applauding madly. The Royal Cook capered. Roxburgh threw back his head and made the Hall ring with his laughter—of course, it had all been a jest, and planned from start to finish. The Dainnan Commander threw a purse to the Cook. A tribe of footmen rolled away the Seven-In-One to be operated on by a bevy of Carvers.

The next course was roasted peacocks, brought forth with wads of burning camphor and wool stuck in their beaks, spitting flames, to be paraded in their jeweled plumage and then devoured. After that, files of liveried servitors triumphantly brought forth pies that, when their pastry lids were cut, released live birds to fly around the hall.

Barring dessert, there could not have been a more complete repast. Many a noble waistline bulged. Pages, footmen, butlers, cup-bearers, all were kept busy scurrying back and forth at the whims of their masters and mistresses. As the last sanap was removed in preparation for the final collation, all entremets disappeared and an orchestra played soft music from the gallery. The musicians gleamed with their own perspiration. Like a field of burning goldenrod flowers, feverish candles blazed, stuck in wrought brackets attached to the sheet-music stands.

The courtiers murmured expectantly.

The Royal Bard rose from his chair. Beckoning to a group of half a dozen boys who had been waiting in the wings, he strode down from the dais to a golden harp that stood there, its frame formed like a giant fish with waves streaming from its scales. All fell silent once more.

"I sing 'The Holly,'" he announced, seating himself at the harp.

Backed by the harmonies of the youthful choir, the Bard sang a traditional song of Imbrol. All those assembled raised their voices in the last verse, and a grand swelling of sound it was—it seemed to rock the walls and lift the very ceiling.

Thomas of Ercildoune waved the choir away and once more touched the strings of his Carp Harp. In a voice both rich and mellow, which carried clearly to all those seated in the Hall, he began a serenade:

My love, though I should never wish that we
Should even by a hair's breadth parted be,
There shall be times when we must dwell apart—
Then would I keep some emblem to my heart;
A token of thee, lady whom I cherish,

That of the lack of thee I may not perish—
A part of thee which no one else could make,
And yet, that would not harm thee for to take;
A pledge of thy return, a treasured thing
More tender than a portrait or a ring;
A part of thee which of thee shall remain.
Thus, sundered we shall never be again;
So if beside thee, love, I cannot be—
I pray thee, spare a lock of hair to me.

Tears brimmed in Rohain's eyes. She forbade them to fall. Had Thorn kept the twist of hair he had stolen from her, or had he tossed it away? The Bard bowed to the High Table and was commended on his performance.

"My apprentice, Toby," said Ercildoune, "has been practicing some epic these last days, methinks. Let us hear it now, Toby."

"If it please Your Majesty, I shall play 'Candlebutter,' " said Toby, bowing low. The courtiers stirred appreciatively. It was one of those old, well-known songs that, although the words bore no relevance to the occasion, was always thought of as indispensable to Imbrol.

"For those who are not aware of the manner of speech used in some regions, candlebutter is an archaic or rustic name for gold," said Toby in a clear voice. "The ballad is made upon the true story of the Dark Daughter, as happened, they say, in days of yore. 'Tis an ancient song and many a minstrel has passed it down through the years. Now it is my turn. I shall try to do it justice." Taking up a lyre for accompaniment, Toby half sang, half chanted a long, strange ballad. As the last liquid notes of the lyre trickled away, the singer bowed. His audience remained, for a time, under the spell of the curious old song.

Hardly had they begun to applaud when a loud explosion and a wizardly cloud of purple smoke from the lower doors heralded the arrival of the Puddings. Upon matching gray steeds, in rode twelve masked equestrians outfitted to represent the twelve months of the Year. Wearing sildron bracelets to bear up the weight, they held aloft flaming spheres of compacted suet, peel, Sugar, brandy, and fruits, whose purpose was to resemble the burning sun in a half-serious attempt to lure the real one back from its Winter retreat in the north. All who viewed these triumphal orbs did so with the anticipation of being fortunate enough to find within their portion one of the lucky silver tokens hidden there. These apparitions jogged once around the Hall, pausing to genuflect to the High Table, the horses having been trained to do the same. They deposited their guttering burdens on the sideboards for subsequent butchery and departed in another burst of smoke and noise.

"La! Uncle never did things by halves!" commented Dianella, covering her ears.

The uncle mentioned, being the Lord High Wizard, Sargoth the Cowled, commenced his customary Imbrol Spectacle directly after dessert. The fame of this man had reached to all the corners of Erith, even to the Tower at Isse, where he had been spoken of with awe and excitement. Rohain soon saw that his reputation had not been overpraised. He demonstrated each of the Nine Arts with utmost skill and aplomb, revealing himself as a true Master of Wizardry. Compared with Sargoth, Zimmuth of Isse Tower seemed but an apprentice.

Servants went around snuffing out candles. The darkened Hall became the scene of wizardly lightning, flame, sparks, and smoke. Between thunders the orchestra played. On the dais below the High Table Sargoth transformed maidens into wolves, wolves into tyraxes, and tyraxes to watch-worms. He sawed men in half; the halves walked around by themselves and were rejoined later. He chopped men into little pieces and restored them to life. He made them disappear, only to reappear where least expected. Inanimate objects came to life. In his ungloved hand, water turned to fire and fire to water. He levitated without a sildron harness. He seemed aflame, he walked through fire unscathed. He performed feats of gramarye that left his audience gawping. In short, he was astounding.

A bell tolled eleven. On the eleventh stroke, the wizard vanished for the last time, leaving a rain of gold, silver, and scarlet sparks to descend slowly into the foggy Hall. A cheer went up—it was time to prepare for Misrule. Footmen scurried to relight the candles. Their light, leaking through the haze, showed that the High Table had already been half-deserted. In order of importance, the courtiers now absented themselves from the Banqueting Hall, repairing to their suites to dress for the Midnight Ball.

With a rustle of silk, Dianella, attired in the costliest of fabrics cut in peasant style, entered Rohain's boudoir. She was followed by her lady's maid.

"Are you almost ready, Dear Heart?" she said with a sweet smile. "The night wears on! Allow me to help you with your coiffure. Servants do not know how to prosecute such affairs successfully. Besides, I have been told your maid's sight is impaired."

Biting her lip, Viviana stepped back. Rohain allowed Dianella to rearrange her curls.

"Like this, see?" said Dianella, teasing out loose strands. "A little messy, like a maid who's forgotten to tidy herself—'twould be true to type, I ween. What a capital costume—it does show your figure to advantage! I see your skivvy-girl here is wearing the one of your gowns I most admire, oh, I could almost be jealous! Yet breeding will tell—the most gracious of raiment cannot enhance a lowborn face. What's this?" She peered closely at Rohain's hair. "What have you done to the roots? Why, I declare!

Griffin, get out of here. You too." She rounded on the two lady's maids, who hastily removed themselves.

Rohain drooped, wine-befuddled, before the looking-glass. "What is the matter with my hair, Dianella?"

"Only that the roots are beginning to grow out gold. How entirely fascinating! Come, come, what are you hiding from us?"

"I hide nothing! If I am Talith, what of it?"

"Of course. What of it indeed! Nobody of any consequence wears their hair yellow these days—only old quizzes like the Dowager Marchioness of Netherby, and cold fish like Maiwenna. Verily, it is out of style. You had better have it seen to quickly—Griffin shall dye it for you on the morrow; she is *taraiz* adept. There's not a moment to lose. Contrasting roots are *so* out of favor!"

She held up a strand of Rohain's hair between finger and thumb.

"La! What emulsion have you used, Heart? Your hair positively glows. Most of the usual black dyestuffs coarsen the tresses something *storfenlent.*"

"I do not know what it was called. My hair was dyed for me by a carlin in White Down Rory."

"I must know her name, this adept witch of the hair-dressing!"

Only half attending, Rohain said, "She is called Maeve One-Eye. Shall the ladies of the Court dance with the Dainnan tonight?"

Dianella laughed her silvery tinkle.

"The ladies of the Court may do many things on *this* night of the Year. All of Roxburgh's stalwarts are *sofine* and unco' gallant—dare I surmise that your eye has rested upon one in particular, *es raith-na?*"

A gong sounded the call to the Ballroom. Dianella glided to the window and peered out. In the darkness below, torches flared.

Rohain rose unsteadily from her seat by the dressing-table.

"Do you know of a Dainnan by the name of Thorn?"

"Thorn?" Dianella paused, without turning around. "Nay, I think not. Nay, I am certain I have not heard that name. Have you asked anyone else?"

"No."

"Well it would be best not to, Dear Heart. It does not look so well, you understand, a lady in your position asking after one of the King-Emperor's hired men, dashing though they be. I am sure you will see this man again, by and by." She lifted from her chatelaine an ivory mirror-case depicting a tournament. Knights jousted while nobles watched from a high gallery. Ivory heralds sounded long trumpets. After a quick glance at her reflection, she snapped it shut. "Is he very much in love with you?"

"I hardly know him."

"But of course! You would be saving yourself for a viscount, at the very least! I am sure your Dainnan loves you from afar, in truest chivalry, with most ardent and *untainted* passion. *Cai dreambliss!* Have you your dance-cards and fan? Come now, take my hand—let us away to the Ball. We must be there before midnight. That is when the best fun begins!"

A great stillness fell, near and far.

In the gardens and courtyards of the palace, bonfires flared, inviting the Winter sun's return. A band of well-wrapped musicians sustained the circles of dancers around each conflagration. Some maidens ran, screaming "Bogles in the hedges!" Someone, it was reported, had seen them—but it turned out to be a mere folly.

The city bells rang a carillon for midnight.

A mighty cheer went up to the starry skies, and a blowing of horns and a rampage of bells and drums. In the Royal

Ballroom, the oboe, the clarinet, the viol, the shawm and hautboy, the serpent, the trumpet, the horn and timpani, the triangle, the gittern, and the double bass struck up.

The Royal Ballroom stood wide and high, its painted, paneled, festooned walls lined with mirrors and chairs, the latter occupied by ladies with fans and gentlemen with snuff-boxes, many of these observers being in various stages of coquetry and flirtation. Dancers packed the floor. It would seem to an onlooker that servant and master, both simple and gentle, mingled without regard to propriety: cup-bearer and countess, minion and marquess, drudge and Dainnan, valet and viscount, laundry-maid and lord, nursery-maid and noble, equerry and earl, squire and seigneur, henchman and high-born lady. With blue glass gleaming at her throat like sapphires, a ragged scullion whirled in the arms of an under-butler with gold-buckled shoes, whose jacket had been turned inside out. A queenly dame in cloth-of-gold partnered an elderly, bewhiskered steward; a kitchen-maid in a stained apron trod the boards with a velveted duke while a baroness danced with a pastry-cook. The Yeoman to the Royal Wine Cellar footed it with the Countess of Sheffield, and the Master of Robes trifled with a gardener's daughter in damson silk and a golden chatelaine. It was all bewildering in the extreme, which indeed was the intention, for the period between midnight and sunrise on Littlesun Day was a dangerous time when anything might happen.

On this the longest night, dark-loving eldritch things roamed abroad—in particular, unseelie entities out to do harm to mortals—and if they should be led astray by appearances, if they should not be able to identify those upon whom they spied, then there was a chance that they would have less power to wreak mischief upon them during the coming year. With reversal in mind, acrobats walked about on their hands, their feet waving in the air, wearing gauntlets over their shoes. Jesters, dressed as birds and butterflies with stars on their heads, toddled here and there; others, wrapped in swaddling to represent the worms of the soil, glissanded near the ceiling.

The lowliest drudge, a young, uncomely maid whose distasteful daily duties included the emptying of chamberpots, presided over the Ball. Smiling in genuine glee, this Queen of Misrule sat on one of the King-Emperor's very thrones, with a paste-and-paint crown stuck askew upon her curls and glass baubles winking on every joint. Ercildoune, who loved such occasions, made great show of falling upon his knees before her, offering tray after tray of sweetmeats and wine. In his joskin's garb, he looked quite the yokel, although rather rakish. His performance, however, was soon eclipsed by Goblet-As-Footman. His powdered wig on sideways, his long-toed shoes tripping him up at the slightest provocation, the Royal Jester fell on many people—judiciously selected. He fell into the lap of the Queen of Misrule and was mortified and begged forgiveness, but, unforgiven, tried to hang himself with a noose whose frayed end he held high in his own hand. When suicide failed, he implored pardon again, she kissed him, and he was so elated that he cut a caper, tripped on his shoes, and landed in her lap once again. In disgust, his fellow jesters heaved him up by the hands and feet and threw him into the multitude, whereupon he was passed from hand to hand over their heads around the room. None scorned to join this activity, least of all those of the Set. In all seasons Goblet was deemed fashionable by the Set, even though he was, by choice, not part of it. His scathing tongue could strip face and facade from those he chose to mock; as jester, he was licensed to lampoon; none bar a very few would not give way before him, and most would not wish to do so. He was popular despite his acerbic wit and because of it; Goblet could say and do almost anything and get away with it. Furthermore, it was deemed lucky to touch a jester on New Year's Eve.

When next seen, Goblet was wearing an elaborate farthingale, with two slightly lopsided puddings squeezed into the bodice and two more in the bustle. In this finery he skipped through the crowd, having perfected the knack of appearing at people's elbows, then kicking up his heels and disappearing with an arch wink before they had time to collect their wits. A trail of children endeavored to follow him.

In the adjacent room, the White Drawing Room, a take-as-you-please supper had been laid out. Gold glittered everywhere: encrusted on the walls and the heavy frames of the paintings that adorned them, on the embroidered chairs, the ornate ceiling, the solid gold firescreens. About the walls, cabinets inlaid with semiprecious stones housed objets d'art. Tall doors gave on to the torchlit gardens. Before these portals posed graceful marble statues and tall ivory vases overflowing with white lilies. Overhead hovered a breathtaking tiered crystal chandelier. The floor was thick with priceless purple and gold carpets that flowed out beyond the White Drawing Room into the length of the red-and-gold East Gallery.

The Yeoman of the Silver Pantry, who compensated for his lack of height with excessive girth, was helping himself generously, piling his plate high with lobster mousse and goose pâté. Nearby, a tipsy butler with a long and equine countenance was performing the most extraordinary antics before an admiring audience of pages and porters, balancing empty plates in aspen stacks upon his head and hands. Not unexpectedly, these ceramic towers ultimately descended with a startling crash, causing the unfortunate Yeoman of the Silver Pantry to jump and inadvertently bestow his victuals on the undeserving purple-and-gold carpets.

Thus deprived, he bristled like an indignant boar.

"You there, Fawcett!" he shouted. "Hold yer noise."

"Shout till yer hoarse, I'll never heed *your* noise," came the flippant reply.

The Yeoman of the Silver Pantry hitched up his belt and rolled his sleeves to his podgy elbows. His cheeks purpled like two generous aubergines.

" 'Tis not I who's horse but you, horse-face—and yet the face of you compares best with the hinder parts of the noble beast."

Sniffing an entertaining discourse, servants gathered around. The Yeoman of the Silver Pantry had struck on an issue sensitive with the butler.

"If horse I be then I can draw the likes of you after me— aye, draw you whithersoever I would choose to go," sneered Fawcett. "Put wheels on and you are a wain— you've the build of it!"

" 'Tis a pity he does *not* wane," interjected the butler's friend waggishly. "He waxes more than he wanes me- thinks—more so than a thousand candles!"

"Nay, no *drawer* you, but an artist," shot back the Yeo- man of the Silver Pantry, ignoring this interruption. "An artist in horse manure." Quickly reconsidering, he added, "Had I but a pair of drawers such as you, you would be the crotch!"

The audience, who had been applauding each sally, cheered this barb of wit. Nonetheless, the butler was not to be deterred. After a brief deliberation as to whether to in- terpret the word "crotch" as "fork" and thus allude to his opponent's disgusting eating habits, he decided on a more threatening approach. Both participants were incisively aware of the retribution that would shortly be exacted from them by the Master of the King's Household in his wrath, as payment for the damage they had occasioned to the car- pets and dishes of the White Drawing Room. Thus they de- cided that it was as well to be hanged for a buck as a fawn.

"A crutch you would fain lean upon once I have bested you!"

"Aye, *leaner* will they call me an you keep me from my dinner," hotly said the Yeoman of the Silver Pantry, who was in fact proud of his bulk. "But I'll dine anon, horse-face, while you shall couch upon the cold ground. Then you'll be the leaner, understand me?"

"Rather do I *over*stand you, base churl." The butler loomed over the short figure of the pantryman, his long chin thrust forward.

"Why then, I'll undermine you!"

While the butler was thinking of a reply, the Yeoman of the Silver Pantry tackled him around the knees and bowled him over.

Fists flew. Rohain and many others prudently withdrew to the comparative safety of the Ballroom. Among the crowd that jostled there she briefly noted a tall man with a scarred face, high cheekbones, and startlingly blue eyes—one of the footmen. Wearing a gorgeous jacket of sapphire velvet lined with white Rimanian bear fur, he was bowing low before a curly-haired chamber-maid, the sixth grand-daughter of the Marquess of Early. The girl took his hand and they began to dance. Their eyes never left each other.

"Love knows no boundaries of rank," murmured Rohain to herself.

Unfolding the pleated leaves of a carved wooden fan, the chicken-skin parchment of which was ostentatiously painted with a scene from the Legend of the Sleeping War-riors, Viviana edged closer to her mistress's elbow.

"I dream—am I truly wearing my lady's cloth-of-silver gown and topaz girdle?"

"Go on with you!" said Rohain, smiling. "You are a lady tonight. You need not attend me."

"Georgiana Griffin attends Dianella—"

"Nonetheless, I insist!"

"A thousand thanks, my lady! I cannot wait to join the dance. This will surely be the best night of my life!"

With a quick curtsy, Viviana made haste to join the ladies waiting for partners.

Rohain's eyes roved the assembly. She fluttered a lacquered fan of brilliant luster, edged with gilt. At her girdle hung a small, slender case containing ivory dance-cards. Made of mother-of-pearl, it was overlaid with gold filigree work and had a matching pencil. Several gentlemen had inscribed its ivory leaves with their names. Having been plagued with offers to dance, each ardent aspirant producing a white lace handkerchief and flourishing it under his nose with a bow, Rohain had accepted a few and refused many. She was an inept dancer, having learned the few steps she knew during impromptu lessons from Viviana—a fact that none of the gallants who whirled her in their arms had seemed to care a whit about. But not one of her partners could match Thorn. She did not wish to dance any more, not with anyone but him. Tired of refusing offers, she had masked her face with a feathered domino borrowed from the Duchess of Roxburgh, dressed herself like a chambermaid, stuck a large pair of artificial moth's wings on her back, and teased out her black hair in a fright.

Dainnan knights were among the crowd in the ballroom, costumed as both aristocrats and servants, but she could not obtain a clear view from where she stood. It occurred to her that from the elevation of the musicians' gallery, one could be sure of commanding the scene. Eluding a dashing young earl who may have penetrated her disguise and was advancing in her direction, Rohain slipped through a service door and found a narrow stair.

As she ascended the stair a chill swept over her. She looked up and flinched. Something barred her way. It was a tall, white object, like a column of pale marble. The flicker of a torch in a sconce showed a long dark shadow stretch-

ing from the pillar's feet and up the wall. She pushed back
her mask to obtain a better view.

"Oh! My lord Sargoth!"

He said nothing. He simply loomed there, looking down
from the added height lent him by the staircase. Torchlight
carved shadows out of his unblemished pallor, his luminous
marble hair. The long face and beard matched the utter col-
orlessness of his wizard's robes. Here was one member of
the Imperial Court not dressed for Misrule. It was all Rohain could do to prevent herself from backing away, turning and fleeing down the stair. She told herself she would
not be intimidated by this man. He was a servant of the
King-Emperor, after all—surely in the Court hierarchy she
was his superior?

"Sir, let me pass."

"My lady—*Rohain,* is it? Is that what you are called?"

"Yes."

"My lady *Rohain,*" he deliberately emphasized the
name. "Far be it from me to impede your upward progress."

He did not move. His eyes glittered oddly. What did he
mean? What could he know?

Her mind groped for some anchor, and found the past.
*Sianadh said never to show fear, never to run. To do so
gives fearsome things power over you.*

"Well then, let me pass," she said, evincing a boldness
she did not feel.

"Assuredly."

He moved, but she thought that instead of stepping aside
he stooped toward her. She recoiled. A voice boomed up the
stairwell from below—"Ho, my fair lady, are you there?"

Ercildoune bounded into sight. With relief, she smiled at
him. When she looked again, Sargoth was gone.

"Oh! Where is he?"

"Who? Have I been so churlish as to interrupt a lovers'
tryst upon the stair? Now, Rohain, you must allow me to

know the name of my rival. And what an enchanting push-broom you make, I declare. Winged to boot!"

"No rival, Your Grace. No rival was here, only Sargoth the Wizard."

"Gadzooks, you tremble like a twanged harpstring, my dear. What, has the old charlatan frightened you? I'll have his gizzards!"

"He has not."

"That is well for him! Never trust a wizard, that's what I say. All that trickery and smoke—bah! There's no more gramarye in the Nine Arts than in a sieve. Come now, were you not directing your steps to the musicians' gallery? I would fain accompany you there. It is a place in which I feel right at ease, if they are playing well."

They ascended together.

Yet, although she leaned long on the parapet looking down, Rohain could not spy the one for whom her eyes ached. And when the red eye of the Winter sun first opened its lid on the late, slate dawn, it seared his absence on a frost-blighted world.

Two days passed.

From the turmoil of festival, the palace was thrown into the upheaval of war. Aggression had flared again at the Nenian Landbridge. This time, the King-Emperor himself was to travel north, with many soldiers and Dainnan, leaving Thomas of Ercildoune in charge at Court. All had been in readiness for this eventuality. In two days more, they were gone. The palace fell silent. The passages echoed with their own emptiness.

A dreariness settled.

Dianella came to Rohain privately, sending the lady's maids away.

"I have tidings."

"What tidings?"

"News for which you have waited long."

"Well, what is it? Prithee, speak!"

"Dear Heart, you seem a trifle peeved these days. Selestorfen thou al Sorrow Isles?"

"No, I am not homesick."

"Now, I insist that you treat me kindly, Heart," scolded Dianella with a smile. "I have done some hunting on your behalf. See how I put myself out to please you?" She pouted. "You know you are dearer than a sister to me."

"If I appeared brusque I ask your pardon, Dianella."

"I forgive easily." Lowering her voice, the courtier went on confidingly, "I have heard somewhat of your Dainnan, Sir Thorn."

Rohain started.

"What? What have you heard?" she said, unable to conceal her eagerness.

"Only that he has gone to the gythe."

"Gone where?"

"To the gythe. He has gone to *war*, Heart, with the last detachment of Dainnan who left here with the King-Emperor. What shall you do now—dress as a soldier-boy and follow him into battle? Oh, but I only tease."

"Then he was here! Are you sure? How can you know? Have you seen him?"

"Patience, patience! You know, Rohain, that I have certain connections here at Court. My uncle is an influential man. He has discreet methods of discovery. You can be assured that no one shall be apprised of your enquiry and that I shall keep you informed of any further word received. No gratitude, please! I have done all this out of friendship."

"But I am grateful, Dianella. You are a worthy friend indeed. I should ask the Duke of Ercildoune to make a heroic song about you."

"Pshaw! How singularly inventive you are. I must take leave of you for now, Heart—duty calls."

"Don't leave—"

"I must."

As Dianella passed through the door, her voice floated back over her shoulder: "Until tomorrow, my—"

The last words were muffled, uttered with a laugh. She must have said "*imaginative* friend." She could not possibly have said "*imaginary.*"

The Letters Patent would soon be finalized, but with the King-Emperor absent for an indefinite period, no date could be set for the official bestowal of Rohain's title. Ercildoune was continually occupied with matters of business, "holding the fort" as he called it, while His Imperial Majesty was absent. The Bard had never a spare moment between receiving and sending dispatches and attending meetings.

Conflicting rumors whirled like maddened insects up and down the streets of Caermelor. The Empire was doomed; it would be smashed apart by a sweeping assault from Namarre. Some barbaric wizard-warlord would then seize governance, and the lands of Erith would be plunged into decades of suffering and strife. Unseelie wights would overrun the cities. All mortal creatures would be destroyed.

Folk cringed, darting uneasy glances northward, as if they expected to see at any moment a tidal wave of unseelie incarnations rolling down to crush them. Like fog, an atmosphere of impending ruin brooded over the city. Many members of the Set dispersed to their country estates. Those who remained became bored and discontented. They quarreled often.

There seemed nothing better for Rohain to do but to repair to her new estate, Arcune. Somberly—in harmony with the weather—she set out with Viviana in the Duchess of Roxburgh's Windship *Kirtle Green*, a topsail schooner, accompanied by that gentlewoman, who, now that her husband had departed once more for the battle zone, was eager to escape the dreary and suspenseful Court climate for the freedom of the countryside. Also on board were the Duchess's eldest child, Rosamonde, her six other children, and her large retinue of servants and nursemaids.

Viviana spent most of the journey below, lying in her cabin. Her normally rosy face had taken on a greenish tinge, like a plum *un*ripening.

"I fear that Windship travel does not truly agree with me, m'lady," she had said woefully. "I never can master the art of walking on aerial decks, and the movement sets my head aspin. Waterships, on the other hand, present no problem."

"That is well. Many folk tremble to board a Watership, fearing the possibility of drowning."

"I have no fear of water voyages at all. I was born with a caul."

"I have heard of such things. A caul is a membrane, is it not? A membrane, sometimes wrapped about the heads of infants newly born. Such articles are supposed to protect against drowning."

"Even so," said Viviana, passing her hand across her perspiring brow, "I carry a piece of my caul everywhere with me, inside this locket-brooch."

"A pretty ornament. I noticed you wear it regularly."

"Oh, ma'am, prithee excuse me. The ship rocks so . . . I must lie down . . ."

Arcune, set in the rolling hinterlands, exceeded its new mistress's expectations. As the schooner docked at the Mooring Mast adjacent to the main house, Rohain leaned over the taffrail, gazing at her lands spread out below. In their Winter raiment they looked fair: fallow fields and green meadows, an orchard, woodlands, a chase abounding in game verts, a cluster of farm buildings, a river, and— most imposing of all—Arcune Hall.

This gracious *chastel*, part castle, part manor house,

stood three or four stories high. Solid as a monolith yet of graceful, aerial architecture, it plumbed the ornamental lake with an exact replica of its columned self. A formal garden skirted the lake: neat flowerbeds, hedged squares of parterre laid out in gravel and sand of different colors in scrolls and arabesques, crossed and bordered by precise lines of trees. Fanning out from the garden walls lay a spacious park, with quiet tracts of velvet lawns, shady copses and spinneys, water like broken panes fallen from the sky's window.

"A fine estate," said Alys-Jannetta of Roxburgh approvingly, "and I shall teach you to be mistress of it."

She did so with a will, hiring more servants, giving orders that the house—which had been unoccupied for several years—should be turned out, aired, polished, dusted, scrubbed, and refurbished. She held consultations with the Steward, the Housekeeper, and the Gamekeeper, and she examined the accounts. For a week, she and Rohain indulged in no recreation, but when all was concluded to her satisfaction, they went riding in the chase.

In this open woodland, stands of leafless birch stood like stiff brooms. Horse-chestnut and elm spread black boughs over a deep, rich leaf-mold on which the horses' hooves dully thudded. A line of ravens in arrowhead formation slid over the gray glass sky. Mist rose in soft streamers, like vaporous shang images of the trees' roots themselves, as if the woodlands could ever grieve or love.

Each breath of the riders hung as a silver cloud. The day was dark. Another storm threatened. From upwind, the dire ululation of a howler rang out, to prove it.

"You have a trustworthy Steward and an honest Housekeeper," said Alys. "I cannot say the same for the Gamekeeper—he'll have to be watched. Howbeit, I would say that this estate, like all good properties, will run smoothly whether you live here or not, although a few unannounced visits by the landlady during the year tends to improve efficiency. On one such visit I shall return to Roxburgh shortly. How I hate these sidesaddles, don't you?"

Rohain, who could not recall ever having sat on a horse before but who felt at ease in the saddle, agreed.

"I do dislike them, yes," replied Rohain. "Next time you visit me here we shall dress like gentlemen and ride like them, like the wind, jumping hedges and ditches wheresoever they fall across our path. But look now, the storm clouds come rolling over. The sky is angry. We must make haste and return before the rain sets in."

The echoing howl of the storm-harbinger again curdled the air.

"Such a Winter it is for tempests!" tutted the Duchess, turning her horse for home. "Such disruption to Windship and Stormrider schedules."

Arcune Hall's most ancient inhabitant was a household bruney known to all as "Wag at the Wa." When no kettle occupied the pot-hook hanging in the kitchen, he would sit there swinging himself to and fro, chuckling. He loved merriment and in particular the company of children, of which, until now, he had lately been deprived. He looked like a grizzled old man with short, crooked legs and a long tail that helped him to keep his seat on the hook. Sometimes he wore a gray cloak, with an old tattered night-cap on his head drawn down over one side of his face, which was always harrowed with toothache, but usually he wore a red coat and blue breeches. He would not approve of any drink stronger than home-brewed ale and used to cough furiously if strong spirits were imbibed in the kitchen. In all other ways he was a benevolent wight despite the toothache, although very fussy about the cleanliness of the house, and the bane of slipshod kitchen-maids. Like most household bruneys he had no fear of cold iron. Swinging the empty

pot-hook would bring him; this the Duchess's children
often did. What with the wight, the children, and the servants, the cavernous old kitchen was the heart of convivial-
ity at Arcune. When beyond the house's thick walls the
wind came in sudden gusts like heavy blows, and sharp,
prickling rain fell and thunder punished the skies with flails
of lightning, all was cosy by the kitchen fire. It was often
there that Rohain, Alys, and the children would spend the
evenings, in the company of the old Housekeeper.

Every day a Relayer of the Noblesse Squadron rode in
with dispatches from Caermelor—communications about
the fighting in the north and, often, snippets of Court doings
in a note from Ercildoune.

"I need to stay informed," said Alys. She looked daily
for tidings of her husband. With equal impatience, Rohain
awaited the incoming reports.

The messenger would be seen coming out of the southeast like some strange bird, his cloak flying, to alight on top
of the spindly Mooring Mast whose structure of pointed
arches was etched against the sky. Soon after, the sildron-
powered lift would begin to descend, carrying both the Relayer and the eotaur with its hoof-crescents unclipped and
flying-girth neutralized by andalum. The ostler of Arcune
would then hasten to take the steed's bridle and lead it to
the stables, while the Stormrider, pulling off his riding
gloves and winged helmet, strode into the house, a butler or
footman hastening before him to open doors and bow pro-
fusely.

True Thomas of Ercildoune corresponded regularly, re-
porting on humorous Court incidents as well as graver matters from the strife-torn north, including descriptions of
battle tactics, which Alys read over and over. The Bard
wrote:

The mounted archers of Namarre are exceeding swift, and they use this to great advantage. Their preferred tactic is encirclement. Even when we outnumber them, they are often speedy enough to surround our troops or outflank us. Aware of this, our commanders try where possible to elect narrow-fronted battlegrounds, protected by natural features of the landscape such as rivers and rocky hills. As additional protection, they keep ready a reserve force in case of cavalry attacks from the rear.

Some days since, the first pitched battle was fought in northwestern Eldaraigne, not far from the Nenian Landbridge. The Luindorn Battalions were marching west in two parallel columns, about four miles apart, when as the first column entered the open fields it was assailed by vast numbers of rebels. In order to provide a secure base from which battle could be waged, the commander ordered his men to set up camp. However, the sorties and continual harassment of the barbarians hampered their efforts, so he sent out the cavalry to stave off the enemy, enabling the infantry to begin establishing an encampment.

However, the Luindorn Drusilliers were unable to engage the rebels in battle and were repeatedly forced to withdraw to avoid being cut off. The barbarian rebels successfully encircled the Imperial troops. Furthermore, our infantry were unable to hold off their lightning strikes and sallies without the Drusilliers beside them, so the Drusilliers gradually fell back until all our troops of the first column were close-packed in a dense and milling confusion, surrounded on all fronts by fast-galloping archers on horseback. Their position was grim. Defeat seemed inevitable, until at last, with a great blowing of horns and clashing of swords on shields, the second column appeared over the horizon behind the rebel forces. It was not long before a Luindorn cavalry charge shattered the Namarrans, scattering them to the four winds.

"The Namarran scouts must have been careless," commented the Duchess, folding the letter and handing it to a footman. "On this occasion, luck was with the first column. It seems these rebels are not to be swiftly defeated."

"I remain puzzled as to their purpose," said Rohain.

"They are rebelling against the Empire," explained the Duchess. "The Namarran population comprises generations of cutthroats and thieves who have been banished to the north as punishment for their crimes. They hate the judicial system that cast them out, and wish to take revenge upon the whole Empire. Theirs is an unstable society in which violence rules. Habitually they quarrel and make war on one another, until the cruelest and most merciless butcher among them claws his way to chieftaincy. But such victories are short-lived. As soon as any flaw appears in the dictator's defences he is attacked, and the conflict begins all over again.

"Plagued by so much strife, the Namarrans cannot prosper. They have come to believe that the answer to their poverty lies in expropriating the wealth of the Empire.

"In the past they have never stopped squabbling for long enough to mount a concerted assault against us. For some unknown reason, they have finally joined forces it seems."

"And still there is no mention of the role of unseelie wights in this conflict," said Rohain in troubled tones. "It seems as if the barbarian commander is keeping them aside, waiting for some significant moment to strike with full force. But why? And what hold could any mortal man, even a great wizard, have over immortal beings so antipathetic to the human race?"

The Duchess shook her head. "Weighty questions," she replied, "and ones that we all ask ourselves often. As yet, no answers have been found."

Some three weeks after they had begun their sojourn at Arcune, there came, in the usual letter from Thomas Rhymer, a paragraph that the Duchess's daughter Rosamonde read aloud.

Unto The Most Noble the Duchess of Roxburgh, Marchioness of Carterhaugh, Countess of Miles Cross, Baroness Oakington-Hawbridge, also to the Lady Rohain of the Sorrows, Mistress of Arcune, I, Your Most Humble Servant Thomas, Duke of Ercildoune, send thee Greetings.

Madam and My Lady,

I send greeting and earnest desires that this missive should find you both hale. Be it known that following the discovery of the wealth amassed at a secret location in the Lofty Mountains and the apprehension of the culprits responsible for its treasonable looting, further questioning has revealed that members of a rival conclave were still at large. One of these, an Ertishman, "Sianadh Kavanagh of County Lochair," also known as "the Bear," was arrested yesterday in Caermelor. The felon has been consigned to the palace dungeons to await His Majesty's pleasure, which may well be execution for treason . . .

"What?" shouted Rohain. "No! It cannot be!"

She rushed to snatch the parchment from Rosamonde's hand but could make nothing of the runes and threw up her hands in despair.

"Alys, I must leave at this instant. Via, pack my chattels, have my horse saddled—nay, the sky would be faster. Is the Relayer still here, he who brought this message? Does he

yet take refreshment in the front parlor? I shall ride up behind him."

The Duchess asked no questions.

"You shall have the use of *Kirtle Green*. Dobben, run
and tell the captain to make ready to sail in haste."

"I thank you, but it will take some time to get her un-
derway—I shall ride behind the Relayer!" cried Rohain
again, in agitation.

"Their rules forbid it. Only Stormriders or the chosen of
the King-Emperor may ride the skies. No need to wring
your hands—the Windship shall be ready as soon as you
are."

The palace dungeons were no worse than the cellars at
Isse Tower. In many ways, they were better, not so damp
and slimy. The passageways had been hewn of clean stone.
They were well-lit and well-ventilated. Still, they were dungeons, and cheerless. Down here, all was stone and iron,
fire and shadow, with little change. The slow decay of time
was signposted by the various laments of prisoners who
came and went. With keys clanking, the Head Jailer led the
way, lurching, down the stairs and along a corridor.

"Hurry, hurry!" urged Rohain.

"Rats," whispered Viviana despairingly at her back. "I
heard them."

Rohain halted, aghast. "Rats? By the Powers, I detest
them more than all the unseelie wights in Erith!" She stared
desperately after the jailer's retreating back. "The guards
will chase them off," she blurted. They ran on and caught
up with the jailer. "Hasten, man!"

"Beg pardon, m'lady, I've a crook knee. I'm goin' as
hasty as I can."

Fume and fret she might, but no more speed could be got
out of him. The clatter of his bunches of keys preceded

them, while the boot-crunches of the two escorting guards brought up the rear, ricocheting off cold stone.

"Obban tesh!" said a voice farther down the passageway. "Can a bloke not get some sleep in here without being woken by yer racket, ye *doch* fly-blown *daruhshie* of a turnkey? Come in here and I'll give ye a right knee to match yer left, ye *sgorrama samrin.*"

"Sianadh!"

Rohain rushed forward, shoving the jailer aside. With both hands, she grasped the iron bars of the cell, gazing inside. There stood a man, bootless, in a ragged tunic of bergamot belted at the waist. His hose were riddled with holes and his cloak of coarse woollen kersey was threadbare. On his head was a taltry, worn beneath a filthy chaperon that ended in an outrageously long liripipe wound under his chin and over the top. From beneath this headgear bristled a red hedge in need of pruning, for it had overgrown to cover the jaw. Scorpions, crudely drawn and almost obliterated by dirt, crawled across the hairy feet.

It was indeed he.

Rohain's tears mingled with laughter. Sianadh stared, his blue eyes bursting from their sockets. For once, he was dumbfounded.

"My lady," said Viviana, "I shall fetch some salts—"

"No." Weakly, Rohain leaned on her maid's shoulder.

"A handkerchief, please. That is all." She wiped her face. The tears disappeared, the smile remained.

"What have ye brought me, jailer?" Sianadh had found his tongue at last, but it rattled hoarsely against his palate. "One of the baobhansith? A siren to tempt and strangle me? Has hanging gone out of fashion?"

"Go," said Rohain, turning to the jailer and the two guards. "I shall be safe here. Wait in the guardroom. I would hold converse with this prisoner."

Baffled, the yeomen warders bowed and obeyed.

"You also, Viviana. Wait around the corner. I have words for his ears alone."

As Viviana departed, Sianadh took a step forward. His eyes squinted, as though he tried to look at something so bright it was too painful to be directly observed.

"What d'ye want of me?"

"Ah, Sianadh! That is the second time I have ever spoken your name and yet it feels not unfamiliar on my lips—I've thought of you so often. I've mourned you. How came you here? I thought you slain—I thought you dead at the foot of Waterstair by the hands of Scalzo. You live! Yes, it is true! If you were some incarnation and not a real man they would have found it out by now."

"Who be you?" His voice was rough with wonder and suspicion.

"I am—Imrhien."

Sianadh's jaw dropped. Then he turned on his heel.

"Trickery," he growled, walking to the far wall of his austere cell.

Her words tumbled out.

"Not trickery. Ask me anything! What happened to the wormskin belt that you won at Crowns-and-Anchors in Luindorn? You unbuckled it so that you could fall out of the sky after we jumped off the pirate brig—now it floats somewhere above Erith. How did we escape the Direath? You fought it until cock-crow. What did you call yourself in Fincastle's Mill? 'My Own Self.' What color were the gowns you ordered for me in Gilvaris Tarv?"

"Enough! Enough! My pate addles. If 'tis in fact Imrhien before me, then by the smoking bones of the Chieftains, her face is somewhat altered and her tongue is making up for lost time." Approaching, he peered through the bars.

"She was kind o' spindly, like ye be. She looked as if she'd snap in twain, with naught but a pin to hold her two halves together. But she was a straw-head."

"I have dyed my hair, *mo scothy gaidair.*"

"Why?"

"It is a long story . . ."

The Ertishman stood with folded arms, shaking his head.

"Nay. It cannot be. I cannot believe what ye say, ye a fine lady and all. Don't be taunting a condemned man."

Rohain seized the bars again and shook them with all her force.

"Listen to me, you stupid, pigheaded Ertishman. Question me about anything!"

He eyed her doubtfully.

"What is the name of my niece?"

"Muirne."

"Ach, ye could have found that out. I have it! What did I, in the Ancient City when the unstorm came?"

"You doffed your taltry. You stood by some stone dragons with your hands upraised and said, *'I be My Own Self, and I be here, so look ye, I have* gilfed *this town with my mark.'*"

Bright-eyed and flushed with expectation, she looked at him. He returned her gaze with a strange one of his own, as if seeing her for the first time. His facial muscles worked in spasms. Very softly, he said, "Your face?"

"Healed by the one-eyed carlin."

"Your voice?"

"That also."

She held her breath.

Beginning deep in his chest, a roar erupted. Sianadh collided with the cell bars at a run. Hurrying up the passageway, Viviana beheld her mistress embracing the prisoner through the grating, the latter still bellowing wordlessly. At the disturbance, other prisoners began to shout.

"Chehrna, chehrna, chehrna!" bellowed Sianadh.

Tearing himself away, he danced around the cell. Guards appeared.

"Silence! You there!"

"Leave him alone," commanded Rohain. Unmoved by the presence of his captors, the Ertishman continued to sing, dance, and leap into the air, which caused his liripipe to unwind and tangle around his legs.

"Let this man out. Unlock this door."

"M'lady, we are forbidden to do that without a release signed by His Imperial Majesty. This man is a treasoner. He is to be hanged."

Sianadh stood quietly now.

"'Tis greeting and farewell, ain't it, *chehrna*," he said.

"Not necessarily," she replied. "My dear friend, you are as innocent as I. I am going to try to have you pardoned. I must go now but I shall soon return."

"Wait! Muirne and Diarmid—do they live?"

"Yes. They thrive at Isenhammer."

"Ceileinh's arms! Take them a message for me, will ye?"

"And have them know you live, condemned? And let them lose you twice?"

"Ach, nay. 'Twill be time enough for to clap eyes on 'em when I be out of this *doch* cage. No use getting 'em worrit. Get me out quicklike, *chehrna*—my throat craves a drenching with a good tavern draft. I'd rather not save 'em the cost of a hangin' by dyin' of thirst."

"I shall get you out, I swear it. Meanwhile, remember—there are two days you ought never to worry about."

They left him grinning. As she moved off, Rohain said to the jailer, "Treat him well. If you do, you shall be rewarded. If you do not, you shall answer to the Duke of Ercildoune and the Duchess of Roxburgh!"

"He must be pardoned. He must not hang."

Rohain stood before the Royal Bard, in a courtyard of Caermelor Palace.

"And why? And why not?" demanded Ercildoune.

"He is a good man, a friend—he saved my honor, my life."

"He is a treasoner."

"As much a treasoner as I!"

"Never say that, Rohain. I forbid it."

"'Tis true. At Waterstair—"

"You took booty to aid you on your return—you confessed it from the first. It has been recognized as no crime. Say no more on't!"

"With what crime is he charged?"

"The thieves we apprehended upon your advice, the men you call Scalzo's—although we did not find one by that name amongst them—they indicted him. It seems that unlike yourself, he returned to Waterstair to pilfer from it. This advice was confirmed by the man's own drunken boasting, overheard in a tavern. 'Tis not the first time a man has hanged himself with a tankard of ale."

"His boasts are empty. The thieves lied."

"You are determined to remain his ally. Yet I have seen this man. I cannot fancy him to be your sweetheart."

"He is not. He is—brother or uncle. Family."

"Since you and no other ask it, I will grant stay of execution. But only His Majesty can grant pardon for such as this."

"Then I must have audience with His Majesty."

"Impossible. He is at the fields of war, as you know."

"And why should I not journey north?"

"My flower, my very bird—you upon the battle-plain? Await His Majesty's return. Until then, your friend, my fellow Ert, may live."

By the grace of the Duke of Ercildoune, Sianadh was allowed, chained and under guard, to ascend daily to one of the parlors. Rohain would converse with him there for hours, regaling him with food and drink to his heart's content.

She told him news of his family, then, having sworn him to secrecy, revealed all of her remembered past that her muteness had kept hidden from him. She had revealed this history to nobody, ever, not even Maeve. She told him of the cruel ivy, *Hedera paradoxis,* and the callous denizens of Isse Tower, and her life as a servant. It was as if a weight had been lifted from her heart, to share such a burden of knowledge.

For his part, Sianadh was tickled to find himself enjoying the hospitality of the King-Emperor's palace, if only conditionally.

" 'Tis the life," he said cheerily, sprawled on a wolfskin rug before the fire. "If I could get these *doch* manacles off I'd be the happiest man. Fortune's smiled on ye, *chehrna.* But ye haven't your past returned to ye, yet."

"No."

"Ye ought to try. It be important to know history. Kings come and go and some remain. To survive, a bloke must know what comes before and after. Things be not what they seem at a given moment. They be the sum of their past and the hope of their future. The smiling stranger may offer ye wine but has he just come from the house of sickness?"

"How am I to find my history?"

"When ye lose summat, ye must retrace your steps to find it."

"Do you say that I should return to Isse Tower?"

"That be what I say. Far as I can tell, 'tis your only hope. I cannot call ye Rohain, or Lady Muck or anything. Find out your real name, eh?"

"I could not go away, leaving you here."

He shrugged.

"I've been worse off. The fare down there in the dungeons be plain but plenty. I be gettin' plenty o' rest and flay me for boots if I've had much of that these past years. From what I ken, the King-Emperor will not be rushing back to pardon me for trying unsuccessfully to steal some of his treasure until after we win this war. Take a Windship to Isse. Ye're wealthy—ye can afford it. Ye will not be gone for long and ye might find out summat."

"No," she repeated, "I could not leave you."

But the dormant questions had reawakened.

"Begging your pardon, m'lady, but I am surprised that you have not been Cut," said Viviana with concern. "There is all this talk of you having family connections with that hairy felon. M'lady, he's Ertish and an outlaw! Dianella and all of them must think it such a quiz and yet they have not Cut you."

"Dianella is saying she thinks it an amusing novelty and she wants a condemned man of her own to keep on a chain."

"Beg pardon, m'lady, but I would not trust her, truly I wouldn't. For all her peacock's plumage, she is nothing but a gray-malkin that tears apart birds and helpless creatures merely for sport. M'lady, until you came here she was generally thought to be the fairest in the land and now she's jilted from her high horse. She does not like it, and that's a fact. But she has not let them Cut you and she worms her way into your affections for her own purposes. She's a cold-hearted one and that's for certain. Her own uncle is unwell, having returned from an excursion black with bruises from a spriggan attack, yet she troubles herself not at all on his behalf."

"You speak truly. Howbeit, I cannot trouble myself with Dianella's meretriciousness."

The meetings with Sianadh brought mixed pleasure and sadness, for the Ertishman could not bring himself to meet

Rohain's eyes very often, and when he did he would hastily avert his gaze. There was none of the easy comradeship of old times. That was all gone, and in its place stood an uncomfortable awareness, as if she were a porcelain figurine on a shelf and he too afraid to touch it lest it break or be sullied by his rough hands. And once or twice she caught him looking at her from the corners of his eyes with an expression of awe, as if he witnessed a vision in which he could not fully have faith.

She desired no reverence, only the banter of good fellowship. Was this distance between them, and the covert duels in the gardens, and the spurious friendship of Dianella part of the real price to be paid for the unwearing of her mask of ugliness? Maeve had said, *"Do not be thankful until you have lived with your changed appearance for a moon-cycle or two. See how you like it then."*

Despite the awkwardness, she looked forward to the company of her friend and used their hours together to discover his recent history.

"The Gailledu saved me," said Sianadh, "as I lay below Waterstair wounded to the bone and almost breathing my last. A life for a life, he repaid me—gathered me up in his arms as if I were no more than a lad. Great strength has he, belied by his looks. It was because of that flower, ye ken, the blue one that Ethlinn preserved in an egg of resin and gave to me. It meant summat.

"He took me to some place in the forest and healed me. When I was well, I returned to Tarv and sheltered with Ethlinn and Roisin. They told me you had set out for Caermelor but that the roads were bad. By then all roads to the west had been declared impassable, wight-struck. My thought was how to swiftly get word to the King-Emperor at Caermelor to inform him of the treasure, so that it could be quickly wrested from Scalzo's cowardly *uraguhnes,* and ye and me could be heroes and Liam, *tambalai* lad, would be avenged. For I had little hope then that ye would get through, the reports being so bad and so many caravans being lost. So I scraped together all the money I could beg or borrow and went to the Stormriders.

"I get sent to a scribe of theirs and I tell him a message to write down, to send to the King-Emperor. Not wanting the world to know about it, like, I don't say exactly what 'tis about, but I give hints. Only one who knew aught could have pieced it together. Anyway, this scribe looks at me kind of strange, and he reminds me of another I saw somewhere, blast his eyes, but I couldn't recall where. I took exception to him from the start. And with good reason, as it turns out later. For when I returned to Tarv Tower with Eochaid at my side, to ask whether the message had been successfully sent for all me trouble and money, we were set upon by ruffians outside the Tower, and hunted through the streets. And in the process, I got separated from Eochaid but the heat was still on me.

"Now, I always had a plan for if something like this should happen—'tis wise to keep a couple of escape plans handy for emergencies, mark you, Imrhien. I have a friend with a boat at Tarv docks. Down there I run, for the lick of me life, but when I get there, the boat is gone. Must've gone out fishing. At this point I remember where I have seen the pox-faced Scribe before—he be one of Scalzo's accomplices. Tarv be full of them—or it was. Anyway, these sons of dogs being hot on me heels, I jump into the nearest boat and head off. This shakes them off me tail because there's a storm brewing which only a silkie or a mad Ertishman would take to the seas in. Being possessed of wondrous seamanship, I sail all the way to Caermelor, and many's the un-*lorraly* tale I could tell about events along the way. But when I finally get here, strike me lucky if the entire population doesn't already know that there's a treasure at Waterstair because some ladyship's found out about it and squawked. It's sleeveless me sayin' aught about what the world already knows and expectin' a reward for it, so there's nothing left for it but to join the army.

"Now, if a lad's going to join the army he wants to make the most of the last of his freedom first. So I makes meself known at the nearest malt-house, where I meet a couple of blokes I used to knock around with in the old days, good mates. We've had a few sessions. Priz—that be his kenning and I wist no other—he was in the lock-up once. He be a fellow always dressed so clean and neat, careful with his clobber, like. Dogga, he don't fuss so much about what's on his back—'tis who's on the end of his fist that counts with him.

"So me and Priz and Dogga be sitting down to dine and Priz tells the story about how in that same malt-house last year there was a fight and the floor was rotten and eight big blokes crashed through the planking into the cellar below, which hadn't been used for fifteen years and was full of slime up to their middles and Priz nearly laughed his well-tailored breeches off at the sight. Then I be telling the story about when old Cauliflower died at the table playing cards, and his hand still on the table, and his mates looked under his hand and there were three aces so they shoved the money in his pockets before they carried him out, 'cos he'd won.

"As I be telling this, in comes Lusco Barrowclough, as loudmouthed a bullying drunkard and want-wit as ever cheated in a hurling match or got thrown out of a Severnesse tavern. I had not had the misfortune to set eyes on the whoreson villain for a year or two—not long enough. Barrowclough's already well-oiled, and it's not long before he starts miscalling the malter and his nice little tarty servant-wenches. I up and tells this gentleman that if I want a disturbance while I be eating, I only have to go and eat at me grandmother's place. He looks down his Feohrkind nose at me, and me wearin' a Finvarnan kilt—and he says with a sneer, 'Nice legs.' 'Would ye like one of 'em up yer backside?' I offers. He starts mouthing off a bit, then Priz says, 'Pipe down while we're trying to eat,' and then Dogga looks up and puts in, 'I've had a gutful of ye.'

"So then Barrowclough, the *uraguhne,* says, 'Well, I've had a gutful of *ye,'* and adds, 'I'll break yer bleedin' neck.' Dogga politely responds, 'Ye couldn't break wind let alone break anyone's neck,' and in less time than it takes to fling a curse across a tavern, the fisticuffs is on. I flatten Barrowclough with much joy and return to my seat. He runs out the door and I politely say 'Pass the salt' and salubriously resume eating with my two mates. Before we have quite finished dining, we look up to see our *shera sethge* gentleman walk *back* in the door. Behind him, another the same. Behind him, another. They keep walking in, until in addition to Barrowclough, there be nine. None of them are comely, I can tell ye—all bull-girthed, solid, bald, scarred, toothless, ugly *skeerdas* to a man, and ropeable as wounded steers. The maltster and the servants went pale, and so did all the other diners.

"Not to be taken by surprise, I punched out one of Barrowclough's cronies with no preamble. As foreseen, a fight began. There were stools being broken across blokes' backs, tables being overturned, crockery smashing, blokes flying through the air, round and round the malt-house for a goodly while. A bloke could have had another square meal and a tankard in the time it took for that fight.

"While this is going on, another two malt-house customers who have been watching with interest see that although 'tis three against ten, the three appear to be winning, so they join in on the winning side. That makes it five against ten, and pretty soon Barrowclough and his nine are being helped out the door by the maltster and his brothers. We three now being five, we returned to our tables and sopped up the last bits of gravy, which had been preserved from ruin more by our own effort than by some stroke of good fortune.

"As we are eating I take time to look at the condition of my mates. Priz, always so immaculate, be missing a boot. The remaining boot be split. One of his sleeves be ripped off at the shoulder, his shirt and every other article on him be torn. Dogga and I be in a similar condition. Heedless of small inconveniences, we are partaking of the last part of our meal when a couple of fellows put their heads around the door and survey the scene. They turn out to be a sheriff and a constable.

" 'Has there been a fight here?' says they.

"We look around in surprise. The malt-house looks a mite untidy.

" 'Fight? I ain't seen no fight,' says we. The maltster says the same as we—so do the serving-wenches.

"The sheriff and the constable look us over once more, while we're licking the gravy off our trenchers and complimenting the maltster's cook on the meal. They warn us against disturbing the peace, we assure them that we shudder to think of the idea ever entering our heads, then they slouch out and leave us be.

"Well, news spread around and the malt-house began to fill up until we found ourselves with a jovial company of drinkers around us. Everyone likes a winner. The night went on and someone brought in a yard of ale, which was a bit of sport, and then more ale all round, and I got to talking about Finvarna and friends I left behind, and then about other friends and relations lost to me—for I thought ye'd been devoured on the Caermelor Road—and then on to what might have been, and the riches I nearly had. I may have said things I wotted not what of. Somehow, the truth got all twisted and next thing the sheriff and his constable be back, with about fifty others, putting the strong-arm on

me and dragging me outside and me throwing punches
while the drink robs me of my strength and then the revels
are over. That be how I ended up here."

Not seven days after Rohain's return to Court, Dianella
again sought a private audience with her. Dressed in a cote-
hardie of red velvet edged with fur, a kirtle of rich
baudekyn, a cloak of blue-green velvet worked with a design in gold and lined with ermine, a reticulated headdress
ornamented with goldsmith's work and jewels, and a hip-
belt of square brooches and jewels, from which depended
an aulmoniere with a baselard thrust through it, alongside a
hand-mirror and a pair of pincers, Dianella looked fair in
the most splendid degree, although, by the frown on her
brow, she was clearly unsettled.

In her glorious plumage, she paced up and down for a
while, pursing her lips and continuing to frown until Rohain said, "Unburden yourself, pray."

"Alas! It is not that simple, Dear Heart. What I have to
say distresses me deeply."

"Thorn—he has not fallen in battle?"

"I know not. But it is not of your Dainnan that I would
speak. It is of yourself. You are discovered."

"What is your meaning?" A seed of apprehension
sprouted in Rohain's mind.

"Ah, what is *yours,* Dear Heart, whoever you may be?
For you are not Rohain of the Sorrows, that has become evident."

A chill sensation ran through Rohain to her fingertips.
Her blood seemed to have frozen in her veins. Dianella
smiled with only her mouth, not her eyes.

"I perceive my words have an effect upon you. Good.
You see, you have been found to be an impostor. Inquiries
have been made, in Severnesse, in the Sorrow Isles. The
family Tarrenys is an old one, granted, yet it has all but died

out. Only a few members are left, all accounted for. Of
them you are not one. Do you deny it?"

After a while, Rohain said, "I do not."

"Well, then!"

Triumph lit Dianella's mien. Rohain itched to slap her
face. If it had not been for the courtier's knowledge of
Thorn, Rohain would have thrust her from the room. Beneath the anger and the fear, a deep sense of shame spread
out, taking root in her very bones. Through clenched teeth
she said, "What now?"

"What now? Dear Heart, there is only one course open
to you. You will not, of course, claim the peerage of Arcune—instead you must leave at once."

It was Rohain's turn to pace now.

"Leave, I say," continued Dianella. "This is not the place
for you. You are above your station. For now, the knowledge of your deception rests with only myself and my
uncle, and I swear to you as a true friend that neither of us
shall expose you if you depart now. But should the word
spread despite our best efforts to keep it secret, there is no
knowing what steps might be taken to punish you for your
wanton guile. For your own safety, go this day, this very
hour."

"You say you will not betray me?"

"La! I am cut to the quick!"

"What do you want in return?"

"More and more ungracious! Really! Do you suggest
that I want payment? Friends do not buy and sell, but gifts
are often passed from one to the other."

"Take my entire wardrobe. Take everything I own in the
Treasury."

"Pshaw! How should it look, if I were to be seen dressed
in your hand-me-downs?"

"Dianella, I need, more than ever now, to retain the influence of my position, if only until the King-Emperor returns. I shall leave Court at first light on the morrow, only to come back one last time for an audience with His Majesty. After that you shall see me nevermore."

"A wise decision on your part, Dearest Heart."

Omitting the courtesies of leave-taking, Dianella sallied from the room with a swish of baudekyn and a clash of implements. Typically, she tossed a parting shot over her shoulder: "Have your maid bring me the costumes now. And the keys to your caskets."

Rohain rang for Viviana.

"I intend to make an excursion from Court," she told the courtier, carefully keeping her tone level. "Have a letter dispatched to Isse Tower. Inform them, at the Seventh House of the Stormriders, to make ready—the Lady Rohain of Arcune sends greetings. She is coming from Caermelor Palace to sojourn for a time."

Her heart felt wrung out like a blood-soaked mop. Now that Dianella had exiled her from Court, she had indeed lost Thorn forever.

Night drew in around Caermelor Palace. Rohain sat gazing drearily into a gold-backed looking-glass framed with ivory and mother-of-pearl. She wondered whether strange visions would trouble her this night, and whether she would wake in fear. Once, back in the cottage of Maeve, she had dreamed of three gentle, loving faces: those of a woman, a man, and a boy-child. Later there had been the Dream of the Rats. Both of these fragments had borne the hallmark of truth—she could not doubt that they were memories in disguise. It was only since Maeve had laid hands upon Rohain that her repose had been disturbed by such images. She suspected something else must have happened at that time, when her face and speech had been restored. The restoration, perhaps, had acted as a catalyst for the beginning of a gradual arousing of memory. In Gilvaris Tarv, Ethlinn had once explained, <<*Sometimes in such cases, all it takes is for the sufferer to come upon something familiar, and then the memories slowly begin to filter back into the mind.*>>

Rohain whispered to her reflection, "My own once-familiar face . . . when I looked upon you, in the mirror of the one-eyed carlin, the sight sparked off an opening of closed doors."

That night, through a chink in one of those doors, there issued a third dream—that of the White Horse.

It was under her, running, the horse—the apotheosis of swiftness and freedom. All was speed, all exhilaration. The wind roared in her ears, the ground passed swiftly by below—were the hooves even touching it? She laughed aloud, but a shape fell out of the sky beating its wings, dark against the sun. It dashed in close—too close—and the laughter turned to screams, but the horse itself was scream-ing and it was a nightmare, because the horizon spun through weightlessness that gathered in the pit of her stom-ach and rose to her gorge, then the hillside came up with a smack and became a spear of white-hot iron that burned through the bone of her leg and she was screaming . . .

Dreams, memories—perhaps she had been better off without them.

4

THE TOWER
Hunt and Hearts' Desire

The twelve mighty Houses from Belfry to Fairlaise,
From Worthing to Outreme, where thunderstorms breed,
Command the four winds on the highest of highways.
The wings of the thoroughbred glory in speed.

> VERSE FROM "SONG OF THE STORMRIDERS"

Uhta: the hour before dawn.

Tidings arrived by carrier pigeon as the Windclipper *Harper's Carp* was being rigged for takeoff. A Dainnan Windship had captured a black pirate brig lurking in the Lofty Mountains, and seized much booty. Desperate and bloody had been the struggle. Few of the reivers had been taken alive. Those who fell had been abandoned, to be devoured by the strange mouths of the forest.

* * *

Winches rattled. Screws rotated. The wooden fish figure-head seemed to leap. As the crew vigorously onhebbed the andalum hull-plates, the Royal Bard's personal clipper began to rise, leaning her silhouette elegantly into the wind. For those on board, there was no feeling of motion forward or upward—rather the impression that the Mooring Mast was leaving the ship and the launch-crew was sinking away below.

Caermelor Palace dwindled. Spreading her canvas wings, the *Harper's Carp* lifted like a long-billed crane through the clouds until she reached cruising altitude. After the first ascent there was no sense of height. The carpet of mist below appeared close and solid, beckoning the passengers to tread upon it. The Windship's shadow skipped along down there, a trick of light-interference painting a colored halo around the keel.

Like a thimbleful of bubbles in the sky, the *Harper's Carp* sailed north along the coastline. By Windship, this journey was almost nine hundred miles. By Seaship across the mouth of the Gulf of Mara the distance would have been considerably shorter. Ercildoune, however, had insisted that Rohain take his private aircraft instead of buying passage on a merchant Seaship, claiming it would provide greater security from eldritch assailants. For the Bard, who was busy with political matters and frequently closeted for hours in discussion with members of the Royal Council, she had contrived an excuse for visiting Isse Tower: "Court is become so dull of late, and I should like to behold with my own eyes one of the famous outposts of the Stormriders."

The captain had no qualms about sailing at night, and so they reached their destination in only four days. Late on the fourth day a jagged stalk began to grow from the horizon, enlarging until it became Isse Tower, fantastically tall, crowned with prongs, its dark shape cutting the sky in half.

A brass trumpet blared—the watchman's signal. Two or

three Skyhorses circled like flies against the raw wound of the western sky. When the sea-breeze had settled, the winches began their keening. The Windship was onhebbed down to the docking stair on the west side, one hundred and twelve feet above ground level. The crew flung out lines. Slowly she was hauled in to her mooring against the Tower's shelf.

Once, a grotesque servant had fled from here—nameless, mute, destitute, despised. Now she had returned, Imrhien-Rohain, to the only home she could remember.

As she descended the gangplank on the captain's arm, a young man in Stormrider uniform greeted her. Hard-faced was he, with the predatory look of a vulture. His hair was severely plastered against his skull and bound at the nape of his neck, his taltry was brazenly thrown back. Here stood Lord Ustorix, Son of the House, the Chieftain's heir, who had once been one of her tormentors.

Ustorix met the arrivals with a deep bow and a calm formality at odds with his demeanor, for his gestures evinced intense excitement and the tension in his face betrayed a desperate covetousness. At his shoulder crowded numerous other Tower gentlefolk in black and silver, led by Ustorix's sister Heligea, herself wide-eyed at the sight of this urbane newcomer.

To the Tower-dwellers, Rohain appeared the paradigm of courtiers. Prudently, she had kept aside half a dozen costumes when she handed over her wardrobe to Dianella. She was dressed in a fur-lined houppelande tightly fitting to the waist, patterned all over with a stitched motif of artichokes and vine-leaves on a ground of dark blue velvet. Dagged sleeves sweeping the ground were folded back to flaunt undersleeves of gold tisshew on deep red velvet, tight to the wrist. Three aerial feathers sprouted from her fur taltry-turban. Her cloak of ciclatoune was fastened at the shoulder by a gold filigree agraffe. From her jeweled girdle depended a sharp-bladed anlace in a decorated sheath, a gold tilhal in the shape of a rooster, whose eyes were pink rubies, and a fringed aulmoniere containing a certain swan's feather.

Two rows of bowing Tower footmen in mustard-and-silver livery lined the way from the gatehall of disembarkation. Servants swarmed deferentially. The honored visitor from Caermelor and her retinue were guided into a wrought-iron lift-cage. Ustorix stood near enough to his guest that nausea overswept her, caused by the familiar odor of his sweat and its past associations. Fighting her illness, she smiled at him, taking note of the way he trembled and flushed. She thought it an interesting effect, as though she brandished a weapon.

"Of course, my father, Lord Voltasus, is in the north, fighting at the King-Emperor's side," he was saying, waving a gloved hand. "I am master here during his absence. My lady mother is on a visit to my sister at the Fifth House, in Finvarna. Yet fear not, all has been made ready for Your Ladyship's arrival, although word of your visit came but two days since. The messenger who delivered it neglected to declare that the visitor would be the fairest flower of the Court. He shall suffer for the omission," he added, with a swaggering bow from which his visitor happened to glance away.

"No doubt," he continued, "Your Ladyship has long desired to admire at first hand the strength of the Seventh House, the magnificence of Isse Tower, forever acclaimed in the accolades of bards."

"No doubt."

Parochial, supercilious man! she thought. *Do you believe the world has nothing better to do than drone endlessly in praise of Stormriders?*

"Be assured, Your Ladyship shall not be disappointed."

"I am certain of that."

High expectations are a necessary prerequisite of disappointment.

*   *   *

The lift-keeper stopped the cage at Floor Thirty-seven, where Ustorix solicitously offered to hand his guest from the cage. Her hands, however, were occupied with lifting the hem of the velvet houppelande. She stepped scrupulously through the door.

"My lady might wish to rest . . . shall be conducted to your quarters . . . obliged if you should sit by my right hand at dinner . . ." The words tumbled out of Ustorix's mouth like fried onion rings—well-oiled, pungent, and hollow. It appeared the Son of the Seventh House waged an inner battle that pitched his innate arrogance against a desire to present himself in what he considered a flatteringly humble manner. He bestowed a second lavish bow. His sister Heligea curtsied. With a brusque nod—she could not bring herself to make polite obeisance to this kindred—Rohain, accompanied by Viviana and a bevy of upper-level servants, left them and entered her designated chambers.

It seemed that the more she scorned Ustorix the more he adored her. Deference would have encouraged his contempt, but ill-usage attracted respect. He, like most bullies, must exist either as a boot-heel to crush, or a doormat to be trodden upon.

At dinner Rohain shone like a peacock among crows— and the crows hung on her every word, copied her every gesture. They presumed that everything she did was the epitome of the latest mode. Of course, they said among themselves, she must be conversant with the latest trends—she had been dwelling at Court. What endeared her to them further was that there was no indecorous laughter from this fashionable courtier, no overt show of emotion to offend their stoicism. A complete model of detachment, she displayed admirable aloofness. Furthermore, she was wealthy, titled, and beautiful into the bargain.

The Greayte Banqueting Hall on Floor Thirty-one seemed small and austere after the glitter of Court. Rohain scrutinized every dish, insisting on learning the name of the cook who was responsible for each. The dishes were numerous, designed to impress. Most she waved aside, barely glancing at them. Beckoning her maid to lean closer, she whispered, "I advise you to partake of nothing prepared by the hands of the cook named Rennet Thighbone. I know he never checks the vegetables for snails. He also cleans his filthy fingernails by kneading pastry, and spits into the sauces—and those are not the worst of his habits."

"Gramercie, m'lady. With gladness I take this advice."

"The masters of this place are unaware of it," added Rohain.

Ustorix fawned, pouring out blandishments. He began intentionally addressing Rohain with the archaic forms "thee" and "thou," whose meaning had evolved from olden times to convey the close association of brotherhood, as between high-ranking Stormriders—or an intimacy of affection, such as between lovers.

"May I tempt thee with a slice of pigeon pie, my lady? The pastry looks interesting—spiced, I fancy, by the spotted look of it. Or perhaps thou wouldst prefer to taste of this dish of cabbage with, I think, rather charming raisins—or baked leveret glazed with quinces and a little of this excellent foaming sauce?"

Rohain said softly to Viviana, "Tell Lord Ustorix's page to instantly inform his master that it is hardly appropriate to address me with such familiarity."

The message having reached its destination, the heir of the House upset his wine in startled mortification, thus adding to his distress. Both he and the page blushed to their ears. Ustorix kicked the lad, sending him sprawling, and bawled a petulant criticism at a passing steward.

The sauce foamed in its pewter boat. Avoiding it, Rohain

sipped the fern-green wine, whose flavor had probably been beneficially influenced by the presence of moss-frogs in the cellar.

"My Lord," Rohain remarked conversationally, turning the twin weapons of her glance on Ustorix, "the fact that Stormriders possess nerves of steel is well-known."

"Of course, my lady. As Riders we are born to it. Courage flows in the bloodline of the Twelve Houses. Howbeit," he added hastily, "an infusion of new blood may sometimes be of benefit, should it be particularly pure."

"As I was saying, the Stormriders' unrivaled reputation for performing death-defying acts has achieved its pinnacle, methinks, with this latest rumor from Isse Tower which has at last reached the Court."

"The tale of my brave ride to Ilian during the storms of Imbrol?" The vulture puffed out its chest. "True, many attempting such a hazardous undertaking would have perished, but I—"

"No. The tale of the Stormriders who stood balanced on sildron, four hundred feet above the ground, wearing no flying-harness or safety ropes."

Ustorix afforded no reply.

"Zounds, what a feat," expounded Rohain, warming to her topic. "We all asked ourselves, *What manner of men are these?* There is naught so charming as a man of heroism and bravery, one who can perform acts of great daring and remain icy cool. Do you not agree, my lady Heligea?"

"Certainly," replied that lady, who until now had exhibited only bored sullenness.

"One must indeed respect such a man," persisted Rohain. "One must adore him. Pray, leave me not in suspense—who were the perpetrators of this rumored exploit?"

"A couple of the servants," drawled Heligea insouciantly, before her brother could reply. "Grod Sheepshorn and Tren Spatchwort."

The knuckles of Ustorix whitened, like a range of snowy peaks. Gimlet-eyed, he shot a glance of pure hatred at Heligea.

"Servants!" Rohain smiled. "Well, if the servants are so remarkable, the masters by rights must be doubly so. I suppose 'tis quite a common feat amongst Stormriders. No doubt you practice it every day. Dearly would I love to witness such a valorous act!"

Am I becoming another Dianella? Oh, but the vulture deserves this, and more.

"May I watch *you* at this trick, my lord?" Rohain asked sweetly. "It would be something to tell them, at Court."

Ustorix's face had grayed. He cleared his throat, attempting a thin smile. The object of his adoration gazed at him expectantly.

"Assuredly . . ."

"Delightful," she said, raising her wineglass in salute. "I look forward to it. By the by, where are these dauntless servants to be found, this Tron Cocksfoot and Garth Sheepsgate?"

"One of them enlisted. The other—well, I am told he joined the crew of a Windship," advised Heligea, who seemed to keep herself informed about all events both Below the dock and Above.

"Was there not talk of some other servant," Rohain continued airily, inwardly remarking on her new persona's ability to dissimulate. "A deformed lad with yellow hair?"

"It is surprising how much talk of Isse Tower's servants reaches the Court," purred Heligea. "One wonders how, since Relayers would hardly bother. Yes, there was once one such as Your Ladyship describes. I know not whence he came, nor where he went. Nobody knows."

"Unfortunately, there may be no time for the sildron demonstration," grittily interjected Ustorix. "I had planned to throw the Tower and demesnes open for a tour of inspection tomorrow, should my lady so condescend."

"Such an undertaking must prove diverting, but do not deny me, my lord, I pray you! I am certain there will be enough time for other diversions. It is not necessary for me to leave here until I receive word of the King-Emperor's return to Caermelor."

And so it was arranged. Before her visit came to an end, the Lady Rohain would be granted the entertainment she desired.

Keeping company with Isse Tower's masters soon palled. After dinner, Rohain pleaded travel fatigue and retired to her rooms. There she instructed Viviana to go discreetly among the Tower servants.

"Find an old drudge-woman called Grethet. She works on Floor Five, around the furnaces. There must be no fuss—concoct some story that I've heard she's skilled at healing and wish to ask her advice, or some such explanation. And discover all you can about another servant who once worked here—a lad, yellow-haired, misshapen."

Shang harbingers prickled Rohain's scalp as she stood in the doorway watching Viviana, gray-cloaked, flit like a thought to the lift-well. There the lady's maid rang the bell and waited. From the deeps, the cage could be heard clunking upward on its rails. The wrought-iron gates slid apart and Dolvach Trenchwhistle burst forth beefily, followed by a quartet of chambermaids bearing laden trays. On beholding Rohain, the Head Housekeeper came to a sudden halt.

"Oh, er, my lady," she stammered with a curtsy, "I was just comin' ter see if there'd be anything Your Ladyship might be wantin'."

"No. Only peace."

"Yes, m'lady. Very good, m'lady."

Dolvach Trenchwhistle turned back toward the lift.

"Trenchwhistle!"

"Yes, m'lady?"

"Carry that tray for that little chambermaid. It is too heavy for her. I am surprised at you. At Court, we hear everything. I had been told that the Head Housekeeper treated her underlings as she would nurture the finest roses. Do not disappoint me."

"Yes, m'lady. Forgive me, m'lady."

Flustered, the Head Housekeeper blundered into a tray, knocking it against the wall. Half the contents spilled. She muttered imprecations. As the lift-gates closed, she crooned aggressively to Viviana, "And what might you be wantin' downstairs, my dear?"

Rohain's skin tautened. The air smacked of lightning. Her dark-dyed hair, relieved of the fur turban, lifted of its own accord. She was alone in her chambers in the Tower.

Her door opened onto a wide passage, at one end of which stood a pair of high and narrow portals. She walked to them, pushed them apart. They gave onto a balcony with a dominite balustrade. Spoutings sprouted winged gargoyles, their tongues protruding. The cool night wind shouldered its way past, bringing a whiff of the sea that knocked at memory's gates. Down below at the dock, the *Harper's Carp* bobbed, waiting to return to Caermelor with the morning breeze, since it could not be spared from duty. The Greayte Southern Star winked like an emerald beacon gemming the horizon. It being the middle of the month, the moon was full. A silver note sounded from somewhere in the crenellations overhead. An impossible silhouette flew across the moon's face—a Stormrider coming in from a Run.

The unstorm traveled close in his wake. Rohain watched it cover the forest, far below, with tiny firefly glows, here and there shining brighter where a tableau pulsed. Isse Harbor was transformed into a carpet of gaudy fish-scales, green and gold. A real Seaship lay at anchor there. A ghostly galleon foundered off the headland, like the Seaship in a song Sianadh had once sung about a vessel caught in the Ringstorm:

> *If ye go forth into the north ye'll see her evermore—*
> *The ship and crew so brave and true, do perish o'er and*
>   *o'er.*
> *Outlin'd in gold from top to hold, each clew and spar*
>   *and cleat—*
> *She founders ever and again in terrible repeat.*

"From whence come I?" Rohain said softly. "From beyond the Ringstorm? Could it be that I sailed from unknown lands beyond the girdle of outrageous winds, and survived?"

The unstorm's terrible splendor rolled by. She walked back toward her chambers but had not yet reached the tall doors when a disquieting occurrence took place, a jarring note in the paean of her triumphant return to Isse Tower.

Almost soundlessly, out of the moonshadows, something limped rapidly across the passageway.

"Stop!" she reprimanded.

It checked, for the space of a heartbeat, then backed away.

"Pod—it is Pod, isn't it?"

A hoarse sob broke from a throat.

"You! You back again! I told you to leave me alone," Pod gasped. "Go away. Go from here. You might bring doom on this place."

"You know me?" She was incredulous. "But how—"

"Yes, I know you. You used to live here. Now you have come back. Come back to bring ruin on us all."

"No, I have not—" but she knew herself to be at his mercy. Pod alone knew her, instantly, when in her altered persona she had scarcely known herself. It lent him a certain power.

"Grethet," she said. "Tell her to come to me. Prithee."

"Cannot do that."

"Why not? I shall pay you."

"I do not want *your* tainted gold. Anyway, the crone's dead—Grethet's cold in her grave."

With that, Pod limped to some hitherto unnoticed slot in a wall and sidled into it. Rohain called into the darkness after him but he did not reappear. Perhaps he was lying . . .

Clouds ate up the moon and a rapid wind slammed the doors shut.

"A rum and gloomy lot they are, m'lady," announced Viviana, "the servants here. All save three of them—the old codger they call the Storyteller, he's all right, and there is a rather strapping strapper among them, by the name of Pennyrigg. He knows how to laugh, at least, not like the rest. And one little girl—she seems ever so nice—name of Caitri Lendoon."

"The daughter of the Keeper of the Keys."

"How clever is my lady, to know all the names of the servants!"

"The yellow-haired lad—what did they say about him?"

"Where he came from and where he has gone are mysteries."

"What did you find out about Grethet?"

"Why, she died, they told me. That's all they said."

Rohain fell silent. Eventually, she sighed. She must not reveal her grief. Inwardly she was crying, aching for the sake of the old woman who had roughly nurtured her, and who had been the last possible link to her old life.

"'Tis late, my lady," said Viviana gently. "Oughtn't you to be abed?"

"I suppose so. You were long away, Via, what else did you hear?"

"Well, the Storyteller, he told a couple of wondrous interesting tales. I could not help listening. He has a way with him; he reels his listeners in like fishes, so to speak."

"Yes. Maybe that old Grethet had a story too. It will never be told now."

The tidings of Grethet's demise caused Rohain to despair about her future. What course should she choose now? She might not return to Caermelor or Arcune. In the absence of any other plans she resolved to remain at Isse Tower until inspiration or opportunity should present itself.

They walked in the demesnes: Rohain, Ustorix, Viviana, the captain and first mate of the *Harper's Carp*, numerous hangers-on and attendants, and the disconsolate Heligea dressed in black, with silver buttons. The solemn shadow of the Tower unrolled itself across the Road and fell into the Harbor. Gulls scourged a cloud-ridden sky.

At Rohain's side, Ustorix raved grandiosely. "These are the hattocking-circuits, m'lady of the Sorrows," he proclaimed, giving an expansive wave. "Smithy and stables are over that way. All that you can see is under my sway. Isse is the keystone of the entire Relay network, and without the network the Kingdom grinds to a halt, the Empire stalls.

"Yeoman Riders, operating at an altitude of three hundred feet, are the younger Sons of the House. They ride for us on miscellaneous errands, or Relay for simple folk with urgent personal messages and enough coin scraped together to pay the fee. The largest squadron, the Regimental, makes its runs at four hundred feet. These are the mercantile wings. They Relay for wealthy merchants, who lavish upon them the appropriate deference and reimbursement, being dependent on our goodwill." He turned eagerly to Rohain. "Knowledge is power," he proclaimed, as though he had invented the phrase. "The merchant who learns of enterprises early might send his own ships ahead to catch his rivals' trade. He who is blessed with first tidings of a shortage might buy up that commodity before prices rise!"

Absently, Rohain acknowledged his words.

"The Noblesse Squadron, of course," he ranted, "rides sky for the peers of the realm—their assigned altitude of five hundred feet is second only to the fastest and highest ranked, the Royals, also known as the King's Emissaries, who are entrusted with state business." Rohain stifled a yawn.

"Would my lady like to see the ornamental gardens?" suggested Heligea halfheartedly, diverting attention from her brother. The visitor's eyes had meanwhile alighted elsewhere.

"For what purpose are those long buildings roofed with slate tiles?"

"They are the workshops of our wizard," smoothly replied Heligea, "Zimmuth, who was introduced to my lady at dinner. Most dull and cluttered are his sheds. Now, the gardens—"

"Let us visit the workshops."

The interior of Zimmuth's main lair was grossly cluttered. Springs, alembics, coils of copper tubing, buckled sheets of metal, gear systems both rack-and-pinion and epicyclic, pendulums, levers, cams, cranks, differentials, bearings, pulleys, assorted tools, and stone jars containing alkahest and corrosive substances crowded every horizontal surface. The well-thumbed pages of a couple of ephemerides flapped weakly, held down by embossed leather bookmarks. Magnetic compasses, theodolites, telescopes, and pocket sundials had been shoved arbitrarily into worn wooden cases with specially shaped satin-lined compartments. Constructions resembling metal innards ticked and whirred. An impossibly configured planetarium dangled from the roof-beams, hitting the heads of all who passed under it. In one corner a clock struck fifteen and fell over with a *sproing*.

Men in skullcaps, with stained taltries and disfigured faces, hammered and filed and sawed. Zimmuth waxed enthusiastic, buzzing like an obsessed bee.

"The sildron hoister project is over here," he spouted, "a new and more efficient lift system. And here is a modern skimmer being built. We had another but it blew asunder in the end. You understand, sildron and andalum will not bind to any other metal—these types of rotors tend to fly apart eventually, like the propellers of Windships. There is inherent instability. And yet I predict that every Tower shall have one someday. And over there, we are developing an improved andalum girth for eotaurs, to make the onhebbing easier."

"Wizard."

Zimmuth broke off his monologue. "Er, yes—um?" Already he had forgotten the visitor's name.

Rohain idly flicked a scrap of iron off a bench. It rang dully on the raddled flagstones.

"Fashion a sildron-powered butterchurn," she suggested.

"What?" Uncouthly, the wizard gaped.

"And try your hand at designing a powered spinning-wheel, or better still, a loom."

He scratched his matted beard. An earwig dropped out. "But what's the point of it? I mean, that is women-servants' work."

"Precisely. Facilitating it would give the women more time."

"To do what?"

"Other things."

"Well, yes, I suppose so. But they do not know how to do other things."

"Such as building precondemned vehicles out of incompatible materials? Doubtless they could work it out if they had time to try, and the inclination."

The wizard had already transferred his attention away from her words. He sucked on his teeth, then jabbed a finger in the air.

"A butterchurn. Yes! It can be done." Like a blinkered horse he trotted away, summoning his henchmen

My lady sows interesting ideas," commented Heligea as the party of gentlefolk moved out of the workshops and toward the gardens. Musingly she twisted her beaded taltry-strings.

"I have heard tell of another, here at Isse, who dabbles in the Arts," said Rohain. "Who is that?"

"A false rumor," interjected Ustorix. "No one here is acquainted with wizardry save Zimmuth."

"That will be Mortier," said Heligea deliberately. "He used to be Master at Swords."

"No longer?"

"No. You see, m'lady, he used to try to transact with wights, outside the demesnes. He thought they would give him power over the unstorm."

"Heligea!" Ustorix rapped.

"One day he was out in the forest with some servants who were a-gathering," his sister went on blandly, "and—"

"We are now come to the gardens," pompously interrupted her brother. A footman ran to open the gate and, bowing, stood aside to let them enter.

"And the unstorm came," persevered Heligea.

"Be silent, chit, or you will answer to me!"

"My lord Ustorix, pray allow dear Heligea to continue," reproved Rohain. In the Stormrider's neck, the tendons popped.

"Well," said Heligea, breaking off a woody stem of poplar and using it to idly thrash its mother tree, "our good

Master Mortier took fright at being caught by the unstorm in the open. He ran away."

The party strolled down a gravel path between uninspiringly leafless hedges. Heligea prodded moodily with her whip-stalk at the groin of a skeletal rosebush, avoiding the furious gaze of her brother.

"We sent out searchers, of course," she went on, "and we finally found him. But it was vile."

"What had happened?"

"We saw his boots first, dangling some way off the ground, swinging slightly. His feet were in them. He was hanging high on a Barren Holly, strung up cruelly on its branches. We cut him down—a wind sprang up as we did so—how the Holly thrashed and hissed!"

"Nay!" exclaimed Rohain in horror and disbelief.

"He was still alive when we cut him down," blithely said young Heligea. "He survived, but he could not speak. His throat was ruined, from hanging there. In truth, his mind was deranged too. He could not teach swordsmanship anymore, but when he recovered partially he took to hammering late at night at some invention he was working on in his chambers. One night as he was working away with only his servant nigh, his rushlight suddenly blew out and the hammer was knocked from his hand. When the servant managed to kindle a light he found Master Mortier pinned to his bench by his own hands. His fingers had to be forced apart to prise him off. After that he lost the use of his hands entirely. Now he has to be fed through a straw. He sits and does nothing. His hair drops out from his scalp until he is smooth and moist. He is no better than a great slug."

The skycaptain and the first mate laughed boorishly. "A sluggard, no less!" they joked.

"Cry pity!" gasped Viviana, grimacing. Her mistress shuddered. She felt the hairs rise on her scalp and recalled

with misgivings a curse she had once mouthed at the Master
at Swords.

A strung-out note pierced the sky from high above. Prim
Heligea craned her neck to catch a glimpse of the incoming
Stormrider.

"I must be informed at once if that Relayer brings word
from the Royal City," said Rohain.

But from Caermelor there came no tidings.

Rohain felt uneasy. Like a sticky cobweb, a restless
melancholy settled over her. It seemed that all plans, all
hopes, had come to a standstill. Sianadh sat alone in a cell,
the shadow of a rope falling across his neck. She, Rohain so-
called, stood un-alone in a tower, the thorn of hopeless passion piercing her heart, the burden of a friend's life weighing
heavily on her shoulders, while the picture she had so fool-
ishly allowed herself to paint, of life as a baroness at Arcune,
was being washed away in the bleak rains of Fuarmis, the
Coldmonth.

Far away in Namarre Thorn was fighting. Perhaps his life
was even now in danger. Worse, perhaps he had been
slain . . . That possibility did not bear contemplation and she
thrust it from her mind. What weird and malignant enemies
might he be facing? And what would happen if the strength
of the Empire's legions should fail and be vanquished?
Stormriders would come hurtling back with messages: *Escape, flee for your lives. The Empire is overthrown, all is
lost* . . .

Rohain envisioned the network of Relayer runs reaching
from point to point across the kingdom like a mightier cobweb, their tension increasing so that they must thrum like
overstretched wires. Dianella crouched like a spider in a corner, waiting. Beside that lady lurked a darkness that was not
her shadow but another like herself, only more heinous: the
wizard Sargoth. At the ganglion of the cobweb loomed the

Tower. At a pitch too high for human hearing, the word *impasse* screamed through Rohain's head.

What would this waiting bring?

"I hope the King-Emperor shall return soon to Caermelor," said Rohain, in a private moment with her maid. "Think you that he will spare Sianadh's life, Viviana? What *kind* of man is he, the King-Emperor? A merciful man?"

Viviana waxed circumspect.

"Wise is how I should describe him, my lady—merciful when mercy is justified, ruthless to warmongers and other evildoers. A shame it is, that he should dwell in widowerhood."

"Ah, yes. Queen-Empress Katharine met her death in terrible circumstances, that much I know. What exactly happened to her? Nobody will enlighten me. Indeed, it seems forbidden to mention the topic, except in the most cursory way."

The girl replied in low tones, "It is not spoken of at Court anymore. But we all know. Leastways, we know the main events, but some tell the tale one way, some tell it another. I can tell it the way I heard it but I know not if 'tis correct in every detail."

"Prithee, say on."

"It happened by the sea. Their two Imperial Majesties were out riding, late, along the strand, when a mist came down and they were separated from their retinue. For a time they rode on, calling to their guards and courtiers, but they could find none. All of a sudden the Queen's horse took fright and bolted. His Majesty spurred his horse and rode after her, hearing her screams through the mist, but when he caught up, he saw her horse in its death throes, mangled, and the Queen being dragged into the sea. He sprang off his steed and ran into the water. Something unspeakably unseelie seized him. It was none other than Nuckelavee, the flayed centaur—no doubt my lady has heard of this terrible monster. His Majesty slashed at it with his sword but it would have dragged him under too, only that with the last of his strength he put his hunting horn to his mouth and blew a long call. At the sound, his attacker loosened its grip and drew back. When his men found him, King James was half-perished, but still trying to drag himself into the waves. They had to pull him out of the water—he would have plunged in after his lady. She was never seen again, and she not yet five-and-twenty.

"That happened some ten years ago, when the Prince was but a lad. Prince Edward seems older than his years, me-thinks, but has grown up fine and handsome." Viviana clasped her hands, staring into some unguessed distance. "His Majesty never took another bride. At that time, all the royal princesses of Erith's lands were either too young or already wed. Besides, it is said he loved Katharine so much that he could never love another."

"A tragic tale."

"Verily. The grief of it changed His Majesty in some ways. He is at once sadder and merrier than before, so they say, although I never knew him aforetimes. I was but a child. They say, too, that sorrow sobered him, for since that time he has thrown all his fervor into ruling well and wisely. The lands of Erith, before this Namarran uprising, have never been so peaceful and prosperous. But then, the House of D'Armancourt has ever been the most powerful dynasty. The historians tell us there has been some special quality, something beyond the ordinary, in all who are born to that line. They say that royal blood is puissant. It sets them apart."

Twice the Winter sun opened its shrunken eye. Both days were soused with rain. The next morning dawned clear. Enclosed within the Tower, daily confronted by its horribly familiar smells and sights, and their painful associations, Rohain grew restless and irritable. She longed to be free of these environs, but had no notion of where she might go.

One evening, after dinner, a wild mood seized her. Leaning toward the sulky Heligea, she asked quietly, "Do you ride?"

"It is my most favored pursuit."

"Do you ride sky?"

"To shoot the blue," said the Daughter of the House, "is of all things what I desire most."

"You are of the Blood."

"It is forbidden. And will ever be."

"Why?"

"It is simply not done."

"Not a good enough reason. Ride sky with me on the very morrow."

Heligea turned disbelieving eyes on Rohain. "Hoy-day! You would never dare!"

"I would. You would too. Wait until your brother is otherwise occupied. The equerries, the grooms, the ostlers—they will not gainsay the daughter of Lord Voltasus."

"'Sblood! 'Tis impossible!" Heligea seemed lit up from within, as if a lamp burned behind the porcelain skin of her face.

Unfolding their mighty wings the next morning, two eotaurs sallied forth from Gate East Three Hundred on the Yeoman Flight level. They circled the demesnes and galloped out across the forest. Beneath flying-helmets, the Riders were masked. They rode astride, demonstrating consummate skill, like Relayers of many years' experience; yet instead of following a Run they branched off, toured the local terrain, and were back in the Tower before noon.

Ustorix's rage was uncontainable.

At first he directed it at his sister, threatening her with

death for breaking one of the most ancient and honored tenets of the Twelve Houses. He scandalized the Tower's occupants with the vulgar raising of his voice, his fiery displays of temper.

When he had finished haranguing his sister, Ustorix rushed unexpectedly through the door of Rohain's suite. His color burned high, his nostrils flared. His hair had escaped its bonds and now draggled in sweaty tendrils.

"What is the meaning of your bursting so rudely in upon me, Lord Ustorix?" demanded Rohain, rising from the chair by the fireplace where she had been seated.

"You know it!" He strode forward, careless in his wrath. "Riding sky is *not* the prerogative of women. Women have not the strength for it. Only noblemen possess the finesse and acuity required to learn the skills of governing eotaurs and the fickle currents of the atmosphere. How will Isse Tower be regarded when word of your folly is spread abroad? It will be said that we of the Seventh House cannot keep our women in their place. It will be said that we are weak, and our women are frolicsome and willful. You have destroyed the reputation of the Seventh House. You have brought ruin upon us all."

"I hardly think so. Take control of yourself, sir. These emotive scenes are scarcely seemly. We ladies can ride sky as featly as any gentleman. No harm has been done. It is a lesson—"

"Hear me!" He gripped her by the arm. "I'll be hanged if you don't need lessoning, and hanged if I'll not teach you."

"Unhand me!"

The young Stormrider glanced down. In his guest's hand, the point of the anlace, still chained to her girdle, jabbed the hard flesh of his stomach. He released his grip on her arm.

"How dare you!" Rohain enunciated carefully. Every ounce of hatred and scorn for him that she had ever stored flung its weight behind those words. Suddenly Ustorix dropped to one knee.

"Forgive me. Forgive me," he gasped over and over. "I was not myself. I did not mean—"

"Depart!"

"Rohain, I am in . . ." He squirmed in anguish, groping for words of apology and excuse.

"Avaunt! Get out!" At the sight of his groveling, Rohain felt only revulsion.

He went.

She wished that she had never thought of riding an eotaur, joyful as the experience had been. She scrubbed her arm raw where he had touched it.

At dinner, Ustorix was all scrupulous politeness. He said, "Tonight I will demonstrate the balancing feat."

"It is not necessary," said Rohain.

"It will be done," he stated tightly.

Gate South Five Hundred gaped, the cusps of its portcullis pointing like daggers. Far below the overhanging threshold, miniature outbuildings were pricked by tiny lights shining from their windows. A light tracery of vapor sculled past, upon a thermal layer, about a hundred feet below. All was black and silver: the forest, as dark as Dianella's hair; the ocean, as silver as a trow's desire; the sky, as colorless as cellar slugs.

Heligea was present, with Ustorix and Rohain and a young Relayer displaying three stars on his epaulettes.

"Lord Ustorix," said Rohain formally, sincerely regretting her taunting, "I beg you not to attempt this."

Now this pompous ass was going to lose his life because she had craved vengeance. It had seemed a good idea at the dinner table, considering her past sufferings, but now that the time had come she wished she had held back her words.

She would not relish witnessing anyone's life being snuffed out. Revenge was supposed to be sweet. This tasted sour.

Her anxiety only served to fuel Ustorix's intent.

"Stand aside," he commanded heroically.

A refractory wind, which had been pummeling the Tower, tapered off. The Stormrider carefully placed the sildron ingots. They hovered. He ran and jumped. Agile and strong from riding sky, he found his footing and, as the momentum transferred to the metal bars, caught his balance. Like an acrobat he stood poised, slowing.

"Well done, sir!" breathed the three-starred Relayer.

"The deed is done," Ustorix called back over his shoulder. His helper tossed him a rope to haul him in. He glided back like a tremulous skater, until, without warning, the quiescent wind reawoke. With a gust forceful enough to shake the Tower walls, it pushed him sideways.

He fell.

Heligea screamed. Rohain squeezed her eyes shut.

"My lord!" The three-starred Relayer peered over the edge. "Are you hale?" he shouted, rather redundantly. The rope hung slack in his hand. The sildron ingots had shot away into the night and were nowhere to be seen.

Ustorix's hand appeared in midair. He had been floating, unharmed.

"The rope." His voice was cracked and strained.

The aide reeled him in. As he clambered onto the salient doorsill, Ustorix pulled off his jacket and began unfastening the buckles of the sildron harness he had worn beneath to provide him with complete safety.

Heligea's laugh was cut short by her brother's virulent scowl.

"I shall do it again," he grated.

"No, Ustor, you are safe now. It does not matter that you cheated," cried Heligea.

Ustorix flung down the harness. "Give me the spare ingots, Callidus."

"Ustorix, you must not!" beseeched Heligea. Gallant Callidus dragged her away.

For the second time that night, the heir of the House threw sildron into the outer airs. He took a deep breath and walked toward the edge. The whole of Eldaraigne yawned below, an expanse so vast and distant that it seemed to suck the very marrow out of his bones.

He collapsed on the floor in a faint.

When a pair of footmen had carried away the young lord, Rohain remained, for a time, alone in the gatehall. The wind was rising. From the core of this thirty-second story, the sound of horses came to her ears. They moved in their stalls, scuffling their hooves. She walked past the alcoves and vestibules leading off to either side, and continued down the wide straw-strewn corridors that circumnavigated the fortress's walls. Eotaurs leaned over their demi-doors to blow their warm breath on her hands, allowing her to scratch their ears and stroke their forelocks.

From the corner of her eye she viewed a small shape edging furtively past.

"Pod."

It shrieked.

"Pod, do not go away. I will depart from here if you tell me something."

"What?"

"Where did Grethet find me? How came I here?"

The lad mumbled.

"I do not understand what you are saying. Prithee, Pod, I returned here to find this out—for that reason only."

"Carters brought you in. Road-caravan."

"Did the carters say anything about me?"

"Said they found you."

"Where?"

"At the old mines—near the accursed place."

"What accursed place?"

"Carter-captain had on a fine cloak, he did. A very fine cloak."

"What accursed place?" she repeated insistently.

"Got to go now."

"Pod! You are my one chance. If there is any kindness left in you, have pity!"

"You had no pity. You made me go on the ship."

Rohain seized Pod's wrist. "Is force the only thing you heed?"

He wriggled. She released him and he scrambled away.

"I shall tell them you hide in the goat-caves," she called.

"No!" wailed the lad, already out of sight. His voice floated back: "Don't tell them where I hide. Huntingtowers. It was at Huntingtowers they found you."

Huntingtowers. Rarely had that place been mentioned by the servants when the yellow-haired lad had lived among them. Like the Fair Realm, like the Unseelie Attriod, it was considered to be a subject that, if discussed openly, attracted ill-fortune in the guise of the wrath of some unspecified agency; yet, like children with an itchy scab, the lowly denizens of the Tower could not leave it quite alone, and sometimes they hinted at it in whispers. It was the name of the haunted crater-lake lying northwest of Isse Tower.

Huntingtowers had another name, but what it was, none of the servants knew. It lay some two days' ride away, toward the Cape of Tides, and it was said to be most evilly infested with unseelie wights—a hub of all things eldritch that irrevocably hated mortal men. A hill rose from the land there, but it had no tall and rounded peak. Instead, its center was sunken and hollow, resembling a giant cauldron. Within this crucible of soil and stone lay a black lake whose level almost reached to the barren rim. Many cone-shaped islands were scattered across this forbidding water, some large, many small. On the central islet, the largest, a strange building had existed for as long as anyone could remember. It was a grim tower surrounded by eight others in a circle, each joined to its two neighbors and the central edifice by the stone arches of several flying bridges. From this fortress, the place had received its kenning, for it was said that an eldritch Hunt dwelt therein, the most terrible Hunt of all, so cruel and merciless that for miles around this black cauldron no mortal folk dared to dwell and even *lorraly* birds and beasts shunned the region. Folk who dwelled on the fringes would speak of their horror as, huddled in their cottages at night, they listened to sounds from high above: the baying of unnatural hounds, the weird and hideous screams of the Hunter, the rush of wind as eldritch steeds careened through the skies.

On nights of a full moon the Wild Hunt would debouch from its stronghold. Indeed, it had sometimes been seen through the spyglasses of the watchmen on the parapets of Isse Tower. So far the unseelie hunters had ignored the heavily fortified House of the Stormriders, but whosoever witnessed the Wild Hunt trembled at the certainty that come morning some road-caravan, or remote-dwelling charcoal-burner or cotter, or someone straying late abroad, would be gone, never to be seen again; or else would be found, far from home, lying torn to pieces in a pool of blood.

Viviana found out from the servants that lately the region of Huntingtowers had fallen into an unusual quietude. The Wild Hunt had not been sighted for many months and it was thought that the dwellers in the black caldera had removed to the north, responding to the mysterious Call; but of that there was no certainty, for no one dared venture there to see.

The moon was just past the full. If from Huntingtowers she had come, reasoned Rohain, then to Huntingtowers she must return. There existed no other clue to her past. From the high windows of the strange edifice in the center of the crater-lake, any aerial approach would doubtless be spied. The only chance for her to reconnoiter undetected in its environs lay in getting there by the deserted and therefore less scrutinized land-routes.

"Viviana."

The lady's maid looked up at her mistress. She had been sewing by candlelight, cocking her head and holding the work at arm's length, peering with utmost concentration as she stitched loose beadwork more securely onto the fringed aulmoniere. Her softly rounded face looked younger in the candle's dandelion glow. Her large and limpid eyes reflected the flame. She held the needle poised for the next stitch.

"Yes, m'lady?"

Rohain seated herself beside the girl.

"I wish to tell you something in the strictest confidence. Viviana, you have been a good servant to me, and a kind friend."

The hand holding the sliver of silver abruptly dropped to its owner's lap.

"Some events have taken place," said Rohain, "which make it impossible for me to keep you on."

"Oh no, my lady, prithee do not say that!" Viviana stuck the needle through the purse and put it aside. "I do not want to leave your service."

"I have with me enough items of value to pay the wages you are owed, and a little extra for a gift, in thanks," said Rohain. "After that I shall not be able to afford a maid."

"But you are a lady! Your estate, your jewels—"

"Are no longer mine. And I am not a gentlewoman—not by birth, I think. I am just like you."

"I cannot believe it!"

"It is true. Furthermore, I am about to embark upon a perilous journey to a perilous place. You cannot come on this path with me, Viviana, and so I am going to send for a Windship to take you back to Caermelor."

"My lady, you could not say anything that would make me more miserable," Viviana said quickly and tremulously. "Send me back? Never. I shall not go."

"There is no choice. You belong at Court, not here."

"I shall be sent back to the Marchioness! Ugh! I'd rather be a scullery maid. No—I shall stay with you."

"But I cannot pay your wages, after this day, and how should you make a living?"

"In the same way as you, I expect," said Viviana, spreading her hands palms upward. "Whatever that may be."

"As for that, I suppose I shall go into service again if I return alive."

Viviana pondered. "Go you into some kind of adventure?"

"Yes—no. It may be a tedious mission or it may be tremendously dangerous and life-threatening."

"Well then, that's not much different from life at Court, m'lady."

Rohain laughed. "It is not necessary to hail me by a courtesy title now."

"I cannot help it, m'lady. Prithee, let me accompany you."

"After what I have told you, do you still wish to come?"

"Yes."

"Why?"

"I'd rather be here than there, if you take my meaning."

"Would you?" It was Rohain who pondered now. "I like you," she said at last, "which is why I'd rather not put you at risk."

"Seeing as how you're not paying my wages anymore, you have no say in the matter," said Viviana primly, picking up the aulmoniere and resuming her sewing. "And now you had better tell me the whole story, m'lady."

So Rohain launched into the tale of her service at Isse Tower, her escape and the finding of the treasure that had allowed her to purchase a cure for her deformity, some fine clothing, and a new identity. She told also of her quest for the past, but, suffering from an ache that throbbed in her heart, she could not bear to mention Thorn—not yet. To her words, Viviana listened with equanimity. At the conclusion she said, "I declare, m'lady, you have been through more adventures than the Dowager Marchioness's crook-tailed tomcat. Yet I have no doubt you are of noble birth, judging by your bearing, and this history you tell has not changed my opinion of you in the slightest. To me, you remain the Lady Rohain."

Rohain shook her head with a nonplussed smile, taken aback at her friend's stubbornness and heartily grateful for it.

No breath of wind ruffled the day. In Isse Harbor, the sea lay satin-smooth, barely moving. Hanging in seaweed valleys far below, countless jellyfish pulsed like glacial moons, blue-white, see-through, finely fimbriated. The Seaship that Rohain had spied from the gargoyled balcony lay becalmed. Its departure had been delayed. This was not the stillness of tranquillity; rather the deadly motionlessness of a predator poised to attack.

Rohain had spun a fabrication to her hosts, made of half-truths, improvisations, and prevarications. She told them that all she had heard about Huntingtowers had piqued her curiosity; that the vogue among the jaded courtiers of Caermelor was to journey in search of novelty and exciting adventure; that the moon was just past the full and therefore this was the best time to explore, or at least to view from the caldera's rim the infamous abode of the Hunt, thus obtaining a delicious thrill of horror. It was a fabrication as full of holes as lace, but it was the best she could concoct on short notice. So bedazzled were they by this living jewel in their midst that her hosts accepted it.

How easily the lies roll out, she thought again, ashamed. *I am no better than Dianella.*

As a groom helped her mount a landhorse Rohain fought a stifling sense of dread. Once in the saddle, she looked around at the other riders. Ustorix in light armor, Viviana, the wizard Zimmuth and one of his scarred henchmen, Dain Pennyrigg, Keat Featherstone from the stables, and Lord Callidus had all wanted to accompany her. Sensing doom, she wished them out of her retinue. If catastrophe struck, their blood would be on her hands.

"Now is your final chance to turn back," she said, "one and all. If I choose to ride into danger, merely for the purpose of satisfying my curiosity concerning this ill-famed place, it is not your responsibility. You have the right to withdraw."

The wizard's henchman made as if to dismount and was stayed by a gesture from Ustorix. Nobody spoke. Like the ship in the harbor, the party's departure had also been delayed. They had set out earlier that morning, but after they had ridden a few miles the wizard's horse had cast a shoe and he had insisted upon them returning to have it reshod. Most of the morning had worn away by the time they set out again.

Ustorix raised his visor. "We shall have to set a good pace now," he said, "if we are to reach the Hill of Rowans by nightfall."

Heligea stood plucking at her brother's cloak.

"Please, Ustor. Take me with you."

"No." He pushed her away with his boot. "Forward," he added over his shoulder.

The twelve landhorses, four of them carrying only packs,

moved off. Heligea stood watching them leave, her hands planted defiantly on her hips.

"I hate you, Ustorix!" she shouted, kicking one of the grooms in the shins.

The party passed through the heavily fortified front gate of the demesnes, turned right, and disappeared from view. The Tower stared out to sea. Behind it, in the servants' graveyard, no wind ruffled the wreath of leaves and berries placed by Rohain beneath the wooden stick marking Grethet's last resting place.

The riders hastened along the beaten dirt of the road. Trees burned black by wintry gales locked fingers overhead, forming a dark tunnel. Every portable precaution against wights accompanied the travelers: bells on bridles, salt, bread, ash keys, the ground-ivy *athair luss,* sprays of dried hypericum tied with red ribbons to rowan staves, tilhals and other charms, self-bored stones, and amber. Every fabric garment was worn inside out, save for the taltries tied closely around their heads. Lords Ustorix and Callidus, flanking Rohain on strong war-horses, had encased themselves in armor of plate and chain. Thus iron-clad, they must surely be invulnerable. The wizard carried a tall, whirring contraption that resembled a windmill, which he said was a modern wight-deterrent and which he cast aside after a couple of miles because it was too heavy for him or his henchman to carry for long.

Their plan was to halt for the night at a hill crowned with rowans, where the serving-men would set up pavilions. Zimmuth was to weave a tight wall of spells about the encampment to keep it safe during the long hours of darkness, the most dangerous time.

After noon the sky darkened with unusual rapidity. The sun became obscured behind a wall of somber gray clouds; its location could only be guessed. Judging by the deepening dusk, it must have been starting to slide toward the horizon when the road began to twist back on itself, climbing steeply.

"We have reached Longbarrow Ridge," announced Callidus, pushing back his talium-lined visor. "On a clear day, the Hill of Rowans can be seen from the summit. Once we have crossed the ridge, we shall be less than an hour's ride from the hill. I'll warrant we'll be there by nightfall."

As he spoke, a heartbeat awoke out of the southeast.

It was an urgent, syncopated throbbing, deep and dire, the supple-wristed thudding of polished wood against goathide stretched over a resounding concavity. The voice of Isse Tower was broadcasting a warning.

"The drums!" exclaimed Ustorix echoingly from within his helm. "The drums of alarum!"

The riders urged forward their horses, hearkening to the compelling rhythm, their pulses rousing to its thrill. The trees thinned and gave way to stunted vegetation. Emerging at the top of a bald ridge, the riders were able to command an unobstructed view. Under clear skies, they might have been able to see the landscape for miles around.

There they reined in, by mutual agreement. Not a word had been spoken, but the presentiment was almost palpable. Why were the drums being sounded? What had the distant Tower watchmen seen? Fear had begun to overtake them all, and they looked to the north from whence, unaccountably, the fear emanated.

Something unseelie was coming.

Swiftly, it was coming.

The evening darkened. Low thunderclouds completely covered the sky like a blanket, from horizon to horizon, and a thick gray mist roiled up from the hollows of the land. Even the sea, so close at hand, was hidden. By now it seemed to the riders that they stood on an island in an ocean of fog, with a heavy ceiling pressing down on their heads and threatening to crush them. They all faced north, straining their eyes to pierce the thickening murk. From that direction came a certainty of sheer horror that enveloped them like some oppressive mantle. Their limbs weighed so heavily they could scarcely move a muscle. It was onerous, in that ghastly miasma, even to think of lifting a hand to guide the horses toward shelter. An unnatural lethargy pinned the riders to the ridgetop.

Their terror increased as sounds approached along the roof of the sky—a baying and yammering, a deep thunder, the crazed hallooing, the berserk screaming of carnivorous horses like the screech of metal ripped asunder. A denser cloud ballooned out of the rest and raced straight toward the watchers. Bursting from its depths loomed the shapes of fire-eyed hounds and dark riders on mounts that snorted flame. Ahead of them plunged their leader—a thing shaped like a man.

Yet it was no true man.

It was a darkness with two sunken sumps for eyes; and, not worn as a helm would be worn, but growing from the head, magnificent when gracing a stag, yet obscene on this human parody—the appalling tines, a pair of wide skullclaws, the antlers.

At the instant these apparitions appeared, Ustorix screamed and launched himself sideways off his horse. In panic, Callidus's steed reared and threw its rider. Zimmuth's mount bolted downhill, followed by the four packhorses. His henchman spurred after him. The Hunt galloped right over the heads of the remaining four riders and receded in the direction of Isse Tower, invisible somewhere in the mist, twenty miles away.

The two men of the stables cursed softly, calming their horses. Rohain's mount shivered beneath her, slippery with the sweat of terror. Leaning over its neck, she murmured into its ear. Keat Featherstone spoke rapidly to his three companions.

"Isse Tower is in dire peril. My lady, forgive us. We are obliged to leave you and return to the aid of our comrades in the Tower. Our lords remain hereabouts—they will guard you."

"I give you leave, Featherstone and Pennyrigg. Wind be with you."

"And with you, lady. We must ride hard. Let those follow who will!"

Without further ado, the two stablemen leapt away down the hill at a great pace.

Clanking, the armor-plated lords lurched on foot after their chargers, whistling and calling. They disappeared down the north side of the ridge, leaving the two damsels alone.

"Well, Viviana," said Rohain. She was dazed and reeling from shock after witnessing such appalling visitations, and was alarmed by their unexpected abandonment. "Well, Viviana, it seems our guardians are otherwise occupied." She mustered her thoughts. "Meanwhile, mayhap we can help our hosts. I vote we follow those who ride to the Tower's aid."

Viviana seemed to shrink. "These things . . ." she said in a low voice. "These things that hunt through the sky . . ."

"We are pinched between a sword and a spear, as the saying goes," said Rohain. "The Tower is beleaguered, for sure, but it is well-manned and fortified. Would you rather we camped on this hill waiting for the Wild Hunt to fly over our heads on its return journey? Or that we continue on to the haunted caldera, two ladies unguarded and alone?"

"Marry," said Viviana in weary disgust, "this is a sorry state of affairs. That Ustorix is a craven bumbler and no mistake. First he falls from his horse in his terror, then he runs away, leaving us vulnerable. So much for his vaunted boldness and chivalry."

"Will you return with me to the House of the Stormriders?"

"I am loathe to do so, m'lady, but we have little choice."

They cast one glance over their shoulders in the direction of the horizon where Huntingtowers brooded unseen, unconquered. Then, pointing the heads of their steeds back toward the stronghold of the Seventh House, they set off at a gallop.

Below the hill, the road dived back under its roof of trees. The dank wall of mist and the obscuring vegetation afforded no view of the Tower to Rohain and Viviana as they rode. The sonorous pattern of the drums continued on for a while, then ceased abruptly, leaving a calm broken only by the hammering of iron-shod hooves on wet clay and leaf-mold.

The pale vapors drew back among the trees and frayed to invisibility. A wind brooming through the upper atmosphere swept most of the dirty clouds away to the west. Only the last rays of the sun lingered by the time the travelers cantered their weary horses along the last stretch of road leading to the demesne-gates of Isse, and a translucent moon was already rising, swimming up into the unfathomable sky like some pale jellyfish. Now rowans crowded in thickly toward the road. To the left, the stone walls of the demesnes rose high, topped with metal spikes and shards.

Through the black lacework of boughs the Tower loured in the half-light, tapering from its wide base to become a slim needle in the sky. So high it soared that its turreted head was hidden in a shredded remnant of cloud. Much winged activity was taking place around the upper stories. Darkly etched on the clouds, dozens of eotaurs whirled in descending spirals, onhebbing toward the ground. Their riders' cloaks billowed up like broken bubbles. Shouts issued from behind the demesne walls, accompanied by the crunch of hooves on gravel. From high above speared shrill, inhuman yells, deep roars, the clash of metal and stone. A howling bundle plummeted from a balcony, its limbs writhing.

Just before a bend in the road that concealed the gate from view, the travelers crossed a stone bridge over a little rill and cantered beneath a long arch of overhanging willows.

"Stop, my lady, I beg you!" They reined in. Rohain glanced quizzically at her companion. "My lady, the Tower is overrun by wights. There is nothing we can do—we must turn back! We must ride for our lives!"

Two more victims hurtled, screaming, from above.

"In good faith—we cannot leave! We must help them fight."

"There is nothing we can do. We are not warriors. To bide here means certain death."

Rohain hesitated. "You have the right of it," she admitted reluctantly, "and yet . . ."

As she faltered, something like a fish-hook raked across her chest. It caught in the fine gold chain of her tilhal, ramming it tight into the flesh of her throat and crushing her windpipe until she could not breathe. Mercifully, the chain snapped. The rooster with pink rubies for eyes shot away into the grasses at the roadside. A scrawny arm whipped like a leather belt across Rohain's eyes, blinding her.

A scrawl of hobyahs had swung down from the willow-boughs overhanging the road. Their grotesque limbs were thin and strong as whipcords. Wrapping them around the heads of the riders, they wrenched off the talium-lined riding hats. Others of their kind dangled by their skinny legs and gripped the damsels by their hair, whereupon their terrified horses ran from underneath them. Both mortals were let fall to the ground.

The hobyahs rushed at their victims. No more than two

feet tall, they leered through bright needles of eyes that slanted upward at the outer corners, narrowing to mere slits. Their noses were large and uptilted. Pointed ears stuck up on either side of their conical caps, and their mouths grinned maliciously. Avoiding contact with turned-out garments or bridle-bells, they hung off the saddles and surcingles, then jumped in twos and threes on the horses' backs and rode them away. Possessed of the hideous strength of eldritch, they hooked their clawlike fingers into their victims' hair and easily dragged them off the road. The struggles of the girls were futile. There could be no escape.

Yet in the next instant, the hobyahs' yodels of victory turned to screeches. Red-and-gold lightning flashed among them, and suddenly there were horsemen brandishing swords. A skirmish broke out. The cold iron blades of the superior force broke the wights' resistance, scattering them, routing them. Staggering to their feet, Rohain and Viviana clung to each other. Blood trickled in runnels from their scalps. Their garments were torn. Hair tumbled over their faces.

"Let us to the safety of the demesnes!" gasped Rohain. But even as they started for the gates, equestrians emerged from both banks of the road ahead, blocking their way. In dismay, the girls whirled about, only to be faced with a second blockade closing in behind.

" 'Tis some eldritch trickery!" cried Viviana. "These men wear the Royal Livery—this cannot be!"

In scarlet jackets and gold braid the riders sat tall and straight. The final thin shafts of sunlight, sword-bright, pierced through disintegrating clouds and struck golden gleams from their face-guards and plumed helms. They appeared like a vision from the Fair Realm.

Five of them rode slowly forward. The damsels exchanged frightened glances.

"We wield iron!" cried Rohain in desperation. "Approach at your peril!"

Calmly, the horsemen reined in a short distance away.

"You mistake us," their leader, a lieutenant, shouted. His tone was grave. "We are cavalry of the Royal Legions."

Wights were incapable of lying.

"Out here it is perilous for mortals," he said. "The lower stories of the Tower are now secured against the enemy. Come. We shall bear you to safety there."

He gestured to two of the cavalrymen. Dismounting, they helped Rohain and Viviana up behind the other two. A black smoke spewed from a southern gate in the Tower, just below the cloud ceiling. Dimly within it, the Wild Hunt soared in outward flight. They seemed this time to be fewer in number. Unseelie hounds and horses swooped around the Tower and struck out northward over the lifting moon, pursued by a company of eotaur-riders who, although great in number, could not match the speed of their eldritch quarry and were sure to be outdistanced.

"Welladay! Huon is driven forth!" exclaimed the lieutenant. His men cheered; several yelled triumphantly and punched the air above their heads.

In perfect formation, six men of the platoon rode up and closed ranks around the officers with the pillion riders. Together, they made toward the gate.

Red-jacketed men-at-arms patrolled throughout the shadowy demesnes. Guards at the Tower doors saluted and allowed the lieutenant to pass through with his wards. He consigned them to the care of some doughty stewards of Isse and returned to his business of scouring the area immediately outside the demesnes.

Within the Tower, all was in uproar. Rohain and Viviana were escorted to a kitchen in one of the lower stories. There they found crowds of house-carls and nobles mingling, making a tremendous hubbub, some chattering, others sobbing.

"Wickedness! Oh, wickedness!"

"'Tis an evil hour that brought these fell fiends upon the House."

"Lend me your kerchief, for I bleed."

"All fate be praised for bringing us our rescuer in time of need!"

"I cannot yet grasp that *he* is among us!"

"And more striking than the stories ever told!"

"Cursed be this day that saw such evil fall on Isse. Yet bless'd it be also . . ."

Some were uncharacteristically shrieking and wringing their hands, and several, in a sorry state, lay prone on the tables while their wounds were tended. Pet capuchins loped about, jabbering and hindering.

Rohain stared at the scene, sickened and appalled. Questions and offers of help surged at her and her companion as soon as they entered. Dolvach Trenchwhistle cleared a path for them with her elbows.

"Make way for the fine ladies from Caermelor! Can't you see that they are hurt, you dolts? Get out of the way."

She seated the fine ladies by the hearth and proffered glasses of brandy. Heligea shouldered her way through the press and stood before them.

"My brother and Callidus! Are they with you?"

"No," said Rohain, sipping brandy to give her strength. "I do not know how they fare."

"Ill tidings, then."

"Yet I would vouch for their safety, encased as they are in all that iron."

"'Sbane! You are wounded, my friend. Blood runs from your hair. You, servant, bring oil." A young girl hastened away.

"What has happened here?" asked Rohain.

"The Tower was attacked at nightfall," said Heligea. "Terrible ravagers they were. Powerful. They landed in at the top stories and went down through the Tower at speed, like rats down a drainpipe. We had no time to escape. Methinks they were hunting for something, or somebody. When they couldn't find their target, they turned on us like boars at bay, and took our people and began to torment them. Then he came."

"Who?"

"Why, none other than the King-Emperor himself!"

"His Imperial Majesty here?" cried Viviana. "I can scarce credit it!"

Heligea's eyes blazed as though with pride, or triumph, or battle-lust. "He came from the south, riding to our rescue, leading the Duke of Roxburgh and others of the Royal Attriod, and regiments of the Royal Legions and *thriesniuns* of the Dainnan, all mounted on Skyhorses. They'd got word that the Scourge was on its way here, and they came. Ah!" Dreamily, she clasped her hands at her throat. "The King-Emperor himself, here at Isse! I never thought to see this hour. Dainnan and men-at-arms swarm all over the Tower. I'll be honest, at first it seemed impossible that even such great fighting men could drive off the Wild Hunt, but victory has been won!"

"Won?" echoed Rohain. "So the wights are all gone and the Tower is safe?"

Heligea waved her hand dismissively. "Yes, yes. Almost safe. A few of the lesser wights that rode with the Hunter remain scattered throughout the upper stories and must be flushed out. We are to remain locked up down here until all things unseelie have been ousted and the Tower thoroughly scoured. As yet I have not set eyes upon His Majesty, but as I am, for the moment, the Mistress of the House, I am sure to be summoned soon by his gentlemen. I confess to a little nervousness, but in good sooth, how I look forward to the moment I am presented!" Lowering her voice, she leaned forward confidentially. "You have seen him at Court. I never have. Is he as fine as they say? Do the images stamped on the coins of the realm do him justice?"

Rohain felt reluctant to admit she had never been in the King-Emperor's presence. She could not know whether the portraits hanging in gilt frames all over the palace were good representations, or the worn and blurred profiles in relief stamped into the coins. Besides, she had only ever seen older coins, depicting the D'Armancourt ancestors. Of the portraits, she recalled only cascades of velvet and brocade. She could barely remember them, not having paid much heed. In any event, she supposed he had aged greatly since those images had been created.

"Via," she said, "tell Heligea what he looks like."

"Well, ma'am, no artist has ever been able to featly capture his likeness," said Viviana. "Just barely do the portraits represent His Majesty. I look forward to seeing him again with all my heart, if only from a distance, for upon my word he is a gentleman any maid or wife would sigh to look upon—a gentleman after every lady's heart. All the ladies at Court are in love with him, I doubt not—every one; and I'd warrant that every woman throughout Erith who has ever set eyes on him would share that passion." Her eyes sparkled. "So handsome is he and so kingly. Just to think of him causes the strangest thrill, as if the shang were passing over." She balked, blushing suddenly. "*Sain* me—I hope you'll not think me impertinent for speaking thus of His Imperial Majesty."

"You *are* impertinent," interrupted Heligea impatiently, "and should be thrashed for presuming to such familiarity, insolent girl. Ah, here comes a servant with the oil."

A girl approached, carrying a stoneware jar. She was young, almost a child, thin and pale-cheeked but vigorous-looking, with large, deep-lidded eyes and a neat, bow-shaped mouth. Rohain recognized that triangular face, surrounded by its abundant cloud of wavy brown locks. The daughter of the Keeper of the Keys, the girl's name was Caitri Lendoon, and she had shown kindness to the deformed, yellow-haired lad.

Before Rohain could acknowledge her former friend, the smell of the oil assaulted her, closing in on her like a dark jail. Her throat and back were on fire. She gagged.

"What is in that jar?" she said hoarsely, holding the folds of her skirts to her nose. "Whatever it is, I beg you to take it away from me. I wonder you don't all expire from the stench."

"'Tis only siedo-pod oil," said Heligea in astonishment. "A pungent scent, aye, but tolerable enough."

"I will not have it near me!"

"It will soothe your hurts, my lady," said the little girl, backing away.

"Mayhap. But I cannot stand the stink of it. I would rather endure the pain of my hurts and take another drop of brandy. You may anoint Viviana, if she is willing, and I will move from her side. Heligea, I must be brought into the King-Emperor's presence as soon as possible."

"None but His Imperial Majesty's gentlemen may attend him now. That is how I am informed."

"Yes, but as soon as the Tower has been secured—"

"Of course. Come, my lady, let these servants bathe you with lavender water if you will not have the oil. And take another sip of the spirit."

There was to be no sleep that night. The moans of the wounded filled the lower halls. Those who had escaped harm spoke of nothing but the disastrous attack, and the unprecedented presence of royalty at the Tower. Occasional noises of belligerence echoed down the stairwells and the lift-shafts as malevolent presences were flushed out of oblique crannies. These became more infrequent, and eventually ceased altogether. Alone in a quiet room of the servants' quarters, Rohain sat by a window embrasure. It was forbidden to open the shutters until the danger had passed, but a cold night breeze crept in through the cracks and this she inhaled with relish.

Viviana approached.

"My lady—"

"Come no closer, Via. I cannot endure the stench of the oil in your hair."

"It is strong, I'll concede, but not truly offensive, surely? Some might consider it pleasant."

"I have ill recollections of the stuff," said Rohain. Her face closed in on itself.

Sensing some inner perturbation, Viviana nodded silently. She curtsied and withdrew.

Rohain remembered: *Here in Isse Tower they use siedopod oil for many purposes, including the assuaging of every hurt from cuts and scratches to bellyaches and warts. Grethet used the stuff for the cuts on my back—yet I detested it well before then. I fought against her but I was too weak. She smeared it on, and as soon as I could I rubbed it off, rolling on rough bags, which opened the wounds afresh; but the stench—the stench clings for ages.*

Restlessly, she stood up and walked to the next window. Along the hairline crack between the shutters, a glimpse of starry sky ran like a black thread stitched with seed pearls. The brandy had warmed her, had taken the edge off the pain of her tortured scalp, but she ached with the longing to go straightaway to the King-Emperor and plead for Sianadh's life. And she blazed with a desire to see which of the Dainnan had accompanied him to the Tower.

All of that lay outside the barred doors.

Around midnight, a hammering on those doors announced the end of the waiting period—the Tower had been cleared of eldritch incarnations.

Chaos resumed. As the Stormriders and their ladies returned to the upper floors, all able-bodied servants were ordered into action preparing billets and provender for the King-Emperor and his attendants and men-at-arms. Heligea disappeared precipitously, in a clanging lift-cage.

Rohain, eluding Viviana to escape the siedo-pod fumes, took another lift-cage up to Floor Thirty-seven. Lords and ladies moved to and fro shouting orders. Overworked servants hurried to obey.

"Where is the King-Emperor?" Rohain asked.

"His Majesty is at the topmost floor, my lady," was the reply. "He may be in conference or at meat. Is there anything you require? A repast is being set out on the tables in the dining halls."

"Thank you—no."

A passing Dainnan knight started at the sight of her face. Simultaneously she jumped, taken by surprise at the sight of his uniform. Recovering his composure, he bowed.

"May I be of assistance, lady? I am Sir Flint."

His unbound hair fountained in bronze filaments to the small of his back.

"The King-Emperor's quarters on the top floor—do you know where they are?"

"His Majesty holds conference there with the Royal Attriod. The while, the Stormriders of the Tower are gathering in the dining halls to take refreshment. May I conduct you there instead? Allow me to call your servants."

Seeing herself suddenly as he must see her, it struck Rohain that she could not kneel at the feet of the King-Emperor dressed in a torn and inside-out riding habit, with her hair tousled. To beg for a man's life, she must appear sleek and well-groomed, as etiquette demanded. She sighed.

"You are kind, Sir Flint. I wish only to retire."

"Your name, my lady?"

Already she was walking away, not wishing to delay.

He bowed again and watched her go.

When she was out of his sight, she ran to her suite. On reaching it, she checked abruptly with her hand on the doorjamb and stared in.

The rooms had been ransacked.

Furniture lay splintered. Chests had been forced open and turned out, then apparently picked up and thrown across the chamber by some agency far stronger than any man, to crash and sprawl open, lids twisted awry, spilling out the remains of their contents. Garments had been strewn, torn to shreds. The looking-glasses lay in splinters on the floor—even their backings had been punched through. Only the frames of their obliterated faces remained. The bed had been reduced to no more than a welter of kindling and rags, scattered with dead leaves and a couple of live loam-worms, dusk pink and jointed. Rohain's jewelery was unrecognizable—misshapen as though melted in a hot fire. Every item she owned had been broken or corrupted. An odor of compost hung over the whole scene.

Softly, she left the scene of the shambles. There was no sign of a door—save for buckled hinges half torn off the door-frame—or she would have closed it.

The hour had grown very late. Dazed, she wandered. The torchlit halls were empty now that the nobles had gone to their supper. Dry leaves eddied along the floors, whispering, blown by a bitterly cold breeze from the gargoyle-wreathed balcony overlooking Isse Harbor. It was there she had stood on the night of the unstorms, watching a ghostly galleon being wrecked off the heads, and wrecked again, over and over.

One of the balcony doors stood open. Beyond, stars dripped thick radiance down the sky and the sight drew her.

Thomas's words came back: *"Go into the wilderness on a clear night and look up. Look long. Then you will have seen something of Faêrie."*

Heedless of the slap and sting of the cold, she stepped out. A wide vista opened across gray water. The moon and the Greayte Southern Star had wheeled out of sight on their inevitable courses and only the fantastic splendor of the other starry realms remained, to draw heart and mind out through the eyes and send them spinning into the void.

Someone else was already on the balcony. A Dainnan leaned on the parapet. Ribbons of black hair rained across his wide shoulders and down his tapered back, reaching to his belt. A sea-draft driving up the walls of the Tower lifted fibers of darkness across the winking stars—the weft from which night itself was woven.

He straightened, turning. He was looking down at Rohain.

Instantly, all her thought was swept away by intense emotion. Speech and movement became impossible under that piercing gaze. Every wish, every hope, had come true in front of her eyes. The sight of him, so often imagined, was hard to invest with reality. For so long had his image existed only in intangible form that she had become accustomed to knowing him as a dream, and could not at first believe what she saw.

As from a distance, a dark, strong voice said:

"So, you came at last to Court, Gold-Hair."

A response was required. Rohain's numbed mind could prepare none. Mechanically, she murmured, "Yes." Her eyes remained wide, fastened on him steadily, drinking him in. The action of speech released her paralyzed thoughts.

"Is it really you . . . ?" She faltered.

"It is I."

She must say something else, something to keep him

here, for the longer he remained the more substantial he became.

"I am glad to see you."

The statement seemed so feeble an offering, compared with the intensity of feeling it represented—as if she'd held oceans in readiness to offer him and instead, through lack of expertise, had handed over only a spoonful of water.

"And I you."

Like Pod, he had known her immediately, despite the complete transformation, and yet he uttered no comment about her hair, her face, her voice.

"How brightly the stars shine tonight," said he, turning again to look out at the spectacle. She, moving to his side, was now blind to the radiant glory of the glittering haze spread across the sky. Only, she was aware of a heat on her left where he stood, like the heat of a beacon-fire, pulsing warmth all down one side of her body while the other was chilled. And so they stood together looking outward, and the rising thermals caught their hair, making it flow out behind them, the dark locks mingling.

An hour passed, or it might have been half an hour, or a minute. It was not forever, although Rohain craved that it should be. Although they kept vigil in silence, it seemed to Rohain that a million words were traced upon the air. They hung there in runes of fire, slowly fading. It was unspeakable to be there beside Thorn at those moments. It was to fall into stars, to ride sky in a thunderstorm, to dance in a riot of jewels at a masquerade ball on the uttermost peak of an ice-mountain, to be swept up on the winds of shang.

"I have searched long for you," Thorn said quietly at last. "Will you come with me to Court?"

"I will." Terror and delight swarmed, fizzing like sweet and savage acid.

"I want you to belong to me, and to no other."

Just like that, with no preamble. She was too stunned to ask questions.

"That I do already. I will be yours for my life." *Did he truly speak those words? Am I sane?*

"Do you swear it?"

"Upon the Star, upon my life, upon anything you wish to name, I swear it."

He held out his hand. She grasped a levin-bolt whose convulsion sizzled from fingers to feet.

"Now we are troth-plighted," he said, as though he had noticed nothing about the effect of his touch. Indeed, she would swear he had felt nothing.

The sound of boots approached, crunching along the corridor. A group of Royal Legionaries came to the open doors. At the sight of the two on the balcony they dropped to their knees, heads bowed.

"Speak," said Thorn.

"Your Imperial Majesty," said the colonel, "the one we seek is here in the Tower—the Lady Rohain."

"You are too tardy to avail me," laughed Thorn, "for I have found her myself."

Have I heard aright? The aftermath of the past day's fear and exertion, which until now Rohain had subjugated, arose again and challenged her consciousness. It mingled with her exhilaration and terror, her pain and confusion. If she allowed it to overwhelm her, she would faint like some overcorseted courtier; it would sunder her from him and when she awoke he would be gone, because this could only be a cruel dream.

She hid her face in her hands. Tears trickled in a pewter rain between her fingers.

Someone caught her up in a hammock of thunder-webs and carried her along. The voice of Thorn, deep and musical, spoke. She could not properly understand the words, but soon a cup was placed in her hands, and she drank, and felt the effects of a sleeping-draft coursing through the pathways of her body. The walls fell in, one by one, and she tumbled in a circle.

Which closed over her head.

He *was* gone, after all.

Music sounded, heartbreakingly sweet and haunting, a piping that described an existence beyond mortal grasp, beyond knowledge, a prize to stretch out and yearn for, unreachable, and she, not knowing what it was, awoke crying because she could not follow.

The sleep-memory troubled her waking mind, and a clear young voice sang:

> I'll sing you nine-O. Heark, how the winds do blow!
> What are your nine-O?
> Nine for the Arts of Gramarye and eight for the notes of
>   singing.
> Seven for the riders in the sky and six for the gamblers'
>   flinging.
> Five for the rings on my love's hand and four for the
>   seasons winging.
> Three, three, the Chances,
> Two, two the lovers' hearts joinèd close together,
> One is one and all alone and shall be so forever.

It was a well-remembered voice, a linnet of a voice that softly sang that old song. It belonged to Caitri, the daughter of the Keeper of the Keys, a daydreamer given to composing ditties that she often hummed to herself. The child seemed oblivious of the world beyond her small horizon, but in fact was the opposite. She sat nearby, playing cat's cradle as she sang. She was dressed in servants' subfusc and smelled of orange blossom.

"Did I dream again?" Bemused, Rohain raised herself on

one elbow. She found herself reclining on a sumptuous couch within a richly decorated, spacious room. In a wide hearth, a fire flamed like evanescent castles of light. The windows were obscured by lengthy velvet draperies emblazoned all over with the Stormrider device, but the curve of the outer wall betrayed the room's status as a Tower chamber.

Young Caitri smiled, still half musing on her song.

"What is dream and what is reality?" she asked, philosophically, rhetorically, and somewhat pedantically for one so young. Such a childish face could not have weathered more than thirteen Winters.

"Where are we?"

"Your Ladyship is at the fortieth story, the most exalted level of the Tower, barring the somewhat cramped turret rooms. The apartments here shall henceforth bear the title 'Royal Suites' and all future guests shall wish to occupy them. I was called upon to attend Your Ladyship and right glad I am to escape, for a time, the sorrow of the misfortune that has descended upon the Seventh House."

"Your mother," said Rohain suddenly, "is she hale?"

"Why yes, my lady," returned the child, frowning her puzzlement. "My mother escaped the scourge . . ." She put aside her string game.

"That is well. Now I must make myself presentable at once."

"Take refreshment, an it please you, lady—here are both victuals and drink. A bath awaits and raiment is laid out. My lady Heligea has gifted part of her own wardrobe, since Your Ladyship's was destroyed by the Antlered One and his unseelie wights. Seamstresses have lengthened the hems in haste, while you slept. Methinks the colors of the Seventh House shall become you. Your Ladyship is to be received by His Majesty this very morning."

"Has the night passed already and is morning come? Where is the King-Emperor?"

"I know not, m'lady. I have not yet beheld His Majesty. Since I was called I have been in a constant state of excitement in case I should happen to glimpse him."

"And Viviana?"

"She was, in sooth, the one called to attend Your Ladyship but she asked me to take her place, since she cannot rid herself of siedo's faithful stench."

"Caitri, I am glad it is you who came."

"Do you know me?"

"Yes. I wist that you are worthy."

"I thank you, m'lady."

"I wist you show kindness to unfortunates, to outcasts."

"I suppose you mean Pod—that I treat him fairly."

"Oh, Pod—yes. A curious lad."

"Your Ladyship has seen him, then? Some say he has the Sight, you know."

"Indeed! That would explain much."

"And somewhat of a gift of prophecy. Yet it is sad, for part of his wit is lacking. Possessing such wondrous gifts, he is unable to use them profitably and is betimes erratic in his augury. Dine now, prithee, or I shall be taken to account for failing to sustain you. I can assure you, our chief cook had no part in the preparation. Confidentially, Rennet Thighbone is a slovenly one."

"What is the Sight, exactly?" asked Rohain, taking up a cup of milk and honey. The girl's talk distracted her from the one thought that churned around and around in her head, threatening to drive her to the brink of madness. She welcomed the distraction.

"Well, I suppose it is the gift of seeing what is real. It is a rare talent—only a very few folk are born possessing it, although the Sight disregards all barriers of social distinction. The rest of us must try to find four-leafed clover, for when its leaves are carried, somewhat of the Sight is acquired, but not always full-blown, and only temporarily." After a pause, she said, "Personally, I think Pod does not have the Sight. I suspect he possesses an extraordinary sense of smell, like animals, or some wights."

Rohain sipped the drink but could barely swallow one mouthful. A tightness knotted the pit of her stomach. Her heart raced. What she had seen last night—was it true? Could she believe her eyes and ears, or had she been overcome with distress and fallen into a strange hallucination? And what had become of her companions on the road?

"Tell me," she said to Caitri. "Featherstone and Pennyrigg, Ustorix and the rest who were with me when I rode out—have they returned?"

"The servant of Master Zimmuth's, he never returned. My lord Callidus was badly wounded. The others are all home and hale, m'lady, which is more than can be said for the many folk of all ranks who were slain or wounded within the Tower's very walls. Truly, doom came among us, and had not the King-Emperor come to succor us we had all perished. 'Twill be long ere we forget."

By the Powers, let my meeting with Thorn not be a mere delusion. If I ask the child and her words prove it an invention of my mind, I shall lose hope. Therefore I shall not ask her.

Rohain bathed. Her assistant helped her dress in Stormrider finery. The black armazine gown, equipped with long, tight sleeves that would have been considered screamingly out of mode at Court, was bordered at the collar, cuffs, and hem with wide bands of black ducape stitched with winged crescents in silver. Caitri pinned a scrollwork brooch at the throat. The folds of the sable cloak displayed richly patterned sarcenet linings, and it was fastened at the front by fine chains laced through small silver bosses at either side. A girdle stitched with silver thread in a diamond pattern on

a black ground passed around Rohain's waist at the back,
but angled down to a V-shape at the front. The shoes were
painstakingly embroidered with a pattern of tiny horses.

Dark tresses flowed rampant down Rohain's back, still
damp. Caitri raked them with a broken-toothed ivory-and-
tortoiseshell comb, then fastened silver stars in the midnight cloud of them, and placed a spangled gauze veil over
all, bound with a fillet encrusted with milk-crystals and tiny
beads of jet.

"They gave me this to put on you," she said, fastening a
golden chain around Rohain's neck. It was a new tilhal—
three bunched hypericum leaves made of jade, clasped in
gold.

"Your Ladyship is indeed comely beyond the ordinary,
as all have been saying," she continued gravely, naively unaware of her boldness. "His Majesty is certain to be pleased
when my lady goes before him."

"Thank you. I am ready now. But I am frightened. I may
have dreamed last night, but which is the more terrifying, to
be awake or asleep, I know not."

Sir Flint of the Third Thriesniun, with a clutch of footmen, escorted Rohain to where the King-Emperor presided
in the Highest Solar. The fortieth floor was heavily
guarded by men-at-arms, but all was calm and serene. It
seemed that the evildoers had passed this level by, leaving
it intact. Ensconced torches shed a warm light on drab
wall-hangings. Their brilliance startling against the black
and silver of the Seventh House, yeomen in scarlet-and-
gold uniforms stood at every door and window, at every
corner. The Royal Standard leaned from wall-brackets, the
crowned lion flaunting its splendid colors.

At the door, the visitor's heart galloped as the sentries
uncrossed their halberds with due ceremony and allowed
her to pass. A wave of dizziness passed over her and she

was forced to pause for an instant. Caitri clutched at her elbow.

"Is my lady hale?" Sir Flint voiced his concern. Rohain nodded.

Across an outer room, through another door. Diagonals of sunlight, mellow and pure as honey-mead, lanced in at the windows.

Rohain looked up. And there he stood, the King-Emperor.

Through the slashed sleeves of his velvet doublet—gold lions worked on a ground of deepest royal purple—black cambric shirtsleeves showed in soft, full gathers, tied at three points. A wide belt of goldwork clasped the calf-length doublet, which was slit at each side in the manner of the Dainnan tunic and worn open at the front to show the shirt. Its wide lapels, lined with black and gold samite, jutted at the shoulders to form a *V* with its point finishing at the waist, just above the belt. Black hose fitted closely to his thighs, tucking into knee-boots turned back at the tops. His cloak, thrown back, flared in many folds from his shoulders. Made from purple velvet, it was worked in crowns and heraldic designs both black and gold, and lined with inky satin. His mane of dark hair spilled from beneath a simple low-crowned cap bearing three soft shadowy plumes.

All this finery could not in any way make him foppish; rather, he was magnificent, clad in splendor as rich and somber as a Summer's evening. His vitality filled the hall as though all light, all darkness radiated from him.

At Rohain's entrance, he regarded her without speaking. Viviana had schooled her in how to meet royalty. Like the servant girl, like the warriors flanking her, she dropped to her knees, bowing her head, noticing with intense clarity the detail of the skyriding design on the slightly worn rugs. This was one of the fringed, hooked rugs she had once been accustomed to punishing, in order to free the dust from it. In a detached way, she wondered who was privileged to undertake that job these days and whether they did it as well as she had.

A weight seemed to be pressing upon her eyelids. Soon she would have to look at him, but it would seem an impossible task.

She waited for him to speak.

Two hands lifted her gently to her feet. Their touch was lightning.

"I'll warrant thou wouldst be more comfortable sitting by me." The voice—rich, tempered, and flawlessly enunciated—a lion's growl. She breathed the cinnamon incense of his presence.

He conducted her to one of two chairs at the head of a table, and seated himself beside her. A timid page took a small key and unreeled the taper of a wax-jack on a little silver stand. He trimmed the wick with a pair of pointed snuffers and tremulously lit it, fumbling with the tinderbox.

Thorn's existence was like a terrible furnace flaming at Rohain's side. She was dimly aware that others were present in the hall—great lords, Roxburgh among them, all standing, facing Thorn. Caitri folded her hands neatly to hide her nervousness at being in the presence of the King-Emperor, and arranged herself against the wall where several pages and wigged footmen made bas-reliefs of themselves in scarlet duretty and gold frogging. High on a pelmet, the goshawk Errantry sat dozing, sometimes nervously flicking his tail from side to side. A whitewash of his mutes streaked and splattered the curtains below, as well as any footmen who happened to be standing in the vicinity. One or two hawk-casts decorated the floor with indigestible bits of bone and feather. Errantry opened one fierce eye and closed it again.

"Fear not," Thorn whispered to Rohain. She found courage to return his smile. "Gentlemen," he said loudly, "here is the Lady Rohain for whom we have all sought high and low."

Still standing, the lords bowed their heads: Richard of Esgair Garthen, Lord High Sea Admiral; Octarus Ogier, Lord High Chieftain of Stormriders; Durand Rivenhall, Lord High Chancellor; Istoren Giltornyr, Lord High Sky Admiral; John Drumdunach, Lord High Commander of the Royal Guard. Thorn introduced the chiefest among them by name to the lady at his side, then dismissed them, along with his Private Secretary, his pages and stewards, the guards, and all the other lords and servants, excepting Caitri. He bade the little girl wait in the anteroom.

Rohain sat utterly still, except that a slight tremor ran through her.

"And now thou shalt want to ask some questions," Thorn said. "Dost thou wish to use handspeak? Hast thou lost thy tongue again? I confess, I was enjoying the novelty of hearing thy voice."

She laughed then, joyously.

<<No, I have not lost my speaking,>> she signed, now at ease.

<<Speak, then!>> his hands signaled.

"Thorn," she said, savoring the name. "Thorn. Your Dainnan name. That is, Your Majesty's Dainnan name."

"Gold-Hair," he said, "it is hardly necessary to address me like that. Or," he added, "to collapse upon the floor when approaching me. Didst thou not pledge thyself to me last night?"

"I did, sir, and most readily."

"Now thou must learn to be our betrothed, rather than a commoner who brazenly declares herself a lady. It is meet that thou shouldst become accustomed to bearing thyself like the future queen."

Her courage returned. "You know all? But how? Did you know I was residing at Court? Why did I not see you? How may a Dainnan be King?"

"Here come the questions, all of a tumble," he said, amused. "But I shall start the tale at the beginning."

"Oh, but before you do," she said quickly, basking in his proximity as if it were Summer sunshine, "I wish to ask you to spare the life of a man imprisoned in your dungeons, condemned to death. His name—"

"He is pardoned, from this moment, whatever his name might be. Now hearken, while I tell the tale. Art thou paying heed?"

"No. I am looking at thee . . ."

Boldly, as though parched and drinking, her eyes traveled over the wiredrawn, flowing lines of his silhouette, the honed planes of his face, stern and laughing at the same time, full of strength, the jawline faintly shadowed with a dark tint, the arch of his throat interrupted by the subtle shadow of the round tumescence midway, and the hollow at the confluence of the collarbone.

His every movement was as graceful and confident as a lion in its prime, his demeanor relaxed yet poised, with the assurance that at need he, as a skilled fighter, could react with speed and power, and there would be only conquest. This time she tried to memorize his flawless beauty. The moment would be ephemeral, as was the wont of moments, and he would vanish soon. *Rare beauty, by nature, must be ephemeral. Without that sting it is no longer rare. But I wish, oh I wish it were not so. I wish that he might endure forever.*

"And I am studying thee," he replied, "and I hope to do so more often and more thoroughly at my leisure. But if thou regard'st men in that manner, thou shalt drive them mad."

"Well, you deserve to be driven mad, sir, for you have already done so to me."

"Now thou must needs hold conversation with me from the other side of the room," he said, flame-eyed. "Else thou might provoke me to encompass and invade thee, here, at this instant."

"In that case," she answered breathlessly, "I remain."

He regarded her with a strange softness, almost sadness.

"Half child, half woman as thou art. For thee, virtuous maiden," he said, "there would be no rightness in that. Not yet."

She forced herself to look away, suddenly understanding; there were rules that *could not* be abrogated, at this place, at this time, in this century, in Erith.

"You must turn your back on me," Rohain commanded the King-Emperor of Erith, knowing him well enough to dare light banter, exulting in the play of words between them and the fragile power she wielded, while still unable to believe it was all true. "Turn your back, whilst you tell me the tale. But look not askance! Ever since I saw you for the first time I have longed to comb my fingers through your hair."

He complied, laughing, sprawling back in the chair and stretching out his long legs. She let the dark veils of his locks flow over her fingertips and was amazed, that the very stuff of midnight could lie soft within her own hands, that what she touched was actually of him; he for whom she had ached throughout eternities.

He spoke.

"Through the glades of Tiriendor I roved in Dainnan fashion, which is my wont when it pleases me, and when needs must. For, Gold-Hair, a good sovereign must gauge the state of his realm, and what better way than to explore it unmarked? Several of my chief lords and advisers are persistently alarmed at this habit, and I must forever persuade them it is safer in the greenwood than in the wilderness of Court where poisonous vipers await the turning of every back.

"I had long studied thee and thy companion, Captain Bruadair, ere thou didst meet with me. I was drawn to thee," he said. "In thee there burned a passion, right from the first moment—a passion of such intensity as I have never encountered. Thou dost possess a capacity for joyousness and for deep sorrow that bedims the torpid ardencies of others. The crests and troughs of their fervor are but the fickle waves of the ocean, whereas thine are like an island mountain, whose head lifts among the clouds, whose foundations are buried far below on the ocean floor. Thou wouldst try to withhold thy fire, but such duplicity was beyond thy means. When it came time for us to part, I was already lost. Thou wouldst not accompany me then, but I was eager to bring thee to my side if not sooner, then later."

"Did it hurt you that I would not go with you?" Rohain asked, surprised. Her heart leapt like a deer.

"Hurt? To a degree. Only as a sword piercing the heart. Thou art kissing my hair."

"Even so." The strands were silk, lying across her mouth.

"When thou didst hasten to the carlin's house," he said, "I ordered guards to be stationed around it, to protect thee, to bring thee to me when your errand was completed. They were to be discreet."

"The watchers—they were men of yours?"

"They were. I ought to have used Dainnan, but I did not suppose that thou wouldst try to slip through my net."

She said, hesitantly, "I was a servant here, once." *Will he now reject me?* He merely nodded, as if it did not matter. Her spirits immeasurably encouraged, she went on: "I escaped and found the wealth of Waterstair. For the sake of it, others wanted me to keep silence. They hounded me. And in Gilvaris Tarv I sought a cure for paradox ivy from the wizard Korguth. It failed and I thought he pursued me to take revenge for his own ill deed. I believed your men watching Maeve's cottage to be those who hunted me for evil purpose."

"Why didst thou not enlighten me concerning your pursuers before we went our separate ways?" he asked, his modulated, laughing tones threaded with a hint of gentle exasperation.

"Why did you not declare your heart's truth?" she parried.

"I asked thee to come with me—is that not enough?"

"It was not plain to me. But you tell me plainly now."

"Because thou hold'st back thine own truth no longer. Thou speakest with thine eyes at last. And thy tongue. And because I would not lose thee a second time."

Her heart seemed to melt like glass in the fire of his intent. "Now I do not fear to have you look upon my face. You read now in my eyes that which has long been written in my heart."

"Thou with thy secret commission to Caermelor—had you but confided to me this tale of treasure-troves, thou hadst saved thyself a deal of toil," he mocked gently.

"I was to impart the tale only to the King-Emperor!"

"And thus 'tis proven that thou hast that rare quality— thou canst guard a secret well. Wilt thou guard thine affairs so readily now that thou hast found thy tongue?"

He laughed. A sudden wave of concern swept through Rohain. There *was* another secret . . . Should he become aware of her strange history as an amnesiac foundling, would he recoil from her? Yet he asked nothing of the past. For him, the present seemed sufficient. Indeed, what could that history matter?

"But tell me," she said, "why did your guards not simply knock at Maeve's door and announce that the King-Emperor summoned me?"

"Thou mightst well have refused, as thou didst once before!"

"I could hardly refuse my sovereign . . ."

"So thou sayest, but how could I have known? Then thou didst disappear. Only once before in my life have I been thwarted so thoroughly. There arose a violent anger in my heart that this should have come to pass, that I should lose thee. All those around me suffered from my rage, which was caused by thee!"

"Say no more!" She tugged playfully at his hair.

"No, thou canst not injure me now," he lightly mocked.

"It was not my fault!"

"Dost thou gainsay me?" he said, feigning to chide her. "When thou didst alter everything about thy appearance and demeanor, thy mode of communication, calling thyself by another name and coming right into my house, which is the last place I would look for thee, while the town criers were bellowing at every gate in the city, morning, noon, and night, to proclaim the King-Emperor's command that anyone who sees a yellow-haired wench called Imrhien should bring her to him instantly, on pain of imprisonment?"

"I heard them shouting, but I never heeded the words."

"They cannot be heard distinctly from the palace, unless the wind is in the right quarter. Which I had always counted pleasant, since their rantings are tiresome."

"Did you have them looking for a yellow-haired wench of exquisite ugliness?"

"No. Thou hadst told me that thou didst want to alter that condition, therefore thou wert bound for the carlin at White Down Rory."

"Yet in the beginning, how could you warm to someone so ill-made?"

He turned his beautiful head and gave her a measuring look.

"Gold-Hair," he said, "I have already told thee."

"Did you *see* my ugliness?"

"I saw it. I saw thee."

"How did you recognize me last night?"

"I say again, I saw *thee*. Thine inner worth."

It was said the D'Armancourt line was set apart from ordinary mortalkind by some puissance of the blood. Likely, that included the Sight; the ability to perceive what lay beneath masks. Thorn looked away, and Rohain resumed her combing. A wonderful silence linked them, filled with unspoken words. *May the Powers of all realms grant that time shall now stand still.*

"I want for nothing now," she said presently.

"Thou shalt change thy mind, in time, as is the wont of women."

"I shall not!" She smiled at his light teasing.

"Dost thou not wish to hear the rest of the story?"

"I do!"

"Behold! Thou hast changed it already."

The goshawk shifted on his perch, shook out his wings, and glided down in a lazy spiral to land upon the back of Rohain's chair. She reached up. Decorously, he nibbled at her hand. Thorn raised his arm and Errantry flew to alight on the leather bracer encircling his wrist. Absently, Thorn stroked the bird's barred plumage.

"We could not find thee," he said. "Your red cockerel of a friend at Isenhammer knew nothing. When there was no sign of thee by Imbroltide, we began in earnest to seek the carlin of White Down Rory."

"I dined in the same hall as you at Imbrol!"

"Alas, that I was unaware of it! My eyes searched beyond the palace walls on that night, my sweet thief of quietude."

"And my eyes did not search at all! What of Maeve?"

"Her cottage was discovered empty."

"Empty! Where had she gone?"

"Curiously, she was nowhere to be found, even though the Dainnan and the most proficient of trackers sought her, and messengers were sent to every land. Then we had to depart for the fields of battle. We had tarried too long because of my quest for thee, but the need grew pressing. During my absence the search continued.

"One evening, afar off in northern Eldaraigne, I was riding out with Roxburgh under the early stars, not far from where our troops were bivouacked. In conversation we chanced to look skywards, which turned us to the topic of beauty. My Lord High Field-Marshal of the Dainnan let slip the fact that a certain beauteous young damsel who had brought tidings of treasure to Caermelor had arrived masked. She had been unaware of particular aristocratic protocols and furthermore had recounted a strange story of traveling in the wilderness with a wild Ert by the kenning of 'The Bear.' That sobriquet had once before come to my ears."

Rohain recalled a conversation by a campfire, Diarmid saying to Thorn: *"When I was a lad, I used to trade words with my—with my uncle."*

To augment his statement, she had signed, <<*Once I heard Sianadh word-fighting against some wicked men. He won.*>>

"He always won. Ertishmen are famous for their skill with words; Finvarna is the birthplace of most of the greatest bards. But the Bear could outspar even his own countrymen."

High in Isse Tower, Thorn again turned the implicit barrage of his gaze upon her.

"I knew then that this 'Rohain Tarrenys of the Sorrows' was thee—changed, healed, as thou hadst desired. 'Rohain' was a name recently brought to my attention at Court. Ercildoune had once or twice bothered me with it. They had described the lady as *dark-haired*. That thou didst go disguised was proof enough that thou didst fear some imminent peril."

"Swee-swit," said the goshawk, dulcet, picking up strands of Thorn's hair in his curved beak.

"Within the hour we departed from the battlefields. The best of our troops rode the skies beside us in haste to Caermelor, with more speed than any Relayer. We were too late—already the Lady of the Sorrows had reached Isse Tower. Pausing only to take fresh eotaurs, we left Caermelor at noon two days since, and rode nonstop, by day and night, arriving here as the festivities of the Antlered One were in full swing."

"Oh, happy chance! Had you not done so, there must have been massacre on an appalling scale."

"In that battle, I went through every blood-splashed hall and stair in this worm-bitten pillar, and my sword Arcturus sang metal's song of death as I wielded him, smiting unseelie heads. Yet, thou hadst once again glided away like sand through my fingers, confounding me. Never to me has woman proved so elusive. No sense could be got out of the incoherent servitors and lords of Isse until at last one of them gathered his wits for long enough to inform me that thou wert away to Huntingtowers and might be lying slain upon the road. Roxburgh, who was already mounted, rode out forthwith. I, about to depart, was compelled to turn back. Someone said they had seen thee in the kitchens. When he was sent to bring thee, thou wert not to be found. Many folk confirmed his report that thou wert here, safe, somewhere. The Tower seethed with folk, but it was secure and I knew I should find thee again, sooner or later. I knew it at last."

He was silent for a while. Then he said, "Who, at Court, guessed thee as Talith?"

"Only the Lady Dianella."

"Say further."

"I told her I was looking for a Dainnan called Thorn. Is your Dainnan name commonly known amongst the courtiers?"

"As well-known as Roxburgh's 'Oak' and Ercildoune's 'Ash.' That lady connives to be Queen, and brooks no rivals. Constantly she flaunts her charms, like the rest, but she is assisted by her plotting uncle who wishes to lever her on the throne and puppet her on his strings. I would hazard she heard the town criers' proclamations. Her kind hang on their every word in the hope of scandal. Hearing that thou didst search for me and I for thee, that jealous deceiver would have found it necessary to ask no further questions. I'll warrant she and the wizard swiftly planned your downfall, before I could discover thee."

"Dianella told me to leave Caermelor."

"I suspect she did so in order that thy demise might occur at a less inconvenient location, and the blame would be looked for elsewhere!" His face darkened. "Those who cross me are punished."

A cloud passed across the sun. Shadows rushed in and dammed the room like thin, dark waters.

Thorn seized a curl of paper and a quill-pen from the table, trimming its point with a porcelain-handled penknife. Dipping the point in ink, he dashed off a missive, blotted it dry, rolled the parchment and tied it with cord, dripped wax from a candle and impressed it with the seal-ring he had not been wearing in the wilderness. Calling to Caitri, he directed her to deliver it to one of the messengers waiting outside the door. When she had departed, he resumed his nonchalant position in the chair, reclining on one elbow.

"But surely," said Rohain earnestly, "Dianella could not guess that the Tower was to be assailed by the Hunt!"

"One would suppose not," said Thorn thoughtfully. "She and her uncle must have prepared some other method of ridding themselves of you, had not Huon intervened."

Rohain thought: *What a curious coincidence, that the Hunt should choose to assail this fortress precisely at the time of my visit here* . . . And then a hand of ice was laid upon her vitals, bestowing a suspicion so terrible she hardly dared to speak it aloud. *Could the wizard Sargoth possibly wield enough power to summon the Wild Hunt? Worse: If he had not summoned it, then who had? And what had the Antlered One hunted for, besides destruction?*

Thorn said, "Didst thou tell the Lady Dianella aught of the carlin?"

"I did!" replied Rohain in consternation. "Cry mercy! Have I endangered the old woman's life? Dianella and her uncle, guessing that Maeve was party to knowledge of Rohain Tarrenys's true identity, might have tried to silence her! Yet surely, mortal men—even the Lord High Wizard's men—could never trace Maeve One-Eye unless she wished it."

"In truth, Gold-Hair. Yet they were not mortal men who went after her."

"Then she must be rescued!"

"She shall be, you may believe it."

"Yet I cannot believe that Sargoth has anything of gramarye at his fingertips, to force unseelie wights to obey him. All his vaunted tricks are only hocus-pocus."

Thorn plucked a loop of light out of the air and waved it over his shoulder.

"Is that hocus-pocus?"

She laughed. "A trick, yes—I'll vouch that it was concealed in your sleeve! I am no country lass from Rosedale, to be gulled by sleight-of-hand!"

The shining thing was a small circle of golden leaves spangled with white gems that glittered, having somehow imprisoned the brilliance of stars within their depths. Thorn pulled down her narrow wrist, printed a kiss on it, and slid the leaf-ring upon her finger. Each axonal fiber along her arm turned to hot wire.

"Thou distract'st me, ever, from the tale," he said, without relinquishing her hand. "My imagination strays. Thou couldst never understand how difficult it is to remain thus, seemingly unmoved."

"Whither do thy thoughts wander?"

He leaned back and whispered in her ear. She murmured a reply. The goshawk, screaming, jumped into the air and flapped around the room, scattering a few loose, downy feathers.

"Out, scapegrace!" said his master, and the bird flew through the window. Thorn rose from the chair. Drawing Rohain to her feet, he followed the hawk to the embrasure. They stood close together, she intensely aware of the light pressure of his arm against her shoulder as they looked out through the archway across a wide land and the curve of a dazzling sea.

Thorn leaned his left hand upon the window-frame. It was long-fingered and strong. Around the ring-finger glinted a thin band—three golden hairs, twisted together.

He has kept the token he seized from me! Ah, what would it be like to wake in the night and see him lying against me, hair rayed out upon the pillow, dark lashes fanned upon his cheek, as soft as a sleeping child's?

Below, high in the abyss, the hawk floated.

"Let us speak no more of the past," murmured Thorn. "Few yellow leaves, or none, cling upon the boughs; stark, dismantled choirs where erst the birds of Summer sang," he said, possibly quoting. "But the dark days of Winter are not unremitting, and clouds have drawn apart on this day to let the sun shine on our contentment."

"As welcome as sunshine is, storm and wind and rain have their beauty also," said Rohain, recalling the rain in the Forest of Tiriendor. "Each season has a virtue to recommend it, not least Winter."

"I' faith, I concur! Fain would I be without these walls, and soon we shall be, for we ride this day to Caermelor."

"By land or sky?"

"By sky. On the wing. Fear'st thou that?" The glance he bestowed on her seemed to fill her bones with water. Her legs would scarcely hold her up.

"On the contrary, I look to it with eagerness! But stay—before I depart from this place, I must first render them aid. Destruction and death have been brought down on innocents. My own apartments were wrecked, although the raiders left this level untouched."

"Not much was destroyed elsewhere, save flesh and bone. Thy lodgings were the worst ravaged. Other inorganic damage was incidental to their more vile pursuits. Among my men there are dyn-cynnils, an apothecary, and other flesh-tailors. As we speak they tend the wounded of Isse, regardless of rank or birth. I myself have recently walked among the injured and to me it seems there is none so badly hurt as will not recover fully. My physicians shall bide here until their work is done. To Caermelor we shall ride without further ado, I insist. There shall our betrothal be announced, and thou shalt meet Prince Edward."

A pure, resonant strum went through and through Rohain. She managed to say, "I approach that meeting with delight."

"A ball shall be held in thine honor, if that should please thee. Should it?"

"If we should dance the gavotte, as before."

"To synchronize with thee is joyousness, no matter the choreography, *caileagh faoileag*," he said lightly.

"Once before you called me that name. What is its meaning?"

" 'Beloved bird of the sea.' The white bird of freedom is an ocean wanderer. It touches no land for seven years in its voyages around the world, flying over vast tracts of open ocean without landmarks. This fairest, most elusive of winged navigators travels far before it finds its rest."

At the back of her mind, a thread snapped, but only a thread. Rohain glanced at her left wrist. Moon-pearls and jet like chips of black ice embraceleted it, in their setting of white metal; a borrowed trinket of Heligea's. They were not what she had looked for.

"Now I have been called a butterfly and a bird," she said. "And Rohain."

"Which means 'beautiful.' Each of us has many names. I have the privilege of possessing such a string of them as might arguably stretch from here to Namarre."

"And one," she said, "is James."

He took her hand. The jolt shook her arm to the shoulder socket.

"Oh!" she said, shivering. "You take my breath away. Your touch has some alchemy in it."

"Think'st thou, indeed? Dost thou tolerate it?"

"It is like a shock, but sweeter than anything I have ever endured."

"How canst thou be certain it is *I* and not *thee* who generates it?"

A silver trumpet sang loudly, somewhere in the machicolations close above. A distant fleck in the southeast shaped itself into a Stormrider.

"A Relayer from Caermelor," said Thorn. "And we must tarry no longer. The day matures. Art thou able to be ready to depart before noon, Distraction? The hour is not far away."

"Easily."

Rohain called for Caitri. A rattle as of small hard objects scattering upon the floor came from the outer room where she waited—the resourceful child had been playing at knucklebones and at the summons had dropped them.

"At your service, my lady."

Caitri, kneeling, had not yet overcome awe sufficiently to glance at her sovereign.

"Tell Viviana to be ready to leave at noon."

"At once, my lady."

"And send a messenger to Roxburgh. I would confer with the Attriod," said Thorn.

"Your Majesty," whispered the maid. Rising, she backed out of the chamber without lifting her eyes.

"I am fond of that child," said Rohain. "May I ask her if she would like to accompany us?"

"There is *nothing* thou needs must ask for. All is thine—take it."

Still clasping her hand, he led her back to the table.

"Is there nought else thou wouldst take from this chimney stack that once housed thee, besides a half-fledged chick?"

His hair held the subtle fragrance of cedar or perhaps wild thyme. Submerged by the barely leashed potency of him, Rohain wrenched her attention away. She recalled a dressing-table in the suite where she had slept on the previous night—one of the many apartments on the fortieth story that had escaped the depredations of the unseelie vandals. The fringed aulmoniere containing Maeve's swan's feather lay there. Beside it lay the crimson vial of Dragon's Blood—Thorn's gift, unchained from around her neck when she had bathed. It had been neglected in the amazement of the morning.

"Yes, there is something. I shall fetch it myself, and return in a trice."

He raised her hand to his lips. Over it, he studied her with speculative tenderness.

"Your kiss is fire," she murmured, blushing.

"Burn, then."

"I do not want to leave your side, even for a trice."

"Remain, then."

"Soon, forever. Now I must go."

He relinquished her hand. Someone's knuckles rapped hesitantly at the outer door. Thorn bade the door-knocker enter, and Rohain fled. Outside in the passageway, a convocation of tall lords stood aside, bowing respectfully, to let her pass. She inclined her head in acknowledgment of their salutes.

In the dressing-chamber a slight figure jerked its head up when she entered in a flurry of silver and black. The dressing table was bereft of all accoutrements save a bowl and ewer.

"Pod! What are you doing here? Where are my purse and vial?"

"I don't know," he rapped out, rather implausibly.

"You have them. Give them to me, please."

He backed away, his hands concealed behind him.

"Prithee, Pod."

The lad's eyes slid from side to side, like loosely strung beads.

"Such as you," he said in a stilted voice, "such as you and such as he shall never find happiness together."

"Say not that!" shouted Rohain vehemently. "Take it back! Wish me well instead. Say it is not so!"

"It is so."

"A king may marry a commoner—why not? He may marry whomsoever he chooses! Why do you hate me?"

"I hate all of you."

"Do you not wish to find friendship?"

"No."

She lunged at him, hoping to catch him off guard and retrieve her belongings. He dodged past, skipping lopsidedly to the door and out.

"Take your pessimistic prophecies hence, base villain!" she cried after him. "They are false, in any event. Never speak to me again!"

She sat before the looking-glass and wiped away a few glassy tears that trembled in her eyes. Pod's prediction had disturbed her deeply. He had stolen the swan's feather and the Dragon's Blood, but it no longer seemed to matter.

A reek of siedo-pods preceded Viviana into the chamber.

"My lady! I am ready to return. I cannot wait to leave this miserable place."

"Stay back, please!" Rohain held a lace kerchief to her nose.

"There is no ridding oneself of it," mourned the lady's maid.

Her mistress waved her away. "Ask Caitri and Pennyrigg and Featherstone and Brand Brinkworth the Storyteller whether they would like to accompany the King-Emperor to Court and abide there. All who wish to do so must assemble at Royal Squadron Level by noon."

Viviana fluttered from the room. Rohain returned to the Highest Solar, before whose door a second crowd milled. Saluting, murmuring, the concourse parted to allow her through. Silver-and-black hat-hedges lined her path. A daunting assembly of lords and attendants now filled the hall, with the King-Emperor at its focus. All fell silent at Rohain's entrance. Boldly she walked to the window embrasure where once again he stood, framed against the sky, with Errantry positioned on his shoulder. Yes, let them witness how it was.

Smiling that brilliant smile which left her weak, he kissed her hand.

"Our business here is concluded. And so to horse," he added to the assembly at large.

They led a procession from the hall. Due to his stature, Thorn's cloak was full-yarded enough to billow from his shoulders like a great banner; as he walked its edges flicked the denizens of the Tower in the passageway, who had shrunk to pilose dwarf borders, having removed their hats and fallen to their knees.

There was a stirring in the stones. The procession halted abruptly when Thorn sidestepped, reached into the bruised shadows of a gouge in the wall, and pulled out a small, yelping figure that stank like a goat-pen. Pod quailed, weakly flapping against Thorn's grip like a half-dead fish on a hook.

"Knave!" said Thorn sternly. "Think you that you can spy on us, hidden, as you erroneously believed?"

Pod hung limply, sullenly.

"Speak!"

The lad pointed an accusing finger.

"She told me not to speak."

"What?" roared Thorn. "Have you been troubling the Lady Rohain? I might have your shape shifted to that of a viper's liver and feed you to my hawk."

"No, no!" squealed Pod pathetically. To Rohain, he looked such a miserable, scrawny thing that compassion and deflection seemed the only possible reaction.

"He has not—" she began then broke off. *He has been troubling me. I would not accuse him, but neither would I lie, especially to Thorn. There have been too many lies, since my tongue was loosened.*

"Any past wrongs are forgiven," said she. "He is able, conceivably, to be an amiable lad."

"He does not look so," said Thorn. "Get yourself some clean clouts, lurker, and a courteous tongue in your head."

He released the boy, who unclotted to a nerveless blob and subsided against the wall.

They moved on.

A phalanx of footmen in mustard livery edged with silver braid stood to attention in straight lines, their gloved hands knotted behind their backs. Saddled and ready, eotaurs cluttered the upper gatehalls with the jangle of their flying-gear and the ring of sildron against stone. Their warm breath scented the air like a harvest.

Lord Ustorix, with Lady Heligea at his elbow, took leave of the King-Emperor and his entourage. The Son of the House croaked his farewells, hoarse with some kind of pent-up emotion.

"Your Majesty has honored our humble abode by this visit and by the succor Your Majesty has bestowed on Your Majesty's undeserving subjects. May Your Majesty and the Lady Rohain ride with the wind at your backs." In his pompous efforts at civility he seemed to be tying clove-hitches with his tongue.

Thorn nodded and leapt astride his steed, thrusting his boots down between the rustling wings and the smooth flanks.

"Lord Ustorix, are you quite recovered from your ordeal?" enquired Rohain.

"No complaint shall escape my lips, most exalted lady," he answered with studied fortitude.

"Until you are, I recommend that Heligea take over your Relayer duties. She is adept at riding sky. In fact, I suggest that she should Relay as often as she wishes."

A murmur of surprise ran through the gathered Household of the Isse Tower. Heligea's grin of triumph eclipsed the scowl of dismay her brother tried to conceal with a low bow.

The sun, at the keypoint of its arch, hung at the center of the sky's dome. The Imperial Flight, a fleet of some three score mighty Skyhorses, burst from an upper gate-hall. Banking to the southwest, they formed an arrowhead and passed away to the distance like charcoaled galleons slowly sinking beneath an azure ocean.

5
CAERMELOR, PART III
Fire and Fleet

If you are the lantern, I am the flame;
If you are the lake, then I am the rain;
If you are the desert, I am the sea;
If you are the blossom, I am the bee;
If you are the fruit, then I am the core;
If you are the rock, then I am the ore;
If you are the ballad, I am the word;
If you are the sheath, then I am the sword.

LOVE SONG OF SEVERNESSE

Viviana and Caitri rode pillion. They had no experience in riding sky, and onhebbing the eotaur flying-gear was too delicate an art for beginners to master. The sliding of andalum chain-plate along the inner courses of the sildron girth-strap to gain or lose altitude took skill born of practice. For the duration of the illicit skyride that had so disjointed the nose of her brother, Heligea—who had secretly practiced for years—had onhebbed like a professional. Rohain, however, had experienced the clumsiness of the novice. Yet this was not the reason Rohain now rode sideways behind Thorn, her arms encircling the wood-hardness of his waist, watching the world dissolve into the flying thunderwrack of his hair.

She leaned against him, almost paralyzed by the exquisite sensation. Later, she could not recall much of that ride save an impression of a storm-whipped shore and a seashell tossed on a dark tide.

Three miles out from Caermelor, the riders heard the trumpets blare. Watchmen on the palace heights had recognized their approach. A mile from the city, the cloud of hugely beating wings began to lose altitude on its long, low final descent. The eotaurs came in over the palace walls, their feathered fetlocks barely clearing the crenellations. They hovered like giant dragonflies over the baileys, churning the air with a backwash as thunderous as a hurricane. From the courtyards below, hats and straw and dust swirled in a chaotic porridge. The cavalcade landed with flawless precision.

Equerries ran to slip off the sildron hoof-crescents and lead away the Skyhorses, to unsaddle them and scrape the sweat from their gleaming flanks, to preen and water and treat the steeds like pampered lords and ladies. Servants hurried to meet the riders, to bear away the jewel-backed riding-gloves they stripped from their hands, to offer fluted cups of wines and cordials. The splendid foot-guards of the Household Division formed two ceremonial columns, creating a human arcade leading to the palace doors. Flowers had been strewn along the cobblestones. Along this arcade walked their sovereign and the dark-haired lady.

As the couple entered the doors of the palace, a slender young man stood upon the flagstones, barring their way. He seemed, in fact, no more than a youth—not much older than Caitri; fourteen or fifteen Summers, a sprout-chinned adolescent. His black hair was impeccably bound into a long horsetail, framing a face that was pale, serious, comely. He bowed briefly to Thorn—a look of understanding flashed between them—and regarded Rohain quizzically from behind soot-colored eyelashes.

There was no need for introductions.

Rohain performed a deep, gracious curtsey. The youth pronounced her current name in the crack-pitched tones of his years and she replied with his royal title. Then they regarded each other. Rohain glimpsed a flicker of what lay behind the starched facade and smiled.

"I am joyed to greet you."

"And I you," he said guardedly, but he smiled too and added, "Well come."

The Heir Apparent stood aside, that the King-Emperor and Rohain might enter first.

The rooms of Rohain's suite burned with frost and flame. Snowy plaster moldings of milky grapes and vine-leaves twined across the ceilings. Brilliant garlands of flowers had been woven into pure white carpets, upon which stood carmine couches and ottomans. A pale marble chimneypiece was drizzled with sparkling ornaments of ruby-red glass. Between the casement windows stretched tall mirrors, polished to perfection.

In one of the three bedchambers—vermilion-carpeted—there stood a bed whose canopy was supported on massive pillars of mahogany. It was hung with curtains of crimson damask embroidered with a twining pattern of clover, over and over. The table at the foot of the bed was muffled in a blood-red cloth. The walls had been painted a soft cream color with a blush of rose in it, and around them were arranged several clothes-chests, lace-draped tables upholding jewel-caskets and chairs of dark, polished mahogany. A tall cushioned chair had been placed near the head of the bed, with a footstool before it.

The main dressing room was sumptuously overfurnished with looking-glasses. Boxes on the dressing table contained numbers of miniature compartments and drawers to hold trinkets and jewelry, with further mirrors fitted to the undersides of the lids, which could be propped open, in case one didn't see enough of oneself elsewhere. In the writing room, an impressive ink stand with a double lid and a central handle dominated the polished jarrah escritoire.

Long fingers of windows, half-disguised by festoons and falls of wine-colored velvet, looked out upon the Winter Garden where crystal wind-chimes had been tied to the boughs, ringing soft and pure, in random melody. Between the green cones of the cypress pines, cornelian fires sprang from high stone dishes, admiring their own fervent lucidity in tarnished ponds.

This, Viviana informed Rohain, was the Luindorn Suite—a vast and exquisitely furnished apartment usually reserved for state visitors.

After breakfast, two height-matched footmen skilled in the art of unobtrusiveness wheeled out the dining trolley and melted quietly away. Caitri, who had rung for them, leaned wide-eyed from a sitting-room window as though she might presently shift to a linnet's shape and fly out into the sky. She appeared oblivious of Rohain and Viviana, who sat head to head, deep in conversation.

"My lady," said Viviana, "that you have found favor in the King-Emperor's eyes is advantageous for us both. As long as his favor lasts, we can *never* be Cut. As for your secret history of service in Isse Tower, why, you can depend on me never to divulge it to anyone. See, you have become a lady after all! I have but one concern—this dresser who has been assigned to you, and this footman also. What next? There is talk that you are to have a noblewoman as your own bodyservant! Are my services to be dispensed with?"

"Of course not. You are to remain as my maid, if you

wish it, as I do. And there are to be no ladies-in-waiting—not yet."

"Ladies-in-waiting?"

As the implications of the term sank in, Viviana's eyes widened. Only a queen would have ladies-in-waiting.

"Six there shall eventually be, chiefed by the Duchess of Roxburgh whenever she is at Court," whispered Rohain.

Simultaneously, maid and mistress burst out laughing. Seizing each other by the hands, they danced the circumference of the floor like children around a beribboned pole on Whiteflower's Day, finally falling breathlessly on two couches of plum-red velvet.

"So 'tis true!" panted Viviana. "His Majesty has asked—"

"Yes! We are troth-plighted, he and I. But it is not generally known—the announcement has yet to be officially made."

"In sooth, rumor has been rife! I did not like to pry, but everyone guesses it. I cannot believe this! My mistress to be Queen-Empress!"

Caitri turned her head, emerging from the haze of her musing. She had been scandalizing at the amount of world that had heretofore been denied her, imprisoned as she had been in Isse Tower.

"Is my lady to be Queen?" She was thunderstruck.

Viviana pranced to the window, grasped the little girl, and whirled her in another polka.

"Yes! Love is the season of the year! What is more, Caitri, when Dain Pennyrigg lifted me from his eotaur just now, he called me his little canary and kissed me. *Kiel varletto!* And he only a stablehand! Oh, but it was *taraiz* delicious. His kiss thrilled me like lightning!"

Rohain nodded. "Passion's current. In both senses of the phrase."

"Skyhorse travel is eminently more pleasurable than Windship travel," pronounced Viviana. "Oh, and Master

Pennyrigg found this in his saddlebags." Rummaging in her pocket, she produced the crimson vial of Dragon's Blood.

Rohain clapped her hands. "Happy day! It is returned to me! Was it companioned by anything else? An aulmoniere perhaps?"

"Why yes, m'lady. Here it is, but it is now putrid with a stink of goats, and I thought to cast it away. I shall have it cleansed for you."

Her mistress took the dirty purse and felt around inside it. "Curses! 'Tis empty! Was there naught else?"

"No, m'lady, there was nothing else which Master Pennyrigg himself did not pack. Only an *ensofell* of smelly hair, tied with string—it comes from a dog or a goat methinks—and the bedraggled feather of some fowl. Shall I throw them away?"

"No, give the feather to me. It is a powerful talisman."

Rohain tucked the feather inside a tapestry aulmoniere, fastened with buttons of jet. It seemed that Pod was at least capable of thanks for his rescue from Thorn's wrath. However, his return of the vial did not hint at a reversal of his dismal prediction. After all, he was supposed to be a prophet, not a maker of curses.

"Come now, my two birds," said Rohain, absently retying a seditious lace on Caitri's gown of forget-me-not blue. "I have been from *his* side for too long. It is fully an hour since we arrived from the Stormrider Tower. That is more than enough time to wash away the stains of travel and recostume ourselves."

"Look at us!" prattled Viviana, ever conscious of appearances. "My lady dark-haired in crimson, I fair in daffodil, and cinnamon Caitri in a sky-colored gown. What a motley bouquet!"

"Yet some among us do not *smell* as a bouquet should," said her mistress, holding a perfumed pomander to her nose to block out the last odorous traces of siedo-pod oil wafting from Viviana's hair. "Hasten!"

A rapping at the door announced the Master of the King's Household, a gray-haired gentleman of middle age. "His Majesty sends greetings, my lady," he said, bending forward from the waist, "and regrets to inform you that he has been called away on a matter of uncommon import."

"So precipitously?" murmured Rohain. "We have only just arrived!"

"These are fickle times," said the gentleman. "Even the best-laid plans may go astray."

"I thank you, sir, for your advice."

The palace seemed suddenly devoid of substance and character during Thorn's unexpected absence. Rohain took the opportunity to visit Sianadh in the dungeons.

"You are to be set free," she told him.

He would not believe her. "'Tis kind of you to try to cheer me," he said in a morose mood. "But these hardhearted *skeerdas* would not free their own grandmother if she was in leg-irons."

"I tell you, I have heard the King-Emperor say so!"

"Ye must have been dreaming," he said mournfully. "Ach! I'd give me right arm for a drop o' the pure stuff."

Thorn returned two days later. He sent a message to Rohain asking her to join him in the Throne Room. Swiftly she made her way through the long galleries and passageways, eager for the reunion.

The columns of the Throne Room aspired to a forty-foot ceiling. This huge space was lit by metallic lusters pendant on thirty-foot chains, and flambeaux on brass pedestals. Twin thrones beneath their dagged and gilded canopy stood atop the grand dais. They were reached by twelve broad stairs.

Around the walls, the history of the world reenacted it-

self perpetually on adjoining tapestries that reached to a
height of twenty feet and represented years of painstaking
stitchery. Above them, every inch of the plasterwork
crawled with painted murals—not scenes, but geometric
designs, stylized flowers, vegetables, flora and fauna, and
fantastic gold-leaf scrollwork that did not stop at the ceiling
merely because that was too high to be easily viewed, but
surged across it in a prolific efflorescence with the vigor of
weeds.

By comparison to this busy overabundance the polished
floor seemed austere, parquetried as it was with wood every
shade of brown between palest blond and burnt umber.
These colored woods formed the heraldic device of the
House of D'Armancourt in repeated tiles six feet square.
The hall was so vast that to enter the doors was to dwindle
immediately to the proportions of a mouse among corn-
stalks.

Rohain entered with her small entourage and a froth of
footmen and alert courtiers who had entangled themselves
in her wake as she sailed through the corridors. Like every
cave in the palace, currently the Throne Room was arrayed
with a flotsam of courtiers and servants. One of the former—a familiar, foppish figure—bowed low before her.

"My Lady Rohain, His Majesty yet walks in the gardens
with the Attriod but will shortly join us here in the Throne
Room."

"Please show me the way to the gardens, Lord Jasper."
He bowed again, but before he could fulfill her request, a
footman, whose wig resembled a white rabbit, dropped to
his knee. He elevated a silver salver from which Lord
Jasper plucked a parchment. The nobleman's brow fur-
rowed as he squinted at the writing of some palace scribe.

"Er—a gentleman begs audience with Your Ladyship. It
appears His Majesty sent for him. An Ertishman with an un-
pronounceable name."

"Send him in," said Rohain.

Uproar and a torrent of Ertish curses emanated from outside the Throne Room, reaffirming Sianadh's contempt for formalities. The doors crashed apart and he burst through like a boulder from a mangonel. Catching sight of Rohain, he stood blinking as though dazed. Two footmen who had been shed from his brawny arms stood helplessly by.

"There ye are, *chehrna,*" said the Ertishman meekly, the bear now a lamb. "The *skeerdas* would not let me through."

"*Mo gaidair,*" said Rohain warmly. She proffered a hand. He took it with the utmost delicacy and a bewildered look. Nothing else being offered in the way of courtesy, she drew it back with an appreciative sigh. "*Mo gaidair,* your lack of etiquette is a refreshing draft."

"*Chehrna,* in one breath I am thinking it might be me last, the next they're turning the key in me cell-door and I am a free man. How is this? What have ye done?"

"Lord Jasper, is there some minor chamber where I can converse with my friend? Somewhere less cavernous and popular?"

Lord Jasper's eyebrows shot up to meet his hairline. "But of course, m'lady," he said, trying to conceal his disapproval by dabbing his brow with a kerchief of embroidered lawn. "Methinks the Hall of Audience is unoccupied for the nonce. Allow me to conduct you there." Calling for footmen to bring lighted tapers, he indicated the Hall's direction with a courtly flourish and a neatly pointed toe.

In a corner of the Hall of Audience, Viviana and Caitri played Cloth-Scissors-Rock. One hundred and sixty candles blazed in gold candlesticks, like banks of radiant flowers. Rohain and Sianadh conversed, she imparting an outline of all that had occurred at Isse Tower. As she spoke, he grew progressively more restive, jubilant at what he was hearing.

"So you see, I did not find what I sought," she concluded, "but I found instead something far dearer to my heart."

"Dear to anyone's heart, the riches of royalty!" he crowed.

"You mistake my meaning. I have no ambition, *mo gaidair.* I did not seek this, I have never desired anything that is theirs—wealth or pomp. Perhaps I have desired respect and ease, who has not? Yet I had hope for an ease that does not live by battening on the toil of others, and a respect that grows from genuine friendship, not social status. I do not need so many jewels, so many costly possessions. All this obsequiousness and etiquette is foreign to me. I suppose I shall get used to it for *his* sake and I doubt not that in time I shall have forgotten that it could be otherwise, and it shall all be enjoyable—for, mistake me not, I am not ungrateful. I entered the world beyond the Tower looking for three things: a face, a voice, a past. In the searching I found the first two, discovered a fourth desire, and lost the third. Now my past matters no longer. The present is all I could desire."

She fell silent. It occurred to her that now, at last, she was at rest, if not at peace—not seeking anymore. Yet even as she surveyed the luxury surrounding her in the Hall of Audience with its one hundred and sixty lighted candles and three times as many waiting to be lit, a musty wind came funneling out of a past she had forgotten that she had forgotten. Troubled by Pod's words, by a couple of abandoned loam-worms, the lingering breath of forest mold, and withered foliage sprinkled like scraps of torn manuscript in the ruined bedchamber, she shuddered and shrank from remembering. History was too dark, far too dark.

"As my first edict," she said briskly, "I shall outlaw the beating of servants throughout Erith."

"Very right-minded of ye, *chehrna*," replied Sianadh, "but ye shall start a rebellion with that kind of thinking."

"My strength shall be used to shield the vulnerable. All *I* need," she concluded, "all I need is air to sustain me, and the one I love."

"And drink," rejoined Sianadh prosaically, jumping up, "and vittles. And him to be good enough for ye."

Unable to restrain his glee, he jumped in the air and danced, as energetically as Rohain had danced with Viviana not long before. To the disgust of the stone-faced footmen and the door-sentries who for years had practiced outfreezing statues, the wild red-haired man performed an Ertish jig.

"Free!" he trumpeted. "Free, and pardoned, and in favor with the Queen Apparent! I could kiss ye, *chehrna,* I could kiss ye!"

A wintry gust, clean and sharp, howled through the chamber. It billowed the wall-hangings and blew out seventy-five candles.

Several Dainnan knights in chain mail had entered the chamber and positioned themselves on either side of the door. Sianadh seized up in midpose. Rohain's maids jumped up and snapped to attention and even the guards ossified further.

Thorn stood in the open doorway, a score of lords at his back.

In Dainnan attire, straight as a sword he stood, and as bright. His hair and *dusken* cloak lifted, like shadowy vanes, in the breath of Winter that had entered with him. That cool current blew across the carpets a scatter of leaves from the gardens, leaves that chased each other and skipped like pagan dancers across the floor's rich patterning. Rohain's heart leapt painfully against her ribs, a bird battering itself against its cage. *His beauty is perilous. I could die merely from beholding it.*

Roxburgh, taciturn, stood behind at his sovereign's shoulder with two or three others of the Attriod. Like the tail of a comet, a glittering train forever attended the King-Emperor.

This tableau shattered when Thorn stepped forward, crunching dry leaves beneath his boots. Sianadh remained standing. A courtier hissed, "On your knees, fellow!"

"I grovel before no man," said Sianadh, "save the King-Emperor himself."

"Behold the King-Emperor, block-brain," muttered Rohain.

"What?" Sianadh jibbed, thrown off balance. Stiffly he sank to his knees, bowing the bushy red head.

"Rise, Kavanagh," said Thorn, calm as a subterranean lake, as cold.

"Ye have pardoned me," said Sianadh, stumbling to his feet and moving to Rohain's side with a mixture of gratefulness and wariness, "and for that I thank ye, Your Majesty. I've a *strong* right arm that has defended Imrhien here and would willingly wield a sword for the Empire, and it has not withered at all despite languishing in your dungeons without so much as a drop of ale to give me fortitude."

The courtiers murmured against his questionable attitude and his unconscionable manner of addressing the King-Emperor using the second-person pronoun. Their sovereign appeared to ignore these mistakes.

"Indeed?" he said, raising one eyebrow. *A captivating trick,* thought Rohain.

"Aye," said Sianadh. Lifting an elbow from beneath, which emanated an odor of stale body fluids, he rolled up a sleeve. "Strong, my arm." Blatantly devoid of finer feeling, he flexed a great pudding of a bicep. Several guards made as if to throw him out for his effrontery. Thorn waved them away.

"Leave us," he commanded his retinue. "Stay you, Rox-burgh, and my page." Bowing, the attendants reluctantly began to trickle out of the Hall of Audience.

"You say that arm has defended the Lady Rohain?" Thorn inquired mildly.

"Aye, and no man has ever beaten me in an arm-wrestle," replied the Ertishman, whose eyes were boldly fixed on Thorn's. Being a few inches shorter, he had to look up to achieve this; an irksome necessity for him.

"Sianadh," admonished Rohain. "Do not be *scothy*. Nothing can rescue you this time."

"Do you make a challenge?" asked Thorn.

"A challenge, by—" Sianadh bit off his words. "Aye, some might call it that, sir. Now I have said it. There it be." His face was a mask of defiance.

The last two departing lords fingered their sword-hilts. "For this insolence his tongue shall be torn out by the roots," muttered one.

"He's for the scaffold," murmured another. Roxburgh folded his arms and looked interested. The heavy doors closed.

The corners of Thorn's mouth twitched slightly. He rolled up his right sleeve and took a seat at a small table. His arm, a tawny mellifluity of waterworn driftwood's smoothly contoured undulations, was vastly different from his opponent's. Sianadh's arm was similarly thewed, but adorned by tattoos, freckles, red bristles, and scars.

Suddenly in his element, Sianadh took the opposite stool. They planted their elbows on the tabletop. Their hands came together. Cords bulged, sinews knotted. Ele-gantly, in the blink of an eye, it was over. Sianadh's hand lay on its back; his shoulders skewed to follow the outward twist of his elbow.

"Two outta three!" he demanded hotly, as though he sat at a tavern table with a drunken caravaner. Shivering beads stood out on his brow. Thorn nodded. The act was repeated, with identical outcome. Sianadh sat stunned as Thorn rolled down his sleeve.

"Well sir, ye've beaten me fair and square," the Ertishman admitted with admiration. "I cannot say as I wasn't ready. I was. But ye might have dignified a man by breaking a sweat. That there is a right arm I'd be proud to fight in the shadow of."

"My sword arm might cast a darker shadow."

The Ertishman threw back his head and shouted with laughter, displaying a crescent of broken teeth like stubs of moldy cheese.

"Call me a blind man," he blurted between guffaws. "Your skian's buckled on the south side. I've made a right *sgorrama* of meself."

"True, but not relevant since you have already proven your worth thrice over," said Thorn. "What boon would you ask of me?"

"Boon? Sir, ye have already extended the numbering of my days, which I am never sure of. I could not ask for better. However . . ." The Ertishman was struck by a sudden awareness of opportunity. He scratched his beard. "D'ye need more men-at-arms?"

"Not at this time."

"Then there's something I have always thought might suit me—to sail on a Windship and trade me way about. Travel, adventure, and wealth. That's my style."

"A clipper lies idle in Finvarna as we speak. I gift her to you. What more? Ask, while I am generous."

"I give ye gramercie, sire. As for more, I may not legally set foot in Finvarna. The High Chieftain, Mabhoneen of Finvarna, has banished me. Yet I have a craving to return."

"You told me he lifted that ban," interjected Rohain.

"I forgot to tell ye," said Sianadh. "He put it back."

"Why?"

"'Tis a long and unjust story, *chehrna*. These days, I yearn for me home something vicious. 'Tis hard to explain—'tis like a sore plague that eats at ye. Aye, I have the homesickness, that which in Finvarna we call the *longari-eth*. I would fain set foot on me native sod again."

"You shall be no longer exiled," Thorn said.

Sianadh digested this. When he looked at Rohain she beheld in his face a light of joy such as she had never seen there.

"Finvarna," crooned Sianadh, as if murmuring a lovename. "Finvarna. I can go back. And a Windship! I shall become a merchant, that I shall. A respectable man. I shall see them, me children, me Granny . . . Ach! The chariot races and the good Ertish cookery—Your Majesty, I cannot find words to show me gratefulness!" He jumped up. "A Windship! It shall be my beast of burden, my donkey. Therefore I shall call it the *Bear's Ass,* or mayhap the *Bear-Ass.*"

"Unfortunately for the rejuvenation of the Register of Ships' Names, she is already titled," said Thorn drily. "Red of canvas, she is called *Rua.*"

"*Rua*—the Red-Haired!" Sianadh chortled.

"You will not return to Finvarna yet?" beseeched Rohain. "You will stay for the Ball and the Tournament of Jousting, *mo gaidair?* There are to be fireworks!"

"I wouldna miss the festivities for gold angels!"

"We shall be happy and remember happy times past."

"Aye, times past." Sianadh quieted abruptly, abashed. "But it cannot be like those times, not now, not never again, with ye looking like that and all." His eyes met hers, open but shielded. In them was written the knowledge that he looked upon a friend now contained within a different vessel, a vessel to which he would have responded differently had he known her in it first. He struggled to come to terms with this, having lived all his life in a world whose mores dictated that friendship should not exist between such a man as he and such a woman as she. The awareness discomfited him and made him feel, somehow, a traitor.

Comeliness is a blade with two edges, mused Rohain.

"Inna shai tithen elion," she said, with a sad smile, recalling their first parting—long ago, it seemed—in Gilvaris Tarv.

"Kavanagh," Thorn said, rising to his foot. "Until you depart you have the freedom of my cellars and my leave to sample their contents in quantities to your liking. This is to indemnify you for the shortages you have ostensibly experienced while living idle at the expense of my Treasury."

"I shall seek them out at once!" said the Ertishman energetically, clapping the King's Page heartily on the shoulder. "I have some drinking to catch up on and I be in need of good fellowship to do it with. Ye look like a good fellow."

The courtier stepped back hastily. Sianadh shrugged.

"Have it your way, jack. I'll warrant the kitchen-hands know how to make merry, if ye do not."

Bowing with more enthusiasm than style, Sianadh took it upon himself to walk backward from the Hall of Audience, to demonstrate his knowledge of etiquette. No sooner had he reached the doors, however, than he was back again. In a sudden, unexpected gesture, he knelt at Thorn's feet a second time, unbidden, wordless.

Briefly, Thorn laid his hand on the Ertishman's head. "*Sain* thee," he said gravely.

This time as Sianadh disappeared around the corner, a high-pitched whoop drifted back.

"Barbarian." The whisper rippled knowingly among the courtiers clustered outside.

"Now," said Thorn to Rohain, turning the twin shafts of his gaze on her to penetrate her eyes and plumb the wellspring of her thought. "Having dispensed with business, my intent, troth-plighted, is to walk with thee beneath the trees."

He took her hand.

Later, as they sauntered together through the gardens, Thorn said, "One man leaves the dungeons, another arrives. The Lord High Wizard is now imprisoned. As for the niece, she is under durance, confined to rooms, with only poor Georgiana Griffin to attend her."

"Good sooth! Are they guilty of conspiring to destroy me, as you suspected?" asked Rohain.

"As sure as drowners fill their lovers' lungs with water. The one has demonstrated it, the other has confessed it," replied Thorn.

"How so?"

"Thou dost recollect I sent a letter from Isse Tower?"

"I do."

"I bade Tom Ercildoune set a watch on the conjuror. When tidings of our success at Isse reached the Court, the swindler and his minions instantly fled. The fool thus betrayed himself, for why should he take flight on hearing the Hunt had been defeated and Dianella's supposed rival found safe, unless he feared reprisal for his part in the fiasco?"

"How did you find him?"

"The Dainnan of the Ninth Thriesniun tracked them to the Well in the Wood's Heart. Hast thou heard of it? No? 'Tis a dry and mossy shaft of ancient stone, forever secure from wickedness, and which the carlin further sealed with the powers of her Wand. But she could not leave. She and the lad, her apprentice, were imprisoned there, under eldritch siege. The conjuror, however, walked unharmed amongst wicked wights winged, tailed, and fanged. Indeed, he was imploring them for aid!"

"Does he wield power over them?" cried Rohain.

"Nay. He is naught but an ill-uttering entertainer, a sly and hollow-hearted man of wax. He had made some pact with them, which ensured his temporary immunity from their wanton wickedness. That is all. When I joined the Ninth Thriesniun we drove back the creatures of unseelie, releasing the two good folk trapped within the Well, and taking the conjuror prisoner. The Dainnan zealously drove the unseelie things far off, whereupon Maeve One-Eye and Tom Coppins went their way on the forest paths again, un-afraid."

"I am glad!"

"The conjurer and his henchmen were brought here to the palace. They were charged with trafficking with wield-ers of maleficent forces. As for the niece, when confronted with the truth she denied it at first, then, perceiving denial to be sleeveless, she told all. Their murderous conspiracy was revealed."

"Murderous conspiracy? Is it a fact that Sargoth sent the Hunt against me? That the infamous Huon should bend to a wizard's will seems incredible, but I fear that the attack on Isse Tower at the time of my visit was more than coinci-dence. Nay," she said, answering her own question, "it can-not be so. Sargoth might have achieved his purpose to equal degree with a well-placed ambush of lesser wights."

"True, *eudail*, no wizard has the power to command Huon. He may have inveigled a hold over some common spriggan or duergar, but no mortal man can govern the Wild Hunt. The conjuror has unwittingly plunged himself into deeper trouble than he knows. His meddling has triggered more than he bargained for. He admitted, when questioned, that he sent some minor unseelie destroyer to slay thee, de-scribing thee as a Talith daughter, a gold-haired damsel with her tresses dyed black. I surmise his words were passed on by eldritch tongues, to reach the ears of a might-ier authority."

Looking directly at Rohain he said gravely, "My bird, something mighty, unseelie, and malevolent came for thee—the Antlered One himself. *Why should Huon wish to hunt at thy heels?"*

His words accorded with her own suspicions. "I know not!" she said, and this was true. *Somehow I have incurred the wrath of the Antlered One. It might be that in my travels I inadvertently spied upon him, or took something that belonged to him or his minions. The Lords of Unseelie require only slight motive to persecute mortalkind.*

In her heart she guessed the reason must lie in her forgotten past, but to herself she denied it, blindly hoping that banning such knowledge would negate that past. There was no place here, now, for sorrow and pain. Here was safety and happiness. Why dig up old miseries?

"What is to become of the prisoners?" she asked.

"Time enough to ponder that later. I have turned my mind to other thoughts. Let those who cross me stew awhile, or rot."

"I would like to visit Dianella."

"As it please thee, *ionmhuinn*. She cannot harm thee now."

Rohain made her way to the rooms of durance.

What did she expect? A brooding, bitter courtier, enthroned in shadow and candlelight, who would not turn her head to look at Rohain?

"Come to gloat, have we?" the prisoner would say. "Come to sneer, now that I am helpless? You have done your work well, have you not? Oh, so successfully!"

"Dianella," the visitor would reply, "I have not come to gloat, to miscall you, or to be miscalled. I do not hate you. I never planned that all this should come to pass, I swear it. Dianella, that you loved him, love him still, I now know. If passion drove you to rash deeds I can at least empathize with that passion. I cannot comprehend how any woman who has looked upon him could be anything but lovestruck."

Then, the courtier might say, "You understand!" and weep, and beg forgiveness.

Rohain's expectations of the meeting, however, were not to be fulfilled.

The only warning may have been a curious expression that flitted across Dianella's face as Rohain entered with her maidservants—that was all. It might have been a look of surprise.

"Rohain! Dear Heart!" The dark-haired beauty glided forward to bestow an embrace on her visitor and kisses on the air. "La! You cannot imagine how glad I am to see you. The boredom has been beyond utterance. Griffin sulks, nobody else says a word, and I scarcely have any callers. The dullness defies description!"

"I am sorry for you . . ." Rohain stammered. Somehow, Dianella in the flesh always disarmed her.

"Of course, you look perfectly lovely!" Dianella purred. "Come—sit by me awhile. Can you spare the time, sweetness? Griffin, we would take a sip. Make arrangements."

Puzzled and wary, Rohain sat at a table of carved walnut inlaid with copper and nacre. The rooms of durance were far from uncomfortable. They were well-furnished and provided with fireplaces in which flames now leaped cheerfully. Seldom used, the rooms were not dungeon cells but apartments set aside for aristocrats who had fallen under suspicion of crimes such as plotting, treason, or spying.

Dianella chattered on as though she entertained at a garden party; as if nothing had ever existed between them besides close friendship.

"You are simply delicious in seed-pearls and point lace. And your hair—still dark-stained! 'Tis *sofine et gloriana!* Wise of you not to have the dye stripped out, Heart. Doubtless the entire country would believe your goldie-yellow to be fake in any case, the sillies, or else you would have had half the Talith population begging at your doorstep, claiming you as cousin." Cocking her head to one side she added pleasantly, "Although in sooth, the yellow would match your skin tones so much more adequately."

She laughed daintily, with her rose of a mouth closed tight as a bud. The color in her cheeks was high. Rohain mumbled a reply as Georgiana Griffin finished pouring the wine, and Dianella's flow ran on with barely a pause.

"How do you like my embroidered surcoat and kirtle? See, the one is worked in motifs of dragonflies and reeds with a border of butterflies, while on the other, worms are stitched in sundry-colored silks, with silver cobwebs and small snails in stumpwork. Different motifs, yet they match so cleverly in design and coloring, don't you think? La! There it is again." Dianella broke off, going to the window. "Did you hear it, sweetness? Oh look—there it is!" She pointed with a tapered fingernail. Joining her, Rohain peered out. She could see nothing but a courtyard below, framed by walls beyond which the ground fell precipitously away to a distant longbow of shoreline melding with a dragon's spine of mountains.

"I suppose it was a spriggan or another of those ghastly little unseelie things," said Dianella from behind Rohain's back. She was already seated at the walnut table again, smiling, her red lips peeled back from her small white teeth. Holding out a chased silver goblet filled with dark liquid she appended, "They have been about so very frequently of late."

As Rohain took the cup, Thorn's leaf-ring on her hand clashed against the metal. The sound reverberated with extraordinary volume. It resonated and hummed sickeningly inside her head, like a tocsin, or perhaps a *toxin*.

"To your health!" cried Dianella, lifting her goblet on high. "No hard feelings, Heart, let's drink to that!"

Rohain raised the vessel.

"No," Georgiana Griffin blurted, "don't drink!"

"Actually, I had no intention of doing so," said Rohain, watching the thin black tongue of liquid drizzle over the rim of her tipped goblet. Spilled on the carpet, it gave off a wisp of steam. She let the vessel fall. Her footman and two guards who had been standing scarcely noticed beside the door—one was never truly alone in the palace—moved swiftly toward Dianella. At the guard-captain's command they stripped her fingers of the empty compartment-ring, and all other rings for good measure. Rohain's maids clustered at her side, both talking at once. Their eyes, round with shock, were turned in accusation on Dianella. That lady returned their stares sadly.

"Alack! I have failed," she drawled. "Yet do not judge me harshly. The decoction would not have harmed you, Dear Heart—it would only have brought upon you a semblance of death. Then, as you lay pale and unmoving in the crypt, my servants would have taken you away. On board a Seaship you would have woken to find yourself banished forever from these domains."

"Did you not mean to slay me?"

"I swear I did not."

Rohain met her adversary's eyes. Deep down in their troubled depths smoldered a faint ember of truth. Dianella tossed her head and looked away as if angry to have been deciphered.

"The House of D'Armancourt is a pure bloodline," she said. "Royal blood—that is the seat of its power. All its brides have been chosen from royal houses or else from aristocrats of great and ancient families such as mine. Your thin serf's blood shall taint it. Worse—you shall be its downfall."

"Hold your tongue!" cried Rohain.

At this, the courtier flushed with fury. Her voice became hard and harsh.

"You think yourself so noble, *selevader uncouthant.* No doubt you thought to come here to these rooms to bring me comfort and show your goodness. Yet when they drag me through the streets next week, you will be watching from the window. You will laugh with the rest."

"What do you mean?"

"Oh, haven't you heard? 'Tis to be the spectacle of a decade! The Lord High Chancellor asked my dear friends Calprisia and Elmaretta to devise a suitable punishment for my so-called crimes. The sweetings suggested that humiliation would be my most dreaded nightmare. My hair is to be shorn off. I am to be dressed in rags and rattled through the streets in a donkey cart. After which, I expect they shall introduce me to the ax. I would prefer it."

"I shall intercede on your behalf."

"How gracious of you! You, whom I have wronged so *dreadfully,* sending you from Caermelor so that my uncle could tell the spriggans to carry you away and play with you. Take your pity elsewhere, *malck-drasp.*" Glowering with sheer hatred at Rohain, the wizard's niece spat words from her mouth like poison. "I will not waste my malison on you. I believe *that* has been done before, and done better."

Rohain departed.

How foolish to have hoped for better.

Later, she said to Thorn, "Dianella's sentence must be commuted. Were I she, to be deprived of proximity to you would be far worse than any infliction of hurt or humiliation."

"Thou art *not* she. Yet if pity moves thee, she shall be merely banished."

"The Sorrow Isles are remote enough, from all accounts. And her uncle?"

"Thou mayst not pity malice."

*   *   *

"Welcome back to Court, Rohain," said Thomas Rhymer. His voice was solemn, but his eyes twinkled. "We have been the worse without you. Dianella is currently indisposed, but, fed on scandal, the Set thrives more hardily than ever. Were I not incapable of even the slightest exaggeration I would swear they add a new word to the drafted courtingle each instant."

"Hail, Sir Thomas," Rohain replied awkwardly.

"Tut. There's no need to be diffident with me, my dear. Of course I guessed as soon as I met you that you had not come from the bleak shores of Sorrow Isles. So did Roxburgh. It mattered little to us—methinks a gentle damsel like you posed no threat to Imperial security! At first your beauty was an intrigue to us both, besides which your manner provided a contrast to the monotonous ways of Court life and the petty obsessions of the so-called Set. It was no time before we found we liked you better, the better we knew you. That you once served in a House of Stormriders does not demean you in our eyes—there is no shame in honest work. Never fear, your secret remains safe. No one else knows."

"Forgive me, sir, for that deception."

"Consider it forgiven. Yet your path, and that of His Majesty, might have proved smoother had you entrusted us with a few meager scraps of knowledge."

"In truth, sir. And I am anguished to think of how much trouble might have been avoided, had I spoken out." *Blood was shed at Isse because of my presence there.*

"Fiddlesticks!" said the Bard, guessing her thoughts. "That was not your doing. It was the work of Huon the Hunter! Come now," he added jovially, "do not be anguished! Is it not consolation that your Dainnan of the wilderness has found you, whom he sought, and you have found him?" He shook his head regretfully. "Had

I known," he said, "had I but known to whom your heart belonged . . ."

"You might have helped me straightway, if I had mentioned the name of Thorn!"

"Indeed, my dear. Howbeit, all that is in the past now. It is time for rejoicing. Come, let me lead you to the Blue Drawing Room. The ladies Rosamonde and Maiwenna would fain keep company with you there, and Alys, with the children of Roxburgh."

The Winter sun shone cold, a pale doubloon. Lacquered against the sky, evergreens layered with fringes of pungent bristles reached out to offer upright cones like rows of squat candles.

It was the twenty-fourth of Fuarmis, just six days until Primrose Amble with its candles, brides, white lace, horseshoes, and procession of ewes garlanded with the first tentative flowers of spring. This year the period of the traditional festival was to be extended. It was to culminate in the celebrations for the royal betrothal, beginning on the fifteenth of Sovrachmis, the Primrosemonth. The lacuna between these dates was wadded with a flurry of activity, a cramming of the palace baileys with carters and their conveyances bringing supplies. Every merchant and pedlar in Caermelor had seized the opportunity of a Royal Ball to hawk his wares, whether or not they had been requisitioned for the occasion. In spite of the continuing belligerence simmering in Namarre, which constantly threatened to spill out across the Nenian Landbridge into northern Eldaraigne, the populace applied themselves to the preparations for this year's festivities with an extra abundance of zeal.

Viewed from a more exalted angle, Court seemed an entirely different place. To Rohain it was as though a screen had dropped from her eyes. She was introduced to aristocrats she had never before encountered, she found herself guided to regions of the palace she had not yet seen, she was treated with a respectfulness so novel she could not accustom herself to it. This new state of dignity was almost unnerving.

Courtiers acknowledged Rohain deferentially wherever she went. Crowds thicker than ever jostled at the gates from early morn until late evening. They were hoping for a glimpse of the chosen bride of the King-Emperor, James XVI of the House of D'Armancourt and Trethe, also titled High King and Emperor of Greater Eldaraigne, Finvarna, Severnesse, Luindorn, Rimany, and Namarre; King of his other Realms and Territories. Those who ran the Court machinery had assiduously put it about that his bride-to-be came of a noble line that, impoverished by ill fortune, had sunk into obscurity. If any disapproval evolved, or any questions were whispered about her birth, they were suppressed and popularly passed over. The King-Emperor might follow any whim he chose, and it would be accepted. As the highest of the high, his actions were beyond the context of convention. Besides, the people were glad their sovereign was to wed again at last.

Dianella's dark dye remained fast in Rohain's hair. It proved difficult to wash out. Rohain considered this fortunate, since to be publicly revealed as Talith would inevitably invite further questions as to her origins, and would surely destroy the careful constructions of the senior members of the King's Household, who so ardently desired that His Majesty's troth-plighted should be accepted by the populace as a gentlewoman.

"Thou dost call me Gold-Hair," she said to Thorn, "though my locks are now as dark as thine."

He shrugged. "Use what paints and colors thou wilt. Thou'rt Gold-Hair, beneath it all."

To the far reaches of the Empire of Erith the tidings of

royal betrothal traveled. Throughout Caermelor, all was noise and traffic, but within the walls of the Palace remained a wonderful, undisturbed tranquillity, an amazing sense of peace. The city whirled, and Rohain was its vortex, the stillness at the storm's eye. To see the evidence of her new authority, her influence as an emblem, took her breath away. Thorn's casual use of power awed her. She wondered how it would be to wield it with such careless assurance.

All this, she would whisper often to herself, *by the Greayte Star—for me?*

And sometimes the prediction of the twisted lad in the Tower would return to tease her.

For her, sheltered, there was no haste, no bustle—only days that slipped by like rain through a colander; days spent sometimes in conversation with Prince Edward, or with Sianadh (when he was not making merry with the butlers, ewerers, and panters in the servants' quarters), or perhaps spent with Thomas Rhymer, or both (the two Ertishmen having formed a drinking and storytelling fellowship), or with the steadfast and ebullient Alys-Jannetta and her lively progeny. Gladly, Rohain was now able to eschew the tiresome company of the Set. Affairs of state took Thorn from her side at times. Then, with her attendants and Maiwenna the Talith gentlewoman and young Rosamonde of Roxburgh, she would ride out in a coach from the Royal Mews, through countryside green-hazed with the buds of an early Spring.

Maiwenna had become a friend. Rohain trusted her almost to the point of revealing her own Talith heritage, but not quite. She asked whether the gentlewoman knew anything of a lost Talith damsel. Maiwenna, however, was nonplussed. She knew of no clues that might lead to discovering Rohain's past. Subsequently, the two spent many hours together, deep in conversation about Avlantia's history.

But most often Rohain's time was spent at the side of he
whom she loved beyond others—loved with a passion so
intense that it was a wound to the heart.

"Let us go out," he would say. "These four walls are like
to suffocate me."

Laughing, chaffing one another, they would saunter in
the gardens, or go riding and hawking through the Royal
Game Reserves in the ancient Forest of Glincuith. He gave
her a sparrowhawk and lessons in archery. He gave her a
crimson rose so very dark that it was almost black, whose
scent was a dream of Midsummer's Night. And his long
hair flowed blacker than Midwinter's Night, glinting with a
red sheen like the dark rose. He gave her a palfrey the hue
of marshmallow frosting, and a diadem of gems like Sugar
crystals. His landhorse, a splendid, swift, and spirited creature that he esteemed as much as he cherished Errantry, was
named Altair. Hers was called Firinn.

These hours together, secluded, afforded Rohain rare
glimpses of a shy tenderness in her beloved, a hesitancy
quite unlike the self-assurance he possessed at other times.
It was like the diffidence of wild creatures, such as birds
and deer. Most often, he would be as a carefree and wanton
youth—zestful, capricious, as merry as a jester, indulging
in whimsy and play and foolish nonsense, in which she par-
ticipated with a footloose joyousness and reckless abandon
that surprised her inner self by springing from it. Gentle,
witty badinage volleyed between them, taking unexpected
turnings. Seldom could he be precognized.

He could be as temperate as the soft winds caressing the
northern valleys, or stern as stone and as grim. And when
this cold mood was on him it did not affect his manner with
Imrhien-Rohain; toward her he was warm always, even
though the unmelting snow of all Winters to others.

She knew full well that in these times of unrest he was
needed at the helm of the Royal Attriod, but as often as pos-

sible he delegated his duties to his commanders and stewards in order to spend time in the company of his betrothed. Fortunately, there had come another unexpected lull in the activities of men and wights in Namarre and northern Eldaraigne. The buildup of minor assaults and skirmishes had again subsided. It seemed they were now gathering their strength, perhaps in readiness for some greater onslaught.

Nonetheless, Thorn could not always be spared from governance. On a day when his duties took him elsewhere, Rohain walked through the palace picture galleries and statue galleries on the arm of the young Prince. They halted beside a window to look out at the dormant Spring Garden with its arches of lichened crab-apples most ancient.

"I should like to see those leafless trees in bloom," she said. "Crab-apples bear exquisite blossoms. I think they are my favorites."

"You shall see them," said Edward, "this and every Spring."

Thorn's silver-clasped hunting-horn was hooked to Edward's belt. As he turned away from the window it chimed against a marble pedestal. Noting the direction of Rohain's gaze, the Prince said, "Traditionally, the Coirnéad is worn by the reigning monarch—however, he has requested that I bear it now and in the future, saying it may stand me in good stead."

"The Coirnéad?"

"A horn of Faêran workmanship. For centuries, an heirloom of the Royal Family."

"A fair ornament."

A frown crumpled the Prince's brow. They walked on. Edward made as if to speak again, but hesitated.

"You are beauteous lady," he stammered suddenly. "Do not think I flatter you, pray, when I tell you your beauty outshines all other beauties. He has chosen his consort well. His recommendation is law to me. My faith in his wisdom and judgment is implicit. I shall be glad to accept you as my—"

"I can never stand in your mother's place. Pray, allow me to be your friend."

"Indeed," he said earnestly, "and I shall be *your* friend and most devoted admirer. Nothing could make me happier than to welcome you into this family, dear Rohain." Raising her hand to his lips, he kissed it. His youthful smile was open, ingenuous.

"So saying, you make my own happiness complete," she said, returning the smile.

The castle hawk-mews was extensive, housing not only hawks but also falcons, and one majestic wedge-tailed eagle named Audax. The Hawkmaster sported eight taut silver scars on his bald dome where the talons of an eagle owl had once gored him when he was stealing her clutch of eggs. In the mornings, he could be seen in the yards with his falconers and austringers, swinging lures to bring half-trained birds back to the fist. The lures were a pair of moorhens' or magpies' wings dried in an open position and fastened back to back, with a fresh piece of tough beef tied onto the end of a line.

Often, the clear ringing of the tail-bell on a returning gyrfalcon tantalized the early light. The bird would scream a welcome as it flew down, jesses trailing, thrusting its feet forward to lock onto the falconer's tasseled glove, the savage joy of flight still purling in its black, gold-rimmed eye.

The Hawkmaster took Rohain among the sounds of the mews—the tiny tintinnabulation of bells, the bird-screams and whistles and chatter, the rasping whirr of rousing wings, the talk among the austringers and falconers. He proudly showed her the clean gravel-floored pens where roosted goshawks or sparrowhawks, merlins, hobbies, ospreys, peregrines, or the great and noble gyrfalcons, tethered to blocks and perches. Boys were assiduously sweeping up casts and scrubbing mutes off the walls. An austringer coped a tiercel goshawk's beak using a small, bone-handled knife and an abrasive stone. Another imped the damaged tail-feather of a hooded gray hawk, carefully attaching a replacement pinion to the base of the broken one. An apprentice weighed a peregrine on a small set of scales.

"Have to cut him down," he said. "He's put on too much."

"Cut him down?" repeated Rohain, astonished.

"Cut down his feed, m'lady," explained the apprentice, with a respectful salute.

"The merry merlins fly at larks," the Hawkmaster said informatively, moving among the birds with Rohain, "but the gay goshawks be the cooks' birds, so we say, for they will tackle fur or feather. A hunting engine they be, the goshawks, swift as arrows—but 'tis their wont to be peevish and contrary betimes. They must be handled with patience."

The eagle sat alone in a magnificent pen, fierce-eyed, his irises silver. He was beautiful: black with a pale nape, wing-coverts, and under-tail coverts. His legs were long, strong, and full-feathered.

"We keeps the hawks and falcons well away from Audax the Great, else he might make a quick meal on 'em," said the Hawkmaster. "He will only come to two men—meself, who trained him, and His Imperial Majesty. Only royalty may fly eagles, but no milk-and-water king could do it. Audax's wing-span be more than seven feet, tip to tip. His weight be nigh on seven pound and his hind claw be as thick as a man's little finger. He can bring down small hounds, ye ken, and deer."

A falconer went past carrying a bucket of day-old chicks

and another of frogs and lizards. The eagle roused and shook himself.

"Coo-ee-el," he whistled. "Pseet-you, pseet-you."

"Soothee, soothee," said the Hawkmaster.

Winter faded. Gone were the moon-spun webs of night, the tinsels of rime lining each edge with glitter, like the shang, and drawing frost feathers on leaf and pane with an exquisite silver pencil. It seemed that every day the sun flew up like a yellow rose and fell down like a red one, and at the end of Winter the stirring of Spring could already be felt as a stirring of the blood; every bare and lichened bough carried the promise of blossom and verdure. The breezes sighed with perfumed breath and sunlight colored them with pale gold. In the Forest of Glincuith, the only sounds were bright gems of birdsong, and baubles of laughter threaded on strange sweet music drifting from the trees; the piping of eldritch things, like the plaint of weird birds. These sounds Thorn made into a necklace and tossed it over the head of his betrothed. It hung about her shoulders, where it mingled with the abundant spirals and falls of heavy gold from which the dye had at last been stripped after many rinsings, along with the natural sheen, so that most folk believed she had bleached her tresses.

Sometimes Rohain and Thorn rode in open country with their entourage and the Hawkmaster and the falconers and the austringers. Then Thorn would fly Audax at ducks and geese and ptarmigan. The eagle was an expert hunter, with many strategies. He soared on thermals, so high that he vanished from human sight. Up there he could easily see everything that moved over a huge area. Once he had chosen his prey, he would appear abruptly from behind a hill where he had deliberately lost height without being noticed, then fly close to the ground until suddenly appearing only a few yards from his quarry, swooping down over the tops of nearby trees. Or he would start his attack with a long, slow descent up to four miles from his victim, or, most spectacular of all, from hundreds of feet above the ground he would stoop, diving with folded wings like a plummeting stone, flattening out at the last moment, spreading out his wings and tail to decelerate efficiently, pulling his head back and throwing his feet forward with talons outstretched to strike and grasp. The remaining shock of impact would be transferred to the prey.

He never missed his target.

Rohain made a discovery.

It was akin to the memory-dreams of the Three Faces, the Rats, the White Horse. Since her return from Isse and the prematurely terminated journey to Huntingtowers, a verity had been clarifying by degrees in her awareness. It was Erith, remembered.

Erith's bones had been dredged up out of the waters of forgetfulness, but not much else. None of the history, none of the character—only the formations of the land and the labels of the countries, cities, villages on the map. The bones, and the names of the bones.

Somehow, the knowledge of three dimensions of the world had seeped through to Rohain. The fourth, which was *time,* was still lacking. Yet it strode on toward her betrothal day.

In the glades of Glincuith, the black fretwork of leafless branches formed, by day, a ceiling of sapphire panes; by night, a roof of smoky glass shattered by a gravel of stars. There, Rohain spent pleasant hours learning the courtly dance steps with a partner who moved so lightly and easily over the springy turf that she could swear their feet trod upon nothingness. Here was a lover who was ready, with extraordinary anticipation, to catch her after every pirouette, to whirl her as if she were a child, her skirts billowing like a full-blown camellia; to sustain and guide her, to hold her pressed so close that she thought his heart was beating within her own breast. The scent of pines was snagged like myrrh in his hair. Beneath her left hand, his shoulder was steel, sliding beneath layers of costly fabric. The dim, crimson light of dying suns gleamed through his hair, and his eyes, fixed upon her, were dark-smoldering coals.

At these times, love's anguish and precipitancy threatened to overwhelm her. It was a torment with a terrible sweetness to it—addictive, unconsumed, consuming. From him raged an answering force, a torrent dammed, a ferocity chained, a storm scarcely suppressed, eager, impatient.

The festival of Primrose Amble having passed by, the betrothal was officially announced and celebrated even while more legions of the Empire were making ready to depart for the north to relieve those that had been stationed there for lengthy periods, or to swell the numbers of the King-Emperor's army. The Royal Ball took place in jeweled splendor, attended by royalty, nobility, and dignitaries from all over Erith; more than a thousand guests. The bride-to-be shone like a piece torn out from the very core of the sun. He who moved beside her seemed by contrast the glorious incarnation of night.

The feast was sumptuous. Rohain sat at the high table beneath the canopy, at Thorn's right hand, sharing with him a cup and plate. At their backs, bright heraldic flags adorned the walls. Before them gleamed a swan-shaped cake covered with three thousand hand-molded Sugarpaste feathers. Below, the Banqueting Hall seethed and glistered.

As he conversed with Rohain, Thorn glanced down the table at Roxburgh, who looked splendid in a dress uniform of royal scarlet and gold. The Dainnan Commander had just cleared his trencher of a mighty helping of meats, and with a purposeful air he was contemplating the other dishes.

"The Commander is a renowned trencherman," said Rohain, noting the object of his gaze.

"Indeed he is!"

Roxburgh having turned aside to speak to his wife, Thorn casually tossed a couple of roasted capons onto his trencher. Roxburgh, helping himself to pie, looked startled at the sight of his erstwhile empty platter. The King's Page made a bursting noise and collapsed behind a gonfalon.

The swan-ship sailed from Waterstair for the occasion, the side of the hill having been knocked out to allow its egress. It was moored over the inner bailey, to the acclamation of the citizens, who could see it from every corner of Caermelor; a giant bird gently lifting in the drafts, bound by iron chains.

In the lists, the jousting knights gave a brave display, sunlight splintering to shards on their harness as their lances shattered on each others' breastplates. The thunderous charge of the armored war-horses and the impact of their meeting shook the ground. The tournament concluded with a night of fireworks.

Fireworks: traditionally a wizard's stock-in-trade. A city wizard, Feuleth, was handling the preparations. Rohain, dressing for the evening feast, her head swimming with the intoxication of these giddy days and nights, became conscious, at last, of overlooking a new wave of apprehension arising in the city.

"Viviana," she said, "what news?"

"A wizard in Gilvaris Tarv, Korguth the Unfeasible or some such, has been Dismantled and struck from the List. And a pirate named Scallywag has been captured."

"Scalzo?"

"Yes, that was it, m'lady."

Can it be that at last my enemies are all undone?

But the lady's maid was still speaking. "And strange things have been happening lately—malign creatures have been creeping into Caermelor. They have been seen in the streets after dark. And in the north, things have gone from bad to worse. They say the barbarian wizard-chieftains and warlords are on the move again. There will be full-scale war, for certain. The times of peace are over."

"As usual you outstrip me with the latest goings-on. How is it that you are aware of these things, Viviana, and I am not?"

The lady's maid blushed delicately. "Of late, you have been occupying yourself with pursuits other than listening to gossip, m'lady," she replied demurely. "We have scarcely seen you. You dismiss us when you go out. You are rarely between walls."

"True enough. What other tidings have been prominent?"

"Only much talk of the forthcoming fireworks!"

After sunset, flaming cressets splashed carnelian light over the city.

Upon the lightless and stony heights of the palace the more privileged crowd waited for the fireworks to begin. The less privileged lingered expectantly beyond the walls, in the streets, on the roofs of houses. Feuleth the Torch-Fingered, a youngish wizard, excitedly prowled the inner bailey. He was setting fuses to last-minute rights in tubes packed with white, prismatic saltpeter, yellow spores of sulfur, and other pyrotechnic generators. For added effect, and to indicate his indispensability, he shouted orders and incantations and waved a staff purportedly imbued with gramarye. Up on the parapets, like a palisade of men, the Royal Attriod surrounded two who stood looking out across the starlit city. She leaned back against him, her head resting next to the base of his throat. He folded his arms around her. Their hands clasped. In the torchlight their profiles formed a double cameo on the somber sky.

With a howl of igniting combustibles, the display commenced. A hundred and eleven colored fountains leaped: rufescent, iridescent, viridescent. Out of them, fast things shot high into the dome of night, where they destroyed themselves spectacularly, bursting into glittering rain, scintillating arrows, brilliant hail, confetti, baubles, sequins, petals, jewels. On the castle wall, vivid pinwheels began to rotate, spurting sparks and making whizzing noises that could barely be heard over the bangs, hisses, whistles, and roars, and the keening of air split by rapid flight. Comets sizzled past.

The assembly cheered wildly.

"Zounds," breathed Thomas of Ercildoune on the parapets. "Old Feu has really outdone himself this time."

That night, another vision came to Rohain. Later, she named it the Dream of the Feast.

A hall, filled with long tables. An assembly of guests, most stunningly beauteous, some offensively grotesque—paragons and parodies, all at one extreme or the other. As Rohain walked the length of the hall, alone, they turned, one by one, to stare, and the pressure of those stares was a threat. Their power was as strong as desire, as indiscriminating and as ruthless. Fear drowned Rohain in its troubled waters. Did they not mock and sneer? Did they not feint and leer, patently, gleamingly observing her walking through their midst, their very presence plucking at her every nerve? Was not their very maintenance of distance a menace, like a steel bar that held them from her but that they could crumple at will, laughing?

At the end of the hall, someone stood waiting, someone whose back was turned. The face could not be discerned. Dreading the sight of it, Rohain yet fastened her gaze upon that one with fascination. At any moment she would see and recognize the face.

The one turned. And turned, and turned again, repeatedly beginning but never completing the rotation. Always, at the moment the first pale curve of the face came into view, the image would flicker and retreat to its opening, like a shang tableau, and there would be the back of the head again, starting to turn.

Rohain knew that in the last instance this someone would be revealed, but even as the face finally swung into view, there was only a great bird with beating wings, black as oblivion.

She woke with a mad yammering in her ears, white pain splitting her skull.

Fell creatures were being seen in the city at night. Not before in this long-hundred of years had they dared to penetrate the walls of Caermelor. A curfew was imposed. The citizens made certain their doors were locked at night, and their abodes well-decked with wight-deterring objects. Wizards and shysters did a brisker trade in charms than usual. Reports came in from outlying areas: The Wild Hunt was active.

The day after the Royal Ball, Thorn came to Rohain and said gravely, "If the city has become unsafe, it will not be long before the palace itself is challenged by the reeking forces of unseelie. The restlessness of the Wild Hunt concerns me. Theirs is an eternal malignity, a deep-rooted ill-will. A dangerous adversary endeavored to get to thee, Gold-Hair, and will likely hunt thee again, for these are immortals and able to pursue forever.

"I must leave Caermelor," he continued. "The north stirs again. This time there is a difference—after many a feint and false rumor, we are certain that the war-chiefs of Namarre are about to push forward at last, and that after all the skirmishes and raids, battle will soon be joined in earnest. More platoons have departed to take up their positions. A group of two hundred and seventy soldiers from the First Cavalry Division is headed from the Ilian army base to Corvath on a merchant Windship. Two more flights are to take out seven hundred troops early tomorrow, with deployment completed in two or three days. To the killing ground I will not take thee, but here thou must not remain. I will take thee and Edward to the one place thou mightst dwell in safety while I am gone."

"So we are to be parted . . ." Rohain's blood fused to lead in her veins.

Thorn drew her closer. The effect was not unexpected, the alchemy turning the lead to molten gold. A clear unscent carried on his breath, like the ether before a storm.

"Dost think I want to leave thee? I want thee by me all ways, day and night, my Pleasure. Yet I will not take thee into danger. A battlefield is no place for thee."

"I care nothing for danger. Take me with you!"

He placed a finger on her mouth and shook his head.

"No. Until I can be by your side again, Gold-Hair, thou shalt bide in another place."

6
THE ISLAND
Green Hair, Dark Sea

On rocky shores there used to stand, windblown,
A lonely tower built of graying stone.
O'er dark and restless seas it shone a light,
And beamed a message through the ageless night,
As if to reach the land where roses bloom,
Whose floral kiss abates despair and gloom.

A VERSE FROM "THE ROSE'S KISS"

Three hundred nautical miles separated Caermelor from that uncertain stretch of water halfway between the Gulf of Mara and the boiling fury of Domjaggar Strait, south of the Cape of Tides and north of the Cape of Winds. Here was a region avoided by Seaship routes, a domain where, no matter how vapid the sky, no matter how placid the sea, mist and cloud gathered their skirts and muffled themselves in their mantles.

The bosun blew his whistle. Blocks squealed overhead as

the main yards were braced round. HIMS *King James XVI* hove to at the frayed edges of this foggy obscurity. It was as if a smoky twilight hovered beyond the bowsprit and the starboard taffrail, while elsewhere the day gleamed as lustrous as polished crystals. A mellow sea-breeze came cantering out of the west to lift among the sails the Royal Heraldry of the pennoncels and the long ribbons of streamers, the gay banners and the swallow-tailed gittons, laying them straight along its flowing mane.

Chunks of charcoal imprisoned crimson heat in a brazier suspended on chains from a tripod on the fo'c'sle. Passengers and crew with their taltries thrown back stood watching as a pitch-smeared arrowhead was touched to the coals. Fiery hair sprang forth from that head. In one swift, sudden movement, Thorn fitted the shaft to the string, bent back his longbow—the shaft sliding through his fingers until his right hand almost met the red blossom—and sent it soaring with a twang and a hissing whine, straight into the twilight's heart.

Standing with feet braced apart at right angles to the target, in the classic archer's stance, he watched it fly, high and far.

It vanished.

And then there came a thinning of the fog, and deep within the murk a form manifested as if seen through frosted glass. Across the waters, past a wild spume that was the white blood of waves suiciding in the jaws of reefs, a mountain loomed, indistinct, crowned with a pale cloud. An island, floating in the sea.

"Release the bird," said Thorn, handing the longbow to his squire. A snowball or a wad of paper scraps was tossed into the air, shaking itself out into the shape of a pigeon. It took wing toward the island. They watched the white chevron disappear, following the red flower. Waves spanked the port side. Ropes creaked, wood complained, and now the faint cries of gulls scratched the wind.

Presently a spark appeared, a brass button against the dark hem of the land.

"There she be!" exclaimed several voices. "The Beacon!"

At this signal, the crew swung into action again, hauling on the braces to swing the main yards back into position. The helmsman spun the wheel and brought the ship about. Sails filled, and with the wind directly behind her the vessel began to pick up speed, skimming the crests, scooting toward the isle.

The mountain towered ever higher.

Along a narrow channel between the reefs sped HIMS *King James XVI,* guided by the Light. She ran between two headlands that held between them a span of vituperative currents called the Rip, until, skating free of those arms, with the Light in the Tower alone on its rocky promontory to the port side, she fell like a gull to its haven into a beautiful harbor, tranquil and still.

Above the harbor, basalt terraces snaked up the cliffs to the cloud-bearded summit dominating all with its formidable presence. This peak let down its shadow to ink the water, dwarfing the tall ship with the lily sails now furled and lashed into long buds. The vessel became a mote of light on a dark pond. By the shore, red birds of fishing boats clustered at their moorings, all facing west. Some of these fishers, and other vessels shaped like seedpods, came out toward the *King James XVI.* Crates of snowflake pigeons and a lumpy bag of letters were uploaded. Few other goods were exchanged—this was not a merchant ship, not a trade visit. Most of the islanders had come to look at the King-Emperor's renowned ship and to try to catch a glimpse of him in person—it had been long since he was last on the island—as well as to welcome Prince Edward and the Lady Rohain, tidings of whom had preceded them.

Thorn's hair swung down to brush Rohain's cheek as he leaned to her. While the clipper's longboats were being lowered into the water, the pair took leave of each other, speaking softly, standing on the fo'c'sle while all others kept a respectful distance. But when for the last time their hands unclasped, Rohain felt it was an agony, as though her flesh had grown to his and was now torn.

"Guard her, Thomas," Thorn had commanded his Bard. "Guard her well." But she had thought it was Thorn who needed vigilance and protection, since he was going to war.

Auspiciously, the wind swung around. A sildron floater took Rohain down the ship's side. In a swathe of rose brocade encrusted with carnelians, she sat in the bow, facing astern like the rowers. At the tiller, the coxswain called out a command. Hemmed in by red birds and seed-husks, the line of boats crawled to shore like oar-legged insects on the sun's glittering path.

The fisher families greeted the Crown Prince, the Lady Betrothed, the Duke of Ercildoune, and the Duchess of Roxburgh and her brood with songs, jonquils, and strings of colored lanterns. They presented them with trinkets and buckles inlaid with mother-of-pearl, all fashioned from carved coral, tusks of walrus, skulls of seals, or teeth of whales. They gave also shell-work bouquets (each shell carefully chosen for its color and shape to replicate a petal of a particular variety of flower), shell-work trinket boxes and glove boxes. The handful of wealthier islanders presented gifts of pearl necklaces, bracelets, and girdles studded with garnets, peridots, and zeolite crystals and containers covered in shagreen. To these they added amber and agate snuff-boxes, nautilus shell cups with pewter rims and feet, porphyry bowls, and a pristine prismatic bowl imprisoning three live leafy sea-dragons: delicate, innocent

creatures that Rohain would later discreetly return to their
habitat.

The village mayor made a speech.

The rumbling strains of a shanty drifted from the royal
ship, out over the water. On the foredeck the men toiled
around the capstan, straining against the bars. The anchor
broke the water like some queer fish, flukes streaming. With
a rattle and a clang it locked into place. Lengths of canvas
dropped from the yardarms and fattened like the bells and
scoops of pale pink shells. A phosphorescent wake awoke.
Cream curled at the prow.

For as long as possible, Rohain held on to the memory
of Thorn in *dusken,* handsome beyond reckoning, resting
his elbows on the taffrail, not waving, merely watching her
steadily, until distance thinned the bond of that mutual gaze
and eventually severed it. Like the tide, terrible grief and
longing then rose in her, and she could not speak, made
mute again by loss. All the light and laughter in the world
was draining out through the Rip, sailing away, far away.

This, then, was the secret island, Tamhania, sometimes
called Tavaal. For hundreds of years it had been the private
retreat of the kings of the House of D'Armancourt. Some
sea-enchantment rendered it safe from all things unseelie.
Furthermore, it was hidden from view by mists engendered,
it was said, by virtue of a herb that grew extensively over its
slopes: *duilleag neoil,* the cloud-leaf, whose effects were
complemented by steam from numerous hot springs. If the
isle was struck by a red-hot arrow fired from beyond its
shores it would become visible for a short time, but no vessel could find the channel through the reefs without the
guidance of the Beacon, and the Light would only be kindled in that gray Tower after the reception of a sealed order
from the King-Emperor, or a secret rune, carried in by messenger birds.

Rohain had taken leave of Sianadh at Caermelor, where he had boarded a merchant Seaship bound for Finvarna. It had been a parting both sorrowful and joyous.

"No tears, *chehrna!*" he had said, tears standing in his own blue eyes, "''Tis not good-bye, in any event! We shall meet again! When the war is over the Queen-Empress must tour the countries of her Empire. Start with the best—the land of the giant elk, and the long rugged shores, and the taverns filled with music and good cheer. Don't ye forget, now!"

He saluted her and swaggered up the gangplank with a jaunty air, waving his cap. That had been the last she had seen of him.

A procession of coaches and riders wound upward along the rutted cliff road from the fishing village on the harbor. Over many an arched bridge of basalt they went, crossing the rills that tumbled down the hillsides, past trees twisted into poetic shapes by salt winds, to the Royal Estate, Tana. High on the mountainside, Tana's castle overlooked the slate roofs of the village, and the cove where flying fish leapt in clear green water.

There the Seneschal of Tana, Roland Avenel, greeted them.

This entire island belonged to the Crown. Of those few Feohrkind folk who had been granted the right to dwell there, some were ancient families, the descendants of generations of islanders: fisher-folk, farmers, and orchardists who for centuries had paid their tithes in services and goods or in gems pried from the gravels and crannies of fissures in the mountain walls. Some had been born on the isle and lived out their span of years on it; others left its cloudy shores when they were full-grown, and never returned. Sometimes, folk came to live on Tamhania who had never set foot there before—men and wives who had sought permission from the official authorities representing the Crown, and been deemed worthy; probably they had some skill or talent to offer the community. Perhaps they themselves longed for peace and seclusion.

The Hall of Tana, the royal residence, was more ethereal by far than the buttressed blocks of Caermelor Palace—a *chastel* out of legend. Its tapering turrets and great ranks of willows rose tier after tier from an ivy-clad plinth that was itself as high as a house—the remains of an old fortress upon which the Hall was founded. Extraordinary masonry adorned the outer walls: pilasters imprisoned in banded stonework, their capitals scrolled or sprouting stone acanthus leaves. Arched niches, ceiled by carvings of giant scallop shells, sheltered statues of mermaids, mermen, porpoises, dolphins, and whales. Over the massive front door loomed the royal coat of arms. Above every ground-floor window, in petrified splendor, the devices of old and noble families were displayed. Swallows darted among the crenellations.

Built upon one of the few level areas on the island, the grounds were parklike. Lawns swept around leafy walks and plantations of ancient, wind-contorted trees that cast their reflections into still ponds, the whole scene overlooking the ocean on the one hand, overlooked by the mountain on the other.

Within, apartments abounded. Huge vaulted cellars with tiled cisterns built into living rock occupied the founding platform. A wide stair led up to the grand salon with its painted wallpaper, heavy-framed portraits, and gilt furniture upholstered in velvet, figured silk, and embroidery. The library was located on this level, as was the dining room, dominated by the marble minstrel's gallery. Higher up, one could find the smaller salons and studies, the bedchambers each with their own sea-theme, and the Hall of the Guards, a gallery one hundred feet long and so wide that ten men could ride abreast through it. Its walls were ornamented with motifs and arabesques in light blues and reds and earthy browns. Throughout the *chastel*, the open-beam ceilings were set with hundreds of paintings of mythic scenes all finished with the highest precision.

In this sumptuous island retreat, the days fled by.

Rohain began to accustom herself to her new environs. It was not like living—it was more like waiting. So she waited, with Prince Edward—as vigorous as Thorn and yet as different from him as father from son—with red-haired Thomas of Ercildoune, and the Duchess Alys, and with Viviana, Caitri, and Georgiana Griffin, who had been dismissed by her invidious mistress and joined Rohain's ever-increasing collection of attendants. Jolly Dain Pennyrigg was with them also, the lad from Isse Tower. He seemed to have become Rohain's equerry by default, even though gray Firinn had not been transported to Tamhania, the steep slopes being unsuitable for thoroughbred riding-horses.

The climate was mild beneath the cloud-blanket, snugged in tepid seas. Turtles the hue of malachite flew under clear waves of jade. Ladybirds crawled or flew everywhere, like tiny buttons, in livery checkered cadmium and black, spotted charcoal and madder.

Fisher-folk plied their nets mainly in the calm band of water betwixt shore and reef, for, once past the reef there was no return, not without the kindling of the Light. Without the Light, all vessels foundered, victims of the rocks. That was part of the island's sea-enchantment. When a fleet was to venture out beyond that barrier, the leader would memorize the day's Pass-Sign and cage a pigeon from the lofts in the Light-Tower. When it came time to return, the rune was daubed minutely on a smidgin of papyrus and fastened to the leg of the patient bird. So that the avian aviator could see its way home, a fiery arrow was shot, to make the island visible. Whosoever forgot the sign, or lost the pigeon or the arrows or the fire, could not return; a boat must be sent out to give them aid. It seemed a troublesome affair, but the islanders had grown accustomed to it, and besides, some arcane property of the Light always ensured calm waters in the channel. Once it was lit, safety was assured, even in the most mettlesome storm.

Time passed, but the hours never hung heavily for the bride-in-waiting. Thomas the Bard taught her how to string a lute and make it sing a little, and how to recognize the runes of writing, beginning with the Thorn Rune, þ, and how to name the stars. She did not know if she had been able to read and write before she lost her memory, but penmanship and deciphering came easily to her. When personal messages arrived from Thorn at the battlefields she allowed no one else to read them, and painstakingly composed replies.

From the fisher-folk she learned how to sail the little boats they called *geolas*—"What language is this you islanders speak in snatches?" she asked. "A version of the Olden Speech. His Majesty is fluent at it," they told her.

But as well as voyaging and making music, it was time to learn to do harm.

Rohain summoned the Seneschal of Tana, Roland Avenel, a silver-maned, doughty ex-legionary of some fifty Winters. She said, "It has come to me that knowledge and the wit to use it are the most powerful weapons. The greatest warrior would fail in the wilderness, did he not understand the seasons and the secret ways to find sustenance and the lore of fire-making. Yet a swift and certain sword-arm would stand anyone in good stead. Will you teach me to fight with weapons?"

So the Seneschal tutored her in wielding a light blade and a skian.

When not fencing, strumming, sailing, or shooting arrows at straw bull's-eyes, Rohain would ride with Edward and their companions. They cantered along dark beaches fringed with black pebbles and rocks twisted like slag. Splendid taltries flapped at their backs. The horses' hooves kicked up black sand flecked with glitter, like dominite. Ferny weeds and strings of succulent beads filled rockpools so clear one would not have guessed there was water in them, save for a shimmer and a blur. The sun cast a golden fretwork on the waves—a limpid mesh over living glass, the wave-rims like the veil-flowers of clematis. On the dunes silvery saltbush clung, and kitten-tail grass, and scented tea-tree with its waxy flowers. After sunset, white wings of spray blew back off the rolling breakers, gleaming phosphorescent in the afterglow.

The sea-wind murmured like Thorn's voice in Rohain's ears.

"While thou dost remain here," he had said, "I will never be far from thee."

Could it be that intense, unremitting longing was powerful enough to bridge distance? Rohain imagined he touched her with every caress of the breeze that occasionally tore the mist into strips, and ruffled her skirts, and played with her tresses. She fancied the soft, warm raindrops on her upturned face might be his kisses. At nights, half waking, she heard the susurration of waves breaking on the boulders below the *chastel,* as the breathing of one who lay in slumber beside her, and she would reach out her hand, but there was only the substance of moonlight where he might have been, and shadow for his hair.

Still, she was embraced by a sense of his nearness. She tried to believe it was not all pretense and, convincing herself, found a kind of contentment.

As for the Antlered One and his Hunt, they were far away, on the other side of the island's enchanted barriers, where they could pose no threat. With each day that elapsed they shrank further back in time, until eventually Rohain abandoned all thought of them.

A secret island, Tamhania-Tavaal was an island of secrets, some of which Rohain came to imperfectly recognize, as days linked together in chains of weeks. Riding or walking along the strand, she and her ladies would often find the fishermen's children playing among the seaweed-fringed rockpools—catching crabs, making coronets of sea-grasses, splashing and laughing. There was one little girl among them who always wore a necklace of perfect pearls that shimmered palest pastel green. Luminous were they, worthy of a princess. Rohain thought it curious that the child of one of the poor fisher-folk should wear such a valuable treasure about her neck as carelessly as if it were no more than a string of common shells.

It was the first of several curious matters, she discovered.

Once, rising early after another restless night, she rode out with her retainers before sunrise. Walking their horses along the shore, they spied a woman sitting on a rock at high-tide mark. She did not notice them, for she was staring out across the sea. As the first glimmer of dawn grayed the waters, a big seal came swimming toward the rock. When he came within a pebble's throw, he raised his head and spoke to the woman.

She replied.

Then he walked up out of the sea with the water sliding off him like moon-drops. He cast off his sealskin as he approached, and met her in the form of a man.

The riders turned their horses and hastened away, leaving the couple alone together on the shore bathed by the glance and glimmer of morning light on the waves.

When Rohain told Roland Avenel about this encounter he nodded and said, "Ah, yes. I too have seen Ursilla once or twice, at early morning, waiting on the rocks. But prithee, bid your attendants to refrain from speaking to anyone about what you and they have witnessed."

"That I shall, if you say discretion is desirable. But who is she, this Ursilla?"

"She is the wife of a farmer here on the isle, a proud, well-favored woman who manages her household, her farm, and her husband well. To all outward appearances she possesses all she could desire. Yet beneath the surface, I fear, she is not happy."

"So I have guessed for myself," acknowledged Rohain.

Avenel paused and scratched his chin thoughtfully, as though searching for words. "All three of Ursilla's children," he went on, "have webbed hands and webbed feet. The membranes of skin between their fingers and toes are so delicate and thin that the light shows through. A horny epidermis grows on the backs of their hands. Every one of them has soft silken hair, the color of the water in the first light of dawn."

"And her lover is one of the island's secrets," concluded Rohain softly. She recalled, then, the little girl with the pearl necklace. "Pray tell me, Master Avenel, why the fishermen's children wear such wonderful jewels when they play. I had imagined them to be poor folk."

"I'll warrant you have seen young Sally," said Avenel with a laugh. "Only one other among the fishers owns such wealth. But nobody envies her, or would try to take the thing from her. Oh, no."

"Why not?"

"Well, because of the way she came by it. 'Tis said that last Summer, Sally was playing with her doll down by the rockpools and when she turned away a mermaid's child stole the toy. Young Sally fled, weeping. On the following day when she returned to look for the doll, the mermaid's child rose from the sea at the edge of the rocks where the spume flies highest."

"A mermaid's child!" interjected Rohain, fascinated. "Have you seen the merfolk, sir? What are they like?"

Avenel smiled and drew breath. The Seneschal of Tana was a fair wordsmith; Rohain loved hearing him speak. Now, as he held forth, he led her to imagine entities resembling young women, with waves of hair like sea-leaves, and half their bodies a graceful, sweeping mosaic of verdigrised copper coins. Their skin was the cream of sea-foam and they had long eyes of cucumber green. Avenel related how the merchild came, and in her shell-white hand she held out the pearl necklace, which she gave to Sally in atonement for the theft. In words of alien accent, she told the mortal child that her mother had bade her do so. Then she looked at Sally with her green eyes before flipping away with a flicker of iridescent scales, to plunge beneath the breakers.

"That has been the most recent sighting of the merfolk," said the Seneschal, "but that one was only a stripling, not yet a harbinger and bringer of storms—at least, not of disastrous ones."

"Are they often glimpsed?"

"Not at all, m'lady. To see a mermaid is rare. In all my years on Tavaal, I have never once set eyes on one, nor, in truth, do I wish to do so. Other sea-wights are seen from time to time, but these sightings too are rarities. None easily let themselves be spied by our kind."

"Who else among the fishers owns a jewel given by sea-folk?"

"The mayor of our village below! In his youth, some thirty years ago, his father was out fishing when one of his comrades caught a wave-maiden on a hook. She promised, if the men let her go, to give them good fortune. The skipper thereupon dropped her over the gunwale and as she swam to her home she sang,

Muckle gude I wid you gie and mair I wid you wish;
There's muckle evil in the sea, scoom weel your fish.

"Then the six fishermen thought they had been cheated.
Only the lad who was later to be our mayor's father took any
notice of the sea-maiden's injunction. He scoomed his fish
very well indeed, and found a splendid pearl among the
scooming, which was kept in the family from that day
forth!"

"Oh, fair fortune!" declared Rohain, pleased with his stories. She added, "I thank you for sharing your knowledge
with me, Master Avenel, and while you are doing so, I beg
you to solve just one more mystery that has us all intrigued.
Last week we rode out to Benvarrey's Bay. There we saw an
ancient apple tree on the cliff, leaning right out over the
water. Ripe fruit aplenty hung on its boughs but no one gathered them. When the wind shook the tree, several apples
dropped into the sea. It seemed a waste. Why do the poor
fisher-folk not harvest the fruit of this tree?"

"There is a story attached to that tree," replied Avenel.
"Years ago, the Sayles were a large fishing family on Tavaal,
with a well-tended croft to supplement their living. They
prospered. Old Sayle had a great liking for apples, and when
they were in season he always took a pile of them in the
boat. But when he became too old to go fishing, the family's
fortunes began to decline. One by one the sons left the island
until only the youngest remained to look after his parents
and the farm. His name was Evan.

"One day after Evan had set the *cleibh-giomach*, the lobster creels, he went climbing on the cliff to look for
seabirds' eggs. He heard a sweet voice calling to him and
when he went down he saw, sitting on a rocky shoal, a
maiden of the benvarrey. Comely she was, so it is told, with
nacreous skin, and eyes like sea anemones, and a slender
waist tapering to a long fluked curve of overlapping scales.

Evan was torn between fear and delight but he greeted her courteously. She asked after his father, and the youth told her about all the family's troubles. When he came home Evan told his parents what had happened and his father was well-pleased with him.

" 'Next time you go fishing,' he said, 'take a pile of apples with you.'

"The white sea daughter was delighted to get the 'sweet land eggs' once more, and good fortune returned to the Sayles. But Evan was smitten, and he spent so much time out in his boat speaking with her when she appeared, and hoping that she might appear when she was absent, that people began to whisper that he had turned idle. When the youth heard these rumors he was so bothered by them that he decided to leave the island, but before he went he planted the apple tree on the cliff and told the sea-daughter that when the tree matured the sweet land eggs would ripen and drop down for her. Although he went, the good luck stayed, but the lovely wight grew weary of waiting for the apples to form and she went off looking for Evan Sayle. In the end the apples ripened, but neither Evan nor the benvarrey ever came back to look for them. Because the tree was planted there for a sea-wight, no mortal will touch the fruit."

When she had listened to this tale, Rohain said, "It seems I have much to learn. You say this sea-girl was a benvarrey, a seelie wight, and yet she had a fish's tail just like a mermaid. How did Evan Sayle recognize she was a benvarrey? And how many kinds of merfolk exist?"

"As to your first question," answered Avenel, "it takes an islander, or one who dwells all his life at the margins of the sea, to be able to discern between the different kinds of fishtailed wights, the half piscean and half mortal-seeming. As for your second question, there are five. There are mermaids with their mermen, there are the benvarreys, the sea-morgans, the merrows, and the *maighdeanna na tu-*

inne, the wave-maidens. The benvarreys do not fail to look kindly on the races of men but the others may be seelie or unseelie or both. Fear not—around the Royal Isle malignity cannot dwell. Unseelie merfolk are repelled from its shores. Indeed, the mermaids of Tavaal *aid* us."

"In what manner?"

"When the men are fishing off the island a mermaid will warn them of forthcoming storms, calling out *'shiaull er thalloo'*—'sail to land.' If they hear this cry, the boats run for shelter at once, or else lose their tackle or their lives. The fishermen fervently hope to never behold a mermaid, for they only show themselves, rising suddenly among the boats, if the forthcoming storm is to be truly terrible, such as the Great Storm of 1079, in which many perished. As you know, m'lady, sea-wights of all kinds dislike being viewed by mortals, and few folk have ever set eyes on any of them, excepting the silkies, who are less wary. Tales of actual sightings are part of island history."

As he finished speaking, Rohain detected a sudden evasiveness, as if he had just then recollected a fact that contradicted his last statement. *I wonder,* she thought, *whether there might be seelie ocean-wights dwelling among us . . .*

"Well," said Rohain, "I have not seen a mermaid, but I have glimpsed a silkie, I think. I hope to see more of the eldritch sea-dwellers."

"Now," said the Seneschal with a change of tone, "I have a question for *you,* m'lady. Would it please you to come down to the shore towards evening? There is to be a party and a music-making. The seals will come near—the true seals, the animals that live on the skerries around the island. You shall see *them,* if not the merfolk."

"Why will they come?"

"They are attracted by any kind of music, even whistling."

"I should be greatly amused by such a spectacle!"

As the day waned, the islanders gathered great piles of driftwood and lit fires along the shoreside, then played their pipes and sang their songs. Out where the breakers arched their toss-maned horses' necks, the seals assembled to listen, their soft fur glistening. Burly, wintry-haired Roland Avenel took his bagpipes and walked along the shore playing traditional airs, splashing his bare feet among bubbled crystal garlands of foam strewn like pear-blossom on the ribbed sand.

This delighted the seals. Their heads stuck up out of the water, and they sat up, perpendicular. An enchanting sight it was for Rohain—eighteen to twenty-five seals gathered, all listening, facing different directions, and Avenel playing the pipes to them.

Annie, a serving-girl from Tana, was among the congregated islanders. She touched Rohain lightly on the elbow, saying, "Most of those creatures out there are *lorraly*, my lady. Others are not."

Rohain "Not *lorraly?*" She glanced eagerly toward the seals. "Are silkies among them?"

"Even so!"

The silkies were the seal-folk, the gentlest of sea-wights. In their seal-form they swam, but in humanlike form they were able to walk on land before returning to the sea. Despite that men were wont to do them great wrong, the silkies had always shown benevolence to mortalkind. They never did harm.

On another day Roland Avenel, knowledgeable in the ways of silkies, took Rohain, Prince Edward, Thomas of Ercildoune, and Caitri down to the strand they called Ronmara. It was a long-light afternoon. The last rays were roseate, the wind temperate, and the tide at its nadir. Not far offshore, out of the sea rose numerous rocky islets formed from tall stacks of hexagonal stones jammed together like honeycomb, a remnant of some past volcanic action. The water was deep on their seaward side and crystalline in shallow bead-fringed pools on the shoreward side.

There, the seal-folk played.

The silkies appeared like a troupe of lithe humans: women and men, youths and maidens and children. All were naked, ivory-skinned. Some lay sunning themselves, while others frolicked and gamboled. Beside them were strewn their downy pelts. Eventually, catching sight of the spies, they seized their sealskins and jumped into the sea in mad haste. Then they swam a little distance before turning, popping up their heads, and, as seals now, gazing at the invaders.

"They are beauteous indeed," exclaimed the young Prince.

"Indeed!" Caitri echoed, boldly.

"'Tis little wonder mortals sometimes fall in love with them," said the Bard.

"Do they?" said the little girl, turning to him in surprise.

"But surely," said Rohain, "such love must be doomed from the outset! One dwells in the sea, the other on the land. When lovers belong to two different worlds, how shall they be happy together?"

"They shall not," said Edward, rather sharply. Avenel nodded, his mien somber.

Rohain was about to ask, *How can you know?* when she thought of Rona Wade. She fell silent. Shallow, flat waves played about her feet, rippling with gold scales of sunlight, each delineated by the kohl-line of its own shadow, as she watched the seal-people swim away.

Three times a week, a fisherman's wife would come to the Hall of Tana with her eldest daughter, delivering fish for the tables. Her husband had a knack for catching the best. The woman's name was Rona Wade, and there was a strangeness about her, like the sea, and as profound.

Rohain liked to try broaching the reticence of this gentle

wife by speaking with her on the occasions they met, but on subjects pithier than island gossip, she would not be drawn. Rohain could not help noticing the webbed fingers of the children of Hugh and Rona Wade. They bore an affinity with those of Ursilla's progeny, however people wisely refrained from commenting on the likeness. The other island children, if they thought anything of these aberrations, envied them. Webbed fingers made for fine swimmers.

It was obvious that Hugh's love for his bonny wife Rona was unbounded, but she returned it only with cool cordiality. Like Ursilla, she had been seen stealing alone to a deserted shore where she would toss a shell or some other object into the water. Upon this signal a large seal would appear, and she spoke to it in an unknown tongue.

But Rona was not really like Ursilla.

After the conversation, the creature would slip back under the waves, its shape unchanged. Rohain guessed that Rona did not love Hugh, but she was fond of her husband and never betrayed him.

There appeared to be much unreturned love on Tamhania, which the arrival of the visitors had served to increase. Within a few days of her arrival, Georgiana Griffin, Dianella's erstwhile servant, had attracted the attention of one of the island's most eligible young men.

Sevran Shaw was a shipmaster and farmer. Island born, he had traveled far over the seas of Erith on his own sloop, trading profitably, before coming home to settle. Shrewd was he, sensible, good-humored, and comfortably well-off. Now in his thirtieth year, he had never married. Several of the island girls had hoped to snare him, but he had not fallen in love until he set eyes on Georgiana Griffin. This refined lady, bred in the rarefied atmosphere of the Court of Caermelor, refused to hear his suit or to accept him as a friend. Weeks passed and his attachment grew only the stronger, although she avoided him and they hardly ever met. It looked as if his love was ill-fated.

Thus proceeded the secrets and the passions of the isle.

Yet there were other mysteries on Tamhania-Tavaal, not of the affective kind, and these seemed to be more easily solved.

Through the island's only village ran crumbling granite walls, and rows of tall wooden piles driven into the ground for no apparent reason. Some stood or leaned like branchless trees, others supported decrepit piers and condemned jetties that stalked toward the water but finished abruptly far short of it, in the middle of the air. Far above the high-tide line, the dried remains of mussels and barnacles encrusted these thick stems.

When Rohain asked about the useless and ruined structures, Avenel told her the village had risen sixteen feet over the last ten years, and the harbor had had to be rebuilt lower down. Local legend asserted that the island had floated at times during the past centuries, traveling on the ocean currents before catching on some submarine reef or snag and taking root again in a new position.

Market day in the uplifted village was a pleasant diversion for Rohain. At the time of full moon, makeshift stalls would be set up in the Old Village Square, and folk would arrive from all over the island to peddle their wares. Riding through the township one market day, with her nineteen ladies and her equerry, Rohain spied a woman dressed in the geranium-colored houppelande commonly adopted by the middle classes. Her head was sheathed in a shawl. Walking among the stalls, she was bartering jars of honey, bunches of hyacinths and watercress, apple cider and apple cider vinegar in ceramic bottles.

Her face drew Rohain's attention. There was a look about this woman that stirred some vague memory. Hope sprang in her heart. Could it be she had at last found someone from her past? Dismounting, she gave the reins to her equerry and approached the woman, who curtsied.

"Do you know me?" asked Rohain.

The woman's eyes were two cups filled with reflections. Weather, years, and sorrow had engraved her face with their etchings, but she was not uncomely. "All on Tamhania know the Lady Rohain Tarrenys, who is to be Queen-Empress."

"But do you *know* me?"

"No, my lady."

"Your face, to me, appears familiar. What is your name?"

"Elasaid. Elasaid of the Groves."

"Are you certain you do not recognize me?"

"Yes."

"What will you take in return for a bag of apples?"

"Cloth. Good cloth for a new cloak."

"Mustardevlys? Rylet? Thick woollen frieze?"

"Ratteen, if it please my lady."

"Give the apples to my equerry. The ratteen shall be sent to you tomorrow."

A bargain was struck. It was a way of being linked to this woman.

At Tana, Rohain again drew Roland Avenel aside. She said, "Today I spoke with a woman in the marketplace. She is called Elasaid of the Groves."

Avenel frowned. "With respect, does my lady deem it seemly for the future Queen-Empress to associate with commoners in marketplaces?"

Rohain arched her brows in surprise.

"Why, sir, I shall speak with whomsoever pleases me!" she responded. "There is nothing indecorous about conversing with an honest person in any place, be it public or private. You forget, sir, I am *not* as the courtiers of Caermelor, so rigid in their hierarchies that they cannot recognize a fellow human creature."

Avenel bowed, murmuring an apology.

"I wish to know," said Rohain, "where she dwells, this Elasaid. I shall visit her."

"She abides low on the eastern slopes above Topaz Bay," answered the Seneschal. "To it, there is a path only fit for donkeys or foot traffic. 'Tis very narrow, and an old stone wall runs all along one side. Those who pass that way must beware of Vinegar Tom. He is not unseelie as wights go— haters of mankind cannot abide here. He is a kind of guardian of the path, that's all. There is a rhyme that you must recite if you want to get by him. If it is not said, Vinegar Tom takes you away and leaves you somewhere on the other side of the island where 'tis remote and prickly, and it can take a fistful of days to get back. When I first came here, they taught me the chant:

Vinegar Tom, Vinegar Tom,
Where by the Powers do you come from?

"I learned this ditty and went, cocksure, along that path. Vinegar Tom came out and he was like a long-legged grey-hound with the head of an ox, with a long tail and huge eyes. When I saw him, I was so flummoxed that I said:

Vinegar Tom, Vinegar Tom,
Where in the world do you come from?

"I said it wrong, but the words rhymed, so Vinegar Tom only tossed me over the wall!"

Rohain took a bolt of ratteen and her retinue and went to visit the lady of the apple groves. The narrow track climbed away from the main road and wound over wooded slopes. To the right, the hillsides dropped sharply to the plane of the sea. To the left they escalated to pathless gullies. There, fern sprays prinked the cracks that ran through spills of ropy, wrinkled rock like the sagging hide of some enormous beast, and mist hovered in ravines walled with strange formations in stone, like frozen waterfalls. Ascending, the party passed spindly towers and pinnacles and needles. They went by a rift in a hillside, which emitted occasional plumes of white steam to augment the ambient brume. In deep gullies, water tumbled noisily over pebbles. A light mist rose from the still surfaces of gray rainpools, and from the puddles lying like shattered pieces of the sky clasped between tree-roots.

They passed Vinegar Tom with no difficulty. When they had repeated the rhyme he turned into the likeness of a four-year-old child without a head, and vanished.

The path led them to a level apron where they beheld a vegetable plot, beehives, and a little freshwater runnel skirted by white-flowered cresses. Here nestled a slate-roofed cot, lapped in gnarled-knuckled trees. Purple hyacinths bloomed among their roots. Small birds twittered, and bees gathered in the foaming pink-and-white confectionery of blossom. From behind fissured, sprouting boles, a waif of a child with green-gold hair spied upon the newcomers, then ran away.

Elasaid welcomed her visitors into her cottage.

"There is more cloth here than the worth of the apples," she said, unfolding a length of ratteen the color of stormwrack.

"Then pay me the balance in histories," said Rohain.

"What would my lady wish to know?"

"The roads you have trod. If it pleases you to tell of them."

"Well, I have trod high roads and low and I don't mind telling at all."

"Tell me first about yon child with the green-gold hair."

"Willingly," said Elasaid of the Groves, "for I love her well. On an evening seven years ago, when the last afterglow of sunset was still reflecting in the sky and the owls were abroad, I heard beautiful singing coming from among the shadows gathering in Topaz Bay. I thought it might be the sea-morgans, and I was eager to see if I could catch a glimpse, so I made my way down to the bay as quietly as I could. However, I was not careful enough—my foot dislodged a pebble, and all I caught was a flash and a glimmer as the sea-morgans dived off the rocks into the tide.

"In their haste and fright, they inadvertently left one of their babies wriggling and laughing beneath the waterfall that splashes from the cliffs above the bay. When I saw the baby I could not do otherwise than love her. I still grieved deeply for my own daughter, so, rightly or wrongly, I took this child created from foam and seaweed and pearls.

"I took her, and I raised her as my own. I called her Liban. She is like any mortal child in most ways, but I can never get her hair completely dry, not even in the sunshine and the breeze, and the tang of the ocean is always in it. She loves to wade and play in my spring-fed pond, and among the wavelets down at the shore. She is a loving daughter, but there are those among the island-dwellers who, recalling their lives outside Tamhania where unseelie mermaids cause shipwrecks, deem it terribly unlucky even to speak of her kind.

"I have tried to make them forget her origin. I have endeavored to put it in their minds that she was born of me, but some do not forget and they wish her ill. Minna Scales is the worst. She had never forgiven me since the colt-pixie chased her son when he tried to steal my Gilgandrias, those apples which are said to be seeded from the land of Faêrie. The wight gave him *'cramp and crooking and fault in his footing'*—it made him the laughingstock of the village. But I'm not to blame for the colt-pixie chasing him. The colt-pixie is a guardian of apple trees. 'Tis a wight. I have no command over such.

"Minna Scales will not let up her niggling," Elasaid continued. " 'Odds fish!' she says to Liban. 'Look how your hair drips water. Go and dry it like a *lorraly* lass!' Liban just laughs at her. We keep to ourselves mostly, on this side of the island. The child is happy. I have learned to treasure every moment of her happiness. I think of the other daughter I had . . ."

Elasaid's hands trembled.

"I have not always lived this simple life," she said. "I voyaged here, to Tavaal, several years ago. Long before I came here, my childhood was spent in a tall and stately house with many servants. I married—perhaps unwisely, but for love. Eight is the number of the children I bore." Her blanks of eyes sank into weary hollows. She rested her still-handsome head on her hand.

"Evil forces took the first seven from me. I took myself away from the last one. To my eternal regret. For, when I tried to return, I could not. My child, my husband, had gone away in their turn, leaving no trace. I was alone. I searched up and down the Known Lands, to no avail. Finally, sick of the world and its heartbreak, I applied to come here, to live out the rest of my days in seclusion. I found Liban. Abiding with her and my freshet of water, and the apples, I open the doors from one day into the next and close them one by one behind me."

It was easy to strike up friendships with the good-natured islanders. Elasaid of the rain-eyes was one of many with whom Rohain liked to pass the time in conversation. Another was Rona Wade, the wife of Hugh, whose children had webbed fingers. Rona could never be persuaded to reveal her thoughts and desires, but she knew all that went on around the island, and was happy to share her knowledge.

On a hazy afternoon, Rona Wade and her web-fingered eldest daughter tarried with Rohain by the kitchen door at the Hall of Tana. Outside waited the surly donkey with the empty fish-baskets, while its mistress discussed island lore.

"Why do the children so often dive near the crescent beach beneath the eastern cliffs?" Rohain wanted to know.

"That is where Urchen Conch threw the chest full of money into the water," said Rona. "They are looking for gold coins. Ah, but I suspect you have not heard that tale, my lady!"

"I have not, and I burn to understand why anyone would throw treasure into the brine! Who is this Conch?"

"Urchen Conch was a somewhat simpleminded fellow," said Rona. "He lived and died a long time ago. Eighty years ago he saved a stranded benvarrey, carrying her back to the sea. He was entitled to three wishes, but did not know to ask, so she rewarded him with information about how to find a treasure. Doing as she bid, he found a chest of antique gold in a great sea-cavern, but he did not know how to dispose of the ancient cash, and at last he threw the coins back into the sea. It is said he threw them from the eastern cliffs."

"What a strange tale!" said Rohain.

She was about to ask further questions when Rona's two younger children came scrambling up the path, apple-cheeked and breathless.

"Mama!" they cried. "Luik what we hae fand under a corn-stack! Ain't it pretty!" Delighted with their prize, they held it high. It shimmered with a downy silverescence—a banner long and wide, rippling in the wind off the slopes. A meadow of moon-grass.

A sealskin.

Gazing at the hide, Rona's dark eyes glistened with rapture. She grasped it, shouting aloud in an ecstasy of joy. The children stood gape-mouthed to see their mother put on such an uncharacteristic display, but she turned to them, her happiness suddenly dimming.

"I love you, my darlings," she said, embracing each one hastily, "I will always love you."

The words hung in memory, long after they had been spoken, as if nailed on emptiness. As soon as she had uttered them, Rona fled down the road toward the sea. The children began to sob. The eldest daughter jumped on the donkey's back.

"I'm gaun tae find Da'!"

She whipped the petulant beast into a headlong run, and the younger ones went wailing after. But they never saw their mama again.

Rohain wept for the family, and brought them food and gifts.

Next morning, in the breakfast room at Tana, the residents sat down to dine.

The sideboard, whose panels were framed by a graceful relief of crayfish and conger eels carved in apple-wood, had been arranged with figurines of water-serpents and merfolk carved from narwhal tusks. The ornaments were inlaid with nacre and the mottled shell of the sea-turtle. Dome-covered chafing-dishes sat atop charcoal braziers. A silver egg-boiler rested over its small spirit lamp. A sand timer was mounted on the lid, showing that the minutes had almost run out.

The Bard sprinkled allspice from a set of lighthouse-shaped porcelain muffineers. The Prince drank from a nautilus-shell beaker mounted in gold. Someone had left a snuff-box lying on the table alongside a miniature ship carved from bone—the box had been made, not unexpectedly, from a deep-bowled, voluted shell, with an engraved silver lid and silver mounts.

Tana's decor tended to be thematic.

"You have heard the news, my lady?" Master Avenel sipped from a polished driftwood mazer reinforced with a silver foot-rim incised with a pattern of scales.

Rohain nodded assent. "Rona Wade has gone."

"Aye, gone back," said the Seneschal, "to her first husband. As Hugh returned from the day's fishing, he saw her greet him in the waves. She called a farewell to him. Hugh is a broken man."

"Well, he was a thief," said Rohain, stirring medlure in a cup whose bowl was embraced by the claws of two coralline crabs.

"Do not judge too harshly, my lady," Avenel reproached gently. "It was love that drove him to the taking of the seal-skin."

"I beg to differ, sir. Love never steals. It does not subjugate."

In the pause that ensued, a housemaid limped past the doorway carrying a dustpan and broom, on her way upstairs to sweep and clean the bedchambers. At first, Rohain had taken pains to avoid this young woman, because her uneven gait reminded her of Pod and his unpleasantries. On further acquaintance, she discovered Molly Chove to be an amiable and cheerful lass, who took it in good part when the other servants teasingly called her "Limpet."

"Master Avenel," she now said to the Seneschal, "is there no help for that lame servant?"

"Molly got her lameness through her own fault," he replied, dabbing at his mouth with a linen serviette. "A couple of lesser wights inhabit the Hall of Tana—whether they benefit it or not there's no telling, but they've become a habit of a few centuries."

"Do they help with household duties?"

"Maybe," said the Seneschal, "but I think not. They are pixies or bruneys, I believe. So I am told; I have not seen them. Howsoever, our housemaids Mollusc and Ann Chove tell me they were kind to these imps, showing them hospitality and so forth, and in return the wights used to drop a silver coin into a pail of clear water that the wenches would place for them in the chimney-corner of the kitchen every night."

"Surely there is water enough for wights in the streams and wells?"

"Domestic wights are loath to budge from their chosen dwelling. They like to have clean water put out for their drinking and washing. Once several years ago, the malus forgot to fill the pail, so the pixies, or whatever they are, went upstairs to their room and shrilly protested about the omission. Annie woke up. She nudged Molly's elbow and recommended that they should both go down to the kitchen to set things aright, but Molly, who likes her sleep, said, 'Leave me be! Would it indulge all the wights on Tavaal, I will not get up.' Annie went down to the yard and pumped clean water into the pail. Incidentally, next morning she found seven silver threepences in it. Meanwhile, as she was going back to bed that night she overheard the wights discussing ways of penalizing lazy Molly. They decided to cripple her in one leg. At the end of seven years, she heard them say, the lameness might be cured by a certain herb that grew on Windy Spur."

"Did they mention the name of this wonderful herb?"

"They did, but 'twas such a lengthy and complicated name, Annie could not grasp it. When Molly got up in the morning she was limping, and she has been perpetually lame to this day."

Prince Edward said, "The island's wizard, Master Lutey, has a reputation as an excellent healer."

"He has not been able to help Molly, sir," replied the Seneschal.

"Then perhaps his reputation is ill-deserved!"

"Do not, I pray you, sir, despise the talent of old Robin Lutey," said Avenel, "for he is skilled—I can vouch for it. Do you know how Lutey came by his powers?"

"Prithee, remind me."

"As a young man he was a fisherman near Lizard Point, farming a little, combing along the beaches after the storms. One evening when the tide was far out he went wandering along the shore seeking for some wreckage-find among the seaweed and rocks. As he turned, empty-handed, to go home, he heard a low moan from among some boulders, and there he discovered a stranded mermaid."

"For a shy race, they are seen surprisingly often," Rohain interjected.

"Only on Tamhania, my lady," said Avenel. "This is a special place."

"I was given to understand that they only showed themselves before storms."

"They only *allow* themselves to be seen when they warn of foul weather. This one was stranded. She could not get back to the sea and had no choice but to be seen, despite the fact that no storm was on the way."

"Next her strange beauty allured him, no doubt?" Rohain was learning the ways of sea-wights.

"Yes, my lady, and he spoke to her, for the sea-folk understand all tongues. She told him that while she combed her long green hair and gazed at herself in the rockpools the tide had gone out without her seeing it. She begged Lutey to carry her over the strip of dry sand, and, giving him her gold-and-pearl Comb as a token, promised him three wishes. She told him that if he was in any trouble, to pass the Comb three times through the sea and call her name, Morvena, and she would come."

"Now you have me puzzled," said Rohain. "How is it that she could not walk, and yet I have heard that some of the sea-damsels when on land have limbs and walk about as well as you or I?"

"That is one of the differences between mermaids and sea-morgans, m'lady."

"So." She nodded. "I continue to learn. And what were Lutey's wishes?"

"The power to break the spells of malign gramarye, to discover thefts, and to cure illness. These she granted, but only to the degree of her own power."

"He was fortunate."

"Indeed, but that was not the end of this fish's tale," said the Seneschal, permitting himself a faint smile at his pun. "As he walked with her over the sands, she clinging to his neck, she told him of all the wonders of her home under the sea and implored him to go with her and share them all. Robin Lutey was fascinated and would undoubtedly have yielded had not a sharp bark of terror from his dog, which had followed him unnoticed, roused him to look back. At the sight of the faithful hound his wits returned to him. Already the clasp of the mermaid was becoming stronger as she touched the waves, and she might have dragged him under into the deep realms of the great kelp-forests, except that this is Tamhania, the isle of kings, and wickedness thrives not here. She relented. But as she swam away she sang to Lutey—and that, he never forgot. It is said that the song of the mermaid sounds forever in his heart, and that one day she will come for him and he will follow her."

"A future not unkind awaits him, then," said the Bard, who had been silent while eating.

"But nay, sir!" said Avenel. "Master Lutey possesses a terrible gift. He has somewhat of prescience, which allows him to garner an inkling of his own doom. I have gathered, although he has never said as much, that although he shall indeed go with the mermaid he shall not live long thereafter, for the dreaded Marool shall come upon him in its domain, the sea, and shall put an end to his life."

Rohain pondered on this. Her eyes were wet. Presently she said, "A mighty wizard is he."

"Officially he may not carry the title of wizard since he

never studied at the College of the Nine Arts, but meanwhile the island benefits from his powers, which are far greater than those of any ordinary wizard."

"Small praise, in sooth," said the Bard drily. "What became of the mermaid's Comb?"

The Seneschal replied, "It is said that whenever he stroked the sea with it she came to him and taught him many things. The old sea-mage still has the Comb."

"But he could not cure Molly's lameness?" Rohain persisted.

"It takes wondrous power to cure anyone who has been wight-struck."

Rohain's hand strayed to her throat. *How true,* she thought. In sudden fear she glanced at her reflection in the mirror-backed sideboard. The face that met her gaze reassured her. *The past is gone. It need not trouble me anymore.*

Days and nights brightened and darkened the shores of Tamhania. They brought a few alterations in life at Tana. On the strand below, the waves washed back and forth, giving and taking. Translucent to the point of transparency were they, only betraying their existence by shadows on the ribbed sand—shadows of floating foam-flecks, the long undulating shadows of ripples, little darknesses made by the water bending the sunlight, robbing the sand of it, throwing it joyously up in brilliant flashes.

One evening Rohain and Viviana entered the kitchens of the Hall of Tana to find Annie and Molly Chove dancing with the cook, while the spit-boy played the fiddle.

"O strange!" cried Rohain, steadying herself against a corner of the well-scrubbed table. "Molly, how do you caper so well? For I see that you dance better than most, and you limping like a henkie only yesterday! It is beyond all belief!"

"I went mushrooming," said Molly, panting and red-cheeked.

Uncertainly, Rohain said, "So you went mushrooming, and that cured you?"

"Nay, mistress! As I were picking a mushroom for me basket an odd-looking boy sprang up out o' the grass, and would not be prevented from smiting me upon the thigh with a sprig of leaves. After that, the pain went right out of me leg and I could walk straight. Now I does the gallopede!"

"Her seven years is over, you see, mistress," explained Annie, as Molly and the cook hoofed it around the kitchen in another mad frenzy. "Wights always keeps their promises."

A new month came in, bringing the Beldane Festival, symbolized by flowers and baskets of eggs and butter-churns. At the Whiteflower's Day Dance, Molly Chove out-footed them all.

After breakfast one morning, Rohain walked beneath the castle walls amid a crowd of attendants. The sea was apple-juice green. White feathers ran down the spine of the sky and a peculiar greenish tinge stained the northwest horizon. Something intangible about the island began to disturb her. She could not identify it, could not quite label it a *wrongness,* but there was something.

"Jewel-toads are on the move, my lady," said young Caitri, "and the goats on the hillsides seek the caves. Master Avenel says these are signs that a bad storm is on the way."

"Storms frighten me," stated Viviana. Nervously she toyed with a silver thimble attached to the well-furnished chatelaine at her waist.

"I had a dream last night," said Georgiana Griffin, "a strange dream. About that islander."

"What islander?" asked Rohain, feigning ignorance.

"Master Shaw."

"I thought you said he was nothing to you."

"He is. But this dream. I thought I was gathering the

primroses and sea-pinks that grow among the saltbushes on
the slope to the west of the Hanging Cave, when I heard a
singing on the rocks below. I looked down and saw Sevran
Shaw lying asleep on the beach and a fair lady watching beside him. Then he was standing beside me and when he
shook the saltbushes, showers of drops fell with a tinkling
sound and turned as they fell into pure gold, and I caught
sight of the lady floating on the water, far out at sea. I woke
then, but just now as we passed that same flowery slope I
could swear I heard the strange singing coming up from the
rocks, as in the dream."

"I have more than heard it," said a male voice. Sevran
Shaw himself was advancing up the path. "I have seen and
conversed with the singer, the eldritch lady of your dream."
A ripple of amazement ran through the assembly of
courtiers. "Greetings and hail, Lady Rohain, Lady Georgiana, ladies!" Shaw addressed them with a gallant bow, his
plumed hat in his hand.

"Greetings, Master Shaw. You say you have seen a mermaid," Rohain said.

"Aye, my lady, and it has been long between such sightings. The last time a mermaid appeared near the Hanging
Cave was just before the terrible storm in which my father
was lost."

"La!" exclaimed Georgiana. "Take care not to repeat the
mermaid's words, sir, for I have heard that they thrive ill
who carry tales from their world to ours."

Shaw returned, "There is no need for fear on my account, for I am the master of this sea-girl." He recounted
how he had risen before dawn on the previous day—having
not closed his eyes all night, for reasons he would not divulge—and walked to the beach to watch the sun rise
across the skerries beyond Seacliffe Head. He had gone
down to the Hanging Cave, a place renowned for its strange
occurrences. As he stood, he heard a low song coming from

a stack of rocks nearby. Moving toward the sound, he saw the singer, a damsel with long green-gold hair falling over her white shoulders, her face turned toward the cave. He knew without a doubt that although for years he had traveled far on the high seas, he was seeing a mermaid for the first time in his life.

Shaw crept toward the rock shelf on which sat this thrilling incarnation, taking cover all the way, but just as he reached it she turned around. Her song changed to a shriek of terror and she attempted to fling herself into the water, but he seized her in his arms. She strove with amazing strength to drag him into the waves with her, but he held her fast and at last bore her down by brute force. She still struggled but at last lay passive on the rock, and as he looked at her he knew he had never seen anything so wild and lovely in all his life.

"Man, what with me?" she had said in a voice sweet and yet so strange that his blood ran cold at the sound.

"Wishes three," he had replied, aware of the traditional formula.

"What did you wish?" breathed Georgiana.

"I wished that neither myself nor any of my friends should perish by the sea, like my father did. Next, I wished that I should be fortunate in all my undertakings. As for the third wish, that is my own business, and I shall never tell anyone but the mermaid."

No one present failed to guess it.

"And she said?" Georgiana murmured.

" 'Quit and have,' was her reply. I slackened my hold then. Raising her hands, palms together, she dived into the sea."

Georgiana scarcely spoke after the tale was done. As they climbed the hillside, returning to the *chastel,* Shaw offered his arm and she leaned on it.

But a mermaid had been seen, for the first time in twelve years. Every islander knew what that meant.

Soon, the elements would rise. A terrible storm was on the way.

That afternoon, Rohain went down to the village. Over the village marketplace the greenish stain in the northern sky had darkened to heavy bruising, spreading across the sky, ominous and threatening. Gusts swatted the stalls in fits and starts, like a vexed housewife with a broom. Folk hurried to finish their market chores so that they could get home and begin battening down. The word was out: Master Shaw had seen a mermaid.

Spying Elasaid of the Groves and her child among the last of the market crowd, Rohain approached them. Liban had plucked a posy of sea-pinks from crevices in the stone walls, and was making them into a chain.

"Why do you not hurry home?" Rohain asked. "Everyone says a storm is on the way."

Elasaid glanced skyward. "On the way, but not yet here," she said. "Liban has told me it will not arrive before nightfall."

As they stood in conversation, a weird song came down the wind. It seemed to approach, keening, from far out at sea.

"Whatever is that?" exclaimed Rohain.

Elasaid fell silent, but the melody was heard again, from close by, and this time it was Liban who sang. "That song is mine," said the green-eyed scrap of a child with sea-pinks in her hair. "Someone is calling me. The storm will come tonight."

"Wisht Liban!" said Elasaid urgently. "Hush now!" But a rope-faced old woman who had been loitering nearby turned and hurried away. "Alas, that was Minna Scales, and she heard what Liban said," said Elasaid sorrowfully.

"She'll be telling the men, those who fear the sea-morgans. What will happen now, I do not know."

Since Rohain had arrived on Tamhania, shang storms had come with their jinking music like tiny discs of thinly beaten silver shaken in a breeze, and they had gone. But this was the first time a "natural" storm had menaced. And, by all the signs, what a storm it promised to be. It would bring the world's winds teeming, screaming forth in long, lean, scavenging fronts bearing tons of airborne water. Its brew of pressures would build up tension in powerful charges for sudden, white-hot release. And with all the ruthlessness of something mindless.

This storm was fast approaching, over the sea. And Rohain felt—she was certain . . .

. . . something *wicked* was coming with it.

As darkness crept across the island, objects rattled in the Hall of Tana. Gorgeously decorated pomanders, pounce boxes, and vinaigrettes were clustered on a small marquetry table. All exuded conflicting scents. To add to the sensory confusion, a porcelain pastille-burner discharged aromatic fumes through its pierced lid. Someone had absentmindedly placed this jumble of fragrant ornaments on the table—Molly perhaps, hastening about her business, distracted by the storm's approach. There they sat, abandoned, and clattered—enamel clunking against metal, wood on ceramic, ivory on bone.

Late in the evening the gale's first outriders hooted eerily in the chimneys and chivvied at the tiles of the chastel's pointed rooves. Thomas of Ercildoune, Roland Avenel, and the Bard's apprentice Toby played loudly for Rohain and the young Prince and Duchess Alys of Roxburgh, but although their music increased in volume so did the storm's music, until nature obtained precedence. Then they put away trumpet and bagpipes and drums and sat in the main salon hearkening to the rising howl.

In a sudden burst of thunder, the castle shuddered. A gauntlet fell off a suit of armor, startling the company. It was like a challenge from the elements: *Behold, I throw down the glove. Brave me if you dare.*

They knew, then, that the storm had reached the island.

"If I retired to bed I would not sleep, with this cacophony ringing in my ears," said the Bard, his tone over-jolly. "I shall bide here until the tempest abates. Wine, Toby! Have them bring more wine!"

"For my part, presently I shall say good night to all and wend upstairs," said the Duchess, yawning behind her hand. "There is no profit in losing sleep." When next Rohain looked toward her, the Duchess had settled back against the cushions of a brocade couch and fallen into a twitchy doze.

Avenel sat brooding.

Rohain and Prince Edward remained at Ercildoune's side. The Prince toyed with an empty cup, while Rohain stared out at the raging weather. The Bard compensated for the sobriety of his companions by quaffing deeply of his own cup, and calling for his squire to refill it. He was the only loquacious member of the party, loudly regaling them with an assortment of boisterous stories.

The main salon, where they kept company, was beautiful. A multitude of candles illuminated its glory. On the ceiling above the window reveal, stenciled swallows dashed across a painted sky. Bullion-fringed swags of heavy blue velvet in stiff folds festooned the pelmet. The tall windows were divided into smaller panes, each with its own shutter daubed with little pictures of rural idyll.

Through the panes of the embrasure, opalescent and salt-glazed, Rohain and Edward looked out across the village, now in darkness. Its lamplit windows were a scatter of square-cut zircons. Beyond it, the harbor now appeared in-substantial, bathed by the raw murk of night and thunder-wrack. The gloom hid any sign of the Light-Tower standing lonely on the ocean's rim. There, the Lightkeeper would be holding vigil, with only the pigeons for company—their cries as soft as dollops of cream—and the great mirrored Light floating at the top of the Tower in its bath of quick silver.

The storm threw an apoplectic fit. Lightning erratically cast blue-white plaster reliefs of the Light-Tower. For the duration of a thought, it blanched the entire landscape with dazzles so intense they printed specters on the vision of the watchers, against the blackness that smacked down after-ward.

The night was at its thickest and the storm had reached an apogee of violence when a brilliant strobe described something *new* out beyond the narrow gap between the headlands. Rohain seized a spyglass, its bronze casing etched with whorls. She trained its lens on the pale thing that seemed to dance there. After a moment, the cylinder dropped from her nerveless fingers. At her side, Edward deftly retrieved the instrument.

"What is toward?" he asked.

"Oh, I cannot bear it. Something must be done. *The Light must be kindled.*"

The Prince applied the spyglass to his eye.

"A ship!" he muttered wonderingly. "And in trouble, it seems—too close to the reefs. But what ship? The glass will not let me descry their ensigns."

By now the Bard had relinquished his winecup and was squinting through a second spyglass. "Why does the Beacon not shine?" he cried, his voice somewhat slurred. "Surely by now the ship's master must have sent the message-birds." Grim-faced, he flung down the instrument. "But in sooth, what birds could fly in this gale? They would be blown away. And with no Light, that ship shall soon be dashed to pieces."

Roused from his reverie, Roland Avenel leapt up and strode to the window. "This is madness," he said, frowning and peering through the metal tube. "No vessels are due to put in. Where is this ship from? And who is she?"

"It matters little! Lives are about to be lost!" expostulated the Bard. "Surely the Lightkeeper knows that. No doubt he'll have seen this ship. It is unavoidable, for the Tower looks out upon the open sea. He is right close to them there—yet inexplicably he remains idle!"

"Has he a heart of ice?" demanded Rohain, pacing the floor, clasping and unclasping her hands.

"He obeys orders," said Avenel.

"A message must be borne swiftly to him, sir," the Bard said, leaning unsteadily toward the prince. "Your orders to light the flame."

The Prince replied, "When an off-island vessel comes in, a foreigner, the command to kindle the Light must bear the Royal Seal. The signet ring bearing that seal is now far from here."

"Of course—it is upon your father's hand," said Rohain. "But do you not wear a similar ring, Edward?"

"No. There is no other."

"Then," said the Bard, "the Lightkeeper must accept the royal command by word of mouth instead! Zounds, methinks the cries of the drowning sailors are already clamoring in my ears. Is that the sound of men calling from the dim and heinous troughs of ocean swell? We must needs hasten!"

"This is madness!" shouted Avenel.

The Duchess Alys woke in fright. "What's amiss?" she said, hastening to join them at the window.

"Ercildoune would have us kindle the Light, despite that the proper procedure is lacking," said the Seneschal angrily.

In a low voice the Prince said, "Good sir, good Thomas, I say to you the Light must not shine on this fell night. Not without the proper directives."

The Bard stared at him in disbelief. "Do I hear aright?" he said indistinctly. "Is Your Highness willing to let those poor folk perish?"

"It may be some trick."

"Edward, how can you say so?" Rohain trembled, hot with indignation. "It might *not* be a trick. Would you lay that on your conscience? On ours?"

The Prince's face was troubled. "Lady, when the Light shines it opens a gate through a shield of gramarye which covers Tamhania like a dome. While that shield is breached, anything unseelie might penetrate."

The Bard said urgently, "For one brief instant only shall it be opened! As soon as the vessel slips through, the Light shall be quenched. Where is your heart, lad? I entreat you— ride with me to the Light-Tower and give your command. The Lightkeeper shall not gainsay the Empire's heir."

"I will ride beside you!" said Rohain.

"May the Powers preserve me from bee-stings and head-strong wenches," muttered the Bard. He tottered slightly, steadying himself against a marquetry table.

The face of the young Prince was ripped to shreds of an-guish and bewilderment. "Mistress Tarrenys, the weather is too wild for thee," he said, taking Rohain by the hand. "Do you not see? Thomas is deep in his cups tonight. The wine leads his thoughts astray. Like many bards he is a passion-ate man, ruled by his heart; the drink amplifies that ten-dency. Were he sober, he would not argue against me, for he understands the rules of the island very well. Prithee, do not even contemplate going out in the storm."

At fourteen, Edward already matched her height. Level with his, her eyes beseeched him. "Won't you come with me to the Light?" she said.

His visage, pale, dark-eyed against the black brushstroke of his hair, softened. With a shuddering sigh, as though torn in twain, he turned out his hands, palms upward as if in surrender. "I will ride with thee."

"Madness!" fumed Avenel.

"Pray think twice!" Alys urged the young man.

"I have made my decision," replied he, and the Duchess could not gainsay the Crown Prince.

A stony road emerged from the northern end of the village. Hugging the line of the shore, it curved around the sweep of the harbor and along the promontory's spine, ending at Light-Tower Point. Along this road seven riders flew through the fangs of the gale, and slanting spears of rain. The darkness was intense, alleviated only by whips of lightning.

They covered the last lap at a gallop. Pounded by the fists of the ocean, the very ground shook beneath the horses' hooves, and salt spray erupted from the base of the cliff to smite them like a beaded curtain. Only the wall on the seaward side of the road saved them from being flung over the edge. Intermittent flickers of light revealed the ill-timed ship, closer now, foundering on the rocks. Its hull was cracking like a monstrous eggshell. Between blasts of thunder and wind, the riders' ears were assailed by cries of fear and misery as thin as the piping of crickets. The ship, hanged on cruel spurs, slumped sideways, dangling.

"We are too late," Ercildoune roared, but the words were snatched from his mouth even as he shouted them. The foundering vessel gave a great lurch. With a last macabre wave of its ragged sails it began to crumple slowly into the corrugated sea. A wave crashed against the rocks and jetted up in a pillar of spray.

The Light-Tower seemed to hover at the end of the

causeway. Over the archway giving onto its courtyard, runes, weather-stained and eroded, spelled out:

> *Here, the Tower of Power.*
> *Ye Who Wander Yonder*
> *Keep the Light in Sight.*

Tossing their reins to the two squires, the riders burst through the Tower's door in a swirl of drenched cloaks and a clatter of squelching boots. The stairs spiraled up and up. At the top, in a round room, an icicle stood.

The Lightkeeper.

Age had plowed severe furrows into the waxen face. Over heavy robes of overcast gray, a gossamer beard hung to his waist. Moonlight hair flowed halfway down his back, from beneath a broad-brimmed, low-crowned hat. Hollowed out of a face as bleached as parian, the eyes were two glass orbs, limpid, almost colorless. The Lightkeeper was an albino of the kindred calling themselves the Arysk: the Icemen.

He unlidded his eyes, like two silver snuff-boxes.

"Welcome, Your Highness," this unlit candle declared above the tumult, his phonetics clicking in the Rimanian accent, "welcome Lords and Ladies." But it sounded like "Veltcome, Yourk Hightness, veltcome, Lorcds ant ladties."

"The ship," shouted the Prince, pushing past the closed eye of the Light on its pedestal in the room's center. He looked down from the latticed windows, barred with chill iron against the ocean's siege.

"Vun ist vrecket alreatty," said the Keeper. "Aknothert comest."

"You have doomed one ship and now you say a second follows the same path, Master Grullsbodnr?" the Bard bellowed angrily.

It was true. The second vessel was smaller than her sister. Lanterns swung from the rigging. Their glow spilled sporadically on flowing-haired figures wearing long gowns. Their mouths were open. They were screaming.

The Bard swore vehemently.

"There are women aboard!"

"And yet . . ." Edward murmured. His voice trailed away.

"No kmessagte. No copmandt," intoned the Lightkeeper glacially.

"Be wary," cried Alys, "I mislike the look of this. What ensigns does the captain hoist? I see none."

"See how the wind has torn the sails! How might ensigns remain untouched?" Ercildoune returned. "They should be ripped to rags!" He and the Duchess disputed, then, like quarreling rooks, in this high nest on its granite tree, until the Bard bawled, "While we stand in discussion, the second ship is driven upon the rocks. Master Grullsbodnr, kindle the Light at once!"

The aged Iceman shook his head. "Ta Light not sheint vidout ta kmessagte."

"Rohain, I appeal to you!" The Bard drove his fist against the Light's pedestal.

"I am of one mind with you, Thomas. Sir?" Rohain turned to Edward.

"I do not know," the Prince shouted against the din, desperately grappling with indecision. "Grullsbodnr is right, and yet if these mariners are indeed mortal and should perish, the shadow of this grievous misdeed will lie heavy on us forever. They might well have been blown off course . . ."

The Duchess Alys plucked at his coat. "Sir," she said, "our own course must not deviate. The mandate is unambiguous. For generations it has obtained security for the royal island. I rode here to prevent folly if I could. The Light must not be kindled this night."

"And I concur," Avenel declared.

As they spoke, another blistering flare displayed a ghastly scene on the rocks below. The second ship had fetched up on their points at last. She tottered. Amid the churning flood, human forms clung to broken spars. Some were overtaken by long valleys, emerging at the summits of crests, sliding down again through dark walls of hyacinth glass, to reappear no more.

"It is too much to be borne," Rohain exclaimed, "two ships destroyed. We might have saved the last. We must send boats without delay, to aid any that survive in the water."

"No boat would live long out there," Avenel said.

On the second ship, the firefly lanterns had all winked out. Only the nautilus curve of her side now lifted and dropped on the storm's pulse, sinking lower in the water, a mere evanescence of bent wood and ruined canvas, in its death throes no longer a ship, merely a broken thing.

Edward touched Rohain's sleeve. His eyes clouded. "Forgive me."

She nodded acknowledgment, unable to speak.

The fenestrations fretted in the gale, the panes rattling in their metal grooves like prisoners shaking the bars of their cells.

"I am sick," the Bard said. "I am sick to my very marrow that we should stand thusly by and let this happen on the chance that it is some ruse of unseelie. If this vision is a forgery, what of it? Do we not have Lutey the mage who breaks spells, do we not have strong men and hounds to hunt down any mischief that should infiltrate?"

"Your heart governs your head, Ercildoune," warned Alys.

"And were that a more prevalent condition, mortalkind must find itself in better state!" he returned warmly. "Drowned, all drowned, those brave folk, and their corpses to wash up, bloated and staring, along the shores of Tamhania this many a day, a mute reproach, the more terrible in its silence."

The windows clattered. Between the leading and the wands of iron, the diamond panes wept salt tears. The Tower room was cold and dreary. Its freeze seeped through Rohain's sodden clothing and into her sinews. The wind's ululation dropped away somewhat, enabling softer speech, but there was nothing to say.

It was after midnight

"We should depart," said Avenel bleakly.

Rohain stole one last glance through the salt-misted lattices, out across the wild sea.

Then, with an altered mien, she turned away from the view. Seizing a candle out of a branch encrusted with dribbles of congealed wax, she stepped up to the Light in its glass cage atop the pedestal.

"Lightkeeper, open the Light's door," she commanded in a clear voice. "I shall kindle it myself, if you shall not."

Edward, filling her place at the window glanced out. Sharply, he said, "Obey, Master Grullsbodnr."

"The future king has spoken," subjoined the Bard, scowling at the Iceman.

The Lightkeeper unfastened the little door. Rohain reached her hand inside. The buttercup candle entered, met the wick, and inflamed it.

The wick was surrounded by polished mirrors. Stark white radiance stood out from them like a solid bar of frost-quartz. Somewhere, clockwork machinery started up. Spring-and-sildron engines whirred and the Light began to rotate. It sent its steely beam through the lattices, far out into the dread of night, over frothing, coughing reefs and farther until, over the trackless ocean, the bounding main, it stretched itself too thin, becoming nothing.

Rohain had espied a third vessel down there—a lifeboat. Its sail seemed as small as a pocket handkerchief.

It was in the channel now. By the Light of the Tower, in protected waters, it steered true—straight for the gap between the headlands. On board were three shipwreck survivors. The young mother stayed at the tiller while two tiny children clung to each other beside the streak of a mast.

The Bard and the Seneschal ran down the stairs, calling to the squires in the stables to launch the Lightkeeper's *geola,* that they might meet the fragile craft as it entered the harbor.

Past the Tower on its northern headland sailed the boat with its three passengers, beneath the single spoke of the wheel of light. The watchers in the upper room could see them clearly, could see their faces now—the courageous, tragic mother, the darling children standing up and spreading their arms wide for balance. But why had they done so? Why let go of the mast? And their arms had a strange look now—they seemed to be stretching . . . the children were growing.

And she was growing too, and changing, the one who no longer held the tiller, who could not hold anything anymore because it had no hands, only terrible wings like two charred fans of night. The two creatures by the mast extended their black pinions. The darkness was pierced by three pairs of incandescent coals—red fires burning holes in beaked skulls. One by one they rose, retracting spurred tridents of talons. The beaks opened.

"Baav!" cawed the first. "Macha!"

"Neman!" croaked the second.

Effortlessly on those outsized kites of wings, slashing the air with slow, powerful downstrokes, the three abominations, crow-things out of a nightmare, flapped away over the lightless harbor. Out of the Light's reach they fled—

shadows winging toward Tamhania's highest point, the mountain's summit.

"Morrigu!" quoth the final corvus in a creaking voice, like the closing of a coffin-lid.

Then the moon came flying in terror from behind the clouds. Her light gleamed down. And there on the opposite headland, on Southern Point just across the Rip from the Light-Tower, was a child. It was Liban, the adopted daughter of Elasaid. She ran, spirited and free, like the ocean. The fear that the Crows had brought was not on her; she was not of mortalkind. Her own pale tresses flew in the storm wind as she ran along the path to the sea, laughing. A handful of men chased after her but they couldn't overtake her, and the last man ran with a crooked gait. That strange sea-song came again, and the waves thundered against the rocks. The men halted in fear, staying where they were up on the cart-track.

The watchers in the Light-Tower heard Liban singing as she ran out along the reef, and then a mighty wave smashed against the reef and reared up. It washed over her, and she was gone.

In fitted bursts of moonlight the tempest subsided, rolling away to the southeast. The wind eased. Utter stillness commenced. Fog snakes came coiling out of the sea-harbor and all along the weed-dashed beaches. Although the hour was well before cock-crow, the villagers were astir in the streets. Lanterns passed to and fro in the dark. Much was amiss. The rough weather had wrought severe damage.

Furthermore, it had been discovered in the village that under cover of the storm, John Scales and his wife had incited some of the more superstitious islanders to form a lynch mob and go after the fey girl sheltered by Elasaid of the Groves. Hearing that trouble was afoot, the mayor had taken charge. He mustered certain law-abiding men who were now riding with him to the road from Southern Point, in order to confront Scales's mob as they returned.

A few islanders—mainly those who were known to have a tendency to be fanciful—claimed to have seen three dark shapes flying from the headlands. They said they were like great birds, traveling in a barbed formation like an arrow-head, and they had ascended toward the mountain peak hanging in the sky. But with more pressing matters to attend to, of the alleged Crows little note was taken.

Seven riders hastened back along the crescent road to the village. They drew rein in the marketplace. Overhead, cloud-tendrils unraveled before the face of the bald moon. Frigid radiance bathed the Old Village Square.

"I must find Elasaid," said Rohain dully. "She will be here, in the village."

Her horse was restless, as if sensing her unease. The cold that weighed her limbs like iron chains was generated more by horror than by her soaked raiment. It was a clammy dread that drained her vitality and painted with a lavender hue her nails and lips. She could think of nothing but the appalling Crows, and the child taken by the wave, Elasaid's loss.

"'Tis folly to remain here," remonstrated the Duchess Alys, quietening her own steed with an expert hand. "I urge you to return with me to hall and hearth."

"I will not be dissuaded."

A man ran up to the party of riders.

"My lords, my ladies," he said, "the mayor's wife bids ye come to his house, if ye will, and be warmed at his fire, and take a sup." He bowed.

Suddenly Elasaid was standing at Rohain's stirrup. Her eyes were dark.

"Have you seen Liban, my lady?" she asked. Her tone was flat, without hope.

"Elasaid," said Rohain, dismounting, "the child is gone back to the sea. Come with us to the house of the mayor. There we will talk."

At the home of the village's chieftain, servants brought wine for the guests. A cherry fire burgeoned amid a heap of driftwood, but Rohain was unable to thaw. She had become as one of the Arysk—a glazed and brittle shard, numb to feeling. When she closed her eyes, three ghastly birds flapped across the linings of her lids.

Edward described to Elasaid the entire story as it had been seen from the Light-Tower.

"We heard Liban singing as she ran out along the rocks," he ended, "and then a great wave came surging up and swept her away. We saw her no more."

After a time, Elasaid murmured, "Another child of mine is gone." She seemed like one who has been struck blind. "But I thank you for bearing these tidings," she went on doggedly. "I do not grieve for her sake—perhaps somewhat for myself, but self-pity bears no merit. She has returned to her own kind as I always knew she would. She was never my child. Liban has been reclaimed, as is fitting, just as Rona Wade returned to her people not long ago. Those two were not born for the land. Yet I never kept Liban here against her will—she was always free to leave. When it was time, they called her, and it was the song, not any act of credulous, craven mortals; it was the song that brought her to the waves."

"Those who harried her shall pay the price," vowed Thomas of Ercildoune, striking his hand against his thigh.

"What of the blackbirds, the outsized hoodie crows?" asked the Prince. "Had the child aught to do with them?"

"No sir," replied Elasaid. "Of this I am certain. Such

creatures are not associated with the sea-morgans—not with any of the merfolk. "

"Do you know their portent?"

"I saw them, the strange birds flying toward the mountain, but I know not from whence these fell things came, or what is their purpose. I know not what they fortoken, but I fear no good will come of this night."

The cherry fire glowed. Somewhere, a cock crowed. *Uhta* waned—the sun's edge ran a line of tinsel along a diaphanous horizon.

In pain, Rohain said, "Elasaid Trenowyn, I understand now why I thought your face was familiar to me. On a glass mountain in Rimany a girl with your face opens a lock with her finger, to free seven enchanted rooks. And in the valley they call Rosedale in Eldaraigne, a fine man waits for you and grieves, as he has waited and grieved this many a year. Do not let him wait much longer."

Elasaid Trenowyn trembled. A spark jumped in her eyes. She picked up her shawl and gave Rohain a wide-eyed look, as though she had never before set eyes on her.

"I hear you."

Saying nothing more, she left the house and went down to the harbor.

No wreckage from drowned ships, no barrels, planks, spars, or corpses washed up on Tavaal's shores. This proved it—eldritch vessels they had indeed been, all three. What mortal understood the workings of such simulacra? Perhaps they had repaired themselves as they sank. Perhaps they were sailing now, deep down among the benthos, phosphorescent lanterns swinging on the rigging to light up the abysmal darkness.

Today the swell rolled long and slow and blank, as if it had grown as heavy as lead, whose sad color it reflected. On the beach, the skeleton of a whale lay as it had lain for years—a behemoth beached a decade earlier. The ribs curved skyward, sand-blasted, wind-scoured. Now the skeleton was a framework of great upturned vaults, a vacant hull, a giant cage of ribs that once housed a heart the size of a horse.

It could be seen from the house of the sea-wizard. Lutey's abode perched like a rickety gull's nest on a low cliff overlooking the village and the harbor. Gulls, in fact, went in and out at the windows like accustomed visitors. They spoke with harsh voices at odds with their lines of loveliness, and when the party of riders arrived, loud was their announcement.

Silhouetted against a souring sky, the company of noble visitors and their retainers waited on horseback. Presently the head of Lutey the Gifted appeared between cliff and sea. He came clambering up over the edge, his robes and hair and plaited beard-ends streaming up over his head, blown by vertical drafts. From a pocket in his clothing peeped a fantastically fashioned Comb of pearls and gold.

The riders dismounted and the mage led them to his house. Bowing, he held open the door. As they entered, the structure trembled like a bird's nest in the wind. From somewhere not far off resounded a deep sound as of drums rolling.

The interior smelled of stale seaweed, yet for all its clutter and avian traffic it was surprisingly clean and orderly. Dried seaweeds—pink, rust, cream, and copper—hung from the rafters. A delicate clepsydra dripped by the window. Beside it lay a brass sextant and a folding pocket-spyglass decorated with lacquer, inscribed with the maker's name: *Stodgebeck of Porthery.*

Shelves held nekton memorabilia. The only two chairs had been carved out of coral broken from the reefs by storms. The bed was a giant clamshell, the table a salvaged captain's table inlaid with nacre and scored by daggers. It was set with sea-urchin candleholders, scallop-shell plates, mussel-shell spoons, and dark amber-green dishes formed from lacquered bull-kelp—a material light and strong, malleable when fresh yet as hard and impermeable as vitreous when dry. Here in Lutey's house were many things of saltwater origin that, like the sea-wind forced by the cliff to alter direction, had suffered a land change.

Like some barnacled, weed-grown sea-creature he seemed, this wizard. His skin was as translucent as a jellyfish, his eyes the windows of an ancient coelacanth. Strung about his throat, a necklace of shark's teeth: scimitars of dentine.

"A force unseelie, a force powerful, has broached our defenses," said the coelacanth, putting a brass astrolabe aside to make a space on the table. "I saw them last night. My strength is not great enough to challenge such foes. I know not where they have gone now, the three dark birds, or what will happen. But ye, Princess, should not bear the guilt of it." He mixed a blue-green potion that he gave to Rohain in a chipped porcelain caudle-cup shaped like an octopus. It burned away the cold dread that had filled her veins with ice since the moment the unseelie entities from the sea had shifted back to their true bird-shapes, and she had at last understood what she had wrought.

"I have Combed the sea," said the sea-mage, "but for the first time in my experience there is no reply." His face was grim. "What became of the masted lifeboat—the vessel that bore the invaders?"

"It spun around three times," the Prince replied, "and then sank, straight down, like a stone."

An echoing boom rolled up all around, and the shelves racketed.

"Be not unduly alarmed," said Lutey, observing the discomfiture of his guests. "It is only the voice of the sea. Alack, that I do not possess its power."

"It sounds from near," said the Prince.

"It is near, sir," said the mage, pulling up a trapdoor set into the floor. Beneath their feet, a great cavern opened out and fell away. Far below, perhaps a hundred feet down in the half-light, a dark swell traveled rapidly toward the inner wall of rock on the last few yards of its journey from the outer ocean.

"The sea-cave undercuts this cliff," explained Lutey as the wave smashed into the wall and another hollow roar shook his house. "It is the same sea-cave where Urchen Conch found a chest of antique gold so many years ago, according to local legend—which I doubt not. Here is a ladder. Sometimes I climb down. I have found no gold there," he added.

He closed the hatch. A gull alighted on his shoulder and wheeled its fierce yellow eye.

"Again I shall Comb the sea this day," said Lutey. "Leave a messenger with me, and I will send word of any tidings."

"What else is to be done?" Avenel asked

"There is naught to be done but watch and wait. Watch and wait, warily and wisely."

Since the night of the storm, those who dwelt in the Hall of Tana, and some who dwelt in the village, would frequently turn their eyes up toward the roof of the island, hidden in white cloud—that remote peak whence the winged creatures of unseelie had vanished. But there was no sign of anything untoward. The peak seemed to float and dream as always; serene, untroubled. No flocks of ravening hoodie crows came swooping like a black rain, talons extended and toothed beaks gaping, to rip the rooftiles off the village houses and devour the inhabitants. As days passed and all appeared unchanged, the people ceased to raise their heads as often. But always the crown of the mountain overhung them, lost in its steamy wreath.

The Seneschal led a band of riders on eotaurs up to the summit. But the roiling vapors were as obdurate as a wall and the sildron-lifted Skyhorses would not, could not enter that blindfold haze. In such a murk, all orientation could easily be lost. Not knowing up from down, horse and rider might fall out of the sky.

One night as she dozed, it seemed to Rohain that she was still in the sea-mage's house, with the waves booming in the sea-cave underneath, slamming against the foundations.

She awoke.

A kind of fine trembling seemed to pass through the canopied bed. The lamps hanging on chains from the ceiling shivered slightly.

A ship came from the mainland. When it sailed away, Elasaid was aboard. The vessel had brought letters, including a hastily written one for Rohain, in Thorn's beautiful, embellished script that was more like an intertwining of leafy vines than characters. This she deciphered by herself. There were tidings of the business of war, and a brief but forceful line, *I think of thee,* the more earnest in its austerity.

News from the war zone was grim—unseelie forces assailed the Royal Legions and the Dainnan by night while Namarran bands harried them by day. The central stronghold of the subversives, hidden somewhere in the Namarran wastelands, could not be found. It was from there that orders were being issued. It was believed that if this fortress could be discovered and scourged of its wizardly leaders, the uprising might be quelled.

"A letter from my mother," said Caitri, waving a leaf of paper. "It seems Isse Tower now harbors a bruney, or a bauchan. It pinches the careless servants and also the masters who beat them. It works hard but Trenchwhistle, now black and blue, is trying to get rid of it, laying out gifts of clothing and so on. It ignores the gifts and won't leave. My mother says the Tower is a better place for it."

Perusing her missives from Court, Viviana let out a scandalized scream.

"*Kiel varletto!* One of the palace footmen has run away with the sixth granddaughter of the Marquess of Early!"

For days, she would not cease talking about the elopement.

Late on an evening, as she lay abed waiting for sleep, Rohain again thought that a vibration came through the floor. It was as if a heavy wagon had passed the Hall of Tana, loaded with boulders—but when she looked from the window, the road beyond the wall was empty.

The apples of Elasaid's abandoned orchards flourished and ripened. The island's gold-hazed humidity seemed lately to be tinged with a slight smell of rotting—imparted perhaps by the cloud-vapors, or by the seaweed cast up by the waves to wither on the shores, or maybe by the *duilleag neoil* itself. As time passed, one became accustomed to the odor and did not notice it at all.

The weather was unusually warm for early Spring, the sea as temperate as bathwater. Rejoicing at this, the village children dived and swam, especially the children of Ursilla and of Rona Wade. Lutey's warning, "wait and watch," had lost its urgency. The people of Tamhania had waited and watched, but nothing had happened. A little, their vigilance relaxed. But if their masters were carefree, the tamed beasts of the island were not. They had grown restless, uneasy. To human eyes all seemed peaceful, all seemed well. Yet beneath this veneer, expectancy thrummed like an overstretched harp-string, drawn taut across land and sea.

On an overcast day, Rohain stood in Tana's library with Roland Avenel. As they conversed, there began a shaking as if an army of armored war-horses charged around the hill, pulling mangonels and other engines of destruction on iron wheels. Ornaments and girandoles rattled. The walls creaked. An ormulu perfume burner toppled from its stand and one book fell out of the shelves. From the coach-house came the noise of the carriages rocking on their springs.

"Mayhap the island floats again!" exclaimed the Seneschal, shaking his gray head in astonishment. "Or it is making ready to do so! Mayhap it has grown weary of this location and has pulled up its ancient sea-anchors or cut them adrift, in order to seek another home."

Tamhania was moving again—at least, that is what they were saying in the village, where the doors and windows of the houses jammed tight in warped frames. And the rainy month of Uiskamis rolled on. On the high spit jutting into the Rip, the grizzled granite Light-Tower seemed to lean into the webs of salt spray, its eye looking far over the silken plain as if it could see past the horizon. At its feet, jagged hunks of rock gripped the uncertain border between land and sea like the Tower's roots, seeming to draw sustenance from both. Perhaps the roots did not go down far enough to fix the island in place.

A minor unstorm went over without much ado. The Scales family and their cohorts stood trial in the village hall. They were fined heavily for their cruel and lawless behavior, after which they became close companions of the stocks in the village square for a couple of days, where, not to waste them, any apples that had rotted in the high humidity were utilized by some of the village lads for target practice. The general opinion was that the sentence had been too lenient.

Meanwhile, Georgiana Griffin began trysting with Master Sevran Shaw.

Rohain went on with her lessons—the study of music and writing, and the warrior's skills. All the while she probed the thin shell enveloping her lost memories. There was that about this place that disquieted her—had disquieted her from the first, even before the coming of the unseelie hoodie crows. Was the island indeed uprooting itself, to float away? If so, where would it go?

Listlessness overlaid all. Along the shores, layers of water came up with a long *swish* as if some sea-lord in metallic robes rushed past in the shallows. Apart from the cry of the wind, that was the only sound. The terns, the sandpipers, gulls, shearwaters, egrets, and curlews seemed to have vanished.

About a week after Whiteflower's Day, Rohain and her companions sat at dinner in the Hall of Tana. Not one diner spoke or lifted a knife. The hounds stood with hackles raised into ridges all along their spines, their lips peeled back off their curved teeth—but it was no intruder they snarled at, only the doors. These moved gently as if guided by an invisible hand. Presently, they began to open and close by themselves. From out in the stables came the hammering of hooves kicking at stalls. On the dinner-table, wine slopped out of the goblets. Salt cellars shuddered, jumped about, and fell over. Above the heads of the diners, high in the bell-tower, the bells shivered, unseen, as if their cold metal sides had caught some ague. The clappers rocked but failed to kiss the inner petals of the bronze tulips. They did not ring. Not yet.

The maid Annie rushed in, incoherent, shouting something about Vinegar Tom. Starting up from his seat and drawing his sword, the Seneschal ran outside in case she was in danger from pursuit. He saw no creature, eldritch or otherwise. When they had soothed the girl she told them *not* what they had thought to hear, that Vinegar Tom had chased or harmed someone. Instead she said that Vinegar Tom was gone.

That which had guarded the path for centuries had deserted its post. And now it came out that the colt-pixie had not been seen for some time either, or the domestic wights of Tana, or the silkies, or any others of seelie ilk.

"Is it possible the wights have left Tamhania?" Alys of Roxburgh asked.

No one could answer her.

Over the ocean, thunder rumbled. Horses screamed and goblets toppled, spilling their blood-red wine across the linen battle-plain of Tana's dinner-table.

"These quakes . . ." said the Duchess. She did not finish her sentence.

"Should we not leave here?" Rohain said. "I fear danger walks the isle."

"I, too, am troubled," nodded the Bard.

"Yet it is his Imperial Majesty's command that we remain," murmured Alys. "A good soldier never disobeys orders. Neither should we."

"'Tis the sea," said the Seneschal overheartily. "'Tis choppy these days. If indeed it floats, the island moves roughly over the waves. We're in for another storm, by the sound of it."

The words fell from his lips like empty husks, and he knew it.

They sat silent again. Still, no one raised a knife. The salt cellar rolled lazily across the table, leaving a silver trail; an arc, a slice of moon, a fragmented sickle.

No mermaid's cry gave warning of what happened next.

Thunder's iron barrel rolled across the firmament, *but there were no thunderclouds*. The seas lurched. Even the warm waters of the sheltered harbor rose in a brisk, pointy dance, but there was no storm—not in the way storms are usually known. For days this went on, and then the ground picked itself up and shook out its mantle. Many villagers rushed outdoors in fright. It became impossible to walk steadily. Windows and dishes broke. At the Hall of Tana, paintings fell from the walls, and in the stables the small bells rang on the bridles hanging from their hooks.

They jingled, those little bells, and then fell silent as the ground stood still again. Next morning, dawn did not come. Beyond its normal bounds, night stretched out like a long black animal.

"Look at the cloud!" cried Viviana, pointing.

The white wreath that continually lurked upon the mountaintop had now darkened to a wrathful gray. It had grown taller, becoming a column. From the top it forked, like the spreading branches of a gigantic, malevolent tree, billowing, blocking sunlight. Beneath its shadow, the mountainsides sloped as green and lush as always, but particles of sand and dirt moved in the tenebrous air, and flecks like black rain or feathers floated—tiny pieces of ash. This dirty wind irritated the eyes, made breathing difficult. The smell of rottenness had increased a hundredfold, and a stink of putrid cabbage invaded everything. To keep out the dust and stench, the islanders wedged shut their doors and windows. They masked their faces.

"Make ready the sea-vessels," said the Bard. "Tell the villagers to prepare to leave."

But Avenel said, "This is the Royal Isle! Naught can harm us here. Besides, most of the villagers refuse to even consider abandoning their homes."

The peculiar storm amplified. Lightning flickered, phosphorescent green, but only within the massive pillar that stood up from the mountain, supporting the sky's congestion. On the island, wells dried up. New ones opened. Streams altered their courses as tremors shook the island to its most profound footings. In the village, the mayor called a meeting.

Thorn had told Rohain: *"Do not leave the island. Wait for me."*

She must do as he had bidden. Yet no longer was Tamhania the safe haven it had been when he had spoken those words. Rohain's own hand had lit the candle in the Light-Tower, opening the island to the bringers of doom—just as, somehow, she had also led death and destruction to Isse Tower.

And once he had asked, *"Why should Huon hunt at thy heels?"*

The question confounded her, haunted her. Recent events once again brought it to the forefront.

The real facts must be confronted. No matter how she tried to deny it, *something* sought her. Now that she was willing to face the truth, it blazed like words written in fire. It seemed incredible she could have overlooked anything so obvious. *Never* had Scalzo's scoundrels sought her, *never* had Korguth's mercenaries plagued her. All the time there had been one enemy—one *other* enemy with unseelie forces under its sway—an enemy far more terrible than any small-time brigand or charlatan of a wizard.

In Gilvaris Tarv, on the day she had saved the seelie waterhorse from enslavement in the marketplace, she had seen a face. Memory now recalled that face in detail. Curious, it had been. In fact, "eldritch" was the word that most described it, and "malevolent." Some unseelie thing in the marketplace had spied her at the very instant her taltry fell back, revealing her extraordinary sun-colored hair. By her hair, perhaps, the creature had recognized her. Perhaps it had known who she had been in her shadowed past. Perhaps, in that past, she had been hunted—but the hunters were thrown off her trail when she lost her face and her voice. Likely, the creature had gone from the marketplace and told of her whereabouts to her true enemy, the Antlered One. It had been after the market-day that suspicious-looking creatures had begun to watch Ethlinn's house. In a stroke of what turned out to be fortune, Rohain had been mistakenly abducted with Muirne. For a time, while they were incarcerated in the *gilf*-house, her whereabouts had passed out of Huon's knowledge.

Rohain pondered on subsequent events. Had the Antlered One got wind of her as she rode with the wagons along the Road to Caermelor? Had he sent the Dando Dogs after the caravan, resulting in the loss of so many lives?

She had eluded him, only to end up at Court where her Talith ancestry was unmasked by Dianella and Sargoth. The wizard had betrayed her to some unseelie minion of the Antlered One, himself not knowing the full extent of what he did, merely wanting her out of the way so that Dianella's path to the throne would be clear. Doubtless, Sargoth had long been allied with the powers of wickedness. He might have known Huon sought for a Talith damsel, and waited until she was out of Caermelor to betray her.

When Sargoth's tidings reached the Hunter, Isse Tower was attacked. Once again Rohain escaped, but now that she had regained both face and voice, Huon knew her. For whatever reason, he had traced her to the haven of Tamhania and knocked on the door. She, in her folly, had opened it and let his foul creatures enter. Why he hunted at her heels, she had forgotten. *He* had not.

"Let us speak no more of the past." Close at her side, Thorn had said these words, while he leaned against a narrow embrasure of Isse Tower and talked with Rohain about Winter, and a hawk had hung suspended in the chalice of the sky.

Those effervescent days had been filled with joyousness. Consequently she, not to spoil it, had not spoken to Thorn of the past, nor told him that it could not be recalled. She had not let him know that in her history there might lie some important, hidden truth.

If he was struck down upon the northern battlefields, he would never know. Swiftly she brushed the thought aside; merely the thought of such loss was like a death-wound to her spirit. But if he triumphed in war, how could she ever return to his side, bringing, as she did, this bane, this curse that shadowed her and touched all those among whom she moved? Thorn was a warrior of extraordinary prowess who had proven his efficacy even against the Wild Hunt, but how long could any mortal man stave off such mighty foes? He and his forces could drive them off once or twice, maybe, but ultimately the immortals, with their unseelie gramarye, must win. This was a peril she would not allow herself to bring upon him.

Thorn—will I ever see thee again? Before I do, I must find out what lies hidden in my past. I must discover why Huon pursues me, so that I, and you, my love, will know how to deal with this peril.

Iron bells clanged inside Rohain's skull.

For three days the sun had not been seen. Under darkness, the air was smothering—a blanket stinking of brimstone. The island held still, or perhaps it gathered itself together one last time. And those who dwelled upon its flanks were still blind to its nature, deaf to its peril. Or perhaps they did not want to see or hear, for the probabilities were too mighty, too awful to comprehend. It is a human trait, to dwell in danger zones and be astonished when catastrophe strikes.

Then the land stirred again.

In Tana's oak-paneled west drawing room, Rohain sat playing at card games with Edward, Alys, and Thomas of Ercildoune, to escape the grit and stench of the outdoors.

On the window-seat beneath wine-hued velvet hangings, Toby plucked a small ivory lute. His fingernails clicked against the frets. Occasionally, distant laughter and squeals drifted in from the nursery, where the children of the Duchess played hide-and-seek.

A butler glided in carrying a tray in his white-gloved hands. He was followed by a replica bearing a similar tray. Placing their burdens on two of a scattering of small, unstable tables, they proceeded to decant hot spike into small porcelain cups. They poured milk from the mouth of a painted jug fashioned as a cow (which had somehow escaped the eye of Tana's majordomo in his thematic pursuit), and offered cherry tarts and cubes of golden Sugar frosted with tiny pictures of sea-pinks.

Candles blazed in lusters and branches—yellow-white shells of light in the gloom. They lit up gilded chairs and tables, couches, silk-upholstered footrests, ottomans with their embroidered bolsters, polished cherrywood cabinets and toy clockwork confections. Roses gushed from porphyry vases.

"Annie saw those flowers today," commented Alys, taking note of the roses, "and was horrified. She said that the blossoming of the burnet rose out of its proper season is an omen of shipwreck and disaster. These small islands breed such superstition."

"Speaking of local vegetation," said the Bard, "I was talking to some coral-fishers the other day. There are some on this island who hold that the surrounding mists are not accumulated, attracted, or given off by cloud-leaf. They hold that *duilleag neoil* has nothing to do with them. The waters around Tamhania are always warm. They say the vapors rise because of"—he picked up a card—"a tremendous heat that burns forever beneath the deeps."

Toby dropped his ox-horn plectrum, then stooped to retrieve it. In the silence, the clockworkings on the mantels clucked like slow insects. Toby resumed playing.

"Did anyone hear anything last night?" asked the Duchess of Roxburgh, leaning forward to put down the Ten of Wands.

"No. I slept well," replied Edward.

"I heard nothing," said the Bard, considering his fan of cards thoughtfully. "But the servants seemed uneasy."

Rohain upturned the Queen of Swords on the tablecloth of turquoise baize.

"I thought," she said, "I dreamed the sound of uncontrollable sobbing."

The Duchess's cards slipped through her fingers to the floor. A footman ran to pick them up.

"Shall we abandon the game at this point?" suggested Edward, folding his rising sun of painted cardboard leaves and tapping them on the table. "And take a cup of best Severnesse spike?"

"An eminently practical idea," replied the Bard diplomatically, stroking his *pique-devant* beard and auburn mustaches. "Who can think of playing cards on a day like this?"

"'Tis a pretty pack." Rohain examined the interlocking swan design on the back of each rectangular wafer. It called to her mind the tale of a swanmaiden stolen by a mortal man, and she was about to remark on this when a tremendous vibration went through the floor and walls, and a deep groan of agony emanated from all around. Almost simultaneously, a further commotion arose from the floors below.

"What is it? What's amiss?" The Prince started from his chair. A tremendous clamor and clatter rushed up the stairway.

Footmen hurried to the door, but as they opened it a horseman rode through in a sudden gale, ducking his head under the high lintel. He wheeled to a halt before them. The stallion reared and curvetted, shrilling, its hooves slicing the carpets. The iron-shod forehooves struck a glancing blow off an ebony table, which flew across the room, its setting of porcelainware and sweetmeats dashing to pieces. Foam flicked from the beast's snorting mouth, showering the crystal vases. In the dark, gusting wind, the curtains of magenta velvet bellied out. The playing cards, all six suits—Wands, Swords, Cups, Coins, Anchors, and Crowns—flew up like frightened seagulls.

"Master Avenel!" cried Edward. He and his companions stared in disbelief.

"Haste, make haste," cried the Seneschal of Tana, controlling his mount with difficulty. "I have just come from the house of Lutey. The island is about to be destroyed."

When the denouement came, it came rapidly. At the Hall of Tana, furniture collapsed. Plaster cracked, loose bricks fell. The belltower shook, from its foundations upward. At last, up in the murky vapors of their eyrie, all by themselves, their ropes dangling untended by any hand, the great bells of Tana's *chastel* began to toll.

Hot and jarred, the sea chopped and changed without rhythm. Up and down the hillsides the fences undulated like serpents. Cracks unseamed their mouths; sand and mud bubbled out. It was almost impossible for anyone to remain on their feet. People stumbled and rolled, clawing at previously fixed objects that proved treacherous. Apple boughs crashed to the ground. Animals ran to and fro in confusion. Amid the black snow, tiny porous stones hailed down, too hot to touch.

Fishing-boats—the entire fleet—made ready to launch.

The false night was so dense now that it was impossible to discern even an outline of the mountain. Where its top should have loomed, there burned a red glare. Over this spurious sunrise strange lightnings snapped continually in an endless display. It looked like a wicker cage of eerie lightworks forming the death-blue, pumping veins of the smoke-tree whose black leaves continued to pour over the nightscape.

The islanders pushed open their doors with difficulty because of the detritus piled up outside. Down from the village to the harbor they fled with their goats, their hounds and horses, their cattle and sheep. Some folk wept; not many—this was a hardy people. Their strings of lamps, like blobs of grazed yellow resin, could hardly be made out in the gloom. Deep drifts of ash and pumice blocked the streets. Larger stones rattled down, causing hurt; a rain of pain. The darkness was so profound, so unnatural, that it was not like night at all. It was a windowless, doorless chamber. Only the tower of coldly flickering lightnings over the mountain could be clearly seen. Generated by tiny fragments of lava in the ash cloud rubbing against each other to build up enormous charges that tore in thundering bolts through the column, it rose to an unguessed ceiling.

The refugees boarded the boats, stepping from the land they knew in their hearts they would never see again. Great waves leapt up as tall as houses and smacked into one another. Through the chaos, the boats bravely put out into the ashen harbor. They sailed across to the Rip and through it, while smoke roiled on the water and fire boiled in the sky. Now blackened by poisonous effluvium, the brass bells of Tana rang out a lonely farewell from the swaying belfry. As the fleet passed the point, a mild glow as of candlelight exuded from the upper room of the Light-Tower.

"The Lightkeeper!" exclaimed Rohain, in the leading ship. "He is still within!"

"He refused to leave," said Avenel, at her side.

Already, while the fleet yet rode out of the harbor, the land woke again and shuddered. As if in answer, the Light beamed forth for the last time, pure and white like a Faêran sword cleaving the murk. Then the mountain roared violently, the scarlet glow flared brightly, and a huge wave opened from the shore, almost swamping the ships, bearing them forward. Bombs of burning rock fell hissing into the sea on all sides. Some went through the rigging and landed, red-hot, on the decks, threatening to set the ships alight before the wary crews scooped them in shovels and tossed them overboard. As the last ship passed through the Rip the island writhed. The Light-Tower itself leaned a little, then, very slowly, as if resisting, it collapsed into the sea. All the way down, the Beacon lanced out courageously, a descending white blade, extinguished only when the waves closed over it.

In a shower of darkness and cinders, the vessels plowed across the deep.

Whether they would escape with their lives or not, none could say.

Behind them, the sea-volcano that was Tamhania had become wildly unstable. Some delicate inner balance had been meddled with. Once it had slept. Now it awakened. A heat so great it was almost inconceivable, hotter than the hottest furnace; a heat that had been lying in wait for more than a millennium at the base of a fracture beneath the island, miles under the sea, now was mobilized. Raising a mindless head, it set its huge shoulders—sinewed with magma, veined with fire—against the scabbed-over crust of soil, to split the lid that held it barely in check. The sea-bed struggled. Deep within the mountain, under tremendous pressure, molten rock welled up through fissures. At temperatures of thousands of degrees, it began to form a dangerous mixture with the volatiles in seawater: venomous fumes to rise like serpents out of vents, stinking sulfurs to belch from fumaroles, asphyxiating exhalations to flow invisibly downhill and gather in hollows, acid vapors to slowly eat through whatever they touched, and strong enough to etch glass, fiery ethers to glow in great veils against the sky, explosive gases to burst open the heart of the volcano with a thunderclap.

Like a chimney catching fire, the central vent began to roar. With each new explosion, blocks the size of palaces hurtled up to the surface, ripped from the throat of the vomiting cone. The air filled with flying rocks. Long streaks of flame arched into the air every few moments. Above the vent a cloud boiled out, convoluted like a brain, its cortex twenty thousand feet above sea level.

A downpour of rain mixed with ash fell on the fishing boats. Some substance in this mud glowed in the dark, and soon the masts and decks looked as if they were covered with myriad tiny embers. Behind the fleet, the steady roar of the dying mountain-island continued, as the boats sailed on through the night—or was it the day? Missiles screamed like unseelie avengers and howled like frights. A subsonic pounding was going on, as though giants worked at their subterranean forges, their hammer blows *thud-thudding* relentlessly on huge anvils, echoing in caverns where nightmarish bellows pulsed, blaring gouts of smoke up through the chimney. Against the blackness of night, roseate fire-curtains gleamed, speckled with gold. Far away on the slopes of tormented Tamhania, jeweled rocks went spitting, spinning over ash wastes where tall fumes leaned now instead of trees. In the harbor, seawater vaporized like immense billows of smoke. Heavy, deadly gases hugged the contours of the mountainsides, streaming down in rivers. Water floated like smoke, gas flowed as if it were liquid.

But the pressure from miles below did not decrease. Tamhania fought, opening new smoking fissures in its flanks, letting the crimson paste ooze out in languid rivers to incinerate and slowly crush the houses of the village. The island bellowed as it threw its guts into the air.

*   *   *

Hours passed. The fleet now sailed under true night, although all celestial lights were extinguished by the tons of ash and fine debris spreading across the upper skies of Erith. The luminous mud scintillated along the boats' rigging. Tamhania was the light of the plenum: a fire-fountain, its noise circling the rim of the world like an iron wheel rolling around a bowl. Floating rocks—porous, gas-filled chunks of pumice like hard, black sponge—made the water hazardous. Infinitesimal specks of ash mixed with spray plastered the faces, clothes, beards, and hair of the refugees. The mixture stung their eyes and curdled to slippery scum on the decks.

As ring-shaped waves rush away from a stone dropped into a pond of still water, so the ocean reacted to the dreadful murmur of the island. The escaping fleet was rocked by ever-larger swells: long copings dividing extreme abysms. As morning was finally reborn, the sun rose dripping out of the sea like a corrupt gem fastened to the sky's filthy cloak. Those who stood on deck looking back, clutching the railings, saw a brilliant burst of light. Soon, over the continual roaring, the sound of a truly enormous explosion came bounding and crashing across the wavetops. It hit the boats with force and passed away to the horizon. The vessels dipped and lurched, but they held together. The passengers did not rejoice. They knew what would follow. Sound travels faster than ripples in water. Heedless of modesty, all the passengers doffed their footwear and outer clothes in case they should be thrown into the water. Many could not swim.

Viviana pinned her locket-brooch to her chemise, and belted on her chatelaine. "When I come ashore," she declared bravely, "I want to have useful articles about me."

The sun climbed higher. In the middle of the morning, a second massive explosion shook the entire region as the side of the volcano's central vent was blown off, engendering spectacular outbursts of tephra and huge clouds of steam. Its reverberation smote the vessels with an open hand.

"Make ready," the word passed from vessel to vessel: "The first wave comes."

The crew raced to douse most of the sails, leaving a stay-sail for steering. As they did so, two helmsmen struggled at the wheel to turn the ship until her bowsprit pointed in the direction of the island, far-off and invisible in a smoky haze wandering ghostlike across the sea. The sailors held the rudder steady, keeping the ship's bow pointed into the volcanic storm.

They saw it, before they heard it—a darkness partitioning the sky.

A wall.

A long, long wall with no end and no beginning that seemed to suck up every drop of water before it. It grew in a beautiful glossy curve, like a shell. Inexorable, stupefying, it approached.

"Hold on!" someone screamed pointlessly against the roaring din of this menace. The helmsmen fought to control the wheel. A swift wind drove against the boats—tons of air displaced by tons of water. The wall rushed across the sea to the fleet, gathered itself up, and hung over like a shelf. Timbers shifted and squeaked under the onslaught of elemental forces. Besmirched with mud, Rohain clung to the mizzenmast. She had been lashed to it, because she was unable to keep her feet against the wind's muscle. The wind screeched in her ears, vacuuming out all other sound. Looking up, she saw tons of coiling water suspended over her head. Bellowing, the wave came on, up and over. Rohain felt the deck drop away as she was lifted into the air. She held her breath.

Down she fell. The boat fell with her. Blood rushed to her feet, and an explosion of water assaulted the decks.

Somehow the valiant little vessel had ridden up to the
crest and down the other side of the wave, gathering so
much speed that she buried her bow in the bottom of the
trough. Behind the mother wave came her daughters, rank
on rank, rearing to a height of ninety feet. Time and again
the boat was wrenched high only to race down and bury
herself in the deadly darkness of the troughs, with only the
stern jutting from the water. There, half-drowned, she
would shudder as though contemplating surrender, eventually raising her bowsprit to lift again. As she came up, tons
of water would come sluicing down the bows onto the deck.

No human cry could be heard against the roar of wind
and sea. Visibility was almost canceled. At a hundred and
thirty-five knots, so strong was the wind that passengers
and crew must close their eyes lest it snatch out their inner
orbits. Closed or open, there was little difference in what
could be seen. Night rode down in the wave-troughs, while
their ridges bubbled with a crust of scorched foam so thick
that it blocked out everything except the tiny rocks that
struck like hammers, and the horizontal daggers of rain or
spray.

When the waves of the aftershock had passed, Rohain
was able to see that the fleet had broken up, dispersed. No
evidence remained of the boat carrying the Duchess of
Roxburgh and her children. It was impossible to know
which vessels had survived. On the far horizon stood a column of gas, smoke, and vapor thirty miles high. And the
second major wave was on its way.

Too soon, it came roaring after its leader. Not a wall, this
was a mountain—a moon-tide altered from the horizontal
to the vertical. Tied securely to various pieces of equipment
on deck, the ladies-in-waiting screamed. Again Rohain's
boat lifted over the crest, borne, incredibly, a hundred and
ten feet high to glide down the mountain's spine. Yet this
time she did not glide—momentum launched her off the top

and thrust her down through the center of the following wave. She emerged on the other side, her passengers and crew struggling for breath, and immediately fell into the next trough, to be submerged again up to the wheel. The battering of noise and water weakened her seams. The boat began to break up, taking in water. Those who were able manned the hand-pumps.

What was it Thomas had said as they boarded? *"Lutey is aboard with us, Rohain. He can never drown."* Did merfolk swim beneath this leaking nut-shell hull, bearing it up, protecting it, keeping the promise they had made? What of the rest of the fleet? There was no sign, now, of any of them— not even a broken plank.

Ahead, Rohain glimpsed, between leaning hills of liquid, a striated coagulation that might have been land. Under ragged remnants of sails like street-beggars' laundry the voyagers traveled on, trying to hold a course for this hopeful sign, largely at the mercy of wind and water. The waves had subsided to sixty feet. On the sloshing decks, Rohain waited anxiously with Edward, Ercildoune, Lutey, the village mayor, Viviana, and Caitri, hoping that it was all over.

Oh, but it is not over, said her heart. *Three crows, there were. That is the eldritch number. Yan, tan, tethera. Third time pays for all, they say.*

Robin Lutey held up the mermaid's Comb. On the ivory, the mesh-patterns of pearls and gold glinted like sunlight through waves, even through the dimness. Bracing himself against the boat's canting, he thrust the Comb into Caitri's hair.

"You are but young," he shouted, his voice barely audible against the wind and sea. "Too young to die."

"Are you suggesting there will be another wave?" yelled Prince Edward. He was standing beside Rohain, among their bodyguards.

Lutey nodded, held up his index finger.

"One more."

"In that event, we must all once again be secured to the boat," called Rohain.

"Nay!" Lutey replied. "Remain free, in case the vessel breaks up."

"If aught should happen, my lady," bellowed the Bard, close to Rohain's ear, "not that aught shall, but should it, thou shalt be safe. Thou'rt protected. It is necessary thou shouldst know this. And the Prince also shall be safe, and now thy little maid also. Rohain, I may never see thee again. There are so many things I cannot say. My heart is full, howbeit by my honor I may not unburden it."

"But no!" she shouted. "How should I be safe and not you? And Viviana, and my ladies!"

"Mayhap Viviana too shall live." His voice sounded hoarse, as if he had swallowed gravel. "She told me she was born with a caul on her head, which is why her mother named her after a sea-witch. If she carries it with her then verily, she shall not die by drowning."

"Thomas . . ."

Rohain's eyes were oceans, overflowing.

Far away, on Tamhania, seawater poured into the volcano's ruined vent and hit the hot magma.

Then the world tore asunder with shocking force.

Such a tumult could only have one source. The whole of the island had been blown upward into the air. Once, long ago, born out of the sea, this strato-volcano had arisen. Now, by the same process, it was being destroyed. After its death, the regulation of the markless sea would disguise its latitude, marching over its former position as though it had never existed.

But for now, the blast traveled out in all directions at more than seven hundred miles per hour. At three hundred and fifty miles per hour, the wave hunted it.

Not so much a wave—the third was an entire ocean standing on end, more than a hundred and fifty feet high. It swamped the entire sky. It was the ocean folding in on itself; the ocean turning inside out. It came, and it picked up Rohain's boat, and the boat traveled on its curling crest in a screaming wind while underneath the sea-bed rose and the water shallowed and the wave gathered until it was a hundred and seventy feet tall and beneath the keel, so dizzyingly far below, there was land.

"Stay close to me!" cried Edward, taking Rohain by the waist. She clutched him tightly.

"Farewell, one and all!" called the Bard through gritted teeth.

Time slowed, or seemed to. In a flash, Rohain realized— a wave like this had happened before. This was not the first time a sea-volcano had erupted in Erith.

. . . to the east, two miles from the sea, lies a thing most curious; the ancient remains of a Watership caught in a cleft between two hills.

Was this to be the fortune of her fishing-boat? To be carried in its entirety, along a river valley for two miles and be deposited, a shattered hulk filled with shattered corpses, far above the level of the distant ocean?

Instead, with a sound curiously reminiscent of the plucking of violin-strings, copper nails began to pull free and pop out of the hull's stressed planking. Timbers burst apart. Caitri clung to Lutey. Viviana's mouth opened like a tunnel of fear. Rohain reached for her, but she and the Prince were flung forth, out into the maelstrom. His hold was wrenched from her waist. Thomas slid away down the vertical deck. Crumbling, capsizing, shattering to fragments, the boat fell down the back of the ocean.

Ash rained down. It rained on and on.
Fine particles infused the air.

The sun, no longer yellow, had metamorphosed to sea-turquoise. A sunset ranged across one third of the sky—such a sunset as had never been seen by the mortal eyes that now beheld it. Flamboyant it was, brilliant, gorgeous. Burning roses formed from rubies were strewn among flaming orange silks, castles of topaz on fire, and great drifts of melting glass nasturtiums. The horizon itself was ablaze.

Long after the sun had disappeared, the dusty air shimmered with rainbows. An emerald nimbus ringed the bitten moon. This then, was Tamhania's epitaph: that its substance would be dispersed all over Erith, bringing night after night of strange beauty, and that wheresoever its fragments touched, the soil would be nourished with the aftermath of its existence, giving rise to new life. And perhaps in that new life would spring an echo of what had once been.

7
THE CAULDRON
Thyme and Tide

Fires in the core of cores lie quiescent;
Once they jetted from its maws, incandescent.
Lava from the magma bath, effervescent,
Nullified all in its path, heat rubescent.
Once upon a cinder cone light flew sparkling—
Now a crater-lake unknown, deep and darkling.
"DORMANCY," A SONG FROM TAPTHARTHARATH

All the time—through the drag and suck, the lift and toss, through the seethe and sudden swell battering ears to deafness, eyes to blindness, skin to numbness, through the forced drafts of brine gulping and gurning in her stomach, the salt stinging her mouth, the dread inbreathing of water provoking a panic of suffocation, her heart racing for air, splashes of red agony on a black ground like an eruption of the lungs; through it all, the object remained beneath Rohain's hand and bore her up: the Hope, the wooden Hope that floated on the top of the ocean.

Another surge, and the buoyant piece of timber scraped on something. Rohain found solidity beneath her feet. She tiptoed on it and it was snatched away, relinquished, abducted, returned. She walked, emerging from the flood. The wood weighed her hand down now—why so faithful? Why could it not leave her? Wiping blur from her eyes with her free hand she looked down. The leaf-ring on her finger was caught in a bent copper nail, partly dislodged and jutting from the fishing boat's figurehead. Thorn's gift had saved her.

Now she leaned over, unhooked the bright metal band, waded to land, and lay down on a muddy knoll above the tide. Her body spasmed as she gave back to the sea the water that had invaded her lungs. Clad only in a pale shift, she sprawled there like a hank of pallid seaweed, long and lank. Somewhere on the sea or under it, her discarded gown floated: a headless, handless specter among specters more truly terrible.

Drying in the mild night within a thin casing of salt and ash, the girl lifted her aching head. She was conscious now of the careless clatter and tinkle of water chuckling down a stony sluice. A brackish freshet bounced down a rock wall, like a handful of silk ribbons. Rohain drank a long and delicious draft. As she leaned, two articles fell forward and swung on front of her face: her jade-leaved tilhal and the vial of *nathrach deirge,* both strung on strong, short chains about her neck. At her waist the tapestry aulmoniere remained firmly attached, though bedraggled. For the retaining of these precious accessories she was grateful.

She sat by the laughing trickle and looked about in wonderment. This was no rocky shore or strand. Farther uphill, trees were growing, with green turf mantling their feet. Perhaps, after all, the ocean had carried her inland. Under the starless sky, its vestigial moon a haloed silver of bluish green, the savage waters that had spat her out were now receding, as though the tide were ebbing. They seemed to clutch at the land as they dragged backward, scoring the turf with their talons. Through the ash haze Rohain saw the mermaid figurehead, wedged between two tree boles. The monstrous wave was shrinking back into itself, leaving behind a swathe of wrenched-up trees, dragged boulders, plowed ground, doomed seaweed, wreckage, flotsam, and a ragged, half-uprooted wattle-bush that shook itself and sprouted a muddy foot whose ankle was encircled with a gold band and whose toenails were painted with rose enamel.

Staggering and slipping through the blowing ash haze, her own feet squelching in sodden turf where alabaster shells lay among bone-white flowers, Rohain seized the foot.

"Via!" she gasped. Relief surged—one other, at least, had survived. Further than that she could not bear to surmise.

Viviana moaned. Rohain helped her from the network of wattle twigs and boughs that had caught her like some flamboyant fish. Scratched and bleeding in her silken shift, the lady's maid could not speak. The only sounds from her were made by the ringing and clashing of the metal chatelettes of the chatelaine fastened to her belt, which had somehow, through the dunking, been spared.

Her mistress supported the court servant, leading her to the freshet.

"Drink now."

She drank, and together they stumbled forward. As the salt water receded, it became clear that the wave had deposited both of them midway up a wall of gentle cliffs sloping down to the original sea level, currently lost beneath the retreating flood.

The brownish mist wafted in streamers that occasionally parted. Rohain strained to look ahead through the haze, trying to glimpse humanlike shapes she had earlier seen or imagined. Staunchly the shapes remained—solidifying, growing larger with every step.

Two embodiments coalesced, dark against umber.

Thorn guaranteed that the leaf-ring would allow its wearer to see the truth and not be tricked by glamour.

The cry that issued from Rohain's throat threatened to tear her flesh in its passing, as lava tears at the walls of its vent. The two incarnations paused in ash night and turned around. One of them, Caitri, ran sobbing and flung herself into Rohain's arms.

"Sweet child," Rohain said over and over, gripping her in a fierce embrace. Presently she asked, "Who is with you?"

Viviana sank to her knees, coughing. The figure accompanying Caitri took on the ragged form of the sea-mage, Lutey, who knelt at Viviana's side.

"Courage," he said. "Courage."

"Have you seen others?" asked Rohain.

"No," Caitri responded.

Lutey said, "A cottage stands yonder, halfway up the cliff. Go there."

"Will they help us?" Viviana choked piteously.

"That steading is long abandoned," said Lutey, "but of those who once dwelled there, one possessed something of the Sight. When she departed, she left behind provisions to succor the needy, for she prophesied that such a dread night as this might come to pass. I know where we have come to land. This entire region, for miles around, is uninhabited by mankind."

"How do you know this, Master Lutey?" asked Rohain quietly, guessing, even before she saw.

The choppy waters had sunk a short distance down the cliff face. There at the border, between the domain of death-cold fishes that lived without breath and the realm of beings who stalked on legs and died without breath, *she* sat. She was shining wet, with the seawater still coursing down her limbs. No ash-dust troubled the luminous splendor of those peacock-feather disks traced in helixes, the shot silk of the great translucent double fin, the marble whiteness of the slender arms, the spun-glass tresses that shone green-gold like new willow leaves and flowed over the full length of her graceful lines.

"She lifted me up," said Caitri, suddenly calm and wondering. "She carried me."

"You must give me the Comb now, little one," said Lutey, holding out his hand for the sparkling thing. "It is time for me to return it."

For the first time, Rohain noticed how aged the sea-mage looked, how wizened and weighed down with years—far more so than when she had first seen him, only days ago.

"You tried to stop it happening, did you not?" she said, understanding. "You tried to work against the birds of unseelie. And it took away your strength."

"Aye, my lady." His face crinkled in a grin. "But sooner or later I'd have been reduced to this, in any event. In some ways"—he glanced at the shining scroll of the sea-girl—"in some ways I'm glad 'tis sooner. She has waited long. So have I."

"But no!" A sob caught in Caitri's throat. "You must not go, sir. Perilous things of the Deep lurk out there. The Marool—"

The old man smiled, and kissed her. Beneath the erosion of years, the face that he turned back toward the vision from the sea was young, brave, and gentle. The little girl fell silent.

Taking the Comb, Lutey clambered down the slope, straight-backed, dignified, moving slowly but with surprising surefootedness. It seemed that time sloughed from him with every tread, until he sprang forward like a lithe young man. He reached her. A sparkle passed between them. She flipped the sinuous tail and was gone without a splash. He turned, raised his hand in a gesture of farewell, and followed, walking.

Caitri wept. The sea lapped at Lutey's ankles, his knees, his hips. A swell rolled in and disintegrated against the land. Finally the water closed over his head, and he was never again seen by mortal eyes.

Whitewashed and slate-roofed, the cottage on the cliff overlooked a little drowned harbor. Bordered by guardian rowans, the abandoned garden, once tamed, had burgeoned into wild dishevelment. Mostly one plant ramped over it: a sharp-scented thyme that smothered most of the other vegetation, save for some parsnips and carrots gone to seed.

The latch lifted easily. The door had not been locked. Weatherproof, to keep out the strong sea-winds, the dwelling had resisted much of the ash-sifted air. Only a fine layer of dust greeted the visitors.

Inside, they found munificence.

A chest that stood in one corner was filled with peasant garb, plain and ill-fitting but clean and serviceable. Another ark held fishermen's oilskins, gloves and taltries, stout boots. A drawer contained two or three knives and bent spoons, candles, a ball of twine, salt, and a tinderbox. There was a hatchet and trowel, a bucket to fetch water from the well—even a sack of musty oats that, boiled up in an old iron cauldron over the fire, made a supper of edible porridge. Beds of desiccated straw lay piled against the walls. Here, by the light of the fire and a single candle, the three companions lay down to rest after bolting the door to keep out the eerie night.

Out in the yard, silence seemed to press so strongly upon the cottage's walls that they bowed inward. No sound came, not even the bark of a fox, the sob of an owl, the moan of a hunting wind. Leaves hung stifled under laminae of ash.

The three companions were deeply affected by all that had happened. To see an entire island destroy itself, to survive a storm beyond their most bizarre invention, to be battered and almost drowned, to be suddenly and utterly wrenched from friends and companions, to find themselves in helpless isolation—all these experiences were too intense to bear close scrutiny. When the madness of the world exceeds its usual bounds there comes a time when the captives of that madness must either slam shut the gates of their minds or else be invaded, transformed, and broken by absurdity, horror, and grief. By some unspoken agreement the three castaways endeavored to avoid the topic of the tragedy in which they had been unwilling participants, with all its disturbing ramifications. They had remained alive; they must persist.

"I suppose the previous occupants must have been wealthy as well as generous, to leave so much behind," mused Caitri, lying back against the straw bedding. "I wonder why they chose such poor lodgings."

"Unless they departed in a hurry. I wonder why they left at all," said Viviana. She glanced quickly toward a window, as though expecting some sudden, malevolent shape to flit secretively past, or dash itself against the panes.

"Somehow I must send word of our survival to His Majesty," said Rohain. "How, I cannot fathom." She swept salty, tousled hair from her forehead. "I am weary beyond belief."

They listened for a while to the oppressive silence, wrapped like a muffler about the cottage's walls. The candle flickered.

"Peril walks near this place, I fancy," said Viviana after a while. "All is too quiet and still. It is uncanny. And the fogs in the air makes it seem more so." She sniffed. "The stench of brimstone and burning clings about us. Phew! Only the smell of the garden thyme overpowers it."

Rohain said, "Yes, there is an uncanny feeling about this place. This night will prove long, I fear. Make the dark hours fly past, Caitri." She went on, forcing a smile, "Tell us a story, prithee."

The little girl settled back against the wall, drawing her cloak around her shoulders. Her vision turned inward as she told of a man who danced with the Faêran for one night only—as he thought—only to discover when day dawned that he had in fact been absent from the world of men for sixty years. As he stepped once more upon the greensward of the mortal realm his footsteps grew lighter and lighter, until he crumbled and fell to the ground as a meager heap of ashes.

Caitri stopped speaking. Outside the cottage, along the sea cliff, no living thing stirred.

She sighed. "You see," she said, "he did not return from the Fair Realm, until long after his mortal span had elsaped. Time there had a pace different from time here, yet mortal time and Faêran time seemed to somehow interlock at moments."

"Entrancing tales," said Vivianna, "but only dreams, in truth—as are all tales of a Fair and Perilous Realm." She yawned.

Forgetting the story, drifting into sleep, Rohain thought of all the other questions she ought to have asked the sea-mage. Where was this coast on which they had been cast ashore? What fate had met the other boats? Why was this region empty of mortal men? Where was Prince Edward? Had any others survived—Alys-Jannetta? Thomas? *Ah, Thomas—am I doomed always to grieve for kindhearted Er-tishmen torn from me? If they have perished, it is in large part because I insisted on the kindling of the Light. The guilt weighs heavily on me . . .*

Caitri's smothered sobs came softly to her ears. So much had been lost to them all.

And then Rohain allowed herself to think of Thorn and a piercing, sweet sorrow flooded through her.

Oh, my dark fire! My knight of chivalrous grace whose joyous temper overlays depths unfathomable, as light leaves float on a forest pool Severely I miss your winning touch, your regard of stern tenderness . . . How shall I send word to thee? Shall I ever again find myself at thy side?

Over all these questions hung another, unanswerable, like a somber mantle. This place, this cottage on the cliff, seemed familiar. *Have I been here before?*

During the night, Rohain woke to silence. Or so it seemed. She fancied she had been roused by the sound of snuffling around the house, as if a dog prowled out there. For a time she lay awake—it made no difference whether she kept her eyes open or not, the darkness was impenetrable.

Abruptly, it gave way to dawn. The color of the air paled to gray and then to the washed-out blue of diluted ink.

"Last night I dreamed that a bird was beating its wings against the cottage door," said Caitri, waking. Instinctively, Rohain looked up at the ceiling, as though she might stare beyond, to the sky. Fear tightened its noose around her neck.

"We must away as soon as possible," she whispered. "Already we have stayed too long."

Below the cliffs, the sea had receded noticeably. Still the air looked burned, like toast, yet it had cleared a little. The sun remained blue-green, like an opal, hanging in a yellowish sky. Southwest of the little harbor, not far from shore, a tall, cone-shaped island lifted its head. Farther west another reared up, and beyond it several more in a great sweeping curve dwindling around to the northwest.

"The Chain of Chimneys," Viviana said, as she stood on the cliff top with Rohain and Caitri. "My governess told me about them when I was a child, in Wytham. I have never seen them before. I think we are on the desolate western coast of Eldaraigne, not far east of—not far from . . ."

"What?" asked Rohain.

"That place. The place we never reached: Hunting-towers."

They searched along the shore, calling, but no other survivors could be found. In the trees farther down, they discovered a few fish that had been caught among the branches and left by the receding wave, to suffocate in the air. These victims they fried for breakfast, since the bag of oats was small and would not feed them for long.

"The oats are our only provisions," said Rohain, "and they will run out after a few days. Time is not limitless either. For now we must rest and regain our strength, but when we leave here on the morrow, you two must take the oat-bag and follow the coastline to the southeast. Make for the Stormriders' Hold at Isse Tower, keeping well away from the Ringroad and its dangers. Tell the Relayers to take word to His Majesty that I am secure."

"Ugh! That Tower is *traiz olc*," muttered Viviana.

"My mother is there, at Isse," said Caitri, fingering the miniature she wore on a chain around her neck. "I would that she and I had been placed in service elsewhere. It is a dreadful pile, that Tower. What has it do with you, my lady? Why did you visit there?"

Rohain told the little girl how she had once served alongside her in the Seventh House of the Stormriders. After the tale ended, Caitri waxed pensive.

"So, you were he," she said at last. Strange events had ceased to astound her.

"Yes."

"There were some marks on your flesh when they brought you in."

"I know. My face was disfigured by paradox ivy. My throat—by something else."

"And your arm also. It looked as though a band or bracelet had dug into your wrist. I could not help noticing. I felt sorry for you. After a time, the weals faded."

"I do not remember any marks on my wrist."

All fell silent.

Evenutally, Rohain said, "I have here a vial of Dragon's Blood, see?" She produced the tapestry aulmoniere, which still enclosed the swan's feather and Thorn's gift. "*Nathrach deirge* it is called, yet 'tis not the blood of dragons but an elixir of herbs. It gives warmth and sustenance. You shall take it with you. Our ways must part here. Viviana, you say Huntingtowers lies close by. I shall go and seek it. No, prithee, do not protest! It would be far more perilous for you to accompany me than to do anything else. I am Huon's quarry. This I have come at last to understand, and I know that he will never give up until he finds me. But I do not know *why*.

"As a vulture in human form once pompously stated, 'Knowledge is power,' and if I can find out why I am Huon's target, perhaps I shall have a better chance of eluding him. After all's said and done, there is only one way for me to discover the reason he hunts me. I must retrace my footsteps in earnest. Once, I tried it, and failed. This time, either I will succeed or Huon will win. But until I meet or defeat my doom there will be no safety for those I love. Those who accompany me anywhere shall become his quarry as much as I."

"But Your Ladyship must come to the Stormriders' Tower yourself, to send the message to Caermelor that you are safe," Viviana said earnestly. "Otherwise, how shall we be believed?"

"I wish that none should know my whereabouts. Not even His Majesty. Tell them that I live, send word to His Majesty, but never reveal my purpose or destination. I do not want others to come seeking after me; they would be seeking their doom." Turning her face away she murmured softly, "Anyway, I am as good as dead already."

"In Caermelor they would never let it rest at that," argued Caitri. "They would extract the truth from us by fair means or foul. And then they will come after you, for your own good."

Rohain was forced to concede the truth of this assertion.

"In that case, do not admit that you have seen me at all. Then they shall have no reason to ask further—" She broke off. "Ah, but to leave His Majesty uninformed cuts me to the quick. Yet if there is no other way to keep them from me . . ."

"We shall not go off without you," burst out Viviana. "We shall not leave you in the wastelands."

"I am able to survive on my own. I have been taught how to find food in the wilderness. This ring I wear, engraved with leaves, has some charm on it, although whether it is strong enough to ward off the Wild Hunt I do not know. I tell you, I must go, and it must be alone and speedily. I am sure that Tamhania's ruin was brought about for the purpose of destroying me or flushing me out of my refuge. My guess is, if such strong forces have been sent against me, wielding the powers of both sea and fire, they will wish to know whether they have succeeded in their mission. Immortal, they will not rest until they are certain of it. Perhaps even now they have learned that I live, and that I walk in this forgotten place. It is possible that as we speak they are drawing nigh. I dare not stay in one place for too long. Haste is imperative."

"But Your Ladyship is to be Queen-Empress!" Viviana burst out in amazement. "What is this talk of pursuit and danger? The Dainnan shall guard you. *His Imperial Majesty* shall be your protector. There can be no greater security than that."

"There is no security against that which threatens me. Do you think mortal arms and wizards' charms can stand against the most malign and feared of eldritch princes? Can the Dainnan blow an island apart?"

"I beg to differ, ma'am. Tamhania was a sleeping volcano. It might have awoken at any time. It destroyed itself with its own life-spirit. I'll warrant the three hoodie crows, great and malevolent though they doubtless are, would not be mighty enough to marshal the elements of heat and pressure."

"Perhaps not, but Huon's birds set the machinery in motion."

"Huon's birds?" repeated Caitri. "My lady is mistaken. Huon commands no birds—at any rate, not in any tale I have heard. His terrible riders and horses and hounds are what he hunts with. Sometimes he enlists spriggans to ride crouching on the cruppers of the fire-eyed shadow-steeds, but no birds. The Crows did not fly at the behest of the Antlered One."

"You are very learned!" exclaimed Rohain, between astonishment and doubt.

"My mother taught me much. She is wise in eldritch lore. Besides, in all of Master Brinkworth's tales there was never a mention of hoodie crows flying with the Wild Hunt."

"Tarry!" said Rohain quickly. "Say no more. Your words discomfit me. I thought I knew my enemy but once again I am thrown into chaos and confusion. If Huon did not send the birds, then what did?"

"I know not, but I do know they might sniff you out," said Caitri. "Spriggans will, at any rate. They have crafty noses and can trace trails in the same way hounds course after scent, only better. I think they might know the scent of you. They ravaged your chamber at the Tower. And by now, they must know your looks."

"Indeed they must," agreed Rohain. "I fear I betrayed myself in the marketplace of Gilvaris Tarv. These are two problems I do not know how to resolve."

"That stytchel-thyme all over the garden has a perfume strong enough to cover any odor," Caitri pointed out. "You might journey incognito, if masked with the fragrance of it."

"Caitri, do not *encourage* Her Ladyship to pursue her wildgoose chase!" said Viviana.

"Nothing can sway me," said Rohain. "I will go to Hunt-ingtowers."

"But the Wild Hunt issues from that place!"

"Usually at the full of the moon, they say. By my reck-oning, we are very early in the month of Duileagmis. The old moon has almost faded. The new moon is yet unborn."

Viviana sighed deeply. "Well then, if you must, m'lady. And if there is anything I can do to keep you safe, I shall do it. So, if 'tis disguise you're after, I can help."

"'Tis not more than six or seven leagues due west of here, by my reckoning," said Viviana, trying to recall the maps her governess had pinned upon the walls of the nurs-ery. "That horrible place, I mean. A swift all-day's walk."

In the lonely cottage above the ocean, the courtier had finished dyeing her mistress's golden hair brown, using a crudely made concoction of boiled tree-bark. Now she set about stitching a half-mask for Rohain's eyes and forehead. Viviana was never one to be unprepared. The versatile chatelaine had come through the shipwreck, still tied to her waist-girdle. From its chains dangled various chatelettes made from rustproof materials: brass scissors, a golden etui with a manicure set inside, a bodkin, a spoon, a vinaigrette, a needle-case, a small looking-glass, a cup-sized strainer for spike-leaves, a timepiece that had stopped, and whose case was inlaid with ivory and bronze, a workbox containing small reels of thread, an enameled porcelain thimble and a silver one, silver-handled buttonhooks and a few spare buttons—glass-topped, enclosing tiny pictures—a miniature portrait of her mother worked in enamels, several rowan-wood tilhals, a highly ornamented anlace, a penknife, an empty silver gilt snuff-box, and a pencil. Only the notecase had been ruined by the salt water.

"'Tis a wonder all that motley didn't pull you down like a millstone," remarked Caitri.

"I carry my caul," Viviana said demurely, returning a needle to its horn case, which was set about with cabuchons. "M'lady, with this half-mask over your eyes, and the lower part of your face well-kohled with chimney-soot, you will look like some filthy country itinerant, begging your pardon. Whether you are lad or wench none will discern, if we bundle you in enough rags. And with a little stytchel-thyme rubbed on, any creature that sees you or catches your scent won't be any the wiser." She cocked her head to one side and gazed critically at Rohain. "I must admit, it seems a shame, ma'am, to spoil a beauty of the rarest sort—for upon my word, never was such a fair face seen at Court or anywhere else for that matter. 'Tis no wonder His Imperial Majesty was smitten."

"Mistress Wellesley!" remonstrated Caitri, now schooled in etiquette. "How boldly you speak before Her Ladyship!"

"Speak plainly before me always, please," said Rohain absently, her mind on other matters. "You should both know I always require frankness and do not consider it an impropriety." She tweaked a lock of her tangled hair over her face to examine its new color.

"Well, if 'tis frankness you are after, my lady," said Viviana, "let me speak my mind now that those other ladies are no longer fluttering about you—*sain* them, I hope they may be safe on land. I do believe you are a lost princess who's slept for a hundred years and been awoken."

Rohain laughed. "Thank you for your kind words. I would it were so, but I fear it is not. I would augur that I am by birth greatly inferior to royalty."

"What exactly do you hope to find at Huntingtowers, m'lady?" asked Caitri.

"I do not know."

"And if you find nothing?"

"I will keep searching. I have no choice. I am driven."

Caitri seemed about to say something else, but thought better of it.

That night the snuffling and sniffing sounds came again around the cottage, and a tapping at the window, soft and insistent. A wordless, muttering drone started up. The three sleepers woke and sat still, not moving so much as a toe. They held their breath until they could hold it no longer, and then expelled it in long, silent sighs, fearful that even the slightest noise would betray them.

Toward dawn, the sounds ceased.

In the morning Rohain bade farewell to her companions. Her sense of loss and desolation was magnified by this parting. Always, the burden of guilt associated with the destruction of the island oppressed her; inwardly she lamented for Edward and Thomas, for Alys and Master Avenel and all the other friends she had lost to the violence of fire and water.

She trudged alone to the top of the cliffs and halted, turning to look back at the brooding expanse of the sea. Beneath a leering sky, it was striped with many shades of gray from ashen to lead. The symmetrical cones of the presumably dormant Chimneys stood sentinel, waves outlining their shores with froth. Two petrels winged across the sky. Far below, the cottage looked tiny, like a mantelshelf ornament.

After a few more steps it was lost to view altogether. Stunted tea-tree scrub grew on the cliff top, spiking the air with the tang of eucalyptus. In the far distance a disused Mooring Mast stood, a dark web sketched against smudged skies.

This is not the first time I have trodden this path, thought Rohain, without knowing why.

The sharp smell of thyme permeated her disguise—her clothes and knapsack, the brown and lusterless hair combed close about her face to obfuscate her features, the half-mask across her eyes and brow, her roughly kohled jaw. In a mustard-colored kirtle and snuff-colored surcoat, a plain leather girdle and an oilskin cloak and taltry, she bore no resemblance to an elegant Court lady. Her slenderness was lost beneath bulky folds.

Is it my fate to go always disguised?

Under the oddly hued sun, whose face had been transformed by the death of Tamhania, it seemed to Rohain that she no longer moved in the world she had known. Duileagmis, the Leaf month of Spring, put forth a bounty of darling buds whose colors appeared altered by the stained atmosphere. Greenish flowers bestarred bilious marram grasses, their perfumes dust-clogged. Rohain stooped swiftly. With a knife obtained from the cottage on the cliff, she sliced at some vegetation, hacking off scurvy grass and the fleshy leaves of samphire. She had recognized this wild food from Thorn's teachings. Chewing some, she tucked the rest into her belt.

Once again, she looked back toward the ash-fogged sea. From this angle it gave the illusion of rising up in a broad band, higher than the land on which she stood. As she hesitated, she spied a movement in the scrub. It issued from behind a dune and made off in the direction of the cottage. The thing had a wightish look, no doubt of it. At the same time, dark dots in the southern sky swelled, proving themselves not to be the sea-eagles she had at first taken them for.

Stormriders!

A desire for concealment gripped her. She dashed for cover in a tea-tree thicket. The company of riders swept over, following the shoreline at a low altitude. Thrice they circled the vicinity of the cottage, swooping in close over the roof.

There was little doubt that the Relayers were scouring the coast for survivors of Tamhania's disaster. Rohain hoped fervently that Viviana and Caitri, wherever they were, would wave down the Stormriders and be taken to safety at the Tower on eotaur-back. But wights were abroad too, it was plain. Even in daylight they were on the move. The creature from behind the dune had headed away with a purposeful air that boded ill. She and her companions had not left the bountiful cottage a moment too soon. As soon as the Stormriders had flown away, Rohain hurried onward.

Farther inland, coastal vegetation gave way to lightly wooded hills. Here grew hypericum with its yellow cymes. Hurriedly she gathered it by the armful for its wight-repellent properties, binding the bunches with twine to hang them about her person alongside the stytchel-thyme. Looking up from her work, she made out the distant trapezium of an apparently flat-topped mountain dominating the murky horizon.

On she went. Under her feet, little tracks were born, ran dipping and climbing through the trees and faded among the turf. Among the bushes, leaves stirred. There came a faint, metallic *ching*. Rohain halted.

"Come forth," she ordered loudly.

More rustlings and a brittle snap were followed by the appearance of Viviana and Caitri from a clump of callistemons.

"You stepped on a twig," Caitri accused Viviana.

"And I did not!"

Rohain said, "Ever since I left the cottage I have been

hearing you two following me. A herd of oxen might have progressed more quietly. You have no woodcraft whatsoever, and Viviana's chatelaine rings like all the bells of Caermelor. I hoped you might give up. I wished you might attract the attention of those Stormriders and go with them. Turn back now, while you are yet far from Huntingtowers."

"No."

"This is to be no picnic in the King's Greenwood."

Sulkily, the two damsels glared at their mistress. They did not reply.

"Those who walk at my side do so at their peril!" fumed Rohain. She then fervently besought them to leave her, in an exchange that lasted a goodly while—time they could ill afford—but they were adamant in their refusals.

It occurred to Rohain that she might easily abandon them and slip away on her own, drawing off the Hunt. She did not entertain the thought for long. Two untutored maidens, roaming out here without even the benefit of her limited knowledge of survival in the wilderness, must surely perish. Either way, there seemed scant hope of saving the lives of these faithful companions. There was no choice—she must accede at last to their wishes.

"Well," she said briskly, "if you are prepared to meet your dooms at such an early age, who am I to stop you? Be it on your own heads. But move discreetly. We are looked for."

"We spied the Stormriders," said Viviana. "Here is your elixir, m'lady."

"Worse things than Stormriders are abroad," replied her mistress, accepting the vial and rehanging it around her neck. "Come. The wind is in the west. We only have to keep our backs to it."

Chains pulled down Rohain's heart. She foresaw the spilling of the blood of her loyal friends, and guilt flooded her conscience. When she faced the direction of Hunting-towers, an undefined fear also began to take root.

As they hastened along the way, to thrust aside dread she pointed out useful wildflowers, and in a low voice imparted knowledge gleaned from Thorn in the wilderness.

"In tales, adventurers merely stroll along through wood and weald, pulling wild berries and nuts off the hedges," said Caitri.

"Yes, I have noticed that," said Rohain. "Obviously, they only go adventuring in Autumn, the season of ripe fruits."

"And they do not die of cold," added Viviana. "In tales they merely lie down to sleep wrapped in their cloaks, even on bitter nights, with no fire or Dragon's Blood to warm them."

"Sheer fiction," said Rohain firmly.

"Common centaury," instructed Rohain, indicating a herb. "A bitter tonic can be made from an infusion of the dried plants. Dock leaves for nettle stings. Loosestrife for henna dyes, pretty hemlock, all lace and poison. Poppies for torpid illusions." She astonished herself with her own erudition. "Here's chicory. The leaves can be eaten, the roots roasted."

"'Tis a veritable pantry out here," marvelled Viviana, "a pharmacopoeia."

"In sooth," affirmed Rohain, "but most of it does not taste very nice."

Everywhere in this pathless land, Spring wildflowers nodded, but there was no time to stop and examine them closely. Instead, Rohain was compelled to rush across the face of the land under unfriendly skies, toward the very bastion of all things unseelie.

"I feel a certain nostalgia for life on the road," she said, brushing with her fingertips the leaves of an overhanging elder-bough.

"You are bold and brave, my lady," said Caitri.

"Mayhap. I am bold but I can be craven, I'm free but I'm caged, I'm joyful but I grieve, Caitri, like everyone else. But do not call me by my title now, or even by my name—we might be overheard."

"What name will you be called instead, my la— my friend?" stuttered Viviana.

"I wish to be called Tahquil. 'Tis a name I heard once, at Court, and did not mislike. It will suffice."

"A strange-sounding, foreign name. It has the ring of Luindorn."

"Indeed, I believe it originates from that country. I heard tell it means 'Warrior,' in feminine form. And warrior I must become. I intend to fight on, despite that fate throws turmoil at me again and again. Whether I will be defeated, I cannot guess."

After a brief halt for an unappealing meal of cold porridge and samphire leaves, the three companions followed a flowery ridge up wooded slopes and over a shoulder of the hills into wild meadows that once had been well-tended farmlands. Abandonment had made wild the overgrown hedges, the deep brakes of flowering briars. Choked drainage-dikes provided a haven for marsh pennywort, bog asphodel, sedges, and rushes. Under the hedges grew foxgloves and tall spikes of woundwort—"A styptic, used to staunch the bleeding of injuries," observed Rohain—and white deadnettles, whose dry hollow stems she collected in a bunch.

"Used in concoctions?" inquired Viviana.

"Used to make whistles."

As she scanned the landscape for provender, words of Thorn's came back to Rohain-Tahquil. He had said, *There is no need to hunger or thirst in the lands of Erith . . . When all else fails, there is always Fairbread.*

The thought brought reassurance.

Later in the afternoon, tattered clouds began to move across the sun's face. A wind gusted, blowing up leaves and dust in sudden spurts. A few spots of dirty rain spattered down. Worse than bad weather, uneasiness crept over the travelers—a cooling of the blood. Rohain-Tahquil shivered, the nape of her neck prickled. Time and time again she would whirl rapidly, knife in hand, only to face emptiness. Yet she could swear she had sensed something following behind. She kept the knife ready in her hand. By unspoken agreement, the companions kept under shelter as much as possible, creeping cautiously from tree to tree or scuttling quickly across open glades. Always their heads turned this way and that as if they expected to see dark shapes of an antlered horseman and other fell manifestations watching them from the shadows, ready to spur forward and ride them down.

Ever ahead loomed the low, flat-topped trapezium of the cauldron-mountain, dark through the haze. The closer they approached it, the heavier was the hush that fell on the landscape. Back along the coast, magpies and larks had warbled their pure bell-tones. From every bush and tree had issued shrill twitterings and pipings. As they pushed farther inland, the birdsong had diminished without the travelers noticing. Now they became aware of a quietude eased only by the murmur of the wind in the leaves.

Acid rain came sluicing down in drowning sheets, hissing in the dust until it made mud of it, before settling down to a steady patter and trickle. Made corrosive by the oxidation of atmospheric nitrogen and brimstone gases from the eruption, water dripped down the collars of the walkers' oilskins, off the edges of their fishermen's taltries, and into their eyes.

"I'd rather an unstorm than this," grumbled Viviana, shouting to be heard above the downpour. "This rain bites. It stings."

"Hush," warned Rohain-Tahquil. "Something might hear us."

As the sun dipped behind their backs, the shower eased. The land had begun to rise steeply. Emerging from a belt of oaks they saw the great sheared-off cone rising ahead of them: the caldera of Huntingtowers, its lower versants leprous with stunted vegetation, pimpled with the low mounds of old, forsaken diggings.

It seemed desolate. Nothing stirred. The ancient caldera lay silent and still. In its mouth, where once deadly fires had raged, the waters of the lake were deep, dark, and cold.

Now that they stood on its slopes, breathless apprehension laid hold of the damsels. It was so strong it was almost intolerable.

The light was fading. In the east, long clouds shredded to black ribbons. No moon came up behind the summit of the blunted cone.

"I shouldn't like to be any closer to that place at night," said Rohain-Tahquil.

They found shelter in a mossy stone ruin that had once, in ages long past, conceivably been a byre. Honeysuckle and traveler's joy formed a roof over the few remaining, slug-haunted walls. Against these they piled dry bracken to serve as a bed. Not daring to light a fire, they unwrapped the last slabs of cold porridge from their dock leaves and dined in silence. Rohain-Tahquil offered a sip of *nathrach deirge* all around. Warmed, but wet and cheerless, they huddled together.

"I did not know it would be like this," complained Viviana. "I hate slugs."

"They like you," said Caitri, subtracting one from Viviana's sleeve. "Anyway, you said you wanted to come," she added primly.

"I said I wanted to come but I never said I would not grumble."

The malachite oval of the sun strayed into a magnificent post-eruption sunset, a drifting flowerscape in a profusion of marigold, carnation, primrose, gentian, and lilac—colors that would bleed softly into the air and hang there in frayed, cymophanous striations like shang-reflections for hours after the sun had wasted away.

"We have been fortunate to discover this niche," said Rohain-Tahquil with a new sense of authority born of her limited knowledge of survival. "Sometimes farmers inscribed runes into the walls of these animal pens—charms to ward off unseelie wights. See here—" With a loose rock she scraped away a thick nap of moss. "Some symbols are cut into the stones. They are worn shallow now and hard to see. Still, they may yet hold some efficacy."

"Of course, all the lesser wights have spied us already," said Caitri. "It is to be hoped that they will be deterred by our iron blades and tilhals and salt, and by these great bunches of hypericum."

"And it is to be hoped they will not go telling their greaters," said Viviana, using a silver needle from her chatelaine to punch holes in a stalk of deadnettle.

"I have been told that eldritch beings do not cooperate like that, not in the way of our kind," said Rohain-Tahquil, crushing yet more thyme leaves to release their penetrating aroma. "Not unless they're forced, by threat or bribe."

"Some have their own leaders," said Caitri. "The siofra bow to their Queen Mab, for example; their little queen no bigger than a man's thumb."

"Even so," replied Rohain-Tahquil, "but fortunately the siofra are given more to glamourish trickery than to war. Their tiny spears would prick no more than a thistle would. Once I traveled with a road-caravan which was dispersed and ravaged by unseelie wights, but I surmise it was not the result of a planned and concerted effort on their part. Many of them happened to be crossing the Road at that time and by ill chance we moved in their way."

It came to her again that perhaps Huon had planned the devastation of the caravan. But no—hindsight and reason told her there were significant differences in the method of attack. The Wild Hunt had mounted a full-scale, coordinated assault directly on the Tower, while the Wights of the Road had appeared at random, following their own hostile instincts rather than obeying a leader.

"Long before that time," she went on, "I learned something of the ways of wights from a fellow traveler. Like all creatures of eldritch, the fell things of unseelie are amoral. Left to their own devices they are arbitrary in their choice of victims, neither punishing the bad nor letting alone the good. Spriggans are trooping wights, to be sure, and they have a chieftain—nominally, at any rate—but most unseelie wights are solitary by nature. They do not hold meetings or discussions, they simply act in accordance with the antipathy that drives them. As such, they are the more terrible, being an ungoverned—I will not say lawless, for they are subject to the rigorous laws of their kind—an ungoverned battalion of man-slayers, a division without a major-general, a corps without a head. Yes, a headless horseman would be an apt symbol. But I have said enough, enough to give you nightmares. Sleep now. I shall take the first watch. Caitri, did you want to tell me something?"

Caitri drew breath and looked at her mistress. Then she shook her head and turned away with a sigh.

There being no moon, and the stars being hidden by the last aerial memories of Tamhania, the night waxed as thick as pitch. The wind had dropped. Strangely hushed was the landscape, and devoid of movement. Time dragged on, with no way to mark the hours. A dark melancholia seeped up from the ground. The thoughts of Rohain-Tahquil strayed to

Thorn, encamped in the north with his men. This night he would speak and laugh, but not with her.

Not with her.

Tears welled at the inner corners of her eyes. They were tears for Thorn, and for the young Prince and the others who had been subjected to the wrath of Tamhania because of her inexcusable stubbornness. Could her culpability ever be absolved? She thought not.

Slugs meandered across her skin. She flicked at them. Toward what she guessed to be midnight, a sound came through the gloom. Something was coming, *brush, brush, brush.*

It stopped.

She ceased to breathe.

It came again, *brush, brush, brush,* and this time she thought it was accompanied by a dull clanking as of several links of a heavy chain striking together. She strained into the darkness until she fancied her eyes must be bulging from their sockets. Nothing was visible. Groping for the sharp knives she had brought from the cottage, she held them ready in both hands. *Brush, brush, brush,* something came, until it stopped right at the doorstep of the ruined shelter.

A sudden wind blasted Rohain's face. In the sky, clouds of vapor and ash parted momentarily. Dimly, the stars shone out. Standing silently in front of the hideaway of crumbling stone was a black dog, huge and shaggy, the size of a calf. It stared with great saucer-eyes as bright as coals of fire.

Tahquil-Rohain's hand groped for the tilhal of jade-carved hypericum leaves that hung beside the vial at her neck. She gripped it tightly. Her thoughts flew to Viviana and Caitri, asleep and innocent at her back.

Let them not wake now, or they will cry out.

There must be no sound, nor sign of fear. This Black Dog might be benign or malign. With luck, it might be a Guardian Black Dog, one of those that had been known to protect travelers. Yet again, it might be one of the unseelie morthadu. In that case, one must not speak or try to strike it, for the morthadu had the power to blast mortals.

She stared back at the apparition and it stared back at her. Her body ached with the tension of keeping perfectly still.

It was said that the sight of the morthadu was a presage of death. Whether the thing now before Tahquil-Rohain represented succor or calamity, there was no way of finding out. She sat, rigid as steel, avoiding the burning scarlet gaze, using every ounce of her strength to prevent herself from betraying her fear by the slightest twitch and thus yielding power to the creature.

Toward midnight, the Black Dog was not there anymore. She kept watch until dawn.

At first light, Tahquil-Rohain roused Viviana to take her turn at the watch. She did not mention their night visitor. No paw marks remained in the sifting ash layer to betray what had come and gone in the night. Tahquil-Rohain surmised there were two possibilities—that the Black Dog was seelie, and had guarded them against some unimaginable menace, or that it was one of the morthadu and had, hopefully, been warded off by one or more of the charms they carried. Either way, she and her friends were safe, for now. She warmed her stiff sinews with a sip of *nathrach deirge,* rolled herself in her cloak, and slept.

When she awoke a third possibility came to her—that the Dog had been unseelie, and had made sure they stayed put all night before going off to spread the news of their whereabouts to others who might be interested. Quickly they departed from the ruin.

Daylight dribbled through clouds and fog. Breakfastless, the travelers climbed among the overgrown mullock heaps of the redundant mines that pocked the foot and heath-covered skirts of the mountain. All the while, the desire to hide pressed on them until it became almost overpowering. Eldritch gramarye seemed to crackle in the air, although nothing untoward could be seen or heard. Nothing was audible at all, in fact, save the wind soughing in their ears. Continually they glanced at the skies and to right and left, every nerve stretched, poised to dive for cover or run for their lives at the first sign of any living thing.

Over their heads, the rim of the caldera hung halfway up the sky. It blocked from view everything within its black walls, including the mysterious architecture of complex towers that, as legend had it, was the stronghold of Huon and his ghastly following. From here the Wild Hunt would put forth on the three nights of every full moon, to sweep out across the countryside and fall upon the unwary, and doing to them what harm they chose.

Or not.

Messages received during the sojourn on Tamhania indicated that since the attack on Isse Tower, the Hunt had not been seen to ride . . .

Viviana said, "My la— Tahquil, there are too many of these slag-heaps—so many pitfalls and potholes. We must be wary. One false step might see one of us toppling down some hidden shaft. The very ground is treacherous. Many places have subsided, while others look to be in danger of collapsing."

"Wisely spoken, Via. You and Caitri must sit here in the shelter of this scrubby brake. I will wander alone awhile."

"It is so perilous, ma'am! What do you seek, exactly?"

"I cannot say."

"Every bush and twig hides something that is ardent to harm us, I am certain. Can we not now go back?"

"I have no choice. I am driven to wander here until I find some clue or key, or perish. There is no life for me in the world if I do not find an answer."

"And maybe if you do," said Viviana.

"My—" Caitri twisted her fingers together.

"What is it, Caitri? If you have something of importance to impart to me, say it now."

"No. No, it is nothing."

"Stay here."

"Where are you going?"

"To the very gates of Huntingtowor. I forbid you to follow. Wait for me. If I am not back by nightfall, leave with all speed."

Tahquil left them sitting with their arms about each other; a pathetic picture, like a charcoal sketch of two orphaned waifs. She walked on, stumbling on clods, rocks, and freshly turned dirt, making sure she walked sunwise—for luck and protection—around the eroded mullock heaps. She recalled from descriptions given to her at Isse Tower that somewhere to the right lay a loop of the Ringroad; a section that was dreaded by road-caravans. But this did not concern her. It did not lie in her path. A low cliff did—she changed direction to walk parallel to it, under its briar-tangled overhang.

A creeper trailed across the ground. Its five-pointed leaves were glossy and dark green. Between them sprouted tiny inflorescences, pale green like the phosphorescence on rotting corpses. The plant attracted her attention. When her ankle brushed against it, fire ripped through her flesh. She jerked away.

Paradox ivy! You cursed leaf!

She avoided it. In doing so, she missed seeing a mine-shaft farther along, teetered on the edge of inviolate darkness, and overbalanced, but in the last instant she was able to throw herself backward. To break her fall she flung out her arms, but stones met her as she landed. She lay winded, her hands scrabbling at rubble and weeds.

Rising to her feet painfully, awkwardly, she noticed a scintilla of gold that winked, once, in the corner of her left eye. Where her hands had clutched the ground, something lay uncovered. She picked it up, brushing away the caked dirt.

And something like a memory spun before her eyes.

The ground emptied from beneath its feet. It hurtled downward, to be brought up on a spear-point of agony. A band around its arm had snagged on a projection. The scrawny thing dangled against the cliff face, slowly swinging like bait on a hook.

Then slowly, with great effort, it lifted its other arm. Bird-boned fingers found the catch and released it. The band sprang open and the creature fell.

The band. A bracelet, gold, with a white bird enameled on it. This she held in her hand.

And knew it belonged to her.

The world faded.

Another took its place.

8
AVLANTIA
Quest and Questions

'Tis rumored that the Piper will come soon
And lead us all to Reason with his tune.
New day shall dawn for those who wait, no doubt—
And through the forests, laughter will ring out.

TRADITIONAL FOLK SONG

In ancient times, when the Ways between the Fair Realm and Erith were still open, of all the races of Men the Talith were most favored by the Faêran—or so it was said. The people of that northern race were tall and golden-haired, eloquent, ardent in scholarship, delighting in poetry, music, and theater, skilled in the sports of field and track, valorous in war. Avlantia was their country, and this sun-beloved land was split into two regions—in the west, Auralonde of the Red Leaves; in the east, Ysteris of the Flowers.

The eringl trees of Auralonde grew nowhere else in Erith. Unlike the thorn bushes shipped from the cooler south to be planted in rows for hedges, their boughs were never bare, for they could not know the touch of snow in these warm climes. Their newly budded leaves glowed briefly green-gold. Unfurling, they swiftly deepened to red-gold, bronze, amber, and scarlet. The roofs of the eringl forests burned deep wine-crimson, and the glossy brown pillars supporting them were wound about with trails of a yellow-leaved vine. Fallen leaves mingled in a bright embroidery on the forest floors, buttoned with fire-bright hemispheres of mushrooms, forming a richly patterned carpet fit for royalty.

Branwyddan, King of the Talith, kept court in Auralonde at Hythe Mellyn, a mighty city built of the golden stone called mellil, which gleamed in the sunlight like pale honey. Tier upon tier, the city's shining roofs, spires, and belfries rose upon the hillside, crowned by the King's palace. Neat shops and taverns bordered the side-streets. Tall and impos-ing houses flanked the city square, which was overlooked also by the domed Law Courts and the gracious columns of the Council Chambers. In stone horse-troughs, white doves flurried on the water like fallen blossoms.

Below the city sprawled a green and fertile river valley, well-tilled, festooned with orchards, and on the other side of this valley the land climbed suddenly to the steep hills of the Dardenon Ranges, well-clad with the flame-colored er-ingls of Auralonde. Hythe Mellyn prospered, as did all of Avlantia.

A plague of rats came to Hythe Mellyn, but though they poured into the city like liquid shadow in a nightmare, it was not their predations that emptied it. The rats were merely the heralds of its doom; many other matters were to come into play before the fate of Hythe Mellyn would be sealed.

At first, when they were few, the needle-eyed, yellow-fanged visitors seemed to be no more than a nuisance. After all, Hythe Mellyn until then had endured no plagues and few vermin. A squeaking and rustling in the night, a chewing of the corners of flour sacks and a depositing of filth in the pantries—these offenses were annoying but could be borne. Traps and baits were laid. It was thought these would eradicate the pests, but the rats' numbers grew steadily despite the efforts of the citizens to destroy them, and they grew bolder. In the hours of darkness they ran across the bedcovers of the citizens. With their septic teeth, they bit people's faces as they lay sleeping, the pain waking them to stare into a mask of horror.

Soon, not only at night were the rats abroad, but also during the hours of daylight. They were to be seen in the street-gutters and on the roofs of houses, scuttling across courtyards, poisoning the carved fountains with their waste. From every cleft and shadow stabbed the knife-point glint of their eyes, and the cold, thin whistling of their squeaks shrilled like spiteful giggling. Never was a pantry door opened without a rain of wriggling black bodies falling from the shelves and scurrying into the corners. Never was the once-sweet air free of the stench of decay and foulness. With sudden bustles of teeth, tails, and spines, the rodents clustered in the cellars like bunches of fat pears. They killed the songbirds in their cages and gnawed unwatched babes in their cradles.

Every countermeasure was tried. More traps and baits were laid, cats were brought in—but for every rodent that was destroyed, two more took its place. In desperation the Lord Mayor posted a reward to whomsoever should rid the city of this scourge—five bags of gold. As the news traveled, it brought in many adventurers from other countries eager to win their fortunes in such an easy way. But it was not easy—in fact, it proved impossible, and the reward grew from five bags to ten, and then to fifteen, as the plague in-

tensified. Rogues and ruffians, itinerants, wizards and con-
jurers—all came with their bags of tricks, each more bizarre
than the last, which they claimed would dispel this curse.
None succeeded. The citizens now lived in a state of siege,
with every cranny in every house sealed. Many people were
too frightened to venture abroad at all, and the city was
seized by paralysis, juddering to a standstill.

On the day the Lord Mayor officially increased the reward to twenty bags of gold, a stranger arrived in Hythe
Mellyn. Foreigners in outlandish garb being by now a common sight, this one caused no more than the raising of an
eyebrow among the few who caught sight of him as he
passed through the rat-infested streets toward the Chambers
of the City Council in his gaily striped doublet, parti-colored
hose, and versicolor cloak, and his cap like a rainbow with
three horns.

But as he entered into the stately oak-paneled halls of the
Council Chambers and bowed before the Lord Mayor and
councilors of Hythe Mellyn, his remarkable comeliness
suddenly became apparent. Dark eyes, upswept at the outer
corners, glittered beneath long lashes. Wavy hair rippled
down his back; it was the color of a blackbird's plumage,
with a gleam of chestnut. The clinging fabric of his doublet
showed his person to be muscular and lithe, slight but well-
proportioned. A faint smile played along his lips, revealing
flawless white teeth. His raiment glowed like the Southern
Lights—a phenomenon never witnessed in Avlantia but
spoken of with awe by travelers who had journeyed to the
low, freezing latitudes of the deep south. They said they had
seen these lights spread across the skies in luminous mantles of living, shifting color—fire red, dawn amber, daffodil
yellow, leaf green, ocean blue, twilight indigo, and violet.
Such was the appearance of the stranger's exotic garb.

Stern-faced, the statesmen of Hythe Mellyn regarded him
as he stood before them. Boldly he returned their gaze, as if

noting their blue eyes and noble features. The ice-white hair
of the elders and the corn-yellow locks of the younger men
fell across broad Talith shoulders richly cloaked in velvet.

"I shall rid you of the plague, my lords," the entrancing
stranger said cheerfully, "for the price of twenty-one bags of
gold."

Among themselves the Lord Mayor and the aldermen
saw no reason why this "colorful fellow," as they called him
in murmured asides, should succeed where others had
failed; and if by some miracle he did, why then they would
be glad to shower him with twenty-one bags of gold, the
freedom of the city, and more! Thus it was that they readily
agreed to his price.

After he heard this, instead of departing to set up traps or
wizardly devices, the handsome youth reached into his
pocket, took out a set of pipes, and began to play a queer,
wild tune. Immediately, the flesh of the listeners crepitated.
Astonished and insulted by this odd behavior, the councilors
were about to order the sentries to cast out this offender
when they were stayed by an even odder sight.

Down from the wall-hangings and across the floor of the
Council Chambers came a thin dark tide, its edges reaching
out like crawling tentacles or threads, directed toward the
Piper where he stood. Silently, as one organism, rats gathered at his feet. He turned and skipped away, still playing,
and they followed him. In sudden fear, the sentries flung
wide the brass-bound, oaken doors.

Outdoors and down the street danced the musician,
trailed by his invidious entourage. Behind them, the officers
of the Council burst out through the doorway. Their shouts
and exclamations mingled with the eerie sound of the piping, which, it seemed, could be heard over the entire city.
Above the city square, shutters banged open and faces
peered out. Rats were gathering—thousands upon thousands
of them. From every storehouse and granary, from every

wainscot and pantry, attic, cellar, and gutter, from drain, cesspit, cistern, and crevice they came scurrying soundlessly, climbing on one another's backs, crushing their fellows in their haste to join the living spate that grew and overflowed the streets in pursuit of the Piper down King's Avenue, through the East Gate, and out of town.

Never before had such a bizarre and loathsome turmoil been seen in Hythe Mellyn. Frozen in wonder, the citizens stared. Children covered their ears against the shrill keening of the pipes. The tune seemed to remain loud and piercing in the heads of the people even as the Piper danced away down the winding road into the valley, across the bridge, and on toward the hills, for it seemed to tell of queer things waiting on the other side of the valley—the dank holds of Seaships filled with sacks of grain, and stinking scrapheaps, and walled darknesses filled with limitless living flesh to feed on. Yet the melody also described dangers that hunted swiftly from behind: steel-jawed engines, swift monsters with rending teeth and claws, and treacherous, irresistible sweetmeats that tasted delicious but burned caustic through the stomach and brought agonizing death. The rate hearkened and followed. The people hearkened, but did not understand.

As the last of the rodents, the maimed, lame, and slow, struggled to catch up with the horde, the Talith slowly emerged from their dwellings and followed, to see where they would go. Through the wrought-iron gates of the city went the people, until they assembled in a great concourse outside the high walls and looked out across Glisswater Vale, while the more venturesome youths gave chase.

The sun was setting in citrine splendor behind the city. Long light lay across the land, sparkling on the distant ribbon of the River Gliss where golden willows leaned. The thin trilling of the pipes interwove with their leaves and echoed down the valley. The black tide followed the road,

with the Piper at its head, and more tributaries ran to join it
from the valley farms, until at last it turned off towards
Hob's Hill.

The rats never returned.

Those brave youths who had continued the chase reported that a portal had yawned suddenly in the green flank
of the hill. There the Piper had entered. The rats followed
him faithfully, every one, and were swallowed up inside. Instantly, a pair of double Doors swung shut, meeting in the
middle. The sound of the pipes ceased abruptly. There remained no crack or disturbance to show where any Doors
had existed. A chill dark wind then blew across the land, and
a solemn watchfulness closed in upon Hob's Hill.

But Hythe Mellyn rejoiced. The spires and belfries gave
voice with their great brass tongues. After throwing open
every gate, door and fenestration, the people danced in the
streets. Not a hale rat remained, only a few crushed and crip-
pled ones, soon to be swept away. King Branwyddan, who
had removed his court to his palace in Ysteris until such
time as the pestilence would be contained, returned soon
after. He commanded the refurbishing of the city, so that all
should be cleansed and repaired. The Lord Mayor ordered
that the coffers be opened and the city's gold be used to buy
in what was needed. Only the Piper's promised payment
was held in reserve, in expectation of his imminent return,
and a hero's welcome was prepared. So began a time of
great industry in Hythe Mellyn, but in their happiness the
workload seemed light to the populace, and in their busy-
ness they did not stop to ask, or perhaps did not want to ask,
where the Piper had gone and why he had not immediately
returned for his reward.

A week slipped by, and another, and another. Still the
Piper did not appear, but if he was mentioned at all, it was
in whispers. He was no mortal creature, that was certain.
Some thought him one of the Faêran; others said he was

naught but an eldritch wight. There was talk of his being unseelie, malicious, and in league with the rats, for one of the
councilors vowed he had spied a small black creature in the
Piper's pocket when he took out his instrument. Iron horseshoes were placed above every archway, and in the gardens
the rowan-trees were hung with bells. But the Piper did not
return and the people began to conjecture that he had been
trapped under Hob's Hill, or had perished, and that by a
stroke of fortune they were rid of this creditor as well as the
rats. Many congratulated themselves on their luck, but others shook their heads.

"He will return," they said quietly among themselves.
"Immortal beings do not forget, nor do they perish so easily.
He will return for his payment."

And they were right.

Seasons changed. Little by little, the gold set aside for the
Piper was borrowed for other purposes. Hythe Mellyn returned to its former glory and the stranger who had saved it
from the rat-plague was almost forgotten. If ever he was
mentioned, it was now postulated that perhaps he had not
drawn off the rats after all—every plague eventually comes
to an end. Besides, there had not been so very many of the
rodents. The baits and traps and cats had wiped most of
them out before the ruffian ever showed his face. But a year
to the day after he had first appeared, the "colorful fellow"
turned up.

Under the judicious rule of William the Wise, Third
King-Emperor of the House of D'Armancourt, no war existed in Erith, and most walled cities did not bother to close
their gates at all. During the rat-plague, Hythe Mellyn's
gates had been sealed at night in an effort to reduce the numbers of invading vermin. Now they stood open again by
night and day. Well-equipped sentries, stationed at the en-

trances, possessed enough force to turn away the few undesirable outlanders who tried to come in.

They never saw the Piper enter.

In the city's heart, the doors of the Council Chambers also stood open, although sentries were always posted for ceremony's sake. These yeomen jumped and thrust forward their pikes as a shadow crossed the stone, but already the Piper walked within the solemn halls, past the statue of King Branwyddan on its pedestal, to stand before the assembled aldermen. In his gorgeous raiment he appeared like a ray of light piercing a stained-glass window. Amid the throes of their discussion, the councilors paused. Heads were raised. Surrounded by the echoing silence of the high-ceilinged hall, the stranger did not bow. He tilted his head cockily. That same faint smile tweaked the corners of his mouth.

"Gentlemen," he said, "I am come to claim my payment. Thrice seven bags of gold."

His words fell into a hollow space of incredulity and were bounced back from the walls and columns.

A mutter of indignation rippled across the chamber. The Lord Mayor rose from his seat.

"Piper, you are come late."

"Late or early, I am come," was the blithe reply.

The Lord Mayor cleared his throat awkwardly.

"But at the time of our bargain, our coffers were full. Now they are depleted, due to the refurbishment of the city. We can ill afford to make such a large payment."

The Piper offered no response.

"For playing a tune," continued the Lord Mayor, "a skilled musician should expect no more than a penny or two. However, we are grateful and not ungenerous, and shall give you a bag of gold. This should be more than enough to keep a thrifty fellow like you in comfort to the end of his days."

"City of Hythe Mellyn," came the cool reply, "you must abide by your promise."

Mutters of outrage and anger rose from the assembly. The Lord Mayor called for silence. Trouble creased his brow.

"Gentlemen," he said to his colleagues, "the Piper speaks truth—a bargain was made."

"Offer half," someone shouted, and argument broke out on all sides. Never in the city's history had the orderly proceedings of the council degenerated into such chaos. Ill feeling toward the jaunty fellow ran strangely high. For the Talith were a wise and just people, but perhaps over time, in the comfort of their prosperity, they had become somewhat arrogant, and their wisdom had become clouded by their love of their city. And perhaps there was some alien quality about the beauty of the Piper that, in some, provoked unreasonable fear and hatred.

Said the Piper, "I do not haggle."

The Secretary sprang to his feet. "Then," he shouted, his face congested with rage, "you are heartless and no true man. You shall receive nought."

A storm of approval greeted his words, against which the Lord Mayor remained silent. The Piper smiled, turned swiftly around, and was gone out through the doors. The aldermen heard a burst of clear laughter fading as he passed quickly through the precincts, and they were seized by a unexplained terror.

"We have done amiss," cried the Lord Mayor in much alarm. "Send the sheriffs and constables after him. He plots some dangerous mischief and must be caught."

Hardly had the messengers sped forth than an uncanny sound was heard throughout Hythe Mellyn.

The Piper was playing a different air.

This time, it promised honey-cakes and ponies, swings and sandcastles, hoops and whistles, rainbows, puppies, and Summer picnics—all lying ahead, on the other side of the valley. No man or woman hearkened to it but they wept, for they were taken as in a nostalgic dream back to the lost days of childhood. No child heard it but they must cease what they had been doing and go in quest of these enchanting delights. Thus, as the Piper danced through the streets, he gathered behind him another entourage. Among the bright-eyed, rose-cheeked faces, not one was above the age of sixteen years. From the houses of merchants and lords, aldermen and tradesmen, they came by the scores and by the hundreds—the sun-haired children of the city, the older ones leading the younger by the hand or carrying the babes. The small tots toddled as fast as they could, but the Piper went slowly. For him there was no need for haste, because all the grown-up citizens stood rooted to the spot. Weeping, they stretched out their arms and called the names of their children, who heeded them not. The children had ears only for the Piper's tune, eager eyes only for some distant place. Their little feet moved as if independent of their owners' control.

The tune, dangerous and irresistible, now told also of nightmares and loss, sickness and pain following hard behind, so that the children lagging at the tail end of the crowd wailed and hurried forward. The Piper danced down the valley road, through orchards bubbling with blushing fruit and fields lush with corn. Slowly the city was emptied of its youth. Along the rutted road between the hawthorn hedges they went, across the ivied stone bridge to the other side of the river where hazel bushes burgeoned and blackbirds sang, and on past the turnip-fields and the cow-meadows.

Unable to move, the parents could only shake their fists and scream and call down every curse on the Piper and beg help from the Faêran, or fate, or any source. For half the day the procession crossed Glisswater Vale, swelled by the children from the farms. The farmers could only reach out their empty hands and watch through brimming eyes. They could not see what happened when the children reached Hob's Hill, but they guessed. The great black Doors gaped, this time to admit the cherished flowering of the Talith. Then they snapped shut, as before, leaving no trace save the footprints of the little ones—a trail that ended halfway up the hillside.

With the closing of the Doors in the hill, the citizens found themselves released. They ran, the third living tide to surge down the valley road and across the bridge. They beat on the hillside. They brought shovels and excavated. They dug with their hands and scratched with their fingernails. Night drew in, and they worked on and on until the sun rose, all the while calling and crying until they were hoarse, but nought did they find save cold stones and soil, roots and worms.

In the weeks and months that followed, they brought every piece of gold and every treasure of Hythe Mellyn and laid it before Hob's Hill, until what was piled there was worth many times twenty-one bags of gold. Still the digging continued, deep into the hill's bowels, but no pick broke through to any secret hole or cavern. Many of the people lay down before the hill among the gold and refused to eat or drink, calling out that they themselves must be taken in exchange for their children. The Secretary of the Council was discovered to have hanged himself from his rafters. King Branwyddan of Avlantia came, bringing chests of treasure as an offering. His own sons had been too old to be taken, yet sorely he grieved for his people.

But no royal gold and no wizard's gramarye or wisdom, and no sacrifice of life or labor could open the Doors of Hob's Hill or even reveal the thinnest hairline crack of an outline.

Hythe Mellyn and all of Avlantia fell into despair.

In later days, travelers who came to the gates of Hythe Mellyn found the city deserted, and went away again. Several explanations were offered. It was reported that a pestilence had arisen and wiped out the population. Some folk said that the children never returned, and the townspeople in their grief hanged themselves on the red trees in the forest, or else traveled to the coast and cast themselves into the sea. Yet others said that the citizens had gone looking for their kin and become trapped under the mountains, and there they wandered still, lost in some strange country. The great Leaving of Hythe Mellyn was a fact, although the manner of the Leaving and the reason behind it were hidden from the knowledge of all, save for a select few.

But the truth of it was this:

When the last child had passed in under Hob's Hill, the Piper, who had stood playing his tune by the Doors as his followers entered, looked back along the road. Far away, just outside the city gates, a small shape crawled in the dust. He played more loudly and the shape moved a little more swiftly, but the sun was setting by this time. The wind bore a faint cry of ineffable sadness and longing over the treetops of the valley. The Piper looked to the sky and laughed, slipping inside the Doors just as they closed.

When the Lord Mayor ran out of the gates he found his little daughter lying in the dust of the road. Gathering her in his arms he brought her home.

Leodogran na Pendran, Lord Mayor of Hythe Mellyn, had given his daughter a pony on her seventh birthday.

"Now, do not let him loose," he had admonished tenderly, "as you did with the songbird."

"Father, he is beautiful!" the child had cried, thanking him with kisses. "And I shall not set him free, for he cannot fly, and might be eaten by wicked wights. But I shall love him and care for him as best I can."

"And ride him, for he is already broken to the saddle."

"Oh no. I shall not ride him unless he wishes it." She stroked the pony's snowy neck. "I do not wish to burden him and make him sad, for he has done no harm. But if he comes to love me as I already love him, then one day he will tell me he enjoys my company. And then, since I cannot run as fast as he, he may let me ride."

Her father shook his head.

"You are too sweet-natured, *elindor*. Be the beast's mistress!"

"Father, pardon me, for I do not wish to be discourteous, but he shall be my friend, and the friend of Rhys too. His name shall be Pero-Hiblinn: Little White Horse in the Olden Speech."

"I see you have studied your lessons, my little bird," stated Leodogran kindly. "But 'Pero-Hiblinn' is a tall name for a short horse."

"Then he shall be 'Peri.'"

"Come, let us take Peri to stable. But do not leave it too long before you ride him!"

And so it was that some weeks later in the last days of Autumn, Ashalind na Pendran rode on Peri's back across the daisy-speckled sward surrounding her father's house, which stood just outside the city walls. By Leodogran's side, young Rhys, Ashalind's brother, clapped his hands, crowing with delight. His sister had crowned him with Autumn daisies and he looked like a merry woodland sprite. As Peri cantered around the field with his tail flying like a white banner, a bird swooped out of the skies like a bolt, close to the pony's head. Startled, the beast reared up, flailing his front legs. The child was thrown to the ground and the bird flew away. Ashalind lay still, as if in a swoon, but when her father rushed to her side, his heart wrung with concern, he saw her eyelids flutter and knew that she lived.

A servant rode for the apothecary, who, after he had performed his ministrations, said: "Sir, such a fall might have proved more serious. Fortune has favored your daughter. She is hale in body save for her left leg, which is broken. I have set it. Let her now rest for three days, but when she rises she will not be able to bear her weight on the limb until it is healed."

A suitable pair of wooden crutches had been commissioned, but before they were ready the Piper had beckoned, and Ashalind had not been able to follow.

Now all the laughter was gone. It had fled from Hythe Mellyn and Auralonde and out of Avlantia altogether. The amber city was all silence and stillness.

From that execrable day when despair had come to Hythe Mellyn, Ashalind was the only child under the age of sixteen dwelling in all the great city, save for the babes who were born thereafter. No jealousy stained the bereaved hearts of the Talith, only love for this child who was the child of them all. A strange and lonely life it was for her, with no playmates of her age and no small brother with whom to frolic— only older youths and maidens, men and wives, graybeards and dowagers with hearts as heavy and eaten-out as old cast-iron cauldrons. Much of her time was spent with the carlin Meganwy, a woman of wisdom who understood the healing arts and taught her many things. Under Meganwy's guidance, the child grew to be a damsel skilled in herb lore and songs.

For Ashalind there was something more than the heartache of missing all those loved ones and watching the world turn gray-haired. For she had been touched by the Piper's call as none of the adults had, and been drawn by it just like the other children. She had been privy, for a moment, to a world beyond the fences of the world. Never could she forget it. In her inner being a longing had awoken, and it smoldered.

Never again, save once, did Ashalind ride upon Peri—

and that was at a time of great need. Her father did not care. He cared little for anything now except his daughter. Nothing she did could displease him. He took off his Lord Mayor's chain of office, for he had not the spirit for it anymore, and his young steward Pryderi Penrhyn, who had been seventeen years old when the children were taken, took over the running of his affairs in the city.

"I have failed in my duty," said Leodogran. "I ought to have spoken for the city and paid the Piper. My silence itself proved to be betrayal."

The delving of Hob's Hill continued at whiles over the years. Graves were raised up there also, for those who had pined away and wished to rest at last near their children. The grass grew over the pits and scars and over the graves, but every year on the first day of Autumn, the Talith of Hythe Mellyn laid on the hillside wreaths of late daisies, leaves, and rowan-berries tied with red ribbons.

The grass grew long on Hob's Hill and the slate-gray hair of Ashalind's father became laced with threads of silver. He withdrew from public life, spending much time in his library—studying, he said, books of lore. But often his daughter would see him there, sitting at the window, staring out into the distance, his eyes clouded like milky opals. His apple orchards, untended, fell into ruin—but his affairs in the city remained well-managed by his trusty steward Pryderi Penrhyn, who did not fail in his duties.

As soon as her leg had healed, Ashalind took to rambling at every chance with her hound Rufus through the wooded hills surrounding Glisswater Vale. Endlessly she sought Rhys and the children or looked for another way into the Piper's realm. Love for her father and brother drove her, no more nor less than that fierce white star of Longing kindled by the pipes, now burning within her.

Rarely were unseelie wights encountered in the eringl forests and Ashalind was not troubled by them in her wanderings, for Avlantia was a domain where evil things seldom strayed. This land was said to be beloved by the Faêran, of whom she had once or twice caught a flicker of a glimpse. Folk who had been visited by them told tales of their strange ways and their beauty.

Seven years Ashalind spent searching, never relinquishing hope when it should, reasonably have long given way to despair.

On her fourteenth birthday, her father gave her a bracelet of gold. Upon it was enameled a white seabird with outstretched wings—the elindor, the bird of freedom, which, after it left the nest, did not touch land for seven years but instead hunted and slept while gliding on the wing or floating on the ocean.

And one evening in late Autumn, just after her birthday, she met a stranger in the woods.

Pale moths were fluttering. A white owl flew into the gathering gloom. There was a glimmer in a clearing. She thought she spied an old gentleman standing there, leaning on a staff and watching her. Approaching without fear, she greeted him courteously.

"Hail to thee, lord."

"Well met, Ashalind, daughter of Leodogran."

His voice was as deep and mellow as dawn.

At this the damsel hesitated, for she was startled not only by his use of her name but by the piercing eyes that bent their gaze to her from under the shadow of his hood, eyes like those of a wild creature, but in what way, she could not say. The whiteness of his robes was as pure and perfect as a snowscape. The hoarfrost of his long hair and beard was like the silver of bedewed cobwebs, a fantasy in crystal lace, a symmetry in ice and diamonds hung with long prisms. His glance was a frozen sword catching the sunlight and stabbing it with brilliant sparks. Yet beneath the snow lay warmth. Now that she viewed him closely, she could not say why she had thought him very old, other than the reason of his pastel coloring, for very few lines were graven upon his face.

His strangeness now engendered in Ashalind an uncertainty bordering on fear. Her fingers touched the tilhal at her throat but the whitebeard said:

"I am no unseelie wight, daughter. You have naught to fear. How should I not know who you are, since you are seen wandering our forests day after day, year by year? Such loyalty as yours should not go unrewarded."

"Sir, I do not know your name but I guess that you are a mighty wizard, such as Razmath the Learned, who fashioned my tilhal."

"I am called Easgathair."

Ashalind seized her opportunity.

"I beg leave to ask of you the same questions I ask of all folk I meet, especially the wise and learned."

"Ask."

Ashalind hesitated again, for there was something thrilling yet almost perilous about this sage, and his presence disquieted her. It came to her, then, that she stood before one of the Faêran. Nonetheless she gathered up her courage, for never yet had she been daunted in her quest, despite that it had forever been fruitless.

"Do the children of Hythe Mellyn still live, and if so, can they be regained?"

The sun had now set and the white moths were clustered more thickly in the air. All around, eringl leaves spread rumors among themselves. A night-hunting bird hooted. The old gentleman shifted his staff.

"Yes," he said, "and yes."

At this reply, Ashalind caught her breath. Many times she had received this same answer from the learned or the optimistic, but this time the words were declared with more than hope or conviction. They were uttered with knowledge.

"If they have taken any food or drink then the children cannot return to you," he continued, "but they may not have done so yet, for seven years of Erith seem shorter than one night to them in the Fair Realm, and they are under the enchantment of their games."

"What is to be done?"

"One alone may go after them and fetch them back. One who has the courage."

"I have it. But I do not know the road."

"Hearken. In view of your faithfulness, and because the treachery of your city was no fault of yours, Ashalind na Pendran, I shall tell you how to find the road. Tomorrow night you must couch yourself beneath the ymp-tree in your father's orchard. Stay awake, and you will find the way. But truly, you are exceeding beauteous and they would keep you, so you must go in disguise. Perhaps they will not expect deception from one so young as you, and may look no deeper. Twine about you sprigs of mint and lavender, so that long-nosed wights may not encounter the fragrance of your skin. Neither speak first, nor give thanks, but show due appreciation. Beware of Yallery Brown and do not reveal your true name."

Ashalind fell to her knees, trembling.

"I will do it all. Pray tell me, good sir, when I go there, how should I make them hearken to me?"

"The moon waxes to the full, and these are feast nights in the halls of the Crown Prince, Morragan, the Fithiach of Carnconnor. At such times he looks mercifully upon petitioners, and may grant favors. He will never vouchsafe the unconditional return of those you seek, but he may vouchsafe the chance to win them."

The staff in the sage's hand was a shaft of moonlight. Moths settled along it like snowflakes. An owl sideslipped low overhead with a whoosh and a whirr of predators' wings. It blurred into the night. The Faêran regarded the damsel with a thoughtful stare.

"Think thrice before you take this chance," he said. "So far, your path has wended across the ordinary hills and dales of humanity. But if you dare to enter the Realm it will change your life forever. Be careful, be very certain before you choose to step across the boundary."

"There is no choice to be made. I must bring them back."

"You are untutored. Beware of the power of gramarye. If on second thought you should decide to continue your normal life, one day perhaps this dream of redemption shall cease to trouble you and you might live in contentment as the years pass by. If you gain entry to the Realm you must pay for it—and the price can be high. No matter which choice you make, you may regret it."

"Sir, no words shall sway me."

"Now thrice have you averred this. Go then. I have warned you."

With that he turned away and went into the shadows under the trees.

"Lord Easgathair, please wait!" she called, following. But he moved swiftly for one so old.

"If you get in, neither eat nor drink until you are out," were the last words he called over his shoulder, and all she saw was the snow-glimmer of his robes vanishing among the eringls ahead and a few white owl-feathers strewn on the ground among the ferns and mosses.

On the following day, Ashalind made the housekeeper, Oswyn, repeat a vow of secrecy. Delighted by the thought of adventure, the woman bustled about following her mistress's instructions, bringing men's rough garb of tunic and breeches, packing the pockets with fragrant herbs as instructed, dyeing Ashalind's hair with black ink and rubbing pig's grease into it until every filament was snarled and tangled. Between them, they pulled the matted locks forward to conceal most of Ashalind's face and bound the rest in a club at the back. The damsel regarded herself critically in the looking-glass. She practiced pulling faces and speaking from the side of her mouth, all the while wondering whether she would have the effrontery to carry this through and whether she ought to walk with an uneven gait, like a farmer's lad accustomed to clod-hopping among furrows.

That night, Leodogran's daughter stole down to the garden and delved her white hands into the soil, tearing her nails on the stones and smearing her face with cinders and clay. Then she went into her father's orchard and lay down beneath the ymp-tree, the most ancient tree of all, the grafted apple. The leaves fell down around her, lightly covering her as she lay wrapped in a blanket. Under the light of the moon and the stars she tried to stay awake but at last slept, dreaming strange dreams of laughter and the ringing of bells, and songs of joy and grief that wounded like swords. But she saw no road. She awoke damp and cold in the blue light of dawn, her thoughts first straying to her own featherbed in its warm chamber, with her hound lying on the rug, and then to young Rhys, lost and crying in the darkness.

None of her friends in the city had ever beheld the sage Easgathair, and when she sought him in the woods she found no sign. The next night she dressed in disguise and kept vigil as before, but again, sleep took her and she discovered nothing. On the third night as she lay, she twined briars and thorns about her wrist to keep herself awake with their pricking: a wild, lacerating bracelet in place of the smooth gold band she usually wore. Late after middle-night she was still awake when she heard at last a heart-stopping sound: the crystal chime of a bridle-bell.

Then it seemed to her that the wind lifted her suddenly and swung her against the night sky.

The jingling approached like the spangle of sequins, like

a woodland of silver bell-flowers rustled by a summer-silk breeze.

Seen indistinctly in the star-watered gloaming between the apple orchard's fretted boughs, a procession of seven score riders was slowly passing by.

A Faêran Rade.

Breathtakingly fair were they, with a shining beauty that was not of Erith. All were arrayed in splendid raiment of green and gold, and mounted on magnificently caparisoned steeds whose bridles glittered with tiny bells, like chains of stars. The knights among them wore golden helmets. Clasped about their limbs were finely chased greaves. Some bore in their hands golden spears like shafts of pale sunlight. To see these riders was startling, like a first glimpse of new blossom in Spring—a sudden enchantment glimmering against boughs that lately stretched stark and black.

To see them was to truly awaken, for the first time.

A knocking started up under Ashalind's ribs, for the yearning within her, born of the Piper's call, had found an answer at last.

The horses were of a splendid breed, surpassing any she had ever seen in the world—noble, milk-white steeds, moving with the grace of the wind. Each possessed the arched neck, the broad chest, the quivering nostril, and the large eyes of a superb hunter. They seemed made of fire and flame, not of mortal flesh. Each was shod with silver, striking silver sparks with each step, and each bore a jewel on his forehead like a star.

The fair riders made the orchard ring with their clear laughter and song, but other horsemen surrounded them—mounted bodyguards or companions. In contrast, these outriders were of hideous form and face and mostly smaller in stature.

When the last of the procession had passed, Ashalind sprang to her feet and followed. Keeping well back so that they would not spy her, she ran after the riders, out through the orchard gate and down Hedgerow Lane and on across the valley. Although the revelers seemed to ride slowly, Ashalind was hard-pressed to keep up. She dropped farther and farther behind. Not once did any face turn back toward her—neither the achingly fair knights and ladies nor the misshapen riders seemed to notice her at all. and thus she grew bolder and more desperate, until after they crossed the bridge there was no more attempt at concealment and she ran openly, gasping for breath, her left leg throbbing deep in the bone.

Ahead loomed Hob's Hill, but now there was a broad road leading to it that had never been there before, and the side of the hill was open. A great light streamed out of the arched Doors. Without pausing, the procession rode inside. Their pursuer was so far behind that she saw the last of them pass within before she could come near. In great fear lest the entrance should disappear before she could reach it, she sprinted forward, sobbing with agony and longing. Her heart banged so loudly in her chest that she thought it would burst. As the monumental Doors finally began to swing to, Ashalind had almost reached the threshold. With a last effort she flung herself through the portal and heard, at her back, the sonorous clang of stone clapping against stone.

All seemed dark at first, but ahead, as if from beyond a corridor or tunnel, shone a pale pink light like the glow of dawn. Recovering her breath, Ashalind hurried toward it. A breeze blew from there, rose-scented, poignant. An extraordinary excitement surged through her, swelled by a sense of yearning and urgency.

The long hallway ended in a second archway. It's single Door stood open.

Beyond, she beheld a staggering view. Under a sapphire sky, a fair land of wooded hills stretched away to mountains of terrible height and majesty, their keen peaks piercing rings of cloud. She had heard tales and songs of the Fair Realm, and the Piper's tune had described it, but the splendor, the seduction, and the fascination of that realm had never yet come home to her. Her heart was possessed, stabbed by enchantment and desire, and she gazed, almost forgetting her mission, at the land beyond dream or invention. She wept, for it was the land of the Piper's tune, and she had only to walk a few steps to reach it. But those steps were forestalled.

Out of a side opening she had not noticed before sprang two small black figures dressed in mail, crossing their pikes to bar her way. Their ears were long, upstanding and pointed, their mouths wide and their noses broad. They stood about three feet tall and exuded a strong odor of leaf-mold.

In accents unfamiliar, these small and evidently dangerous adversaries demanded, "Halt stranger. Who trespasses here and on what business?" A gleam darted from their slits of eyes. Their barbed and whiplike tails switched aggressively from side to side.

Ashalind drew herself up to her full height and tried to gain a moment to ponder, for she had not remembered to make a new name for herself. She shrank from giving them the name of anyone she knew in case it brought the owner into danger. Thoughts quarreled in her head—the kenning her father called her, and her golden bracelet, now lying on the dressing-table at home. She spoke in a gruff voice, mumbling.

"I am called Elindor. I am come to ask a boon of the Lord Morragan of Carnconnor."

Distastefully, the spriggans eyed the filthy peasant lad.

"Steenks," they agreed, exchanging nods. They spoke to each other in their own creaking tongue.

"Follow," they said at last, and one entered into the opening from which they had appeared, where a stair led upward. With one last longing glance at the land *beyond* the hill, Ashalind started to climb, and the second spriggan came after.

The stair soared up and up, and opened into a corridor from which led many branches and portals leading to rooms and other stairways, one of which the leading guard climbed. At the top of this second flight was a third. By now Ashalind had been rendered once again breathless, for it was difficult to ascend so far and fast. Fortunately she was not hampered by skirts or a feigned limp, although in the leg that had been broken the bone ached. Already weary from the race across the valley, she was also troubled by thirst.

The wights led her finally to a high room in a tower. The door stood open and a resplendently furnished room lay within. The walls were clad with bright tapestries and leafy vines; the chairs and tables were wrought of gold, embellished with jewels and living flowers. One of the tables was set with goblets and jugs, and dishes piled high with fruits and sweetmeats. Warm air blew softly in at the open windows. What had at first seemed to be a blaze in the hearth was no fire, but a heap of roses so red they seemed aflame. Ashalind had never seen such a splendid room and hardly dared venture in.

"Enter," said the creaking voice of the leading spriggan sentry.

She went in, but the speaker was no longer to be seen, nor was the other who had been following behind. After examining the room in amazement, she moved to the windows and looked out. There below she saw the spreading of a great garden ringed by a greenwood. Birds and fountains made music, a sea of roses surged and broke like waves against the garden walls, and on the long lawns children played.

The children of Hythe Mellyn.

Unchanged, not a day older than when they had departed seven years before, they frolicked there, lit by brilliant sunlight that seemed peculiarly clear and pink, as if viewed through a pane of roseate quartz. Ashalind dared not call to them, disguised as she was, but tears of joy and pain stung her eyes when she spied Rhys among them. Leaning from the window, she stretched out her arms, but a sound at her back made her start and turn around.

The spriggans had returned. They led her through the thundering halls and extravagant galleries of a fantastic palace, until they came at last to the most amazing hall of all.

Therein, the air was charged.

Lofty trees grew along the walls—indeed they constituted the walls, intersticed by greenery. Their boughs made a serpentine roof of leaves, forming arches laced together by the mellow breeze, tiled by glimmers of azure sky. Flamboyant birds winged across this ceiling and owls perched as if carved.

Merriment resounded, and music of harps and flutes. Long, narrow tables stretched the length of the hall, set with gold-wrought bowls of flowers and platters of food. Seated along them was a splendid company.

At the sight, Ashalind's head spun. For a long instant she thought she fell upward from on a rocky height into a dizziness of open sky where points of light glistered, thick as salt. The song of the stars seemed to choir in her head.

She was among the Faêran.

A faint shimmer of radiance surrounded them. Their voices fell like flower petals on water, as musical as birdsong in the morning. They spoke in a language Ashalind did not understand: a tongue as smooth as polished silver, as rich as the jewel-hoards of dragons. Some wore scarlet and gold and amber like leaping flames, some were clad in green and silver like moonlight on leaves, some in soft gray like curling smoke. Others among them appeared to be as naked as needles, graced only with the beauty of their comely forms and their flowing hair, which was threaded with jewels and flowers.

Courageously, Ashalind stepped forward. Instantaneously, silence fell and all eyes turned to her.

Justly were they called the Fair Folk. Indeed, they were the fairest of all, possessing a beauty that was intoxicating, almost paralyzing. Ashalind had barely caught sight of them through the half-leafless boughs of the apple trees, but now that she was so close, it seemed to her as if her heart and brain had stopped functioning and she could think of nothing to say.

They seemed at first if formed of air and light, yet as strong and living as trees, as lively as wind and fire and swift-flowing waters. Clean and finely drawn were their features, with high cheekbones and sculpted chins. At the outer corners, their eyebrows and their eyes swept up, slanting ever so slightly, as if everything about them was suspended from above and only whimsy anchored them to the ground. Tall and straight as spears were they, the lines of their forms clean and hard. Taut was their peach-blossom skin. Always they smiled and laughed. Indeed, it seemed that gravity and other weighty matters never touched these flower-ladies—fragile and slender, almost waiflike—or these virile lords possessed of the strength and grace of warrior heroes, who were beautiful in another way entirely—not as flowers, but as lions and eagles of immense power. Ashalind thought some among the assembly were older, some younger, but how they gave this impression was hard to say. No heavy jowl, no sagging chin gave evidence of accumulated years. Perhaps the effect of age was lent by an air of greater wisdom and tempered gaiety, in addition to some indefinable aspect of appearance.

Appearing stiff and awkward by comparison with the

easy grace of the Faêran, eldritch wights sat among them. These seemed to be mortal men and women, but were not. Some were lovely to look upon, others ordinary—but all were betrayed by some deformity, no matter now minor. Others not so beauteous also mingled with this astonishing company: dangerous fuaths and murderous duergars, un- seelie wights of assorted hideousness whose spindly shanks and outsized extremities made a screamingly grotesque con- trast to the beauty of their companions. To Ashalind they ap- peared like fungoid growths and molds sprouting amid wildflowers.

Woodland beasts she saw also—the mask of a narrow- eyed fox, the curve of a deer's neck, lop-eared hares pale as curd flitting over the roots of the wall-trees, a raven on a high branch.

A voice announced, "Elindor of Erith comes to beg audi- ence of His Royal Highness, Morragan, Crown Prince of the Realm, Fithiach of Carnconnor."

Bright, melodious laughter rippled around the hall as Ashalind approached the high table and knelt, hardly daring to raise her eyes.

"His Royal Highness bids me welcome you, stranger," said a corrosive voice. "Come, drink the guest-cup with us."

The fellow who had spoken gave a rictus of a smile. He was small and thin, with bloodless lips, a savage, wrinkled face of a yellowish-brown hue, a greasy beard sprouting from his chin. His hair hung lank and stringy, like tangled rats' tails, but it was striped with the colors of dandelions and mud. Clothed in shades of tan and yellow, he stood be- hind the shoulder of a tall Faêran lord who was seated at the center of the high table.

As Ashalind dared to lift her gaze for a moment to this lord, a cool, keen wind gusted through the hall.

Or so it seemed.

With eyes as gray as the cold southern seas, *he* was the

most grave and comely of all the company. Hair tumbled down in waves to his elbows, and it was the blue-black shade of a raven's wing. The heartbreakingly handsome face betrayed no sign of any passion. Leaning his elbow on the table with the relaxed poise of the omnipotent, he regarded his petitioner, but said nothing.

Bending forward, the wrinkled fellow at the lord's shoulder poured a draft into a jeweled horn and offered it to the newcomer, along with a knowing leer.

"Drink, *erithbunden*."

"Sir, I respectfully decline your hospitality, but let it be no cause for ill will, I beg of you. I am come but for one task, and I have vowed not to eat or drink until I have accomplished it."

It was a sore trial to Ashalind to say this, for the wine was sweet-scented, clear and pale green like the new leaves of Spring in Ysteris, and thirst shriveled her palate.

"You are as discourteous as you are decorated with the dirt of your country," reprimanded the rat-haired fellow, handing the horn to a gargoyle-like creature, which gulped the drink. "And what may be that task?"

Undaunted she bowed, replying, "I have come to win back the children of Hythe Mellyn."

The crowd of Faêran murmured among themselves, and the sound was a brook in Spring, or wind through the cornfields.

"And why do you wish to take them away from this happy place?" barked Rat-Hair. "For mark you, they dwell in bliss."

Ashalind found no words for reply but bowed her head in silence, afraid of causing insult and losing her chance to redeem the lost ones.

"His Royal Highness's Piper should have been paid," continued the puckered fellow. "A bargain is a bargain. The brats are our playthings now, to toy with as we please. Mayhap we will keep them forever. Mayhap on a whim we will send them back"—with a sudden grin he cocked his head to one side—"in a hundred Erith years"—his head jerked, bird-like, to the other side—"and watch them wither with accumulated age, crumbling to dust as soon as they set foot on Erith's soil!"

This drollery was greeted with joy by several of the more insanely hideous unseelie wights.

Then for the first time the raven-haired prince spoke. His voice was deep and beautiful, like a storm's song.

"What shalt thou give, to earn these children?"

Ashalind, still kneeling, heard her blood thump behind her ears. She chose her words carefully before she made reply.

"Your Royal Highness, ask of me what you will and I will endeavor to provide it—if such is within my power and causes no evil."

"Think you, that you can make conditions, *cochal*-eater?" snapped the ocher-faced fellow. As he spoke a large rat ran across his shoulders and disappeared, and the warm wind from the window-arches turned chill, lifting the gray-eyed lord's fall of hair as if he were undersea in a current, spreading the strands like dark wings.

But the prince-lord smiled.

"Elindor of Erith thinks to consider his words wisely," he said. "Consider this. If thou canst solve three questions of me, then thou shalt take away thy noisy brats. If not, then they shall stay forever, and thou also."

Ashalind bowed low.

"Sir, your offer is accepted as graciously as it is given, and I am ready for the three questions."

"First, tell me how many stars shine in the skies of Erith. Next, tell me what I am thinking. Last, thou must consider two of the Doors which lead from the chamber below this hall, and tell me which one leads to Erith."

At these words the ratty fellow laughed hideously, but his master's face still revealed nothing.

Despair threatened to overwhelm Ashalind. She tried to play for time.

"Those questions are . . ." she fumbled for words, "not easy, sir. I beg leave of you to take time to ponder them anon."

"Beg, snivel, grovel," said the servant. "Now or never."

"Hold thy tongue, Yallery Brown," said his master. "Or I shall have thee again imprisoned beneath the stone. Go then, mortal, I grant thee the time. But speak no word, scribe no symbol, and make no sign until thy return, for the answers must be of thine own inspiration and not of others. Return when the moon of thy land waxes full again. Give me the answers then or my servant Yallery Brown shall have thee too." He turned away, to drink from a goblet he held in his hand.

Then the spriggans seized her and rushed her down from that place, and when she came out from Hob's Hill she found herself alone in the night and the falling rain. But the moon was crescent and three weeks had already passed.

When Leodogran's daughter was discovered to have vanished, the city had roused to uproar. She was sought high and low, until Oswyn in fear and shame confessed a garbled version of all that had passed—that Ashalind had met a wizard named Easgathair who had told her how to find a way to the Perilous Realm.

"Alas," mourned Leodogran, "for now she too is lost."

He fell into a fit and would not allow a morsel of food to pass his lips. Oswyn had expected dismissal, but Leodogran told her she was blameless, whereupon she fell to her knees and thanked him for his mercy and justice.

The learned wizard Razmath was consulted.

"Easgathair is not a wizard but the Gatekeeper of the

Faêran," said he. "Mayhap Ashalind has been ensnared because, after all, she is the One Who Would Not Follow when the Piper played his dire tune. The laws of the Faêran, so it is said, are absolute. It may be that she was marked as their own from the very moment the Piper blew the first note."

In the house of na Pendran, one rainy eve, Pryderi the loyal young steward sat by the fireside with Leodogran. All the servants were abed, for the hour was late, when the hound Rufus began joyously to bark and there came a knocking on the door. There on the threshold stood Ashalind—wet, dark, dirty, dazed, unspeaking. From her black hair, ink ran in rivulets down her face and her ill-fitting men's garb. Leodogran clasped her in his arms.

"Never shall I let you from my sight again, Elindor mine," said he. "My bird, my precious bird is come home."

But she spoke no reply.

A cool wind was blowing from the south. Leodogran's daughter left her father's lore-books where she had been studying them in the library. Throwing her cloak about her shoulders, she unlatched and opened the front door, but her father, appearing at her elbow, closed it again and took her hand.

"Ashalind, you must not go out."

He studied her face. He could see that a great conflict was happening within her, and knowing this hurt him grievously.

"How can I help you? Why do you not speak?"

But his daughter was afraid to make any sign, even to shake her head, for the power of the Faêran was everywhere. Somehow they would know, and the chance would be lost forever. She turned again to the door.

"Wait. I shall walk beside you." Concerned only for her welfare, Leodogran took up his own cloak and his walking-stick. If, in her sickness, she needed to wander, so be it— only he would never let her from his sight.

Thus, every day at dusk in the wooded hills about the city, Ashalind walked with Leodogran and Pryderi, while the dog Rufus followed close in her footsteps. Tears ran unstaunched down the damsel's face, for she sought there Easgathair, believing he might help her in some way, and she feared he would not appear before her unless she walked alone. Yet her father would not leave her nor could she ask it of him. Her hope was that Easgathair would tell her the answers to the three questions without even being asked, for it was certain he would know of the bargain she had struck in the hall under the hill. But all that passed through the eringl woods were the white moths and owls. Without the help of Easgathair, she and the children must be doomed.

The third problem set by the Faêran prince at first appeared not to be difficult. She had seen two Doors leading out from a chamber below the Hall of Feasts, one made of polished silver and the other made of oak. It would seem simple enough to recognize the portal leading to Erith—but perhaps over-simple. Faêran things were often not as they seemed, and that task might prove the most treacherous of all. For the Erith Door to be fashioned of wood was too obvious. It was a trick—yet what if it were a double trick? Believing she would choose the silver Door, they would make sure the wooden one barred the way to Erith. Or perhaps not . . . Alas, that question might be more formidable than she had supposed, after all. For the second question she had prepared an answer—whether it would prove acceptable or not was another matter. But for the first there seemed no solution.

Every night, returning to the house, Ashalind gazed up at the sky. To look up and suddenly see the majesty of the far-flung net of stars burning blue-white in their trillions, that was an awesome experience. Always that moment of first seeing them was like the moment when, after silence in an echoing hall, a choir of hundreds burst into song, high and deep, accompanied by the rumbling growl of a pipe organ. The stars, indeed, seemed a heavenly choir if only she could hear their music. The Longing for the Fair Realm ached in her more gnawingly than before, ever since she had scented the rosy breeze at the end of the tunnel in the hill and walked the halls of Carnconnor. The sight of the stars in their quietude and utterness eased that pain yet exacerbated anxiety. How could they possibly be counted?

The swiftly waxing moon rode high in the heavens, pooling shadows in Leodogran's eyes. The glory of the stars blazed like diamonds thickly sprinkled on velvet. As soon as Ashalind began to count them, some faded and others twinkled forth, and they moved as on a great slow wheel, dying and being born.

On the night of the full moon, Ashalind stole secretly from the house and crept to the stables. There she had hidden a cloak that laced down the front. With this she covered her gown, adding a close-fitting wimple to hide her golden hair and a hood to overshadow her features. She smeared her face and hands with filth as before, and embraced the white pony standing in his stall. Silently, in thought only, she bade him farewell, not daring to even whisper his name. Win or lose, she must now honor her promise to return to the place beyond the hill. And lose she must, for should she solve the last two problems to the satisfaction of the Faêran, the first she could not answer.

"First, tell me how many stars shine in the skies of Erith. Next, tell me what I am thinking. Last, thou must consider two of the Doors which lead from the chamber below this hall, and tell me which one leads to Erith."

The final hour was come. She would be separated forever from her father, Pryderi, Meganwy, Oswyn, and her home. She would fall prey to the unseelie, unspeakable thing called Yallery Brown. Imagining what sport he might have with her, she quailed, hesitating. Should she go back, knowing she would fail? What if she never returned to those legendary halls—would they pursue her? Would they hunt her to the fences of Erith, or would they merely laugh at her impotency and faintheartedness, turning their backs on her forever? She had promised to return. *Honor your word,* her father always said. *Honor your word.* She must keep her promise to return to the Faêran hall. And, though it should be pointless, she must also honor the condition not to speak, scribe, or show sign. No farewell could be spoken, no letter could be left for her father.

She might vanish without clue and spend eternity in the rose garden with Rhys, or in the clutches of Yallery Brown, but in her perverse and willful heart, despite her misgivings, sorrow was mingled with excitement. Since her first glimpse of the Realm the white-hot Longing had begun to excoriate her mind more stringently than ever. That land was the vision of her waking hours and filled all her dreaming, and the pull of it was like the moon to the ocean. The Piper's tune had told all. It was indeed the world wherein lay all the hidden forests of fable, the soaring peaks of dreams, sudden chasms of weird adventure: a land at once dangerous and wild, yet filled with joy and wonders unguessed.

She muffled Peri's hooves, tying on rags. When she ran her fingers through his mane, one or two coarse hairs slid free to cling to her sleeve. One or two more would grow to replace them. The pony swung his head around to look at her. His brown eyes seemed full of wisdom, and as she gazed into them the answer came to her and she knew what to do. From the nearby tack room she fetched a sharp knife and hacked clumps of hair from the mane in several places, letting them fall into the straw. Haltering the now unlovely pony, she led him from the stall.

Beneath the silver penny of the moon went the cloaked damsel and the white horse, among the outbuildings to the overgrown apple orchard. For there was only one way Ashalind could be certain of finding the Doors under Hob's Hill once again. She lay down under the ymp-tree.

Middle-night approached. Gnarled lichen-covered trunks leaned, their leafless boughs reaching out to cast shadow-nets on weedy aisles. Feeling the spell of drowsiness coming over her, Ashalind clutched a clump of thistles. Needles of pain shot up her arm, awakening her to the sound of sweetly tinkling bells. The Faêran Rade passed through the trees like shimmering ghosts. Peri whickered softly and pricked up his ears. Climbing on his back, Ashalind followed.

As before, the Doors of Hob's Hill opened and the light from within revealed a paved way. Lagging several paces behind the end of the procession, Ashalind rode in. The Doors rumbled to, and she slid down to stand beside her steed, who strained toward the far archway. Beyond it now lay a landscape of purple night bejeweled with giant stars of every hue. The everdawn day of Faêrie had altered to soft silver-blue, a sonata in moonlight.

Would Rhys now be sleeping in a bower of blossom somewhere in the Fair Realm? Or would he and the other children still be playing their enchanted games in the rose garden under the canopy of stars? With a rush of tenderness a picture of his face came to mind: his skin soft as a ripe peach, his eyes wide and trusting. Always he had looked to Ashalind as a mother, since their own mother, Niamh, had died giving him birth.

The two spriggan sentries appeared and, complaining, commenced to escort the visitor away.

"Garfarbelserk, Scrimscratcherer," remarked one, hefting his pike in a knobble-jointed hand.

"Untervoderfort, Spiderstalkenhen," agreed the other with a nod and a scowl.

Peri snorted and tried to kick the wights, at which they struck at him with the butts of their pikes, screeching. Ashalind-as-Peasant-Lad shouldered her way between the weapons and the pony.

"Stay away from my steed! Hush, hush, Peri. You must come with me."

His mistress took the tilhal from around her neck and tied it to his halter for protection. This time the sentries led her by a divergent route with no stairs up or down.

Gathering force as she approached, the presence of the Faêran broke over her like a wave.

On this occasion she was brought to a different hall, whose walls were lined with silver trees. The ceiling was high, or else there was no ceiling. Overhead gleamed the shadows and strange fires of the night sky, a fever of stars. To a wild song of fiddles the Faêran danced, clad in rustling silk or living flowers, their hair spangled with miniature lights. Many wights, both seelie and unseelie, danced among them garbed in robes of zaffre and celadon. Repulsive beings, scaled, mailed, leathered, feathered, beastlike, or bizarre, mingled with the beauteous. Lace-moths drifted everywhere like bits of torn-up gauze tossed into the air. In the shadows, a pair of agates opened, watched, closed—the eyes of a great black wolf.

When the music ceased the dancers seated themselves around the hall, laughing, conversing in their marvelous language or in the common tongue. The contemptuous sentries beckoned and Ashalind stepped forward, keeping her cloak close-wrapped around her. Instantly a hush fell on the gathering. She felt herself to be truly alien here, a gauche, awkward thing, bound to the soil, bound to ordinariness and eventual mortality. How they must despise her. From under the shadow of her hood, her eyes scanned the gathering. A frisson of excitement surprised her when she saw him. It might have been fear or it might not.

Brighter than the rest was the soft radiance surrounding the gray-eyed lord. He stood on a dais at the far end of the hall, in the midst of a bevy of lords and ladies. Nearby, Yallery Brown sat with some ill-favored companions of assorted shapes and sizes, some resembling cruel-faced men and others so truly goblinesque as to approximate no living creature Ashalind had ever seen.

From somewhere to the right, a mellow voice announced her presence: "Elindor of Erith returns to beg audience of His Royal Highness, Morragan of Carnconnor, Crown Prince among the Faêran."

Whereupon Yallery Brown and his cohorts howled and hooted, prancing with glee. Ashalind waited on bended knee, her head bowed, firmly gripping Peri's halter. Thistledown, like thousands of tiny, pale dancers on tiptoe, floated through the air.

Morragan turned upon her cool, mocking eyes, eyes the color of smoke. "Elindor!" he said in his beautiful storm's voice. "Are they in truth naming young churls after birds in Erith?"

Her blood halted in icy veins. Could it be he saw through her disguise? Was a reply expected?

After a moment he laughed and said:

"No matter. Speak."

"Sir, I have returned with the answers to Your Royal Highness's three questions. The first was, 'How many stars are in the skies of Erith?' And I answer, that there are as many stars as there are living hairs growing on the body of my horse. See here, if it please my lord—it was necessary for me to cut some off to ensure that the total was exact. If anyone doubts this, they may count the hairs themselves and they will find that I do not lie."

A burst of laughter and applause greeted her words. Yallery Brown gave a shriek and his comrades yowled like cats. The Faêran lord did not smile, but Ashalind's hopes leapt, for he said:

"A clever reply, *erithbunden,* and amusing. So the first question is answered. What of the second? Canst thou tell me what I am thinking?"

"Yes sir," said Ashalind bravely, using her own clear voice for the first time. "Your Royal Highness is thinking his humble petitioner is a peasant lad, Elindor of Erith. But your Royal Highness is misled. I am Ashalind na Pendran."

At this, in a desperate and daring gambit, she threw off her disguise. Bright locks spilled down her back. Using the discarded wimple she wiped her face clean, then stood proud and straight before the astonished assembly, clad in her linen gown. The prince regarded her consideringly. Applause rang louder this time, and praises were shouted from all sides of the hall.

"E'en so!" some of the courtiers cried. "'Tis none other." For they knew of her, they had seen her wandering on the borders of the Realm, searching, and but for her hound Rufus, she might have been stolen years since.

All eyes turned to the prince, but he offered not a word. Then stepped forth a lady of the Faêran, and her loveliness was a poem. Her dark hair, bound in a silver net laced with glints, reached to her ankles. Her gown was cloth-of-silver overlaid with a kirtle of green lace wrought in a pattern of leaves. Laughing, she said, "Ashalind, we love clever riddles and tricks—you bring us much merriment this night. We would welcome thee to dwell among us."

"The golden hair of the Talith is much to our taste," added another Faêran lady, smiling.

Great wisdom was written in their beautiful faces. Ashalind wondered how such as they could traffic with unseelie things, but she recalled a passage from the lore-books:

"The laws, ethics, customs, and manners of the Realm

are in many ways unlike those of Erith and are strange to us."

"That," said Yallery Brown suddenly, pointing straight toward Ashalind, "is ours anyway. It was intended to be part of the city's payment." With unnerving swiftness he crossed to her side, reached up, and spitefully tugged her hair. The pony's eyes rolled and he shied nervously. Icy fire flowed down the damsel's spine. She noted a dandelion flower, yellow as cowardice, peeping from the wight's hideously knotted hair. It might have been growing there, rooted in his skull.

From among the gathering, a Faêran lord spoke. Like the others of his kind, he was comelier than the comeliest of men. A gold-mounted emerald brooch clasped his mantle at the shoulder, and on his head was a velvet cap with a swathe of long spinach-green feathers trailing down to one side.

"In order to find this way in to our country, thou hast spied upon our Rade from under the boughs of the ymp-tree. We of the Realm do not love spies. Other meddlers such as thee have paid the price."

"My fingers itch to tear out the eyes of this false-tongue mortal, my liege," said Yallery Brown, turning beseechingly to the prince.

"Yet this smacks of Faêran help and advice," interjected another Faêran lord. He was garbed in a gaily striped doublet, parti-colored hose, and versicolor cloak, his cap a rainbow of three horns. Ashalind thought she recognized him.

"Even this clever deceiver," Three-Horn-Cap continued, "could not have come here without the aid of one of our own people—so there can be no forfeit to pay. The Erithan brats were taken because of the perfidy of her kind, those same Men who delved the green slopes of the sithean with iron, and scarred it. But she did not follow me, and thus she is not part of the fee."

He smiled, showing dazzling white teeth.

"Yes, gentle maid," he added, "I am the Piper."

Of course, Ashalind hated the Piper, and yet looking upon him she was forced to admit she loved him, as one must love all the Faêran, even while abhorring them at the same time.

Said Prince Morragan, breaking his silence at last, "I desire no truck with mortals save for sport, and even that becometh tedious eventually."

"Never for me, my liege," whispered the rat-faced Yallery Brown. "Oh, never for me."

"She is not thine yet," replied his master. "Thus we come to the last question. If this *erithbunden* chooses aright, she and the others shall go free, and it shall be *their* loss. But if she chooses the wrong door, she and they will take the road to doom, Yallery Brown, and perhaps thou shalt be the architect of that doom or perhaps it shall be myself. Behold the Hall of Three Doors!"

As he spoke, the dancers parted, and behold! they stood already in that chamber Ashalind had seen previously. A pathway opened among the crowd revealing not only the Door by which she had entered, but also two closed portals. The Doors of silver and oak faced each other from opposite sides of the hall, and beside each one waited a doughty, grim-faced young man, in ragged plaid and heavy leather, feet planted firmly apart, each holding a pike twined with the dripping red filaments of spirogyra. These door-wardens stared into the distance, looking neither to right nor left. Their raiment too was wet—indeed water streamed from it in droplets and rivulets to pool around their feet. Seaweed was tangled in their lank hair.

"One of these Doors," said Yallery Brown, "leads to Erith. The other leads to your downfall." He played a little tune on a fiddle and added, "Think you that you and the brats be the only mortals in the Realm? Not so. For these pikemen of the Doors be Iainh and Caelinh Maghrain, twin sons of the Chieftain of the Western Isles, believed drowned with their comrades in the waters of Corrievreckan. Foolish and arrogant were they, to think they could ride the back of the finest steed in Aia. Now they have learned their lesson well, for they have served in the domain of the Each Uisge this many a long year. Lucky men are these, for their five comrades were torn apart and only their livers washed to shore. And although they look as alike as two peas in a pod they are as different as day from night, for one is forced to be an honest man, while the other never spoke a true word since my lord the Each Uisge became his master. Speak ye the truth, man?"

The guard of the silver Door said, "Yea."

"And speak ye also the truth?"

"Yea," said the guard of the oaken Door.

"You see, it is as I have said," Yallery Brown continued. "And this is quite curious to us, for lying is a skill possessed only by mortals. False wench, do not think that we shall tell you which man is which!"

A very pale, exceedingly charming fellow now came forward. He wore close-fitting green armor like the shell of a sea-creature, with a fillet of pearls on his brow and a dagged mantle of brown-green like the leaves of bull-kelp, but he moved like a horse, and despite his finery an unspeakable malevolence hung about him like a ragged shadow.

For a brief moment the mortal damsel looked into his terrible eyes. Cold and expressionless, they stared at her, as devoid of emotion or pity as fathomless water, as a drowning pool, as cold rocks and waves that relentlessly smash ships to splinters. Whatever his true shape, here was a thing of horror. She thought: *I am beholding the Each Uisge himself, the Prince of Waterhorses. May all that is benevolent preserve me.*

He said, "My servants only speak two words—yea and nay. They may never say more." His voice, booming like waves surging in subterranean caverns, ended in the hint of a whicker.

Then said Prince Morragan, "The mortal may ask one question of one pikeman only."

Ashalind turned as pale as the Each Uisge and clutched at her pony for support. She had hoped for more clues than this. The wights surrounding Yollery Brown screamed with laughter and leaped about, cutting the most fantastic capers, but the Faêran lady with ankle-length hair said softly:

"Ashalind, fairest, there exists a question which would reveal all to you, if only you could deduce it. We may not aid you in this, but do not despair."

"When the music stops," said the raven-haired Fithiach, "thou must needs choose."

The dulcet melodies began again, and a whirlpool of dancers flew around Ashalind and the pony, their feet in truth scarcely touching the floor. Time passed, but how much time she could not tell—whether it was a few moments or hours or days. There must be some question she could ask one of the guards, the answer to which would tell her with certainty which was the right Door. If she could not find it out she must choose at random and take a chance, as recklessly as tossing a coin: a chance of losing all, forever—not only for herself but for Hythe Mellyn and the children, for Rhys and their father and for Pryderi. Had she come this far only to fail?

The music and movement distracted her cogitations. She buried her face in the pony's ruined mane and covered her ears. In the darkness her mind raced with a thousand questions, and permutations of what their answers would reveal.

It is like pondering a move in a chess game, she thought. *If I ask this, then if he is the truth-teller he will say that, but if he is the liar he will say the other, and how should that help me in the end?*

With a flash of inspiration she lifted her head. She saw

that amid all the motion one tall figure stood and looked down at her and knew the triumph in her eyes.

"Thou hast another choice, Ashalind Elindor," said Prince Morragan softly. "To go out by neither Door. I have no love for mortals and would not be grieved if thy race all should perish, but thou'rt passing fair among mortals, and faithful, and acute. Bide here now, and I swear no harm shall come to thee under my protection."

Beneath straight eyebrows, the smoke-gray eyes were keen and searching. Strands of black-blue hair wafted across his arresting features. This Faêran was indeed comely beyond the dreams of mortals, and he possessed terrible power. The Longing for the Realm pained Ashalind like a wound. He spoke again, more softly than ever:

"I can take thee through fire as through castles of glass. I can take thee through water as through air, and into the sky as through water, untrammeled by saddle or steed or sildron. Flight thou shalt have, and more. Thou hast never known the true wonder of the favor of the Faêran."

For moments the damsel struggled, pinned by the piercing blade of his gaze, and then her pony blew on her neck and nuzzled her shoulder. At the sudden warmth of his hay-scented breath, she sighed and lowered her eyes.

"Sir, I must take the children home."

Instantly the gray eyes blazed with a bleak and cold flame. The prince turned away, his cloak flaring, sweeping a shadowy swathe through the air.

The music stopped. The dancers stood still.

"Now choose!" cried the Piper.

Ashalind went to the guard at the oaken Door and asked her question. He replied:

"Nay."

And she said, "Then I choose your Door."

Immediately the Door opened to reveal a long green tunnel of overarching trees beyond which shone the hills of

Avlantia in the saffron morning, and the larks were singing, and a merlin hovered in the sky, and the hedges were bare and black along the fallow fields, and blue smoke stenciled the distant skies. And from the city came the sound of bells: "Awake! Awake!"

But Prince Morragan grasped Ashalind by the hair, pulling her head back so that she must look up at him.

"Thou hast won this game," he said evenly. "Thou canst walk the green way and return to thy home. The children will come behind you, but only those who have not tasted of our food and drink. To them it will seem as though they have passed but one hour in the Realm. Go now, but if thou turnest back, even once, thou shalt return here and never leave." Abruptly he released her.

Tears pricked her eyes as she took the pony by the halter and stepped through the Door. The rumor of a multitude of footsteps came from behind, and childish voices.

Slowly she paced along the vaulted avenue, and soon the first of the children passed her, running down the road, calling to one another in joyful voices. She glanced to the side and saw many whose names she knew, but Rhys was not among them. Had her brother, then, been one of those who had eaten the food of Faêrie?

"Ashalind!" called the compelling voice of the gray-eyed prince. She stumbled, but plodded on. He called her name a second time and she halted and stood, but only for an instant. Onward she went, and now she was halfway along the arched way. More and more children ran past, like leaves blown by an Autumn gale, and there were hundreds of them, but still she could not find her brother, and she thought of Yallery Brown and his flesh-devouring rats, and her courage almost failed her.

"Ashalind."

This time she fell to her knees and could not arise. The children hurried by. To look over her shoulder, to see one who governed gramarye standing there with the whole of the Fair Realm at his back and that world promised to her—it would be so easy. So sweet it would be, to watch him pivot on his heel and walk away, and to follow. Slowly she clambered to her feet. Despite her desire, she neither looked back nor turned around. She pressed on, her feet and legs heavy, as though she waded through honey. Now the end of the avenue was near, and crowds of children streamed down into the valley, and rushing to meet them down the road from Hythe Mellyn to the bridge flew another crowd—the men and wives of Hythe Mellyn come to bring their children home. Forward into the sunlight went Ashalind.

Then, farther back, she heard the piping tones of her own brother:

"Sister, turn and help me, for I am afraid."

At that, with a rush of relief, she almost spun about, but she said, "Do not be afraid, Rhys." And still she faced toward Erith.

"Sister, turn and help me, for I cannot walk." Her heart was wrenched, but she hardened it.

"Then, Rhys, you must crawl, for I may not turn back."

His sobs turned to screams—"Sister, a monster is upon me!"

For the third time, Ashalind stopped, right under the eaves of the last tree, and her neck ached from the effort of not turning her head, and she cried out:

"No, you are not my brother, for he never addressed me as 'Sister'!"

Then she heard a crash of thunder and the angry scream of Yallery Brown, and wild laughter. A freezing gust of wind tore leaves from the trees. But her brother came up beside her and she recognized that this time it was he in truth. She set him on the pony's back and they followed the last of the children down the valley.

Sitting on a mullock heap beneath a briar-hung cliff, the young woman blinked. It had been a long time since she had done so and her eyes were filmed with mist, gritty. She looked at the bracelet in her hand, her father's gift. She slipped it on her wrist. Closing, the catch went *click*.

And the memories kept flooding back.

9
THE LANGOTHE
The Longing for Leaving;
the Leaving of Longing

> *What is Longing that it never lets go? Would that joy could grip us*
> *so!*
> *Even the strong oak falls at last, having withstood the south wind's*
> *blast.*
> *What is Longing that it never runs out? Even a well may fail in*
> *drought.*
> *What is Longing that it never ages, like leaves to dust and youths to*
> *sages?*
> *What is Longing that it will not depart and let peace descend on*
> *mortal heart?*
>
> MADE BY LLEWELL, SONGMAKER OF AURALONDE

The tale of the Return of the Children was recounted far and wide in Avlantia. The entire country feted and praised Ashalind na Pendran. A wealth of gifts and the highest honors in the land were bestowed upon her. Bards made songs about the brave maiden who had ventured into the Secret Country, facing not only the Faêran but also the most dangerous of wights, and, against all odds, outwitting them all. The King of Avlantia himself bestowed upon her the title "Lady of the Circle," with the rank of baroness. Glory and honor paved her way, and happiness ought to have followed—but it was not to be. There remained something the people of Hythe Mellyn had not reckoned with.

"Langothe," said the wizard Razmath, reading from a lore-book before an Extraordinary Assembly of the citizens of Hythe Mellyn. "The Green Book of Flandrys describes it as the Longing, or Yearning, for the Fair Realm. All who have visited Tirnan Alainn—as some of the ancients called it—all who have so much as *glimpsed* that country, wish to return. They do no good in the mortal world thereafter. They cannot forget it, even for a little while, and continually search for a Way to return. In severe cases they pine away to their deaths, having no interest in meat or drink and no desire for life in Erith."

Gravely he raised his eyes to survey the men and women seated before him.

"There is no known cure." He closed the book.

Stiffly, Leodogran rose to speak. He stood with shoulders bowed.

"Never has there been such joy in this city as on the day our children returned after seven years in the Perilous Realm. On that morn I rose from my couch to find my daughter's bed empty and foesaken. But there came to my door a messenger from Easgathair, Gatekeeper of the Faêran, saying, 'Ring the bells and rouse the city, for your daughter is bringing the children home.'"

He paused, fighting some inward battle, momentarily unable to speak.

"And on that day we believed all our dreams had come true. The children had indeed been restored to us, but alas, what was lost has never been entirely regained. The Langothe is upon them despite all we have tried. Not love nor gold nor wizardry can bring our children's hearts back to their native land. Though they love us and were overjoyed to be reunited with us, their thoughts constantly stray far away. Ever they wander, ever they search. We have consulted the histories and books of wisdom to no avail. In truth, there is no cure.

"Some lads and lasses never returned from the Perilous Realm because they had partaken of its food or drink. To add to the city's grief, their families have mourned long. My ladies, my lords and gentlemen, we lived in sorrow for seven years, and now for seven long weeks we have watched our neighbors grieve afresh while our children languish and fade. What say ye?"

Then Meganwy, the Carlin of the Herbs, rose to her feet saying, "I speak for most of us when I declare, we must put an end to sorrow. We cannot let the children's well-being continue to decline, nor can we bear to be separated from our darlings. Only one path lies open to us. Together we must seek a way to leave Hythe Mellyn, yea, to leave Erith's dear lands, and journey to dwell in the Realm. How we shall find that place, and whether those that dwell there will admit us, I know not."

This proposition was greeted with a great outcry, and fiery debate ensued, and continued throughout the many assemblies that followed.

Like the other mortal visitors to the Fair Realm, Ashalind had been brushed by the strange pull of the land beyond the stars. As with them, her interest in the meats of Erith had declined, and her flesh waned, losing the soft curve of youth and conforming closer to the angles of her bones. She did not speak of her own anguish, of the severity with which the Langothe seared her spirit. However, they guessed, her father and Pryderi. Rhys knew only too well; at whiles she and the ailing child would hold one another in a tight embrace.

"What is to be done, Ashli?" he would sigh. "What is to be done?"

At a loss, she could only shake her head.

The snowy lace of blossom was on the hawthorn when overnight, it seemed, there came a sudden increase in eldritch and Faêran activity throughout all the lands of Erith. Wights of all kinds were abroad in unprecedented numbers, and the Fair Folk were glimpsed much more frequently than ever before, in woodlands and meadows, in high places, and by water. Rumors seethed. It was said that some great catastrophe loomed, such as war or the end of the world. People whispered that the King-Emperor in Caermelor knew all about it, for he was in the confidence of the Faêran sovereign, and that they both struggled to avert the mysterious calamity. Many stories circulated, but none knew for certain what the truth might be.

A delegation of wizards, aldermen, and elders of Hythe Mellyn met on many occasions with Branwyddan, King of Avlantia, and his privy council in the palace that crowned the golden city. The fourteen-year-old Lady Ashalind and Pryderi Penrhyn, ten years her senior, were included among them. Hours toiled past in discussion.

"Your Majesty," said Meganwy of the Herbs, "in Hythe Mellyn there have been many gatherings of the people, and much ado. The Langothe sorely afflicts our children, and some have died of it. Families yearn vainly for their lost youngsters. Life burdened with this curse is unbearable for many—they wish to leave the city and find a Way into the Fair Realm, there to dwell in peace with their loved ones."

"How many wish to go?" the king asked, somber of countenance.

Razmath the Learned, wizard of Hythe Mellyn, replied,

"About one third part of the city's population, Your Majesty—those whose children are most severely affected or who never returned."

"That is many," sighed the king, "yet we have looked long upon these silent children and their wan faces. Even the sternest heart could not remain unmoved. I have pondered much on this matter and spoken of it at length with my advisers. Gravely it concerns me, that I cannot furnish contentment for my subjects. Grievously it troubles me that the goodly flower of my people would leave Hythe Mellyn. Yet their sovereign shall not stand in the way of their happiness. So it shall be. If they wish to go, I, Branwyddan, will not gainsay my people, though to lose them will surely be a devastating blow to this land. For many years now the numbers of our race have been dwindling. Sorrow waxes heavy within me—I fear that a Leaving such as this will herald the final days of the Talith." He added, "Perhaps only a hastening of the inevitable."

Leodogran said, "Your Majesty is gracious and just, and we thank you for your favor. But sire, we need your help, for we do not know how to discover a way to return. My daughter has lain awake beneath the ymp-tree night after night, yet no Faêran procession rides by, no Doors appear in the hillside. Methinks the Hob's Hill traverse is now permanently closed to mortalkind. I have scant knowledge of the Ways between the worlds. What say ye, Orlith?"

The king's wizard spoke. "Oak coppices, rings of mushrooms, the turf-covered sitheans, circles of standing stones, high places, green roads of leaf and fern, certain wells and tarns, stands of thorn or ash or holly—all these and more are sites where a Way may be found. It is said that these Ways into the Secret Realm, all so different, are each guarded by a Gateway configured like a short passage with a Door at either end, one leading to Erith, the other to the Fair Realm. They are not always doors as we recognize them, with posts and hinges, but Faêran portals that may bear many guises. These Gateways cannot be traversed without the aid or permission of the Faêran."

Then spoke Gwyneth, Queen of Avlantia:

"William the Wise, King-Emperor in Caermelor, has commerce with the Fair Folk, I believe. It is said that a great friendship exists between them."

"A messenger shall be dispatched forthwith, asking his help in this matter," said Branwyddan, "although I vigorously emphasize that it sorely grieves me to think of losing any of our people." Sorrow clouded his brow. "But hearken also to this—of late, unusual occurrences have disturbed all of Erith, as you are well aware, and they have shaken the very foundations of the Royal City in Eldaraigne. An answer from there may come late or not at all, for we hear that William, King-Emperor, is greatly occupied and hardly sleeps. Caermelor has issued orders to open new dominite mines, so that as much of this stone as possible may be dug out of the ground for two purposes: to line the walls of buildings, and to extract the base metal talium for the making of chain mesh. Furthermore, news has been received that heavily guarded shipments of a new kind of metal are being received at the King-Emperor's treasure-houses. What this all means, I may not yet say. But I tell you—time is not unlimited and you must not delay in making your move. Now is the hour to act. Speedily find a Way to the Perilous Realm if that is your desire, citizens of Hythe Mellyn, and end the suffering before it is too late."

In the soft spring twilight the air was heavy with honey fragrance. Leodogran remained at the palace in discussion with the wizards Orlith and Razmath, while his daughter walked in the company of Meganwy and Pryderi down the winding streets, through Hythe Mellyn toward the city walls. Ashalind was thinking of her little brother; at the house of na Pendran, the stolen and regained Rhys lay in his bed under Oswyn's care, dreaming of an enchanted rose garden.

"Pray tell us Mistress Ashalind," said Pryderi, forgetting, as always, her new title of Lady of the Circle. "What is the question you asked to find out the Door leading to Erith? For we have all pondered upon it until we are ready to tear out our hair and 'tis most unfair of you to make us suffer so."

Meganwy said to him, "But Pryderi, if you had studied the lore-books you would have found it! For although Ashalind reckoned out the answer herself, the riddle is an ancient one, and has been asked and solved before."

"Do not chide me with ignorance!" returned Pryderi good-naturedly. "I do not spend my days with my nose buried in books, that is all. There are better things to do. Now, Ashlet, you must relieve me of my misery."

"Not until you promise not to tease my Meganwy so."

"Oh, balderdash!" laughed the carlin, her eyes crinkling with merriment. "'Tis merely banter among friends. He only teases those he loves. Besides, I am used to it—after all, I have put up with it since the lad's knees were scabby as two tortoises. And that was a full day ago, at the least."

Pryderi snorted.

"The question," interrupted Ashalind, before he could respond with a clever retort, "which was in fact the *answer,* was, 'Would the other guard tell me that this is the door to freedom?' "

They walked awhile in silence, then Pryderi spoke again.

"I see. Well said. Acute, if I may say so. 'Tis fortunate you had perused the same moldy tomes as Meganwy."

"I had not! It is news to me that this is an old riddle. As Meganwy said, I fathomed it myself!"

"The more credit to you, child," said Meganwy gently.

"How strange it is," mused Pryderi, "that not so long ago

we would have given everything we owned if only the children could escape from the Fair Realm. Now we are desperately seeking a Way for them to return. Truly it is said, 'Misguided are mortals.'"

A pale, hollow-eyed child leaning from a casement called out to them. There was an ache in her voice.

"My lady, have you found a Way?"

"Nay," Ashalind returned, "not yet."

A gaunt, lethargic youth lounged beneath the wall by the city gates, looking out across the valley. A reed pipe hung from his belt. As though begging for his life he asked Ashalind, "Are you bound for Faêrie, my lady? Shall we return now?"

His name was Llewell, and he was one of the returned youths, a brilliant musician and songmaker. He was being driven mad by the Langothe. In his delusion he often believed he was truly one of the Faêran.

"Nay, Llewell," Ashalind said again, turning away lest the sight of his forlorn and desolate aspect should crush her heart. "Soon, maybe. Meanwhile, make us a song so that we might forget, for a time."

So it was, always, with the children. They turned to Ashalind in their blind and urgent need. They clung to hope in the form of her native wit, by which, once, she had achieved the impossible. They wanted to believe she could do it again. And like them, she had been *There*. She understood how they suffered with the Longing.

Outside the gates there was a stirring among the trees, a susurration in the leaves. The rumor of things unseen was everywhere: muffled laughter, scamperings, squeakings, shrill whistles, low mutterings, and far-off singing. The lands of Erith were alive with the denizens of Faêrie as never before—the Fair Folk themselves, often heard or sighted but rarely seen clearly, eldritch wights trooping and solitary, wights of water and wood, hill and house, cave and field; incarnations both seelie and unseelie.

"Eldritch creatures lurk all about us," said Meganwy. "Surely there must be one who can take a message to Easgathair. From your account, Ashalind, the Faêran sage seemed to hold you in high regard."

"Then the misguided are not only mortals," said Pryderi, striding ahead.

Ashalind smiled, as she still sometimes did, despite the dull, sustained pain of unfulfilled yearning. "Pryderi loves me!" she cried after him chaffingly.

"I do!" he called back over his shoulder.

Ashalind took Meganwy's arm.

"What you say is true, Wise Mother," she said. "Let us go direct to the orchard. It is said that apple blossom delights all creatures of gramarye, particularly the Faêran."

Soft wind, as warm as love, whispered sweet nothings to budding leaves. From far away scraped the raucous hubbub of jackdaws coming home to roost. A skein of swans stitched its way slowly across the mellow west. Passing under the trees and half-hidden by blossom, the urisk was unnoticeable at first, but a flicker of movement caught Meganwy's eye. Silently the carlin took Ashalind by the sleeve, indicating with her forefinger. A small, seelie manthing moved between the trees on hairy, goatlike legs.

"In the name of Easgathair," Ashalind called out urgently, "I bid you tarry."

With a rustle, the wight jumped away into the trees and was seen no more.

That evening after supper, Ashalind personally set out the pail of clean water and the dish of cream for the household bruney, a task usually carried out by Oswyn. The dark hours came creeping. She sat in the kitchen's inglenook, waiting, waking, and at midnight the bruney came stealing. Its face was ugly and rough, with a stubbly gray beard and wide mouth; its hands were outsized. A conical cap of soft brown deer's hide covered its head; its other clothing consisted of a threadbare coat, patched knee breeches, coarse woollen hose, and large boots. The damsel watched the wight begin its chores, sweeping and scrubbing, scouring the pans to mirror-brightness with preternatural speed and efficiency.

"Bruney," she said softly into the shadows, never taking her eyes from it, never meeting its gaze. The little manlike thing ceased its industry.

"What are ye doin' sae late awake, Mistress Ashalind?"

"I seek your help, hearth-wight of my home."

"I seen ye grow up from a bairn no bigger 'n meself, and yer father before ye and his father before that. Have I ever failed this house?"

"No, you've never failed this house. You've been good to us—never a dollop of sour cream, never a drop of unclean water. In return, we've looked after you. Bruney, I seek audience with the Lord Easgathair of the Faêran. Can you bring me before him?"

"I have ways to send messages to the Faêran, Mistress Ashalind, but I wist the Lord Easgathair will nae heed me at this time, if ever, for ill deeds and evil tidings have come upon us all."

"Of what do you speak?"

"Fell doings and ill fortune," said the bruney obscurely, "but there be nocht that such as I can do to change things. Alack that I should see such times as these. Alack for the folly of the great and noble. The world shall be mightily changed and what's tae come of it I know not."

"But you will try this for me?"

"Aye, that I will, hearth-daughter. Now get ye abed as is proper and leave me to my doings. They's my hours now, not yourn." He shook his little besom broom at her.

"Good night," she said, lifting the hems of her skirts as she flitted upstairs.

Toward morning, just before cock-crow, Rufus woke up and began to bark frantically at the bedroom door. Leaping half-awake from her bed, in her linen nightgown, Ashalind collared him.

"Hush, sir. Stay."

The bruney's head appeared around the door's edge and spoke. "'Tis only me, Rufus. What are ye groazling and bloostering about, ye great lummox?" Lowering his ears sheepishly, the dog wagged his tail. "Mistress Ashalind," the bruney went on, "I hae a message for ye."

"Yes?"

"Next middle-night ye mun gae to Cragh Tor."

The head disappeared.

Steep, thickly wooded hills rose close on every side, dark against the star-salted dome of night. Streamlets splashed like threads of spun moonlight down their shoulders. A path wound its way up Cragh Tor, overhung by a cliff on one hand, dropping away precipitously on the other. As the party of three walkers climbed higher, they saw, looking back through a gap in the hills, a scattering of yellow lights shining like fireflies in a dusky dell: the lamplit windows of the city.

Finding the hilltop deserted, they sat down on mossy stones to wait, uneasily. Cragh Tor's summit was flat. No trees grew there; instead it was crowned by a half-circle of granite monoliths, thirty feet high, a ruined cromlech whose other half had collapsed in centuries past. Of the stones that stood, three were still connected by lintels while the others leaned lazily, painted with lichens in rouge, celadon, and fawn. Grass grew over the fallen monoliths, which lay partially buried. Usually this place was dismal and unwelcoming, and this night was no exception. An unquiet breathing of the night soughed and grieved its way in eddies around the angles and edges of the rocks. From somewhere below the ground came the gushing hum of running water. Glowing eyes peered out from shadows near ground level, but no voice answered the inquiries of the incongruous mortals. No Faêran lord or lady appeared.

Ashalind and her companions felt the presence of wights massing thickly all around. The night was full of their mutterings, their lascivious snickerings, sudden wild laughter and unnerving yells. A sneering bogle jumped out, then leapt, spry as a toad, over the rim of the hill. Gray-faced trow-wives peered from shadows and tall tussocks, whispering and pointing, their eyes protruding like onion-bulbs, their oversized heads bound in dun shawls. One of them was clutching a ragged baby. The slight weight of the tilhals at the throats of the mortals felt reassuring, yet inadequate. The trows melted away as slowly the hours of darkness stretched on. The mortals huddled drowsily into their cloaks for warmth.

It was about an hour before dawn when soft music came stealing out of the darkness, subtle but permeating, like jasmine's fragrance. Simultaneously, a rose-petal glow bathed Cragh Tor Circle, like the dawn but untimely. A fox ran across the grass. The monoliths were shining with an inner radiance, like crystal with a heart of fire, and now strange flowers sprang in the turf. Two people of the Faêran were seated upon a fallen monolith while a third stood, one foot braced upon a stone, strumming a small golden harp.

He was like a sudden bird of the night, this harpist, an orchid of many colors, a tonal melody. Twined about his neck was a live snake, slender as grass, yellow-green as unripe lemons. Blinking away the blur of weariness, Ashalind started up, biting off a low cry before it had left her lips.

The harpist was also the Piper.

She turned away, wisely concealing her anger and indignation.

The musician laid down the instrument and spoke softly to his companions. Then the whitebeard with the staff spoke.

"Hail and well met, fair company," said Easgathair, greeting by name each of the three who now stood before him. He looked indefinably older and more careworn than before, and at this, Ashalind wondered, for the Faêran were said to be immortal, and unaffected by the passage of time.

The three petitioners bowed.

"At your service, Lord Easgathair," Ashalind said.

"We know your names." She who uttered these words was seated at Easgathair's right hand—the Faêran lady with the calm and lovely face Ashalind had seen in the halls of the Fithiach of Carnconnor, she whose dark hair reached to her ankles. Green gems now winked like cats' eyes on her hair and girdle. The fox that had run across the grass sat elegantly beside her, looking out from narrow slits of amber. "But you do not know ours," she went on. "I am called Rithindel of Brimairgen."

"My lady, you gave me courage when I needed it most," said Ashalind with a curtsy.

"That which is already possessed need not be given."

"I, Cierndanel, the Royal Bard, greet you, mortals," said the slender young harpist-Piper, bowing with a white smile that seemed, to Ashalind, mocking.

"The musicianship of Cierndanel is renowned amongst our people," Easgathair said.

While Meganwy and Pryderi saluted the musician, Ashalind faltered, filled with conflicting desires for vengeance and courtesy. Here before her stood the one who had originated all her troubles, with his irresistible pipe-tunes.

The Faêran bard turned an inquiring eye upon the young woman. Like a nail, it transfixed her.

"Have I offended thee, comeliest of mortals?" (A voice like rain on leaves.) "Say how, that I might ask forgiveness. A frown blights thy loveliness like late frost upon the early sprouts of Spring."

"Can you not guess, sir? Yet offended, I have no wish to offend. I will say no more."

"Tell on. Our discourse cannot progress until I am satisfied."

"Well, then." Ashalind took a deep breath and blurted out, "You, sir, are the perpetrator of the most heinous thievery of all. You are the Piper. You stole the children. That's your offense."

"I am all astonishment," said Cierndanel.

At Ashalind's tidings, Pryderi took an impetuous step forward, raising his fists. Meganwy's eyes snapped fire.

Before they could take issue, Easgathair held up his hand. "Wait," he said. "Cierndanel, thou know'st not the ways of mortals as I do. In their eyes, your accomplishment was not a meting out of justice but a misdeed. Understand, mortals, that Cierndanel was acting on behalf of the justice of the Realm when he led away the children with the music of the Pipes Leantainn. 'Twas not done for revenge or spite, 'twas a lessoning and an upholding of what is just; a fair treatment and due punishment in accordance with equity."

"Faêran equity," said Pryderi tightly.

Meganwy said, "We can hardly applaud the Piper's actions, but let us not quarrel. I have studied somewhat of Faêran customs and mores, and while I cannot approve, I acknowledge. Our moral code is not yours."

"You all seem to forget," pursued Cierndanel, the bardic snake sliding around his neck like a pouring of liquid jade and topaz, "that I piped away your plague of rodents also."

"But did not Yallery Brown send the rats to begin with?" cried Ashalind.

"The wight Yallery Brown has nought to do with me, sweet daughter. He, like many of his kind, mingles freely with those of our people who tolerate such types, but what mischief they may choose to make outside the Fair Realm is no concern of ours. The crime, the betrayal of promise, was the city's," he added, stroking the seashell curve of his harp with a long and elegant hand. "Why hold a grudge against me for being the instrument, so to speak, of retribution?"

The corners of his mouth quirked. A smile tugged at them, as ever.

Said Easgathair, "Condemned mortals ever rail against the executioner, though 'tis only his given task, and had there been no transgression, there would be no punishment."

"It seems immortals shall never understand why," said Pryderi bitterly.

"Immortals we be, yes," returned Easgathair, "but filled with passion; swift to laugh and love, swift to anger, slow to weep. We can, like you, be bowed by grief."

"No, never like us," replied Pryderi. There was a harsh edge to his tone. "Never like us, since you cannot know death."

"An immeasurable gulf," acknowledged the Lady Rithindel, after a pause, "sunders our races, one from the other."

"Nonetheless," said Meganwy, "we must let grudges shrivel and be blown away like the leaves of past seasons, for now we are come to ask for your help. Knowing the Fair Ones to be an equitable and just people, we are certain you will not deny us."

"Indeed, we will not deny that we are equitable and just!" said Easgathair. "Seat yourselves before us now. We wait to hear what you shall say, although perhaps we have guessed already."

"We wish to speak of the Langothe," said Ashalind, guardedly taking a seat beside Pryderi on a mossy stone.

Easgathair nodded.

"We cannot abide with it," she continued, "and we beg you to let the children return to the Fair Realm with their families, there to remain. We ask that they may receive protection against unseelie wights such as mingle with the retinue of the Fithiach of Carnconnor, and that they should dwell far from his halls."

"Far and near do not mean the same in the Realm as they do here," said Cierndanel lightly. "Thou mightst cross from one end of Faêrie to the other and still be close to the place from whence thou proceeded. Indeed, there are no ends or beginnings as thou know'st them."

The Lady Rithindel said, "Angavar, our High King, has always welcomed the gold-haired Talith whenever they have entered our country. You people of the gold have often been a source of delight, aye, and help to us, and this occasion, I wot, would be no exception—despite that he is grievously burdened at this time."

Ashalind saw Easgathair's fist clench as he gripped his staff. Raising his silver-white head, he directed a calm gaze at the mortals.

"Ashalind," he said, "for seven years thou didst wander in the hills and those eringl woodlands where the Faêran take delight in riding and hunting. Thy kindness and loyalty of spirit were marked by those who saw thee pass and that is why I helped thee when thou first asked. For that same reason I will help thee a second time, for it is the way of my people to reward goodness. Also, there are some among us who would perhaps opine that at this time we need, more than ever, a quota of humankind to abide among us. As Gatekeeper to the Realm, I will grant your request. You and your friends and families shall have your admittance, as well as protection against wights. Against Prince Morragan I cannot shield you, but I think he will not harm you."

The mortal folk jumped up and embraced each other, smiling, bowing deeply to the three Faêran. "Lord Easgathair, Lady Rithindel, Lord Cierndanel—we greet your generous words with joy!" they cried, mindful, even in the midst of their exultation, to refrain from thanking them, as custom decreed.

A meteor arced down the glistering sky, scoring a trail as fine as diamond-dust. Chaste breezes raced across open spaces, lifting the white silk strands of the Gatekeeper's hair. His proud face, with the erudition of eternity engraved into it, hardened to an uncharacteristic severity.

"It delights us to behold your happiness," he said, "but many things you must now learn—for a dire event has come to pass in Aia, and a more disastrous one shall yet befall. Sit yourselves down once more. I must relate to you now a history of Three Contests."

Perplexed and intrigued, Ashalind and her friends did as he had bid. When they were comfortably settled, the sage began. "Know first that I, Easgathair White Owl, am the Gatekeeper, the overseer of all the Ways between the Realm and Erith. Some while ago—time runs out of kilter in your country, but it was about the season when Angavar High King traded places with one of your kings for a year and a day, and the two of them became friends—some while ago, I was challenged to a game of Kings-and-Queens, or Battle Royal, as it is sometimes known. The Talith entitle the game 'chess.' My challenger was the younger brother of the High King—Prince Morragan, the Raven Prince, who is called the Fithiach. Morragan has long been my friend, and such a challenge was not unprecedented. We often vied with one another in amiable gaming."

"Indeed," interjected Cierndanel as the whitebeard

paused, "and the prince's bard Ergaiorn follows his lead, for it was then that he won from me in a wager the Pipes Leantainn, the Follow Pipes as mortals might name them, and the very instruments with which thou wouldst have quarrel, sweet maid."

"Then, sir, I would venture to say that you are well rid of them," rejoined Ashalind with feeling. "But prithee, Lord Easgathair, do not halt the tale."

"Alas," continued the Gatekeeper grimly, "I did not see then the dark current that ran deep, far below the surface of the charm and wit and mirthfulness of Prince Morragan. I did not suspect the iron acrimony that had become lodged in his once-blithe heart, hardening it over the years, feeding the fires of his pride and arrogance.

"He gifted me with a beautiful Kings-and-Queens set made of gold and jewels, beautifully wrought by Liriel, jewelsmith of Faêrie, and challenged me to find anywhere in the Realm a fairer or cleverer assemblage of pieces for the board. We played the game and, as was our wont, we bet on the outcome.

"Lately the Fithiach had been lamenting the fact that always I must abide near to my post in the Watchtower, from which I can oversee all the rights-of-way, and if I step into Erith I must not stray too far lest I am needed. Until he spoke of this, I had not resented my duties, but when he conjured these ideas I was persuaded perhaps they were at whiles a trifle irksome, and I might enjoy a brief respite, if only for a change.

" 'If thou shouldst win the contest,' said Morragan, 'I shall take thy place in the Watchtower for a space of a year and a day, while thou sojourn'st as thou wishest.'

" 'But sir,' said I, 'what stake may I offer thee? Thou dost already possess all thou couldst desire.'

" 'Wilt thou grant me a boon?' said he, and I made answer—'Provided it is within my scope.'

"Eventually we settled that if I should lose I would grant him a boon as yet unasked; that I would pay him whatever he should desire, were it within my power. We played and I defeated him. He assumed my role at the Watchtower for a year and a day.

"Some time later, I in my turn gifted the prince with an equipage of Kings-and-Queens, the pieces being the size of siofra, those diminutive wights who love to mimic our forms and customs.

" 'Skillfully is this wrought, I'll allow, my friend,' said he, 'and 'tis larger than the Golden Set I bestowed on thee, yet no prettier or more artful.'

"Then I showed him how at the touch of a golden wand the pieces moved by themselves, by internal clockworks, and walked to their positions as bid.

"Thus, with the Mechanical Set a second game was played. On this occasion we both wagered the same stake: 'The loser shall pay what the winner shall desire,' and Prince Morragan ended up the victor.

" 'One victory to each of us! This time I have defeated thee, Easgathair,' he said, laughing, 'but I must beg for time to consider before I ask for what I desire.'

" 'Sir, thou mightst enjoy as much time as thou wishest,' I boasted—'And whilst thou art at it, thou mayst take time also to search high and low for a cleverer or more beautiful set than this, which I'll warrant thou shalt never find in the Realm.' At that the brother of the High King smiled and agreed, but added, 'Yet I will bring thee a more marvelous collection and there shall be a third trial. This shall decide the champion.'

"Fool that I was to play for unspecified boons," said Easgathair bitterly. "And yet how could I suspect? I believed him free of jealous thought. One day, not long—in our reckoning—after thou, Ashalind, hadst taken away the children, he brought me to a glade where a platform was raised. It was inlaid with squares of ivory and ebony and upon it stood sixteen dwarrows in mail, armed, and twelve lords and ladies of Erith, including four mounted knights, also a quartet of stone-trolls, all enchanted, all alive. At the player's spoken command they obeyed!"

"But how cruel," protested Meganwy, "to enslave living creatures in that way!"

"They were trespassers in the Realm," explained Cierndanel the Faêran bard with a shrug. "Those who trespass may, by rights, be taken."

The mortals looked askance, but held their tongues.

"With this Living Set we played a game," said the Gatekeeper, "and once more the Fithiach defeated me. He is an adept player and I began to wonder whether he had allowed me to win the first time. As before, we agreed that the loser must pay what the winner should desire—but this time, having won, he immediately asked for what he wanted. He asked, did the Raven Prince, and I was bound to honor my word. I did not guess it had already become a bitterbynde."

Easgathair rose and paced around the circle. His feet crushed no blade nor pressed any flower.

"It was then that I discovered the thoughts he harbored. For he made a terrible demand, which was truly anathema to my expectation. I alone am in charge of the Keys to each Gate. If the Ways and the Gates are invisible to you it is because they are merely closed. Rarely are they locked. Once locked, they remain shut forever, according to our Law, as happened to one Gateway after the theft from Lake Coumluch on Whiteflower's Day." The Gatekeeper shook his silver-maned head. "I recall precisely the words the Fithiach used when he described the boon he would ask of me. He proclaimed:

" *'Upon thy word, Easgathair White Owl, thou shalt grant me this deed. Thou shalt lock the Gates to the Ways between the Realm and Erith, barring the passage of*

Faêran, eldritch wights both seelie and unseelie, unspeaking creatures, and all mortal Men. No more shall traffic pass to and from the Realm, which shall remain properly for the Faêran and not be sullied by humankind. At the instant when the Gates finally close, those who bide within the Realm shall remain within and those who bide without shall remain without. After the locking, all the Keys shall be placed in the Green Casket, whose lid shall be sealed by my Password.' "

Pryderi jumped up in a panic.

"Are the Ways to be closed forever? Then we must hasten!"

"I asked him," said Easgathair, "for grace of a year and a day. For friendship's sake he granted it."

" *'Thou mightst enjoy grace of a year and a day,'* he said, *'but do not conjecture that the passage of time shall change my heart. Never shall I retract this demand.'* "

"Why should the prince wish to cut Aia in twain, to sunder Erith from the Fair Realm?" asked Meganwy. "Why does he so despise mingling with mortals?"

"Prince Morragan has no love for your race. There are deeds done by mortals which have aroused his ire, and also stirred the anger of others of our kind—deeds such as spying and stealing, the breaking of promises, slovenly habits, lying, greed, captiousness, the snaring of a Faêran bride by a mortal man. Morragan loves only the Faêran, but traffics also with eldritch wights. His hatred of mortals is not like the bloodthirsty savagery of unseelie wights but rather a desire to shun your kind, to shut them away from his sight."

"So," Pryderi summarized, "it is purely out of contempt for mortal folk that he would lock the Gates to Faêrie."

"That, and more," said Easgathair. "Know that Morragan is the younger brother of Angavar, called Iolaire, High King of the Realm, who is friend to mortals. Your own King-Emperor William once helped Angavar to bring about the fall of the Waelghast, the Chieftain of the Unseelie Hosts, who was a supporter of Prince Morragan. The Waelghast used to plague Angavar in days of yore. Methinks, perhaps Morragan, in his jealousy, encouraged this. Without the Waelghast the unseelie wights are leaderless, but more and more nowadays they are foraying into Erith to harass mortals and mayhap Morragan is behind this also.

"Angavar is powerful. Morragan is the younger and so he must be Crown Prince, instead of King. 'Twould be unwise for me to reveal more, here in this place—even stones may have ears. Suffice to say that rivalry between siblings causes strife in many races, and jealousy is not a trait monopolized by mortals. It hurts Angavar to Close the Ways."

Clouds of moths gathered around the luminous stones, spattering their tiny X-shaped shadows in evanescent patterns on the lichen. The fox gave a grating, silvery yap like the beat of a wire brush against metal. Down in the mosses, a small stone bobbed up and down as though something were pushing up from underneath it.

"Get thee hence!" said Easgathair, pushing the stone with his foot. It wailed thinly and dropped with a clunk.

An eggshell of silence closed around the Circle, brittle and fragile. Ashalind and her friends were dumbfounded at what they had heard.

"We begged the Fithiach to reconsider," said Rithindel in low tones, "but he would not listen. Many of our folk applaud his plan, especially those who have ever given him loyalty and love. Now ill will sunders the Faêran and many go forth to visit Erith, knowing it shall be for the last time. For there are a multitude of things in Erith that please many of us—not least, its mortalkind."

"Angavar High King," Cierndanel the Piper said, "has ordered Giovhnu the Faêran Mastersmith to forge a special metal with which to make gifts of farewell for William of Erith—a metal such as has not before been seen in Aia, a metal with which gramarye is alloyed. *Sildron,* it is called. Your people shall deem it precious."

"Why then are we mining the yellow metal, the native talium?" asked Pryderi.

"Never have all the Gates been locked," said Cierndanel. "It is feared that when the Day of Closing comes, a weaving might be torn; a balance might be shifted. The imbalance may well let loose wild winds of gramarye. Strong forces surround the places where our two countries intersect, and they will be thrown into confusion, striving one against the other. It is possible they will go howling around Erith forever, without guide or purpose. Untamed winds of gramarye can create shape and image out of the thoughts of Men. Only talium can block them out."

"On the Day of Closing," said Easgathair with a sigh, "Midwinter's Day in Erith, three warning calls will be sounded throughout both worlds. On the last call, the Gates shall swing shut, and remain so, seamlessly and forever."

"Unless Prince Morragan should later reconsider and open the Green Casket of Keys using the Password," said Meganwy, "and return the Keys to you, sir."

"He has vowed never to change his decision once he is sealed within the Realm. What's more, he would have no reason to do so. He is a denizen of the Realm and believes all his happiness can be found therein, throughout eternity. Indeed, he is not mistaken. The delights and adventures of Faêrie are limitless. I can assure you, never shall Morragan change his mind."

"But might you not divine or guess the Password?"

"There are words and words, in a multitude of tongues. In the Realm, time is infinite. But should the wrong Password be spoken to the Casket three times, its Lock will melt and fuse so that nothing may ever open it, alas."

"And alas for the Langothe," said Ashalind resentfully, "for dearly do I love the good soil of Erith. Had I not heard your tune, Piper, and glimpsed that place, I had rather eat of a fresh-baked brown cob than all the sweet fruits of the Fair Realm. I had rather walk in the briar-tangled woods than the ever-blooming rose gardens, and wear the good linen and coarse wool than dress in Faêran gossamer and moonlight. But now I have no choice, for my blood is changed."

"Hush, Ashalind," warned Meganwyr; but the Piper laughed.

"We take no insult that a damsel should declare her love for her native land."

The Lady Rithindel reached down and caressed the ears of the restless fox. She looked out across the land below, its valleys now drowned in mist. The skies were bleaching in the east. A frigid blue light waxed all around.

"The cock crows soon," she said, "and we must away."

"In the morning of Midwinter's Day," said Easgathair to Ashalind, "gather together all those who wish to dwell forever in the Realm. Take the way leading west from the city. When you come to the crossroads, take the Green Road."

"I know of no Green Road," said Pryderi.

"On that day, those who seek it shall find it. Follow that path to the land of your desire. For now, return to your homes. Farewell."

Ashalind and her friends took their leave. As they passed beyond the ring of stones they turned back for one last glance, but the Circle was empty. A sense of desolation and abandonment overtook them, as if the last light had faded from the world. They shivered; something more penetrating than chill puncturing their bones. A cock crowed in the distance and the sun peeped over the rim of the world, lighting the dew on the mossy stones and the grass, making jewelry of it.

Thus began the Leaving of Hythe Mellyn, the exodus that no war, plague, or pestilence had brought about. Instead, this migration was initiated by the Langothe; that yearning for a place which all mortals strive to find, in their own way, whether consciously or not, an estate sought either within the known world or beyond.

Throughout Erith in the weeks that remained before the closing of the Gates there was unprecedented mingling of Faêran, mortal, and wight. The Talith families who had resolved to depart set their arrangements in order, and packed the belongings they wished to take with them. As the day drew nearer, more and more of their friends and relations, unable to bear the thought of parting forever, decided to join them.

Thus it happened that early in the morning of Midwinter's Day an immense procession left the golden city by the Western Gate and proceeded down the road, their shadows lying long before them. Of the entire population, only a handful remained behind.

Piled high with boxes and chests, the horses and carriages and wains trundled along. Hounds ran alongside, or rode in the wains with the children. Some folk were mounted, others went on foot. All were singing. Every voice lifted in the clear morning air, and the song they sang was the love for the green hills, the sun-warmed stone, and the red trees of the homeland they were leaving behind. "Farewell to Erith," they sang, "land of our birth. No more shall we tread your wandering paths or look out across the fields to the sea."

They smiled as they wept, and hardly knew whether it was gladness or sorrow that they felt; indeed, pain and joy seemed, on that journey, to be one and the same.

Behind the procession the city stood almost empty on the hill. Blank windows stared out over deserted courtyards and the streets lay silent, but the amber mellil stone glowed as ever in the sunlight.

At the crossroads where usually roads radiated in four

directions, there was now a fifth. A winding Green Road,
smooth and unmarked by wheel ruts, stretched out, disappearing over the hills. Bordered with ferns, it was paved not
with stone but with pliant turf. Down this path the convoy
turned. Those folk who remained standing at the city gates
with the Avlantian royal family and their retainers saw them
dwindle into the distance, their singing still carried faintly
on the breeze. The watchers strained their eyes until they
could see their kinsmen no more, but some said later that
they had seen a bright light burning white on the horizon
and that the procession had passed right into the center of
it.

The King moved his Court from Hythe Mellyn to Filori,
in the land called Ysteris of the Flowers. The abandoned
city rang hollow, like a great bell. With the Leaving of
Hythe Mellyn, the spirit had gone out of the people. As the
years passed, fewer children were born to the Talith. Their
race dwindled; the last of the royal family died without
heirs and the Talith civilization passed into legend. No
Feohrkind or Erts or Icemen came from the southern lands
to Avlantia, to settle in the abandoned Talith Kingdom—or
if they came, they did not remain. Therefore the cities lay
dreaming in their crumbling splendor, visited only by the
tawny lions and the dragon-lizards that basked in the sun.
In later days it was said that a plague or pestilence or unseelie gramarye had emptied the cities of Avlantia. The real
reason was forgotten.

Ashalind, riding sidesaddle on the black mare Satin—a
gift from the city—lagged behind even the most reluctant
travelers on the Green Road, despite the urgings of her
friends. Only Rufus trotted beside her, alert, reveling in the
myriad scents only a hound's nose could trace. Ahead, Rhys
rode with their father on the big roan gelding with Peri following on a rope, bearing light packs. Leodogran was glad-

dened to see how vitality was returning to his young son as they traversed farther along the Road, and color bloomed in the boy's cheeks.

Pryderi's spirited horse pranced forward eagerly, fighting restraint.

"Don't dally, Ashalind," the young man called merrily over his shoulder. "You have made your choice like the rest of us. Lingering only protracts regret. Look forward—we shall be happy when we arrive!"

Leodogran's daughter would not listen, heeding no one. Tugging gently on Satin's reins, she looked up and thought she spied, out toward the coast, a white bird flying.

"I am torn," she said to herself, "between the land of my heart and the realm that's infiltrated my blood."

And she glanced back at the lonely city on the hill.

But her family and friends were advancing down the Road, and so she flicked the reins and rode on. Her hood fell back from her fair head and the edges of her traveling cloak opened like flower petals to reveal her riding-habit, a long-sleeved gown of blond and turquoise saye, worn beneath a short, fitted jacket of ratteen. About her throat was wound a white cambric neckcloth. Nostalgically, she had garlanded her wrists with eringl leaves in place of briars. Beneath the leaves her bracelet glowed on her left arm, like a flame reflected in the rim of a goblet of golden glass.

As they traveled, the road began, imperceptibly, to alter. It became a sunken lane of deep banks, and thick, overhanging hedges. Bright flowers flecked its grassy borders, yet they were not the blooms of Erith.

To either side of the Road, stands of eringls gave way to thick forests, simultaneously bearing fruit and blossom. Rufus ran ahead to join the other hounds frisking and tumbling on the green verge. When Ashalind looked back at the city again, it was gone. Hythe Mellyn, the trees with their leaves of somber crimson and bronze, the hills—all had vanished. Landscapes fair and foreign unrolled behind the travelers on all sides, and they were not the hills of home.

The terrible heartache of the Langothe fell away like a discarded mantle, whereupon a form of delirium overswept the mortals. They ran and rode on as though nothing could touch them. Their mood was euphoric, as if they had become invulnerable giants who strode at the top of the world and perceived, through vast gulfs of air, the immensity of a mountain range suspending its ancient blocks from horizon to horizon, each peak stamped on the sky so clearly that they could step out and tread them all.

Now that she had entered the Fair Realm with all of her loved ones and the Langothe was assuaged, it almost seemed to Ashalind that there was naught she could ever lack again. Happiness surrounded her, within her reach, only waiting until she took a sip or sup of Faêran food, when she would possess that happiness and be possessed by it completely. Only the *memory* of the Langothe remained, a fading knowledge that it had once existed. But there was also, still, the memory of Erith, which must be relinquished, wiped out by the act of consuming a part of this new land, in order to be consumed, to gain the utter peace that stems from utter lack of yearning.

A memory too precious?

Afterward, she could never clearly recall those hours in Faêrie when, for a brief efflux, time ran synchronously with time in Erith.

She and her people had come into a marvelous countryside. Here the trees were taller, their foliage denser; the valleys were sharper, the mountains steeper, the shadows more mysterious, thrilling, and menacing. All colors were of greater intensity and brilliance, yet at the same time softer and more various. Through everything ran a promise of excitement that profoundly stirred the psyche.

Avenues of towering trees like rows of pencils led to glimpsed castles of marble and adamant, flecked rose-gold by an *alien* sun. Exuberant brooks flowed through meadows, and on the lower slopes of the hills deer grazed beneath great bowery trees in pastures of flowery sward. Orchards, where fruit hung like lanterns, were yet snowed with full blossom. In the boughs, songbirds trilled melodies to shatter the heart with their poignancy.

Even as the Talith pushed deeper into the Realm, the rosember light paled in the glimmering blue of evening.

The newcomers perceived that a feast was laid out on the starlit lawns, beneath spreading boughs heavy with scalloped leaves. There were pies and puddings, flans and flummeries, saffron seed-cakes, cloudy white bread and soft yellow butter, raspberries, pears, strawberries and honeyed figs, creamy curd, truffles, and crystal goblets encircling dark wine. The children who had eaten Faêran food and remained in the Fair Realm now came running forth. Ecstatic families were reunited. Beasts of burden, unhitched from rein and shaft, ran free. Bundles, chests, and boxes were left beside still-laden wains, all abandoned, all *unnecessary* now.

Entranced by the music of fiddle and harp, the yellow-haired people of Hythe Mellyn danced and feasted in the mellow evening. Their cares had been discarded with their belongings on the flower-starred lawns. Caught in the ecstasy of the moment, Ashalind cast off her traveling cloak and prepared to join in. Yet at the last, she did not.

The mortals were being watched. Faêran forms moved among the trees.

When she glimpsed them, something within Ashalind lurched and turned over.

At her elbow, handsome Cierndanel said, "Thou art honored, Lady of Erith. The most noble and exalted Lady of the

Realm has sent for thee. Come." He flashed his mercurial grin.

It seemed then to Ashalind that she followed him, or else was transported by some unfathomed means, to another location. In this new place there reclined a Faêran lady; surely a queen among her race. And as Ashalind beheld her she was given to know her name also: Nimriel of the Lake.

Nimriel's tranquillity was that of the calmness of a vast loch at dawn. Her mystery was that of a solitary black tarn in the forest, where, like a breath of steam, a creature of legend comes to drink, its single diamond spire dipping to send swift rings expanding out across the surface. Her beauty bewitched like moonlit reflections of swans moving on water. She was mistress of all the wisdom hidden in deep places; in drowned valleys and starlit lagoons; beneath mountain meres where salmon cruised in the dim, peaty fathoms.

Ashalind looked into a pair of wells, dark and clear.

It was said among mortals that if you stand at the bottom of a deep shaft and look up, then even on a sunny noon you will see the stars shining against pure shadow. That is what it was like to meet the gaze of the Lady of the Lake.

As Ashalind made her duty on bended knee, a darkhaired maiden, lissom as a stemmed orchid, stepped forward: the Lady Rithindel. She offered a two-handled cup.

"Thou art welcome among us, Ashalind na Pendran! My lady Nimriel invites thee to drink."

Ashalind's hands reached out to take the cup. The red eringl leaves encircling her wrists brushed against it, rustling. Releasing the cup, she drew back with a sigh.

"The Lady Nimriel is generous, but I have promised myself that I shall neither eat nor drink until the last Gate is closed and all links between our two worlds are severed forever."

On an inland sea the weather might change suddenly. Blinding fogs might form without warning, a wind might come gusting from nowhere to whip up white-capped waves.

The Lady Nimriel spoke, soft and low.

"Many fear me, Ashalind na Pendran."

"Ought I to be amongst them, my lady?"

"Thou hast refused my cup. I do not lightly brook refusal of my hospitality. Nevertheless, because thou speakest from thine heart, thou hast no cause to be afraid."

Ashalind bowed in acknowledgment.

"My custom is to gift newcomers. If thou wilt not accept food or drink, perhaps thou wilt accept other gifts. On thy journeyings, thou mayst need to cheat the moon." Briefly the lake-queen leaned forward and brushed her fingertips across Ashalind's dagger-slender waist.

"My lady speaks of journeys," exclaimed the damsel. "I believed mine to be over."

"Thy voyage is only just beginning, daughter of Erith. This I see, although as yet I know not the reason. Thou need'st not much in the way of gifts. Thou dost possess many of thine own. Yet mine is bestowed now."

Confused, at a loss for words, Ashalind stammered a reply. She could not understand what it was the lady had given her.

The two reservoirs of lucency regarded her gravely, as though from a distance.

"Know this, daughter of Erith. The Faêran are in great strife and turmoil at this very hour. Our eyes, from all over the Realm, are turned now towards your country. The time of Closing draweth near, but *all is not as it should be.* Part of the plan goes awry. Go now to Easgathair and thou shalt view, from the Windows of the Watchtower, what the eyes of all who dwell here can see without aid. Farewell."

Cierndanel escorted Ashalind to the Watchtower. Again, they traveled by some esoteric, indescribable method.

Light, as if filtered through geranium-tinted glass,

washed over a stone building. It was a tower, intricately carved all over, whose slender flying buttresses soared to pointed arches and singing spires. Glossy-leaved ivy climbed there among the rosettes and gargoyles and pinnacles.

Inside the tower, stairs led upward to a chamber where the Gatekeeper stood amid a gathering of the Faêran. Leodogran and Rhys were among them. Eight tall windows reached from floor to ceiling, each facing a different direction. Their crystal panes did not hinder the birds flying in and out. At times these windows would cloud over like breath-misted mirrors. When they cleared, different landscapes would lie beyond them.

Between these fenestrations soared slender golden pillars twined with living ivy leaves and carved ones of peridot, jade, and emerald. The golden ceiling too was festooned with these leaves, and with clusters of jeweled fruit and flowers. In the center of the room stood a raised plinth draped with mossy velvet, gilt-embroidered. Thereon rested a large gold-clasped green casket with a high-arched lid. The lid was closed.

Easgathair greeted Ashalind, saying grimly, "I would that I could welcome you here in a happier hour." His glacial hair and the voluminous folds of his white robes fanned out as he swung around to glance at the Northwest Window, then settled around him again.

"I too, my lord," replied Ashalind, but her father said gladly:

"Sir, there could be no happier hour."

Rhys, laughing, chased birds around the hall.

"The Windows may look onto any right-of-way according to my command," said the Gatekeeper. "See, the South Window shows the Gate at Carnconnor, that thou call'st the Hob's Hill."

A curious thought struck Ashalind.

"Does it show the passage which divides the outer Door in the side of Hob's Hill from the inner Door to the Fair Realm? Does that passage lie in Erith or in Faêrie?"

Distracted, Easgathair glanced over his shoulder. "I must return to the Northwest Window."

"Allow me to explain." The fetching Cierndanel, who seemed to be everywhere at once, took the Gatekeeper's place. "Every Gateway comprises two Doors, an inner and an outer, with a short passageway between. Time flows at different speeds in Erith and the Realm. A Gate-passage is needed to adjust the flow when something passes from one stream to the other. It operates like a lock in a canal."

"Suppose someone was trapped in there!" said the damsel, thinking of the Gatehouse at the palace in Hythe Mellyn, with its fortified barbican and its ceiling pierced by murder-holes for the destruction of invaders.

"There exists a safeguard to prevent such an accident. When they are locked, the Gates at each end will still open outwards only, permitting traffic to flow *out* of the Gate-passage in either direction."

"Like eel traps backwards," put in Rhys, intrigued. Recognizing the Piper, drawn by him, he had ceased his vain attempts to capture a bird in his hands.

"Just so, perspicacious lad. But from this hour, such engines are of use no longer. Already has each Key been turned in each Lock. All Keys, great and small, have been remitted to Easgathair White Owl—from the emerald Key of Geata Duilach, the Leaf Gate, with its intricate wards, to the silver-barreled crystal Key of the Moon Gate; the shell and jade of Geata Cuan's Key and the great basalt Key of Geata Ard. They lie, indestructible but untouchable, in the Green Casket, which is even now sealed by the Password of the Fithiach." He gestured toward the casket on the plinth. "Every bond on every Door has been set to lock and link, and now it only remains to join them at the appointed and immutable hour of the Closing. Listen! Do you not hear? The winds of gramarye are awakening at this outrage, the winds of Ang. They flare from the Ringstorm at Erith's rim. Soon they might prowl the lands of thy world, dyed by the imprints of men's designs."

The smile that usually played about his lips had left him. A shadow crossed his attractive face.

"But something's amiss. Thou seest how the crowds cluster about the Northwest Window, with White Owl at their fore. They look upon a Gate we call the *Geata Poeg na Déanainn,* awaiting Angavar High King and Prince Morragan, who still ride within Erith's boundaries. The royal brothers dare to ride late, as the Closing draws nigh. The first Call is about to sound!"

"Why do they tarry?" asked Ashalind, craning her neck for a better view of the Northwest Window.

"The Fithiach and his followers were returning from a last Rade in Erith, hawking I was informed—but the King and his knights have ridden out to detain them, blocking their path."

In the Northwest Window a scene revealed itself with startling detail and clarity. A hush fell on the assembly in the Watchtower. Beyond the Window the skies of Erith sheeted storm gray and a strong wind drove the clouds at a cracking pace. Thunderheads boiled over darkly.

Two companies of riders faced each other, one led by Prince Morragan, whose sculpted face could clearly be seen framed by the long dark hair and cloak billowing out behind him. His followers, about a hundred tall Faêran knights, sat motionless upon their horses. Harsh-faced, they gazed upon the King's retinue, which was massed between them and the traverse called the Geata Poeg na Déanainn. The Faêran King's voice could clearly be heard, by the enchantment of the Watchtower Window.

"Brother, renounce thy boon of the Gatekeeper. Shall I

drive thee forth before the Gates close and shalt thou be exiled forever from the Realm?"

The watchers cried out in shock and dismay, but the Crown Prince betrayed no sign of disquiet. Calmly, he replied:

"Dost think me a fool? 'Tis a game of bluff."

"Nay," replied the King, "there is no more time for games."

For an instant, anger flashed from the Crown Prince's eyes, then he smiled and lifted a hand in a signal to his knights. They split into two groups and sprang away, one to the right, the other to the left. Immediately the King's knights spread out to block them, but some broke through and were harried and pursued, and wrestled from their steeds. Faêran-wrought metal flashed up silver against the purple stormwrack of the furious skies. Desperately, the followers of the Fithiach raced to elude their hunters, to reach the portal between the worlds, the Geata Poeg na Déanainn. Among all these knights, two stood out—the High King and his brother. These two, so noble of bearing, strove hardest each against the other. The wind was howling, running before the storm.

Suddenly, cutting across the milling confusion, the sound of a horn rang out, dulcet and virginal, piercing both worlds. Faêran, mortal, and wight alike paused and lifted their eyes.

"The First Call to Faêrie," cried Easgathair White Owl. "The appointed hour approaches. Hasten home!"

Some among the assembled Faêran exclaimed to one another in consternation, "They must hurry! 'Tis too odious a fate they are hazarding!"

Cierndanel said to Ashalind, "The Sundering of Aia will wreak great changes in Erith, many of which cannot be foretold. The very Gates themselves might become distorted or dislocated beyond recognition. As the instant of

Closing draws upon us, Time, habitually unsynchronized, begins to run awry. *The King and the Prince risk misjudging the moment of their return.*"

"Ah," murmured Ashalind, whose thoughts were far away. "How I crave to return to *my* home. I cannot bear that this should be my final view of it. Yet, should I return, I would pine away swiftly. The Langothe, incurable, would destroy me."

"Not necessarily," said Cierndanel in surprise, wresting his gaze from the Window, "for there is a cure for the Langothe." At his throat the eyes of the slender serpent glared, twin peridots, coldly insulted by humanity.

"A cure!" Ashalind whirled to confront him. "Lord Easgathair never told us!"

"You did not ask for the cure, my lady, but instead for entry into the Realm, which was granted."

"A cure!" Oppression unchained Ashalind's spirit and she laughed weakly, too stunned at this revelation to be vexed at Faêran literalness. "Where is this cure? How can I obtain it?"

"Perhaps it is not commonly known amongst mortals, but the High King of the Realm has the power to take away the Langothe. He is the only one who can do so. Simply by saying the words, *'Forget desire and delight in the Land Beyond the Stars,'* he can annul the Longing."

"Then I must go now to him before it is too late! Alas, would that I had known before! Would that this fact had been noted in the books of lore, for pity's sake!" she exclaimed passionately.

"It is already too late. There is no time. The Closing is imminent. Besides," said Cierndanel, "he does not lightly grant the cure."

Beyond the Northwest Window, a red-haired rider called to the High King.

"Turn back, sir! Turn back now for home."

The King's company drew together and swerved, but as they rode toward the Geata Poeg na Déanainn, the riders of Morragan the Fithiach galloped close at their heels. At a shout from the High King, his company wheeled and urged their horses against those who followed, driving them back. Directly over their heads now, lightning struck repeatedly. Hundreds of bolts flashed within the space of a few heartbeats, scalding the sky to white brilliance. A distant pine tree exploded into a living torch.

"Renounce thy boon!" the High King roared to his brother, his voice strong above battle and thunder. His demand was answered by Morragan's mocking laugh.

"The Fithiach knows that the King in desperation tries to trick him," whispered Cierndanel on breath of lavender. "I too believe our sovereign is bluffing. He never would banish his brother from the Realm—he is not as ruthless as that—and if his words be examined closely, it will be found that he has not in fact said that he would do so. But what is this madness that overtakes them? They must all make greater haste now!"

From beyond the Window echoed deep-throated yells of anger, the clash of battle, the shrill neighing of Faêran horses. The two sides were evenly matched. They fought magnificently, not to wound or kill, but to prevent progress, and in so doing each impeded the other. Their fighting was a dance of strength and skill, like the clashing of stags in a forest glade, or two thunderstorms meeting to tear open the sky. Conceivably, it was their Faêran rage that now disturbed Erith's elements.

Presently the Call came for the second time, its haunting echoes lifting high overhead—the long, pure notes of the horn, a two-note hook on which to suspend the moment.

"Turn back—the hour is upon us!" cried the High King's captains.

As one, the Faêran lords swung around and began a race,

but as before they would not leave off harrying and hunting one another until, nearing the right-of-way, the High King's entourage turned in fury again to assail and drive off their rivals.

"Leave well alone!" shouted Easgathair. About him, the gathering parted as he strode closer to the Window, his white hair flying like shredded gossamer. He seemed taller, and fierce as a hunting owl.

"Can those beyond the traverse see and hear us?" wondered Rhys, at his sister's side.

"They could do so if they wished," answered Cierndanel, hovering nearby, "for there is little beyond the power of such mighty ones. But in the heat of this moment it seems they have eyes only for the conflict at hand."

"We must make the choice now!" said many of the Faêran who watched. "If Angavar High King does not return in time, we choose exile with him." In the next blink they were gone.

Others protested that it was unthinkable that the royal brothers and their knights would not return in time. Nevertheless many fled the Watchtower; soon a flood of Faêran, wights, birds, and animals poured through the Geata Poeg na Déanainn to aid the King's return. There was scant chance that they would reach him before the Closing—the combatants fought, in fact, more than a mile from the Gate.

Silently, Ashalind battled an agony of indecision. She lifted her gaze once more toward the knights beyond the Window, staring at the melee. And all at once she forgot to breathe. In that instant her spirit fled out of her eyes and into Erith.

"Father, forgive me," she cried suddenly, "I must try to return . . ."

Aghast, Leodogran cried, "But why?"

"Only that—" His daughter struggled to find words. "My future lies in Erith, I think. If the High King does not return in time, I will beg him to cure my Langothe, for he has the power so to do."

"My Elindor, my dearling—would you be parted from us forever?"

"Oh, I do not want that, but it must happen, for just now I have learned where my heart lies, or else my heart has been torn from my body, for I feel a rupture there, as if it were no longer here with me."

His face was stricken. "Why do you decide now, at the terminal stroke, to leave forever all the people you love, all you have worked for, in the hour of your triumph? What strange perversity has overtaken you?"

"Father—" She struggled for words, her feet of their own accord stepping away from him as she spoke. "I do not want to hurt you. This bird must fly the nest, dear Father, or else it will never fly at all. Forgive me. You shall be happy, you and the others I love. Mayhap you shall forget me, here in this land of bliss. My duty is over now. My path is my own. Furthermore, and more importantly—"

"I forbid it!"

Father and daughter opposed one another, the only motionless figures among the swirling multitude.

"Have I not done enough?" Ashalind begged. *My ears strain to hear that last Call. Let it not be now!*

Slowly, Leodogran bowed his head. After a pause he took a pouch, a horn-handled knife, and a dagger from his belt and handed them to his daughter. His movements were stiff, his voice was roughened with grief. "These heirlooms and this gold, which I bethought in my naivety we would need in this place, I give to you with my benison. They are of no use here. They may do you some good, if you go. But I hope you will not. There must be more to this, more than you have told. I do not understand you."

He kissed her and quickly turned away.

"Father, when Rhys came back from Faêrie I vowed that

I should never weep again, unless it were for happiness. I shed no tears now, but I will carry your loving words with me."

She leaned to embrace Rhys, whispering comfort in his ear. Rufus had somehow eagerly pushed his way in and she bent down to pet him. Excitement and sadness flooded through her. Her words rose strongly, angerly.

Tell Pryderi, Meganwy, and Oswyn I hold them always dear in my heart. And Satin, who is free here—whisper the same in her ear. Cierndanel! If the High King does not turn back in time, I would return to Erith through the Geata Poeg na Déanainn."

The Faêran Piper looked at her wonderingly, yet knowingly.

Woe the while! thought Ashalind, in an agony of impatience. *The Faêran Herald puts the clarion to his lips.*

"In truth?" said the Piper. "But the King shall return, he *must* return. The Iolaire is the very quintessence of the Fair Realm. Without him its virtue would be greatly diminished. And those that accompany him right now are the flower of Faêran knighthood, who, if they do not reach the Gateway soon, would be banished until the end of time. But thou, fair damsel, thou mayst not leave, for hast thou not eaten our food and drunk our wine?"

"I have not."

His comely face sharpened. She caught a spark of anger in his eyes.

"Stay here," he said.

"As you love life, Cierndanel, benefactor and malefactor of my people, aid me now!"

He paused, as if considering. Then he smiled.

"Very well. Follow me to the right-of-way if you wish, but I think you will never pass through it."

As the Piper grasped Ashalind's hand, she saw, through the milling crowd, Pryderi. Flailing desperately like a drowning swimmer, he was pushing his way toward her. His jaw knotted, his eyes aghast and fixed, he gasped and lunged forward, but then was gone in what seemed the blink of an eye, and the Watchtower, the assembly vanished with him.

Cierndanel led her to an avenue of trees in blossom, whose boughs arched to intertwine overhead. At the far end of this tunnel, two stone columns capped with a sarsen lintel framed a scene. Thunderstorms raged in the skies of Erith and the maelstrom of Faêran knights did battle. Behind them, distant peaks reared their heads to the racing clouds. Ice-crystals clung to the grainy surface of the Erith Door, but the perfumed trees of the Realm Door swayed gently. Ashalind and Cierndanel found themselves surrounded by a crowd of Faêran and wights, who paid them no heed, being engrossed in staring through the Gateway toward Erith.

"Thou seest, every traverse has two Doors," said Cierndanel, speaking quickly, "and a passage which lies between. Before thee lies the Geata Poeg na Déanainn. In the common speech of Erith, that means the 'Gate of Oblivion's Kiss.'

"Mark thee, it bears this name for a reason," he added. "Over the centuries, several mortal visitors have departed the Realm through this right-of-way and all have been given the same warning. The Gate of Oblivion's Kiss imposes one condition on all those who use it. After passing through into Erith, if thou shouldst ever be kissed by one who is Erith-born, thou shalt lose all memory of what has gone before. The kiss of the *erithbunden* would bring oblivion upon thee, so beware, for then there is no saying whether the bitterbyndings of such a covenant may ever crumble, whether memory ever would return. I think it would not."

She nodded, trembling. "I heed."

"Furthermore," he insisted, "the Geata Poeg na Déanainn is a Wandering Gate with no fixed threshold in Erith. When open, it behaves like any other traverse and remains fixed in its location. But when the Gate is shut it shifts at random, as a butterfly flits erratically from blossom to blossom. Therefore, one is never able to predict its next position. Chiefly it is wont to give onto the country of Eldaraigne, in the north, somewhere in that region known as Arcdur. Always, that was a land uninhabited by your people, but perhaps no longer. Knowing these truths, dost thou still desire to pass through this perilous portal?"

"I do."

Unexpectedly, the Faêran Piper folded around Ashalind's shoulders a long, hooded cloak the color of new leaves. He whispered closely in her ear, his words carried on a fragrance of musk roses:

"Fear not, brave daughter of Erith. The Gates are perilous only in the rules by which they exist. If you abide by these, not so much as a hair of your head shall be harmed."

Ashalind closed her eyes to the strange beauties and perils of the Fair Realm, reaching for the scent of wet soil, the tang of pine, the chill of a storm wind, the cry of elindors on the wing. Her head spun and her mouth was parched taut with a terrible thirst. Easgathair's voice roared from nowhere in the mortal world:

"Return instantly, ye knights, for the time is nigh! The Gates are Closing!"

Ashalind looked through the Gate-passage. At the Erith Gate, one or two of the knights from both sides broke away and rode hard, sparks zapping from their horses' hooves.

"Forget this quarrel!" Easgathair's cavear boomed from somewhere indeterminate. "Set aside your pride and ride for the Realm!" But the High King and the Crown Prince, intent on their purpose, continued to ignore his warning.

Then red lightning smote from the High King's upraised

hand, splitting the sky, and all who looked on heard him shout, "By the Powers, I will not again petition thee, Crow-Lord. Now thou hast truly stirred my wrath. Consequently, I swear I *shall* exile thee."

"No!" Hoarse and harsh came Morragan's vehement denial, and for the first time there was a note of alarm in his tone. He flung a zigzag bolt of blue energy from his palm. Confronted with his brother's fury, he gave ground, but even as they battled, the long, clear warning sounded for the third time, rising like a ribbon of bronze over the tree-tops.

" 'Tis too late!" thundered the Gatekeeper.

Now at last the High King and the Raven Prince were riding together, flying for the Gateway at breakneck speed with their knights flanking them, and nothing stood in the path of their headlong rush; they spoke not, nor looked to left or right, and all quarrels were abandoned as the threat of permanent expatriation became imminent. Dread fell on the hearts of the assembled audience. A crash like the world's end shook the floor of the Watchtower, the horizon shuddered, and a shadowy veil drew across the vault above. There arose a loud keening and clamor of voices fair and harsh from near and far, and as the beautiful riders almost gained the Gate, a cataclysmic tumult filled the sky and seemed to burst it asunder. The voices of the Faêran joined in a lament like a freezing wind that blights the Spring, for the Gates were swinging shut, and those they loved most would be exiled for eternity.

A sudden terrible gust slammed through the Gate of Oblivion's Kiss with a mighty concussion, snatching mortal breath. It was all over. The Faêran royalty and their companions were forever excluded from the Realm. The Watchtower Windows shattered and fell out in shards, leaving shadowy apertures that stared sorrowfully across the

long lawns where the Talith dancers stood poised as if in a
frozen tableau.

But with a pang of regret for the land of desire and delight, which spoke of the Langothe already reawakening to
haul on its chains, Ashalind had slipped into the Gate of
Oblivion's Kiss.

10
DOWNFALL

There's a place that I can tell of, for I've glimpsed it once or
   twice,
As I've wandered by a misty woodland dell.
I believe I almost saw it on the green and ferny road,
Or beside the trees that shadow the old well.
And I've never dared to whisper, and I've never dared to shout,
Even though it always comes as a surprise,
For I fear that by my movement or the sounding of my voice
I might make it disappear before my eyes.

'Tis a place of great enchantment and wild gramarye: a fair,
Everlasting haunt of timeless mystery,
You'll find danger there, and beauty; strange adventure curs'd
   and bless'd,
That will seem to wake a longing memory.
But I've heard that if you go there you might stay for far too long,
And you may forget the road by which you came.
Some folk never learn the way. If you should find it then beware,
For if you return, you'll never be the same.

FOLK SONG OF ERITH

For immeasurable moments, all was confusion. Something fluttered and battered softly about her head in the colorless half-light. Ashalind could not comprehend her status. Had she fallen off Peri's back, or perhaps Satin's? Her leg ached. Should it not heal, she would not be able to follow the Piper—oh, the anguish of hearing that call and not being able to respond! She would drag herself through the dust . . . Such a hard bed to lie on, this, and why was everything so hushed and still?

Stung by sudden recollection she sat bolt upright. She looked around for the stony land she had seen at the end of the Gate-passage, and the Faêran knights embattled there. But there was no open sky above her head, no Erith, no tall riders, only a dim, distorted passageway, an arched and twisted tunnel sealed by a Door at either end. The vaulted ceiling was cracked. In places it sagged down like a bag of water. The Gate-passage had been biased, damaged by the unprecedented sundering of the worlds between which it lay. Yet its structure remained viable.

For how long?

In each half of the chamber the walls were different. As they approached one Door they resembled living trees growing closely together, their boughs meeting to interweave as a ceiling. Toward the other portal they merged into rough-hewn rock.

This, then, was the Gate-passage between the Other Country and Erith.

The distraction beat her around the head again, with soft wings. It was a hummingbird. She recalled it rushing by her as she had leapt through the Realm Gate. Now in agitation the tiny creature darted about, seeking escape.

"Which Door shall I open for you?"

But the bird flew up to the wracked ceiling and perched in a niche there.

"Little bird, which Door shall I open for myself? I still have a choice—how odd. I may go out from here to either place, but once out, I may never come back." She empathized with mailed crustaceans entering a wicker trap: a one-way entrance with no return.

The Lords of Faêrie had been trapped in Erith after all. In her native land, they lingered. Gently, Ashalind pushed the stone Erith Door with one finger. It floated open easily under the slight pressure. Beyond stretched a land of towering rocks: Arcdur, empty of all signs of life. Night reigned.

The hummingbird dashed past. Once outside, it rebelled against the darkness and tried to return, but some invisible barrier prevented this. It flew away, leaving Ashalind bereft.

She let her hand follow it, gingerly, through the Erith Door, out into the airs of home. Her fingertips tingled and she snatched them back. How interesting—it seemed that one could be partway out and still get back in, but if, like the bird, one made a complete exit, a barrier was thrown up. Withdrawing, she allowed the Door to close itself and sat leaning against the wall to ponder, touching the dying eringl leaves that covered the bracelet on her wrist.

The Door would not harm a thing of flesh by closing on it.

Now that this truth was apparent, a plan began to evolve.

She fancied she could hear, at the other end of the Gate-passage, beyond the silver Realm Door with its golden hinges, the sound of sweet, sad singing. If she could somehow prop open the Erith Door then even if she ventured into Erith she could return through the Gate-passage and thus into the Realm whenever she wished. The Gate of Oblivion's Kiss would let no one else pass through it, now that its Key had been turned in its Lock. Prince Morragan's edict had ensured that: "... *barring the passage of Faêran, el-*

*dritch wights both seelie and unseelie, unspeaking creatures
and all mortal men . . ."* Yet she fitted none of those descriptions! Ashalind laughed, as it came to her that the
Raven Prince had overlooked mortal women—overlooked
and underestimated. Doubtless, Meganwy would have said,
A common trait among males.

Enchantments must always be carefully worded. The
Raven Prince had not been careful enough. The thought of
this made the smile linger on Ashalind's lips, and she recalled the remnant of some old tale she had heard in childhood, the story of a man who had outwitted a Lord of
Unseelie by hiding in the walls of his home. She thought:
*Here in the walls where I now dwell, I am neither within the
Realm nor without it . . . Indeed, borders are mysterious, indeterminate places.*

Furthermore, if the Doors could be propped open and the
Gate could be duped to allow the unhindered passage to and
fro of the only living creature (bar the hummingbird) who
had been locked neither in Faêrie nor in Erith, then she
might be able to carry a message from one place to the other.
What if, in Erith, she could discover the Password to the
Green Casket; the Password that would release the Keys to
open all the Gates again? Then the High King might be reunited with his Realm!

The preternaturally attractive Prince Morragan, whose
dark male beauty cloaked acid and steel, had asked his boon
and it had been fulfilled exactly. Once fulfilled, all boons
lost their power over whosoever had promised them.

There remained only the danger of the second pledge, the
unasked boon that Morragan had cleverly won from the
Gatekeeper. But if she, Ashalind, could only find the High
King, surely he would be able to put all things to rights, to
force his brother to reveal the Password and renounce his
second boon in exchange for his own return to the Realm.

Surely the Crown Prince would do anything to be reunited with his beloved homeland.

Was it possible? Could she return the generosity of the Faêran by reuniting them with their High King? She would search in Erith for him—surely it was not possible for him to have gone too far away in such a short time—and when she found him, she would beg him to cure the Langothe, which had begun again, of course, to eat at her. Then she would tell him of her secret way back into the Fair Realm and all would be well! The only peril would lie in preventing Prince Morragan from discovering the secret first.

But the Fithiach did not know she was in Erith. No one in Erith knew.

Her fingertip pushed open the stone Erith Door for the second time.

The landscape had changed dramatically. Weather had eroded some monoliths, while others looked sharp and new, as if they had but lately been thrust up from subterranean workshops in some violent upheaval of the ground. It was no longer nighttime. Sunset tinged the air with the delicate pink of blood diluted in water. Puzzled, it took her a moment to work out what was happening, and when she did her insides crawled like cold worms, her stomach flopped like a fish.

Time in Erith was racing past while she remained in the Gate-passage. She must delay no longer—how many years might have passed already? In a panic, she tried to think quickly. Cierndanel, or someone else, had said that time was running all awry because of the Closing. There was no telling how many years might have elapsed by the time she finally slipped through the Door into Erith—perhaps seven years, perhaps a hundred. All the mortals she had known, who had remained behind, might be long dead. Her world might be altered in many other undreamed-of ways. It might have evolved into a place unknown.

"I shall be a stranger in my own land," croaked Ashalind, with difficulty forcing words from dehydrated lips.

The Faêran, however, could not be slain; they were immortal. They could choose or be forced by serious injury to pass away into a lesser form, but unchallenged, the exiled knights, the royal lords of the Realm and the lords and ladies who had fled to join them would live on, whatever else.

With a sense of overwhelming urgency she propped her father's knife in the open Erith Door. As soon as she let go, the Door snapped shut, breaking it.

A living hand could keep the Door open, but not an object of metal. If only she could delude this enchanted valve, make it believe that she was partway through it, perpetually half in, half out, it would stay open for her, and her alone. Some part of her must remain in the doorway, to prop it open. A finger? No, that was too gruesome to contemplate. Other measures must be taken. She worked quickly.

For the third and last time she opened the Erith Gate. Arcdur's stony bones leaned up, even more skewed and corroded, shouting against the low-slung sky. A storm was raging, but Ashalind could not wait for it to abate—already too much time had passed. Her preparations were made. Pulling Cierndanel's gift-cloak closer around her shoulders, she stepped out of the quiet passage.

Chaos assailed her. Reflexively she flung herself back against an upright stone pillar, one of the Gateposts. Torrents of rain lashed all around and wind screamed through darkness. Crouching in the lee of the rock, she let the waters of Erith run down her face into her parched mouth, drinking greedily of the chill deluge, feeling it irrigate her body and send silver channels running along her veins, until she had her fill.

Already her riding-habit was sodden. It was strange to recall this was the very costume in which she had made the

journey from Hythe Mellyn to the Perilous Realm. That
journey now seemed so long ago and far away. The words of
Nimriel came back: *"Thy voyage is only just beginning,
daughter of Erith."* Ashalind wrapped herself more tightly
in the Faêran cloak. Lightning ripped open the belly of the
sky and its dazzle revealed in a black-and-white instant a
world of tumbled rocks and oblique crags utterly different
from the realm she had departed from moments earlier.
Looking back, she noted that on this side the Geata Poeg na
Déanainn looked to be no more than a tall crevice between
leaning boulders, perilously inviting, its secret recesses
wrapped in deep shadow. Intermittent flashes illuminated
slanting water-curtains pleated suddenly by gusts of wind.
Her thirst slaked, Ashalind felt a great weariness coming
over her. She crawled under an overhang, out of the storm's
fury. Desiccated leaves flaked from her wrists and turned to
dust. The Faêran cloak was warm. Briefly she wondered
how this Erithan storm compared to the one in which Morragan had battled against his brother, maybe a hundred years
ago.

Then she slept.

Pale dawn revealed a nacreous veil over the sun. Rivulets
chattered swiftly over pebbles, droplets fell tinkling from
ledges. Boulders had piled themselves high everywhere in
fantastic, towering shapes. Water and granite surrounded
Ashalind. The only signs of life were mosses and pink
lichens.

She drank again, from a rocky cascade, wishing that she
had a flask in which to carry water. She was alone in an uncertain place, probably far from human habitation, and she
knew nothing of wilderness survival, but good sense told her
that thirst and exposure were her two most immediate enemies, and against them she must be prepared. First—survive. Next—fulfill her quest. She decided not to proceed

until she had memorized the surroundings in the vicinity of
the Geata Poeg na Dèanainn, to ensure future recognition.

The furor of the Closing had distorted and dislodged the
entire Gate, including both of its Doors. The portal had been
blasted out of alighment. Fallen rocks partially covered the
Erith Door.

*I think the Faêran would no longer know this Gate. Only
I am here, to record it in memory.*

She began to take careful note of her surroundings,
preparing to imprint every detail of the Gate's identity and
location on her consciousness. Something nagged, diverting
her attention, like a fly buzzing about her ears. She lost concentration . . .

"*—hain?*"

Crackling voices, someone calling out a name.

She took no notice. It was not her name. Or was it?

What was her name?

The interruption faded. A fancy.

She shook her head to rid her ears of the buzzing. The
voices faded, giving way to memories.

The Faêran cloak now appeared to be mottled gray in
color, exactly like granite. Its fabric, soft and strong, was
unidentifiable and had remained dry, although rain and
wind had bedraggled her riding-gown and other garments.
Leodogran's dagger and pouch of gold swung from her belt.
Ashalind emptied the water out of her riding-boots, braided
her long hair, and bound it around her head for convenience,
then took a deep breath of the pure, silver-tinged air. It set
her blood ringing. The soft luminescence that indicated the
sun's position was still low in the sky, behind dully gleaming crags that stood up like pointed teeth.

Northeast of Arcdur, she knew, lay the strait that separated Eldaraigne from Avlantia. Besides having no means of
crossing it she was reluctant to return to her homeland lest
devastating changes had been wrought on it by the winds of

Closing, or by Time. Never had she traveled out of Avlantia, but her thorough education had included studying the maps of the Known Lands of Erith. These she now recalled.

South, a long way south, lay the Royal City, Caermelor, and the Court of the King-Emperor of Erith. It might be the best place to glean news of the whereabouts of Faêran royalty. Besides, the Geata Poeg na Déanainn had spilled her out toward the south, so it seemed somehow meet to continue in the same direction.

Now that excitement, fatigue, and thirst were behind her, Ashalind was aware that hunger, like a rat, gnawed her belly. Worse than that, the Langothe, which had coiled up like a snake temporarily dormant, now hit her with full force, redoubled now that she had not only breathed the air of the Fair Realm but also left her loved ones there. Retching, she staggered and clutched at an outcrop, half turning toward the Gate.

Now was the time to leave, and leave quickly, before the Langothe's cruel pull drew her back to the Fair Realm at the very outset of her quest. With an effort, as though walking through water rather than air, she forced herself to set out, step by step, aching to turn back, at least to take one extra glance over her shoulder at the Geata Poeg na Déanainn. Instead, as she rounded a granite shoulder she quickened her pace. To deflect her thoughts from hunger and longing she determined to focus her mind on her final glimpse of the Gate, to recall every detail so as to engrave its image deeply into memory. She must never forget.

The Door she left behind, seemingly just another rocky crevice among many, stood still and unnoticeable in the deep shadows of morning, as it had stood for many years. Yet not quite as it had previously stood—a crack was penciled down one side, where it remained slightly ajar. Only a thin crack; a hairline, one might say, as wide as the thickness of three strands of gold, three thin braids of hairs torn out, one by one, from the roots and weighed down at one end by a rock and at the other by a broken knife. A girl's fingernail might have slid into that gap, as it had indeed slid not long before, to test it.

A girl's fingernail could open that Door, as long as the girl was the owner of the hair.

"—hain! Rohain!"

The girl on the mullock heap opened her eyes to darkness. Spicy, intoxicating night enclosed her in its embrace. Someone was calling. Fear drilled her brain, lacerating it with cold skewers.

"Rohain . . ."

How can one move, with wooden limbs?

Closer now: "Where are you?"

Where indeed? On the slopes of Huntingtowers.

She stood up too late—they were upon her, two white masks of terror in the gloom.

"She's here!"

"My lady, hasten!"

The young woman stared at the masks, unseeing.

" 'Tis us, Viviana and Caitri—we have been searching for you all day! Quickly—night is come and danger is upon us! Wights are everywhere and not a seelie one amongst them!"

The urgent tones shattered meditation. An insubstantiality floated away from the dreamer's grasp. Her reverie had been interrupted just as she was about to recreate a visualization of the portal to Faêrie.

Now I shall never recall it.

As her lady's maids grabbed her by the elbows, the damsel had enough presence of mind left to ensure that the bracelet securely encircled her wrist. Then they were off, stumbling through the mountainside's witchy darkness.

Wicked and eldritch indeed was the night. The three mortals were tripped and tricked at every turn, taunted and haunted, jeered at, leered at by the hideous, the horrible, the hateful. Unseelie energies hummed electric in the air like charged wires, for the wind or eldritch fingers to pluck or to slide down with fiendish screams; like cords to snake across their path, to catch in webs at their ankles, transmitting the throbbing menace of the darkness in thin metal slices of pain. On ran the three mortal maidens, expecting at any time to be cut down from behind, or beside, or in front, but there was a globe of soft luminosity illuminating their path.

This light traveled with them. It radiated from the ring worn on the finger of one of them. Things that lunged at the escapers were brushed by the edge of this orb. They yelped and ricocheted away. The boots of the three damsels hammered on the surface of a road as they crossed. On the other side a bank ascended steeply into a wood. Panting, they climbed up into the tangle of undergrowth, pushing in under muffling trees until one of them, the smallest, fell.

"Caitri!"

"I can run no further. Go on without me."

Green eyes, long and narrow, popped up like sudden lamps. A skinny, pale hand reached for Caitri. Her mistress slashed at it with a knife. Black blood spurted. The screech was like a white-hot arrow through the eardrums. Encouraged, she slashed right and left, back and forth. On her hand, Thorn's leaf-ring flared. Shadows leaped up and away from it, and so did the mad things of the night. Some of the screaming was pouring from the knife-wielder's own mouth, a wordless battle cry of which she had not known she was capable, a song of frenzy. Her knife was everywhere, flashing in a kind of whirling cocoon of steel within which her two charges huddled.

When she stopped, arms hanging by her sides, the blade no longer gleamed. Inky blood covered it, splashed her arms and dripped from her clothing. Silence on silver chains hung suspended from somewhere far above. The damsel wiped the knife, ineffectually, on her sleeve.

"Trouble us no more!" she shouted into the quiescent shadows—or tried to shout. The words emerged in a strangled whisper. She sank to her knees on a whispering carpet of leaves.

"You saved us." said Viviana, awed. "Are you hurt?"

"Is there any water?"

In the woods, the night was long. She whose memories had been reborn did not sleep. She sat with her back to her dozing friends, holding a knife in each hand. The ring shone. Strangely, wights' blood had never smeared it.

I must recall the image of the Gate.

Somehow, as she sat through the night, she happened to glance again at the golden bracelet that symbolized her kenning-name. Her eyes began to cloud over. More memories returned . . .

Arcdur. She had traveled through it.

Avlantian riding-habits had not been designed for hard walking. The skirts of blond and turquoise saye tangled about Ashalind's legs and caused her to stumble. On her feet, the soft leather boots yielded to sharp angles of adamant. Only the amazing Faêran cloak flowed with her movements, never snagging on projections, conforming to her body with a gentle caress.

Jumbled stones and scree slopes made progress even slower and more difficult. Constant water and wind kept the rocks swept clean of silt in this region—only in the deepest cracks it found refuge, and there the mosses grew, or the tenacious roots of the blue-green arkenfir.

The cadence of the wind amplified as Ashalind approached the summit of a hill, and it was as if she were at the edge of the world, for there was only the deep sky beyond. In a few steps, a majestic vista of far-flung hills and stacks stalking into the distance unfolded unexpectedly at her feet, and the wind came up over the hill to meet her, soughing in her ears. She paused, looking out over lonely Arcdur, devoid of human habitation. Choughs on the wing caught updrafts. Cloaking the opposite ridge was a dark patch of conifers. To her right, a glint on the horizon suggested the sea. She picked her way down the hill and lay flat to drink at a clear beck, then went on, hoping to reach the shelter of the trees before nightfall. The Faêran cloak provided extraordinary warmth and protection, and without it she must surely have perished by now, but fallen pine needles would be a softer cushion than rock.

She stepped from stone to stone, conscious always of keeping her footing, aware that her next enemy in this remote region was injury. She kept going on a course due south, memorizing landmarks along the way: a stack of flat rocks like giant pancakes, another like loaves of bread . . . most of the constructions reminded her of food, and she wondered how long it was since she had eaten. Searching her memory, she recalled honeyed pears poached in a cardamom and anise sauce, followed by buttered griddle-cakes, eaten for breakfast on the morning of the Leaving. The memory tied knots in her belly, and she turned her musing elsewhere.

She pondered all the strange events that had brought her here, and the foolishness of Men and Faêran that had caused them. Images of her loved ones in the Fair Realm made her choke with longing and she suddenly stopped and hurled herself down among the boulders, digging her fingers into gravel.

"I cannot go on. I must go back."

There she lay, rigid, while the sun moved a little farther across the pearly sky and the choughs wheeled, inquisitive, above. Eventually, out of her confusion arose a conclusion: She had decided to attempt this venture in order to be rid of the Langothe and to bring the High King back to his Realm. Yet even as she reached this disposition she knew the answer was not really that simple; there was more, if only she had the courage to admit it. For now, however, the important point was that she had freely chosen her own path. No one had coerced her. She had elected to pursue this quest, and all pain, all longing, must be contained and controlled if it were to be achieved.

Hence, with a new strength born of despair, she climbed to her feet again and resumed her journey.

There was no food. It was very beautiful, this land of stone and pine so close to the sky; clear and clean, embroidered with joyous, glimmering waters. But day followed day and Ashalind could find nothing to eat, not even mushrooms down among the gnarled roots of the arkenfirs. Chitinous beetles sometimes crawled in crevices, but she had no mind to consume them. When they opened their wingcases and became airborne, the choughs swooped to snatch them instead.

The light-headedness and aching she had experienced in the first two days vanished, leaving her with a sense of remarkable calm and vigor. She held her course, but on the sixth day of her journey the land to the east started to climb in ragged notches, more precipitous and sheer, while to the west it gentled, and groves of pine and fir marched over undulating hills.

Using a castle-shaped crag as a landmark for her turning-point, she was now forced to veer westward. Somewhere ahead, she knew, lay the northwest coast of Eldaraigne that looked out over a vast sea whose end was in the storm-ring that encircled the rim of the world. A deep ocean current, the Calder Flow, journeyed from the icy southern latitudes past the island country of Finvarna to touch that coast with its chill fingers and keep Arcdur cooler, year-round, than the rest of the country.

On the seventh day she gathered a few handfuls of watercress and wild sage, the first edible plants she had seen. But she noticed that her hands and feet were always cold, and her limbs quaked. Her strength was failing. At night, proper sleep would not come, only a trancelike state, similar to floating on water, buoyed up and unable to sink. She wondered how long anyone could continue to travel without proper sustenance. Perhaps if she could reach the seashore she would find food. If she did not, then she must lie down there and die, within sight of elindors flying over the waves.

Would elindors still navigate the airs of Erith? How many years had passed? Would Men still walk the world, or would their cities lie in ruin? She stumbled, then shook her head to clear it, but could not focus, and recalled vaguely that she had fallen many times that day and her hands were bleeding.

The sky turned from pearl to grape. Another storm blew out of the west that night, bringing strong winds and lashing rain. It lasted all night and through the next day. The Faêran clothes were waterproof, but moisture insinuated itself past the edges to dampen her neck and wrists.

By nightfall on the ninth day the rain had dissipated to the southeast. The falling sun had at last broken through the clouds, and as the traveler plodded up the side of a grassy dune she saw it, low on the horizon, scattering a fish-scale path across the sea. Lulled by the susurration of the waves, she sat among saltbushes and watched the evening's glory fade. Stars appeared. A gibbous moon looked down at the long pale beach, but Ashalind, wrapped in her cloak, her head pillowed on her arms, was already dozing.

It was a fitful sleep, disturbed by dreams of Faêran feasts. The first gleam of dawn wakened her suddenly, and, raising her head, she looked out to sea. A stifled cry escaped her lips, and in the next instant she had sprung to her feet and, drawing on her last reserves, was running down to the water's edge, waving and calling.

Triangular sails floated, saffron, in the dawnlight. A boat, not far from shore, was silently heading south toward a headland. Onward it tacked without deviation, seeming unaffected by her cries, and she thought it would pass from sight forever and leave her stranded to become, washed by time and tide, sunbleached bones in the sand. But the angle of the hull changed. It had turned, and now cut through water toward her; she could see the curl of white foam beneath the prow. When the vessel was within earshot, she hove to. Her keel prevented her from venturing into the shallows. A man on board dropped anchor and shouted, honoring the time-worn cliché of mariners:

"Ahoy there!"

"Help me," Ashalind answered. "I have no food. I am alone."

The man hesitated.

"Please help me." The damsel's voice cracked and she sank to the sand, heedless of the lace-edged waves swirling around her knees. Perhaps he did not believe her, or thought she was a decoy for some brigand's ambush, which indicated that *wherever* she was, danger lurked still.

There was a splash. He had stripped to his breeches and was swimming to the beach, towing something buoyant on a rope. A strong swimmer, he soon rose out of the water, dripping, and waded out. He was thickset and bearded, with hair as brown as his body. Bright eyes peered from a weathered face.

"Gramercie. I am grateful," was all she could think of to say. She tried to stand but collapsed again. He gave her a measuring stare, then asked, in unfamiliar but clear accents:

"Can you swim?"

She nodded, unclasping the cloak and throwing off the ragged gown and jacket.

"Come on now," the man said to the gaunt, hollow-eyed damsel shivering in hose and gipon. Securing her to the cluster of inflated bladders, he towed her out to the boat and dragged her aboard, then tossed a dry blanket over her while he returned to retrieve her riding-habit and mantle.

There was a small cabin on board, and wicker baskets filled with luminous shells like pale rainbows. An older, grizzle-bearded sailor in the boat handed her a bottle of water and some food: stale bread, cheese, and pickles in a stoneware jar.

"Eat slowly," he advised.

On his return the younger man dressed himself. Then without another word he dragged in the anchor. The old man hauled on the jibsheet and took the tiller. The favorable breeze bellied out the lateens against an azure sky. Ashalind lay back on a pile of stinking nets and watched the horizon rise and fall.

"Where are you from? Where are you going?"

"My name is Ashalind na Pendran. I am a traveler, seeking the High King of the Fair Folk. I lost my way."

This was the truth, as far as it went. She trusted them, these brown sailors—their faces were open and honest. Nonetheless, the secret of the Gate was too precious to be revealed to any save the High King of the Faêran.

"My name is William Javert," said the younger man, "and this is my father, Tom. Never have I known a young lass like you to travel alone, but such practices may be common in outlandish regions, I suppose. I doubt not that you seek whom you say you seek, but we have never seen any such people as those you call the Fair Folk. It is not our habit to pay heed to tales and legends of the Strangers. If such folk do exist, maybe 'tis better they remain hidden. To my mind, the less trouble that is stirred up, the better. Some old tales what folks make up when they got nothin' useful to do, tell of a King of the Strangers—the Gentry, as some calls 'em—who sleeps with his warriors under a hill, but I don't put much faith in that. I believe in what I see. In wights I believe, for mickle trouble they do give us. Thought you was one, at first."

"Old folk used to tell tales of a Perilous Kingdom," Tom said, squinting at the damsel, "but I do not know where it was supposed to be. Under the sea perhaps, or under the ground. The Strangers dwelled there, it was said, and their King too. But nowt has been seen of that country since ages long gone, when folks was more ignorant and believed in such fancies. Then again, the world's a queer place."

The son, William, took his turn at the helm. The boat changed tack and they rounded another headland, still keeping the coastline in view to the left. The hull rocked on a gentle swell. As they sailed southward, the distant landscape changed from the barren rocks of Arcdur to wooded hills.

"Caermelor . . . who is King there?" asked the passenger.

William regarded her with a quizzical stare.

"Where have you come from, that you don't know our sovereign's name? Your manner of speaking sounds foreign . . ."

"I come from far away. North."

"Ach, I wouldna have believed any folk did not know of our good King-Emperor, the Sixteenth James D'Armancourt!"

Ashalind fell silent. In her time the sovereign had been William the Wise, who was grandson of the great Unitor, son of James the Second. Had thirteen generations passed? Two or three centuries? It was difficult to credit that such a vast span of time had elapsed.

"How old is the dynasty of D'Armancourt?" she asked.

"Why," said old Tom, "it is traced back, they say, a thousand years, that was the first King James. But not all were called James. Some of the D'Armancourt kings bore other names."

Shocked at this crushing of her hopes, Ashalind clenched her hands. In a spasm of frustration she hammered her fist on a wooden water-barrel. A millennium! It was too much to contemplate. What far-reaching changes had taken place in Erith during such a long period? Why were the exiled Faêran lost or forgotten?

A flock of shearwaters flew overhead. In the water several yards from the keel, something splashed. Instantly the attention of the men was fixed on the spot.

"'Tain't *she,* is it?" William asked in a low voice.

"Nay, 'tis one of the *maighdeans,*" said his father. "But which kind I cannot tell."

Through the aquamarine depths Ashalind caught a fleeting glimpse of a long, glittering curve, a drifting skein of pale hair, an eldritch face. Then the subaquatic visitor was gone.

"A *maighdean na tuinne,*" explained Tom to the ignorant northerner, "a damsel of the waves. 'Twould be a good thing to befriend one of them, a seelie one, for they can give warning of storms. The last few days, we were diving for coral and nacris-shell on the northern reefs—that storm blew us off course and away from the fleet. The anchor dragged and we were caught out. Had to run for hours before the wind."

An eerie crooning of music came blowing to their ears along the wind. Ashalind saw, on the distant beach, half a dozen figures swaying in dance. The men shaded their eyes with their hands.

William became oddly quiet and appeared to pay a lot of attention to his steering. The distant dancers must have caught sight of the boat. With cries and shouts, they pulled on garments that had lain beside them on the rocks, and slid into the water. The dark shapes of them arrowed toward the small vessel. The young sailor loosened the jib and the sails hung flapping. When the swimmers came cavorting close, the heads that broke the surface were those of seals. William leaned over and spoke to them in a tongue Ashalind could not recognize. He spoke lovingly, gently, and the seals replied in the same language.

"One of the Roane was once wife to Will," Tom mur murmured to Ashalind. "He stole her sealskin while she was dancing, and hid it. 'Tis unlike him to do such a thing, but she were very comely and he were fair taken with her. She begged him to return it, for without it she couldna return to the skerries out in the ocean. But he would not give in and at last persuaded her to marry him. She made a good and dutiful wife to him for three years, although she always had a wistful eye on the sea. One day she chanced to find the skin and then she was off in haste, down to the sea never to return. Will allus asks for news of her. But you see, unions between mortals and immortals allus end in breach and bereavement. Everyone knows that. Will should ha' known."

"Please, Will, ask the Roane if they know aught of the High King of the Fair Folk."

William spoke again in the seal language.

"They say they never speak to mortals about the Fair Folk," he translated, when the seals had given their answer, "but the eldritch wights of Huntingtowers may be able to tell."

The Roane went undulating away through the waves, and Tom turned the sail so that the wind filled it. The patched canvas snapped taut as the air crammed into it. Foam creamed at the prow.

Ashalind asked, "Huntingtowers—what is that?"

"A dreadful unseelie place it is, a caldera infested with powerful wights of gramarye," said Tom. "It lies on the other side of the old magmite mines, not more than seven leagues west of a cottage belonging to a good family of fisher-folk known to us—the Caidens. That family lives in fear of the wicked things that issue from the place from time to time."

"Have you seen any of the creatures that dwell therein?"

"No. But Tavron Caiden has told us of them. And they're not pretty, most of 'em. There's nasty little spriggans and trows as creeps about, and white pigs and hares, but the Caidens wear wizard-*sained* tilhals and the lesser wights don't bother them much—they keep away from the rowan and the iron. The worst things . . ." Here the shell-diver paused and scanned the horizon with a troubled air. "The worst things is them that goes hunting. Fuaths and duergars and such. Some of them are worse than any nightmare. Others of them look like Men, even right noble and kingly Men, but there's something wrong about them . . ."

"Kingly Men, you say? Then Faêran may be amongst them!" cried Ashalind, dropping the bread on which she had been biting. Her face was flushed.

"That may be so, but there is no mercy in the creatures that infest Huntingtowers, and that place is not where you should seek your King. It is a hub of evil and death. I do not even like to speak of it on a fair day such as this. Leave that sinkhole to the wicked wights, lass. Caermelor's the place for you. News always flows toward big cities."

"This cottage of your friends—is it far from here?" Ashalind asked.

"'Tis near Isse Harbor. It stands alone on the northern coast of the Cape of Tides—twelve to fourteen days away depending on the wind, and if we do not call in at our village on the Isle of Birds. But we have a good haul of nacris-shell already on board, as you can see, and we are heading home to unload it. Besides, we'll not put a slip of a thing like you ashore at the Cape of Tides, not in the shadow of Huntingtowers."

"If you do, I shall give you gold." Their passenger rattled the pouch her father had given her, then took some coins from it. The antique disks in her palm glinted, flashing in the sunlight. "I beg of you—take me there."

Astonishment registered on the ingenuous faces of the shell-divers, quickly replaced by suspicion.

"How did you come by such wealth? Is it honest gold?"

"It is honest gold, not stolen, nor gold of gramarye to change into leaves and blow away. But it has lain hidden this past millennium and now it is uncovered."

"Ye'd be better off coming with us to the Isle of Birds. From there you might take the ferry to Finvarna, and thence find passage south to Caermelor on one of the regular shipping runs."

"Sir, I am grateful for your advice but I will not be dissuaded."

Putting their heads together, the two boatmen murmured earnestly to one another. From time to time they glanced at their passenger, who lowered her eyes and endeavored to look as if she took no heed of their discussion.

"Be you steadfastly set on this course, lass?" said Tom at last. "Is there naught that will change your mind?"

"I am steadfast. If you will not take me to the Cape of Tides, I shall seek another ferryman, in any case."

A troubled expression clouded the brow of the shell-diver. "This goes against my better judgment. If you be set on going near Huntingtowers, we will transport you, but not for payment. 'Twould not be right, to bring a starving waif like you into danger and take her gold as well. If you change your mind when you get to Tavron Caiden's place, you might make your way to the Royal City from there."

"Gramercie!"

Privately, Ashalind decided she would leave payment with them despite their protestations. They had given her food and passage, and it was evident they were not rich folk.

* * *

They made landfall thrice during the next fourteen days, entering profound inlets where steps were crudely hewn into the cliffs. William replenished their water supplies from thin waterfalls that trailed like the frayed ends of silk down these walls of adamant, but they met no man there.

"These lands of the northwest coast are deserted," William said. "Here dwell only the birds and beasts, and wicked things, and the wind."

Rugged and rocky was the coastline. The sheer cliffs that lined it were pierced by deep channels and wild, wave-churned sounds cutting far back into the land. For some miles, huge trees crowded down to the very cliff tops. Dense shadows were netted beneath their boughs.

On sighting these ancient woodlands, William remarked in a grim undertone, "There ends the westernmost arm of the terrible forest."

At length, the voyagers sailed between islands and arrived on the coast of the mainland at an area where cliffs sloped gently to a tiny harbor. There they tied up the boat and came ashore. The salt breeze stung their faces with a hint of chill. "Winter's here," said Tom.

The cottage of the Caidens, whitewashed and slate-roofed, overlooked the neat harbor. Behind it was a large, well-tended vegetable patch, the inevitable bee-skeps, and racks for drying fish. Stunted rowans and plum trees grew all around. A few sea-pinks straggled in the window-boxes facing east. Tavron's wife, Madelinn, kept chickens, goats, and a sheep whose wool she spun.

There were children—a boy, Darvon, and a girl, Tansy. This family welcomed the boatmen and the yellow-haired stranger into their midst, sharing their home and provender, begrudging nothing. Tom and William returned their greetings and hospitality with amiability, but it was evident that the two men were uneasy.

"The lass here had some notion about Huntingtowers," explained William, "but instead she may go on to Caermelor, with the next road-caravan that comes this way, or take ship."

Tom advised, "Do not be too hasty, lass. Wait until you hear more about that place."

The next morning the choll divers sailed away to the Isle of Birds, carrying the gold coins Ashalind had slipped into their pockets while they were not looking.

"Stay awhile, lass," Tavron Caiden said, "before you travel on. 'Tis few enough folk who pass this way and we would be glad of the company. Besides, by the look of you, if you don't mind me saying so, a rest would do you good."

Indeed, the turmoil of the Leaving and the Closing, the shock of finding she had been gone from Erith for a thousand years, and the toilsomeness of hard travel across Arcdur without nourishment had taken their toll. For the first two days the newcomer slept a great deal, woke to eat, and slept again. Good health began to return. The Langothe was on her, nevertheless, pulling toward the north where lay the Gate to the Fair Realm, but she felt driven to quest on, to be rid of the terrible longing at its root. The Caidens bade her tarry longer with them, until strength fully returned. When they saw that she was bent on departing with all haste, they would not tell her the way to Huntingtowers.

"Stay awhile," they begged. "Bide just a few days more, then we will tell you the way and set you rightly on it."

Indeed, their guest was in no state to argue and must submit. They set the best of their simple provender before her. Although she hungered, she had seen Faêran food and breathed its fragrance. No Erithan victuals gave off much flavor in her mouth now, and, above all, the eating of flesh had come to seem abhorrent.

The fisher-folk had never before seen golden hair, and by

this she learned for the first time—to her secret sorrow—
that the Talith Kingdom was no more. The race had ebbed.
Its few remaining representatives were scattered throughout
Erith, and in Avlantia red-and bronze-leaved vines grew
over the ruins of the cities. Throughout the Known Lands
the stockier brown-haired Feorhkind predominated now, far
outnumbering even the red Erts of Finvarna. One or two
small Feorhkind villages had been established on the fringes
of Avlantia, but generally that kindred preferred the cooler
southern lands.

Without revealing her origins, Ashalind gleaned much
more information from the conversation of her hosts. She
learned about the fine talium chain mesh that lined the taltry
hoods, used to protect against that wind of gramarye they
called the shang, which burned Men's emotions into the
ether. She found out about sildron, which (it could only be
she who remembered) had been the gift of the High King of
the Fair Realm to the D'Armancourt Dynasty. In this new
era, sildron lifted Windships and the Skyhorses whose
routes never passed over the remote region where the cottage stood. She discovered much concerning the Stormriders and the King's warriors, the Dainnan, and the strifes of
past history, and the current unrest in the northeast lands that
was wont to erupt into skirmishes.

She was fascinated, numbed by the changes that had happened over a millennium. There seemed so many—yet so
few, when such an incredible span of time was considered.
Conceivably, the enchantment of the Gate allowed those
who passed through it to adapt to alterations in language
over the years. As for the evolution of technology, the centuries of ignorance and strife known as the Dark Era had
checked the progress of civilization in Erith, or even
dragged it backward. Apart from sildron, taltries, and the
shang, there seemed little difference between the world as
she had known it and the world as she saw it now. Perhaps

she would not feel like so much of a misfit in this new age after all.

Yet she marveled and she grieved. A thousand years; it might as well have been forever.

The Caiden children, who had been restraining their curiosity with difficulty begged their mother to tell them stories of her travels in the north. After the tale of her hardships in Arcdur was related, they wanted another, and another. Ashalind was happy to oblige as best she could without revealing her secret, so she delved into her hoard of tales learned from Meganwy, and from wandering Storytellers, until Madelinn bade the children cease their pestering and leave the guest some peace.

At night by the fireside, with the pet whippet lying before the hearth and the sea-sound booming beyond the walls, Ashalind regaled her hosts with all the gestes and songs she could recall. In return they told her about the hollow hill where, it was said, Faêran knights and ladies lay in enchanted sleep with their horses, hounds, and hawks and their treasures of untold wealth, and of how it was supposed to be possible to wake them by certain means if one could find the entrance to their underground halls. But none knew which hills they were, or if the stories were true.

Only one event marred the harmony of these times.

The child Tansy had a tuneful singing voice. Ashalind taught her many songs, including one named "The Exile," which had been made by Llewell, the young songmaker who had been among those brought out of Faêrie by Ashalind. Well did she remember that youth calling to her at the gates of Hythe Mellyn. He had been driven mad by the Langothe and sometimes believed he was one of the Faêran. But he had never returned to the Fair Realm, for he pined and died before the Leaving. His songs remained.

Full many leagues of foreign soil I've trod.
At last, I would reclaim my native sod.
Alas, it seems I cannot find the way.
Exiled, my heart grows heavy, day by day.
And wondrous as these hills and vales may be,
They're not the mystic realms I crave to see—
The dream'd-of world in childhood's state of bliss—
My land of birth; that is the place I miss.
So am I doomed to seek, forever banned?
A stranger wandering in this strange land?
The strongest measures cannot ease the pain.
Oh, will I ever see my home again?

When she first heard it, Tansy was so taken with this song that she stood on tiptoe to offer Ashalind a kiss. In fright, Ashalind jumped back, covering her face with her hands.

"Oh no! You must not do that!"

The family stared at her, astonished at this peculiar behavior.

The guest stammered her apologies.

"I must not be kissed. It is a bitterbynde, a geas. It must not be broken."

The awkward moment passed. A geas must be respected, no matter how strange, and so must the wishes of a guest.

It was a pleasure to help with the many tasks demanded by this solitary life: bread-baking, cheesemaking, drying and salting barrels of fish, gardening, washing, tending the hives and the animals. Immersion in the work of this family temporarily ameliorated the nostalgia Ashalind felt for her own, but always the Langothe corroded the core of her.

One night she was woken with crackling hair, feeling for the first time the prickling exhilaration of the unstorm.

Opening the shutters she saw, below the cliff, every wave-crest foaming with stars. Near at hand, the vegetable

patch was powdered with emerald-dust, and even the tethered goat watched with blazing topaz eyes, its horns
sculpted of polished agate. It was just as Cierndanel had
said—*"The winds of gramarye are awakening at this outrage, the winds of Ang. They flare from the Ringstorm at
Erith's rim. Soon they shall prowl the lands of thy world,
dyed by the imprints of men's designs."*

On other days the shang came, dimming sunlight, frosting the land and sea with strange lights, but there were no
tableaux here in this far-flung outpost.

"Why do you live alone?" Ashalind asked her benefactress as they mended nets down by the harbor. "Is it not perilous?"

"We have no choice," replied Madelinn. "No other folk
will live so close to the place of dread. Unseelie things roam
near here. Men who venture to the caldera never return, or if
they do, they come back raving mad and perish soon after.
Sometimes when the moon is full, dark skyriders come to
Huntingtowers from the northeast and after that a ghastly
Hunt issues from that place. Its leader is Huon, the unseelie
prince from whose skull grows a set of antlers like those of
a stag, and he is called the Hunter."

"I have heard the name," murmured Ashalind. "Who has
not?"

"When the Hunt is abroad, we lock ourselves inside the
house, barring all the doors and windows, but the bars do not
keep out the horrible baying of black hounds with fiery eyes,
and the beating of hooves. It's enough to make your blood
curdle."

"Why then do you live here?"

"Because it is our own." Madelinn spoke with quiet dignity. "Eight years ago, when the children were small, we
sailed here, from Gilvaris Tarv on the east coast. Tavron and
I were raised among fisher-folk, but poverty had forced us
to seek employment in that city. It was a terrible life." She

shook her head, frowning. "Bad conditions; cruelty. Never enough pay to feed the family properly. The children were forever hungry. My uncle lived in this cottage on the cliffs. He died and I inherited it. Here we came, and here we rule ourselves and seldom go hungry, even if it is sometimes fish day after day. We have learned to live in the shadow of Huntingtowers."

"Will you tell me of that place?"

Madelinn stretched her arm out in a wide gesture to the sea. A tall cone-shaped island reared its peak not far from the shore, southwest of the little harbor. Farther west another thrust up, and beyond it several more in a great sweeping curve dwindling around to the northwest.

"That's what we call the Chain of Chimneys," she said, "a line of fire-mountains, ages old, that once lifted themselves out of the sea."

"I have heard of them by repute," said Ashalind. "Called by the old Feorhkind name of Eotenfor, the Giant's Stepping-Stones."

"Aye," said Madelinn. "One of these fire-heads pushed up under the land instead of the sea, and became Huntingtowers Hill. In its top is a vast cauldron more than a mile wide, and inside that are a dozen or so small hills. Ash cones they were. Now they are islands in a lake, for the crater has filled with water. The biggest island is right smack in the middle of it all, but spans and causeways have been built everywhere, it is said, so that the eldritch creatures may cross over. On this central hill is a keep of stone, surrounded by eight other towers all linked by flying bridges."

Madelinn paused thoughtfully and pushed a stray strand of hair back from her face.

"Well," she continued, "I suppose some folk must have gone there to see it all and returned with some wit left, else we wouldn't know what the place looked like, would we? Don't say as how I'd recommend a sightseeing tour, though.

The lesser unseelie wights there can be put off with charms, but them things that go a hunting—they are full wicked."

But Ashalind was only half listening. Her mind was on Huntingtowers Hill.

If some of the exiled Faêran dwelt there, they must surely know the whereabouts of King Angavar. But by what Madelinn had said it seemed that they shunned mortals, and would be hardly likely to welcome her in, answer her questions, and wave good-bye. She must approach with caution and try to glean information using stealth. What if they were not Faêran? Wights such as the Each Uisge were able to take on a form resembling Men or Faêran, duping those who did not look too closely. Nonetheless, they could never make the transformation complete and always bore some inconspicuous but betraying sign such as webbed fingers or animal's feet, and when in man-shape they moved like Men, not with Faêran grace.

Prince Morragan had mingled with unseelie wights at Carnconnor. Perhaps it was he who was master at Huntingtowers. At this notion a surge of something akin to shock or exhilaration coursed through Ashalind.

Beside her, the fisherwoman sighed. "One day we might leave this place. We grow no richer here. The merchants of the road-caravans are miserly in their bartering for dried fish and only come by once a year. And it is not right for the children to be raised in the shadow of fear. One day . . . I don't know where we'd go."

There came an evening when the moon was almost full. The wind screamed at the gray-green sea and whipped the white-horse crests out beyond the harbor. Inside the cottage, ruby light flickered from the fire, casting deceptive shadows on rough walls.

Ashalind placed the purse of gold sovereigns on the table and loosened the drawstring of its mouth. Coins spilled out, gleaming softly across scored wood. The fisher-folk stared, struck dumb by the sight of so much wealth.

"This is for you," their guest explained, "save only for seven pieces, which I may need on my journey. If I do not return within three days take all of it and leave this place, for my efforts might inadvertently arouse the wrath of unseelie wights, and you might find yourselves in peril. If my quest is successful I may not return. If unsuccessful I will ask you to take me in your boat to Caermelor. I go now to Hunting-towers to seek the High King of the Fair Folk."

The silence was broken by Tavron clearing his throat.

"We shall not take your gold," he said gruffly. "Return it to the pouch. Our hospitality asks no fee."

"I do not mean to insult you," stammered Ashalind. "Only, if I do not return I shall not need it. With this you might buy land elsewhere and start a new life."

Sensing her distress, the white whippet jumped into her lap. Fondly, she caressed it, thinking of her faithful Rufus.

"If you must go, I shall accompany you as your guard," said Tavron. "Charms are not enough to ward off such wickedness as lurks there."

"Would you leave your family unprotected?" asked Ashalind.

"There will be no going to the place of dread, especially now," interrupted Madelinn. "Have you not heeded our warnings? The moon will be full tomorrow night, and it is then the Wild Hunt goes forth to scour the surrounding lands. All mortals who love life ought to stay safe behind rowan and iron."

"I have heeded your words," replied Ashalind, "but I am driven. A certain longing burns in me and daily eats me away—longing that can only be appeased when I have found the one I seek. It is the Langothe, and those who have never felt it cannot understand. Nothing you can say will alter my course. I have no choice."

"You must fight it," pleaded Tansy. "Stay with us. Teach us more songs."

"I must go."

The next morning, covered by the Faêran mantle, which had subtly altered its hues to match the surroundings, Ashalind left the cottage. She took her father's iron dagger, a wallet of food, some charms, and a leather water-bottle that was a gift from Tavron. The ragged riding-habit lay folded in a wooden chest inside the cottage; in place of it she wore worsted galligaskins, a pair of boys' buskins, and a tunic of brown bergamot, all gifts from the Caidens.

"These garments are old, but fit for traveling," Tavron Caiden said. "Unfortunately we have no taltry for you. If an unstorm should come, you must become still, eschew passion—otherwise your image will be painted on the airs for all passersby to see."

"It may be that the curious cloak you wear has the power to protect from the shang," suggested Madelinn. "Cover your head with the hood. It might work."

At the cottage door the fisherwife made one last appeal.

"Do not go, Ashalind," she said, looking the damsel squarely in the eyes. "My mother was a carlin and I possess some of her foresight. I tell you that if you go to Hunting-towers you go to your doom. I tell you that you will be defeated there, and that it will be the end of you as we know you now. You will die or, at best, you will be altered in some terrible, inexplicable way."

Her entreaties were in vain.

With embraces but no kisses, the family bade farewell. They turned their harrowed faces aside to hide their horror at this obvious suicide.

The damsel set out in a westerly direction toward the tip of the Cape of Tides. She climbed the slope behind the cottage, breathing hard from the exertion. Shreds of morning mist were dissolving in tatters. At the top of the cliff she halted, surveying the satin expanse of the sea. The waters were striped with shades of blue from milky to intense, under a cornflower sky. The perfect cones of the Chimneys stood like guardians, waves creaming on their beaches. A shag perched on a rock, transfixed and cruciform, drying its wings. As yet, Ashalind had seen no elindors in this new era. This morning only shearwaters and petrels rode the sky.

The whippet had followed her. Stoically, she sent it back with a harsh word. The cottage looked tiny, far below. In a few steps it was lost to view.

Low tea-tree scrub grew on the cliff top, spiking the air with the tang of eucalyptus. In the distance, a disused Mooring Mast stood dark against the skyline. Rain had fallen the night before, and puddles made mirrors on the ground.

Despite a growing feeling of trepidation, the traveler made swift progress along the cliffs and past the overgrown mullock heaps of the abandoned mines. Toward nightfall she reached the foot of the long-dead volcano. Its heath-covered flanks rose in a long slow sweep to a brooding summit that appeared flat from her vantage point. Hairs prickled on her arms and neck. The prescience of danger pressed down like the weight of a mountain. Dark clouds clustered over the sun's face and the air stilled. No birds sang here. Stopping in the shelter of a scrubby brake, Ashalind took a draft of water. Her stomach roiled with trepidation; she could not eat a bite. After tugging the Faêran hood more firmly around her face, she began to ascend as noiselessly and unobtrusively as possible.

As she climbed the hillside, she sensed she was being watched. Bushes rustled furtively, and twin points of viridescent light gleamed out from many an enigmatic shadow. Close by, a shout of loud laughter made her jump. Sweating with more than effort, she labored on, eyes darting from side

to side, trying to make sense out of the odd shapes in the
gathering darkness. What a fool she had been, she realized
too late, to challenge a domain of wights at night. Most of
these creatures were nocturnal, and she had placed herself at
a grave disadvantage. She ought to have found a sheltered
place to sleep and await the dawn. Had she lost her wits already, in her eagerness to be rid of the wearisome Langothe?
But there would be no turning back now that she had come
so far, and she toiled on until she reached the lip of the
caldera.

The waxing moon, risen early, extruded ghostlike shafts
through a gash in the cumulus. Its crepuscular light reflected
back from the expansive lake that lay stretched out far
below Ashalind's feet, strewn with the dark humps of islets
like solemn tortoises. The top of the central island rose up
level with the caldera's rim, and from it soared, attenuated,
the fantastic structure Madelinn Caiden had described, with
its towers and flying bridges. From within these towers
bluish light pierced the slit windows at many levels. The
slits glowed eerily, like blue gas; weird optics watching the
night. To the right, a road came through a cutting in the rim
and crossed several bridges to reach the towers.

From somewhere to the left a crow harshly said "cark-
cark." Surely it was unusual for diurnal birds to be calling
out at this time of night. The intruder took a deep breath and
started to move quietly down the inside wall toward the first
bridge.

Her fall was caused by a white hare that ran under her
feet. In the next instant, something small but with the
strength of a coiled spring landed heavily on her, gouging,
beating, pummeling, until her hand found the iron dagger's
hilt and she wrenched it from its sheath.

The thing sprang away, shrieking falsetto alarm as it fled
into the night. Blood dripped into the damsel's eyes and she
wiped it away with her sleeve.

"Cold iron will not serve you far, 'ere," said a voice like two dry branches rubbing together.

"It serves me well enough," she said to the spriggan who stood six paces away.

"Only foolish mortals trespass in the domain of 'Uon, the Prince of 'Unters," the spriggan said, answering her first question before she had asked it. "Especially when *he* is on his way. For this, you must die."

It flinched, blinking as she flicked the dagger to reflect moonlight from the blade into its squinty eyes. This was partly to disguise the fact that her hands were shaking.

"Ah, but if I die, you will not benefit," Ashalind said steadily. "In return for certain information, I am prepared to pay gold. True gold."

She rattled the purse.

"Pah," sneered the spriggan. "What use is that yellow metal to me, eh? I 'ave no need of gold, true or otherwise. It cannot buy me juicy caterpillars or sweet cocoons and spiders' eggs." The wight pranced around, switching its tail restlessly. "What else does the *erithbunden* offer?"

"Do you like maggots?"

"Love 'em."

"I passed a dead bird not long ago . . ."

She broke off—the wight had already disappeared in the direction she indicated. Something bit her knee. Reflexively, she kicked it away. With a sigh of relief and disappointment, she decided to retrace her steps after all, and wait on the lower slopes until morning.

As she turned away a nuggety, grotesque shape detached itself from obscurity. Here was a wight even more sinister and repulsive than a spriggan. Ashalind backed away, clutching the charms at her belt, for she recognized this small, manlike being as a black dwarf—a duergar. Battling a sinking feeling, the damsel hoped the rowan and iron charms had some potency against such a dangerous entity.

"What else *do* you offer?" the duergar asked casually.

"I am come to buy information. I offer nothing until I can be sure that you are a trusted henchman of Huon the Hunter, who would have knowledge such as I seek," she countered. Her hand shivered, gripping the charms. This thing was not to be trifled with—duergars were quick to anger and quicker to strike. She wondered why it had not already torn her hand off. Maybe the immutable laws of eldritch forbade it until she showed fear, or else some protective spell of the Lady Nimriel lingered.

"For instance," she continued, trying to trick the wight into revealing the information she was after, "do you know the whereabouts of Angavar High King?"

Out of its puddle of inky shadow, the duergar took a step closer.

"If you want information, I can smuggle you secretly into the Keep of Huon the Horned," it offered, flexing grimy fingernails and baring long, pointed teeth, "on the wains that come tonight. First, give us a little suck of your blood."

Ashalind recalled stories of benighted travelers found by roadsides in the morning, desiccated husks.

"No!" Wildly she cast her mind about, desperate for something with which to buy off this manifestation of iniquity. Fumbling at her wrist, she said, "A golden bracelet inlaid with a white bird . . . gold coins . . . poppyseed biscuits and blackberry cakes . . ."

"Ignorant flax-wench! How dare you offer trash!"

"If you dislike my offerings, then we cannot do business." She grew still, but she was too wise to turn her back and walk away.

Noise ceased while the night condensed under a grinning moon.

"Cut off your hair and I will get you into the Keep," said the duergar eventually.

"The Central Keep? Unharmed and in secret? Yes!"

A whip snaked from the wight's powerful hand. Before the damsel could recoil, it lashed her throat like a tongue of white-hot steel. The duergar emitted a strange mewling noise, which may have been laughter, and muttered, "Yea indeed."

Ignoring the searing pang at her throat, Ashalind unbound the long heavy braid from her head and cut it off close to the scalp. She tossed the rope of hair into the wight's hands just as the sound of horses' hooves and wooden wheels came clopping and rattling out of the darkness.

"The bird may enter the cage but it will never sing the songs it learns, and when it pops out its head—pigeon pie!" were the black dwarf's last words. The wicked thing rushed away and Ashalind followed as fast as possible, knowing it was bound to keep its promise to her. Around the caldera's upjutting rim the duergar led her, to the cutting where the road came through from the gentler slopes. Along that road, a convoy of wagons was entering the volcanic basin. The vile creature leaped up beside the driver of the lead wain. What it did to him, Ashalind could not be certain, but the wain and those in procession behind it stopped long enough for her to climb swiftly aboard. As the train moved off again, she found a deep, wooden chest half full of some pungent dried pods and concealed herself inside.

She could tell by the numbness now in her throat that the treacherous duergar had stolen her voice, and she knew by the jolting and swaying and the hollow ring and thud of hooves that the wagons were passing over bridges from island to island. When the wain stopped, the chest was unloaded and propelled upward with nauseating speed before being transferred a second time and left alone in utter silence.

Bleakly the smuggled girl pondered over the loss of her voice, the latest setback of so many in her life. If she could only learn the whereabouts of the King and find him, he might provide some Faêran cure.

After a long while she dared to lift the lid. The chest had been abandoned among others in a dim storeroom, but the door of the room was ajar, admitting a streak of cyanic light. Having ventured out of the redolent container, she nervously peeped around the door. There was only an empty stone flagged hallway with other recessed doors leading off to either side. A faint smell of charred meat permeated the air.

Waves of weariness washed over Ashalind. She had walked far that day. Fear had kept her senses sharp, but now, in this tomblike quiet, she was overwhelmed by the need for sleep. After withdrawing into the half-empty storeroom she curled herself in the farthest corner, among a stack of boxes, then pulled the Faêran cloak around her and closed her eyes.

Severing themselves from nightmare, faint echoes woke her. They had sprung from the mutter of distant voices. Feeling in need of sustenance, she took a swig from the water-bottle hanging at her belt and ate the blackberry cakes she had, in desperation, offered the duergar. Refreshed, she emerged from her niche and followed the undercurrent of sound. It led her along deserted passageways, up spiral stairs, and onto another floor more sumptuously decorated. Tapestries hung along the walls of the galleries, and rushes strewed the floors. Blue lamps glowed. Hearing the *pad-pad* of multiple footsteps approaching, Ashalind pressed herself into a recessed doorway. Her Faêran cloak adopted the dusky hues of bluestone and old oak, and without noticing her, half a dozen assorted creatures went past in the wake of a manlike figure with billowing cloak.

"Stinks of siedo-pods up 'ere," a creaking voice commented as the bevy disappeared around a corner.

Fine droplets beaded the damsel's brow. It dawned on her that siedo-pods' strong odor might well mask the scent of mortal flesh. Following quietly behind the group, she peered around the corner. The mutterings she had been hearing emanated from a doorway farther along, and were accompanied by a clinking of pottery and metal. Beyond that doorway, a grating voice deeper than the tones of spriggans was giving orders to select certain wines and convey them in haste: ". . . and hoof it, you spigot-nosed kerns," it rasped. "His Royal Highness will soon be here."

At these words tempests of blood beat about the temples of the spy. She could have screamed for sheer delight and terror. Such good fortune, such evil luck! By "His Royal Highness," the speaker could mean only Prince Morragan. It seemed the Crown Prince was not, after all, comatose beneath a hill, surrounded by Faêran knights. Doubtless he would know the whereabouts of his brother. Had he remained unsleeping throughout the years? Or had he woken not long since? How dreary, how weary, how slow-dragging and tedious would be a millennium of banishment!

But tragedy must follow, if this royal exile should discover and identify her. Instantly he would guess she had come recently from the Fair Realm. How else might a mortal have survived for a thousand years?

That the Prince must recognize her the moment he set eyes on her she had no doubt. He would not forget the mortal maid who had entered his dominions, answered his challenges, reclaimed his captives, refused his invitations, and thwarted his desires. He would be fully aware she had accompanied the Talith in their migration to the Realm before the Closing. All these years, he had supposed her locked away in Faêrie with her family. If she had appeared in Erith, there could be only one explanation. Against all possibility, *somewhere*, a Door had been opened.

Assuredly the unseelie wights of Huntingtowers would torment her until she revealed the secret of the Gateway, and then all would be lost. Morragan would send her back to

Faêrie with the Password, and when Easgathair opened the Gates, the Prince would be there waiting to enter the Realm in place of his brother, his rival. Then would Morragan use the remaining unasked boon to exile the High King from the Fair Realm, this time truly forever. He would rule in his brother's place. And it would be her fault.

But no, she would not permit discovery. She would be careful. She would listen, and learn what she could.

"Get rid of those miserable slaves below," a voice bellowed. "If he finds any cursed mortals here, your heads will roll on the flagstones, then I shall kick 'em out the windows. And while he visits, utter only the common speech, on pain of disembowelment. I will not have the Fithiach disturbed by your squawkings and squeakings. I will cut out the tongue of the first dung-gobbler that disobeys."

Bowed figures hurried out of the doorway bearing laden trays, and ascended yet another stair.

Soon after, Ashalind's cloaked form glided after them. She had no idea how long the mantle's special qualities might let her remain undetected, but a relatively quick death was preferable to years spent slowly perishing from the agony of the Langothe, and she must persist in her quest.

Thick rugs carpeted the floors of this upper level. More brightly lit, the walls were hung with arras of richer textiles, and shields emblazoned with wonderful devices. The last of the wightish menials entered a chamber by way of richly carved doors inlaid with bronze. The bellowing voice had spoken of mortal slaves in the lower regions of the Keep. Ashalind wondered whether she might possibly pose as a servitor, and thus move freely with less chance of discovery. But no—it was clear that when the Fithiach visited, all mortals were banished from his sight. Nonetheless, he must endure mortal speech, for according to what she had overheard, he despised the guttural wightish languages but would not permit them to sully the Faêran tongue by employing it. So far, within these walls she had heard only common-speak.

Meanwhile, judging by the sounds in the carved-door chamber, further preparations were being made for the arrival of the Raven Prince.

A small insignificant portal was sunk into a niche almost opposite the carved doors, across the passageway from them. When Ashalind pushed, it's hinges obeyed with a groan. Inside nestled another dark storage cubicle—a good enough vantage point for surveillance when the door was left ajar. Dust arose like phantom brides, and a spider dropped on her face. She might have yelped in surprise, had the duergar not stolen her power of speech.

Her narrow field of vision through the carved doors across the corridor showed lofty arched windows looking out from the larger chamber, which was bustling with activity. A tall, manlike figure moved past one window. Its head was crowned by the branching antlers of a stag. A graceful lady was standing with her back to Ashalind, dressed in a lace-edged green velvet gown sewn thickly all over with peridots. Dark hair cascaded down her back. Gold ornaments glittered on her svelte arms. She might have been a damsel of the Faêran, since several ladies of the Fair Realm had been riding among the ill-fated hawking party exiled on the Day of Closing, and others had fled into Erith as the last Call sounded, when the exile of the royal brethren was in no doubt. But when this green-clad belle turned around, the hem of her dress swished aside. The spy flinched. The "woman" was neither Faêran nor mortal, but an eldritch wight. How doubly hideous it seemed, that such a fair form should walk upon woolly sheep's hooves.

A glow of firelight to the right illuminated polished furniture and tableware. Nothing else in that room could be observed.

*   *   *

A familiar voice came pummeling like a blow to the stomach:

"Set those goblets aright, nasty little hoglin, or I shall have you flayed like your sniveling cousin whose hide hangs above the Gate of Horn."

Never had Ashalind erased from memory the coarse tones of Yallery Brown.

Commotion arose to the left. She could not see what caused it.

"Get out," commanded the unseelie rat-wight. "His Highness arrives."

A motley collection of wights hastened from the chamber, disappearing down the corridor. A chill draft followed them, and the clatter of hooves on stone.

"My liege . . ." Yallery Brown's tone was fawning. He had broken off as if in fear or awe.

Several tall figures crossed quickly past the doorway. The carved doors were slammed shut—in the instant before they met, Ashalind discerned a stunning profile that could only be Morragan's. He and his retainers must have entered at the arched windows, which were as vast and high as the front gates of a castle.

Through a gap at the threshold drifted the conversation of those sequestered within. Listening with intense concentration, Ashalind could glean most of what they were saying, but it made little sense. Either they discussed matters far removed from her knowledge, or else she was too tired to comprehend. Eventually she succumbed again to sleep.

By the fluctuations in the window-light when the carved doors were open, Ashalind could tell night from day. She remained concealed hungrily in the spider-haunted cell, sipping her water, and the next night Morragan met again with his followers in the chamber.

There was scant liquid remaining in her leather bottle,

and the siedo-pod odor was fading. The Faêran hated spies, and the Raven Prince in particular detested mortals. She began to think that if she were caught there, the manner of her demise at the mercy of unseelie wights might prove more horrible than the Langothe. But she stayed, and she listened, wishing heartily that there were some way of prompting the gathering to speak of the High King.

On the third night, by strange fortune, they did—but it was not as she had hoped. The heavy doors stood ajar. A low buzz of conversation had been proceeding for a good while, when Morragan's Faêran voice carried clearly across the corridor, rich, deep, and melodious in contrast to the harsh, throaty tones and raucous squeaks of the wights.

Gooseflesh raked the listener's spine.

"There has been a restlessness of late," he said musingly, "a breath of finer air, as from the Realm. This dusk, I rode down by the fisherman's cot and heard a maid within, warbling a song I have never heard before. In faith, it moved me not a little, although poorly versed."

Ashalind held her breath. From the unseen fireplace on the right sparks flew into her field of vision and hung dying in midair.

"A song of exile," said Morragan.

"If it displeased my lord," murmured Yallery Brown, "the cottage shall be razed, and those who have dwelt there for far too long shall be punished."

The eavesdropper stiffened. She must return as soon as possible to warn the Caidens!

"A song of exile," repeated Morragan, "reminding me of my own."

A thicker spray of sparks exploded, as if someone had kicked a burning log.

"Cursed be Angavar, may his reign end!" said the marvelous Faêran voice. "May his knights rot in their hill grave. Cursed be the White Owl and his Keys. Cursed be the moment the Casket snapped shut with the Word. Might I but live those times over again . . ."

Ashalind, eyes tightly shut, clasped her hands together. Her lips moved soundlessly.

The King, speak again of the High King! Where is this hill beneath which he sleeps amid his noble companions?

"Behold, Your Highness, they bring up the steeds." said the winter-wind voice of Huon, Prince of Hunters and steward of the stronghold. "Tonight we hunt."

A rush of biting air swung the carved doors open on their hinges. Morragan stood at a window, looking out at the night. The full moon was rising, outlining the statuesque shape of him, the wide shoulders from which his cloak eddied like a piece of darkness.

"The Realm," he said.

Then softly he spoke, but the night airs carried his voice back to the ears of the eavesdropper. It was a rhyme. The words were Faêran and she did not know what they meant, but their implication was haunting, lyrical, and strummed her Langothed heart with pain.

A half-shang gust lifted Morragan's cloak and hair like a wave. The inked-in outline of a horse appeared at the window. Then the Prince was gone, and several motley figures followed. Bridles jingled, boots scraped on bluestone, and commands were shouted. Far below, hounds began to yelp. A horn sounded. With a dissonance of shrill whoops and strident shouts the Hunt was away, borne aloft on invisible airstreams through the silver-sprayed vaults of darkness.

Abruptly, the fire went out.

Soon afterward, the spy heard two wightish servants come shuffling out of the chamber. As they came through the carved doors, one hoarsely muttered something.

"Shut your snout, clotpoll," the other wheezed, "or I'll roll your head in the fire. I'll teach you to speak the low tongue when the Crown Prince is honoring your dunghill with a visit!"

"So high and mighty are you not?" returned the hoarse one sarcastically. "You may have been chosen for his royal household, scumbag, but you do not deserve it and as soon as they see through you, you'll be thrown out on your muleish ear."

The wights had by now come to a halt in the corridor.

"You cap of all fools alive!" berated the wheezer. "And do you plot to take my place? I was chosen for wit and wisdom far beyond the grasp of your greasy claws, boiled-brains."

"Ha!" retorted Hoarse-Throat. "The jumped-up feather-goose is even more contemptible when it struts!"

His antagonist could scarcely contain his ire. "You know not to whom you speak," he hissed between gritted teeth. "Be wary, parasite, for your folly outweighs your fat head. I'll warrant you do not even have a notion of the Faêran words spoken this night by his Royal Highness!"

The other spluttered incoherently.

"Anyone with a jot of wit knows the meaning," said Wheezer triumphantly. "Even the merfolk sing it in the Gulf of Namarre. It is a riddle, an easy one, but too hard for the likes of *you,* you foul, undigested hodge-pudding."

"You're full of air!"

"Nay, noisome stench, and I'll prove it!"

Wheezer cleared its throat noisily and began to translate, slowly, as if every word was an effort.

"*Nor bound to dust, ye ocean's bird, the word's thy name, the Key's the word.* So? What's the answer, goat-face?"

But before goat-face could reply a voice thundered out from down the corridor: "Get along there, you rump-fed idlers, chattering like parrots outside the door! If you utter another word I'll have your lungs!"

With a rattling of spilled trays, the servants fled.

*   *   *

After that there was no more sound, except the wind whining around the Keep and the loud drumming of Ashalind's heart. The riddle was indeed easy. The answer was the elindor, or white bird of freedom, which spent seven years on the wing or water without touching land—her kenning-name. And there was another answer "Flindor" was the Password that opened the Green Casket of the Keys, in the Fair Realm.

Like syrup, silence poured forth from the recently vacated chamber. Surely the room was empty. Pulling the hood of the Faêran cloak over her head and tying it securely, Ashalind crossed the corridor, crept inside, and looked around. Indeed, they were all gone. There was no sign of Morragan's erstwhile presence. She was, again, bereft. Perversely, she had hoped for some evidence of him—what, she could not say. But fingering the enameled bracelet on her wrist, she exulted. She had discovered a fact of tremendous significance! She now knew the Password! The elindor, the white bird of freedom—how ironic that Morragan should have chosen it as the master key. The jest was manifold—the bird that lived free of the bonds of Erith's soil, the kenning of she who had freed the children, the Password to free the Keys from the Green Casket. But she must make haste and escape from Huntingtowers Keep—the danger was too great.

Her ears, strained to the limits of hearing, caught scuffling noises approaching along the corridor. It was too late to leave the chamber through the heavy carved doors. What measure of camouflage the cloak offered, she could not guess. Wildly she looked for a place of concealment among the furnishings, but none offered itself. Nor were there any other exits, save the wide, high openings of the windows, which led to a ledge over sheer nothingness, looking out on lands far below and dark horsemen riding the sky, fell shapes etched against crystal. A huge raven that had been watching her from the sill flapped slowly away. At that moment, enraged screaming broke out in the corridor, just beyond the doors. Terrified, Ashalind ran out to the ledge and dropped down over the side.

For a mere instant she hung by her sliding fingers over a void, knowing full well she would inevitably lose her grip. The chamber above was filled with a cacophony of raucous braying, piercing screeches, and the crashes of laden tables being overturned. Her kicking feet found a toehold just as her left hand lost its grip. Leaves brushed her face, thick tendrils of common ivy. It grew thickly, latticed all over the outer wall, great ancient, arthritic stems of it. Grabbing hold, she began to climb down.

Silent sobs of fear shook her body. Terror melted her sinews like wax and drained them of power, so that her fingers, nerveless, could scarcely grip. The half-shang wind buffeted erratically, alternately flattening her against the wall and wrenching her away, outlining each ivy leaf with green-and-gold rime. Claws of dead stems hooked themselves in her garments. There was no time to disengage them, so they tore great rents in the fabric.

Down she scrambled, seeking blindly for footholds and not knowing when her toes might scrabble against naked bluestone. Farther and farther down she maneuvered, sliding one quivering foot after another, one sweat-slicked hand after another, her heart pounding like a pestle in her chest. How far she must descend she did not know for certain, but the central Keep had looked to be hundreds of feet high. From the corners of her eyes, she could see other towers with their watchful blue-gas windows, and glimpse a couple of soaring spans over an abyss. It was like being a beetle clinging to an open wall, so vulnerable, for all eyes to see, for any predator to pick off with ease.

A chair came hurtling down from above, passed her within a hairsbreadth, and went spinning down to shatter far below. Doggedly she continued to descend. They had discovered her presence. It was only a matter of time before they hunted her down. The water-bottle hampered her. She dropped it.

When her fingers would obey her no longer, she let go of the ivy. After falling a surprisingly short distance, she lay in a crumpled heap, dazedly trying to comprehend that she still lived and had reached the ground safely after all. She tried to stand, but her legs gave way, so she began to crawl, passing by the smashed shards of the fallen chair. Common ivy sprawled all over the ground, covering small bushes and shrubs. Something became hooked on it—her bracelet. Carefully she freed it. The white bird shone in the moonlight, and somehow, the sight of this icon gave her strength and courage. Standing up, she broke into a run.

In the rising unstorm, scarlet and silver sparks flew from her iron-shod boots as she fled from island to islet, from bridge to bridge. Shang afterimages pulsed here and there, and the edge of every leaf on every bush was spangled. Up and over the caldera rim she ran, and down the other side, using the iron dagger to slash wildly at small things that sprang, yellow-eyed and malevolent, from the darkness. Away back, the hue and cry gathered momentum. Onward she sped, until she reached the mining grounds, and as she darted in among the heaps she heard the Wild Hunt catching up at her heels. The fire-eyed hounds were baying weirdly now, but there was a jarring note too, a sound that didn't belong. It sounded like a small dog yapping, and its source was up ahead. Rounding a mullock heap, she beheld the white whippet from the cottage of the Caidens. It barked frantically, ran a little distance, then turned to see if she was fol-

lowing. Placing all her faith in the brave little dog, she hastened after it.

The ululation of the pack crescendoed, soon augmented
by the deafening blare of horns. She dared not look back, but
it seemed as if the Hunt must be almost on her shoulders,
when without warning the whippet disappeared into a hole
in a hillock. Ashalind followed suit, not a moment too soon,
and the horde thundered past overhead.

Gasping for life, the damsel lay with outflung arms in the
umbra of a deep cavern whose floor sloped gradually downward. Her throat and chest burned. Somewhere nearby, the
little dog whimpered uneasily, and she sensed that it was trying to communicate. Still panting, she crawled in the direction of the sound.

The quietude outside was split by a roar and a concussion
that made the ground shake. Handfuls of clay nodules and
damp soil showered onto her hair and ragged clothes. After
springing up in blind panic, the refugee ran farther into the
cave, only to feel the floor drop away beneath her feet. She
started to slide. The dagger was still in her hands—swivel-
ing her body like an acrobat, she jammed the blade into the
soil to halt her progress. Loose pebbles slipped past and
down—she must have stumbled, in her mad rush, over the
edge of a shaft. The dagger stayed firmly embedded and she
realized she had not fallen far. Her feet dangled over some
unguessable depth. She hung from the weapon's hilt. Just
above her head the whippet stood, whining. When she
looked up she saw its anxious form backlit by gray light
from the cave's entrance.

The bellowing roar blared again, and heavy steps caused
the ground to vibrate. Something monstrous and massive
was approaching, and everything trembled before it. Its
weight might cause a cave-in, burying her and the whippet.

Doubtless the giant, or whatever it was, intended to do just that. In an agony of effort Ashalind heaved herself up, slid down, tried again, and finally inched herself up over the edge of the shaft. As she crawled up and over, on her elbows, her face level with the dog's muzzle, she saw it wag its tail with delight to see her safe.

"No!" she moaned in helpless exhaustion. The animal trotted toward her.

"No, no!" she tried to scream; but no words came from her wight-whipped throat, and, unchastised, the white whippet licked her face in innocent and loving greeting—the kiss of the Erith-born.

Acknowledgments

Yallery Brown: The tale of Yallery Brown is inspired by an article in "Legends of the Cars" by Mrs. Balfour. *Folk-Lore* 11, 1891.

McKeightley and the Antlered One: Inspired by "The Devil at Ightfield," collected in *English Legends,* by Henry Bett. Batsford, London, 1952. This traditional tale has many variants.

Perdret Olvath: Inspired by "The Fairy Widower," from *Popular Romances of the West of England,* by Robert Hunt. London, 1865.

Eilian: Inspired by a traditional tale collected in *Celtic Folklore, Welsh and Manx, Vol. 1,* by John Rhys. Oxford University Press, 1901. Also inspired by an account of a Faërie Rade in *Remains of*

Nithsdale and Galloway Song, collected by R. H. Cromek. Cadell & Davies, London, 1810.

The Midwife and the Faêran: Inspired by a tale in *Celtic Folklore, Welsh and Manx* (vol. 1), collected by John Rhys. Oxford University Press, 1901.

The Stolen Child: Inspired by and partially quoted from the old folktale "The Stanhope Fairies," collected in *Folk-Tales of the North Country,* by F. Grice. Nelson, London and Edinburgh, 1944.

Lake Coumluch: Inspired by the traditional tale "The World Below the Water," collected in *Legendary Stories of Wales,* by E. M. Wilkie. George G. Harrap & Co. Ltd., London, Bombay, Sydney, 1934.

Meroudys and Orfeo: Inspired by MS. Ashmole 61, reproduced in *Illustrations of the Fairy Mythology of Shakespeare,* by Halliwell, reprinted by W. C. Hazlitt in *Fairy Tales, Legends and Romances Illustrating Shakespeare,* 1875.

The Enchanted Knight: Inspired by a traditional ballad recorded in No. 39a, *The English & Scottish Popular Ballads,* edited by F. J. Child. The Folklore Press in Association with the Pagent Book Co., New York, 1957.

Bevan Shaw and the Mermaid: Inspired by and partially quoted from "The Mermaid of Gob-Ny-Ooyl," a folktale collected by Sophia Morrison for *Manx Fairy Tales*. Nutt, London, 1911.

Vinegar Tom: Inspired by a folktale collected by the late Ruth Tongue and reproduced in *County Folklore VIII, Somerset Folklore*. Folklore Society, 1965. The rhyme is a traditional quotation.

Liban: Inspired by and partially quoted from the folktale "The Sea-Morgan's Baby," collected by the late Ruth Tongue for her book *Forgotten Folk-Tales,* 1970.

Evan Sayle and the Mermaid: Inspired by and partially quoted from the folktale "John Reid and the Mermaid," in *Scenes and Legends of the North of Scotland*. Hugh Miller, Edinburgh, 1872.

Scoom Weel Your Fish: Inspired by and partially quoted from the folktale "The Mermaid Released," *County Folklore III, Orkney and Shetland Islands*. Edited by G. K. Black. Folklore Society, 1903.

The Piper and the Rats: Inspired by "The Pied Piper," by Joseph Jacobs, from *More English Fairy-tales,* 1894.

Lutey and the Mermaid: Inspired by a folktale collected in *Traditional and Hearthside Stories of West Cornwall,* 1st series. William Bottrell, Penzance, 1870.

Lazy Molly: Inspired by a folktale collected in *A Book of Folklore,* by Sabine Baring-Gould. Collins, London, n.d.

The Swanmaiden: Inspired by and partially quoted from "The Fairy Maiden," a traditional tale collected in *Legendary Stories of Wales,* by E. M. Wilkie. George Harrap & Co., 1934.

The Guardian Black Dog: Inspired by a passage in *My Solitary Life,* p. 188, by Augustus Hare, n.d., n.p.

The Unseelie Black Dog: Inspired by the traditional tale "The Mauthe Doog of Peel Castle," collected in *Minstrelsy of the Scottish Border,* with notes and introduction by Sir Walter Scott. Edited by T. F. Henderson. Oliver & Boyd, Edinburgh, 1932.

ABOUT THE AUTHOR

CECILIA DART-THORNTON's interests include playing music, oil painting, computer image-making, photography, and clay sculpture. She lives in Australia, and welcomes reader e-mail at www.dartthornton.com.

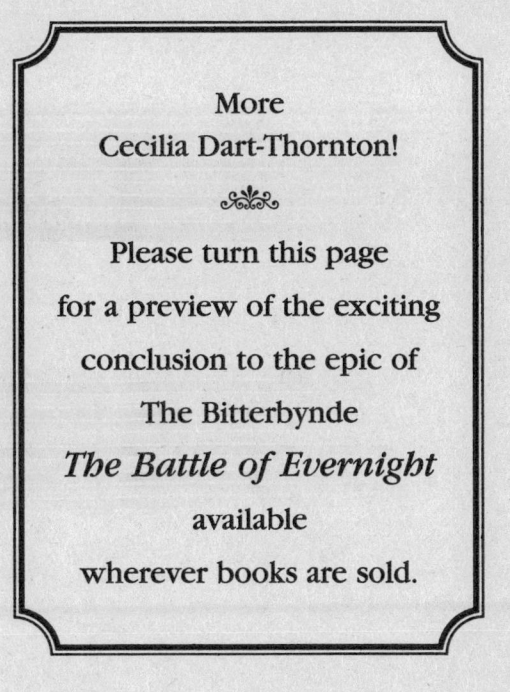

More
Cecilia Dart-Thornton!

Please turn this page
for a preview of the exciting
conclusion to the epic of
The Bitterbynde
The Battle of Evernight
available
wherever books are sold.

1

KHAZATHDAUR
The Masts of Shadow

Pale rings of smoke come floating through the trees,
Clear voices thread like silver on the breeze,
And as I look towards the west I grieve,
For in my heart, I'm crying out to leave.
MADE BY LLEWELL, SONGMAKER OF AURALONDE

The rain was without beginning and without end. It pattered on incessantly, a drumming of impatient fingers. There was only the sound of the rain and the rasp of breathing while the girl, mute, amnesiac, shorn, and wasted, climbed out over the brink of the mine-shaft. She was alone, with no concept of her own identity, no memory of how she had come to this place. In subterranean darkness she crawled blindly, until, reaching an opening, she tumbled out among javelins of rain. Over levels of harsh stone and through dripping claws of vegetation she drove herself on limbs emaciated by weeks of the Langothe and days of starvation in the wilderness and lack of appetite for the food of Erith after the sight and fragrance of Faêran fare. Sometimes she slept momentarily, or perhaps lost consciousness.

Pleasantly, even the Langothe had been forgotten then.

With stiffening limbs she moved slowly through the mud and wet stone of the abandoned mine, oblivious of its beauties or horrors, blind to obstacles that tore at her. Reaching level ground, she rose onto trembling legs and walked, an action her limbs seemed to remember by some instinct of their own.

The little dog was gone. The girl had lain a long time underground after the cave-in, at whiles licking at water-droplets that oozed from the rock. Buried alive, she was presumed dead. The Hunt had been abandoned because the hunters had not known who she was, believing her to be merely some foolish spy, some unlucky wanderer or thief, now punished by death beneath the rock fall. Yet she had survived, whether due to the Lady Nimriel's mysterious gift or some inherent strength, or something else, unfathomable.

The ground had emptied from beneath her feet. She hurtled downward, to be brought up on a spear-point of agony. Her bracelet had snagged on a dead twig. She released the catch and fell into a thicket of *Hedera paradoxis.*

Hours passed.

Later, lying ivy-poisoned by the roadside, the shorn-haired waif in tattered masculine attire had been discovered by a passing carter. He had stolen her Faêran cloak and delivered her into the hands of Grethet.

Much had happened since then . . .

Now, as memories flooded back like sap rising in Spring, a strange euphoria blossomed within the damsel lying in a semi-trance beneath the night-bound woods near Huntingtowers. The experience of recall imbued her with power. She felt like a winged being looking down on the world from an impossible height, while a light of glory crayonned her pinions in gold. So expanded was she in this virtual form that if she held out her hand she could cup the rain. Clouds brushed her cheek with cold dew, and should she raise her arms she could catch the sun like a golden ball. Mankind moved like beetles around her feet, and nothing could touch her. She had endured it all and been borne through, shining. She was winning.

So far.

Her shoulder hurt. It was being shaken in an iron claw. Her entire body quaked. She thrust off the claw, uttering an inarticulate groan.

"Rohain! Mistress!" Hazel eyes in a rounded, dimpled face appeared, framed by bobbing yellow curls with brown roots.

Sitting up, the dreamer took a swig from the water-bottle. Like any warrior, she rinsed her mouth and spat, then wiped her lips on her bloodstained sleeve.

"Via, I told you not to call me that. And cut your fingernails." She rubbed her shoulder. "Are we alive?"

"Yes, all three. You saved us."

"I would like to agree, but I have this ornament on my finger which is responsible for our current state of health." Her hands wandered up to her face, lightly touching the forehead, the nose, the chin. She examined a strand of dark hair. "Am I as I was? Am I ugly or beautiful? Boy or girl?"

Viviana and Caitri exchanged meaningful looks.

"Your experience at Huntingtowers has unsettled you, er . . . Tahquil," said Caitri. "Come, let us help you to your feet. We must get away from here. We are still too close to that place."

As they stood up, the one they called Tahquil swayed, clutching at her heart. Leaning against a linden tree, she closed her eyes and grimaced.

"Zooks, ma'am, what is amiss?" asked Viviana, full of concern.

"Ah, no, it cannot be. Alas, it has me again. This, then, is the price."

"*What* has you?"

"The Langothe. There's no salve for it." The sufferer gulped down her pain. "Let us go on." *I must endure the unendurable.*

She wondered how long it would take to destroy her.

It was the second of Duileagmis, the Leafmonth, viminal last month of Spring. In the woods, every leaf was a perfect spear-blade chipped from lucent emerald, fresh from the bud. As yet the new foliage was unbitten by insect, unparched by wind, untorn by rain.

The travelers walked through a glade striped with slender silver-paper poles marked at spaced intervals with darker notches that accentuated the clean smooth paleness of the bark. The tops of the poles were lost overhead in a yellow-stippled haze of tenderest green.

The damsel called Tahquil twisted the golden leaf-circle on her finger. Her thoughts fled to he who had bestowed it upon her. *I miss thee. I have come full circle. Here I am once more. And thee, my love, shall I ever see thee again?*

The damsel, Tahquil. Her insides ached. Yearning chewed at them.

Thus she thought: *I am a thousand and seventeen and a half years old. I am Ashalind na Pendran, Lady of the Circle. I come from a time before the shang, before Windships and sildron. The kingdom of my birth has crumbled to nothing. One of the most powerful Faêran in Aia pursues me—but why? Is it simply because I committed the crime of eavesdropping and survived his vengeance, or does he guess I have found a way back to the Realm? Is he after my life or my knowledge? And all the while the other powerful Faêran, his royal brother, sleeps forever amongst a great company of knights beneath some unmarked hill.*

One Gate to Faêrie remains passable: the Gate of Oblivion's Kiss. Only I may enter it, only I might recognize it, if I could recall. But the past has returned imperfectly to me. The most important recollection of all, that of the Gate's location, is still hidden in oblivion's mists—mayhap 'tis hidden forever. Indeed, some other events surrounding my time in the Gate-passage lack clarity.

If I could return to the Fair Realm with the Password "elindor," the Keys could be released from the Green Casket. The Gates might be opened once more. The Faêran would be able to send a discreet messenger to where their High King lies—for surely they could guess where he would be, or find him by means of gramarye—to tell him to return in all haste and secrecy to the Realm. Yet, if the Raven Prince discovers that the Gates are open and enters the Fair Realm before his brother, he might use his second boon to close them again and condemn the High King to continuing, everlasting exile.

Back and forth shuttle my thoughts, my confusion. This is like playing a game of Kings-and-Queens: if this, then thus, but if that, then the other.

Nonetheless, many matters are now clarified. Now I understand truly who it is that hunts at my heels—it is not the Antlered One, after all. Huon is only one of Morragan's minions. Huon's powers are nought by comparison with his master's. Now I un-

derstand whose henchman noticed my Talith hair in the marketplace of Gilvaris Tarv, and who lost track of me after the attack on the road-caravan, and who found me again when Dianella and Sargoth betrayed me. I understand who it was that ordered the Wild Hunt to assail Isse Tower, who sent the Three Crows of War through the Rip of Tamhania. I know who pursues me with destruction wherever I may go—the Raven Lord, Morragan, Fithiach of Carnconnor, Crown Prince of Faêrie.

Somberly, as she walked through the birch woods, the traveler with the dark-dyed hair and the festoons of thyme dwelled again on the moment she had first set eyes on him in the halls of Carnconnor under Hob's Hill.

With eyes as gray as the cold southern seas, he was the most grave and comely of all the present company. His hair tumbled down in waves to his elbows, the blue-black shade of a raven's wing . . . he regarded her, but said naught.

I dismiss that personage from my contemplation, she said to herself. *He brings sorrow. The Faêran! I have met with them, spoken with them! Sorrow they bring to mortals but delight also, and they are so joyous and goodly to behold as I would not have believed possible.* Again she caressed the golden ring on her finger, smiling sadly, her eyes misted with reflections. *Indeed, had I not seen with my own eyes Thorn wielding cold iron in his very hand, I would have said he must be of Faêran blood. Beloved heart-*

hreaker! I am fervently glad he is no Faêran—but I must banish thoughts of him now.

When I walked from the Geata Poeg na Déanainn, it was my thought to embark on a quest to restore the Faêran High King to his Realm. I won-der—how long had he reigned in the Iuln Realm, the High King of all Immortals, bearded with his pride swollen with power, overripe with glory in his failing years? For how many centuries did he sit upon his hoary throne in Faêrie, toying with the lives of mor-tals, before he met his own exile? And would it truly matter to me if this ancient King and his dormant warriors were to lie forever entombed under Erith's eroding mountains?

She sighed. She already knew the answer.

Yes, it would matter. Those who sleep might waken, one day.

In this era, I have heard more tales of the Faêran than I knew in the past. Those tales have illustrated a race that is dazzling, but callous and cruel. Like all mortals I am drawn to them, but now that I recall history, my abhorrence is confirmed. I dislike the Faêran, almost as heartily as the Raven Prince hates mortalkind. I could not endure it if Faêran warriors should awaken and, undying, walk in my Erith. It is the fault of the Fair Ones and their quarrels, and their heartless laws, that I am here now in this per-ilous place, separated from those I love. I am fully aware of the trouble they may wreak, if they rouse from their enchanted sleep.

She who I once was, Ashalind of my memories—

*she loved them. I, her future incarnation, am wiser.
Oh, they are beauteous, fascinating—it is impossible
not to be attracted by them. But I, Tahquil-Rohain,
loathe and fear their alien ways, their weird moral-
ity, their immutable laws, their arrogant use of
power. 'Tis true that sometimes, when it suits them,
they may behave with kindness—but the tales reveal
them to be haughty, proud, contemptuous, and cruel.
They are users and punishers of my race. Rightly do
folk name the Faêran "the Strangers." Strange indeed
are they, scorching flames of gramarye. They ought to
be shut out of our world.*

*This is my conclusion: that the Sleepers must
awaken and depart. They must go back to where they
belong. Every Faêran now in Erith must be repatri-
ated.*

*If the Langothe is not too swift in its deadly work,
I shall go back to Arcdur and seek the Gate. Then I
shall return through it to the Perilous Realm and use
the Password to unlock their Casket of Keys so that the
Faêran of the Realm may go forth and find the hill in
Erith where their King sleeps. Some shall waken him
and his noble company, and take them away. Others
shall take away the beautiful Raven Prince who frets
and rails so passionately against his exile. When they
and all their shadowy, sparkling, fair, and terrible
kind are gone, then the Gates must truly be locked
forever. I shall not rest until that is accomplished.*

This is my predicament and my undertaking.

Colored spindles of lupins, as high as a man's knee, marched between the boles of the silver birches. Each one flaunted a different hue, ranging from salmon, peach, and apricot to mauve, maroon, and lavender. Clusters of flower-turrets sprang from their own green coronas of frondescence. Now at the height of their blossoming they stood so erect, so tapered and symmetrical, each petal so crisp and painted and perfect, that they seemed artificial. The petals brushed the garments of the travelers as they passed.

"Where are we going?" asked Caitri, not unreasonably.

"Northeast. Then north." *Nearer to Thorn, in fact. Yet never shall I seek thee, my beloved, never shall I bring my hunters upon thee.*

"Did you find what you wanted at Hunting-towers?"

"I did. Tonight, if we find a safe place to rest, I shall tell you everything."

"Tonight you shall sleep," admonished Viviana in a motherly manner, "since you did not do so last night. We thought you were in a trance. We believed you were bewitched."

"Why are we heading north?" Caitri wanted to know.

"The region called Arcdur lies to the north. I must find something there—a Gate. The first time we see Stormriders overhead, you must wave them down and go with them, feigning that you have not seen me. You two have suffered enough. This new quest of mine is not for courtiers."

"Your words insult us," said Viviana.

"I am sorry, but it is true."

In silence they walked on.

"We will not see Relayers," said Caitri. "We are traveling far from the lands over which the Skyroads run, which are their usual routes. Besides, they have searched this coast already. They shall believe us lost, and they will not return."

"Is there any road to Arcdur from here?" Viviana queried.

"Not that I know of. The King's High Way used to go there, but it has long since been swallowed by the forest, or fallen into the sea. I know only that Arcdur's western shores lie along the northwest coast of Eldaraigne."

"Then we ought to keep to the sea's margins," Viviana said. "If we keep the ocean to our left we will be sure to come to Arcdur eventually."

"It would be impossible," said Tahquil-Ashalind, once Rohain. "The cliffs along here are rugged, pierced by deep inlets thrusting far back into the land. Without a boat we cannot go that way."

Viviana stopped by some low tree ferns. She plucked out some whorls of fiddle-heads, tightly coiled, like pale green clockwork springs. Other greenery and assorted vegetation hung on lengths of twine from her waist, her shoulders, and her elbows, obscuring the articles swinging and clanking from her chatelaine.

"You have not eaten since the day before yester-day, *auradonna*," the courtier reminded Tahquil from behind her matted, bleached curls. " 'Tis little wonder your belly pains you."

The euphoria dissipated. Tahquil looked at the dead and wilting leaves she herself carried, and the dirty, worm-eaten tubers. A forgotten tendril of some-thing akin to hunger stirred within her. One could not live on memories. The three companions sat beneath the lissome poles of the birches and kindled a fire. Vi-viana unbound bunches of edible roots, seed-pods, and herbage.

"Via has become adept at finding food," explained Caitri with a touch of reproach, "especially since you went off on your own. She's remembered all you've taught us. She has an eye for it."

"Even courtiers can learn," said Viviana haughtily, "to be useful."

"Then let me teach you how to cook," offered Tahquil. It would be a distraction from the hurt within.

These wooded, gently undulating hills were named the Great Western Forest, but, more innocuous than a forest, they were actually one vast woodland of beech, budding birch, oak, and rustling, new-leafed poplars, hung with leafy creepers. The trees were in-terspersed with brakes of hazel and wild currant bushes veiled with a diaphanous lace of blossoms. Rivulets chuckled through shady dells. Bluebells sprang in a lapis lazuli haze, attractive and perilous.

Directed by a dim, smoke-bleared sun glimpsed

through the woodland canopy, the travelers walked on through the reddish-brown smog of the day, and at evenfall, when weariness threatened to sweep Tahquil from her feet, they climbed to shelter in a huge and ivied weather beech, pulling themselves up on vegetable cables to rest in a scoop at the junction of three great boughs.

Twittering like sparrows in the undergrowth and fallen leaves, a gaggle of small wights came tumbling and capering over the knotted roots below. They were grigs. No more than eight inches tall were they, apple-cheeked, their eyes dark brown with no whites, their small mouths grinning. On their heads perched fungus-red caps, terminating in tasseled points. Their knee breeches were bark brown, their coats the fern green of trooping wights. In this typical eldritch attire they performed cartwheels and other acrobatic feats that they apparently considered hilarious, and which in their audience's opinion were tediously uninspired.

"I should like to throw something at the little *uncouthants*," said Viviana peevishly.

Nestling into the spoon of the tree, Tahquil slept. Oblivion descended, total again. She slept through the shang wind when it came, but Viviana, watching, pulled her mistress's taltry over her head lest she dreamed. In the unstorm, the cindery air transmuted to minuscule sequins.

"I shall have to inform her soon," said Caitri.

VISIT WARNER ASPECT ONLINE!

THE WARNER ASPECT HOMEPAGE
You'll find us at: www.twbookmark.com then by clicking on Science Fiction and Fantasy.

NEW AND UPCOMING TITLES
Each month we feature our new titles and reader favorites.

AUTHOR INFO
Author bios, bibliographies and links to personal websites.

CONTESTS AND OTHER FUN STUFF
Advance galley giveaways, autographed copies, and more.

THE ASPECT BUZZ
What's new, hot and upcoming from Warner Aspect: awards news, bestsellers, movie tie-in information . . .